Guy Rivers

Guy Rivers: A Tale of Georgia

Selected Fiction of William Gilmore Simms
Arkansas Edition

John Caldwell Guilds
Editor

The University of Arkansas Press
Fayetteville 1993

Copyright 1993 by John Caldwell Guilds

Manufactured in the United States of America

97   96   95   94   93   5   4   3   2   1

This book was designed by John Coghlan using the Minion typeface.

The paper used in this publication meets the minimum requirements of the American National Standard for Permanence of Paper for Printed Library Materials Z39.48-1984. ⊛

Library of Congress Cataloging-in-Publication Data

Simms, William Gilmore, 1806–1870.
Guy Rivers : a tale of Georgia / John Caldwell Guilds.
p. cm. — (Selected fiction of William Gilmore Simms : Arkansas Edition)
Includes bibliographical references.
ISBN 1-55728-274-9 (alk. paper)
1. Georgia—History—1775–1865—Fiction. 2. Georgia—Gold discoveries—Fiction. I. Guilds, John Caldwell, 1924– .
II. Title. III. Series.
PS2848.G8   1993
813' .3—dc20
                                                    92-31614
                                                    CIP

ACKNOWLEDGMENT

I am grateful for the assistance of Caroline Collins in preparing the explanatory notes and the historical and textual data in the appendices.

Contents

Preface to the Arkansas Edition

William Gilmore Simms needs to be read to be appreciated, and he can be neither read nor appreciated unless his works are made available. Thus I am pleased to edit for the University of Arkansas Press *Selected Fiction of William Gilmore Simms: Arkansas Edition,* beginning with *Guy Rivers: A Tale of Georgia. Selected Fiction* will include novels originally designated by Simms as Border Romances, selected novels from his Revolutionary War Series, his three novels dealing with pre-colonial and colonial warfare with Native Americans, and several volumes of his best shorter fiction, including *The Wigwam and the Cabin.* In these volumes, Simms depicts the American frontier from pre-colonial times in sixteenth-century Florida in its ever-westward movement across the Appalachian Mountains to the Mississippi River Valley in the early nineteenth century.

Though the Arkansas Edition of Simms will not be a critical edition in the strictest sense, the principles in establishing copy-text are those recommended by the Committee on Scholarly Editions of the Modern Language Association. For each volume copy-text has been selected under the following procedures: (1) if the author issued a revised edition, such edition becomes copy-text; (2) if there was no revised edition, the original publication is the copy-text; (3) if a critical text (established under CEAA or other comparable standards) exists, such text is the copy-text. In each volume of *Selected Fiction* there will be explanatory as well as textual notes, with a list of the more significant substantive revisions made by the author in preparing the text for a revised edition. Simms's nineteenth-century spelling remains unmodernized; all emendations in the text of typographical errors, redundancies, or omissions are recorded.

    Each volume will contain both an Introduction and an Afterword. I am indebted to the University of Arkansas Press for permission to incorporate relevant portions of my *Simms: A Literary Life* for the Introductions; the Afterwords analyze the works by Simms in more detail and depth than was possible in the limited scope of a biography.

    JCG

WILLIAM GILMORE SIMMS CHRONOLOGY

1806   Born in Charleston, South Carolina, April 17, the son of William Gilmore Simms, an Irish immigrant, and Harriet Ann Augusta Singleton Simms

1808   Mother died; left in the custody of his maternal grandmother by his father, who, frustrated by personal tragedy and business failure, deserted Charleston for the Southwest

1812–16   Attended public schools in Charleston

1816   At age ten made momentous decision to remain in Charleston with grandmother rather than join now-wealthy father in Mississippi

1816–18   Concluded formal education at private school conducted in buildings of the College of Charleston

1818   Apprenticed to apothecary to explore medical career

1824–25   Visited father in Mississippi; witnessed rugged frontier life

1825   Began study of law in Charleston office of Charles Rivers Carroll; edited (and published extensively in) the *Album*, a Charleston literary weekly

1826   Married Anna Malcolm Giles, October 19

1827   Admitted to bar; appointed magistrate of Charleston; published two volumes of poetry; first child, Anna Augusta Singleton Simms, born November 11

1832   Anna Malcolm Giles Simms died, February 19; made first visit to New York, where he met James Lawson, who became his literary agent and lifelong friend

1833 Published first volume of fiction, *Martin Faber: The Story of a Criminal*

1834 Published first "regular novel," *Guy Rivers: A Tale of Georgia*

1835 Published *The Yemassee: A Tale of Carolina* and *The Partisan: A Tale of the Revolution*

1836 Married Chevillette Eliza Roach, November 15, and moved to Woodlands, the plantation owned by her father; published *Mellichampe: A Legend of the Santee*

1837 Birth of Virginia Singleton Simms, November 15; first of fourteen children born to Chevillette Roach Simms

1838 Published *Richard Hurdis: or, The Avenger of Blood. A Tale of Alabama*

1840 Published *Border Beagles: A Tale of Mississippi* and *The History of South Carolina*

1841 Published *The Kinsmen: or, The Black Riders of Congaree: A Tale* (later retitled *The Scout*) and *Confession: or, The Blind Heart. A Domestic Story*

1842 Published *Beauchampe, or, The Kentucky Tragedy. A Tale of Passion* (later retitled *Charlemont*)

1842–43 Editor, *Magnolia*, Charleston literary magazine

1844 Elected to South Carolina legislature for 1844–46 term; published *Castle Dismal: or, The Bachelor's Christmas. A Domestic Legend*

1845 Published *The Wigwam and the Cabin* and *Helen Halsey: or, The Swamp State of Conelachita. A Tale of the Borders;* editor, *Southern and Western* (known as "Simms" Magazine)

1846   Published *Views and Reviews in American Literature History and Fiction, First Series* (dated 1845)

1847   Published *Views and Reviews, Second Series* (dated 1845)

1849–55 Editor, *Southern Quarterly Review*

1850   Published *The Lily and the Totem, or, The Huguenots in Florida*

1851   Published *Katharine Walton: or, The Rebel of Dorchester. An Historical Romance of the Revolution in Carolina* and *Norman Maurice; or, The Man of the People, An American Drama*

1852   Published *The Sword and the Distaff; or, "Fair, Fat and Forty," A Story of the South, at the Close of the Revolution* (retitled *Woodcraft*); *The Golden Christmas: A Chronicle of St. John's, Berkeley; As Good as a Comedy; or, The Tennessean's Story;* and *Michael Bonham: or, The Fall of Bexar. A Tale of Texas*

1853   Published *Vasconselos. A Romance of the New World* and a collected edition of *Poems*

1855   Published *The Forayers or the Raid of the Dog-Days*

1856   Published *Eutaw. A Sequel to The Forayers . . . ; Charlemont or The Pride of the Village. A Tale of Kentucky;* and *Beauchampe, or the Kentucky Tragedy. A Sequel to Charlemont;* disastrous lecture tour of North, in which he voiced strong pro-South Carolina and pro-Southern views

1858   Death of two sons to yellow fever on the same day, September 22: the "crowning calamity" of his life

1859   Published *The Cassique of Kiawah. A Colonial Romance*

1860   Vigorously supported the secessionist movement

1862   Woodlands burned; rebuilt with subscription funds from friends and admirers; birth of last child, Charles Carroll Simms, October 20

1863	Chevillette Roach Simms died September 10: "bolt from a clear sky"
1864	Eldest son William Gilmore Simms, Jr., wounded in Civil War battle in Virginia, June 12; most intimate friend in South Carolina, James Henry Hammond, died November 13
1865	Woodlands burned by stragglers from Sherman's army; witnessed the burning of Columbia, described in *The Sack and Destruction of the City of Columbia, S.C.*
1866	Made arduous but largely unsuccessful efforts to reestablish relations with Northern publishers
1867	Published "Joscelyn; A Tale of the Revolution" serially in the magazine *Old Guard*
1869	Published "The Cub of the Panther; A Mountain Legend" serially in *Old Guard;* published "Voltmeier, or the Mountain Men" serially in *Illuminated Western World* magazine
1870	Delivered oration on "The Sense of the Beautiful" May 3; died, after a long bout with cancer, at the Society Street home of his daughter Augusta (Mrs. Edward Roach) in Charleston, June 11, survived by Augusta and five of the fourteen children from his second marriage

INTRODUCTION TO *GUY RIVERS*

William Gilmore Simms's ambivalence about his future is illustrated in a single paragraph from a letter of January 19, 1833, to his ever more intimate friend, James Lawson. "Things go wildly in this quarter," Simms wrote, "and I only linger in So. Caro. until something takes place. My uncle in Mississippi writes earnestly after me, and I shall only wait until the first of February is well over, when I shall probably bend my course to the stabling place of the Sun." Simms was ready, it would seem, to heed the earlier pleadings of his father, now echoed by his uncle as well, to leave South Carolina for Mississippi. His next sentence, however, reveals why he was never to forsake the city of his birth: "I have sent to the Harpers' the first volume of a novel,[1] on which as yet I hear nothing" (*L*, I, 49). The implications of this statement are important: Simms has sent a partially completed *novel* to the Harper brothers—a novel, for the first time, after six consecutive volumes of poetry. Although there is some doubt about whether the reference is to *Martin Faber* or to *Guy Rivers,* both of which Simms was working on at the time and both of which were eventually published by Harpers, the thrust is nevertheless clear: Simms's "main work" (*L*, I, 45) is now the novel, not poetry as in the past. Ultimately, it was the publication of *Martin Faber* that changed a poet into a novelist. It was *Martin Faber* rather than *Guy Rivers* only because the former preceded the latter in publication by some nine or ten months—the difference between September 1833 and June–July 1834; either work alone could have changed Simms's life. At age twenty-six William Gilmore Simms had found the genre for which his talents best suited him. That literature was to be his life's work was never again a question; and if literature was his profession, Charleston—or, at least, the Atlantic seaboard, not the Southwest frontier—was to be his home. Thereafter, although he never ceased writing poetry and experimenting with other literary forms, he was primarily a writer of fiction. The success of *Martin Faber* (to be followed quickly by *Guy Rivers*) catapulted the young Charlestonian into the public eye of literary America and spurred him into an amazingly fertile and imaginative decade in which he produced no fewer than twelve novels and two collections of short stories.

The major share of Simms's energy in the fall of 1833 went into the writing of *Guy Rivers,* the first of the novels influenced by his trips to the Southwest, and the first in the series known as the Border Romances. On November 27, 1833, he wrote that "'Guy Rivers,' a story of the South, in two volumes, by the author of 'Martin Faber'—'Atalantis'— &c is in rapid progress" (*L*, I, 53). Actually, Simms had been concentrating on *Guy Rivers* for more than a year, having remarked in November 1832, in apparent reference to the novel, that "the first volume, in rough, is completed" (*L*, I, 45). By the end of December 1833 Simms had the work "finished—bating corrections," but reported to James Lawson that "it still remains in my hands." He then noted "a small blunder" in the advance notices of *Guy Rivers* in that the novel "does not relate in any degree to the late political difficulties in So. Carolina." Before closing his letter of December 29, 1833, to his New York friend, the Charlestonian informed him that "it is not improbable that you shall see me in New York before the winter is well over," after he ascertained "the period most proper for . . . publication" (*L*, I, 55). Whether Simms got to the North during the winter months is unknown, but we do know that he was there by June 12, 1834, awaiting the publication of *Guy Rivers,* which occurred between that date and July 19. On the latter date, after reading the first reviews, Simms wrote from New Haven to the New Yorker: "Of course, the success of 'Guy' is not less grateful to me than to my friends; but you have not surely estimated only my strength of mind and character, when you suggest caution as to the manner in which I speak of its success and of my own. . . . As far as I have seen all the papers speak well of 'Guy'" (*L*, I, 59).

Among the most enthusiastic of the newspaper reviews were those in the *Charleston Courier* of July 19, 1834, and the *New York American*[2] of a few days earlier. The Charleston paper stated that "Mr. Simms has entered a new field . . . whose untrodden paths afford a large scope for his fine imaginative mind and he has used the materials . . . with a master's hand." The *American* proclaimed that "no American novel since the days when the appearance of Mr. Cooper's *Spy* created such a sensation . . . has excited half the interest that will attend the circulation of

Guy Rivers. . . ." Perhaps the most significant magazine review of *Guy Rivers* was written by Henry William Herbert, editor of the *American Monthly Magazine,* for the July 1834 number of his journal. Herbert heaped praise on every aspect of the novel and, like the reviewer in the *American,* focused upon a comparison of the accomplishments of Cooper and Simms: "There is more acquaintance, displayed in these two volumes, with secret springs of human action," Herbert asserted, "than in all the novels Cooper ever has written, or will ever write. . . ." It is "in depicting character that the author of Guy Rivers is most happy," the reviewer continued; ". . . we unhesitatingly assign to Guy Rivers a high place in the scale of fiction . . . above every American novel that has met our eye. . . ." Herbert concluded that Cooper, "great as he is in graphic detail, could not have written Guy Rivers had he died for it . . ." (II, 295–304).

Even more than *Martin Faber,* then, *Guy Rivers: A Tale of Georgia* added luster to the growing reputation of William Gilmore Simms. Whereas *Martin Faber* was at best a short novel based largely upon an earlier short story, *Guy Rivers* represented, in Simms's own words, "the first of my regular novels."[3] Rather than springing from an earlier story, it was conceived from the beginning as a novel in two volumes; and for the first time Simms unloosened his verve and narrative power into sustained creation of a distinctively American theme. It was with the publication of *Guy Rivers,* Simms was to write twenty years later, that he "commenced a professional career in literature which has been wholly unbroken since . . ." (7). With *Guy Rivers* Simms "abandoned the profession of the patriot and politician" and adopted his "first love," literature, as his "proper vocation" (9–10). *Martin Faber* had made Simms known to literary America for the first time, primarily as a promising young writer of fiction; *Guy Rivers* built upon that reputation and established him as one of the major American novelists of the time, rivaled in popularity only by Cooper.

As its subtitle indicates, *Guy Rivers* (to quote the author) "is a tale of Georgia—a tale of the miners—of a frontier and wild people, and the events are precisely such as may occur among a people & in a region of that character" (*L,* I, 55). It was this raw, fresh quality of *Guy Rivers* (a quality that was to mark the other Border Romances as well) that most offended Simms's first biographer, William P. Trent.[4] Stating that Simms's series of novels "laid in nearly all the Southwestern States, are sometimes as rough in their construction as the people described were in their manners and customs," he noted: "All are marred by a slipshod style, by a repetition of incidents, and by the introduction of an unnecessary amount of the horrible and the revolting." Although he seemed to accept Simms's response to critics who objected to "the lavish oaths put in the mouths of his characters," noting that "he could not change for the better a backwoodsman's vocabulary," Trent charged that Simms "might have avoided, at least, introducing brutal murders not necessary to the action of the story," suggesting that "he might have remembered that a good artist is not called upon to exercise his powers upon subjects not proper to his art, simply because such subjects belong to the realm of the real and the natural." How much his own taste intruded upon his review can be seen in his summary:

> He [Simms] might have remembered that nobility is that quality of a romance which is essential to its permanence; and that the fact he was describing accurately the life of a people whom he thoroughly understood would not alone preserve his work for the general reader. When all is said, one is forced to wish that Simms had written fewer or none of these stories, and that he had spent the time thus saved in polishing the really excellent historical romances. . . . But he had to make a living, and the public liked sensational tales, so there is great excuse for him.[5]

This review is important because it clearly reveals the strong artistic and critical bias that permeates and negates Trent's assessment of Simms's frontier writing. It is not difficult for the modern reader or critic to see that what Trent considered Simms's most glaring faults might well be praised now as his main strengths: his ability to depict "accurately" the "real and the natural" life (and vocabulary) of Southern backwoodsmen "whom he thoroughly understood."

Guy Rivers is a powerful, if flawed novel. It reveals Simms's gusto in portraying the chase, the battle, the violence of the frontier: swiftmoving, action-packed narrative flows from Simms's pen with ease and naturalness; it captures the reader's imagination and interest and holds them until Simms moves the action from the woods and hills to the drawing room, where stilted, pretentious language replaces the salty vernacular of the ruffian and backwoodsman. What vitality there is in characterization comes in the portraits of untutored frontiersmen like Mark Forrester. The plot is episodic rather than symphonic, and many narrative threads dangle loosely without context rather than intertwine into a closely woven carpet. The hero and the heroine,

Ralph and Edith Colleton, seldom rise above the cardboard artificiality of the Southern gentleman and gentlewoman either in their hackneyed speech or in their almost unbelievably heroic and unselfish actions.

There is at least one instance, however, in which Edith's strict adherence to a principle of self-worth seems almost the object of Simms's satire. When Guy Rivers offers to spare Ralph Colleton from death if Edith will agree to marry the outlaw, she immediately refuses: she is unwilling to adjust her concept of personal integrity and virtue even to save the life of the man she loves. In contrast, the other leading female character in *Guy Rivers*, Lucy Munro, who is also in love with Colleton, would have given herself to the outlaw, as Rivers himself points out, to protect her lover from death. In this respect, Lucy Munro seems much more humanized, much more capable of love and concern, than the proudly inflexible heroine Edith. Perhaps the fact that Lucy does not belong to the South Carolina aristocracy frees her from the rigid code of conduct and honor at the center of Southern chivalry. Her father had been a respectable man, but at his death Lucy became the ward of her uncle, Wat Munro, a fellow criminal with Guy Rivers. Lucy, then, has an interestingly complicated background of a well-bred father on the one hand and an outlaw foster-father on the other, and emerges as one of Simms's most believable heroines. She possesses ladylike reticence in going to Colleton's room at midnight to warn him of his danger, but once again her human concern outweighs her sense of protocol and she does go, despite her embarrassment, and helps him escape. She also makes a daring escape from Guy Rivers' fortress after she learns that her testimony may save Colleton from being falsely convicted of murder, though her confusion at having to reveal her presence in Colleton's room and at having to implicate her foster-father in the crime renders her testimony useless. For the reader she is much more realistically conceived than most of Simms's inordinately lifeless ingenues. A possible flaw in Lucy Munro's characterization occurs, however, near the end of the novel. She has contended for Ralph Colleton's love, but has lost to Edith, to whom Colleton is betrothed. It seems inconsistent with Lucy's independence and free spirit, as previously drawn, that she would accept the invitation of Ralph and Edith Colleton that she come to live with them after their marriage.[6]

Simms's portrait of the title character comes from a mixture of influences: the Gothic tradition that had also helped to produce *Martin Faber;* Simms's own experiences in the frontier Southwest, where he either saw, or heard about at first hand, the leaders of a criminal gang who ruled with terror and horror; and a perverse desire on the author's part to create a well-educated lawyer-outlaw—with many of the traits of an aristocrat—whose own satanic nature and love of cruelty were abetted by burning resentment of his rejection by the gentry. Unfortunately, Simms fails to bring these diverse characteristics together into an artistic whole, and Guy Rivers comes through as a stiff, morose Byronic villain consumed with hate, too one-dimensional to be credible. Simms's attempt to humanize his criminal—and to offer insight into the psychology of crime—does not fully succeed because Rivers' attribution of his criminality to an undisciplined environment comes without prior build-up or subsequent development of data. Near the end of the novel the outlaw denounces his mother for having nurtured in him those qualities that led him to a life of crime: ". . . I charge it all upon her . . . twenty years of crime and sorrow, and a life of hate, and probably a death of ignominy—all owing to the first ten years of my infant education, where the only teacher I knew was the woman who gave me birth!" (404).

Although his judgment of *Guy Rivers* was too harsh, and was so, one might add, for self-serving reasons, Trent was nevertheless correct in attributing the novel's startling success with American readers and critics alike to Simms's discovery of a literary theme and a literary technique for which in 1834 America hungered. "Undiluted Americanism was what many readers were crying for, and they got it in 'Guy Rivers,'" Trent wrote; "excitement, sentimentality, bombast were what others were crying for, and they got all three in 'Guy Rivers.' What wonder, then, that the book was popular" (86). But in patronizingly dismissing *Guy Rivers* as a vulgar popular novel unworthy of serious consideration, Trent reflects the condescending attitude spawned by a latent Victorian idealism that blinded him to any recognition of literary merit in the graphic portrayal of a squalid, untamed backwoods devoid of "nobility." In *Guy Rivers* for the first time in our literature the ugliness, the lawlessness, the brutality of the early nineteenth-century American frontier were fully exposed. Long before Howells, Simms perceived the necessity of replacing belles-lettres' "ideal grasshopper, . . . the good old romantic card-board grasshopper" with a "real grasshopper . . . simple, honest, and natural."[7] Simms's frontier, like Howells' grasshopper, is ugly and real—not ideal and uplifting; but it is deserving of belated recognition of its authenticity.

Notes

1. Simms's reference to a "first volume" seems to suggest *Guy Rivers* (published in two volumes) rather than *Martin Faber* (published in a single volume). Simms's reference, however, is of course to his manuscript, not to the printed version, the format of which was probably determined by J. & J. Harper. *L,* I, 45, 49, first identifies *Martin Faber* as the manuscript Simms was referring to; but *L,* V, 435, changes the attribution to *Guy Rivers,* probably correctly. Regardless, the impact on Simms's career of his decision to concentrate on fiction is unquestionable.

2. Undated, but before July 19 because the *Courier* of that date quotes the *American* review.

3. "Dedicatory Epistle to Charles R. Carroll, Esq. of South Carolina," dated November 15, 1854, and published as the preface to the "new and revised" Redfield edition of *Guy Rivers* (New York, 1855). Subsequent quotations from this "Dedicatory Epistle" or other portions of *Guy Rivers* are indicated within parenthesis in the text by page number[s] in the Arkansas Edition.

4. William P. Trent, *William Gilmore Simms* (Boston: Houghton Mifflin, 1892).

   For an assessment of Trent's influence see my "'Long Years of Neglect': Atonement at Last?" in *Long Years of Neglect: The Work and Reputation of William Gilmore Simms* (Fayetteville: University of Arkansas Press, 1988). See also John McCardell, "Trent's Simms: The Making of a Biography," in *A Master's Due: Essays in Honor of David Herbert Donald* (Baton Rouge: Louisiana State University Press, 1985).

5. Trent, *Simms,* 88–89.

6. For a more extended discussion of Lucy Munro, see Afterword, 460–62.

7. See William Dean Howells, *Editor's Study* [December 1887], ed. James W. Simpson (Troy, New York: Whitson, 1983), 112.

GUY RIVERS

A

TALE OF GEORGIA

By W. Gilmore Simms, Esq.
AUTHOR OF "THE YEMASSEE" — "THE PARTISAN" — "MELLICHAMPE"—
"KATHARINE WALTON" — "THE SCOUT" — "WOODCRAFT," ETC.

"Who wants
A sequel, may read on. Th' unvarnished tale
That follows, will supply the place of one."
Rogers' *Italy.*

New and Revised Edition

REDFIELD
34 BEEKMAN STREET, NEW YORK
1855

STEREOTYPED BY C. C. SAVAGE,
13 Chambers Street, N.Y.

CHARLES R. CARROLL, ESQ.
OF SOUTH CAROLINA.

MY DEAR CARROLL.—

The task of revising my earlier writings, for a new and uniform edition of my works, brings naturally back to memory, and recalls, with vivid effect, the experiences of my youth, the agreeable and the disagreeable, the hopeful and discouraging, which I knew when they were severally written. In this labor, none of these works occasions more lively reminiscences than this novel of Guy Rivers, first published twenty years ago, and then dedicated to you. It was then that I commenced a professional career in literature which has been wholly unbroken since; and, in its reperusal, I retrace, with a saddening satisfaction, the events, public and personal, which made for us an almost mutual life at that period. Little, then, did either of us foresee or conjecture the changes which Providence had in store for both. Then we rode and ran together—read, and mused, and wrote together—and, in a vague and misty light of the fancy—the Indian summer of the soul— seeing nothing certainly of our future, yet hoping much, we indulged in our several dreams—which were scarcely several—which, in fact, were nearly entertained in common;—confiding in our youth—in the sky and sunshine—and brooding little upon those gradual developments of the coming time, which were to bring with them such a world of change. Then we were lawyers and politicians upon a small scale:— lawyers, with quite too little devotion to Themis to win many of her favors;—politicians, with a too small knowledge of men to make politics a profitable investment; and, more amusing still, politicians with at least one conclusive argument against every hope of personal progress, that we both entertained a wild fancy of patriotism—dreaming that our little world needed reformation, and that we were, in some degree, the very persons allotted to put the house of state in order!

I suppose, by this time, you are quite as well satisfied as myself, that we were somewhat mistaken; and that our poor little world of home, however needing reformation, was yet very far from being in that very bad state in which our youthful patriotism fancied that she groaned. At all events, we both discovered that she had quite too many self-sacrificing patriots, in whose eyes the toils of office had no terrors, to render necessary any services or sacrifices of ours. One lesson, besides, we have both learned from the experience of those days. We have seen that the mere government of a state has but little power to endanger the securities of any people so long as society is true to itself; that society is, in fact, the only safe guaranty for government; and that, so long as a community remains decently firm in its morals, pure enough to submit to no outrage of propriety, energetic enough to prosecute its toils of progress without looking back, having a sturdy zeal in the prosecution of common objects, and manhood enough to adhere with determination to the objects avowed; just so long will it remain secure against the vagaries of mere politicians. We need never despair, in short, of the safety of any society which is working, honest and courageous. Government may annoy and afflict such a people; may harass their minds, and, in some degree, retard their successes; but can neither destroy their fortunes, nor usurp their liberties. After some twenty-five years of active observation, a looker-on rather than a sharer in the strife, I have come to the conclusion that politicians rarely destroy anything—but themselves and one another! They supersede each other—succeed each other—as the sparks fly upward—doing a little mischief while they remain—leaving an unpleasant smell behind them when they depart—but exercising just as little influence upon the world's progress as the fly upon the wagon-wheel! Society, however unconsciously, sucks out the little sweet that they possess, along with the sour and the bitter, and then flings away the skin, with as little heed as we do that of the orange, after we have drawn from it all its juices! In giving up the profession of patriotism, therefore, we are both consoled with the conviction that our little world is, at no time, in much danger from the machinations of little politicians.

I need not remind you that the fruit of our first connection with the political struggles of our youth, was fatal to our personal prospects in such a career. The final overthrow of the party with which we were allied, was a perpetual closing of the doors of public life to us. I say perpetual, though, truth to speak, we were only under the ban some few years, and the "era of good feelings," in process of time, was the natural result of the necessity for a new political organization. But five years lost to a young politician, might as well be an eternity! To remain, for that period, in waiting upon the benches of equal hope and mortification, would wear out the inexpressibles of the best patriot living. It would argue, besides, a degree of stolidity to which I had not the slightest pretension. With a few sighs, therefore, not so profound as those of Othello, I abandoned the profession of the patriot and politician. My occupation, for the time, was gone; for, cut off from politics, I was equally cut off from law. The prejudices which a young beginner incurs in politics, will necessarily follow him into the courts where his talents have been untried. Besides, I had never heartily embraced the profession—had never studied *con amore*—and, after two years wasted in the dreary life of a political editor, I was not in training for the resumption of the severe and systematic methods which the law demands of its votaries. Literature was my only refuge, as it had been my first love, and, as I fancied, my proper vocation; and "Guy Rivers," the first volume of which was written before I was of age, was the first of my regular novels.

To you, my dear Carroll, who watched my early beginnings with so much friendly interest, I need not say that "Guy Rivers"—crude of plan, in many respects—awkward, in consequence of the measured and stiltish style of an unpractised hand—with many faults of taste, and some, perhaps, of moral—was yet singularly successful with the public. Its rapid popularity, however unmerited, seemed to justify me in the new profession I had chosen; and the young lawyer and the patriot politician were naturally very soon sunk in the novelist and romancer.

Since then—"I am afraid to think of what I've done!"

It is not a subject upon which I can properly expatiate; but it will be permitted to me, regarding "Guy Rivers," as my first deliberate attempt in prose fiction, to linger over its pages, and in an address to you, with more than ordinary parental interest. I could wish *now*—were this proper or possible—to remould the whole of the first half of the story, both as respects plan and style; for this portion was written under a false, or, rather, an imperfect, conception of what was demanded by such a work. The reader will, no doubt, readily detect the difference of manner which exists between the first and latter half of the story. But nothing now can be done toward the amendment of the halting portions, except to trim and pare away some of the cumbering foliage;— lop off, here and there, the truant twigs and branches, clear away the excess of undergrowth, and smoothe, in some degree, the easy passage of the reader through its over-massed intricacies.

No one can, better than myself, detect the mistakes and excesses of this performance. I can now see where new trees might have been set out with profit; where finer effects might be produced by changing the face of the landscape and conducting the spectator to the survey of the scene from other points of vision. But the mind, however willing and resolute, revolts at the alteration, whatever its promise of improvement. The labor of such a performance grows absolutely terrible even to contemplate; and, in very degree with the ability of the artist to repair or improve the ancient structure, is his capacity to design and build anew. It is also very questionable whether any attempt to amend or correct the errors in an old plan might not expose the whole fabric to the censure of rude and wretched joinery. Any person who has undertaken the repairs of an old house, without duly knowing, at the outset, what is exactly wanted, will readily conceive how much more serious must be the task of remodelling a work of art, in supplying defects in the original conception, and making such alterations in the finish, as would be demanded by improving tastes, a more matured experience, and higher aims in the mind of the artist. Something has been done—nay, a great deal, I may say— toward the pruning of the style—the removal of the rank undergrowth, the verbiage, the excrescences, and supplying the deficient finish. The reader would perhaps be surprised by a comparison of the new with the old edition in this respect. Something, too, I have done toward the elaboration of the idea, and the better development of occasional scenes. More than this could not be attempted. With the hope, my dear Carroll, that what has been done will suffice to render "Guy Rivers" more acceptable than before to the public and yourself, I surrender him to your hands. May the perusal of the story now, prove as grateful to you as it did twenty years ago, and recall to you as vividly as to me, those days of grateful struggle and not less grateful illusion.

With ancient regard,
Ever faithfully yours, &c.,
W. GILMORE SIMMS.

WOODLANDS, S. C.
November 15, 1854.

Guy Rivers

CHAPTER ONE

The Sterile Prospect and the Lonely Traveller

Our scene lies in the upper part of the state of Georgia, a region at this time fruitful of dispute, as being within the Cherokee territories. The route to which we now address our attention, lies at nearly equal distances between the main trunk of the Chatahoochie and that branch of it which bears the name of the Chestatee, after a once formidable, but now almost forgotten tribe. Here, the wayfarer finds himself lost in a long reach of comparatively barren lands. The scene is kept from monotony, however, by the undulations of the earth, and by frequent hills which sometimes aspire to a more elevated title. The tract is garnished with a stunted growth, a dreary and seemingly half-withered shrubbery, broken occasionally by clumps of slender pines that raise their green tops abruptly, and as if out of place, against the sky.

The entire aspect of the scene, if not absolutely blasted, wears at least a gloomy and discouraging expression, which saddens the soul of the most careless spectator. The ragged ranges of forest, almost untrodden by civilized man, the thin and feeble undergrowth, the unbroken silence, the birdless thickets,—all seem to indicate a peculiarly sterile destiny. One thinks, as he presses forward, that some gloomy Fate finds harbor in the place. All around, far as the eye may see, it looks in vain for relief in variety. There still stretch the dreary wastes, the dull woods, the long sandy tracts, and the rude hills that send out no voices, and hang out no lights for the encouragement of the civilized man. Such is the prospect that meets the sad and searching eyes of the wayfarer, as they dart on every side seeking in vain for solace.

Yet, though thus barren upon the surface to the eye, the dreary region in which we now find ourselves, is very far from wanting in resources, such as not only woo the eyes, but win the very soul of civilization. We are upon the very threshold of the gold country, so famous for its prolific promise of the precious metal; far exceeding, in the contemplation of the knowing, the lavish abundance of Mexico and of Peru, in their palmiest and most prosperous condition. Nor, though only the frontier and threshold as it were to these swollen treasures, was the portion of country now under survey, though bleak, sterile, and uninviting, wanting in attractions of its own. It contained indications which denoted the fertile regions, nor wanted entirely in the precious mineral itself. Much gold had been already gathered, with little labor, and almost upon its surface; and it was perhaps only because of the limited knowledge then had of its real wealth, and of its close proximity to a more productive territory, that it had been suffered so long to remain unexamined.

Nature, thus, in a section of the world seemingly unblessed with her bounty, and all ungarnished with her fruits and flowers, seemed desirous of redeeming it from the curse of barrenness, by storing its bosom with a product, which, only of use to the world in its conventional necessities, has become, in accordance with the self-creating wants of society, a necessity itself; and however the bloom and beauty of her summer decorations may refresh the eye of the enthusiast, it would here seem that, with an extended policy, she had planted treasures, for another and a greatly larger class, far more precious to the eyes of hope and admiration than all the glories and beauties in her sylvan and picturesque abodes. Her very sterility and solitude, when thus found to indicate her mineral treasures, rise themselves into attractions; and the perverted heart, striving with diseased hopes, and unnatural passions, gladly welcomes the wilderness, without ever once thinking how to make it blossom like the rose.

Cheerless in its exterior, however, the season of the year was one—a mild afternoon in May—to mollify and sweeten the severe and sterile aspect of the scene. Sun and sky do their work of beauty upon earth, without heeding the ungracious return which she may make; and a rich warm sunset flung over the hills and woods a delicious atmosphere of beauty, burnishing the dull heights and the gloomy pines with golden hues, far more bright, if far less highly valued by men, than the metallic treasures which lay beneath their masses. Invested by the lavish bounties of the sun, so soft, yet bright, so mild, yet beautiful, the waste put on an appearance of sweetness, if it did not rise into the picturesque. The very uninviting and unlovely character of the landscape, rendered the sudden effect of the sunset doubly effective, though, in a colder moment, the spectator might rebuke his own admiration with question of that lavish and indiscriminate waste which could clothe, with such glorious hues, a region so little worthy of such bounty; even as we revolt at sight of rich jewels about the brows and neck of age and ugliness. The solitary group of pines, that, here and there, shot up suddenly like illuminated spires;— the harsh and repulsive hills, that caught, in differing gradations, a glow and glory from the same bright fountain of light and beauty;—even the low copse, uniform of height, and of dull hues, not yet quite caparisoned for spring, yet sprinkled with gleaming eyes, and limned in pencilling beams and streaks of fire; these, all, appeared suddenly to be subdued in mood, and appealed, with a freshening interest, to the eye of the traveller whom at midday their aspects discouraged only.

And there is a traveller—a single horseman—who emerges suddenly from the thicket, and presses forward, not rapidly, nor yet with the manner of one disposed to linger, yet whose eyes take in gratefully the softening influences of that evening sunlight.

In that region, he who travelled at all, at the time of which we write, must do so on horseback. It were a doubtful progress which any vehicle would make over the blind and broken paths of that uncultivated realm. Either thus, or on foot, as was the common practice with the mountain hunters; men who, at seventy years of age, might be found as lithe and active, in clambering up the lofty summit as if in full possession of the winged vigor and impulse of twenty-five.

Our traveller, on the present occasion, was apparently a mere youth. He had probably seen twenty summers—scarcely more. Yet his person was tall and well developed; symmetrical and manly; rather slight, perhaps, as was proper to his immaturity; but not wanting in what the backwoodsmen call *heft*. He was evidently no milksop, though slight; carried himself with ease and grace; and was certainly not only well endowed with bone and muscle, but bore the appearance, somehow, of a person not unpractised in the use of it. His face was manly like his person; not so round as full, it presented a perfect oval to the eye; the forehead was broad, high, and intellectual—purely white, probably because so well shadowed by the masses of his dark brown hair. His eyes were rather small, but dark and expressive, and derived additional expression from their large, bushy, overhanging brows, which gave a commanding, and, at times, a somewhat fierce expression to his countenance. But his mouth was small, sweet, exquisitely chiselled, and the lips of a ripe, rich color. His chin, full and decided, was in character with the nobility of his forehead. The *tout ensemble* constituted a fine specimen of masculine beauty, significant at once of character and intelligence.

Our traveller rode a steed which might be considered, even in the South, where the passion for fine horses is universal, of the choicest parentage. He was blooded, and of Arabian, through English, stocks. You might detect his blood at a glance, even as you did that of his rider. The beast was large, high, broad-chested, sleek of skin, wiry of limb, with no excess of fat, and no straggling hair; small ears, a glorious mane, and a great lively eye. At once docile and full of life, he trod the earth with the firm pace of an elephant, yet with the ease of an antelope; moving carelessly as in pastime, and as if he bore no sort of burden on his back. For that matter he might well do so. His rider, though well developed, was too slight to be felt by such a creature—and a small portmanteau carried all his wardrobe. Beyond this he had no *impedimenta;* and to those accustomed only to the modes of travel in a more settled and civilized country—with bag and baggage—the traveller might have appeared—but for a pair of moderately-sized twisted barrels which we see pocketed on the saddle—rather as a gentleman of leisure taking his morning ride, than one already far from home and increasing at every step the distance between it and himself. From our privilege we make bold to mention, that, strictly proportioned to their capacities, the last named appurtenances carried each a charge which might have rendered awkward any interruption; and it may not be saying too much if we add, that it is not improbable to this portion of his equipage our traveller was indebted for that security which had heretofore obviated all necessity for their use. They were essentials which might or might not, in that wild region, have been put in requisition; and the prudence of all experience, in our border country, is seldom found to neglect such companionship.

So much for the personal appearance and the equipment of our young traveller. We have followed the usage among novelists, and have dwelt thus long upon these details, as we design that our adventurer shall occupy no small portion of the reader's attention. He will have much to do and to endure in the progress of this narrative.

It may be well, in order to the omission of nothing hereafter important, to add that he seems well bred to the *manège*—and rode with that ease and air of indolence, which are characteristic of the gentry of the south. His garments were strictly suited to the condition and custom of the country—a variable climate, rough roads, and rude accommodations. They consisted of a dark blue frock, of stuff not so fine as strong, with pantaloons of the same material, all fitting well, happily adjusted to the figure of the wearer, yet sufficiently free for any exercise. He was booted and spurred, and wore besides, from above the knee to the ankle, a pair of buckskin leggins, wrought by the Indians, and trimmed, here and there, with beaded figures that gave a somewhat fantastic air to this portion of his dress. A huge cloak strapped over the saddle, completes our portrait, which, at the time of which we write, was that of most travellers along our southern frontiers. We must not omit to state that a cap of fur, rather than a fashionable beaver, was also the ordinary covering of the head—that of our traveller was of a finely-dressed fur, very far superior to the common fox-skin cap worn by the plain backwoodsmen. It declared, somewhat for the superior social condition of the wearer, even if his general air and carriage did not sufficiently do so.

Our new acquaintance had, by this time, emerged into one of those regions of brown, broken, heathery waste, thinly mottled with tree and shrub, which seem usually to distinguish the first steppes on the approach to our mountain country. Though undulating, and rising occasionally into hill and crag, the tract was yet sufficiently monotonous; rather saddened than relieved by the gentle sunset, which seemed to gild in mockery the skeleton woods and forests, just recovering from the keen biting blasts of a severe and protracted winter.

Our traveller, naturally of a dreamy and musing spirit, here fell unconsciously into a narrow footpath, an old Indian trace, and without pause or observation, followed it as if quite indifferent whither it led. He was evidently absorbed in that occupation—a very unusual one with youth on horseback—that "chewing of the cud of sweet and bitter thought"—which testifies for premature troubles and still gnawing anxieties of soul. His thoughts were seemingly in full unison with the almost grave-like stillness and solemn hush of everything around him.

His spirit appeared to yield itself up entirely to the mournful barrenness and uninviting associations, from which all but himself, birds and beasts, and the very insects, seemed utterly to have departed. The faint hum of a single woodchuck, which, from its confused motions, appeared to have wandered into an unknown territory, and by its uneasy action and frequent chirping, seemed to indicate a perfect knowledge of the fact, was the only object which at intervals broke through the spell of silence which hung so heavily upon the sense. The air of our traveller was that of one who appeared unable, however desirous he might be, to avoid the train of sad thought which such a scene was so eminently calculated to inspire; and, of consequence, who seemed disposed, for this object, to call up some of those internal resources of one's own mind and memory, which so mysteriously bear us away from the present, whatever its powers, its pains, or its pleasures, and to carry us into a territory of the heart's own selection. But, whether the past, in his case, were more to be dreaded than the present; or whether it was that there was something in the immediate prospect which appealed to sterile hopes, and provoking memories, it is very certain that our young companion exhibited a most singular indifference to the fact that he was in a wild empire of the forest—a wilderness— and that the sun was rapidly approaching his setting. The bridle held heedlessly, lay loose upon the neck of his steed; and it was only when the noble animal, more solicitous about his night's lodging than his rider, or rendered anxious by his seeming stupor, suddenly came to a full stand in the narrow pathway, that the youth seemed to grow conscious of his doubtful situation, and appeared to shake off his apathy and to look about him.

He now perceived that he had lost the little Indian pathway which he had so long pursued. There was no sign of route or road on any side. The prospect was greatly narrowed; he was in a valley, and the trees had suddenly thickened around him. Certain hills, which his eyes had hitherto noted on the right, had disappeared wholly from sight. He had evidently deflected greatly from his proper course, and the horizon was now too circumscribed to permit him to distinguish any of those guiding signs upon which he had relied for his progress. From a bald tract he had unwittingly passed into the mazes of a somewhat thickly-growing wood.

"Old Blucher," he said, addressing his horse, and speaking in clear silvery tones—"what have you done, old fellow? Whither have you brought us?"

The philosophy which tells us, when lost, to give the reins to the steed, will avail but little in a region where the horse has never been before. This our traveller seemed very well to know. But the blame was not chargeable upon Blucher. He had tacitly appealed to the beast for his direction when suffering the bridle to fall upon his neck. He was not willing, now, to accord to him a farther discretion; and was quite too much of the man to forbear any longer the proper exercise of his own faculties. With the quickening intelligence in his eyes, and the compression of his lips, declaring a resolute will, he pricked the animal forward, no longer giving way to those brown musings, which, during the previous hour, had not only taken him to remote regions, but very much out of his way besides. In sober earnest, he had lost the way, and, in sober earnest, he set about to recover it; but a ten minutes' farther ride only led him to farther involvements; and he paused, for a moment, to hold tacit counsel with his steed, whose behavior was very much that of one who understands fully his own, and the predicament of his master. Our traveller then dismounted, and, suffering his bridle to rest upon the neck of the docile beast, he coursed about on all sides, looking close to the earth in hopes to find some ancient traces of a pathway. But his search was vain. His anxieties increased. The sunlight was growing fainter and fainter; and, in spite of the reckless manner, which he still wore, you might see a lurking and growing anxiety in his quick and restless eye. He was vexed with himself that he had suffered his wits to let fall his reins; and his disquiet was but imperfectly concealed under the careless gesture and rather philosophic swing of his graceful person, as, plying his silent way, through clumps of brush, and bush, and tree, he vainly peered along the earth for the missing traces of the route. He looked up for the openings in the tree-tops—he looked west, at the rapidly speeding sun, and shook his head at his horse. Though bold of heart, no doubt, and tolerably well aware of the usual backwoods mode of procedure in all such cases of embarrassment, our traveller had been too gently nurtured to affect a lodge in the wilderness that night—its very "vast contiguity of shade" being anything but attractive in his present mood. No doubt, he could have borne the necessity as well as any other man, but still he held it a necessity to be avoided if possible. He had, we are fain to confess, but small passion for that "grassy couch," and "leafy bower," and those other rural felicities, of which your city poets, who lie snug in garrets, are so prone to sing; and always gave the most unromantic preference to comfortable lodgings and a good roof;

so, persevering in his search after the pathway, while any prospect of success remained, he circled about until equally hopeless and fatigued; then, remounted his steed, and throwing the bridle upon his neck, with something of the indifference of despair, he plied his spurs, suffering the animal to adopt his own course, which we shall see was nevertheless interrupted by the appearance of another party upon the scene, whose introduction we reserve for another chapter.

CHAPTER TWO

The Encounter—
The Chevalier D'industrie

Thus left to himself, the good steed of our traveller set off, without hesitation, and with a free step, that promised, at least, to overcome space hurriedly, if it attained not the desired destination. The rider did not suffer any of his own doubts to mar a progress so confidently begun; and a few minutes carried the twain, horse and man, deeply, as it were, into the very bowels of the forest. The path taken by the steed grew every moment more and more intricate and difficult of access, and, but for the interruption already referred to, it is not impossible that a continued course in the same direction, would have brought the rider to a full stop from the sheer inaccessibleness of the forest.

The route thus taken lay in a valley which was necessarily more fertile, more densely packed with thicket, than the higher road which our rider had been pursuing all the day. The branches grew more and more close; and, what with the fallen trees, the spreading boughs, the undergrowth, and broken character of the plain, our horseman was fain to leave the horse to himself, finding quite enough to do in saving his eyes, and keeping his head from awkward contact with overhanging timber. The pace of the beast necessarily sunk into a walk. The question with his rider was, in what direction to turn, to extricate himself from the mazes into which he had so rashly ridden? While he mused this question,

Blucher started suddenly with evidently some new and exciting consciousness. His ears were suddenly lifted—his eyes were strained upon the copse in front—he halted, as if reluctant to proceed. It was evident that his senses had taken in some sights, or sounds, which were unusual.

Of course, our traveller was by no means heedless of this behavior on the part of the beast. He well knew the superior keenness of the brute senses, over those of the man; and his own faculties were keenly enlisted in the scrutiny. There might be wolves along the track—the country was not wanting in them; or, more to be feared, there might be a panther lurking along some great overhanging forest bough. There was need to be vigilant. Either of these savages would make his propinquity known, at a short distance, to the senses of an animal so timid as the horse. Or, it might be, that a worse beast still—always worst of all when he emulates the nature of the beast—man!—might be lurking upon the track! If so, the nature of the peril was perhaps greater still, to the rider if not the steed. The section of the wild world in which our traveller journeyed was of doubtful character; but sparingly supplied with good citizens; and most certainly infested with many with whom the world had quarrelled—whom it had driven forth in shame and terror.

The youth thought of all these things. But they did not overcome his will, or lessen his courage. Preparing himself, as well as he might, for all chances, he renewed his efforts to extricate himself from his thick harborage; pressing his steed firmly, in a direction which seemed to open fairly, the sky appearing more distinctly through the opening of the trees above. Meanwhile, he kept his eyes busy, watching right and left. Still, he could see nothing, hear nothing, but the slight footfall of his own steed. And yet the animal continued uneasy, his ears pricked up, his head turning, this way and that, with evident curiosity; his feet set down hesitatingly, as if uncertain whether to proceed.

Curious and anxious, our traveller patted the neck of the beast affectionately, and, in low tones, endeavored to soothe his apprehensions:

"Quietly, Blucher, quietly? What do you see, old fellow, to make you uneasy? Is it the snug stall, and the dry fodder, and the thirty ears, for which you long. I'faith, old fellow, the chance is that both of us will seek shelter and supper in vain to-night."

Blucher pricked up his ears at the tones, however subdued, of his rider's voice, which he well knew; but his uneasiness continued; and, just when our young traveller, began to feel some impatience at his restiffness and coyness, a shrill whistle which rang through the forest, from the copse in front, seemed at once to determine the correctness of sense in the animal, and the sort of beast which had occasioned his anxieties. He was not much longer left in doubt as to the cause of the animal's excitement. A few bounds brought him unexpectedly into a pathway, still girdled, however, by a close thicket—and having an ascent over a hill, the top of which was of considerable elevation compared with the plain he had been pursuing. As the horse entered this pathway, and began the ascent, he shyed suddenly, and so abruptly, that a less practised rider would have lost his seat.

"Quiet, beast! what do you see?"

The traveller himself looked forward at his own query, and soon discovered the occasion of his steed's alarm. No occasion for alarm, either, judging by appearances; no panther, no wolf, certainly—a man only—looking innocent enough, were it not for the suspicious fact that he seemed to have put himself in waiting, and stood directly in the midst of the path that the horseman was pursuing.

Our traveller, as we have seen, was not wholly unprepared, as well to expect as to encounter hostilities. In addition to his pistols, which were well charged, and conveniently at hand, we may now add that he carried another weapon, for close quarters, concealed in his bosom. The appearance of the stranger was not, however, so decided a manifestation of hostility, as to justify his acting with any haste by the premature use of his defences. Besides, no man of sense, and such we take our traveller to be, will force a quarrel where he can make his way peacefully, like a Christian and a gentleman. Our young traveller very quietly observed as he approached the stranger—

"You scare my horse, sir. Will it please you to give us the road?"

"Give you the road?—Oh! yes! when you have paid the toll, young master!"

The manner of the man was full of insolence, and the blood, in a moment, rushed to the cheeks of the youth. He divined, by instinct, that there was some trouble in preparation for him, and his teeth were silently clenched together, and his soul nerved itself for anticipated conflict. He gazed calmly, however, though sternly, at the stranger, who appeared nothing daunted by the expression in the eyes of the traveller. His air was that of quiet indifference, bordering on contempt, as if he knew his duties, or his man, and was resolved upon the course he was appointed to pursue. When men meet thus, if they are persons of even ordinary intelligence, the instincts are quick to conceive and act, and the youth was now more assured than ever, that the contest awaited him which should try his strength. This called up all his resources, and we may infer that he possessed them in large degree, from his quiet forbearance and deliberation, even when he became fully sensible of the insolence of the person with whom he felt about to grapple.

As yet, however, judging from other appearances, there was no violence meditated by the stranger. He was simply insolent, and he was in the way. He carried no weapons—none which met the sight, at least, and there was nothing in his personal appearance calculated to occasion apprehension. His frame was small, his limbs slight, and they did not afford promise of much activity. His face was not ill favored, though a quick, restless black eye, keen and searching, had in it a lurking malignity, like that of a snake, which impressed the spectator with suspicion at the first casual glance. His nose, long and sharp, was almost totally fleshless; the skin being drawn so tightly over the bones, as to provoke the fear that any violent effort would cause them to force their way through the frail integument. An untrimmed beard, run wild; and a pair of whiskers so huge, as to refuse all accordance with the thin diminutive cheeks which wore them; thin lips, and a sharp chin;—completed the outline of a very unprepossessing face, which a broad high forehead did not tend very much to improve or dignify.

Though the air of the stranger was insolent, and his manner rude, our young traveller was unwilling to decide unfavorably. At all events, his policy and mood equally inclined him to avoid any proceeding which should precipitate or compel violence.

"There are many good people in the world"—so he thought—"who are better than they promise; many good Christians, whose aspects would enable them to pass, in any crowd, as very tolerable and becoming ruffians. This fellow may be one of the unfortunate order of virtuous people, cursed with an unbecoming visage. We will see before we shoot."

Thus thought our traveller, quickly, as became his situation. He determined accordingly, while foregoing none of his precautions, to see farther into the designs of the stranger, before he resorted to any desperate issues. He replied, accordingly, to the requisition of the speaker; the manner, rather than the matter of which, had proved offensive.

"Toll! You ask toll of me? By what right, sir, and for whom do you require it?"

"Look you, young fellow, I am better able to ask questions myself, than to answer those of other people. In respect to this matter of answering, my education has been wofully neglected."

The reply betrayed some intelligence as well as insolence. Our traveller could not withhold the retort.

"Ay, indeed! and in some other respects too, not less important, if I am to judge from your look and bearing. But you mistake your man, let me tell you. I am not the person whom you can play your pranks upon with safety, and unless you will be pleased to speak a little more respectfully, our parley will have a shorter life, and a rougher ending, than you fancy."

"It would scarcely be polite to contradict so promising a young gentleman as yourself," was the response; "but I am disposed to believe our intimacy likely to lengthen, rather than diminish. I hate to part over-soon with company that talks so well; particularly in these woods, where, unless such a chance come about as the present, the lungs of the heartiest youth in the land would not be often apt to find the echo they seek, though they cried for it at the uttermost pitch of the pipe."

The look and the language of the speaker were alike significant, and the sinister meaning of the last sentence did not escape the notice of him to whom it was addressed. His reply was calm, however, and his mind grew more at ease, more collected, with his growing consciousness of annoyance and danger. He answered the stranger in a vein not unlike his own.

"You are pleased to be eloquent, worthy sir—and, on any other occasion, I might not be unwilling to bestow my ear upon you; but as I have yet to find my way out of this labyrinth, for the use of which your facetiousness would have me pay a tax, I must forego that satisfaction, and leave the enjoyment for some better day."

"You are well bred, I see, young sir," was the reply, "and this forms an additional reason why I should not desire so soon to break our acquaintance. If you have mistaken your road, what do you on this?—why are you in this part of the country, which is many miles removed from any public thoroughfare?"

"By what right do you ask the question?" was the hurried and unhesitating response. "You are impertinent!"

"Softly, softly, young sir. Be not rash, and let me recommend that you be more choice in the adoption of your epithets. Impertinent is an ugly word between gentlemen of our habit. Touching my right to ask this or that question of young men who lose the way, that's neither here nor there, and is important in no way. But, I take it, I should have some right in this matter, seeing, young sir, that you are upon the turnpike, and I am the gate-keeper who must take the toll."

A sarcastic smile passed over the lips of the man as he uttered the sentence, which was as suddenly succeeded, however, by an expression of gravity, partaking of an air of the profoundest business. The traveller surveyed him for a moment before he replied, as if to ascertain in what point of view properly to understand his conduct.

"Turnpike! this is something new. I never heard of a turnpike and a gate for toll, in a part of the world in which men, or honest ones at least, are not yet commonly to be found. You think rather too lightly, my good sir, of my claim to that most vulgar commodity called common sense, if you suppose me likely to swallow this silly story."

"Oh, doubtless—you are a very sagacious young man, I make no question," said the other, with a sneer—"but you'll have to pay the turnpike for all that."

"You speak confidently on this point; but, if I am to pay this turn-pike, at least, I may be permitted to know who is its proprietor."

"To be sure you may. I am always well pleased to satisfy the doubts and curiosity of young travellers who go abroad for information. I take you to be one of this class."

"Confine yourself, if you please, to the matter in hand—I grow weary of this chat," said the youth with a haughty inclination, that seemed to have its effect even upon him with whom he spoke.

"Your question is quickly answered. You have heard of the Pony Club—have you not?"

"I must confess my utter ignorance of such an institution. I have never heard even the name before."

"You have not—then really it is high time to begin the work of enlightenment. You must know, then, that the Pony Club is the propri-etor of everything and everybody, throughout the nation, and in and about this section. It is the king, without let or limitation of powers, for sixty miles around. Scarce a man in Georgia but pays in some sort to its support—and judge and jury alike contribute to its treasuries. Few dis-pute its authority, as you will have reason to discover, without suffering condign and certain punishment; and, unlike the tributaries and agents of other powers, its servitors, like myself, invested with jurisdiction over certain parts and interests, sleep not in the performance of our duties; but, day and night, obey its dictates, and perform the various, always laborious, and sometimes dangerous functions which it imposes upon us. It finds us in men, in money, in horses. It assesses the Cherokees, and they yield a tithe, and sometimes a greater proportion of their ponies, in obedience to its requisitions. Hence, indeed, the name of the club. It relieves young travellers, like yourself, of their small change— their sixpences; and when they happen to have a good patent lever, such a one as a smart young gentleman like yourself is very apt to carry about him, it is not scrupulous, but helps them of that too, merely by way of *pas-time.*"

And the ruffian chuckled in a half-covert manner at his own pun.

"Truly, a well-conceived sort of sovereignty, and doubtless, sufficiently well served, if I may infer from the representative before me. You must do a large business in this way, most worthy sir."

"Why, that we do, and your remark reminds me that I have quite as little time to lose as yourself. You now understand, young sir, the toll you have to pay, and the proprietor who claims it."

"Perfectly—perfectly. You will not suppose me dull again, most candid keeper of the Pony Turnpike. But have you made up your mind, in earnest, to relieve me of such trifling encumbrances as those you have just mentioned?"

"I should be strangely neglectful of the duties of my station, not to speak of the discourtesy of such a neglect to yourself, were I to do otherwise; always supposing you burdened with such encumbrances. I put it to yourself, whether such would not be the effect of my omission."

"It most certainly would, most frank and candid of all the outlaws. Your punctiliousness on this point of honor entitles you, in my mind, to an elevation above and beyond all others of your profession. I admire the grace of your manner, in the commission of acts which the more tame and temperate of our kind are apt to look upon as irregular and unlovely. You, I see, have the true notion of the thing."

The ruffian looked with some doubt upon the youth—inquiringly, as if to account in some way for the singular coolness, not to say contemptuous scornfulness, of his replies and manner. There was something, too, of a searching malignity in his glance, that seemed to recognise in his survey features which brought into activity a personal emotion in his own bosom, not at variance, indeed, with the craft he was pursuing, but fully above and utterly beyond it. Dismissing, however, the expression, he continued in the manner and tone so tacitly adopted between the parties.

"I am heartily glad, most travelled young gentleman, that your opinion so completely coincides with my own, since it assures me I shall not be compelled, as is sometimes the case in the performance of my duties, to offer any rudeness to one seemingly so well taught as yourself. Knowing the relationship between us so fully, you can have no reasonable objection to conform quietly to all my requisitions, and yield the toll-keeper his dues."

Our traveller had been long aware, in some degree, of the kind of relationship between himself and his companion; but, relying on his defences, and perhaps somewhat too much on his own personal capacities of defence, and, possibly, something curious to see how far the love of speech in his assailant might carry him in a dialogue of so artificial a character, he forbore as yet a resort to violence. He found it excessively difficult, however, to account for the strange nature of the transaction so far as it had gone; and the language of the robber seemed so inconsistent with his pursuit, that, at intervals, he was almost led to doubt whether the whole was not the clever jest of some country sportsman, who, in the guise of a levyer of contributions upon the traveller, would make an acquaintance, such as is frequent in the South, terminating usually in a ride to a neighboring plantation, and pleasant accommodations so long as the stranger might think proper to avail himself of them.

If, on the other hand, the stranger was in reality the ruffian he represented himself, he knew not how to account for his delay in the assault—a delay, to the youth's mind, without an object—unless attributable to a temper of mind like that of Robin Hood, and coupled in the person before him, as in that of the renowned king of the outlaws, with a peculiar freedom and generosity of habit, and a gallantry and adroitness which, in a different field, had made him a knight worthy to follow and fight for Baldwin and the Holy Cross. Our young traveller was a *romanticist,* and all of these notions came severally into his thoughts. Whatever might have been the motives of conduct in the robber, who thus audaciously announced himself the member of a club notorious on the frontiers of Georgia and among the Cherokees for its daring outlawries, the youth determined to keep up the game so long as it continued such. After a brief pause, he replied to the above politely-expressed demand in the following language:—

"Your request, most unequivocal sir, would seem but reasonable; and so considering it, I have bestowed due reflection upon it. Unhappily, however, for the Pony Club and its worthy representative, I am quite too poorly provided with worldly wealth at this moment to part with much of it. A few shillings to procure you a cravat—such as you may get of Kentucky manufacture—I should not object to. Beyond this, however (and the difficulty grieves me sorely), I am so perfectly incapacitated from doing anything, that I am almost persuaded, in order to the bettering of my own condition, to pay the customary fees, and applying to your honorable body for the privilege of membership, procure those means of lavish generosity which my necessity, and not my will, prevents me from bestowing upon you."

"A very pretty idea," returned he of the road; "and under such circumstances, your jest about the cravat from Kentucky is by no means wanting in proper application. But the fact is, our numbers are just now complete—our ranks are full—and the candidates for the honor are so numerous as to leave little chance for an applicant. You might be compelled to wait a long season, unless the Georgia penitentiary and Georgia guard shall create a vacancy in your behalf."

"Truly, the matter is of very serious regret," with an air of much solemnity, replied the youth, who seemed admirably to have caught up the spirit of the dialogue—"and it grieves me the more to know, that, under this view of the case, I can no more satisfy you than I can serve myself. It is quite unlucky that your influence is insufficient to procure me admission into your fraternity; since it is impossible that I should pay the turnpike, when the club itself, by refusing me membership, will not permit me to acquire the means of doing so. So, as the woods grow momently more dull and dark, and as I may have to ride far for a supper, I am constrained, however unwilling to leave good company, to wish you a fair evening, and a long swing of fortune, most worthy knight of the highway, and trusty representative of the Pony Club."

With these words, the youth, gathering up the bridle of the horse, and slightly touching him with the rowel, would have proceeded on his course; but the position of the outlaw now underwent a corresponding change, and, grasping the rein of the animal, he arrested his farther progress.

"I am less willing to separate than yourself from good company, gentle youth, as you may perceive; since I so carefully restrain you from a ride over a road so perilous as this. You have spoken like a fair and able scholar this afternoon; and talents, such as you possess, come too seldom into our forests to suffer them, after so brief a sample, to leave us so abruptly. You must come to terms with the turnpike."

"Take your hands from my horse, sirrah!" was the only response made by the youth; his tone and manner corresponding with the change in the situation of the parties. "I would not do you harm willingly; I want no man's blood on my head; but my pistols, let me assure you, are much more readily come at than my purse. Tempt me not to use them—stand from the way."

"It may not be," replied the robber, with a composure and coolness that underwent no change; "your threats affect me not. I have not taken my place here without a perfect knowledge of all its dangers and consequences. You had better come peaceably to terms; for, were it even the case that you could escape *me*, you have only to cast your eye up the path before you, to be assured of the utter impossibility of escaping those who aid me. The same glance will also show you the tollgate, which you could not see before. Look ahead, young sir, and be wise in time, and let me perform my duties without hindrance."

Casting a furtive glance on the point indicated by the ruffian, the youth saw, for the first time, a succession of bars—a rail fence, in fact, of more than usual height—completely crossing the narrow pathway and precluding all passage. Approaching the place of strife, the same glance assured him, were two men, well armed, evidently the accomplices of the robber who had pointed to them as such. The prospect grew more and more perilous, and the youth, whose mind was one of that sort which avails itself of its energies seemingly only in emergencies, beheld his true course, with a moment's reflection, and hesitated not a single moment in its adoption. He saw that something more was necessary than to rid himself merely of the ruffian immediately before him, and that an unsuccessful blow or shot would leave him entirely at the mercy of the gang. To escape, a free rein must be given to the steed, on which he felt confident he could rely; and, though prompted by the most natural impulse to send a bullet through the head of his assailant, he wisely determined on a course which, as it would be unlooked for, had therefore a better prospect of success.

Without further pause, drawing suddenly from his bosom the bowie-knife commonly worn in those regions, and bending forward, he aimed a blow at the ruffian, which, as he had anticipated, was expertly eluded—the assailant, sinking under the neck of the steed, and relying on the strength of the rein, which he still continued to hold, to keep him from falling, while at the same time he kept the check upon the horse.

This movement was that which the youth had looked for and

desired. The blow was but a feint, for, suddenly turning the direction of the knife when his enemy was out of its reach, he cut the bridle upon which the latter hung, and the head of the horse, freed from the restraint, was at once elevated in air. The suddenness of his motion whirled the ruffian to the ground; while the rider, wreathing his hands in the mane of the noble animal, gave him a free spur, and plunged at once over the struggling wretch, in whose cheek the glance of his hoof left a deep gash.

The steed bounded forward; nor did the youth seek to restrain him, though advancing full up the hill and in the teeth of his enemies. Satisfied that he was approaching their station, the accomplices of the foiled ruffian, who had seen the whole affray, sunk into the covert; but, what was their mortification to perceive the traveller, though without any true command over his steed, by an adroit use of the broken bridle, so wheel him round as to bring him, in a few leaps, over the very ground of the strife, and before the staggering robber had yet fully arisen from the path. By this manœuvre he placed himself in advance of the now approaching banditti. Driving his spurs resolutely and unsparingly into the flanks of his horse, while encouraging him with well-known words of cheer, he rushed over the scene of his late struggle with a velocity that set all restraint at defiance—his late opponent scarcely being able to put himself in safety. A couple of shots, that whistled wide of the mark, announced his extrication from the difficulty—but, to his surprise, his enemies had been at work behind him, and the edge of the copse through which he was about to pass, was blockaded with bars in like manner with the path in front. He heard the shouts of the ruffians in the rear—he felt the danger, if not impracticability of his pausing for the removal of the rails, and, in the spirit which had heretofore marked his conduct, he determined upon the most daring endeavor. Throwing off all restraint from his steed, and fixing himself firmly in the stirrup and saddle, he plunged onward to the leap, and, to the chagrin of the pursuers, who had relied much upon the obstruction, and who now appeared in pursuit, the noble animal, without a moment's reluctance, cleared it handsomely.

Another volley of shot rang in the ears of the youth, as he passed the impediment, and he felt himself wounded in the side. The wound gave him little concern at the moment, for, under the excitement of the strife, he felt not even its smart; and, turning himself upon the saddle, he drew one of his own weapons from its case, and discharging it, by way of taunt, in the faces of the outlaws, laughed loud with the exulting spirit of youth at the successful result of an adventure due entirely to his own perfect coolness, and to the warm courage which had been his predominating feature from childhood.

The incident just narrated had dispersed a crowd of gloomy reflections, so that the darkness which now overspread the scene, coupled as it was with the cheerlessness of prospect before him, had but little influence upon his spirits. Still, ignorant of his course, and beginning to be enfeebled by the loss of blood, he moderated his speed, and left it to the animal to choose his own course. But he was neither so cool nor so sanguine, to relax so greatly in his speed as to permit of his being overtaken by the desperates whom he had so cleverly foiled. He knew the danger, the utter hopelessness, indeed, of a second encounter with the same persons. He felt sure that he would be suffered no such long parley as before. Without restraining his horse, our young traveller simply regulated his speed by a due estimate of the capacity of the outlaws for pursuit a-foot; and, without knowing whither he sped, having left the route wholly to the horse, he was suddenly relieved by finding himself upon a tolerably broad road, which, in the imperfect twilight, he concluded to be the same from which, in his mistimed musings he had suffered his horse to turn aside. He had no means to ascertain the fact, conclusively, and, in sooth, no time; for now he began to feel a strange sensation of weakness; his eyes swam, and grew darkened; a numbness paralyzed his whole frame; a sickness seized upon his heart; and, after sundry feeble efforts, under a strong will, to command and compel his powers, they finally gave way, and he sunk from his steed upon the long grass, and lay unconscious;—his last thought, ere his senses left him, being that of death! Here let us leave him for a little space, while we hurriedly seek better knowledge of him in other quarters.

CHAPTER THREE

Young Love—The Retrospect

It will not hurt our young traveller, to leave him on the greensward, in the genial spring-time; and, as the night gathers over him, and a helpful insensibility interposes for the relief of pain, we may avail ourselves of the respite to look into the family chronicles, and show the why and wherefore of this errant journey, the antecedents and the relations of our hero.

Ralph Colleton, the young traveller whose person we have described, and whose most startling adventure in life, we have just witnessed, was the only son of a Carolinian, who could boast the best blood of English nobility in his veins. The sire, however, had outlived his fortunes, and, late in life, had been compelled to abandon the place of his nativity—an adventurer, struggling against a proud stomach, and a thousand embarrassments—and to bury himself in the less known, but more secure and economical regions of Tennessee. Born to affluence, with wealth that seemed adequate to all reasonable desires—a noble plantation, numerous slaves, and the host of friends who necessarily come with such a condition, his individual improvidence, thoughtless extravagance, and lavish mode of life—a habit not uncommon in the South—had rendered it necessary, at the age of fifty, when the mind, not less than the body, requires repose rather than adventure, that he should emigrate from the place of his birth; and with resources diminished to a cipher, endeavor to break ground once more in unknown forests, and commence the toils and troubles of life anew. With an only son (the youth before us) then a mere boy, and no other family, Colonel Ralph Colleton did not hesitate at such an exile. He had found out the worthlessness of men's professions at a period not very remote from the general knowledge of his loss of fortune: and having no other connection claiming from him either countenance or support, and but a single relative from whom separation might be painful, he felt, comparatively speaking, but few of the privations usually following such a removal. An elder brother, like himself a widower, with a single child, a daughter, formed the whole of his kindred left behind him in Carolina; and, as between the two brothers there had existed, at all times, some leading dissimilar points of disposition and character, an occasional correspondence, due rather to form than to affection, served all necessary purposes in keeping up the sentiment of kindred in their bosoms. There were but few real affinities which could bring them together. They never could altogether understand, and certainly had but a limited desire to appreciate or to approve many of the several and distinct habits of one another; and thus they separated with but few sentiments of genuine concern. William Colleton, the elder brother, was the proprietor of several thousand highly valuable and pleasantly-situated acres, upon the waters of the Santee—a river which irrigates a region in the state of South Carolina, famous for its wealth, lofty pride, polished manners, and noble and considerate hospitality. Affluent equally with his younger brother by descent, marriage had still further contributed toward the growth of possessions, which a prudent management had always kept entire and always improving. Such was the condition of William Colleton, the uncle of the young Ralph, then a mere child, when he was taken by his father into Tennessee.

There, the fortune of the adventurer still maintained its ancient aspect. He had bought lands, and engaged in trade, and made sundry efforts in various and honorable ways, but without success. Vocation after vocation had with him a common and certain termination, and after many years of profitless experiment, the ways of prosperity were as far remote from his knowledge and as perplexing to his pursuit, as at the first hour of his enterprise. In worldly concerns he stood just where he had started fifteen years before; with this difference for the worse, however, that he had grown older in this space of time, less equal to the tasks of adventure; and with the moral energies checked as they had been by continual disappointments, recoiling in despondency and gloom, with trying emphasis, upon a spirit otherwise noble and sufficiently daring for every legitimate and not unwonted species of trial and occasion. Still, he had learned little, beyond *hauteur* and querulousness, from the lessons of experience. Economy was not more the inmate of his dwelling than when he was blessed with the large income of his birthright; but, extravagantly generous as ever, his house was the abiding-place of a most lavish and unwise hospitality.

His brother, William Colleton, on the other hand, with means hourly increasing, exhibited a disposition narrowing at times into a selfishness the most pitiful. He did not, it is true, forego or forget any of those habits of freedom and intercourse in his household and with those about him, which form so large a practice among the people of the south. He could give a dinner, and furnish an ostentatious entertainment—lodge his guest in the style of a prince for weeks together, nor exhibit a feature likely to induce a thought of intrusion in the mind of his inmate. In public, the populace had no complaints to urge of his penuriousness; and in all outward shows he manifested the same general characteristics which marked the habit of the class to which he belonged.

But his selfishness lay in things not so much on the surface. It was more deep and abiding in its character; and consisted in the false estimate which he made of the things around him. He had learned to value wealth as a substitute for mind—for morals—for all that is lofty, and all that should be leading, in the consideration of society. He valued few things beside. He had different emotions for the rich from those which he entertained for the poor; and, from perceiving that among men, money could usurp all places—could defeat virtue, command respect denied to morality and truth, and secure a real worship when the Deity must be content with shows and symbols—he gradually gave it the chief place in his regard. He valued wealth as the instrument of authority. It secured him power; a power, however, which he had no care to employ, and which he valued only as tributary to the maintenance of that haughty ascendency over men which was his heart's first passion. He was neither miser nor mercenary; he did not labor to accumulate— perhaps because he was a lucky accumulator without any painstaking of his own: but he was, by nature an aristocrat, and not unwilling to compel respect through the means of money, as through any other more noble agency of intellect or morals.

There was only one respect in which a likeness between the fortunes of the two brothers might be found to exist. After a grateful union of a

few years, they had both lost their wives. A single child, in the case of
each, had preserved and hallowed to them the memories of their mothers. To the younger brother Ralph, a son had been born, soothing the
sorrows of the exile, and somewhat compensating his loss. To William
Colleton, the elder brother, his wife had left a single and very lovely
daughter, the sweet and beautiful Edith, a girl but a few months younger
than her cousin Ralph. It was the redeeming feature, in the case of the
surviving parents, that they each gave to their motherless children, the
whole of that affection—warm in both cases—which had been enjoyed
by the departed mothers.

Separated from each other, for years, by several hundred miles of
uncultivated and untravelled forest, the brothers did not often meet;
and the bonds of brotherhood waxed feebler and feebler, with the swift
progress of successive years. Still, they corresponded, and in a tone and
temper that seemed to answer for the existence of feelings, which neither, perhaps, would have been so forward as to assert warmly, if challenged to immediate answer. Suddenly, however, when young Ralph was
somewhere about fifteen, his uncle expressed a wish to see him; and,
whether through a latent and real affection, or a feeling of self-rebuke
for previous neglect, he exacted from his brother a reluctant consent
that the youth should dwell in his family, while receiving his education
in a region then better prepared to bestow it with profit to the student.
The two young cousins met in Georgia for the first time, and, after a
brief summer journey together, in which they frequented the most
favorite watering places, Ralph was separated from Edith, whom he had
just begun to love with interest, and despatched to college.

The separation of the son from the father, however beneficial it
might be to the former, in certain respects of education, proved fatal to
the latter. He had loved the boy even more than he knew; had learned to
live mostly in the contemplation of the youth's growth and development; and his absence preyed upon his heart, adding to his sense of
defeat in fortune, and the loneliness and waste of his life. The solitude
in which he dwelt, after the boy's departure, he no longer desired to disturb; and he pined as hopelessly in his absence, as if he no longer had a
motive or a hope to prompt exertion. He had anticipated this, in some
degree, when he yielded to his brother's arguments and entreaties; but,
conscious of the uses and advantages of education to his son, he felt the
selfishness to be a wrong to the boy, which would deny him the benefits
of that larger civilization, which the uncle promised, on any pretexts. A

calm review of his own arguments against the transfer, showed them to be suggested by his own wants. With a manly resolution, therefore, rather to sacrifice his own heart, than deny to his child the advantages which were held out by his brother, he consented to his departure. The reproach of selfishness, which William Colleton had not spared, brought about his resolve; and with a labored cheerfulness he made his preparations, and accompanied the youth to Georgia, where his uncle had agreed to meet him. They parted, with affectionate tears and embraces, never to meet again. A few months only had elapsed when the father sickened. But he never communicated to his son, or brother, the secret of his sufferings and grief. Worse, he never sought relief in change or medicine; but, brooding in the solitude, gnawing his own heart in silence, he gradually pined away, and, in a brief year, he was gathered to his fathers. He died, like many similarly-tempered natures, of no known disorder!

The boy received the tidings with a burst of grief, which seemed to threaten his existence. But the sorrows of youth are usually short-lived, particularly in the case of eager, energetic natures. The exchange of solitude for the crowd; the emulation of college life; the sports and communion of youthful associates—served, after a while, to soothe the sorrows of Ralph Colleton. Indeed, he found it necessary that he should bend himself earnestly to his studies, that he might forget his griefs. And, in a measure he succeeded; at least, he subdued their more fond expression, and only grew sedate, instead of passionate. The bruises of his heart had brought the energies of his mind to their more active uses.

From fifteen to twenty is no very long leap in the history of youth. We will make it now, and place the young Ralph—now something older in mind as in body—returned from college, finely formed, intellectual, handsome, vivacious, manly, spirited, and susceptible—as such a person should be—once again in close intimacy with his beautiful cousin. The season which had done so much for him, had been no less liberal with her; and we now survey her, the expanding flower, all bloom and fragrance, a tribute of the spring, flourishing in the bosom of the more forward summer.

Ralph came from college to his uncle's domicil, now his only home. The circumstances of his father's fate and fortune, continually acting upon his mind and sensibilities from boyhood, had made his character a marked and singular one—proud, jealous, and sensitive, to an extreme which was painful not merely to himself, but at times to others.

But he was noble, lofty, sincere, without a touch of meanness in his composition, above circumlocution, with a simplicity of character strikingly great, but without anything like puerility or weakness.

The children—for such, in reference to their experience, we may venture to call them—had learned to recognise in the progress of a very brief period but a single existence. Ralph looked only for Edith, and cared nothing for other sunlight; while Edith, with scarcely less reserve than her bolder companion, had speech and thought for few besides Ralph. Circumstances contributed not a little to what would appear the natural growth of this mutual dependence. They were perpetually left together, and with few of those tacit and readily-understood restraints, unavoidably accompanying the presence of others older than themselves. Residing, save at few brief intervals, at the plantation of Colonel Colleton, they saw little and knew less of society; and the worthy colonel, not less ambitious than proud, having become a politician, had left them a thousand opportunities of intimacy which had now become so grateful to them both. Half of his time was taken up in public matters. A leader of his party in the section of country in which he lived, he was always busy in the responsibilities imposed upon him by such a station; and, what with canvassing at election-polls and muster-grounds, and dancing attendance as a silent voter at the halls of the state legislature, to the membership of which his constituents had returned him, he saw but little of his family, and they almost as little of him. His influence grew unimportant with his wards, in proportion as it obtained vigor with his faction—was seldom referred to by them, and, perhaps, if it had been, such was the rapid growth of their affections, would have been but little regarded. He appeared to take it for granted, that, having provided them with all the necessaries called for by life, he had done quite enough for their benefit; and actually gave far less of his consideration to his own and only child than he did to his plantation, and the success of a party measure, involving possibly the office of doorkeeper to the house, or of tax-collector to the district. The taste for domestic life, which at one period might have been held with him exclusive, had been entirely swallowed up and forgotten in his public relations; and entirely overlooking the fact, that, in the silent goings-on of time, the infantile will cease to be so, he never seemed to observe that the children whom he had brought together but a few years before might not with reason be considered children any longer.

Children, indeed! What years had they not lived—what volumes of experience in human affections and feelings had the influence and genial warmth of a Carolina sun not unfolded to their spirits—in the few sweet and uninterrupted seasons of their intercourse. How imperious were the dictates of that nature, to whose immethodical but honest teachings they had been almost entirely given up. They lived together, walked together, rode together—read in the same books, conned the same lessons, studied the same prospects, saw life through the common medium of mutual associations; and lived happy only in the sweet unison of emotions gathered at a common fountain, and equally dear, and equally necessary to them both. And this is love—they loved!

They loved, but the discovery was yet to be made by them. Living in its purest luxuries—in the perpetual communion of the only one necessary object—having no desire and as little prospect of change—ignorant of and altogether untutored by the vicissitudes of life—enjoying the sweet association which had been the parent of that passion, dependent now entirely upon its continuance—they had been content, and had never given themselves any concern to analyze its origin, or to find for it a name. A momentary doubt—the presages of a dim perspective—would have taught them better. Had there been a single moment of discontent in their lives at this period, they had not remained so long in such ignorance. The fear of its loss can alone teach us the true value of our treasure. But the discovery was at hand.

A pleasant spring afternoon in April found the two young people, Ralph and Edith—the former now twenty years of age, and the latter in the same neighborhood, half busied, half idle, in the long and spacious piazza of the family mansion. They could not be said to have been employed, for Edith rarely made much progress with the embroidering needle and delicate fabric in her hands, while Ralph, something more absorbed in a romance of the day, evidently exercised little concentration of mind in scanning its contents. He skimmed, at first, rather than studied, the pages before him; conversing occasionally with the young maiden, who, sitting beside him, occasionally glanced at the volume in his hand, with something of an air of discontent that it should take even so much of his regard from herself. As he proceeded, however, in its perusal, the story grew upon him, and he became unconscious of her occasional efforts to control his attention. The needle of Edith seemed also disposed to avail itself of the aberrations of its mistress, and to rise in rebellion; and, having pricked her finger more than once in the effort to proceed with her work while her eyes wandered to her companion, she at length threw down the gauzy fabric upon which she had been so partially employed, and hastily rising from her seat, passed into the adjoining apartment.

Her departure was not attended to by her companion, who for a time continued his perusal of the book. No great while, however, elapsed, when, rising also from his seat with a hasty exclamation of surprise, he threw down the volume and followed her into the room where she sat pensively meditating over thoughts and feelings as vague and inscrutable to her mind, as they were clear and familiar to her heart. With a degree of warm impetuosity, even exaggerated beyond his usual manner, which bore at all times this characteristic, he approached her, and, seizing her hand passionately in his, exclaimed hastily—

"Edith, my sweet Edith, how unhappy that book has made me!"

"How so, Ralph—why should it make you unhappy?"

"It has taught me much, Edith—very much, in the last half hour. It has spoken of privation and disappointment as the true elements of life, and has shown me so many pictures of society in such various situations, and with so much that I feel assured must be correct, that I am unable to resist its impressions. We have been happy—so happy, Edith, and for so many years, that I can not bear to think that either of us should be less so; and yet that volume has taught me, in the story of parallel fortunes with ours, that it may be so. It has given me a long lesson in the hollow economy of that world which men seek, and name society. It has told me that we, or I, at least, may be made and kept miserable for ever."

"How, Ralph, tell me, I pray you—how should that book have taught you this strange notion? Why? What book is it? That stupid story!" was the gasping exclamation of the astonished girl—astonished no less by the impetuous manner than the strong language of the youth; and, with the tenderest concern she laid her hand upon his arm, while her eyes, full of the liveliest interest, yet moistened with a tearful apprehension, were fixed earnestly upon his own.

"It is a stupid book, a very stupid book—a story of false sentiment, and of mock and artificial feelings, of which I know, and care to know, nothing. But it has told me so much that I feel is true, and that chimes in with my own experience. It has told me much besides, that I am glad to have been taught. Hear me then, dear Edith, and smile not carelessly at my words, for I have now learned to tremble when I speak, in fear lest I should offend you."

She would have spoken words of assurance—she would have

taught him to think better of her affections and their strength; but his impetuosity checked her in her speech.

"I know what you would say, and my heart thanks you for it, as if its very life depended upon the utterance. You would tell me to have no such fear; but the fear is a portion of myself now—it is my heart itself. Hear me then, Edith—*my* Edith, if you will so let me call you."

Her hand rested on his assuringly, with a gentle pressure. He continued—

"Hitherto we have lived with each other, only with each other—we have loved each other, and I have almost only loved you. Neither of us, Edith (may I believe it of you?) has known much of any other affection. But how long is this to last? that book—where is it? but no matter—it has taught me that, now, when a few months will carry us both into the world, it is improper that our relationship should continue. It says we can not be the children any longer that we have been—that such intercourse— I can now perceive why—would be injurious to you. Do you understand me?"

The blush of a first consciousness came over the cheek of the maiden, as she withdrew her hand from his passionate clasp.

"Ah! I see already," he exclaimed: "you too have learned the lesson. And is it thus—and we are to be happy no longer!"

"Ralph!"—she endeavored to speak, but could proceed no further, and her hand was again, silently and without objection, taken into the grasp of his. The youth, after a brief pause, resumed, in a tone, which though it had lost much of its impetuousness, was yet full of stern resolution.

"Hear me, Edith—but a word—a single word. I love you, believe me, dear Edith, I love you."

The effect of this declaration was scarcely such as the youth desired. She had been so much accustomed to his warm admiration, indicated frequently in phrases such as these, that it had the effect of restoring to her much of her self-possession, of which the nature of the previous dialogue had a little deprived her; and, in the most natural manner in the world, she replied—perhaps too, we may add, with much of the artlessness of art—

"Why, to be sure you do, Cousin Ralph—it would be something strange indeed if you did not. I believe you love me, as I am sure you can never doubt how much you are beloved by me!"

"*Cousin* Ralph—*Cousin* Ralph!" exclaimed the youth with something of his former impetuosity, emphasizing ironically as he spoke the unfortunate family epithet—"Ah, Edith, you *will not* understand me— nor indeed, an hour ago, should I altogether have understood myself. Suddenly, dear Edith, however, as I read certain passages of that book, the thought darted through my brain like lightning, and I saw into my own heart, as I had never been permitted to see into it before. I there saw how much I loved you—not as my cousin—not as my sister, as you sometimes would have me call you, but as I *will not* call you again—but as—as—"

"As what?"

"As my *wife,* Edith—as my own, own wife!"

He clasped her hand in his, while his head sunk, and his lips were pressed upon the taper and trembling fingers which grew cold and powerless within his grasp.

What a volume was at that moment opened, for the first time, before the gaze and understanding of the half-affrighted and deep-throbbing heart of that gentle girl. The veil which had concealed its burning mysteries was torn away in an instant. The key to its secret places was in her hands, and she was bewildered with her own discoveries. Her cheeks alternated between the pale and crimson of doubt and hope. Her lips quivered convulsively, and an unbidden but not painful suffusion overspread the warm brilliance of her soft fair cheeks. She strove, ineffectually, to speak; her words came forth in broken murmurs; her voice had sunk into a sigh; she was dumb. The youth once more took her hand into his, as, speaking with a suppressed tone, and with a measured slowness which had something in it of extreme melancholy, he broke silence:—

"And have I no answer, Edith—and must I believe that for either of us there should be other loves than those of childhood—that new affections may usurp the place of old ones—that there may come a time, dear Edith, when I shall see an arm, not my own, about your waist; and the eyes that would look on no prospect if you were not a part of it, may be doomed to that fearfullest blight of beholding your lips smiling and pressed beneath the lips of another?"

"Never, oh never, Ralph! Speak no more, I beseech you, in such language. You do me wrong in this—I have no such wish, no such thought or purpose. I do not—I could not—think of another, Ralph. I will be yours, and yours only—if you really wish it."

"If I wish! Ah! dear Edith, you are mine, and I am yours! The world shall not pass between us."

She murmured—

"Yours, Ralph, yours only!"

He caught her in his passionate embrace, even as the words were murmured from her lips. Her head settled upon his shoulder; her light brown hair, loosened from the comb, fell over it in silky masses. Her eyes closed, his arms still encircled her, and the whole world was forgotten in a moment;—when the door opened, and a third party entered the room in the person of Colonel Colleton.

Here was a catastrophe!

CHAPTER FOUR

A Rupture—
The Course of True Love

Colonel Colleton stood confounded at the spectacle before him. Filled with public affairs, or rather, with his own affairs in the public eye, he had grown totally heedless of ordinary events, household interests, and of the rapid growth and development of those passions in youth which ripen quite as fervently and soon in the shade as in the sun. These children—how should they have grown to such a stature! His daughter, at this moment, seemed taller than he had ever seen her before! and Ralph!—as the uncle's eyes were riveted upon the youth, he certainly grew more than ever erect and imposing of look and stature. The first glance which he gave to the scene, did not please the young man. There was something about the expression of the uncle's face, which seemed to the nephew to be as supercilious, as it certainly was angry. Proud, jealous of his sensibilities, the soul of the youth rose in arms, at the look which annoyed him. That Edith's father should ever disapprove of his passion for his cousin, never once entered the young man's brain. He had not, indeed, once thought upon the matter. He held it to be a thing of course that the father would welcome a union which promised to strengthen the family bond, and maintain the family name and blood in perpetuity. When, therefore, he beheld, in his uncle's face, such an expression of scorn mixed with indignation, he resented it with the fervor of his whole soul. He was bewildered, it is true, but he was also chafed, and it needed that he should turn his eyes to the sweet cause of his offence, before he could find himself relieved of the painful feelings which her father's look and manner had occasioned him.

Poor Edith had a keener sense of the nature of the case. Her instincts more readily supplied the means of knowledge. Besides, there were certain family matters, which the look of her father suddenly recalled—which had never been suffered to reach the ears of her cousin;—which indicated to her, however imperfectly, the possible cause of that severe and scornful expression of eye, in the uncle, which had so confounded the nephew. She looked, with timid pleading to her father's face, but dared not speak.

And still the latter stood at the entrance, silent, sternly scanning the young offenders, just beginning to be conscious of offence. A surprise of any kind is exceedingly paralyzing to young lovers, caught in a situation like that in which our luckless couple were found on this occasion. It is probable, that, but for this, Ralph Colleton would scarcely have borne so meekly the severe look which the father now bestowed upon his daughter.

Though not the person to trouble himself much at any time in relation to his child, Colonel Colleton had never once treated her unkindly. Though sometimes neglectful, he had never shown himself stern. The look which he now gave her was new to all her experience. The poor girl began to conceive much more seriously of her offence than ever;—it seemed to spread out unimaginably far, and to involve a thousand violations of divine and human law. She could only look pleadingly, without speech, to her father. His finger silently pointed her to withdraw.

"Oh, father!"—the exclamation was barely murmured.

"Go!" was the sole answer, with the finger still uplift.

In silence, she glided away; not, however, without stealing a fond and assuring glance at her lover.

Her departure was the signal for that issue between the two remaining parties for which each was preparing in his own fashion. Ralph had not beheld the dumb show, in which Edith was dismissed, without a rising impulse of choler. The manner of the thing had been particularly offensive to him. But the father of Edith, whatever his offence, had suddenly risen into new consideration in the young man's mind, from the moment that he fully comprehended his feelings for the daughter. He was accordingly, somewhat disposed to temporize, though there was still a lurking desire in his mind, to demand an explanation of those supercilious glances which had so offended him.

But the meditations of neither party consumed one twentieth part of the time that we have taken in hinting what they were. With the departure of Edith, and the closing of the door after her, Colonel Colleton, with all his storms, approached to the attack. The expression of scorn upon his face had given way to one of anger wholly. His glance seemed meant to penetrate the bosom of the youth with a mortal stab—it was hate, rather than anger, that he looked. Yet it was evident that he made an effort to subdue his wrath—its full utterance at least—but he could not chase the terrible cloud from his haughty brow.

The youth, getting chafed beneath his gaze, returned him look for look, and his brows grew dark and lowering also; and, for anger, they gave back defiance. This silent, but expressive dialogue, was the work of a single moment of time. The uncle broke the silence.

"What am I to understand from this, young man?"

"Young man, sir!—I feel it very difficult to understand you, uncle! In respect to Edith and myself, sir, I have but to say that we have discovered that we are something more than cousins to each other!"

"Indeed! And how long is it, I pray, since you have made this discovery?"

This was said with a dry tone, and hard, contemptuous manner. The youth strove honestly to keep down his blood.

"Within the hour, sir! Not that we have not always felt that we loved each other, uncle; only, that, up to this time, we had never been conscious of the true nature of our feelings."

The youth replied with the most provoking simplicity. The uncle was annoyed. He would rather that Ralph should have relieved him, by a conjecture of his own, from the necessity of hinting to him that such extreme sympathies, between the parties, were by no means a matter of course. But the nephew would not, or could not, see; and his surprise, at the uncle's course, was perpetually looking for explanation. It became necessary to speak plainly.

"And with what reason, Ralph Colleton, do you suppose that I will sanction an alliance between you and my daughter? Upon what, I pray you, do you ground your pretensions to the hand of Edith Colleton?"

Such was the haughty interrogation. Ralph was confounded.

"My pretensions, sir?—The hand of Edith!—Do I hear you right, uncle? Do you really mean what you say?"

"My words are as I have said them. They are sufficiently explicit. You need not misunderstand them. What, I ask, are your pretensions to the hand of my daughter, and how is it that you have so far forgotten yourself as thus to abuse my confidence, stealing into the affections of my child?"

"Uncle, I have abused no confidence, and will not submit to any charge that would dishonor me. What I have done has been done openly, before all eyes, and without resort to cunning or contrivance. I must do myself the justice to believe that you knew all this without the necessity of my speech, and even while your lips spoke the contrary."

"You are bold, Ralph, and seem to have forgotten that you are yet but a mere boy. You forget your years and mine."

"No, sir—pardon me when I so speak—but it is you who have forgotten them. Was it well to speak as you have spoken?" proudly replied the youth.

"Ralph, you have forgotten much, or have yet to be taught many things. You may not have violated confidence, but—"

"I *have not* violated confidence!" was the abrupt and somewhat impetuous response, "and will not have it spoken of in that manner. It is not true that I have abused any trust, and the assertion which I make shall not therefore be understood as a mere possibility."

The uncle was something astounded by the almost fierce manner of his nephew; but the only other effect of this expression was simply, while it diminished his own testiness of manner in his speeches, to add something to the severity of their character. He knew the indomitable spirit of the youth, and his pride was enlisted in the desire for its overthrow.

"You are yet to learn, Ralph Colleton, I perceive, the difference and distance between yourself and my daughter. You are but a youth, yet— quite too young to think of such ties as those of marriage, and to make any lasting engagement of that nature; but, even were this not the case, I am entirely ignorant of those pretensions which should prompt your claim to the hand of Edith."

Had Colonel Colleton been a prudent and reflective man—had he, indeed, known much, if anything, of human nature—he would have withheld the latter part of this sentence. He must have seen that its effect would only be to irritate a spirit needing an emollient. The reply was instantaneous.

"My pretensions, Colonel Colleton? You have twice uttered that word in my ears, and with reference to this subject. Let me understand you. If you would teach me by this sentence the immeasurable individual superiority of Edith over myself in all things, whether of mind, or heart, or person, the lesson is gratuitous. I need no teacher to this end. I acknowledge its truth, and none on this point can more perfectly agree with you than myself. But if, looking beyond these particulars, you would have me recognise in myself an inferiority, marked and singular, in a fair comparison with other men—if, in short, you would convey an indignity; and—but you are my father's brother, sir!" and the blood mounted to his forehead, and his heart swelling, the youth turned proudly away, and rested his head upon the mantel.

"Not so, Ralph; you are hasty in your thought, not less than in its expression," said his uncle, soothingly. "I meant not what you think. But you must be aware, nephew, that my daughter, not less from the fortune which will be exclusively hers, and her individual accomplishments, than from the leading political station which her father fills, will be enabled to have a choice in the adoption of a suitor, which this childish passion might defeat."

"Mine is no childish passion, sir; though young, my mind is not apt to vary in its tendencies; and, unlike that of the mere politician, has little of inconsistency in its predilections with which to rebuke itself. But, I understand you. You have spoken of her fortune, and that reminds me that I had a father, not less worthy, I am sure—not less generous, I feel—but certainly far less prudent than hers. I understand you, sir, perfectly."

"If you mean, Ralph, by this sarcasm, that my considerations are those of wealth, you mistake me much. The man who seeks my daughter must not look for a sacrifice; she must win a husband who has a name, a high place—who has a standing in society. Your tutors, indeed, speak of you in fair terms; but the public voice is everything in our country. When you have got through your law studies, and made your first speech, we will talk once more upon this subject."

"And when I have obtained admission to the practice of the law, do you say that Edith shall be mine?"

"Nay, Ralph, you again mistake me. I only say, it will be then time enough to consider the matter."

"Uncle, this will not do for me. Either you sanction, or you do not. You mean something by that word *pretensions* which I am yet to understand; my name is Colleton, like your own, and—"

There was a stern resolve in the countenance of the colonel, which spoke of something of the same temper with his impetuous nephew, and the cool and haughty sentence which fell from his lips in reply, while arresting that of the youth, was galling to the proud spirit of the latter, whom it chafed nearly into madness.

"Why, true, Ralph, such is your name indeed; and your reference to this subject now, only reminds me of the too free use which my brother made of it when he bestowed it upon a woman so far beneath him and his family in all possible respects."

"There again, sir, there again! It is my mother's poverty that pains you. She brought my father no dowry. He had nothing of that choice prudence which seems to have been the guide of others of our family in the bestowment of their affections. He did not calculate the value of his wife's income before he suffered himself to become enamored of her. I see it, sir—I am not ignorant."

"If I speak with you calmly, Ralph, it is because you are the indweller of my house, and because I have a pledge to my brother in your behalf."

"Speak freely, sir; let not this scruple trouble you any longer. It shall not trouble me; and I shall be careful to take early occasion to release you most effectually from all such pledges."

Colonel Colleton proceeded as if the last speech had not been uttered.

"Edith has a claim in society which shall not be sacrificed. Her father, Ralph, did not descend to the hovel of the miserable peasant, choosing a wife from the inferior grade, who, without education, and ignorant of all refinement, could only appear a blot upon the station to which she had been raised. Her mother, sir, was not a woman obscure and uneducated, for whom no parents could be found."

"What means all this, sir? Speak, relieve me at once, Colonel Colleton. What know you of my mother?"

"Nothing—but quite as much as your father ever knew. It is sufficient that he found her in a hovel, without a name, and with the silly romance of his character through life, he raised her to a position in society which she could not fill to his honor, and which, finally, working upon his pride and sensibility drove him into these extravagances which in the end produced his ruin. I grant that she loved him with a most perfect devotion, which he too warmly returned, but what of that?—she was still his destroyer."

Thus sternly did the colonel unveil to the eyes of Ralph Colleton a

portion of the family picture which he had never been permitted to survey before.

Cold drops stood on the brow of the now nerveless and unhappy
youth. He was pale, and his eyes were fixed for an instant; but, suddenly
recovering himself, he rushed hastily from the apartment before his
uncle could interpose to prevent him. He heard not or heeded not the
words of entreaty which called him back; but, proceeding at once to his
chamber, he carefully fastened the entrance, and, throwing himself
upon his couch, found relief from the deep mental agony thus suddenly
forced upon him, in a flood of tears.

For the first time in his life, deriving his feeling in this particular
rather from the opinions of society than from any individual consciousness of debasement, he felt a sentiment of humiliation working in
his breast. His mother he had little known, but his father's precepts and
familiar conversation had impressed upon him, from his childhood, a
feeling for her of the deepest and most unqualified regard. This feeling
was not lessened, though rebuked, by the development so unnecessarily
and so wantonly conveyed. It taught a new feeling of distrust for his
uncle, whose harsh manner and ungenerous insinuations, in the
progress of the preceding half-hour, had lost him not a little of the
youth's esteem. He felt that the motive of his informer was not less
unkind than was the information painful and oppressive; and his mind,
now more than ever excited and active from this thought, went on discussing, from point to point, all existing relations, until a stern resolve
to leave, that very night, the dwelling of one whose hospitality had been
made a matter of special reference, was the only and settled conclusion
to which his pride could possibly come.

The servant reminded him of the supper-hour, but the summons
was utterly disregarded. The colonel himself condescended to notify the
stubborn youth of the same important fact, but with almost as little
effect. Without opening his door, he signified his indisposition to join
in the usual repast, and thus closed the conference.

"I meet him at the table no more—not at his table, at least," was the
muttered speech of Ralph, as he heard the receding footsteps of his
uncle.

He had determined, though without any distinct object in view, upon
leaving the house and returning to Tennessee, where he had hitherto
resided. His excited spirits would suffer no delay, and that very night was
the period chosen for his departure. Few preparations were necessary.

With a fine horse of his own, the gift of his father, he knew that the course lay open. The long route he had more than once travelled before; and he had no fears, though he well knew the desolate character of the journey, in pursuing it alone. Apart from this, he loved adventure for its own sake. The first lesson which his father had taught him, even in boyhood, was that braving of trial which alone can bring about the most perfect manliness. With a stout heart, and with limbs not less so, the difficulties before him had no thought in his mind; there was buoyancy enough in the excitement of his spirit, at that moment, to give even a pleasurable aspect to the obstacles that rose before him.

At an early hour he commenced the work of preparation: he had little trouble in this respect. He studiously selected from his wardrobe such portions of it as had been the gift of his uncle, all of which he carefully excluded from among the contents of the little portmanteau which readily comprised the residue. His travelling-dress was quickly adjusted; and not omitting a fine pair of pistols and a dirk, which, at that period, were held in the south and southwest legitimate companions, he found few other cares for arrangement. One token alone of Edith—a small miniature linked with his own, taken a few seasons before, when both were children, by a strolling artist—suspended by a chain of the richest gold, was carefully hung about his neck. It grew in value, to his mind, at a moment when he was about to separate, perhaps for ever, from its sweet original.

At midnight, when all was silent—his portmanteau under his arm—booted, spurred, and ready for travel—Ralph descended to the lower story, in which slept the chief servant of the house. Cæsar was a favorite with the youth, and he had no difficulty in making himself understood. The worthy black was thunderstruck with his determination.

"Ky! Mass Ralph, how you talk! what for you go dis time o'night? What for you go 't all?"

The youth satisfied him, in a manner as evasive and brief as possible, and urged him in the preparation of his steed for the journey. But the worthy negro absolutely refused to sanction the proceeding unless he were permitted to go along with him. He used not a few strong arguments for this purpose.

"And what we all for do here, when you leff? 'speck ebbery ting be dull, wuss nor ditch-water. No more fun—no more shuffle-foot. Old maussa no like de fiddle, and nebber hab party and jollication like udder people. Don't tink I can stay here, Mass Ra'ph, after you gone;

'spose, you no 'jection, I go 'long wid you? You leff me, I take to de swamp, sure as a gun."

"No, Cæsar, you are not mine; you belong to your young mistress. You must stay and wait upon her."

"Ha!" was the quick response of the black, with a significant smirk upon his lip, and with a cunning emphasis; "enty I see; wha' for I hab eye ef I no see wid em? I 'speck young misses hab no 'jection for go too—oh, Mass Ra'ph! all you hab for do is for ax em!"

The eye of the youth danced with a playful light, as if a new thought, and not a disagreeable one, had suddenly broken in upon his brain; but the expression lasted but for an instant. He overruled all the hopes and wishes of the sturdy black, who, at length, with a manner the most desponding, proceeded to the performance of the required duty. A few moments sufficed, and with a single look to the window of his mistress, which spoke unseen volumes of love, leaving an explanatory letter for the perusal of father and daughter, though addressed only to the latter—he gave the rough hand of his sable friend a cordial pressure, and was soon hidden from sight by the thickly-spreading foliage of the long avenue. The reader has been already apprized that the youth, whose escape in a preceding chapter we have already narrated, and Ralph Colleton, are one and the same person.

He had set forth, as we have seen, under the excitation of feelings strictly natural; but which, subtracting from the strong common sense belonging to his character, had led him prematurely into an adventure, having no distinct purposes, and promising largely of difficulty. What were his thoughts of the future, what his designs, we are not prepared to say. His character was of a firm and independent kind; and the proba- bility is, that, looking to the profession of the law, in the study of which noble science his mind had been for some time occupied, he had con- templated its future practice in those portions of Tennessee in which his father had been known, and where he himself had passed some very pleasant years of his own life. With economy, a moderate talent, and habits of industry, he was well aware that, in those regions, the means of life are with little difficulty attainable by those who are worthy and will adventure. Let us now return to the wayfarer, whom we have left in that wildest region of the then little-settled state of Georgia—doubly wild as forming the debatable land between the savage and the civilized—par- taking of the ferocity of the one, and the skill, cunning, and cupidity of the other.

CHAPTER FIVE

Mark Forrester—The Gold Village

There were moments when Ralph Colleton, as he lay bruised and wounded upon the sward, in those wild woods, and beneath the cool canopy of heaven, was conscious of his situation, of its exposure and its perils—moments, when he strove to recover himself—to shake off the stupor which seemed to fetter his limbs as effectually as it paralyzed his thoughts;—and the renewed exercise of his mental energies, brought about, and for a little while sustained, an increased consciousness, which perhaps rather added to his pain. It taught him his own weakness, when he strove vainly to support himself against the tree to which he had crawled; and in despair, the acuteness of which was only relieved by the friendly stupor which came to his aid, arising from the loss of blood, he closed his eyes, and muttering a brief sentence, which might have been a prayer, he resigned himself to his fate.

But he was not thus destined to perish. He had not lain many minutes in this situation when the tones of a strong voice rang through the forest. There was a whoop and halloo, and then a catch of a song, and then a shrill whistle, all strangely mingled together, finally settling down into a rude strain, which, coming from stentorian lungs, found a ready echo in every jutting rock and space of wood for a mile round. The musician went on merrily from verse to verse of his forest minstrelsy as he continued to approach; describing in his strain, with a ready ballad-facility, the numberless pleasures to be found in the life of the woodman. Uncouthly, and in a style partaking rather more of the savage than the civilized taste and temper, it enumerated the distinct features of each mode of life with much ingenuity; and, in stanzas smartly epigrammatic, did not hesitate to assign the preference to the former.

As the new-comer approached the spot where Ralph Colleton lay, there was still a partial though dim light over the forest. The twilight was richly clear, and there were some faint yellow lines of the sun's last glances lingering still on the remote horizon. The moon, too, in the opposite sky, about to come forth, had sent before her some few faint harbingers of her approach; and it was not difficult for the sturdy woodman to discern the body of the traveller, lying, as it did, almost in his path. A few paces farther on stood his steed, cropping the young grass, and occasionally, with uplifted head, looking round with something like human wonderment, for the assertion of that authority which heretofore had him in charge. At the approach of the stranger he did not start, but, seeming conscious of some change for the better in his own prospects, he fell again to work upon the herbage as if no interruption had occurred to his repast.

The song of the woodman ceased as he discovered the body. With an exclamation, he stooped down to examine it, and his hands were suffused with the blood which had found its way through the garments. He saw that life was not extinct, and readily supposing the stupor the consequence of loss of blood rather than of vital injury, he paused a few moments as in seeming meditation, then turning from the master to his unreluctant steed, he threw himself upon his back, and was quickly out of sight. He soon returned, bringing with him a wagon and team, such as all farmers possess in that region, and lifting the inanimate form into the rude vehicle with a tender caution that indicated a true humanity, walking slowly beside the horses, and carefully avoiding all such obstructions in the road, as by disordering the motion would have given pain to the sufferer, he carried him safely, and after the delay of a few hours, into the frontier, and then almost unknown, village of Chestatee.

It was well for the youth that he had fallen into such hands. There were few persons in that part of the world like Mark Forrester. A better heart, or more honorable spirit, lived not; and in spite of an erring and neglected education—of evil associations, and sometimes evil pursuits— he was still a worthy specimen of manhood. We may as well here describe him, as he appears to us; for at this period the youth was still insensible—unconscious of his deliverance as he was of his deliverer.

Mark Forrester was a stout, strongly-built, yet active person, some six feet in height, square and broad-shouldered—exhibiting an outline, wanting, perhaps, in some of the more rounded graces of form, yet at the same time far from symmetrical deficiency. There was, also, not a little of ease and agility, together with a rude gracefulness in his action, the result equally of the well-combined organization of his animal man and of the hardy habits of his woodland life. His appearance was youthful, and the passing glance would perhaps have rated him at little more than six or seven-and-twenty. His broad, full chest, heaving strongly with a consciousness of might—together with the generally athletic muscularity of his whole person—indicated correctly the possession of prodigious strength. His face was finely southern. His features were frank and fearless—moderately intelligent, and well marked—the *tout ensemble* showing an active vitality, strong, and usually just feelings, and a good-natured freedom of character, which enlisted confidence, and seemed likely to acknowledge few restraints of a merely conventional kind. Nor, in any of these particulars, did the outward falsely interpret the inward man. With the possession of a giant's powers, he was seldom so far borne forward by his impulses, whether of pride or of passion, as to permit of their wanton or improper use. His eye, too, had a not unpleasing twinkle, promising more of good-fellowship and a heart at ease than may ever consort with the jaundiced or distempered spirit. His garb indicated, in part, and was well adapted to, the pursuits of the hunter and the labors of the woodman. We couple these employments together, for, in the wildernesses of North America, the dense forests, and broad prairies, they are utterly inseparable. In a belt, made of buckskin, which encircled his middle, was stuck, in a sheath of the same material, a small axe, such as, among the Indians, was well known to the early settlers as a deadly implement of war. The head of this instrument, or that portion of it opposite the blade, and made in weight to correspond with and balance the latter when hurled from the hand, was a pick of solid steel, narrowing down to a point, and calculated, with a like blow, to prove even more fatal, as a weapon in conflict, than the more legitimate member to which it was appended. A thong of ox-hide, slung over his shoulder, supported easily a light rifle of the choicest bore; for there are few matters indeed upon which the wayfarer in the southern wilds exercises a nicer and more discriminating taste than in the selection of a companion, in a pursuit like his, of the very last importance; and which, in time, he learns to love with a passion almost comparable to his love of woman. The dress of the woodman was composed of a coarse gray stuff, of a make sufficiently *outré*, but which, fitting him snugly, served to set off his robust and well-made person to the utmost advantage. A fox-skin cap, of domestic manufacture, the tail of which, studiously preserved, obviated any necessity for a foreign tassel, rested slightly upon his head, giving a unique finish to his appearance, which a fashionable hat would never have supplied. Such was the personage, who, so fortunately for Ralph, plied his craft in that lonely region; and who, stumbling upon his insensible form at nightfall, as already narrated, carefully conveyed him to his own lodgings at the village-inn of Chestatee.

The village, or town—for such it was in the acceptation of the time and country—may well deserve some little description; not for its intrinsic importance, but because it will be found to resemble some ten out of every dozen of the country towns in all the corresponding region. It consisted of thirty or forty dwellings, chiefly of logs; not, however, so immediately in the vicinity of one another as to give any very decided air of regularity and order to their appearance. As usual, in all the interior settlements of the South and West, wherever an eligible situation presented itself, the squatter laid the foundation-logs of his dwelling, and proceeded to its erection. No public squares, and streets laid out by line and rule, marked conventional progress in an orderly and methodical society; but, regarding individual convenience as the only object in arrangements of this nature, they took little note of any other, and to them less important matters. They built where the land rose into a ridge of moderate and gradual elevation, commanding a long reach of prospect; where a good spring threw out its crystal waters, jetting, in winter and summer alike, from the hillside or the rock; or, in its absence, where a fair branch, trickling over a bed of small and yellow pebbles, kept up a perpetually clear and undiminishing current; where the groves were thick and umbrageous; and lastly, but not less important than either, where agues and fevers came not, bringing clouds over the warm sunshine, and taking all the hue, and beauty, and odor from the flower. These considerations were at all times the most important to the settler when the place of his abode was to be determined upon; and, with these advantages at large, the company of squatters, of whom Mark Forrester, made one, by no means the least important among them, had regularly, for the purposes of gold-digging, colonized the little precinct into which we have now ventured to penetrate.

Before we advance farther in our narrative, it may be quite as well to say, that the adventurers of which this wild congregation was made up were impelled to their present common centre by motives and influences as various as the differing features of their several countenances. They came, not only from all parts of the surrounding country, but many of them from all parts of the surrounding world; oddly and confusedly jumbled together; the very *olla-podrida* of moral and mental combination. They were chiefly those to whom the ordinary operations of human trade or labor had proved tedious or unproductive—with whom the toils, aims, and impulses of society were deficient of interest; or, upon whom, an inordinate desire of a sudden to acquire wealth had exercised a sufficiently active influence to impel to the novel employment of gold-finding—or rather gold-*seeking,* for it was not always that the search was successful—the very name of such a pursuit carrying with it to many no small degree of charm and persuasion. To these, a wholesome assortment of other descriptions may be added, of character and caste such as will be found ordinarily to compose everywhere the frontier and outskirts of civilization, as rejected by the wholesome current, and driven, like the refuse and the scum of the waters, in confused stagnation to their banks and margin. Here, alike, came the spendthrift and the indolent, the dreamer and the outlaw, congregating, though guided by contradictory impulses, in the formation of a common caste, and in the pursuit of a like object—some with the view to profit and gain; others simply from no alternative being left them; and that of gold-seeking, with a better sense than their neighbors, being in their own contemplation, truly, a *dernier* resort.

The reader can better conceive than we describe, the sorts of people, passions, and pursuits, herding thus confusedly together, and with these various objects. Others, indeed, came into the society, like the rude but honest woodman to whom we have already afforded an introduction, almost purely from a spirit of adventure, that, growing impatient of the confined boundaries of its birthplace, longs to tread new regions and enjoy new pleasures and employments. A spirit, we may add, the same, or not materially differing from that, which, at an earlier period of human history, though in a condition of society not dissimilar, begot the practices denominated, by a most licentious courtesy, those of chivalry.

But, of whatever stuff the *morale* of this people may have been made up, it is not less certain than natural that the mixture was still incoherent—the parts had not yet grown together. Though ostensibly in the pursuit of the same interest and craft, they had anything but a like fortune, and the degree of concert and harmony which subsisted between them was but shadowy and partial. A mass so heterogeneous in its origin and tendency might not so readily amalgamate. Strife, discontent, and contention, were not unfrequent; and the laborers at the same instrument, mutually depending on each other, not uncommonly came to blows over it. The successes of any one individual—for, as yet, their labors were unregulated by arrangement, and each worked on his own score—procured for him the hate and envy of some of the company, while it aroused the ill-disguised dissatisfaction of all; and nothing was of more common occurrence, than, when striking upon a fruitful and productive section, even among those interested in the discovery, to find it a disputed dominion. Copartners no longer, a division of the spoils, when accumulated, was usually terminated by a resort to blows; and the bold spirit and the strong hand, in this way, not uncommonly acquired the share for which the proprietor was too indolent to toil in the manner of his companions.

The issue of these conflicts, as may be imagined, was sometimes wounds and bloodshed, and occasionally death: the field, we need scarcely add—since this is the history of all usurpation—remaining, in every such case, in possession of the party proving itself most courageous or strong. Nor need this history surprise—it is history, veracious and sober history of a period, still within recollection, and of events of almost recent occurrence. The wild condition of the country—the absence of all civil authority, and almost of laws, certainly of officers sufficiently daring to undertake their honest administration, and shrinking from the risk of incurring, in the performance of their duties, the vengeance of those, who, though disagreeing among themselves, at all times made common cause against the ministers of justice as against a common enemy—may readily account for the frequency and impunity with which these desperate men committed crime and defied its consequences.

But we are now fairly in the centre of the village—a fact of which, in the case of most southern and western villages, it is necessary in so many words to apprize the traveller. In those parts, the scale by which towns are laid out is always magnificent. The founders seem to have calculated usually upon a population of millions; and upon spots and sporting-grounds, measurable by the olympic coursers, and the ancient fields of combat, when scythes and elephants and chariots made the warriors, and the confused cries of a yelping multitude composed the conflict itself. There was no want of room, no risk of narrow streets and pavements, no deficiency of area in the formation of public squares. The houses scattered around the traveller, dotting at long and unfrequent intervals the ragged wood which enveloped them, left few stirring apprehensions of their firing one another. The forest, where the land was not actually built upon, stood up in its primitive simplicity undishonored by the axe.

Such was the condition of the settlement at the period when our hero so unconsciously entered it. It was night, and the lamps of the village were all in full blaze, illuminating with an effect the most picturesque and attractive the fifty paces immediately encircling them. Each dwelling boasted of this auxiliar and attraction; and in this particular but few cities afford so abundantly the materials for a blaze as our country villages. Three or four slight posts are erected at convenient distances from each other in front of the building—a broad scaffold, sufficiently large for the purpose, is placed upon them, on which a thick coat of clay is plastered; at evening, a pile is built upon this, of dry timber and the rich pine which overruns and mainly marks the forests of the south. These piles, in a blaze, serve the nightly strollers of the settlement as guides and beacons, and with their aid Forrester safely wound his way into the little village of Chestatee.

Forming a square in the very centre of the town, a cluster of four huge fabrics, in some sort sustained the pretensions of the settlement to this epithet. This ostentatious collection, some of the members of which appeared placed there rather for show than service, consisted of the courthouse, the jail, the tavern, and the shop of the blacksmith— the two last-mentioned being at all times the very first in course of erection, and the essential nucleus in the formation of the southern and western settlement. The courthouse and the jail, standing directly opposite each other, carried in their faces a family outline of sympathetic and sober gravity. There had been some effect at pretension in their construction, both being cumbrously large, awkward, and unwieldy; and occupying, as they did, the only portion of the village which had been stripped of its forest covering, bore an aspect of mutual and ludicrous wildness and vacancy. They had both been built upon a like plan and equal scale; and the only difference existing between them, but one that was immediately perceptible to the eye, was the superfluous abundance of windows in the former, and their deficiency in the latter. A moral agency had most probably prompted the architect to the distinction here hit upon—and he felt, doubtless, in admitting free access to the light in the house of justice, and in excluding it almost entirely from that of punishment, that he had recognised the proprieties of a most excellent taste and true judgment. These apertures, clumsily wrought in the logs of which the buildings were made, added still more to their generally uncouth appearance. There was yet, however, another marked difference between the courthouse and jail, which we should not omit to notice. The former had the advantage of its neighbor, in being surmounted by a small tower or cupola, in which a bell of moderate size hung suspended, permitted to speak only on such important occasions as the opening of court, sabbath service, and the respective anniversaries of the birthday of Washington and the Declaration of Independence. This building, thus distinguished above its fellows, served also all the purposes of a place of worship, whenever some wandering preacher found his way into the settlement; an occurrence, at the time we write, of very occasional character. To each of the four vast walls of the jail, in a taste certainly not bad, if we consider the design and character of the fabric, but a single window was allotted—that too of the very smallest description for human uses, and crossed at right angles with rude and slender bars of iron, the choicest specimens of workmanship from the neighboring smithy. The distance between each of these four equally important buildings was by no means inconsiderable, if we are required to make the scale for our estimate, that of the cramped and diminished limits accorded to like places in the cities, where men and women appear to increase in due proportion as the field lessens upon which they must encounter in the great struggle for existence. Though neighbors in every substantial respect, the four fabrics were most uncharitably remote, and stood frowning gloomily at one another—scarcely relieved of the cheerless and sombre character of their rough outsides, even when thus brightly illuminated by the glare thrown upon them by the several blazes, flashing out upon the scene from the twin lamps in front of the tavern, through whose wide and unsashed windows an additional lustre, as of many lights, gave warm indications of life and good lodgings within. At a point equidistant from, and forming one of the angles of the same square with each of these, the broader glare from the smith's furnace streamed in bright lines across the plain between, pouring through the unclayed logs of the hovel, in which, at his craft, the industrious proprietor was even then busily employed. Occasionally, the sharp click of his hammer, ringing upon and resounding from the anvil, and a full blast from the capacious bellows, indicated the busy animation, if not the sweet concert, the habitual cheerfulness and charm, of a more civilized and better regulated society.

Nor was the smith, at the moment of our entrance, the only noisy member of the little village. The more pretending establishment to which we are rapidly approaching, threw out its clamors, and the din of many voices gathered upon the breeze in wild and incoherent confusion. Deep bursts of laughter, and the broken stanza of an occasional catch roared out at intervals, promised something of relief to the dull mood; while, as the sounds grew more distinct, the quick ear of Forrester was enabled to distinguish the voices of the several revellers.

"There they are, in full blast," he muttered, "over a gallon of whiskey, and gulping it down as if 'twas nothing better than common water. But, what's the great fuss to-night? There's a crowd, I reckon, and they're a running their rigs on somebody."

Even Forrester was at a loss to account for their excess of hilarity to-night. Though fond of drink, and meeting often in a crowd, they were few of them of a class—using his own phrase—"to give so much tongue over their liquors." The old toper and vagabond is usually a silent drinker. His amusements, when in a circle, and with a bottle before him, are found in cards and dice. His cares, at such a period, are too considerate to suffer him to be noisy. Here, in Chestatee, Forrester well knew that a crowd implied little good-fellowship. The ties which brought the gold-seekers and squatters together were not of a sort to produce cheerfulness and merriment. Their very sports were savage, and implied a sort of fun which commonly gave pain to somebody. He wondered, accordingly, as he listened to yells of laughter, and discordant shouts of hilarity; and he grew curious about the occasion of uproar.

"They're poking fun at some poor devil, that don't quite see what they're after."

A nearer approach soon gave him a clue to the mystery; but all his farther speculations upon it were arrested, by a deep groan from the wounded man, and a writhing movement in the bottom of the wagon, as the wheel rolled over a little pile of stones in the road.

Forrester's humanity checked his curiosity. He stooped to the sufferer, composed his limbs upon the straw, and, as the vehicle, by this time, had approached the tavern, he ordered the wagoner to drive to the rear of the building, that the wounded man might lose, as much as possible, the sounds of clamor which steadily rose from the hall in front. When the wagon stopped, he procured proper help, and, with the tenderest care, assisted to bear our unconscious traveller from the vehicle, into the upper story of the house, where he gave him his own bed, left him in charge of an old negro, and hurried away in search of that most important person of the place, the village-doctor.

CHAPTER SIX

Code and Practice of the Regulators

Forrester was fleet of foot, and the village-doctor not far distant. He was soon procured, and, prompt of practice, the hurts of Ralph Colleton were found to be easily medicable. The wound was slight, the graze of a bullet only, cutting some smaller blood-vessels, and it was only from the loss of blood that insensibility had followed. The moderate skill of our country-surgeon was quite equal to the case, and soon enabled him to put the mind of Mark Forrester, who was honestly and humanely anxious, at perfect rest on the subject of his unknown charge. With the dressing of his wound, and the application of restoratives, the consciousness of the youth returned, and he was enabled to learn how he had been discovered, where he was, and to whom he was indebted for succor in the moment of his insensibility.

Ralph Colleton, of course, declared his gratitude in warm and proper terms; but, as enjoined by the physician, he was discouraged from all unnecessary speech. But he was not denied to listen, and Forrester was communicative, as became his frank face and honest impulses. The brief questions of Ralph obtained copious answers; and, for an hour, the woodman cheered the solitude of his chamber, by the narration of such matters as were most likely to interest his hearer, in respect to the new region where he was, perforce, kept a prisoner. Of Chestatee, and the people thereof, their employment, and the resources of the neighborhood, Forrester gave a pretty correct account; though he

remained prudently silent in regard to the probable parties to that
adventure in which his hearer had received his hurt.

From speaking of these subjects, the transition was natural to the
cause of uproar going on below stairs. The sounds of the hubbub penetrated the chamber of the wounded man, and he expressed some
curiosity in respect to it. This was enough for the woodman, who had
partially informed himself, by a free conversation with the wagoner
who drove the vehicle which brought Ralph to the tavern. He had
caught up other details as he hurried to and fro, when he ran for the
doctor. He was thus prepared to satisfy the youth's inquiry.

"Well, squire, did you ever see a live Yankee?"

The youth smiled, answering affirmatively.

"He's a pedler, you know, and that means a chap what can wheedle
the eyes out of your head, the soul out of your body, the gould out of
your pocket, and give you nothing but brass, and tin, and copper, in the
place of 'em. Well, all the hubbub you hear is jest now about one of
these same Yankee pedlers. The regilators have caught the varmint—
one Jared Bunce, as he calls himself—and a more cunning, rascally, pre-
sumptious critter don't come out of all Connecticut. He's been a
cheating and swindling all the old women round the country. He'll pay
for it now, and no mistake. The regilators caught him about three hours
ago, and they've brought him here for judgment and trial. They've got
a jury setting on his vartues, and they'll hammer the soul out of him
afore they let him git out from under the iron. I don't reckon they kin
cure him, for what's bred in the bone, you know, won't come out of the
flesh; but they'll so bedevil bone and flesh, that I reckon he'll be the last
Yankee that ever comes to practice again in this Chestatee country.
Maybe, he ain't deserving of much worse than they kin do. Maybe, he
ain't a scamp of the biggest wethers. His rascality ain't to be measured.
Why, he kin walk through a man's pockets, jest as the devil goes through
a crack or a keyhole, and the money will naterally stick to him, jest as ef
he was made of gum turpentine. His very face is a sort of kining [coin-
ing] machine. His look says dollars and cents; and its always your dollars and cents, and he kines them out of your hands into his'n, jest with
a roll of his eye, and a mighty leetle turn of his finger. He cheats in
everything, and cheats everybody. Thar's not an old woman in the
country that don't say her prayers back'ards when she thinks of Jared
Bunce. Thar's his tin-wares and his wood-wares—his coffeepots and
kettles, all put together with saft sodder—that jest go to pieces, as ef

they had nothing else to do. And he kin blarney you so—and he's so quick at a mortal lie—and he's got jest a good reason for everything—and he's so sharp at a 'scuse [excuse] that it's onpossible to say where he's gwine to have you, and what you're a gwine to lose, and how you'll get off at last, and in what way he'll cheat you another time. He's been at this business, in these diggings, now about three years. The regilators have swore a hundred times to square off with him; but he's always got off tell now; sometimes by new inventions—sometimes by bible oaths—and last year, by regilarly *cutting dirt* [flight]. He's hardly a chance to git cl'ar now, for the regilators are pretty much up to all his tricks, and he's mighty nigh to ride a rail for a colt, and get new *scores* ag'in old scores, laid on with the smartest hickories in natur.'"

"And who are the regulators?" asked the youth, languidly.

"What! you from Georgy, and never to hear tell of the regilators? Why, that's the very place, I reckon, where the breed begun. The regilators are jest then, you see, our own people. We hain't got much law and justice in these pairts, and when the rascals git too sassy and plentiful, we all turn out, few or many, and make a business of cleaning out the stables. We turn justices, and sheriffs, and lawyers, and settle scores with the growing sinners. We jine, hand in hand, agin such a chap as Jared Bunce, and set in judgment upon his evil-doings. It's a regular court, though we make it up ourselves, and app'ints our own judges and juries, and pass judgment 'cordin' to the case. Ef it's the first offence, or only a small one, we let's the fellow off with only a taste of the hickory. Ef it's a tough case, and an old sinner, we give him a belly-full. Ef the whole country's roused, then Judge Lynch puts on his black cap, and the rascal takes a hard ride on a rail, a duck in the pond, and a perfect seasoning of hickories, tell thar ain't much left of him, or, may be, they don't stop to curry him, but jest halters him at once to the nearest swinging limb."

"Sharp justice! and which of these punishments will they be likely to bestow upon the Yankee?"

"Well, thar's no telling; but I reckon he runs a smart chance of grazing agin the whole on 'em. They've got a long account agin him. In one way or t'other, he's swindled everybody with his notions. Some bought his clocks, which only went while the rogue stayed, and when he went they stopt forever. Some bought ready-made clothes, which went to pieces at the very sight of soap and water. He sold a fusee to old Jerry Seaborn, and warranted the piece, and it bursted into flinders, the very first fire, and tore little Jerry's hand and arm—son of old Jerry—almost to pieces. He'll never have the right use of it agin. And that ain't all. Thar's no counting up his offences."

"Bad as the fellow is, do you think it possible that they will torture him as you describe, or hang him, without law, and a fair trial?"

"Why, Lord love you, ha'n't I told you that he'll have a fair trial, afore the regilators, and thar'll be any number of witnesses, and judges, and sheriffs, and executioners. But, ef you know'd Bunce, you'd know that a fair trial is the very last marcy that he'd aix of Providence. Don't you think now that he'll git anything worse than his righteous desarvings. He's a fellow that's got no more of a saving soul in him than my whip-handle, and ain't half so much to be counted on in a fight. He's jest now nothing but a cheat and a swindle from head to foot; hain't got anything but cheat in him—hain't got room for any principle—not enough either to git drunk with a friend, or have it out, in a fair fight, with his enemy. I shouldn't myself wish to see the fellow's throat cut, but I ain't slow to say that I shall go for his tasting a few hickories, after that a dip in the horse-pond, and then a permit to leave the country by the shortest cut, and without looking behind him, under penalty of having the saft places on his back covered with the petticoats of Lot's wife, that we hear of in the Scriptures."

Ralph Colleton was somewhat oppressed with apathy, and he knew how idle would be any attempt to lessen the hostility of the sturdy woodman, in respect to the wretched class of traders, such as were described in Jared Bunce, by whom the simple and dependent borderers in the South and West, were shockingly imposed upon. He made but a feeble effort accordingly, in this direction, but was somewhat more earnest in insisting upon the general propriety of forbearance, in a practice which militated against law and order, and that justice should be administered only by the proper hands. But to this, Mark Forrester had his ready answer; and, indeed, our young traveller was speaking according to the social standards of a wholly different region.

"There, again, 'squire, you are quite out. The laws, somehow or other, can't touch these fellows. They run through the country a wink faster than the sheriff, and laugh at all the processes you send after them. So, you see, there's no justice, no how, unless you catch a rogue like this, and wind up with him for all the gang—for they're all alike, all of the same family, and it comes to the same thing in the end."

The youth answered languidly. He began to tire, and nature craved repose, and the physician had urged it. Forrester readily perceived that the listener's interest was flagging—nay, he half fancied that much that he had been saying, and in his best style, had fallen upon drowsy senses. Nobody likes to have his best things thrown away, and, as the reader will readily conceive, our friend Forrester had a sneaking consciousness that all the world's eloquence did not cease on the day when Demosthenes died. But he was not the person to be offended because the patient desired to sleep. Far from it. He was only reasonable enough to suppose that this was the properest thing that the wounded man could do. And so he told him; and adjusting carefully the pillows of the youth, and disposing the bedclothes comfortably, and promising to see him again before he slept, our woodman bade him good night, and descended to the great hall of the tavern, where Jared Bunce was held in durance.

The luckless pedler was, in truth, in a situation in which, for the first time in his life, he coveted nothing. The peril was one, also, from which, thus far, his mother-wit, which seldom failed before, could suggest no means of evasion or escape. His prospect was a dreary one; though with the wonderful capacity for endurance, and the surprising cheerfulness, common to the class which he belonged, he beheld it without dismay, though with many apprehensions.

Justice he did not expect, nor, indeed, as Forrester has already told us, did he desire it. He asked for nothing less than justice. He was dragged before judges, all of whom had complaints to prefer, and injuries to redress; and none of whom were over-scrupulous as to the nature or measure of that punishment which was to procure them the desired atonement. The company was not so numerous as noisy. It consisted of some twenty persons, villagers as well as small farmers in the neighborhood, all of whom, having partaken *ad libitum* of the whiskey distributed freely about the table, which, in part, they surrounded, had, in the Indian phrase, more tongues than brains, and were sufficiently aroused by their potations to enter readily into any mischief. Some were smoking with all the industrious perseverance of the Hollander; others shouted forth songs in honor of the bottle, and with all the fervor and ferment of Bacchanalian novitiates; and not a few, congregating about the immediate person of the pedler, assailed his ears with threats sufficiently pregnant with tangible illustration to make him understand and acknowledge, by repeated starts and wincings, the awkward and uncomfortable predicament in which he stood. At length, the various disputants for justice, finding it difficult, if not impossible, severally, to command that attention which they conceived they merited, resolved themselves into something like a committee of the whole, and proceeded to the settlement of their controversy, and the pedler's fate, in a manner more suited to the importance of the occasion. Having procured that attention which was admitted to be the great object, more by the strength of his lungs than his argument, one of the company, who was dignified by the title of colonel, spoke out for the rest.

"I say, boys—'tisn't of any use, I reckon, for everybody to speak about what everybody knows. One speaker's quite enough in this here matter before us, Here's none of us that ha'n't something to say agin this pedler, and the doings of the grand scoundrel in and about these parts, for a matter going on now about three years. Why, everybody knows him, big and little; and his reputation is so now, that the very boys take his name to frighten away the crows with. Now, one person can jist as well make a plain statement as another. I know, of my own score, there's not one of my neighbors for ten miles round, that can't tell all about the rotten prints he put off upon my old woman; and I know myself of all the tricks he's played at odd times, more than a dozen, upon 'Squire Nichols there, and Tom Wescott, and Bob Snipes, and twenty others; and everybody knows them just as well as I. Now, to make up the score, and square off with the pedler, without any flustration, I move you that Lawyer Pippin take the chair, and judge in this matter; for the day has come for settling off accounts, and I don't see why we shouldn't be the regulators for Bunce, seeing that everybody agrees that he's a rogue, and a pestilence, and desarves regilation."

This speech was highly applauded, and chimed in admirably with all prejudices, and the voice that called Lawyer Pippin to preside over the deliberations of the assembly was unanimous. The gentleman thus highly distinguished, was a dapper and rather portly little personage, with sharp twinkling eyes, a ruby and remarkable nose, a double chin, retreating forehead, and corpulent cheek. He wore green glasses of a dark, and a green coat of a light, complexion. The lawyer was the only member of the profession living in the village, had no competitor save when the sitting of the court brought in one or more from neighboring settlements, and, being thus circumstanced, without opposition, and the only representative of his craft, he was literally, to employ the slang phrase in that quarter, the "cock of the walk." He was, however, not so much regarded by the villagers a worthy as a clever man. It required not erudition to win the credit of profundity, and the lawyer knew how to make the most of his learning among those who had none. Like many other gentlemen of erudition, he was grave to a proverb when the occasion required it, and would not be seen to laugh out of the prescribed place, though "Nestor swore the jest was laughable." He relied greatly on saws and sayings—could quote you the paradoxes of Johnson and the infidelities of Hume without always understanding them, and mistook, as men of that kind and calibre are very apt to do, the capacity to repeat the grave absurdities of others as a proof of something in himself. His business was not large, however, and among the arts of his profession, and as a means for supplying the absence of more legitimate occasions for its employment, he was reputed as excessively expert in making the most of any difficulty among his neighbors. The egg of mischief and controversy was hardly laid, before the worthy lawyer, with maternal care, came clucking about it; he watched and warmed it without remission; and when fairly hatched, he took care that the whole brood should be brought safely into court, his voice, and words, and actions, fully attesting the deep interest in their fortunes which he had manifested from the beginning. Many a secret slander, ripening at length into open warfare, had been traced to his friendly influence, either *ab ovo,* or at least from the perilous period in such cases when the very existence of the embryo relies upon the friendly breath, the sustaining warmth, and the occasional stimulant. Lawyer Pippin, among his neighbors, was just the man for such achievements, and they gave him, with a degree of shrewdness common to them as a people, less qualified credit for the capacity which he at all times exhibited in bringing a case into, than in carrying it out of court. But this opinion in nowise affected the lawyer's own estimate of his pretensions. Next to being excessively mean, he was excessively vain, and so highly did he regard his own opinions, that he was never content until he heard himself busily employed in their utterance. An opportunity for a speech, such as the present, was not suffered to pass without due regard; but as we propose that he shall exhibit himself in the most happy manner at a later period in our narrative, we shall abridge, in few, the long string of queerly-associated words in the form of a speech, which, on assuming the chair thus assigned him, he poured forth upon the assembly. After a long prefatory, apologetic, and deprecatory exordium, in which his own demerits, as is usual with small speakers, were strenuously urged; and after he had exhausted most of the commonplaces about the purity of the ermine upon the robes of justice, and the golden scales, and the unshrinking balance, and the unsparing and certain sword, he went on thus:—

"And now, my friends, if I rightly understand the responsibility and obligations of the station thus kindly conferred upon me, I am required to arraign the pedler, Jared Bunce, before you, on behalf of the country, which country, as the clerk reads it, you undoubtedly are; and here let me remark, my friends, the excellent and nice distinction which this phrase makes between the man and the soil, between the noble intellect and the high soul, and the mere dirt and dust upon which we daily tread. This very phrase, my friends, is a fine embodiment of that democratic principle upon which the glorious constitution is erected. But, as I was saying, my friends, I am required to arraign before you this same pedler, Jared Bunce, on sundry charges of misdemeanor, and swindling, and fraud—in short, as I understand it, for endeavoring, without having the fear of God and good breeding in his eyes, to pass himself off upon the good people of this county as an honest man. Is this the charge, my friends?"

"Ay, ay, lawyer, that's the how, that's the very thing itself. Put it to the skunk, let him deny that if he can—let him deny that his name is Jared Bunce—that he hails from Connecticut—that he is a shark, and a pirate, and a pestilence. Let him deny that he is a cheat—that he goes about with his notions and other rogueries—that he doesn't manufacture maple-seeds, and hickory nutmegs, and ground coffee made out of rotten rye. Answer to that, Jared Bunce, you white-livered lizard."

Thus did one of his accusers take up the thread of the discourse as concluded in part by the chairman. Another and another followed with like speeches in the most rapid succession, until all was again confusion; and the voice of the lawyer, after a hundred ineffectual efforts at a hearing, degenerated into a fine squeak, and terminated at last in a violent fit of coughing, that fortunately succeeded in producing the degree of quiet around him to secure which his language had, singularly enough, entirely failed. For a moment the company ceased its clamor, out of respect to the chairman's cough; and, having cleared his throat with the contents of a tumbler of Monongahela which seemed to stand permanently full by his side, he recommenced the proceedings; the offender, in the meantime, standing mute and motionless, now almost stupified with terror, conscious of repeated offences, knowing perfectly the reckless spirit of those who judged him, and hopeless of escape from their hands, without, in the country phrase, the loss at least of "wing and tail feathers." The chairman with due gravity began:—

"Jared Bunce—is that your name?"

"Why, lawyer, I can't deny that I have gone by that name, and I guess it's the right name for me to go by, seeing that I was christened Jared, after old Uncle Jared Withers, that lives down at Dedham, in the state of Massachusetts. He did promise to do something for me, seeing I was named after him, but he ha'n't done nothing yet, no how. Then the name of Bunce, you see, lawyer, I got from my father, his name being Bunce, too, I guess."

"Well, Jared Bunce, answer to the point, and without circumlocution. You have heard some of the charges against you. Having taken them down in short-hand, I will repeat them."

The pedler approached a few steps, advanced one leg, raised a hand to his ear, and put on all the external signs of devout attention, as the chairman proceeded in the long and curious array.

"First, then, it is charged against you, Bunce, by young Dick Jenkins, that stands over in front of you there, that somewhere between the fifteenth and twenty-third of June—last June was a year—you came by night to his plantation, he living at that time in De Kalb county; that you stopped the night with him, without charge, and in the morning you traded a clock to his wife for fifteen dollars, and that you had not been gone two days, before the said clock began to go whiz, whiz, whiz, and commenced striking, whizzing all the while, and never stopped till it had struck clear thirty-one, and since that time it will neither whiz, nor strike, nor do nothing."

"Why, lawyer, I ain't the man to deny the truth of this transaction, you see; but, then, you must know, much depends upon the way you manage a clock. A clock is quite a delicate and ticklish article of manufacture, you see, and it ain't everybody that can make a clock, or can make it go when it don't want to; and if a man takes a hammer or a horsewhip, or any other unnatural weapon to it, as if it was a house or a horse, why, I guess, it's not reasonable to expect it to keep in order, and it's no use in having a clock no how, if you don't treat it well. As for its striking thirty-one, that indeed is something remarkable, for I never heard one of mine strike more than twelve, and that's zactly the number they're regulated to strike. But, after all, lawyer, I don't see that Squire Jenkins has been much a loser by the trade, seeing that he paid me in bills of the Hogee-nogee bank, and that stopped payment about the time, and before I could get the bills changed. It's true, I didn't let on that I knowed anything about it, and got rid of the paper a little while before the thing went through the country."

"Now, look ye, you gingerbread-bodied Yankee—I'd like to know what you mean about taking whip and hammer to the clock. If you mean to say that I ever did such a thing, I'll lick you now, by the eternal scratch!"

"Order, order, Mr. Jenkins—order! The chair must be respected. You must come to order, Mr. Jenkins—" was the vociferous and urgent cry of the chairman, repeated by half a dozen voices; the pedler, in the meanwhile, half doubting the efficacy of the call, retreating with no little terror behind the chair of the dignified personage who presided.

"Well, you needn't make such a howling about it," said Jenkins, wrathfully, and looking around him with the sullen ferocity of a chafed bear. "I know jist as well how to keep order, I reckon, as any on you; but I don't see how it will be out of order to lick a Yankee, or who can hinder me, if I choose it."

"Well, don't look at me, Dick Jenkins, with such a look, or I'll have a finger in that pie, old fellow. I'm no Yankee to be frightened by sich a lank-sided fellow as you; and, by dogs, if nobody else can keep you in order, I'm jist the man to try if I can't. So don't put on any shines, old boy, or I'll darken your peepers, if I don't come very nigh plucking them out altogether."

So spake another of the company, who, having been much delectified with the trial, had been particularly solicitous in his cries for order. Jenkins was not indisposed to the affray, and made an angry retort, which provoked another still more angry; but other parties interfering, the new difficulty was made to give place to that already in hand. The imputation upon Jenkins, that his ignorance of the claims of the clock to gentle treatment, alone, had induced it to speak thirty-one times, and at length refuse to speak at all, had touched his pride; and, sorely vexed, he retired upon a glass of whiskey to the farther corner of the room, and with his pipe, nursing the fumes of his wrath, he waited impatiently the signal for the wild mischief which he knew would come.

In the meanwhile, the examination of the culprit proceeded; but, as we can not hope to convey to the reader a description of the affair as it happened, to the life, we shall content ourselves with a brief summary. The chair went on rapidly enumerating the sundry misdeeds of the Yankee, demanding, and in most cases receiving, rapid and unhesitating replies—evasively and adroitly framed, for the offender well knew that a single unlucky word or phrase would bring down upon his shoulders a wilderness of blows.

"You are again charged, Bunce, with having sold to Colonel Blundell a coffee-pot and two tin cups, all of which went to pieces—the solder melting off at the very sight of the hot water."

"Well, lawyer, it stands to reason I can't answer for that. The tin wares I sell stand well enough in a northern climate: there may be some difference in yours that I can't account for; and I guess, pretty much, there is. Now, your people are a mighty hot-tempered people, and take a fight for breakfast, and make three meals a day out of it: now, we in the north have no stomach for such fare; so here, now, as far as I can see, your climate takes pretty much after the people, and if so, it's no wonder that solder can't stand it. Who knows, again, but you boil your water quite too hot? Now, I guess, there's jest as much harm in boiling water too hot, as in not boiling it hot enough. Who knows? All I can say is, that the lot of wares I bring to this market next season shall be calkilated on purpose to suit the climate."

The chairman seemed struck with this view of the case, and spoke with a gravity corresponding with the deep sagacity he conceived himself to have exhibited.

"There does seem to be something in this; and it stands to reason, what will do for a nation of pedlers won't do for us. Why, when I recollect that they are buried in snows half the year, and living on nothing else the other half, I wonder how they get the water to boil at all. Answer that, Bunce."

"Well, lawyer, I guess you must have travelled pretty considerable down east in your time and among my people, for you do seem to know all about the matter jest as well and something better than myself."

The lawyer, not a little flattered by the compliment so slyly and evasively put in, responded to the remark with a due regard to his own increase of importance.

"I am not ignorant of your country, pedler, and of the ways of its people; but it is not me that you are to satisfy. Answer to the gentlemen around, if it is not a difficult matter for you to get water to boil at all during the winter months."

"Why, to say the truth, lawyer, when coal is scarce and high in the market, heat is very hard to come. Now, I guess the ware I brought out last season was made under those circumstances; but I have a lot on hand now, which will be here in a day or two, which I should like to trade to the colonel, and I guess I may venture to say, all the hot water in the country won't melt the solder off."

"I tell you what, pedler, we are more likely to put you in hot water than try any more of your ware in that way. But where's your plunder?—let us see this fine lot of notions you speak of"—was the speech of the colonel already so much referred to, and whose coffee-pot bottom furnished so broad a foundation for the trial. He was a wild and roving person, to whom the tavern, and the racecourse, and the cockpit, from his very boyhood up, had been as the breath of life, and with whom the chance of mischief was never willingly foregone. But the pedler was wary, and knew his man. The lurking smile and sneer of the speaker had enough in them for the purposes of warning, and he replied evasively:—

"Well, colonel, you shall see them by next Tuesday or Wednesday. I should be glad to have a trade with you—the money's no object—and if you have furs, or skins, or anything that you like to get off your hands, there's no difficulty, that I can see, to a long bargain."

"But why not trade now, Bunce?—what's to hinder us now? I sha'n't be in the village after Monday."

"Well, then, colonel, that'll just suit me, for I did calkilate to call on you at the farm, on my way into the nation where I'm going looking out for furs."

"Yes, and live on the best for a week, under some pretence that your nag is sick, or you sick, or something in the way of a start—then go off, cheat, and laugh at me in the bargain. I reckon, old boy, you don't come over me in that way again; and I'm not half done with you yet about the kettles. That story of yours about the hot and cold may do for the pigeons, but you don't think the hawks will swallow it, do ye? Come—out with your notions!"

"Oh, to be sure, only give a body time, colonel," as, pulled by the collar, with some confusion and in great trepidation, responded the beleaguered dealer in clocks and calicoes—"they shall all be here in a day or two at most. Seeing that one of my creatures was foundered, I had to leave the goods, and drive the other here without them."

The pedler had told the truth in part only. One of his horses had indeed struck lame, but he had made out to bring him to the village with all his wares; and this fact, as in those regions of question and inquiry was most likely to be the case, had already taken wind.

"Now, look ye, Bunce, do you take me for a blear-eyed mole, that never seed the light of a man's eyes?" inquired Blundell, closely approaching the beset tradesman, and taking him leisurely by the neck. "Do you want to take a summerset through that window, old fellow, that you try to stuff us with such tough stories? If you do, I *rether* reckon you can do it without much difficulty." Thus speaking, and turning to some of those around him, he gave directions which imparted to the limbs of the pedler a continuous and crazy motion, that made his teeth chatter.

"Hark ye, boys, jist step out, and bring in the cart of Jared Bunce, wheels and all, if so be that the body won't come off easily. We'll see for ourselves."

It was now the pedler's turn for speech; and, forgetting the precise predicament in which he personally stood, and only solicitous to save his chattels from the fate which he plainly saw awaited them, his expostulations and entreaties were rapid and energetic.

"Now, colonel—gentlemen—my good friends—to-morrow or the next day you shall see them all—I'll go with you to your plantation—"

"No, thank ye. I want none of your company—and, look ye, if you know when you're well off, don't undertake to call me your friend. I say, Mr. Chairman, if it's in order—I don't want to do anything disorderly—I move that Bunce's cart be moved here into this very room, that we may see for ourselves the sort of substance he brings here to put off upon us."

The chairman had long since seemingly given up all hope of exercising, in their true spirit, the duties of the station which he held. For a while, it is true, he battled with no little energy for the integrity of his dignity, with good lungs and a stout spirit; but, though fully a match in these respects for any one, or perhaps any two of his competitors, he found the task of contending with the dozen rather less easy, and, in a little while, his speeches, into which he had lugged many a choice *ad captandum* of undisputed effect on any other occasion, having been completely merged and mingled with those of the mass, he wisely forbore any further waste of matter, in the stump-oratory of the South usually so precious; and, drawing himself up proudly and profoundly in his high place, he remained dignifiedly sullen, until the special reference thus made by Colonel Blundell again opened the fountains of the oracle and set them flowing.

The lawyer, thus appealed to, in a long tirade, and in his happiest manner, delivered his opinion in the premises, and in favor of the measure. How, indeed, could he do otherwise, and continue that tenacious pursuit of his own interests which had always been the primary aim and object, as well of the profession as the person. He at once sagaciously beheld the embryo lawsuit and contingent controversy about to result from the proposition; and, in his mind, with a far and free vision, began to compute the costs and canvass the various terms and prolonged trials of county court litigation. He saw fee after fee thrust into his hands—he beheld the opposing parties desirous to conciliate, and extending to him sundry of those equivocal courtesies, which, though they take not the shape of money are money's worth, and the worthy chairman had no scruples as to the propriety of the measure. The profits and pay once adjusted to his satisfaction, his spirit took a broad sweep, and the province of human fame, circumscribed, it is true, within the ten mile circuit of his horizon, was at once open before him. He beheld the strife, and enjoyed the triumph over his fellow-laborers at the bar—he already heard the applauses of his neighbors at this or that fine speech or sentiment; and his form grew insensibly erect, and his eye glistened proudly, as he freely and fully assented to the measure which promised such an abundant harvest. Vainly did the despairing and dispirited pedler implore a different judgment; the huge box which capped the body of his travelling vehicle, torn from its axle, without any show of reverential respect for screw or fastening, was borne in a moment through the capacious entrance of the hall, and placed conspicuously upon the table.

"The key, Bunce, the key!" was the demand of a dozen.

The pedler hesitated for a second, and the pause was fatal. Before he could redeem his error, a blow from a hatchet settled the difficulty, by distributing the fine deal-box cover, lock and hinges, in fragments over the apartment. The revelation of wares and fabrics—a strange admixture, with propriety designated "notions"—brought all eyes immediately around, and rendered a new order, for common convenience, necessary in the arrangement of the company. The chairman, chair and man, were in a moment raised to a corresponding elevation upon the table, over the collection; and the controversy and clamor, from concentrating, as it did before, upon the person of the pedler, were now transferred to the commodities he brought for sale. Order having been at length obtained, Colonel Blundell undertook the assertion of his own and the wrongs of his fellow-sufferers, and kept uninterrupted possession of the floor.

"And now, Mr. Chairman, I will jist go a little into the particulars of the rogueries and rascalities of this same Yankee. Now, in the first place, he is a Yankee, and that's enough, itself, to bring him to punishment—but we'll let that pass, and go to his other transactions—for, as I reckon, it's quite punishment enough for that offence, to be jist what he is. He has traded rotten stuffs about the country, that went to pieces the first washing. He has traded calico prints, warranted for fast colors, that ran faster than he ever ran himself. He has sold us tin stuffs, that didn't stand hot water at all; and then thinks to get off, by saying they were not made for our climate. And let me ask, Mr. Chairman, if they wasn't made for our climate, why did he bring 'em here? let him come to the scratch, and answer that, neighbors—but he can't. Well, then, as you've all hearn, he has traded clocks to us at money's worth, that one day ran faster than a Virginny race-mare, and at the very next day, would strike lame, and wouldn't go at all, neither for beating nor coaxing—and besides all these doings, neighbors, if these an't quite enough to carry a skunk to the horsepond, he has committed his abominations without number, all through the country high and low—for hain't he lied and cheated, and then had the mean cowardice to keep out of the way of the *regilators,* who have been on the look-out for his tracks for the last half year? Now, if these things an't *desarving* of punishment, there's nobody fit to be hung—there's nobody that ought to be whipped. Hickories oughtn't to grow any longer, and the best thing the governor can do would be to have all the jails burnt down from one eend of the country to the other. The proof stands up agin Bunce, and there's no denying it; and it's no use, no how, to let this fellow come among us, year after year, to play the same old hand, take our money for his rascally goods, then go away and laugh at us. And the question before us is jist what I have said, and what shall we do with the critter? To show you that it's high time to do something in the matter, look at this calico print, that looks to be sure, very well to the eye, except, as you see, here's a tree with red leaves and yellow flowers—a most ridiculous notion, indeed, for who ever seed a tree with sich colors here, in the very beginning of summer?"

Here the pedler, for the moment, more solicitous for the credit of the manufactures than for his own safety, ventured to suggest that the print was a mere fancy, a matter of taste—in fact, a notion, and not therefore to be judged by the standard which had been brought to decide upon its merits. He did not venture, however, to say what, perhaps, would have been the true horn of the difficulty, that the print was an autumn or winter illustration, for that might have subjected him to condign punishment for its unseasonableness. As it was, the defence set up was to the full as unlucky as any other might have been.

"I'll tell you what, Master Bunce, it won't do to take natur in vain.

If you can show me a better painter than natur, from your pairts, I give up; but until that time, I say that any man who thinks to give the woods a different sort of face from what God give 'em, ought to be licked for his impudence if nothing else."

The pedler ventured again to expostulate; but the argument having been considered conclusive against him, he was made to hold his peace, while the prosecutor proceeded.

"Now then, Mr. Chairman, as I was saying—here is a sample of the kind of stuff he thinks to impose upon us. Look now at this here article, and I reckon it's jist as good as any of the rest, and say whether a little touch of Lynch's law, an't the very thing for the Yankee!"

Holding up the devoted calico to the gaze of the assembly, with a single effort of his strong and widely-distended arms, he rent it asunder with little difficulty, the sweep not terminating, until the stuff, which, by-the-way, resigned itself without struggle or resistance to its fate, had been most completely and evenly divided. The poor pedler in vain endeavored to stay a ravage that, once begun, became epidemical. He struggled and strove with tenacious hand, holding on to sundry of his choicest bales, and claiming protection from the chair, until warned of his imprudent zeal in behalf of goods so little deserving of the risk, by the sharp and sudden application of an unknown hand to his ears which sent him reeling against the table, and persuaded him into as great a degree of patience, as, under existing circumstances, he could be well expected to exhibit. Article after article underwent a like analysis of its strength and texture, and a warm emulation took place among the rioters, as to their several capacities in the work of destruction. The shining bottoms were torn from the tin-wares in order to prove that such a separation was possible, and it is doing but brief justice to the pedler to say, that, whatever, in fact, might have been the true character of his commodities, the very choicest of human fabrics could never have resisted the various tests of bone and sinew, tooth and nail, to which they were indiscriminately subjected. Immeasurable was the confusion that followed. All restraints were removed—all hindrances withdrawn, and the tide rushed onward with a most headlong tendency.

Apprehensive of pecuniary responsibilities in his own person, and having his neighbors wrought to the desired pitch—fearing, also, lest his station might somewhat involve himself in the meshes he was weaving around others, the sagacious chairman, upon the first show of violence, roared out his resignation, and descended from his place. But this movement did not impair the industry of the *regulators*. A voice was heard proposing a bonfire of the merchandise, and no second suggestion was necessary. All hands but those of the pedler and the attorney were employed in building the pyre in front of the tavern some thirty yards; and here, in choice confusion, lay flaming calicoes, illegitimate silks, worsted hose, wooden clocks and nutmegs, maplewood seeds of all descriptions, plaid cloaks, scents, and spices, jumbled up in ludicrous variety. A dozen hands busied themselves in applying the torch to the devoted mass—howling over it, at every successive burst of flame that went up into the dark atmosphere, a savage yell of triumph that tallied well with the proceeding.

"Hurrah!"

The scene was one of indescribable confusion. The rioters danced about the blaze like so many frenzied demons. Strange, no one attempted to appropriate the property that must have been a temptation to all.

Our pedler, though he no longer strove to interfere, was by no means insensible to the ruin of his stock in trade. It was calculated to move to pity, in any other region, to behold him as he stood in the doorway, stupidly watching the scene, while the big tears were slowly gathering in his eyes, and falling down his bronzed and furrowed cheeks. The rough, hard, unscrupulous man can always weep for himself. Whatever the demerits of the rogue, our young traveller above stairs, would have regarded him as the victim of a too sharp justice. Not so the participators in the outrage. They had been too frequently the losers by the cunning practice of the pedler, to doubt for a moment the perfect propriety—nay, the very moderate measure—of that wild justice which they were dealing out to his misdeeds. And with this even, they were not satisfied. As the perishable calicoes roared up and went down in the flames, as the pans and pots and cups melted away in the furnace heat, and the painted faces of the wooden clocks, glared out like those of John Rogers at the stake, enveloped in fire, the cries of the crowd were mingled in with a rude, wild chorus, in which the pedler was made to understand that he stood himself in a peril almost as great as his consuming chattels. It was the famous ballad of the *regulators* that he heard, and it smote his heart with a consciousness of his personal danger that made him shiver in his shoes. The uncouth doggrel, recited in a lilting sort of measure, the peculiar and various pleasures of a canter upon a pine rail. It was clear that the mob were by no means satisfied

with the small measure of sport which they had enjoyed. A single verse
of this savage ditty will suffice for the present, rolled out upon the air,
from fifty voices, the very boys and negroes joining in the chorus, and
making it tell terribly to the senses of the threatened person. First one
voice would warble

"Did you ever, ever, ever!"—

and there was a brief pause, at the end of which the crowd joined in
with unanimous burst and tremendous force of lungs:—

"Did you ever, ever, ever, in your life ride a rail?
    Such a deal of pleasure's in it, that you never can refuse:
You are mounted on strong shoulders, that'll never, never fail,
    Though you pray'd with tongue of sinner, just to plant you
where they choose.
Though the brier patch is nigh you, looking up with thorny faces,
    They never wait to see how you like the situation,
But down you go a rolling, through the penetrating places,
    Nor scramble out until you give the cry of approbation.
Oh! pleasant is the riding, highly-seated on the rail,
    And worthy of the wooden horse, the rascal that we ride:
Let us see the mighty shoulders that will never, never fail,
    To lift him high, and plant him, on the crooked rail astride.
            The seven-sided pine rail, the pleasant bed of briar,
            The little touch of hickory law, with a dipping in the
            mire.
"Did you ever, ever, ever," &c.,

from the troupe in full blast!

The lawyer Pippin suddenly stood beside the despairing pedler, as
this ominous ditty was poured upon the night-winds.

"Do you hear that song, Bunce?" he asked. "How do you like the
music?"

The pedler looked in his face with a mixed expression of grief,
anger, and stupidity, but he said nothing.

"Hark ye, Bunce," continued the lawyer. "Do you know what that
means? Does your brain take in its meaning, my friend?"

"Friend, indeed!" was the very natural exclamation of the pedler as
he shrank from the hand of the lawyer, which had been affectionately
laid upon his shoulder. "Friend, indeed! I say, Lawyer Pippin, if it hadn't
been for you, I'd never ha' been in this fix. I'm ruined by you."

"Ruined by me! Pshaw, Bunce, you are a fool. I was your friend all the time."

"Oh, yes! I can see how. But though you did stop, when they began, yet you did enough to set them on. That was like a good lawyer, I guess, but not so much like a friend. Had you been a friend, you could have saved my property from the beginning."

"Nay, nay, Bunce; you do me wrong. They had sworn against you long ago, and you know them well enough. The devil himself couldn't stop 'em when once upon the track. But don't be down in the mouth. I can save you now."

"Save me!"

"Ay! don't you hear? They're singing the regulation song. Once that blaze goes down, they'll be after you. It's a wonder they've left you here so long. Now's your time. You must be off. Fly by the back door, and leave it to me to get damages for your loss of property."

"You, lawyer? well, I should like to know how you calkilate to do that?"

"I'll tell you. You know my profession."

"I guess I do, pretty much."

"Thus, then—most of these are men of substance; at least they have enough to turn out a pretty good case each of them—now all you have to do is to bring suit. I'll do all that, you know, the same as if you did it yourself. You must lay your damages handsomely, furnish a few affidavits, put the business entirely in my hands, and—how much is the value of your goods?"

"Well, I guess they might be worth something over three hundred and twenty dollars and six shillings, York money."

"Well, give me all the particulars, and I venture to assure you that I can get five hundred dollars damages at least, and perhaps a thousand. But of this we can talk more at leisure when you are in safety. Where's your cart, Bunce?"

"On t'other side of the house—what they've left on it."

"Now, then, while they're busy over the blaze, put your tackle on, hitch your horse, and take the back track to my clearing; it's but a short mile and a quarter, and you'll be there in no time. I'll follow in a little while, and we'll arrange the matter."

"Well, now, lawyer, but I can't—my horse, as you see, having over eat himself, is struck with the founders and can't budge. I put him in

'Squire Dickens' stable, 'long with his animals, and seeing that he hadn't had much the day before, I emptied the corn from their troughs into his, and jest see what's come of it. I hadn't ought to done so, to be sure."

"That's bad, but that must not stop you. Your life, Bunce, is in danger, and I have too much regard for you to let you risk it by longer stay here. Take my nag, there—the second one from the tree, and put him in the gears in place of your own. He's as gentle as a spaniel, and goes like a deer. You know the back track to my house, and I'll come after you, and bring your creature along. I 'spose he's not so stiff but he can bring me."

"He can do that, lawyer, I guess, without difficulty. I'll move as you say, and be off pretty slick. Five hundred dollars damage, lawyer—eh!"

"No matter, till I see you. Put your nag in gears quickly—you have little time to spare!"

The pedler proceeded to the work, and was in a little while ready for a start. But he lingered at the porch.

"I say, lawyer, it's a hard bout they've given me this time. I did fear they would be rash and obstropulous, but didn't think they'd gone so far. Indeed, its clear, if it hadn't been that the cretur failed me, I should not have trusted myself in the place, after what I was told."

"Bunce, you have been rather sly in your dealings, and they have a good deal to complain of. Now, though I said nothing about it, that coat you sold me for a black grew red with a week's wear, and threadbare in a month."

"Now, don't talk, lawyer, seeing you ha'n't paid me for it yet; but that's neither here nor there. If I did, as you say, sell my goods for something more than their vally, I hadn't ought to had such a punishment as this."

The wild song of the rioters rang in his ears, followed by a proposition, seemingly made with the utmost gravity, to change the plan of operations, and instead of giving him the ride upon the rail, cap the blazing goods of his cart with the proper person of the proprietor. The pedler lingered to hear no further; and the quick ear of the lawyer, as he returned into the hall, distinguished the rumbling motion of his cart hurrying down the road. But he had scarcely reseated himself and resumed his glass, before Bunce also reappeared.

"Why, man, I thought you were off. You burn daylight; though they do say, those whom water won't drown, rope must hang."

"There is some risk, lawyer, to be sure; but when I recollected this box, which you see is a fine one, though they have disfigured it, I thought I should have time enough to take it with me, and anything that might be lying about;" looking around the apartment as he spoke, and gathering up a few fragments which had escaped the general notice.

"Begone, fool!" exclaimed the lawyer, impatiently. "They are upon you—they come—fly for your life, you dog—I hear their voices."

"I'm off, lawyer"—and looking once behind him as he hurried off, the pedler passed from the rear of the building as those who sought him re-entered in front.

"The blood's in him—the Yankee will be Yankee still," was the muttered speech of the lawyer, as he prepared to encounter the returning rioters.

CHAPTER SEVEN

The Yankee Outwits the Lawyer

It was at this moment that Forrester entered the tavern-hall, curious to know the result of the trial, from which his attendance upon Ralph had unavoidably detained him. The actors of the drama were in better humor than before, and uproarious mirth had succeeded to ferocity. They were all in the very excess of self-glorification; for, though somewhat disappointed of their design, and defrauded of the catastrophe, they had nevertheless done much, according to their own judgment, and enough, perhaps, in that of the reader, for the purposes of justice. The work of mischief had been fully consummated; and though, to their notion, still somewhat incomplete from the escape of the pedler himself, they were in great part satisfied—some few among them, indeed—and among these our quondam friend Forrester may be included—were not sorry that Bunce had escaped the application of the personal tests which had been contemplated for his benefit; for, however willing, it was somewhat doubtful whether they could have been altogether able to save him from the hands of those having a less scrupulous regard to humanity.

The sudden appearance of Forrester revived the spirit of the transaction, now beginning somewhat to decline, as several voices undertook to give him an account of its progress. The lawyer was in his happiest mood, as things, so far, had all turned out as he expected. His voice was loudest, and his oratory more decidedly effective than ever.

The prospect before him was also of so seductive a character, that he yielded more than was his wont to the influences of the bottle-god; who stood before him in the shape of the little negro, who served forth the whiskey, in compliance with the popular appetite, from a little iron-hooped keg, perched upon a shelf conveniently in the corner.

"Here Cuffee, you thrice-blackened baby of Beelzebub!—why stand you there, arms akimbo, and showing your ivories, when you see we have no whiskey! Bring in the jug, you imp of darkness—touch us the Monongahela, and a fresh tumbler for Mr. Forrester—and, look you, one too for Col. Blundell, seeing he's demolished the other. Quick, you terrapin!"

Cuffee recovered himself in an instant. His hands fell to his sides—his mouth closed intuitively; and the whites of his eyes changing their fixed direction, marshalled his way with a fresh jug, containing two or more quarts, to the rapacious lawyer.

"Ah, you blackguard, that will do—now, Mr. Forrester—now, Col. Blundell—don't be slow—no backing out, boys—hey, for a long drink to the stock in trade of our friend the pedler."

So spoke Pippin; a wild huzza attested the good humor which the proposition excited. Potation rapidly followed potation, and the jug again demanded replenishing. The company was well drilled in this species of exercise; and each individual claiming caste in such circle, must be well prepared, like the knight-challenger of old tourney, to defy all comers. In the cases of Pippin and Blundell, successive draughts, after the attainment of a certain degree of mental and animal stolidity, seemed rather to fortify than to weaken their defences, and to fit them more perfectly for a due prolongation of the warfare. The appetite, too, like most appetites, growing from what it fed on, ventured few idle expostulations; glass after glass, in rapid succession, fully attested the claim of these two champions to the renown which such exercises in that section of the world had won for them respectively. The subject of conversation, which, in all this time, accompanied their other indulgences, was, very naturally, that of the pedler and his punishment. On this topic, however, a professional not less than personal policy sealed the lips of our lawyer except on those points which admitted of a general remark, without application or even meaning. Though drunk, his policy was that of the courts; and the practice of the sessions had served him well, in his own person, to give the lie to the *"in vino veritas"* of the proverb.

Things were in this condition when the company found increase in the person of the landlord, who now made his appearance; and, as we intend that he shall be no unimportant auxiliar in the action of our story, it may be prudent for a few moments to dwell upon the details of his outward man, and severally to describe his features. We have him before us in that large, dark, and somewhat heavy person, who sidles awkwardly into the apartment, as if only conscious in part of the true uses of his legs and arms. He leans at this moment over the shoulders of one of the company, and, while whispering in his ears, at the same time, with an upward glance, surveys the whole. His lowering eyes, almost shut in and partially concealed by his scowling and bushy eyebrows, are of a quick gray, stern, and penetrating in their general expression, yet, when narrowly observed, putting on an air of vacancy, if not stupidity, that furnishes a perfect blind to the lurking meaning within. His nose is large, yet not disproportionately so; his head well made, though a phrenologist might object to a strong animal preponderance in the rear; his mouth bold and finely curved, is rigid however in its compression, and the lips, at times almost woven together, are largely indicative of ferocity; they are pale in color, and dingily so, yet his flushed cheek and brow bear striking evidence of a something too frequent revel; his hair, thin and scattered, is of a dark brown complexion and sprinkled with gray; his neck is so very short that a single black handkerchief, wrapped loosely about it, removes all seeming distinction between itself and the adjoining shoulders—the latter being round and uprising, forming a socket, into which the former appears to fall as into a designated place. As if more effectually to complete the unfavorable impression of such an outline, an ugly scar, partly across the cheek, and slightly impairing the integrity of the left nostril, gives to his whole look a sinister expression, calculated to defeat entirely any neutralizing or less objectionable feature. His form—to conclude the picture—is constructed with singular power; and though not symmetrical, is far from ungainly. When impelled by some stirring motive, his carriage is easy, without seeming effort, and his huge frame throws aside the sluggishness which at other times invests it, putting on a habit of animated exercise, which changes the entire appearance of the man.

Such was Walter, or, as he was there more familiarly termed, Wat Munro. He took his seat with the company, with the ease of one who neither doubted nor deliberated upon the footing which he claimed among them. He was not merely the publican of his profession, but better fitted

indeed for perhaps any other avocation, as may possibly be discovered in
the progress of our narrative. To his wife, a good quiet sort of body, who,
as Forrester phrased it, did not dare to say the soul was her own, he
deputed the whole domestic management of the tavern; while he would
be gone, nobody could say where or why, for weeks and more at a time,
away from bar and hostel, in different portions of the country. None
ventured to inquire into a matter that was still sufficiently mysterious to
arouse curiosity; people living with and about him generally entertaining a degree of respect, amounting almost to vulgar awe, for his person
and presence, which prevented much inquiry into his doings. Some few,
however, more bold than the rest, spoke in terms of suspicion; but the
number of this class was inconsiderable, and they themselves felt that the
risk which they incurred was not so unimportant as to permit of their
going much out of the way to trace the doubtful features in his life.

As we have already stated, he took his place along with his guests;
the bottles and glasses were replenished, the story of the pedler again
told, and each individual once more busied in describing his own
exploits. The lawyer, immersed in visions of grog and glory, rhap-
sodized perpetually and clapped his hands. Blundell, drunkenly happy,
at every discharge of the current humor, made an abortive attempt to
chuckle, the ineffectual halloo gurgling away in the abysses of his
mighty throat; until, at length, his head settled down supinely upon his
breast, his eyes were closed, and the hour of his victory had gone by;
though, even then, his huge jaws opening at intervals for the outward
passage of something which by courtesy might be considered a laugh,
attested the still anxious struggles of the inward spirit, battling with the
weaknesses of the flesh.

The example of a leader like Blundell had a most pernicious effect
upon the uprightness of the greater part of the company. Having the
sanction of authority, several others, the minor spirits it is true, settled
down under their chairs without a struggle. The survivors made some
lugubrious efforts at a triumph over their less stubborn companions,
but the laborious and husky laugh was but a poor apology for the
proper performance of this feat. Munro, who to his other qualities
added those of a sturdy *bon-vivant,* together with Forrester, and a few
who still girt in the lawyer as the prince of the small jest, discharged
their witticisms upon the staggering condition of affairs; not forgetting
in their assaults the disputatious civilian himself. That worthy, we
regret to add, though still unwilling to yield, and still striving to retort,

had nevertheless suffered considerable loss of equilibrium. His speeches were more than ever confused, and it was remarked that his eyes danced about hazily, with a most ineffectual expression. He looked about, however, with a stupid gaze of self-satisfaction; but his laugh and language, forming a strange and most unseemly coalition, degenerated at last into a dolorous sniffle, indicating the rapid departure of the few mental and animal holdfasts which had lingered with him so long. While thus reduced, his few surviving senses were at once called into acute activity by the appearance of a sooty little negro, who thrust into his hands a misshapen fold of dirty paper, which a near examination made out to take the form of a letter.

"Why, what the d—l, d—d sort of fist is this you've given me, you bird of blackness! where got you this vile scrawl?—faugh! you've had it in your jaws, you raven, have you not?"

The terrified urchin retreated a few paces while answering the inquiry.

"No, mass lawyer—de pedler—da him gib um to me so. I bring um straight as he gib um."

"The pedler! why, where is he?—what the devil can he have to write about?" was the universal exclamation.

"The pedler!" said the lawyer, and his sobriety grew strengthened at the thought of business; he called to the waiter and whispered in his ears—

"Hark ye, cuffee; go bring out the pedler's horse, saddle him with my saddle which lies in the gallery, bring him to the tree, and, look ye, make no noise about it, you scoundrel, as you value your ears."

Cuffee was gone on his mission—and the whole assembly, aroused by the name of the pedler and the mysterious influence of the communication upon the lawyer, gathered, with inquiries of impatience, around him. Finding him slow, they clamored for the contents of the epistle, and the route of the writer—neither of which did he seem desirous to communicate. His evasions and unwillingness were all in vain, and he was at length compelled to undertake the perusal of the scrawl; a task he would most gladly have avoided in their presence. He was in doubt and fear. What could the pedler have to communicate, on paper, which might not have been left over for their interview? His mind was troubled, and, pushing the crowd away from immediately about him, he tore open the envelope and began the perusal—proceeding with a measured gait, the result as well of the "damned cramp hand" as of the still foggy intellect and unsettled vision of the reader. But as the characters and their signification became more clear and obvious to his gaze, his features grew more and more sobered and intelligent—a blankness overspread his face—his hands trembled, and finally, his apprehensions, whatever they might have been, having seemingly undergone full confirmation, he crumpled the villanous scrawl in his hands, and dashing it to the floor in a rage, roared out in quick succession volley after volley of invective and denunciation upon the thrice-blasted head of the pedler. The provocation must have been great, no doubt, to impart such animation at such a time to the man of law; and the curiosity of one of the revellers getting the better of his scruples in such matters—if, indeed, scruples of any kind abode in such a section—prompting him to seize upon the epistle thus pregnant with mortal matter, in this way the whole secret became public property. As, therefore, we shall violate no confidence, and shock no decorum, we proceed to read it aloud for the benefit of all:—

"DEAR LAWYER: I guess I am pretty safe now from the *regilators,* and, saving my trouble of mind, well enough, and nothing to complain about. Your animal goes as slick as grease, and carried me in no time out of reach of rifle-shot—so you see it's only right to thank God, and you, lawyer; for if you hadn't lent me the nag, I guess it would have been a sore chance for me in the hands of them savages and beasts of prey.

"I've been thinking, lawyer, as I driv along, about what you said to me, and I guess it's no more than right and reasonable I should take the law on 'em; and so I put the case in your hands, to make the most on it; and seeing that the damages, as you say, may be over five hundred dollars, why, I don't see but the money is jest as good in my hands as theirs, for so it ought to be. The bill of particulars I will send you by post. In the meanwhile, you may say, having something to go upon, that the whole comes to five hundred and fifty dollars or thereabouts, for, with a little calculation and figering, I guess it won't be hard to bring it up to that. This don't count the vally of the cart, for, as I made it myself, it didn't cost me much; but, if you put it in the bill, which I guess you ought to, put it down for twenty dollars more—seeing that, if I can't trade for one somehow, I shall have to give something like that for another."

"And now, lawyer, there's one thing—I don't like to be in the reach of them 'ere regilators, and guess 'twouldn't be altogether the wisest to stop short of fifteen miles to-night: so, therefore, you see, it won't be in my way, no how, to let you have your nag, which is a main fine one, and goes slick as a whistle—pretty much as if he and the wagon was made for one another; but this, I guess, will be no difference to you, seeing that you can pay yourself his vally out of the damages. I'm willing to allow you one hundred dollars for him, though he a'n't worth so much, no how; and the balance of the money you can send to me, or my brother, in the town of Meriden, in the state of Connecticut. So no more, dear lawyer, at this writing, from

  "Your very humble sarvant
   "to command, &C."

  The dismay of the attorney was only exceeded by the chagrin with which he perceived his exposure, and anticipated the odium in consequence. He leaped about the hall, among the company, in a restless paroxysm—now denouncing the pedler, now deprecating their dissatisfaction at finding out the double game which he had been playing. The trick of the runaway almost gave him a degree of favor in their eyes, which did not find much diminution when Pippin, rushing forth from the apartment, encountered a new trial in the horse left him by the pedler; the miserable beast being completely ruined, unable to move a step, and more dead than alive.

CHAPTER EIGHT

New Friends in Strange Places

Ralph opened his eyes at a moderately late hour on the ensuing morning, and found Forrester in close attendance. He felt himself somewhat sore from his bruises in falling, but the wound gave him little concern. Indeed, he was scarcely conscious of it. He had slept well, and was not unwilling to enter into the explanatory conversation which the woodman began. From him he learned the manner and situation in which he had been found, and was furnished with a partial history of his present whereabouts. In return, he gave a particular account of the assault made upon him in the wood, and of his escape; all of which, already known to the reader, will call for no additional details. In reply to the unscrupulous inquiry of Forrester, the youth, with as little hesitation, declared himself to be a native of the neighboring state of South Carolina, born in one of its middle districts, and now on his way to Tennessee. He concluded with giving his name.

"Colleton, Colleton," repeated the other, as if reviving some recollection of old time—"why, 'squire, I once knew a whole family of that name in Carolina. I'm from Carolina myself, you must know. There was an old codger—a fine, hearty buck—old Ralph Colleton—Colonel Ralph, as they used to call him. He did have a power of money, and a smart chance of lands and field-niggers; but they did say he was going behindhand, for he didn't know how to keep what he had. He was always buying, and living large; but that can't last for ever. I saw him first at a muster. I was then just eighteen, and went out with the rest, for the first time. Maybe, 'squire, I didn't take the rag off the bush that day. I belonged to Captain Williams's troop, called the 'Bush-Whackers.' We were all fine-looking fellows, though I say it myself. I was no chicken, I tell you. From that day, Mark Forrester wrote himself down '*man.*' And well he might, 'squire, and no small one neither. Six feet in stocking-foot, sound in wind and limb—could outrun, outjump, outwrestle, outfight, and outdo anyhow, any lad of my inches in the whole district. There was Tom Foster, that for five long years counted himself cock of the walk, and crowed like a chicken whenever he came out upon the ground. You never saw Tom, I reckon, for he went off to Mississippi after I sowed him up. He couldn't stand it any longer, since it was no use, I licked him in sich short order: he wasn't a mouthful. After that, the whole ground was mine; nobody could stand before me, 'squire, that a'n't slow at raising game chickens."

At the close of this rambling harangue, Mark Forrester, as we may now be permitted to call him, looked down upon his own person with no small share of complacency. He was still, doubtless, all the man he boasted himself to have been; his person, as we have already briefly described it, offering, as well from its bulk and well-distributed muscle as from its perfect symmetry, a fine model for the statuary. After the indulgence of a few moments in this harmless egotism, he returned to the point, as if but now recollected, from which he set out.

"Well, then, Master Colleton, as I was saying, 'twas at this same muster that I first saw the 'squire. He was a monstrous clever old buck now, I tell you. Why, he thought no more of money than if it growed in his plantation—he almost throwed it away for the people to scramble after. That very day, when the muster was over, he called all the boys up to Eben Garratt's tavern, and told old Eben to set the right stuff afloat, and put the whole score down to him. Maybe old Eben didn't take him at his word. Eben was a cunning chap, quite Yankee-like, and would skin his shadow for a saddle-back, I reckon, if he could catch it. I tell you what, when the crop went to town, the old 'squire must have had a mighty smart chance to pay; for, whatever people might say of old Eben, he knew how to calculate from your pocket into his with mon-strous sartainty. Well, as I was saying, 'squire, I shouldn't be afraid to go you a little bet that old Ralph Colleton is some kin of your'n. You're both of the same stock, I reckon."

"You are right in your conjecture," replied the youth; "the person of whom you speak was indeed a near relative of mine—he was no other than my father."

"There, now—I could have said as much, for you look for all the world as if you had come out of his own mouth. There is a trick of the eye which I never saw in any but you two; and even if you had not told me your name, I should have made pretty much the same calculation about you. The old 'squire, if I rightly recollect, was something stiff in his way, and some people did say he was proud, and carried himself rather high; but, for my part, I never saw any difference 'twixt him and most of our Carolina gentlemen, who, you know, generally walk pretty high in the collar, and have no two ways about them. For that matter, however, I couldn't well judge then; I may have been something too young to say, for certain, what was what, at that time of my life."

"You are not even now so far advanced in years, Mr. Forrester, that you speak of your youth as of a season so very remote. What, I pray, may be your age? We may ask, without offence, such a question of men: the case where the other sex is concerned is, you are aware, something different."

The youth seemed studiously desirous of changing the direction of the dialogue.

"Man or woman, I see, for my part, no harm in the question. But do call me Forrester, or Mark Forrester, whichever pleases you best, and not mister, as you just now called me. I go by no other name. Mister is a great word, and moves people quite too far off from one another. I never have any concern with a man that I have to mister and sir. I call them 'squire because that's a title the law gives them; and when I speak to you, I say 'squire, or Master Colleton. You may be a 'squire yourself, but whether you are or are not, it makes no difference, for you get the name from your father, who is. Then, ag'in, I call you master—because, you see, you are but a youth, and have a long run to overtake my years, few as you may think them. Besides, master is a friendly word, and comes easy to the tongue. I never, for my part, could see the sense in mister, except when people go out to fight, when it's necessary to do everything a little the politest; and, then, it smells of long shot and cold business, 'squire. 'Tisn't, to my mind, a good word among friends."

The youth smiled slightly at the distinction drawn with such nicety by his companion, between words which he had hitherto been taught to conceive synonymous, or nearly so; and the reasons, such as they were, by which the woodman sustained his free use of the one to the utter

rejection of the other. He did not think it important, however, to make
up an issue on the point, though dissenting from the logic of his companion; and contented himself simply with a repetition of the question
in which it had originated.

"Why, I take shame to answer you rightly, 'squire, seeing I am no
wiser and no better than I am; but the whole secret of the matter lies in
the handle of this little hatchet, and this I made out of a live-oak sapling
some sixteen years ago—Its much less worn than I, yet I am twice its
age, I reckon."

"You are now then about thirty-two?"

"Ay, just thirty-two. It don't take much calculating to make out that.
My own schooling, though little enough for a large man, is more than
enough to keep me from wanting help at such easy arithmetic."

With the exception of an occasional and desultory remark or two,
the conversation had reached a close. The gravity—the almost haughty
melancholy which, at intervals, appeared the prevailing characteristic
of the manners and countenance of the youth, served greatly to dis-
courage even the blunt freedom of Mark Forrester, who seemed piqued
at length by the unsatisfactory issue of all his endeavors to enlist the
familiarity and confidence of his companion. This Ralph soon discovered. He had good sense and feeling enough to perceive the necessity of
some alteration in his habit, if he desired a better understanding with
one whose attendance, at the present time, was not only unavoidable
but indispensable—one who might be of use, and who was not only
willing and well-intentioned, but to all appearance honest and harmless, and to whom he was already so largely indebted. With an effort,
therefore, not so much of mind as of mood, he broke the ice which his
own indifference had suffered to close, and by giving a legitimate excuse
for the garrulity of his companion, unlocked once more the treasure-
house of his good-humor and volubility.

From the dialogue thus recommenced, we are enabled to take a farther glance into the history of Forrester's early life. He was, as he
phrased it, from "old So. Ca." pronouncing the name of the state in the
abridged form of its written contraction. In one of the lower districts he
still held, in fee, a small but inefficient patrimony; the profits of which
were put to the use of a young sister. Times, however, had grown hard,
and with the impatience and restlessness so peculiar to nearly all classes
of the people of that state, Mark set out in pursuit of his fortune among

strangers. He loved from his childhood all hardy enterprises; all employments calculated to keep his spirit from slumbering in irksome quiet in his breast. He had no relish for the labors of the plough, and looked upon the occupation of his forefathers as by no means fitted for the spirit which, with little besides, they had left him. The warmth, excitability, and restlessness which were his prevailing features of temper, could not bear the slow process of tilling, and cultivating the earth—watching the growth and generations of pigs and potatoes, and listening to that favorite music with the staid and regular farmer, the shooting of the corn in the still nights, as it swells with a respiring movement, distending the contracted sheaves which enclose it. In addition to this antipathy to the pursuits of his ancestors, Mark had a decided desire, a restless ambition, prompting him to see, and seek, and mingle with the world. He was fond, as our readers may have observed already, of his own eloquence, and having worn out the patience and forfeited the attention of all auditors at home, he was compelled, in order to the due appreciation of his faculties, to seek for others less experienced abroad. Like wiser and greater men, he, too, had been won away, by the desire of rule and reference, from the humble quiet of his native fireside; and if, in after life, he did not bitterly repent of the folly, it was because of that lighthearted and sanguine temperament which never deserted him quite, and supported him in all events and through every vicissitude. He had wandered much after leaving his parental home, and was now engaged in an occupation and pursuit which our future pages must develop. Having narrated, in his desultory way to his companion, the facts which we have condensed, he conceived himself entitled to some share of that confidence of which he had himself exhibited so fair an example; and the cross-examination which followed did not vary very materially from that to which most wayfarers in this region are subjected, and of which, on more than one occasion, they have been heard so vociferously to complain.

"Well, Master Ralph—unless my eyes greatly miscalculate, you cannot be more than nineteen or twenty at the most; and if one may be so bold, what is it that brings one of your youth and connections abroad into this wilderness, among wild men and wild beasts, and we gold-hunters, whom men do say are very little, if any, better than them?"

"Why, as respects your first conjecture, Forrester," returned the youth, "you are by no means out of the way. I am not much over twenty, and am free to confess, do not care to be held much older. Touching your further inquiry, not to seem churlish, but rather to speak frankly and in a like spirit with yourself, I am not desirous to repeat to others the story that has been, perhaps, but learned in part by myself. I do not exactly believe that it would promote my plans to submit my affairs to the examination of other people; nor do I think that any person whomsoever would be very much benefited by the knowledge. You seem to have forgotten, however, that I have already said that I am journeying to Tennessee."

"Left Carolina for good and all, heh?"

"Yes—perhaps for ever. But we will not talk of it."

"Well, you're in a wild world now, 'squire."

"This is no strange region to me, though I have lost my way in it. I have passed a season in the county of Gwinnett and the neighborhood, with my uncle's family, when something younger, and have passed, twice, journeying between Carolina and Tennessee, at no great distance from this very spot. But your service to me, and your Carolina birth, deserves that I should be more free in my disclosures; and to account for the sullenness of my temper, which you may regard as something inconsistent with our relationship, let me say, that whatever my prospects might have been, and whatever my history may be, I am at this moment altogether indifferent as to the course which I shall pursue. It matters not very greatly to me whether I take up my abode among the neighboring Cherokees, or, farther on, along with them, pursue my fortunes upon the shores of the Red river or the Missouri. I have become, during the last few days of my life, rather reckless of human circumstance, and, perhaps, more criminally indifferent to the necessities of my nature, and my responsibilities to society and myself, than might well beseem one so youthful, and, as you say, with prospects like those which you conjecture, and not erroneously, to have been mine. All I can say is, that, when I lost my way last evening, my first feeling was one of a melancholy satisfaction; for it seemed to me that destiny itself had determined to contribute towards my aim and desire, and to forward me freely in the erratic progress, which, in a gloomy mood, I had most desperately and, perhaps, childishly undertaken."

There was a stern melancholy in the deep and low utterance—the close compression of lip—the steady, calm eye of the youth, that somewhat tended to confirm the almost savage sentiment of despairing indifference to life, which his sentiments conveyed; and had the effect of eliciting a larger degree of respectful consideration from the somewhat uncouth but really well-meaning and kind companion who stood beside him. Forrester had good sense enough to perceive that Ralph had been gently nurtured and deferentially treated—that his pride or vanity, or perhaps some nobler emotion, had suffered slight or rebuke; and that it was more than probable this emotion would, before long, give place to others, if not of a more manly and spirited, at least of a more subdued and reasonable character. Accordingly, without appearing to attach any importance to, or even to perceive the melancholy defiance contained in the speech of the young man, he confined himself entirely to a passing comment upon the facility with which, having his eyes open, and the bright sunshine and green trees for his guides, he had suffered himself to lose his way—an incident excessively ludicrous in the contemplation of one, who, in his own words, could take the tree with the 'possum, the scent with the hound, the swamp with the deer, and be in at the death with all of them—for whom the woods had no labyrinth, and the night no mystery. He laughed heartily at the simplicity of the youth, and entered into many details, not so tedious as long, of the various hairbreadth escapes, narrow chances, and curious enterprises of his own initiation into the secrets of wood-craft, and to the trials and perils of which, in his own probation, his experience had necessarily subjected him. At length he concluded his narrative by seizing upon one portion of Ralph's language with an adroitness and ingenuity that might have done credit to an older diplomatist; and went on to invite the latter to quarter upon himself for a few weeks at least.

"And now Master Colleton, as you are rambling, as you say, indifferent quite as to what quarter you turn the head of your creature—suppose now you take up lodgings with me. I have, besides this room, which I only keep for my use of a Saturday and Sunday when I come to the village—a snug place a few miles off, and there's room enough, and provisions enough, if you'll only stop a while and take what's going. Plenty of hog and hominy at all times, and we don't want for other and better things, if we please. Come, stay with me for a month, or more, if you choose, and when you think to go, I can put you on your road at an hour's warning. In the meantime, I can show you all that's to be seen. I can show you where the gold grows, and may be had for the gathering. We've snug quarters for the woods, plenty of venison; and, as you must

be a good shot coming from Carolina, you may bring down at day-
dawn of a morning a sluggish wild turkey, so fat that he will split open
the moment he strikes the ground. Don't fight shy, now, 'squire, and
we'll have sport just so long as you choose to stay with us."

The free and hearty manner of the woodman, who, as he concluded
his invitation, grasped the hand of the youth warmly in his own, spoke
quite as earnestly as his language; and Ralph, in part, fell readily into a
proposal which promised something in the way of diversion. He gave
Forrester to understand that he would probably divide his time for a
few days between the tavern and his lodge, which he proposed to visit
whenever he felt himself perfectly able to manage his steed. He signified
his acknowledgment of the kindness of his companion with something
less of hauteur than had hitherto characterized him; and, remembering
that, on the subject of the assault made upon him, Forrester had said
little, and that too wandering to be considered, he again brought the
matter up to his consideration, and endeavored to find a clue to the persons of the outlaws, whom he endeavored to describe.

On this point, however, he procured but little satisfaction. The
description which he gave of the individual assailant whom alone he
had been enabled to distinguish, though still evidently under certain
disguises, was not sufficient to permit of Forrester's identification. The
woodman was at a loss, though evidently satisfied that the parties were
not unknown to him in some other character. As for the Pony Club, he
gave its history, confirming that already related by the outlaw himself;
and while avowing his own personal fearlessness on the subject, did not
withhold his opinion that the members were not to be trifled with:—

"And, a word in your ear, 'squire—one half of the people you meet
with in this quarter know a leetle more of this same Pony Club than is
altogether becoming in honest men. So mind that you look about you,
right and left, with a sharp eye, and be ready to let drive with a quick
hand. Keep your tongue still, at the same time that you keep your eyes
open, for there's no knowing what devil's a listening when a poor weak
sinner talks. The danger's not in the open daylight, but in the dark.
There's none of them that will be apt to square off agin you while you're
here; for they know that, though we've got a mighty mixed nest, there's
some honest birds in it. There's a few of us here, always ready to see that
a man has fair play, and that's a sort of game that a scamp never likes to
take a hand in. There's quite enough of us, when a scalp's in danger,
who can fling a knife and use a trigger with the best, and who won't wait

to be asked twice to a supper of cold steel. Only you keep cool, and wide awake, and you'll have friends enough always within a single whoop. But, good night now. I must go and look after our horses. I'll see you soon—I reckon a leetle sooner than you care to see me."

Ralph Colleton good humoredly assured him that could not be the case, and with friendly gripe of the hand, they parted.

CHAPTER NINE

More of the Dramatis Personæ

In a few days, so much for the proper nursing of Mark Forrester, and of the *soi-disant medico* of the village, Ralph Colleton was able to make his appearance below, and take his place among the *habitués* of the hotel. His wound, slight at first, was fortunate in simple treatment and in his own excellent constitution. His bruises gave him infinitely more concern, and brought him more frequent remembrances of the adventure in which they were acquired. A stout frame and an eager spirit, impatient of restraint, soon enabled our young traveller to conquer much of the pain and inconvenience which his hurts gave him, proving how much the good condition of the physical man depends upon the will. He lifted himself about in five days as erectly as if nothing had occurred, and was just as ready for supper, as if he had never once known the loss of appetite. Still he was tolerably prudent and did not task nature too unreasonably. His exercises were duly moderated, so as not to irritate anew his injuries. Forrester was a rigid disciplinarian, and it was only on the fifth day after his arrival, and after repeated entreaties of his patient, in all of which he showed himself sufficiently *impatient,* that the honest woodman permitted him to descend to the dinner-table of the inn, in compliance with the clamorous warning of the huge bell which stood at the entrance.

The company at the dinner-table was somewhat less numerous than that assembled in the great hall at the trial of the pedler. Many of the persons then present were not residents, but visiters in the village from the neighboring country. They had congregated there, as was usually the case, on each Saturday of the week, with the view not less to the procuring of their necessaries, than the enjoyment of good company. Having attended in the first place to the ostensible objects of their visit, the village tavern, in the usual phrase, "brought them up;" and in social, yet wild carousal, they commonly spent the residue of the day. It was in this way that they met their acquaintance—found society, and obtained the news; objects of primary importance, at all times, with a people whose insulated positions, removed from the busy mart and the stirring crowd, left them no alternative but to do this or rust altogether. The regular lodgers of the tavern were not numerous therefore, and consisted in the main of those laborers in the diggings who had not yet acquired the means of establishing households of their own.

There was little form or ceremony in the proceedings of the repast. Colleton was introduced by a few words from the landlord to the landlady, Mrs. Dorothy Munro, and to a young girl, her niece, who sat beside her. It does not need that we say much in regard to the former—she interferes with no heart in our story; but Lucy, the niece, may not be overlooked so casually. She has not only attractions in herself which claim our notice, but occupies no minor interest in the story we propose to narrate. Her figure was finely formed, slight and delicate, but neither diminutive nor feeble—of fair proportion, symmetry, and an ease and grace of carriage and manner belonging to a far more refined social organization than that in which we find her. But this is easily accounted for; and the progress of our tale will save us the trouble of dwelling farther upon it now. Her skin, though slightly tinged by the sun, was beautifully smooth and fair. Her features might not be held regular; perhaps not exactly such as in a critical examination we should call or consider handsome; but they were attractive nevertheless, strongly marked, and well defined. Her eyes were darkly blue; not languishingly so, but on the contrary rather lively and intelligent in their accustomed expression. Her mouth, exquisitely chiselled, and colored by the deepest blushes of the rose, had a seductive persuasiveness about it that might readily win one's own to some unconscious liberties; while the natural position of the lips, leaving them slightly parted, gave to the mouth an added attraction in the double range which was displayed beneath of pearl-like and well-formed teeth; her hair was unconfined, but short; and rendered the expression of her features more youthful and girl-like than might have been the result of its formal arrangement—it was beautifully glossy, and of a dark brown color.

Her demeanor was that of maidenly reserve, and a ladylike dignity, a quiet serenity, approaching—at periods, when any remark calculated to infringe in the slightest degree upon those precincts with which feminine delicacy and form have guarded its possessor—a stern severity of glance, approving her a creature taught in the true school of propriety, and chastened with a spirit that slept not on a watch, always of perilous exposure in one so young and of her sex. On more than one occasion did Ralph, in the course of the dinner, remark the indignant fire flashing from her intelligent eye, when the rude speech of some untaught boor assailed a sense finely-wrought to appreciate the proper boundaries to the always adventurous footstep of unbridled licentiousness. The youth felt assured, from these occasional glimpses, that her education had been derived from a different influence, and that her spirit deeply felt and deplored the humiliation of her present condition and abode.

The dinner-table, to which we now come, and which two or three negroes have been busily employed in cumbering with well-filled plates and dishes, was most plentifully furnished; though but few of its contents could properly be classed under the head of delicacies. There were eggs and ham, hot biscuits, hommony, milk, marmalade, venison, *Johnny,* or journey cakes, and dried fruits stewed. These, with the preparatory soup, formed the chief components of the repast. Everything was served up in a style of neatness and cleanliness, that, after all, was perhaps the best of all possible recommendations to the feast; and Ralph soon found himself quite as busily employed as was consistent with prudence, in the destruction and overthrow of the tower of biscuits, the pile of eggs, and such other of the edibles around him as were least likely to prove injurious to his debilitated system.

The table was not large, and the seats were soon occupied. Villager after villager had made his appearance and taken his place without calling for observation; and, indeed, so busily were all employed, that he who should have made his *entrée* at such a time with an emphasis commanding notice, might, not without reason, have been set down as truly and indefensibly impertinent. So might one have thought, not employed in like manner, and simply surveying the prospect.

Forrester alone contrived to be less selfish than those about him, and our hero found his attentions at times rather troublesome.

Whatever in the estimation of the woodman seemed attractive, he studiously thrust into the youth's plate, pressing him to eat. Chancing, at
one of these periods of polite provision on the part of his friend, to
direct his glance to the opposite extreme of the table, he was struck with
the appearance of a man whose eyes were fixed upon himself with an
expression which he could not comprehend and did not relish. The
look of this man was naturally of a sinister kind, but now his eyes wore
a malignant aspect, which not only aroused the youth's indignant retort
through the same medium, but struck him as indicating a feeling of
hatred to himself of a most singular character. Meeting the look of the
youth, the stranger rose hurriedly and left the table, but still lingered in
the apartment. Ralph was struck with his features, which it appeared to
him he had seen before, but as the person wore around his cheeks,
encompassing his head, a thick handkerchief, it was impossible for him
to decide well upon them. He turned to Forrester, who was busily intent
upon the dissection of a chicken, and in a low tone inquired the name
of the stranger. The woodman looked up and replied—

"Who that?—that's Guy Rivers; though what he's got his head tied
up for, I can't say. I'll ask him;" and with the word, he did so.

In answer to the question, Rivers explained his bandaging by charg-
ing his jaws to have caught cold rather against his will, and to have
swelled somewhat in consequence. While making this reply, Ralph
again caught his glance, still curiously fixed upon himself, with an
expression which again provoked his surprise, and occasioned a gathering sternness in the look of fiery indignation which he sent back in
return.

Rivers, immediately after this by-play, left the apartment. The eye
of Ralph changing its direction, beheld that of the young maiden
observing him closely, with an expression of countenance so anxious,
that he felt persuaded she must have beheld the mute intercourse, if so
we may call it, between himself and the person whose conduct had so
ruffled him. The color had fled from her cheek, and there was something of warning in her gaze. The polish and propriety which had distinguished her manners so far as he had seen, were so different from
anything that he had been led to expect, and reminded him so strongly
of another region, that, rising from the table, he approached the place
where she sat, took a chair beside her, and with a gentleness and ease,
the due result of his own education and of the world he had lived in,
commenced a conversation with her, and was pleased to find himself

encountered by a modest freedom of opinion, a grace of thought, and a general intelligence, which promised him better company than he had looked for. The villagers had now left the apartment, all but Forrester; who, following Ralph's example, took up a seat beside him, and sat a pleased listener to a dialogue, in which the intellectual charm was strong enough, except at very occasional periods, to prevent him from contributing much. The old lady sat silently by. She was a trembling, timid body, thin, pale, and emaciated, who appeared to have suffered much, and certainly stood in as much awe of the man whose name she bore as it was well fitting in such a relationship to permit. She said as little as Forrester, but seemed equally well pleased with the attentions and the conversation of the youth.

"Find you not this place lonesome, Miss Munro? You have been used, or I mistake much, to a more cheering, a more civilized region."

"I have, sir; and sometimes I repine—not so much at the world I live in, as for the world I have lost. Had I those about me with whom my earlier years were passed, the lonely situation would trouble me slightly."

She uttered these words with a sorrowful voice, and the moisture gathering in her eyes, gave them additional brightness. The youth, after some commonplace remark upon the vast difference between moral and physical privations, went on—

"Perhaps, Miss Munro, with a true knowledge of all the conditions of life, there may be thought little philosophy in the tears we shed at such privations. The fortune that is unavoidable, however, I have always found the more deplorable for that very reason. I shall have to watch well, that I too be not surprised with regrets of a like nature with your own, since I find myself constantly recurring, in thought, to a world which perhaps I shall have little more to do with."

Rising from her seat, and leaving the room as she spoke, with a smile of studied gayety upon her countenance, full also of earnestness and a significance of manner that awakened surprise in the person addressed, the maiden replied—

"Let me suggest, sir, that you observe well the world you are in; and do not forget, in recurring to that which you leave, that, while deploring the loss of friends in the one, you may be unconscious of the enemies which surround you in the other. Perhaps, sir, you will find my philosophy in this particular the most useful, if not the most agreeable."

Wondering at her language, which, though of general remark, and fairly deducible from the conversation, he could not avoid referring to some peculiar origin, the youth rose, and bowed with respectful courtesy as she retired. His eye followed her form for an instant, while his meditations momentarily wrapped themselves up more and more in inextricable mysteries, from which his utmost ingenuity of thought failed entirely to disentangle him. In a maze of conjecture he passed from the room into the passage adjoining, and, taking advantage of its long range, promenaded with steps, and in a spirit, equally moody and uncertain. In a little time he was joined by Forrester, who seemed solicitous to divert his mind and relieve his melancholy, by describing the country round, the pursuits, characters, and conditions of the people— the habits of the miners, and the productiveness of their employ, in a manner inartificial and modest, and sometimes highly entertaining.

While engaged in this way, the eye of Ralph caught the look of Rivers, again fixed upon him from the doorway leading into the great hall; and without a moment's hesitation, with impetuous step, he advanced towards him, determined on some explanation of that curious interest which had become offensive; but when he approached him with this object the latter hastily left the passage.

Taking Forrester's arm, Ralph also left the house, in the hope to encounter this troublesome person again. But failing in this, they proceeded to examine the village, or such portions of it as might be surveyed without too much fatigue to the wounded man—whose hurts, though superficial, might by imprudence become troublesome. They rambled till the sun went down, and at length returned to the tavern.

This building, as we have elsewhere said, was of the very humblest description, calculated, it would seem, rather for a temporary and occasional than a lasting shelter. Its architecture, compared with that even of the surrounding log-houses of the country generally, was excessively rude; its parts were out of all proportion, fitted seemingly by an eye the most indifferent, and certainly without any, the most distant regard, to square and compass. It consisted of two stories, the upper being assigned to the sleeping apartments. Each floor contained four rooms, accessible all, independently of one another, by entrances from a great passage, running both above and below, through the centre of the structure. In addition to the main building, a shed in the rear of the main work afforded four other apartments, rather more closely constructed, and in somewhat better finish than the rest of the structure: these were in the occupation of the family exclusively. The logs, in this work, were barbarously uneven, and hewn only to a degree barely sufficient to permit of a tolerable level when placed one upon the other. Morticed together at the ends, so very loosely had the work been done, that a timid observer, and one not accustomed to the survey of such fabrics, might entertain many misgivings of its security during one of those severe hurricanes, which, in some seasons of the year, so dreadfully desolate the southern and southwestern country. Chimneys of clay and stone intermixed, of the rudest fashion, projected from the two ends of the building, threatening, with the toppling aspect which they wore, the careless wayfarer, and leaving it something more than doubtful whether the oblique and outward direction which they took, was not the result of a wise precaution against a degree of contiguity with the fabric they were meant to warm, which, from the liberal fires of the pine woods, might have proved unfavorable to the protracted existence of either.

The interior of the building aptly accorded with its outline. It was unceiled, and the winds were only excluded from access through the interstices between the remotely-allied logs, by the free use of the soft clay easily attainable in all that range of country. The light on each side of the building was received through a few small windows, one of which only was allotted to each apartment, and this was generally found to possess as many modes of fastening as the jail opposite—a precaution referable to the great dread of the Indian outrages, and which their near neighborhood and irresponsible and vicious habits were well calculated to inspire. The furniture of the hotel amply accorded with all its other features. A single large and two small tables; a few old oaken chairs, of domestic manufacture, with bottoms made of ox or deer skin, tightly drawn over the seat, and either tied below with small cords or tacked upon the sides; a broken mirror, that stood ostentatiously over the mantel, surmounted in turn by a well-smoked picture of the Washington family in a tarnished gilt frame—asserting the Americanism of the proprietor and place—completed the contents of the great hall, and were a fair specimen of what might be found in all the other apartments. The tavern itself, in reference to the obvious pursuit of many of those who made it their home, was entitled "The Golden Egg"—a title made sufficiently notorious to the spectator, from a huge signboard, elevated some eight or ten feet above the building itself, bearing upon a light-blue ground a monstrous egg of the deepest yellow, the effect of which was duly heightened by a strong and thick shading of sable all round it—the artist, in this way, calculating no doubt to afford the object so encircled its legitimate relief. Lest, however, his design in the painting itself should be at all questionable, he had taken the wise precaution of showing what was meant by printing the words "Golden Egg," in huge Roman letters, beneath it; these, in turn, being placed above another inscription, promising "Entertainment for man and horse."

But the night had now closed in, and coffee was in progress. Ralph took his seat with the rest of the lodgers, though without partaking of the feast. Rivers did not make his appearance, much to the chagrin of the youth, who was excessively desirous to account for the curious observance of this man. He had some notion, besides, that the former was not utterly unknown to him; for, though unable to identify him with any one recollection, his features (what could be seen of them) were certainly not unfamiliar. After supper, requesting Forrester's company in his chamber, he left the company—not, however, without a few moments' chat with Lucy Munro and her aunt, conducted with some spirit by the former, and seemingly to the satisfaction of all. As they left the room, Ralph spoke:—

"I am not now disposed for sleep, Forrester, and, if you please, I should be glad to hear further about your village and the country at large. Something, too, I would like to know of this man Rivers, whose face strikes me as one that I should know, and whose eyes have been haunting me to-day rather more frequently than I altogether like, or shall be willing to submit to. Give me an hour, then, if not fatigued, in my chamber, and we will talk over these matters together."

"Well, 'squire, that's just what pleases me now. I like good company, and 'twill be more satisfaction to me, I reckon, than to you. As for fatigue, that's out of the question. Somehow or other, I never feel fatigued when I've got somebody to talk to."

"With such a disposition, I wonder, Forrester, you have not been more intimate with the young lady of the house. Miss Lucy seems quite an intelligent girl, well-behaved, and virtuous."

"Why, 'squire, she is all that; but, though modest and not proud, as you may see, yet she's a little above my mark. She is book-learned, and I am not; and she paints, and is a musician too, and has all the accomplishments. She was an only child, and her father was quite another sort of person from his brother who now has her in management."

"She is an orphan, then?"

"Yes, poor girl, and she feels pretty clearly that this isn't the sort of country in which she has a right to live. I like her very well, but, as I say, she's a little above me; and, besides, you must know, 'squire, I'm rather fixed in another quarter."

They had now reached the chamber of our hero, and the servant having placed the light and retired, the parties took seats, and the conversation recommenced.

"I know not how it is, Forrester," said the youth, "but there are few men whose looks I so little like, and whom I would more willingly avoid, than that man Rivers. What he is I know not—but I suspect him of mischief. I may be doing wrong to the man, and injustice to his character; but, really, his eye strikes me as singularly malicious, almost murderous; and though not apt to shrink from men at any time, it provoked something of a shudder to-day when it met my own. He may be, and perhaps you may be able to say, whether he is a worthy person or not; for my part, I should only regard him as one to be watched jealously and carefully avoided. There is something creepingly malignant in the look which shoots out from his glance, like that of the rattlesnake, when coiled and partially concealed in the brake. When I looked upon his eye, as it somewhat impertinently singled me out for observation, I almost felt disposed to lift my heel as if the venomous reptile were crawling under it."

"You are not the only one, 'squire, that's afraid of Guy Rivers."

"Afraid of him! you mistake me, Forrester; I fear no man," replied the youth, somewhat hastily interrupting the woodman. "I am not apt to fear, and certainly have no such feeling in regard to this person. I distrust, and would avoid him, merely as one who, while possessing none of the beauty, may yet have many of the propensities and some of the poison of the snake to which I likened him."

"Well, 'squire, I didn't use the right word, that's certain, when I said afraid, you see; because 'tan't in Carolina and Georgia, and hereabouts, that men are apt to get frightened at trifles. But, as you say, Guy Rivers is not the right kind of man, and everybody here knows it, and keeps clear of him. None cares to say much to him, except when it's a matter of necessity, and then they say as little as may be. Nobody knows much about him—he is here to-day and gone to-morrow—and we never see much of him except when there's some mischief afoot. He is thick with Munro, and they keep together at all times, I believe. He has money, and knows how to spend it. Where he gets it is quite another thing."

"What can be the source of the intimacy between himself and Munro? Is he interested in the hotel?"

"Why, I can't say for that, but I think not. The fact is, the tavern is nothing to Munro; he don't care a straw about it, and some among us do whisper that he only keeps it a-going as a kind of cover for other practices. There's no doubt that they drive some trade together, though what it is I can't say, and never gave myself much trouble to inquire. I can tell you what, though, there's no doubt on my mind that he's trying to get Miss Lucy—they say he's fond of her—but I know for myself she hates and despises him, and don't stop to let him see it."

"She will not have him, then, you think?"

"I know she won't if she can help it. But, poor girl, what can she do? She's at the mercy, as you may see, of Munro, who is her father's brother; and he don't care a straw for her likes or dislikes. If he says the word, I reckon she can have nothing to say which will help her out of the difficulty. I'm sure he won't regard prayers, or tears, or any of her objections."

"It's a sad misfortune to be forced into connection with one in whom we may not confide—whom we can have no sympathy with—whom we can not love!"

"'Tis so, 'squire; and that's just her case, and she hates to see the very face of him, and avoids him whenever she can do so without giving offence to her uncle, who, they say, has threatened her bitterly about the scornful treatment which she shows him. It's a wonder to me how any person, man or woman, can do otherwise than despise the fellow; for, look you, 'squire, over and above his sulky, sour looks, and his haughty conduct, would you believe it, he won't drink himself, yet he's always for getting other people drunk. But that's not all: he's a quarrelsome, spiteful, sore-headed chap, that won't do as other people. He never laughs heartily like a man, but always in a half-sniffling sort of manner that actually makes me sick at my stomach. Then, he never plays and makes merry along with us, and, if he does, harm is always sure, some-how or other, to come of it. When other people dance and frolic, he stands apart, with scorn in his face, and his black brows gathering clouds in such a way, that he would put a stop to all sport if people were only fools enough to mind him. For my part, I take care to have just as little to say to him as possible, and he to me, indeed; for he knows me just as well as I know him: and he knows, too, that if he only dared to crook his finger, I'm just the man that would mount him on the spot."

Ralph could not exactly comprehend the force of some of the objections urged by his companion to the character of Rivers: those, in particular, which described his aversion to the sports common to the people, only indicated a severer temper of mind and habit, and, though rather in bad taste, were certainly not criminal. Still there was enough to confirm his own hastily-formed suspicions of this person, and to determine him more fully upon a circumspect habit while in his neighborhood. He saw that his dislike and doubt were fully partaken of by those who, from circumstance and not choice, were his associates; and felt satisfied—though, as we have seen, without the knowledge of any one particular which might afford a reasonable warranty for his antipathy—that a feeling so general as Forrester described it could not be altogether without foundation. He felt assured, by an innate prediction of his own spirit, unuttered to his companion, that, at some period, he should find his anticipations of this man's guilt fully realized; though, at that moment, he did not dream that he himself, in becoming his victim, should furnish to his own mind an almost irrefutable argument in support of that incoherent notion of relative sympathies and antipathies to which he had already, seemingly, given himself up.

The dialogue, now diverted to other topics, was not much longer protracted. The hour grew late, and the shutting up of the house, and the retiring of the family below, warned Forrester of the propriety of making his own retreat to the little cabin in which he lodged. He shook Ralph's hand warmly, and, promising to see him at an early hour of the morning, took his departure. A degree of intimacy, rather inconsistent with our youth's wonted haughtiness of habit, had sprung up between himself and the woodman—the result, doubtless, on the part of the former, of the loneliness and to him novel character of his situation. He was cheerless and melancholy, and the association of a warm, well-meaning spirit had something consolatory in it. He thought too, and correctly, that, in the mind and character of Forrester, he discovered a large degree of sturdy, manly simplicity, and a genuine honesty—colored deeply with prejudices and without much polish, it is true, but highly susceptible of improvement, and by no means stubborn or unreasonable in their retention. He could not but esteem the possessor of such characteristics, particularly when shown in such broad contrast with those of his associates; and, without any other assurance of their possession by Forrester than the sympathies already referred to, he was not unwilling to recognise their existence in his person. That he came from the same part of the world with himself may also have had its effect—the more particularly, indeed, as the pride of birthplace was evidently a consideration with the woodman, and the praises of Carolina were rung, along with his own, in every variety of change through almost all his speeches.

The youth sat musing for some time after the departure of Forrester. He was evidently employed in chewing the cud of sweet and bitter thought, and referring to memories deeply imbued with the closely-associated taste of both these extremes. After a while, the weakness of heart got seemingly the mastery, long battled with; and tearing open his vest, he displayed the massive gold chain circling his bosom in repeated folds, upon which hung the small locket containing Edith's and his own miniature. Looking over his shoulder, as he gazed upon it, we are enabled to see the fair features of that sweet young girl, just entering her womanhood—her rich, brown, streaming hair, the cheek delicately pale, yet enlivened with a southern fire, that seems not improperly borrowed from the warm eyes that glisten above it. The ringlets gather in amorous clusters upon her shoulder, and half obscure a neck and bosom of the purest and most polished ivory. The artist had caught from his subject something of inspiration, and the rounded bust seemed to heave before the sight, as if impregnated with the subtlest and sweetest life. The youth carried the semblance to his lips, and muttered words of love and reproach so strangely intermingled and in unison, that, could she have heard to whom they were seemingly addressed, it might have been difficult to have determined the difference of signification between them. Gazing upon it long, and in silence, a large but solitary tear gathered in his eye, and finally finding its way through his fingers, rested upon the lovely features that appeared never heretofore to have been conscious of a cloud. As if there had been something of impiety and pollution in this blot upon so fair an outline, he hastily brushed the tear away; then pressing the features again to his lips, he hurried the jewelled token again into his bosom, and prepared himself for those slumbers upon which we forbear longer to intrude.

CHAPTER TEN

The Black Dog

While this brief scene was in progress in the chamber of Ralph, another, not less full of interest to that person, was passing in the neighborhood of the village-tavern; and, as this portion of our narrative yields some light which must tend greatly to our own, and the instruction of the reader, we propose briefly to record it. It will be remembered, that, in the chapter preceding, we found the attention of the youth forcibly attracted toward one Guy Rivers—an attention, the result of various influences, which produced in the mind of the youth a degree of antipathy toward that person for which he himself could not, nor did we seek to account.

It appears that Ralph was not less the subject of consideration with the individual in question. We have seen the degree and kind of espionage which the former had felt at one time disposed to resent; and how he was defeated in his design by the sudden withdrawal of the obnoxious presence. On his departure with Forrester from the gallery, Rivers reappeared—his manner that of doubt and excitement; and, after hurrying for a while with uncertain steps up and down the apartment, he passed hastily into the adjoining hall, where the landlord sat smoking, drinking, and expatiating at large with his guests. Whispering something in his ear, the latter rose, and the two proceeded into the adjoining copse, at a point as remote as possible from hearing, when the explanation of this mysterious caution was opened by Rivers.

"Well, Munro, we are like to have fine work with your accursed and blundering good-nature. Why did you not refuse lodgings to this youngster? Are you ignorant who he is? Do you not know him?"

"Know him?—no, I know nothing about him. He seems a clever, good-looking lad, and I see no harm in him. What is it frightens you?" was the reply and inquiry of the landlord.

"Nothing frightens me, as you know by this time, or should know at least. But, if you know not the young fellow himself, you should certainly not be at a loss to know the creature he rides; for it is not long since your heart was greatly taken with him. He is the youth we set upon at the Catcheta pass, where your backwardness and my forwardness got me this badge—it has not yet ceased to bleed—the marks of which promise fairly to last me to my grave."

As he spoke he raised the handkerchief which bound his cheeks, and exposed to view a deep gash, not of a serious character indeed, but which, as the speaker asserted, would most probably result in a mark which would last him his life. The exposure of the face confirms the first and unfavorable impression which we have already received from his appearance, and all that we have any occasion now to add in this respect will be simply, that, though not beyond the prime of life, there were ages of guilt, of vexed and vexatious strife, unregulated pride, without aim or elevation, a lurking malignity, and hopeless discontent—all embodied in the fiendish and fierce expression which that single glimpse developed to the spectator. He went on—

"Had it been your lot to be in my place, I should not now have to tell you who he is; nor should we have had any apprehensions of his crossing our path again. But so it is. You are always the last to your place;—had you kept your appointment, we should have had no difficulty, and I should have escaped the mortification of being foiled by a mere stripling, and almost stricken to death by the heel of his horse."

"And all your own fault and folly, Guy. What business had you to advance upon the fellow, as you did, before everything was ready, and when we could have brought him, without any risk whatever, into the snare, from which nothing could have got him out? But no! You must be at your old tricks of the law—you must make speeches before you cut purses, as was your practice when I first knew you at Gwinnett county-court; a practice which you seem not able to get over. You have got into such a trick of making fun of people, that, for the life of me, I can't be sorry that the lad has turned the tables so handsomely upon you."

"You would no doubt have enjoyed the scene with far more satisfaction, had the fellow's shot taken its full effect on my skull—since, besides the failure of our object, you have such cause of merriment in what has been done. If I did go something too much ahead in the matter, it is but simple justice to say you were quite as much aback."

"Perhaps so, Guy; but the fact is, I was right and you wrong, and the thing's beyond dispute. This lesson, though a rough one, will do you service; and a few more such will perhaps cure you of that vile trick you have of spoiling not only your own, but the sport of others, by running your head into unnecessary danger; and since this youth, who got out of the scrape so handsomely, has beat you at your own game, it may cure you of that cursed itch for tongue-trifling, upon which you so much pride yourself. 'Twould have done, and it did very well at the county sessions, in getting men out of the wood; but as you have commenced a new business entirely, it's but well to leave off the old, particularly as it's now your policy to get them into it."

"I shall talk as I please, Munro, and see not why, and care not whether, my talk offends you or not. I parleyed with the youth only to keep him in play until your plans could be put in operation."

"Very good—that was all very well, Guy—and had you kept to your intention, the thing would have done. But he replied smartly to your speeches, and your pride and vanity got to work. You must answer smartly and sarcastically in turn, and you see what's come of it. You forgot the knave in the wit; and the mistake was incurable. Why tell him that you wanted to pick his pocket, and perhaps cut his throat?"

"That was a blunder, I grant; but the fact is, I entirely mistook the man. Besides, I had a reason for so doing, which it is not necessary to speak about now."

"Oh, ay—it wouldn't be lawyer-like, if you hadn't a reason for everything, however unreasonable," was the retort.

"Perhaps not, Munro; but this is not the matter now. Our present object must be to put this youth out of the way. We must silence suspicion, for, though we are pretty much beyond the operation of law in this region, yet now and then a sheriff's officer takes off some of the club; and, as I think it is always more pleasant to be out of the halter than in it, I am clear for making the thing certain in the only practicable way."

"But, are you sure that he is the man? I should know his horse, and shall look to him, for he's a fine creature, and I should like to secure him; which I think will be the case, if you are not dreaming as usual."

"I am sure—I do not mistake."

"Well, I'm not; and I should like to hear what it is you know him by?"

A deeper and more malignant expression overspread the face of Rivers, as, with a voice in which his thought vainly struggled for mastery with a vexed spirit, he replied:—

"What have I to know him by? you ask. I know him by many things—and when I told you I had my reason for talking with him as I did, I might have added that he was known to me, and fixed in my lasting memory, by wrongs and injuries before. But there is enough in this for recollection," pointing again to his cheek—"this carries with it answer sufficient. You may value a clear face slightly, having known none other than a blotted one since you have known your own, but I have a different feeling in this. He has written himself here, and the damned writing is perpetually and legibly before my eyes. He has put a brand, a Cain-like, accursed brand upon my face, the language of which can not be hidden from men; and yet you ask me if I know the executioner? Can I forget him? If you think so, Munro, you know little of Guy Rivers."

The violence of his manner as he spoke well accorded with the spirit of what he said. The landlord, with much coolness and precision, replied:—

"I confess I do know but little of him, and have yet much to learn. If you have so little temper in your speech, I have chosen you badly as a confederate in employments which require so much of that quality. This gash, which, when healed, will be scarcely perceptible, you speak of with all the mortification of a young girl, to whom, indeed, such would be an awful injury. How long is it, Guy, since you have become so particularly solicitous of beauty, so proud of your face and features?"

"You will spare your sarcasm for another season, Munro, if you would not have strife. I am not now in the mood to listen to much, even from you, in the way of sneer or censure. Perhaps, I am a child in this, but I can not be otherwise. Besides, I discover in this youth the person of one to whom I owe much in the growth of this very hell-heart, which embitters everything about and within me. Of this, at another time, you shall hear more. Enough that I know this boy—that it is more than probable he knows me, and may bring us into difficulty—that I hate him, and will not rest satisfied until we are secure, and I have my revenge."

"Well, well, be not impatient, nor angry. Although I still doubt that the youth in the house is your late opponent, you may have suffered wrong at his hands, and you may be right in your conjecture."

"I am right—I do not conjecture. I do not so readily mistake my man, and I was quite too near him on that occasion not to see every feature of that face, which, at another and an earlier day, could come between me and my dearest joys—but, why speak I of this? I know him: not to remember would be to forget that I am here; and that he was a part of that very influence which made me league, Munro, with such as you, and become a creature of, and a companion with, men whom even now I despise. I shall not soon forget his stern and haughty smile of scorn—his proud bearing—his lofty sentiment—all that I most admire—all that I do not possess—and when today he descended to dinner, guided by that meddling booby, Forrester, I knew him at a glance. I should know him among ten thousand."

"It's to be hoped that he will have no such memory. I can't see, indeed, how he should recognise either of us. Our disguises were complete. Your whiskers taken off, leave you as far from any resemblance to what you were in that affair, as any two men can well be from one another; and I am perfectly satisfied he has little knowledge of me."

"How should he?" retorted the other. "The better part of valor saved you from all risk of danger or discovery alike; but the case is different with me. It may be that, enjoying the happiness which I have lost, he has forgotten the now miserable object that once dared to aspire—but no matter—it may be that I am forgotten by him—he can never be by me."

This speech, which had something in it vague and purposeless to the mind of Munro, was uttered with gloomy emphasis, more as a soliloquy than a reply, by the speaker. His hands were passed over his eyes as if in agony, and his frame seemed to shudder at some remote recollection which had still the dark influence upon him. Munro was a dull man in all matters that belong to the heart, and those impulses which characterize souls of intelligence and ambition. He observed the manner of his companion, but said nothing in relation to it; and the latter, unable to conceal altogether, or to suppress even partially his emotions, did not deign to enter into any explanation in regard to them.

"Does he suspect anything yet, Guy, think you?—have you seen anything which might sanction a thought that he knew or conjectured more than he should?" inquired Munro, anxiously.

"I will not say that he does, but he has the perception of a lynx—he is an apt man, and his eyes have been more frequently upon me to-day than I altogether relish or admire. It is true, mine were upon him—as how, indeed, if death were in the look, could I have kept them off! I caught his glance frequently; turning upon me with that stern, still expression, indifferent and insolent—as if he cared not even while he surveyed. I remember that glance three years ago, when he was indeed a boy—I remembered it when, but a few days since, he struck me to the earth, and would have ridden me to death with the hoofs of his horse, but for your timely appearance."

"It may be as you believe, Guy; but, as I saw nothing in his manner or countenance affording ground for such a belief, I can not but conceive it to have been because of the activity of your suspicions that you discovered his. I did not perceive that he looked upon you with more curiosity than upon any other at table; though, if he had done so, I should by no means have been disposed to wonder; for at this time, and since your face has been so tightly bandaged, you have a most villanously attractive visage. It carries with it, though you do regard it with so much favor, a full and satisfactory reason for observance, without rendering necessary any reference to any more serious matter than itself. On the road, I take it, he saw quite too little of either of us to be able well to determine what was what, or who was who, either then or now. The passage was dark, our disguises good, and the long hair and monstrous whiskers which you wore did the rest. I have no apprehensions, and see now that you need have any."

"I would not rest in this confidence—let us make sure that if he knows anything he shall say nothing," was the significant reply of Rivers.

"Guy, you are too fierce and furious. When there's a necessity, do you see, for using teeth, you know me to be always ready; but I will not be for ever at this sort of work. If I were to let you have your way you'd bring the whole country down upon us. There will be time enough when we see a reason for it to tie up this young man's tongue."

"I see—I see!—you are ever thus—ever risking our chance upon contingencies when you might build strongly upon certainties. You are perpetually trying the strength of the rope, when a like trouble would render it a sure hold-fast. Rather than have the possibility of this thing being blabbed, I would—"

"Hush—hark!" said Munro, placing his hand upon the arm of his companion, and drawing him deeper into the copse, at the moment that Forrester, who had just left the chamber of Ralph, emerged from

the tavern into the open air. The outlaw had not placed himself within
the shadow of the trees in time sufficient to escape the searching gaze of
the woodman, who, seeing the movement and only seeing one person,
leaped nimbly forward with a light footstep, speaking thus as he
approached:

"Hello! there—who's that—the pedler, sure. Have at you, Bunce!"
seizing as he spoke the arm of the retreating figure, who briefly and
sternly addressed him as follows:—

"It is well, Mr. Forrester, that he you have taken in hand is almost as
quiet in temper as the pedler you mistake him for, else your position
might prove uncomfortable. Take your fingers from my arm, if you
please."

"Oh, it's you, Guy Rivers—and you here too, Munro, making love
to one another, I reckon, for want of better stuff. Well, who'd have
thought to find you two squatting here in the bushes! Would you
believe it now, I took you for the Yankee—not meaning any offence
though."

"As I am not the Yankee, however, Mr. Forrester, you will I suppose,
withdraw your hand," said the other, with a manner sufficiently
haughty for the stomach of the person addressed.

"Oh, to be sure, since you wish it, and are not the pedler," returned
the other, with a manner rather looking, in the country phrase, to "a
squaring off for a fight"—"but you needn't be so gruff about it. You are
on business, I suppose, and so I leave you."

"A troublesome fool, who is disposed to be insolent," said Rivers,
after Forrester's departure.

"Damn him!" was the exclamation of the latter, on leaving the
copse—"I feel very much like putting my fingers on his throat; and shall
do it, too, before he gets better manners!"

The dialogue between the original parties was resumed.

"I tell you again, Munro—it is not by any means the wisest policy to
reckon and guess and calculate that matters will go on smoothly, when
we have it in our own power to make them certainly go on so. We must
leave nothing to guess-work, and a single blow will readily teach this
youth the proper way to be quiet."

"Why, what do you drive at, Guy. What would you do—what
should be done?"

"Beef—beef—beef! mere beef! How dull you are to-night! were you
in yon gloomy and thick edifice (pointing to the prison which frowned

in perspective before them), with irons on your hands, and with the prospect through its narrow-grated loopholes, of the gallows-tree, at every turning before you, it might be matter of wonder even to yourself that you should have needed any advice by which to avoid such a risk and prospect."

"Look you, Guy—I stand in no greater danger than yourself of the prospect of which you speak. The subject is, at best, an ugly one, and I do not care to hear it spoken of by you, above all other people. If you want me to talk civilly with you, you must learn yourself to keep a civil tongue in your head. I don't seek to quarrel with anybody, but I will not submit to be threatened with the penalties of the rogue by one who is a damned sight greater rogue than myself."

"You call things by their plainest names, Wat, at least," said the other, with a tone moderated duly for the purpose of soothing down the bristles he had made to rise—"but you mistake me quite. I meant no threat; I only sought to show you how much we were at the mercy of a single word from a wanton and head-strong youth. I will not say confidently that he remembers me, but he had some opportunities for seeing my face, and looked into it closely enough. I can meet any fate with fearlessness, but should rather avoid it, at all risks, when it's in my power to do so."

"You are too suspicious, quite, Guy, even for our business. I am older than you, and have seen something more of the world: suspicion and caution are not the habit with young men like this. They are free enough, and confiding enough, and in this lies our success. It is only the old man—the experienced in human affairs, that looks out for traps and pitfalls. It is for the outlaw—for you and me—to suspect all; to look with fear even upon one another, when a common interest, and perhaps a common fate, ought to bind us together. This being our habit, arising as it must from our profession, it is natural but not reasonable to refer a like spirit to all other persons. We are wrong in this, and you are wrong in regard to this youth—not that I care to save him, for if he but looks or winks awry, I shall silence him myself, without speech or stroke from you being necessary. But I do not think he made out your features, and do not think he looked for them. He had no time for it, after the onset, and you were well enough disguised before. If he had made out anything, he would have shown it to-night; but, saving a little stiffness, which belongs to all these young men from Carolina, I saw nothing in his manner that looked at all out of the way."

"Well, Munro, you are bent on having the thing as you please. You will find, when too late, that your counsel will end in having us all in a hobble."

"Pshaw! you are growing old and timid since this adventure. You begin to doubt your own powers of defence. You find your arguments failing; and you fear that, when the time comes, you will not plead with your old spirit, though for the extrication of your own instead of the neck of your neighbor."

"Perhaps so—but, if there be no reason for apprehension, there is something due to me in the way of revenge. Is the fellow to hurl me down, and trench my cheek in this manner, and escape without hurt?"

The eyes of the speaker glared with a deadly fury, as he indicated in this sentence another motive for his persevering hostility to Colleton—an hostility for which, as subsequent passages will show, he had even a better reason than the unpleasing wound in his face; which, nevertheless, was in itself, strange as it may appear, a considerable eyesore to its proprietor. Munro evidently understood this only in part; and, unaccustomed to attribute a desire to shed blood to any other than a motive of gain or safety, and without any idea of mortified pride or passion being productive of a thirst unaccountable to his mind, except in this manner, he proceeded thus, in a sentence, the dull simplicity of which only the more provoked the ire of his companion—

"What do you think to do, Guy—what recompense would you seek to have—what would satisfy you?"

The hand of Rivers grasped convulsively that of the questioner as he spoke, his eyes were protruded closely into his face, his voice was thick, choking and husky, and his words tremulous, as he replied,

"His blood—his blood!"

The landlord started back with undisguised horror from his glance. Though familiar with scenes of violence and crime, and callous in their performance, there was more of the Mammon than the Moloch in his spirit, and he shuddered at the fiendlike look that met his own. The other proceeded:—

"The trench in my cheek is nothing to that within my soul. I tell you, Munro, I hate the boy—I hate him with a hatred that must have a tiger-draught from his veins, and even then I will not be satisfied. But why talk I to you thus, when he is almost in my grasp, and there is neither let nor hinderance? Sleeps he not in yon room to the northeast?"

"He does, Guy—but it must not be! I must not risk all for your

passion, which seems to me, as weak as it is without adequate provocation. I care nothing for the youth, and you know it; but I will not run
the thousand risks which your temper is for ever bringing upon me.
There is nothing to be gained, and a great deal to be lost by it, at this
time. As for the scar—that, I think, is fairly a part of the business, and is
not properly a subject of personal revenge. It belongs to the adventure,
and you should not have engaged in it, without a due reference to its
possible consequences."

"You shall not keep me back by such objections as these. Do I not
know how little you care for the risk—how little you can lose by it?"

"True, I can lose little, but I have other reasons; and, however it may
surprise you, those reasons spring from a desire for your good rather
than my own."

"For my good?" replied the other, with an inquiring sneer.

"Yes, for your good, or rather for Lucy's. You wish to marry her. She
is a sweet child, and an orphan. She merits a far better man than you;
and, bound as I am to give her to you, I am deeply bound to myself and
to her, to make you as worthy of her as possible, and to give her as many
chances for happiness as I can."

An incredulous smile played for a second upon the lips of the outlaw, succeeded quickly, however, by the savage expression, which, from
being that most congenial to his feelings, had become that most habitual to his face.

"I can not be deceived by words like these," was his reply, as he
stepped quickly from under the boughs which had sheltered them and
made toward the house.

"Think not to pursue this matter, Guy, on your life. I will not permit it; not now, at least, if I have to strike for the youth myself."

Thus spoke the landlord, as he advanced in the same direction.
Both were deeply roused, and, though not reckless alike, Munro was a
man quite as decisive in character as his companion was ferocious and
vindictive. What might have been the result of their present position,
had it not undergone a new interruption, might not well be foreseen.
The sash of one of the apartments of the building devoted to the family
was suddenly thrown up, and a soft and plaintive voice, accompanying
the wandering and broken strains of a guitar, rose sweetly into song
upon the ear.

"'Tis Lucy—the poor girl! Stay, Guy, and hear her music. She does
not often sing now-a-days. She is quite melancholy, and it's a long time

since I've heard her guitar. She sings and plays sweetly; her poor father had her taught everything before he failed, for he was very proud of her, as well he might be."

They sunk again into the covert, the outlaw muttering sullenly at the interruption which had come between him and his purposes. The music touched him not, for he betrayed no consciousness; when, after a few brief preliminary notes on the instrument, the musician breathed forth the little ballad which follows:—

Lucy's Song.
I.
"I met thy glance of scorn,
    And then my anguish slept,
But, when the crowd was gone,
    I turned away and wept.
II.
"I could not bear the frown
    Of one who thus could move,
And feel that all my fault,
    Was only too much love.
III.
"I ask not if thy heart
    Hath aught for mine in store,
Yet, let me love thee still,
    If thou canst yield no more.
IV.
"Let me unchidden gaze,
    Still, on the heaven I see,
Though all its happy rays
    Be still denied to me."

A broken line of the lay, murmured at intervals for a few minutes after the entire piece was concluded, as it were in soliloquy, indicated the sad spirit of the minstrel. She did not remain long at the window; in a little while the song ceased, and the light was withdrawn from the apartment. The musician had retired.

"They say, Guy, that music can quiet the most violent spirit, and it seems to have had its influence upon you. Does she not sing like a mocking-bird?—is she not a sweet, a true creature? Why, man! so forward and furious but now, and now so lifeless! bestir ye! The night wanes."

The person addressed started from his stupor, and, as if utterly

unconscious of what had been going on, *ad interim*, actually replied to
the speech of his companion made a little while prior to the appearance
and music of the young girl, whose presence at that moment had most
probably prevented strife and, possibly, bloodshed. He spoke as if the
interruption had made only a momentary break in the sentence which
he now concluded:—

"He lies at the point of my knife, under my hands, within my
power, without chance of escape, and I am to be held back—kept from
striking—kept from my revenge—and for what? There may be little
gain in the matter—it may not bring money, and there may be some
risk! If it be with you, Munro, to have neither love nor hate, but what
you do, to do only for the profit and spoil that come of it, it is not so
with me. I can both love and hate; though it be, as it has been, that I
entertain the one feeling in vain, and am restrained from the enjoyment
of the other."

"You were born in a perverse time, and are querulous, for the sake
of the noise it makes," rejoined his cool companion. "I do not desire to
restrain your hands from this young man, but take your time for it. Let
nothing be done to him while in this house. I will run, if I can help it,
no more risk for your passions; and I must confess myself anxious, if
the devil will let me, of stopping right short in the old life and beginning a new one. I have been bad enough, and done enough, to keep me
at my prayers all the rest of my days, were I to live on to eternity."

"This new spirit, I suppose, we owe to your visit to the last camp-
meeting. You will exhort, doubtless, yourself, before long, if you keep
this track. Why, what a prophet you will make among the crop-haired,
Munro! what a brand from the burning!"

"Look you, Guy, your sarcasm pleases me quite as little as it did the
young fellow, who paid it back so much better than I can. Be wise, if you
can, while you are wary; if your words continue to come from the same
nest, they will beget something more than words, my good fellow."

"True, and like enough, Munro; and why do you provoke me to say
them?" replied Rivers, something more sedately. "You see me in a passion—you know that I have cause—for is not this cause enough—this
vile scar on features, now hideous, that were once surely not unpleasing."

As he spoke he dashed his fingers into the wound, which he still
seemed pleased to refer to, though the reference evidently brought with
it bitterness and mortification. He proceeded—his passion again rising
predominant—

"Shall I spare the wretch whose ministry defaced me—shall I not have revenge on him who first wrote villain here—who branded me as an accursed thing, and among things bright and beautiful gave me the badge, the blot, the heel-stamp, due the serpent? Shall I not have my atonement—my sacrifice—and shall you deny me—you, Walter Munro, who owe it to me in justice?"

"I owe it to you, Guy—how?"

"You taught me first to be the villain you now find me. You first took me to the haunts of your own accursed and hell-educated crew. You taught me all their arts, their contrivances, their lawlessness, and crime. You encouraged my own deformities of soul till they became monsters, and my own spirit such a monster that I no longer knew myself. You thrust the weapon into my hand, and taught me its use. You put me on the scent of blood, and bade me lap it. I will not pretend that I was not ready and pliable enough to your hands. There was, I feel, little difficulty in moulding me to your own measure. I was an apt scholar, and soon ceased to be the subordinate villain. I was your companion, and too valuable to you to be lost or left. When I acquired new views of man, and began, in another sphere, that new life to which you would now turn your own eyes—when I grew strong among men, and famous, and public opinion grew enamored with the name, which your destiny compelled me to exchange for another, you sought me out—you thrust your enticements upon me; and, in an hour of gloom, and defeat, and despondency, you seized upon me with those claws of temptation which are even now upon my shoulders, and I gave up all! I made the sacrifice—name, fame, honor, troops of friends—for what? Answer *you*! You are rich—you own slaves in abundance—secure from your own fortunes, you have wealth hourly increasing. What have I? This scar, this brand, that sends me among men no longer the doubtful villain—the words are written there in full!"

The speaker paused, exhausted. His face was pale and livid—his form trembled with convulsion—and his lips grew white and chalky, while quivering like a troubled water. The landlord, after a gloomy pause, replied:—

"You have spoken but the truth, Guy, and anything that I can do—"

"You will not do!" responded the other, passionately, and interrupting the speaker in his speech. "You will do nothing! You ruin me in the love and esteem of those whom I love and esteem—you drive me into exile—you lead me into crime, and put me upon a pursuit which teaches me practices that brand me with man's hate and fear, and—if the churchmen speak truth, which I believe not—with heaven's eternal punishment! What have I left to desire but hate—blood—the blood of man—who, in driving me away from his dwelling, has made me an unrelenting enemy—his hand everywhere against me, and mine against him! While I had this pursuit, I did not complain; but you now interpose to deny me even this. The boy whom I hate, not merely because of his species, but, in addition, with a hate incurred by himself, you protect from my vengeance, though affecting to be utterly careless of his fate—and all this you conclude with a profession of willingness to do for me whatever you can! What miserable mockery is this?"

"And have I done nothing—and am I seeking to do nothing for you, Guy, by way of atonement? Have I not pledged to you the person of my niece, the sweet young innocent, who is not unworthy to be the wife of the purest and proudest gentleman of the southern country? Is this nothing—is it nothing to sacrifice such a creature to such a creature? For well I know what must be her fate when she becomes your wife. Well I know you! Vindictive, jealous, merciless, wicked, and fearless in wickedness—God help me, for it will be the very worst crime I have ever yet committed! These are all your attributes, and I know the sweet child will have to suffer from the perpetual exercise of all of them."

"Perhaps so! and as she will then be mine, she must suffer them, if I so decree; but what avails your promise, so long as you—in this matter a child yourself—suffer her to protract and put off at her pleasure. Me she receives with scorn and contempt, you with tears and entreaties; and you allow their influence; in the hope, doubtless, that some lucky chance—the pistol-shot or the hangman's collar—will rid you of my importunities. Is it not so, Munro?" said the ruffian, with a sneer of contemptuous bitterness.

"It would be, indeed, a lucky event for both of us, Guy, were you safely in the arms of your mother; though I have not delayed in this affair with any such hope. God knows I should be glad, on almost any terms, to be fairly free from your eternal croakings—never at rest, never satisfied, unless at some new deviltry and ill deed. If I did give you the first lessons in your education, Guy, you have long since gone beyond your master; and I'm something disposed to think that Old Nick himself must have taken up your tuition, where, from want of corresponding capacity, I was compelled to leave it off."

And the landlord laughed at his own humor, in despite of the hyena-glare shot forth from the eye of the savage he addressed. He continued:—

"But, Guy, I'm not for letting the youth off—that's as you please. You have a grudge against him, and may settle it to your own liking and in your own way. I have nothing to say to that. But I am determined to do as little henceforth toward hanging myself as possible; and, therefore, the thing must not take place *here*. Nor do I like that it should be done at all without some reason. When he blabs, there's a necessity for the thing, and self-preservation, you know, is the first law of nature. The case will then be as much mine as yours, and I'll lend a hand willingly."

"My object, Munro, is scarcely the same with yours. It goes beyond it; and, whether he knows much or little, or speaks nothing or everything, it is still the same thing to me. I must have my revenge. But, for your own safety—are you bent on running the risk?"

"I am, Guy, rather than spill any more blood unnecessarily. I have already shed too much, and my dreams begin to trouble me as I get older," was the grave response of the landlord.

"And how, if he speaks out, and you have no chance either to stop his mouth or to run for it?"

"Who'll believe him, think you?—where's the proof? Do you mean to confess for both of us at the first question?"

"True—," said Rivers, "there would be a difficulty in conviction, but his oath would put us into some trouble."

"I think not; our people know nothing about him, and would scarcely lend much aid to have either of us turned upon our backs," replied Munro, without hesitation.

"Well, be it then as you say. There is yet another subject, Munro, on which I have just as little reason to be satisfied as this. How long will you permit this girl to trifle with us both? Why should you care for her prayers and pleadings—her tears and entreaties? If you are determined upon the matter, as I have your pledge, these are childish and unavailing; and the delay can have no good end, unless it be that you do in fact look, as I have said, and as I sometimes think, for some chance to take me off, and relieve you of my importunities and from your pledges."

"Look you, Guy, the child is my own twin-brother's only one, and a sweet creature it is. I must not be too hard with her; she begs time, and I must give it."

"Why, how much time would she have? Heaven knows what she considers reasonable, or what you or I should call so; but to my mind she has had time enough, and more by far than I was willing for. You must bring her to her senses, or let me do so. To my thought, she is making fools of us both."

"It is, enough, Guy, that you have my promise. She shall consent, and I will hasten the matter as fast as I can; but I will not drive her, nor will I be driven myself. Your love is not such a desperate affair as to burn itself out for the want of better fuel; and you can wait for the proper season. If I thought for a moment that you did or could have any regard for the child, and she could be happy or even comfortable with you, I might push the thing something harder than I do; but, as it stands, you must be patient. The fruit drops when it is ripe."

"Rather when the frost is on it, and the worm is in the core, and decay has progressed to rottenness! Speak you in this way to the hungry boy, whose eyes have long anticipated his appetite, and he may listen to you and be patient—I neither can nor will. Look to it, Munro: I will not much longer submit to be imposed upon."

"Nor I, Guy Rivers. You forget yourself greatly, and entirely mistake me, when you take these airs upon you. You are feverish now, and I will not suffer myself to grow angry; but be prudent in your speech. We shall see to all this to-morrow and the next day—there is quite time enough—when we are both cooler and calmer than at present. The night is something too warm for deliberation; and it is well we say no more on the one subject till we learn the course of the other. The hour is late, and we had best retire. In the morning I shall ride to hear old Parson Witter, in company with the old woman and Lucy. Ride along with us, and we shall be able better to understand one another."

As he spoke, Munro emerged from the cover of the tree under which their dialogue had chiefly been carried on, and reapproached the dwelling, from which they had considerably receded. His companion lingered in the recess.

"I will be there," said Rivers, as they parted, "though I still propose a ride of a few miles to-night. My blood is hot, and I must quiet it with a gallop."

The landlord looked incredulous as he replied—"Some more deviltry: I will take a bet that the cross-roads see you in an hour."

"Not impossible," was the response, and the parties were both lost to sight—the one in the shelter of his dwelling, the other in the dim shadow of the trees which girdled it.

CHAPTER ELEVEN

Forest Preaching

At an early hour of the ensuing morning, Ralph was aroused from his slumbers, which had been more than grateful from the extra degree of fatigue he had the day before undergone, by the appearance of Forrester, who apologized for the somewhat unseasonable nature of his visit, by bringing tidings of a preacher and of a preaching in the neighborhood on that day. It was the sabbath—and though, generally speaking, very far from being kept holy in that region, yet, as a day of repose from labor—a holyday, in fact—it was observed, at all times, with more than religious scrupulosity. Such an event among the people of this quarter was always productive of a congregation. The occurrence being unfrequent, its importance was duly and necessarily increased in the estimation of those, the remote and insulated position of whom rendered society, whenever it could be found, a leading and general attraction. No matter what the character of the auspices under which it was attained, they yearned for its associations, and gathered where they were to be enjoyed. A field-preaching, too, is a legitimate amusement; and, though not intended as such, formed a genuine excuse and apology for those who desired it less for its teaching than its talk—who sought it less for the word which it brought of God than that which it furnished from the world of man. It was a happy cover for those who, cultivating a human appetite, and conscious of a human weakness, were solicitous, in respecting and providing for these, not to offend the Creator in the presence of his creatures.

The woodman, as one of this class, was full of glee, and promised Ralph an intellectual treat; for Parson Witter, the preacher in reference, had more than once, as he was pleased to acknowledge and phrase it, won his ears, and softened and delighted his heart. He was popular in the village and its neighborhood, and where regular pastor was none, he might be considered to have made the strongest impression upon his almost primitive and certainly only in part civilized hearers. His merits of mind were held of rather an elevated order, and in standard far over-topping the current run of his fellow-laborers in the same vineyard; while his own example was admitted, on all hands, to keep pace evenly with the precepts which he taught, and to be not unworthy of the faith which he professed. He was of the methodist persuasion—a sect which, among those who have sojourned in our southern and western forests, may confidently claim to have done more, and with motives as little questionable as any, toward the spread of civilization, good habits, and a proper morality, with the great mass, than all other known sects put together. In a word, where men are remotely situated from one another, and can not well afford to provide for an established place of worship and a regular pastor, their labors, valued at the lowest standard of human want, are inappreciable. We may add that never did laborers more deserve, yet less frequently receive, their hire, than the preachers of this particular faith. Humble in habit, moderate in desire, indefatigable in well-doing, pure in practice and intention, without pretence or ostentation of any kind, they have gone freely and fearlessly into places the most remote and perilous, with an empty scrip, but with hearts filled to overflowing with love of God and good-will to men—preaching their doctrines with a simple and an unstudied eloquence, meetly characteristic of, and well adapted to, the old groves, deep primitive forests, and rudely-barren wilds, in which it is their wont most commonly to give it utterance: day after day, week after week, and month after month, finding them wayfarers still—never slumbering, never reposing from the toil they have engaged in, until they have fallen, almost literally, into the narrow grave by the wayside; their resting-places unprotected by any other mausoleum or shelter than those trees which have witnessed their devotions; their names and worth unmarked by any inscription; their memories, however, closely treasured up and carefully noted among human affections, and within the bosoms of those for whom their labors have been taken; while their reward, with a high ambition cherished well in their lives, is found only in that better abode where they are promised a cessation from their labors, but where their good works still follow them. This, without exaggeration, applicable to the profession at large, was particularly due to the individual member in question; and among the somewhat savage and always wild people whom he exhorted, Parson Witter was in many cases an object of sincere affection, and in all commanded their respect.

As might readily be expected, the whole village and as much of the surrounding country as could well be apprized of the affair were for the gathering; and Colleton, now scarcely feeling his late injuries, an early breakfast having been discussed, mounted his horse, and, under the guidance of his quondam friend Forrester, took the meandering path, or, as they phrase it in those parts, the old *trace*, to the place of meeting and prayer.

The sight is something goodly, as well to the man of the world as to the man of God, to behold the fairly-decked array of people, drawn from a circuit of some ten or even fifteen miles in extent, on the sabbath, neatly dressed in their choicest apparel, men and women alike well mounted, and forming numerous processions and parties, from three to five or ten in each, bending from every direction to a given point, and assembling for the purposes of devotion. No chiming and chattering bells warn them of the day or of the duty—no regularly-constituted and well-salaried priest—no time-honored fabric, round which the old fore-fathers of the hamlet rest—reminding them regularly of the recurring sabbath, and the sweet assemblage of their fellows. We are to assume that the teacher is from their own impulses, and that the heart calls them with due solemnity to the festival of prayer. The preacher comes when the spirit prompts, or as circumstances may impel or permit. The news of his arrival passes from farm to farm, from house to house; placards announce it from the trees on the roadside, parallel, it may be, with an advertisement for strayed oxen, as we have seen it numberless times; and a day does not well elapse before it is in possession of everybody who might well avail themselves of its promise for the ensuing Sunday. The parson comes to the house of one of his auditory a night or two before; messages and messengers are despatched to this and that neighbor, who despatch in turn to other neighbors. The negroes, delighting in a service and occasion of the kind—in which, by-the-way, they generally make the most conspicuous figures—though somewhat sluggish as couriers usually, are now not merely ready, but actually swift of foot. The place of worship and the preacher are duly designated, and, by the time appointed, as if the bell had tolled for their enlightenment, the country assembles at the stated place; and though the preacher may sometimes fail of attendance, the people never do.

The spot appointed for the service of the day was an old grove of gigantic oaks, at a distance of some five or six miles from the village of Chestatee. The village itself had not been chosen, though having the convenience of a building, because of the liberal desire entertained by those acting on the occasion to afford to others living at an equal distance the same opportunities without additional fatigue. The morning was a fine one, all gayety and sunshine—the road dry, elevated, and shaded luxuriantly with the overhanging foliage—the woods having the air of luxury and bloom which belonged to them at such a season, and the prospect, varied throughout by the wholesome undulations of valley and hill, which strongly marked the face of the country, greatly enlivened the ride to the eye of our young traveller. Everything contributed to impart a cheering influence to his senses; and with spirits and a frame newly braced and invigorated, he felt the bounding motion of the steed beneath him with an animal exultation, which took from his countenance that look of melancholy which had hitherto clouded it.

As our two friends proceeded on their way, successive and frequent groups crossed their route, or fell into it from other roads—some capriciously taking the by-paths and Indian tracks through the woods, but all having the same object in view, and bending to the same point of assemblage. Here gayly pranced on a small cluster of the young of both sexes, laughing with unqualified glee at the jest of some of their companions—while in the rear, the more staid, the antiques and those rapidly becoming so, with more measured gait, paced on in suite. On the road-side, striding on foot with step almost as rapid as that of the riders, came at intervals, and one after the other, the now trimly-dressed slaves of this or that plantation—all devoutly bent on the place of meeting. Some of the whites carried their double-barrelled guns, some their rifles—it being deemed politic, at that time, to prepare for all contingencies, for the Indian or for the buck, as well as for the more direct object of the journey.

At length, in a rapidly approaching group, a bright but timid glance met that of Colleton, and curbing in the impetuous animal which he rode, in a few moments he found himself side by side with Miss Munro, who answered his prettiest introductory compliment with a smile and speech, uttered with a natural grace, and with the spirit of a dame of chivalry.

"We have a like object to-day, I presume," was, after a few compli-
mentary sentences, the language of Ralph—"yet," he continued, "I fear
me, that our several impulses at this time scarcely so far resemble each
other as to make it not discreditable to yours to permit of the comparison."

"I know not what may be the motive which impels you, sir, to the
course you take; but I will not pretend to urge that, even in my own
thoughts, my route is any more the result of a settled conviction of its
high necessity than it may be in yours, and the confession which I
shame to make, is perhaps of itself, a beginning of that very kind of self-
examination which we seek the church to awaken."

"Alas, Miss Lucy, even this was not in my thought, so much are we
men ignorant of or indifferent to those things which are thought of so
much real importance. We seldom regard matters which are not of
present-enjoyment. The case is otherwise with you. There is far more
truth, my own experience tells me, in the profession of your sex,
whether in love or in religion, than in ours—and believe me, I mean
this as no idle compliment—I feel it to be true. The fact is, society itself
puts you into a sphere and condition, which, taking from you much of
your individuality, makes you less exclusive in your affections, and
more single in their exercise. Your existence being merged in that of the
stronger sex, you lose all that general selfishness which is the strict result
of our pursuits. Your impulses are narrowed to a single point or two,
and there all your hopes, fears and desires, become concentrated. You
acquire an intense susceptibility on a few subjects, by the loss of those
manifold influences which belong to the out-door habit of mankind.
With us, we have so many resources to fly to for relief, so many attractions to invite and seduce, so many resorts of luxury and life, that the
affections become broken up in small, the heart is divided among the
thousand; and, if one fragment suffers defeat or denial, why, the pang
scarcely touches, and is perhaps unfelt by all the rest. You have but few
aims, few hopes. With these your very existence is bound up, and if you
lose these you are yourselves lost. Thus I find that your sex, to a certain
age, are creatures of love—disappointment invariably begets devotion—and either of these passions, for so they should be called, once
brought into exercise, forbids and excludes every other."

"Really, Mr. Colleton, you seem to have looked somewhat into the
philosophy of this subject, and you may be right in the inferences to
which you have come. On this point I may say nothing; but, do you

conceive it altogether fair in you thus to compliment us at our own expense? You give us the credit of truth, a high eulogium, I grant, in matters which relate to the affections and the heart; but this is done by robbing us entirely of mental independence. You are a kind of generous outlaw, a moral Robin Hood, you compel us to give up everything we possess, in order that you may have the somewhat equivocal merit of restoring back a small portion of what you take."

"True, and this, I am afraid, Miss Lucy, however by the admission I forfeit for my sex all reputation for chivalry, is after all the precise relationship between us. The very fact that the requisitions made by our sex produce immediate concession from yours, establishes the dependence of which you complain."

"You mistake me, sir. I complain not of the robbery—far from it; for, if we do lose the possession of a commodity so valuable, we are at least freed from the responsibility of keeping it. The gentlemen, nowadays, seldom look to us for intellectual gladiatorship; they are content that our weakness should shield us from the war. But, I conceive the reproach of our poverty to come unkindly from those who make us poor. It is of this, sir, that I complain."

"You are just, and justly severe, Miss Munro; but what else have you to expect? Amazon-like, your sex, according to the quaint old story, sought the combat, and were not unwilling to abide the conditions of the warfare. The taunt is coupled with the triumph—the spoil follows the victory—and the captive is chained to the chariot-wheel of his conqueror, and must adorn the march of his superior by his own shame and sorrows. But, to be just to myself, permit me to say, that what you have considered a reproach was in truth designed as a compliment. I must regret that my modes of expression are so clumsy, that, in the utterance of my thought, the sentiment so changed its original shape as entirely to lose its identity. It certainly deserved the graceful swordsmanship which foiled it so completely."

"Nay, sir," said the animated girl, "you are bloodily-minded toward yourself, and it is matter of wonder to me how you survive your own rebuke. So far from erring in clumsy phrase, I am constrained to admit that I thought, and think you, excessively adroit and happy in its management. It was only with a degree of perversity, intended solely to establish our independence of opinion, at least for the moment, that I chose to mistake and misapprehend you. Your remark, clothed in any other language, could scarcely put on a form more consistent with your meaning."

Ralph bowed at a compliment which had something equivocal in it, and this branch of the conversation having reached its legitimate close, a pause of some few moments succeeded, when they found themselves joined by other parties, until the cortége was swollen in number to the goodly dimensions of a cavalcade or caravan designed for a pilgrimage.

"Report speaks favorably of the preacher we are to hear today, Miss Munro—have you ever heard him?" was the inquiry of the youth.

"I have, sir, frequently, and have at all times been much pleased and sometimes affected by his preaching. There are few persons I would more desire to hear than himself—he does not offend your ears, nor assail your understanding by unmeaning thunders. His matter and manner, alike, are distinguished by modest good sense, a gentle and dignified ease and spirit, and a pleasing earnestness in his object that is never offensive. I think, sir, you will like him."

"Your opinion of him will certainly not diminish my attention, I assure you, to what he says," was the reply.

At this moment the cavalcade was overtaken and joined by Rivers and Munro, together with several other villagers. Ralph now taking advantage of a suggestion of Forrester's, previously made—who proposed, as there would be time enough, a circuitous and pleasant ride through a neighboring valley—avoided the necessity of being in the company of one with respect to whom he had determined upon a course of the most jealous precaution. Turning their horses' heads, therefore, in the proposed direction, the two left the procession, and saw no more of the party until their common arrival at the secluded grove—druidically conceived for the present purpose—in which the teacher of a faith as simple as it was pleasant was already preparing to address them.

The venerable oaks—a goodly and thickly clustering assemblage—forming a circle around, and midway upon a hill of gradual ascent, had left an opening in the centre, concealed from the eye except when fairly penetrated by the spectator. Their branches, in most part meeting above, afforded a roof less regular and gaudy, indeed, but far more grand, majestic, and we may add, becoming, for purposes like the present, than the dim and decorated cathedral, the workmanship of human hands. Its application to this use, at this time, recalled forcibly to the mind of the youth the forms and features of that primitive worship, when the trees bent with gentle murmurs above the heads of the rapt worshippers, and a visible Deity dwelt in the shadowed valleys, and whispered an auspicious acceptance of their devotions in every breeze. He could not help acknowledging, as, indeed, must all who have ever been under the influence of such a scene, that in this, more properly and perfectly than in any other temple, may the spirit of man recognise and hold familiar and free converse with the spirit of his Creator. Here, indeed, without much effort of the imagination, might be beheld the present God—the trees, hills and vales, the wild flower and the murmuring water, all the work of his hands, attesting his power, keeping their purpose, and obeying, without scruple, the order of those seasons, for the sphere and operation of which he originally designed them. They were mute lessoners, and the example which, in the progress of their existence, year after year, they regularly exhibited, might well persuade the more responsible representative of the same power the propriety of a like obedience.

A few fallen trees, trimmed of their branches and touched with the adze, ranging at convenient distances under the boughs of those along with which they had lately stood up in proud equality, furnished seats for the now rapidly-gathering assemblage. A rough stage, composed of logs, rudely hewn and crossing each other at right angles, covered, when at a height of sufficient elevation, formed the pulpit from which the preacher was to exhort. A chair, brought from some cottage in the neighborhood, surmounted the stage. This was all that art had done to accommodate nature to the purposes of man.

In the body of the wood immediately adjacent, fastened to the overhanging branches, were the goodly steeds of the company; forming, in themselves, to the unaccustomed and inexperienced eye, a grouping the most curious. Some, more docile than the rest, were permitted to rove at large, cropping the young herbage and tender grass; occasionally, it is true, during the service, overleaping their limits in a literal sense; neighing, whinnying and kicking up their heels to the manifest confusion of the pious and the discomfiture of the preacher.

The hour at length arrived. The audience was numerous if not select. All persuasions—for even in that remote region sectarianism had done much toward banishing religion—assembled promiscuously together and without show of discord, excepting that here and there a high stickler for church aristocracy, in a better coat than his neighbor, thrust him aside; or, in another and not less offensive form of pride, in the externals of humility and rotten with innate malignity, groaned audibly through his clenched teeth; and with shut eyes and crossed hands, as in prayer, sought to pass a practical rebuke upon the less devout exhibitions of those around him. The cant and the clatter, as it prevails in the crowded mart, were here in miniature, and Charity would have needed something more than a Kamschatka covering to have shut out from her eyes the enormous hypocrisy of many among the clamorous professors of that faith, of which they felt little and knew less. If she shut her eyes to the sight, their groans were in her ears; and if she turned away, they took her by the elbow, and called her a back-slider herself. Forrester whispered in the ears of Ralph, as his eye encountered the form of Miss Munro, who sat primly amid a flock of venerables—

"Doesn't she talk like a book? Ah, she's a smart, sweet girl; it's a pity there's no better chance for her than Guy Rivers. But where's he—the rascal? Do you know I nearly got my fingers on his throat last night. I felt deusedly like it, I tell you."

"Why, what did he to you?"

"Answered me with such impudence! I took him for the pedler in the dark, and thought I had got a prize; it wasn't the pedler, but something worse—for in my eyes he's no better than a polecat."

But, the preacher had risen in his place, and all was silence and attention. We need scarcely seek to describe him. His appearance was that of a very common man; and the anticipations of Colleton, as he was one of those persons apt to be taken by appearances, suffered something like rebuke. His figure was diminutive and insignificant; his shoulders were round, and his movements excessively awkward; his face was thin and sallow; his eyes dull and inexpressive, and too small seemingly for command. A too-frequent habit of closing them in prayer contributed, no doubt, greatly to this appearance. A redeeming expression in the high forehead, conically rising, and the strong character exhibited in his nose, neutralized in some sort the generally-unattractive outline. His hair, which was of a deep black, was extremely coarse, and closely cropped: it gave to his look that general expression which associated him at once in the mind of Ralph, whose reading in those matters was fresh, with the commonwealth history of England—with the puritans, and those diseased fanatics of the Cromwell dynasty, not omitting that profound hypocrite himself. What, then, was the surprise of the youth, having such impressions, to hear a discourse unassuming in its dictates, mild in its requisitions, and of a style and temper the most soothing and persuasive!

The devotions commenced with a hymn, two lines of which, at a time, having been read and repeated by the preacher, furnished a guide to the congregation; the female portion of which generally united to sing, and in a style the sweetness of which was doubly effective from the utter absence of all ornament in the music. The strains were just such as the old shepherds, out among the hills, tending their charges, might have been heard to pour forth, almost unconsciously, to that God who sometimes condescended to walk along with them. After this was over, the preacher rose, and read, with a voice as clear as unaffected, the twenty-third psalm of David, the images of which are borrowed chiefly from the life in the wilderness, and were therefore not unsuited to the ears of those to whom it was now addressed. Without proposing any one portion of this performance as a text or subject of commentary, and without seeking, as is quite too frequently the case with small teachers, to explain doubtful passages of little meaning and no importance, he delivered a discourse, in which he simply dilated upon and carried out, for the benefit of those about him, and with a direct reference to the case of all of them, those beautiful portraits of a good shepherd and guardian God which the production which he read furnished to his hands. He spoke of the dependence of the creature—instanced, as it is daily, by a thousand wants and exigencies, for which, unless by the care and under the countenance of Providence, he could never of himself provide. He narrated the dangers of the forest—imaging by this figure the mazes and mysteries of life—the difficulty, nay, the almost utter impossibility, unless by His sanction, of procuring sustenance, and of counteracting those innumerable incidents by fell and flood, which, in a single moment, defeat the cares of the hunter and the husbandman—setting at naught his industry, destroying his fields and cattle, blighting his crops, and tearing up with the wing of the hurricane even the cottage which gives shelter to his little ones. He dwelt largely and long upon those numberless and sudden events in the progress of life and human circumstance, over which, as they could neither be foreseen nor combated with by man, he had no control; and appealed for him to the Great Shepherd, who alone could do both. Having shown the necessity of such an appeal and reference, he next proceeded to describe the gracious willingness which had at all times been manifested by the Creator to extend the required protection. He adverted to the fortunes of all the patriarchs in support of this position; and, singling out innumerable instances of this description, confidently assured them, in turn, from these examples, that the same Shepherd was not unwilling to provide for them in like manner. Under his protection, he assured them, "they should not want." He dilated at length, and with a graceful dexterity, upon the truths—the simple and mere truths of God's providence, and the history of his people—which David had embodied in the beautiful psalm which he had read them. It was poetry, indeed—sweet poetry— but it was the poetry of truth and not of fiction. Did not history sustain its every particular? Had not the Shepherd made them to lie down in green pastures—had he not led them beside the still waters—restored he not their souls—did he not lead them, for his name's sake, in the paths of righteousness—and though at length they walked through the valley where Death had cast his never-departing shadow, was he not with them still, keeping them even from the fear of evil? He furnished them with the rod and staff; he prepared the repast for them, even in the presence of their enemies; he anointed their heads with oil, and blessed them with quiet and abundance, until the cup of their prosperity was running over—until they even ceased to doubt that goodness and mercy should follow them all the days of their life; and, with a proper consciousness of the source whence this great good had arisen, they determined, with the spirit not less of wise than of worthy men, to follow his guidance, and thus dwell in the house of the Lord for ever. Such did the old man describe the fortunes of the old patriarchs to have been; and such, having first entered into like obligations, pursuing them with the same fond fixedness of purpose, did he promise should be the fortunes of all who then listened to his voice.

As he proceeded to his peroration, he grew warmed with the broad and boundless subject before him, and his declamation became alike bold and beautiful. All eyes were fixed upon him, and not a whisper from the still-murmuring woods which girded them in was perceptible to the senses of that pleased and listening assembly. The services of the morning were closed by a paraphrase, in part, of the psalm from which his discourse had been drawn; and as this performance, in its present shape, is not to be found, we believe, in any of the books devoted to such purposes, it is but fair to conclude that the old man—not unwilling, in his profession, to employ every engine for the removal of all stubbornness from the hearts of those he addressed—sometimes invoked Poetry to smile upon his devotions, and wing his aspirations for the desired flight. It was sung by the congregation, in like manner with the former—the preacher reading two lines at a time, after having first gone through the perusal aloud of the piece entire. With the recognised privilege of the romancer, who is supposed to have a wizard control over men, events, and things alike, we are enabled to preserve the paraphrase here:—

"Shepherd's Hymn.

"Oh, when I rove the desert waste, and 'neath the hot sun pant,
The Lord shall be my shepherd then—he will not let me want—
He'll lead me where the pastures are of soft and shady green,
And where the gentle waters rove the quiet hills between.

"And when the savage shall pursue, and in his grasp I sink,
He will prepare the feast for me, and bring the cooling drink—
And save me harmless from his hands, and strengthen me in toil,
And bless my home and cottage-lands, and crown my head with oil.

"With such a Shepherd to protect—to guide and guard me still,
And bless my heart with every good, and keep from every ill—
Surely I shall not turn aside, and scorn his kindly care,
But keep the path he points me out, and dwell for ever there."

The service had not yet been concluded—the last parting offices of prayer and benediction had yet to be performed—when a boy, about fourteen years of age, rushed precipitately into the assembly. His clothes were torn and bloody, and he was smeared with dirt from head to foot. He spoke, but his words were half intelligible only, and comprehended by but one or two of the persons around him. Munro immediately rose and carried him out. He was followed by Rivers, who had been sitting beside him.

The interruption silenced everything like prayer; there was no further attention for the preacher; and accordingly a most admired disorder overspread the audience. One after another rose and left the area, and those not the first to withdraw followed in rapid succession; until, under the influence of that wild stimulant, curiosity, the preacher soon found himself utterly unattended, except by the female portion of his auditory. These, too, or rather the main body of them at least, were now only present in a purely physical sense; for, with the true characteristic of the sex, their minds were busily employed in the wilderness of reflection which this movement among the men had necessarily inspired.

Ralph Colleton, however, with praiseworthy decorum, lingered to the last—his companion Forrester, under the influence of a whisper from one over his shoulder, having been among the first to retire. He, too, could not in the end avoid the general disposition, and at length took his way to the animated and earnest knot which he saw assembled in the shade of the adjoining thicket, busied in the discussion of some concern of more than common interest. In his departure from the one gathering to the other, he caught a glance from the eye of Lucy Munro, which had in it so much of warning, mingled at the same time with an expression of so much interest, that he half stopped in his progress, and, but for the seeming indecision and awkwardness of such a proceeding, would have returned—the more particularly, indeed, when, encountering her gaze with a corresponding fixedness—though her cheek grew to crimson with the blush that overspread it—her glance was not yet withdrawn. He felt that her look was full of caution, and inwardly determined upon due circumspection. The cause of interruption may as well be reserved for the next chapter.

CHAPTER TWELVE

Trouble Among the Trespassers

Ralph now made his way into the thick of the crowd, curious to ascertain the source of so much disquiet and tumult as now began to manifest itself among them. The words of peace which they had just heard seemed to have availed them but little, for every brow was blackened, and every tongue tipped with oaths and execrations. His appearance attracted no attention, if, indeed, it were not entirely unobserved. The topic in hand was of an interest quite too fresh and absorbing to permit of a single glance toward any other of more doubtful importance, and it was only after much delay that he was enabled at length to get the least insight into the mystery. All were speakers, counsellors, orators—old and young, big and little, illustrious and obscure—all but the legitimate and legal counsellor Pippin, who, to the surprise of the youth, was to be seen galloping at the uttermost stretch of his horse's legs toward the quiet of his own abode. The lawyer was known to have a particular care of number one, and such a movement excited no remark in any of the assembly. There was danger at hand, and he knew his value—besides, there might be business for the sessions, and he valued too highly the advantages, in a jury-case of a clean conscience, not to be solicitous to keep his honor clear of any art or part in criminal matters, saving only such connection as might come professionally.

That the lawyer was not without reason for his precaution, Ralph had soon abundant testimony himself. Arms and the munitions of war, as if by magic, had been rapidly collected. Some of the party, it is true, had made their appearance at the place of prayer with rifles and fowling-pieces, a practice which occasioned no surprise. But the managers of the present movement had seemingly furnished all hands with weapons, offensive and defensive, of one kind or another. Some were caparisoned with pistols, cutlasses, and knives; and, not to speak of pickaxes and clubs, the array was sufficiently formidable. The attitude of all parties was war-like in the extreme, and the speeches of those who, from time to time, condescended to please themselves by haranguing their neighbors, teemed with nothing but strife and wounds, fight and furious perfor-mance.

The matter, as we have already remarked, was not made out by the youth without considerable difficulty. He obtained, however, some par-ticulars from the various speakers, which, taken in connection with the broken and incoherent sentences of Forrester, who dashed into speech at intervals with something of the fury of a wounded panther in a cane-brake, contributed at length to his full enlightenment.

"Matter enough—matter enough! and you will think so too—to be robbed of our findings by a parcel of blasted 'coons, that haven't soul enough to keep them freezing. Why, this is the matter, you must know: only last week, we miners of Tracy's diggings struck upon a fine heap of the good stuff, and have been gathering gold pretty freely ever since. All the boys have been doing well at it; better than they ever did before—and even Munro there, and Rivers, who have never been very fond of work, neither of them, have been pretty busy ever since; for, as I tell you, we were making a sight of money, all of us. Well now, somehow or other, our good luck got to the ears of George Dexter and his men, who have been at work for some time past upon old Johnson's diggings about fourteen miles up on the Sokee river. They could never make much out of the place, I know; for what it had good in it was pretty much cleaned out of it when I was there, and I know it can't get better, seeing that gold is not like trees, to grow out every year. Well, as I say, George Dexter, who would just as lief do wrong as right, and a great deal rather, got tired, as well as all his boys, of working for the fun of the thing only; and so, hearing as I say of our good luck, what did they do but last night come quietly down upon our trace, and when Jones, the old man we kept there as a kind of safeguard, tried to stop 'em, they shot him through the body as if he had been a pig. His son got away when his father was shot, though they did try to shoot him too, and come post haste to tell us of the transaction. There stands the lad, his clothes all bloody and ragged. He's had a good run of it through the bushes, I reckon."

"And they are now in possession of your lands?"

"Every fellow of 'em, holding on with gun in hand, and swearing to be the death of us, if we try for our own. But we'll show them what's what, or I can't fling a hatchet or aim a rifle. This, now, Master Colleton, is the long and the short of the matter."

"And what do you propose to do?" asked Ralph, of his informant.

"Why, what should we do, do you think, but find out who the best men are, and put them in possession. There's not a two-legged creature among us that won't be willing to try that question, any how, and at any time, but more particularly now, when everything depends upon it."

"And when do you move, Forrester?"

"Now, directly—this very minute. The boys have just sent for some more powder, and are putting things in readiness for a brush."

The resolution of Ralph was at once adopted. He had nothing, it is true, to do with the matter—no interest at stake, and certainly no sympathy with the lawless men who went forth to fight for a property, to which they had not a jot more of right than had those who usurped it from them. But here was a scene—here was incident, excitement—and with all the enthusiasm of the southern temper, and with that uncalculating warmth which so much distinguishes it, he determined, without much regard to the merits of the question, to go along with the party.

"I'll ride with you, Forrester, and see what's going on."

"And stand up with us, 'squire, and join in the scuffle?" inquired his companion.

"I say not that, Forrester. I have no concern in this matter, and so long as I am let alone myself, I see no reason for taking part in an affair, of the merits of which I am almost entirely ignorant."

"You will take your arms with you, I suppose. You can lend them to those who fight, though you make no use of them yourself."

"Yes—I never go without arms in travelling, but I shall not lend them. A man should no more lend his arms than he should lend his coat. Every man should have his own weapons."

"Yes; but, 'squire, if you go along with us, you may be brought into the scrape. The other party may choose to consider you one of us."

"It is for this reason, not less than others, that I would carry and not lend my arms."

"Well, 'squire, you might lend them to some of us, and I would answer for them. It's true, as you say, that every man should have his own weapons; but some among us, you see, ha'n't got 'em, and it's for that we've been waiting. But come, it's time to start; the boys are beginning to be in motion; and here come Munro and that skunk Rivers. I reckon Munro will have the command, for he's thought to be the most cunning among us."

The party was now ready for departure, when a new interruption was experienced. The duties of the pastor were yet to begin, and, accordingly, sallying forth at the head of his remaining congregation, Parson Witter placed himself in front of the seceders. It is unnecessary that we should state his purpose; it is as little necessary that we should say that it was unavailing. Men of the kind of whom we speak, though perhaps not insensible to some of the bolder virtues, have no sympathy or love for a faith which teaches forbearance under wrong and insult, and meekness under blows. If they did not utterly laugh in his face, therefore, at his exhortations, it was because, at the very first, they had to a man turned their backs upon him, and were now generally mounted. Following the common lead, Ralph approached the group where stood his fair friend of the morning; and acknowledged, in an under-tone, to herself, the correctness of her opinion in regard to the merits of the sermon. She did not reply to the observation, but seeing his hand upon the bridle, asked hurriedly—

"Do you, sir—does Mr. Colleton go with this party?"

"I do; the circumstances are all so novel, and I am curious to see as much of manners and events foreign to those to which I have been accustomed, as may be practicable."

"I fear, sir, that those which you may behold on occasions such as these, and in this country, though they may enlighten you, will do little toward your gratification. You have friends, sir, who might not be willing that you should indulge in unnecessary exposure, for the satisfaction of a curiosity so unpromising."

Her manner was dignified, and though as she spoke a something of rebuke came mingled with the caution which her language conveyed, yet there was evidently such an interest in his fortunes embodied in what she said, that the listener whom she addressed could not feel hurt at the words themselves, or the accompanying expression.

"I shall be a mere looker-on, Miss Munro, and dare to disregard the caution which you bestow, though duly sensible of the kindness which gives it utterance. Perhaps, too, I may be of service in the way of peace-making. I have neither interest nor wish which could prompt me to any other course."

"There is every need for caution among young travellers, sir; and though no astrologer, it seems to me your planet is full of unfavorable auguries. If you will be headstrong, see that you have your eyes about you. You have need of them both."

This was all in by-play. The group had passed on, and a single nod of the head and a doubtful smile, on her part, concluded the brief dialogue we have just narrated. The youth was puzzled to understand the significant warnings, which, from time to time, she had given him. He felt unconscious of any foe in particular, and though at that time sojourning with a people in whom he could repose but little confidence, he yet saw no reason to apprehend any danger. If her manner and words had reference simply to the general lawlessness of the settlement, the precaution evidently conveyed no compliment to his own capacities for observation. Whatever might have been her motive, the youth felt its kindness; and she rose not a little in his esteem, when he reflected with how much dignity and ladylike propriety she had given, to a comparative stranger, the counsel which she evidently thought necessary to his well-being. With a free rein he soon overtook Forrester, and with him took his place in the rear of the now rapidly-advancing cavalcade.

As Forrester had conjectured, the command of the party, such as it was, was assigned to the landlord. There might have been something like forty or fifty men in all, the better portion of them mounted and well armed—some few on foot struggling to keep pace with the riders—all in high spirits, and indignant at the invasion of what they considered their own. These, however, were not all hunters of the precious metal, and many of them, indeed, as the reader has by this time readily conjectured, carried on a business of very mixed complexion. The whole village—blacksmith, grocer, baker, and clothier included, turned out *en masse*, upon the occasion; for, with an indisputable position in political economy, deriving their gains directly or indirectly from this pursuit, the cause was, in fact, a cause in common.

The scene of operations, in view of which they had now come, had to the eye all the appearance of a moderate encampment. The intruding force had done the business completely. They had made a full transfer, from their old to their new quarters, of bag and baggage; and had possessed themselves of all the log-houses in and about the disputed region. Their fires were in full heat, to use the frontier phrase, and the water was hissing in their kettles, and the dry thorns crackling under the pot. Never had usurpers made themselves more perfectly at home; and the rage of the old incumbents was, of course, duly heightened at a prospect of so much ease and felicity enjoyed at their expense.

The enemy were about equal in point of number with those whom they had so rudely dispossessed. They had, however, in addition to their disposable force, their entire assemblage of wives, children, slaves, and dependants, cattle and horses, enough, as Forrester bitterly remarked, "to breed a famine in the land." They had evidently settled themselves *for life*, and the ousted party, conscious of the fact, prepared for the *dernier* resort. Everything on the part of the usurpers indicated a perfect state of preparedness for an issue which they never doubted would be made; and all the useless baggage, interspersed freely with rocks and fallen trees, had been well-employed in increasing the strength of a position for which, such an object considered, nature had already done much. The defences, as they now stood, precluded all chance of success from an attack by mounted men, unless the force so employed were overwhelming. The defenders stood ready at their posts, partly under cover, and so arrayed as easily to put themselves so, and were armed in very nearly the same manner with the assailing party. In this guise of formidable defence, they waited patiently the onset.

There was a brief pause after their arrival, on the part of the invading force, which was employed principally in consultation as to the proper mode of procedure, and in examination of the ground. Their plan of attack, depending altogether upon the nature of circumstances yet to be seen, had not been deliberated upon before. The consultation lasted not long, however, and no man's patience was too severely tried. Having deputed the command to the landlord, they left the matter pretty much to that person; nor was their choice unhappy.

Munro had been a partisan well-taught in Indian warfare; and it was said of him, that he knew quite as well how to practise all their subtleties as themselves. The first object with him, therefore, in accordance with his reputation, was to devise some plot, by which not only to destroy the inequality of chances between the party assailing and that defending a post now almost impregnable, but to draw the latter entirely out of their defences. Still, it was deemed but courteous, or prudent at least, to see what could be done in the way of negotiation; and their leader, with a white handkerchief attached to a young sapling, hewn down for the purpose, by way of apology for a flag, approached the besieged, and in front of his men demanded a conference with the usurping chief.

The demand was readily and at once answered by the appearance of the already named George Dexter; a man who, with little sagacity and but moderate cunning, had yet acquired a lead and notoriety among his fellows, even in that wild region, simply from the reckless boldness and fierce impetuosity of his character. It is useless to describe such a person. He was a ruffian—in look and manner, ruffianly—huge of frame, strong and agile of limb, and steeled against all fear, simply from a brute unconsciousness of all danger. There was little of preliminary matter in this conference. Each knew his man, and the business in hand. All was direct, therefore, and to the point. Words were not to be wasted without corresponding fruits, though the colloquy began, on the part of Munro, in terms of the most accredited courtesy.

"Well, George Dexter, a pleasant morning to you in your new accommodations. I see you have learned to make yourself perfectly at home when you visit your neighbors."

"Why, thank you, Wat—I generally do, I reckon, as you know of old. It's not now, I'm inclined to think, that you're to learn the ways of George Dexter. He's a man, you see, Wat, that never has two ways about him."

"That's true, friend George, I must say that for you, were I to have to put in on your tombstone."

"It's a long ride to the Atlantic, Wat; and the time is something off yet, I reckon, when my friends will be after measuring me for a six-foot accommodation. But, look you, Wat, why are all your family here?—I did think, when I first saw them on the trail, some with their twisted and some with smooth bores, tomahawks, and scalping-knives, that they took us for Indians. If you hadn't come forward now, civilly, I should have been for giving your boys some mutton-chops, by way of a cold cut."

"Well, George, you may do that yet, old fellow, for here we have all come to take our Sunday dinner. You are not in the notion that we shall let you take possession here so easily, without even sending us word, and paying us no rent—no compensation?"

"Why, no, Wat—I knew you and your boys too well for that. I did look, you see, to have a bit of a brush, and have made some few preparations to receive you with warmth and open arms," was the response of

Dexter, pointing as he spoke to the well-guarded condition of his intrenchments, and to his armed men, who were now thickly clustering about him.

Munro saw plainly that this was no idle boast, and that the disposition of his enemy's force, without some stratagem, set at defiance any attack under present circumstances. Still he did not despair, and taught in Indian warfare, such a position was the very one to bring out his energies and abilities. Falling back for a moment, he uttered a few words in the ear of one of his party, who withdrew unobserved from his companions, while he returned to the parley.

"Well, George, I see, as you have said, that you have made some preparations to receive us, but they are not the preparations that I like exactly, nor such as I think we altogether deserve."

"That may be, Wat—and I can't help it. If you will invite yourselves to dinner, you must be content with what I put before you."

"It is not a smart speech, Dexter, that will give you free walk on the high road; and something is to be said about this proceeding of yours, which, you must allow, is clearly in the teeth of all the practices prevailing among the people of the frontier. At the beginning, and before any of us knew the value of this or that spot, you chose your ground, and we chose ours. If you leave yours or we ours, then either of us may take possession—not without. Is not this the custom?"

"I tell you what, Munro, I have not lived so long in the woods to listen to wind-guns, and if such is the kind of argument you bring us, your dumpy lawyer—what do you call him?—little Pippin, ought to have been head of your party. He will do it all day long—I've heard him myself, at the sessions, from mid-day till clean dark, and after all he said nothing."

"If you mean to persuade yourself, George, that we shall do no more than *talk* for our lands and improvements, you are likely to suffer something for your mistake."

"Your 'lands and improvements!' Well, now, I like that—that's very good, and just like you. Now, Wat, not to put you to too much trouble, I'd like to look a little into your title to the lands; as to the improvements, they're at your service whenever you think proper to send for them. There's the old lumber-house—there's the squatter's house—there's where the cow keeps, and there's the hogsty, and half a dozen more, all of which you're quite welcome to. I'm sure none of you want 'em, boys—do you?"

A hearty laugh, and cries in the negative, followed this somewhat technical retort and reply of the speaker—since, in trespass, according to the received forms of law, the first duty of the plaintiff is to establish his own title.

"Then, George, you are absolutely bent on having us show our title? You won't deliver up peaceably, and do justice?"

"Can't think of such a thing—we find the quarters here quite too comfortable, and have come too far to be in a hurry to return. We are tired, too, Wat; and it's not civil in you to make such a request. When you can say 'must' to us, we shall hear you, but not till then; so, my old fellow, if you be not satisfied, why, the sooner we come to short sixes the better," was the response of the desperado.

The indifferent composure with which he uttered a response which was in fact the signal for bloodshed, not less than the savage ferocity of his preparations generally, amply sustained his pretension to this appellative. Munro knew his man too well not to perceive that to this "fashion must they come at last;" and simply assuring Dexter that he would submit his decision to his followers, he retired back upon the anxious and indignant party, who had heard a portion, and now eagerly and angrily listened to the rest of the detail.

Having gone over the matter, he proceeded to his arrangements for the attack with all the coolness, and certainly much of the conduct of a veteran. In many respects he truly deserved the character of one; his courage was unquestionable, and aroused; though he still preserved his coolness, even when coupled with the vindictive ferocity of the savage. His experience in all the modes of warfare, commonly known to the white man and Indian alike, in the woods, was complete; everything, indeed, eminently fitted and prepared him for the duties which, by common consent, had been devolved upon him. He now called them around him, under a clump of trees and brushwood which concealed them from sight, and thus addressed them, in a style and language graduated to their pursuits and understandings:—

"And now, my fine fellows, you see it is just as I told you all along. You will have to fight for it, and with no half spirit. You must just use all your strength and skill in it, and a little cunning besides. We have to deal with a man who would just as lief fight as eat; indeed, he prefers it. As he says himself, there's no two ways about him. He will come to the scratch himself, and make everybody else do so. So, then, you see what's before you. It's no child's play. They count more men than we—not to speak of their entrenchments and shelter. We must dislodge them if we can; and to begin, I have a small contrivance in my head which may do some good. I want two from among you to go upon a nice business. I must have men quick of foot, keen of sight, and cunning as a black-snake; and they musn't be afraid of a knock on the head either. Shall I have my men?"

There was no difficulty in this, and the leader was soon provided. He selected two from among the applicants for this distinction, upon whose capacities he thought he could best rely, and led them away from the party into the recess of the wood, where he gave them their directions, and then returned to the main body. He now proceeded to the division, into small parties, of his whole force—placing them under guides rather than leaders, and reserving to himself the instruction and command of the whole. There was still something to be done, and conceiving this to be a good opportunity for employing a test, already determined upon, he approached Ralph Colleton, who surveyed the whole affair with intense curiosity.

"And now, young 'squire, you see what we're driving at, and as our present business wo'nt permit of neutrality, let us hear on which side you stand. Are you for us or against us?"

The question was one rather of command than solicitation, but the manner of the speaker was sufficiently deferential.

"I see not why you should ask the question, sir. I have no concern in your controversy—I know not its merits, and propose simply to content myself with the position of a spectator. I presume there is nothing offensive in such a station."

"There may be, sir; and you know that when people's blood's up, they don't stand on trifles. They are not quick to discriminate between foes and neutrals; and, to speak the truth, we are apt, in this part of the country, to look upon the two, at such moments, as the same. You will judge, therefore, for yourself, of the risk you run."

"I always do, Mr. Munro," said the youth. "I can not see that the risk is very considerable at this moment, for I am at a loss to perceive the policy of your making an enemy of me, when you have already a sufficient number to contend with in yonder barricade. Should your men, in their folly, determine to do so, I am not unprepared, and I think not unwilling, to defend myself."

"Ay, ay—I forgot, sir, you are from Carolina, where they make nothing of swallowing Uncle Sam for a lunch. It is very well, sir; you take your risk, and will abide the consequences though I look not to find you when the fray begins."

"You shall not provoke me, sir, by your sneer; and may assure yourself, if it will satisfy you, that though I will not fight for you, I shall have no scruple of putting a bullet through the scull of the first ruffian who gives me the least occasion to do so."

The youth spoke indignantly, but the landlord appeared not to regard the retort. Turning to the troop, which had been decorously attentive, he bade them follow, saying

"Come on, boys—we shall have to do without the stranger; he does not fight, it seems, for the fun of the thing. If Pippin was here, doubtless, we should have arguments enough from the pair to keep *them* in whole bones, at least, if nobody else."

A laugh of bitter scorn followed the remark of Munro, as the party went on its way.

Though inwardly assured of the propriety of his course, Ralph could not help biting his lip with the mortification he felt from this circumstance, and which he was compelled to suppress; and we hazard nothing in the assertion when we say, that, had his sympathies been at all enlisted with the assailing party, the sarcasm of its leader would have hurried him into the very first rank of attack. As it was, such was its influence upon him, that, giving spur to his steed, he advanced to a position which, while it afforded him a clear survey of the whole field, exposed his person not a little to the shot of either party, as well from without as from within the beleaguered district.

The invading force soon commenced the affair. They came to the attack after the manner of the Indians. The nature of forest-life, and its necessities, of itself teaches this mode of warfare. Each man took his tree, his bush, or stump, approaching from cover to cover until within rifle-reach, then patiently waiting until an exposed head, a side or shoulder, leg or arm, gave an opportunity for the exercise of his skill in marksmanship. To the keen-sighted and quick, rather than to the strong, is the victory; and it will not be wondered at, if, educated thus in daily adventure, the hunter is enabled to detect the slightest and most transient exhibition, and by a shot, which in most cases is fatal, to avail himself of the indiscretion of his enemy. If, however, this habit of life begets skill in attack and destruction, it has not the less beneficial effect in creating a like skill and ingenuity in the matter of defence. In this way we shall account for the limited amount of injury done in the Indian

wars, in proportion to the noise and excitement which they make, and
the many terrors they occasion.

The fight had now begun in this manner, and, both parties being at
the outset studiously well sheltered, with little or no injury—the shot
doing no more harm to the enemy on either side than barking the
branch of the tree or splintering the rock behind which they happened
individually to be sheltered. In this fruitless manner the affray had for a
little time been carried on, without satisfaction to any concerned, when
Munro was beheld advancing, with the apology for a flag which he had
used before, toward the beleaguered fortress. The parley he called for
was acceded to, and Dexter again made his appearance.

"What, tired already, Wat? The game is, to be sure, a shy one; but
have patience, old fellow—we shall be at close quarters directly."

It was now the time for Munro to practise the subtlety which he had
designed, and a reasonable prospect of success he promised himself
from the bull-headed stupidity of his opponent. He had planned a
stratagem, upon which parties, as we have seen, were despatched; and
he now calculated his own movement in concert with theirs. It was his
object to protract the parley which he had begun, by making propositions for an arrangement which, from a perfect knowledge of the men
he had to deal with, he felt assured would not be listened to. In the
meantime, pending the negotiation, each party left its cover and, while
they severally preserved their original relationships and were so situated
as, at a given signal, to regain their positions, they drew nearer to one
another, and in some instances began a conversation. Munro was cautious yet quick in the discussion, and, while his opponent with rough
sarcasms taunted him upon the strength of his own position, and the
utter inadequacy of his strength to force it, he contented himself with
sundry exhortations to a peaceable arrangement—to a giving up of the
possessions they had usurped, and many other suggestions of a like
nature, which he well knew would be laughed at and rejected. Still, the
object was in part attained. The invaders, becoming more confident of
their strength from this almost virtual abandonment of their first resort
by their opponents, grew momently less and less cautious. The rifle was
rested against the rock, the sentinel took out his tobacco, and the two
parties were almost intermingled.

At length the hour had come. A wild and sudden shriek from that
part of the beleaguered district in which the women and children were
congregated, drew all eyes in that direction, where the whole line of

tents and dwellings were in a bright conflagration. The emissaries had done their work ably and well, and the devastation was complete; while the women and children, driven from their various sheltering-places, ran shrieking in every direction. Nor did Munro, at this time, forget his division of the labor: the opportunity was in his grasp, and it was not suffered to escape him. As the glance of Dexter was turned in the direction of the flames, he forgot his precaution, and the moment was not lost. Availing himself of the occasion, Munro dashed his flag of truce into the face of the man with whom he had parleyed, and, in the confusion which followed, seizing him around the body with a strength equal to his own, he dragged him, along with himself, over the low table of rock on which they had both stood upon the soft earth below. Here they grappled with each other, neither having arms, and relying solely upon skill and muscle.

The movement was too sudden, the surprise too complete, not to give an ascendency to the invaders, of which they readily availed themselves. The possession of the fortress was now in fact divided between them; and a mutual consciousness of their relative equality determined the two parties, as if by common consent, quietly to behold the result of the affair between the leaders. They had once recovered their feet, but were both of them again down, Munro being uppermost. Every artifice known to the lusty wrestlers of this region was put in exercise, and the struggle was variously contested. At one time the ascendency was clearly with the one, at another moment it was transferred to his opponent; victory, like some shy arbiter, seeming unwilling to fix the palm, from an equal regard for both claimants. Munro still had the advantage; but a momentary pause of action, and a sudden evolution of his antagonist, now materially altered their position, and Dexter, with the sinuous agility of the snake, winding himself completely around his opponent, now whirled him suddenly over and brought himself upon him. Extricating his arms with admirable skill, he was enabled to regain his knee, which was now closely pressed upon the bosom of the prostrate man, who struggled, but in vain, to free himself from the position.

The face of the ruffian, if we may so call the one in contradistinction to the other, was black with fury; and Munro felt that his violation of the flag of truce was not likely to have any good effect upon his destiny. Hitherto, beyond the weapons of nature's furnishing, they had been unarmed. The case was no longer so; for Dexter, having a momentary use of his hand, provided himself with a huge dirk-knife, guarded by a string which hung around his neck, and was usually worn in his bosom: a sudden jerk threw it wide, and fixed the blade with a spring.

It was a perilous moment for the fallen man, for the glance of the victor, apart from the action, indicated well the vindictive spirit within him; and the landlord averted his eyes, though he did not speak, and upraised his hands as if to ward off the blow. The friends of Munro now hurried to his relief, but the stroke was already descending—when, on a sudden, to the surprise of all, the look of Dexter was turned from the foe beneath him, and fixed upon the hills in the distance—his blow was arrested—his grasp relaxed—he released his enemy, and rose sullenly to his feet, leaving his antagonist unharmed.

CHAPTER THIRTEEN

New Parties to the Conflict

This sudden and unlooked-for escape of Munro, from a fate held so inevitable as well by himself as all around him, was not more a matter of satisfaction than surprise with that experienced personage. He did not deliberate long upon his release, however, before recovering his feet, and resuming his former belligerent attitude.

The circumstance to which he owed the unlooked-for and most unwonted forbearance of his enemy was quickly revealed. Following the now common direction of all eyes, he discerned a body of mounted and armed men, winding on their way to the encampment, in whose well-known uniform he recognised a detachment of the "Georgia Guard," a troop kept, as they all well knew, in the service of the state, for the purpose not merely of breaking up the illegal and unadvised settlements of the squatters upon the frontiers, upon lands now known to be valuable, but also of repressing and punishing their frequent outlawries. Such a course had become essential to the repose and protection of the more quiet and more honest adventurer whose possessions they not only entered upon and despoiled, but whose lives, in numerous instances, had been made to pay the penalty of their enterprise. Such a force could alone meet the exigency, in a country where the sheriff dared not often show himself; and, thus accoutred, and with full authority, the guard, either *en masse*, or in small divisions like the present, was employed, at all times, in scouring, though without any great success, the infested districts.

The body now approaching was readily distinguishable, though yet at a considerable distance—the road over which it came lying upon a long ridge of bald and elevated rocks. Its number was not large, comprising not more than forty persons; but, as the squatters were most commonly distrustful of one another, not living together or in much harmony, and having but seldom, as in the present instance, a community of interest or unity of purpose, such a force was considered adequate to all the duties assigned it. There was but little of the pomp or circumstance of military array in their appearance or approach. Though dressed uniformly the gray and plain stuffs which they wore were more in unison with the habit of the hunter than the warrior; and, as in that country, the rifle is familiar as a household thing, the encounter with an individual of the troop would perhaps call for no remark. The plaintive note of a single bugle, at intervals reverberating wildly among the hills over which the party wound its way, more than anything beside, indicated its character; and even this accompaniment is so familiar as an appendage with the southron—so common, particularly to the negroes, who acquire a singular and sweet mastery over it, while driving their wagons through the woods, or poling their boats down the streams, that one might fairly doubt, with all these symbols, whether the advancing array were in fact more military than civil in its character. They rode on briskly in the direction of our contending parties—the sound of the bugle seeming not only to enliven, but to shape their course, since the stout negro who gave it breath rode considerably ahead of the troop.

Among the squatters there was but little time for deliberation, yet never were their leaders more seriously in doubt as to the course most proper for their adoption in the common danger. They well knew the assigned duties of the guard, and felt their peril. It was necessary for the common safety—or, rather, the common spoil—that something should be determined upon immediately. They were now actually in arms, and could no longer, appearing individually and at privileged occupations, claim to be unobnoxious to the laws; and it need occasion no surprise in the reader, if, among a people of the class we have described, the measures chosen in the present exigency were of a character the most desperate and reckless. Dexter, whose recent triumph gave him something in the way of a title to speak first, thus delivered himself:—

"Well, Munro—you may thank the devil and the Georgia guard for getting you out of that scrape. You owe both of them more now than you ever calculated to owe them. Had they not come in sight just at the lucky moment, my knife would have made mighty small work with your windpipe, I tell you—it did lie so tempting beneath it."

"Yes—I thought myself a gone chick under that spur, George, and so I believe thought all about us; and when you put off the finishing stroke so suddenly, I took it for granted that you had seen the devil, or some other matter equally frightful," was the reply of Munro, in a spirit and style equally unique and philosophical with that which preceded it.

"Why, it was something, though not the devil, bad enough for us in all conscience, as you know just as well as I. The Georgia guard won't give much time for a move."

"Bad enough, indeed, though I certainly ought not to complain of their appearance," was the reply of Munro, whose recent escape seemed to run more in his mind than any other subject. He proceeded:—

"But this isn't the first time I've had a chance so narrow for my neck; and more than once it has been said to me, that the man born for one fate can't be killed by another; but when you had me down and your knife over me, I began to despair of my charm."

"You should have double security for it now, Wat, and so keep your prayers till you see the cross timbers, and the twisted trouble. There's something more like business in hand now, and seeing that we shan't be able to fight one another, as we intended, all that we can do now is to make friends as fast as possible, and prepare to fight somebody else."

"You think just as I should in this matter, and that certainly is the wisest policy left us. It's a common cause we have to take care of, for I happen to know that Captain Fullam—and this I take to be his troop—has orders from the governor to see to us all, and clear the lands in no time. The state, it appears, thinks the land quite too good for such as we, and takes this mode of telling us so. Now, as I care very little about the state—it has never done me any good, and I have always been able to take care of myself without it—I feel just in the humor, if all parties are willing, to have a tug in the matter before I draw stakes."

"That's just my notion, Wat; and d—n 'em, if the boys are only true to the hub, we can row this guard up salt river in no time and less. Look you now—let's put the thing on a good footing, and have no further disturbance. Put all the boys on shares—equal shares—in the diggings, and we'll club strength, and can easily manage these chaps. There's no reason, indeed, why we shouldn't; for if we don't fix them, we are done up, every man of us. We have, as you see and have tried, a pretty strong fence round us, and, if our men stand to it, and I see not why they shouldn't, Fullam can't touch us with his squad of fifty, ay, and a hundred to the back of 'em."

The plan was feasible enough in the eyes of men to whom ulterior consequences were as nothing in comparison with the excitement of the strife; and even the most scrupulous among them were satisfied, in a little time, and with few arguments, that they had nothing to gain and everything to lose by retiring from the possessions in which they had toiled so long. There was nothing popular in the idea of a state expelling them from a soil of which it made no use itself; and few among the persons composing the array had ever given themselves much if any trouble, in ascertaining the nice, and with them entirely metaphysical distinction, between the *mine* and *thine* of the matter. The proposition, therefore, startled none, and prudence having long since withdrawn from their counsels, not a dissenting voice was heard to the suggestion of a union between the two parties for the purpose of common defence. The terms, recognising all of both sides, as upon an equal footing in the profits of the soil, were soon arranged and completed; and in the space of a few moments, and before the arrival of the newcomers, the hostile forces, side by side, stood up for the new contest as if there had never been any other than a community of interest and feeling between them. A few words of encouragement and cheer, given to their several commands by Munro and Dexter, were scarcely necessary, for what risk had their adherents to run—what to fear— what to lose? The courage of the desperado invariably increases in proportion to his irresponsibility. In fortune, as utterly destitute as in character, they had, in most respects, already forfeited the shelter, as in numberless instances they had not merely gone beyond the sanction, but had violated and defied the express interdict, of the laws: and now, looking, as such men are apt most usually to do, only to the immediate issue, and to nothing beyond it, the banditti—for such they were— with due deliberation and such a calm of disposition as might well comport with a life of continued excitement, proceeded again, most desperately, to set them at defiance.

The military came on in handsome style. They were all fine-looking men; natives generally of a state, the great body of whose population are well-formed, and distinguished by features of clear, open intelligence.

They were well-mounted, and each man carried a short rifle, a sword, and pair of pistols. They rode in single file, following their commander; a gentleman, in person, of great manliness of frame, possessed of much grace and ease of action. They formed at command, readily, in front of the post, which may be now said to have assumed the guise of a regular military station; and Fullam, the captain, advancing with much seeming surprise in his countenance and manner, addressed the squatters generally, without reference to the two leaders, who stood forth as representatives of their several divisions.

"How is this, my good fellows? what is meant by your present military attitude? Why are you, on the sabbath, mustering in this guise— surrounded by barricades, arms in your hands, and placing sentinels on duty. What does all this mean?"

"We carry arms," replied Dexter, without pause, "because it suits us to do so; we fix barricades to keep out intruders; our sentinels have a like object; and if by attitude you mean our standing here and standing there—why, I don't see in what the thing concerns anybody but ourselves!"

"Indeed!" said the Georgian; "you bear it bravely, sir. But it is not to you only that I speak. Am I to understand you, good people, as assembled here for the purpose of resisting the laws of the land?"

"We don't know, captain, what you mean exactly by the laws of the land," was the reply of Munro; "but, I must say, we are here, as you see us now, to defend our property, which the laws have no right to take from us—none that I can see."

"So! and is that your way of thinking, sir; and pray who are you that answer so freely for your neighbors?"

"One, sir, whom my neighbors, it seems, have appointed to answer for them."

"I am then to understand, sir, that you have expressed their determination on this subject, and that your purpose is resistance to any process of the state compelling you to leave these possessions!"

"You have stated their resolution precisely," was the reply. "They had notice that unauthorized persons, hearing of our prosperity, were making preparations to take them from us by force; and they prepared for resistance. When we know the proper authorities, we shall answer fairly—but not till then."

"Truly, a very manful determination; and, as you have so expressed yourself, permit me to exhibit my authority, which I doubt not you will readily recognise. This instrument requires you, at once, to remove from these lands—entirely to forego their use and possession, and within forty-eight hours to yield them up to the authority which now claims them at your hands." Here the officer proceeded to read all those portions of his commission to which he referred, with considerable show of patience.

"All that's very well in your hands, and from your mouth, good sir; but how know we that the document you bear is not forged and false— and that you, with your people there, have not got up this fetch to trick us out of those possessions which you have not the heart to fight for? We're up to trap, you see."

With this insolent speech, Dexter contrived to show his impatience of the parley, and that brutal thirst which invariably prompted him to provoke and seek for extremities. The eye of the Georgian flashed out indignant fires, and his fingers instinctively grasped the pistol at his holster, while the strongly-aroused expression of his features indicated the wrath within. With a strong and successful effort, however, though inwardly chafed at the necessity of forbearance, he contrived, for a while longer, to suppress any more decided evidence of emotion, while he replied:—

"Your language, sirrah, whatever you may be, is ruffianly and inso-lent; yet, as I represent the country and not myself in this business, and as I would perform my duties without harshness, I pass it by. I am not bound to satisfy you, or any of your company, of the truth of the com-mission under which I act. It is quite enough if I myself am satisfied. Still, however, for the same reason which keeps me from punishing your insolence, and to keep you from any treasonable opposition to the laws, you too shall be satisfied. Look here, for yourselves, good peo-ple—you all know the great seal of the state!"

He now held up the document from which he had read, and which contained his authority; the broad seal of the state dangling from the parchment, distinctly in the sight of the whole gang. Dexter approached somewhat nearer, as if to obtain a more perfect view; and, while the Georgian, without suspicion, seeing his advance, and supposing that to be his object, held it more toward him, the ruffian, with an active and sudden bound, tore it from his hands, and leaping, followed by all his group, over his defences, was in a moment close under cover, and out of all danger. Rising from his concealment, however, in the presence of the officer, he tore the instrument into atoms, and dashing them toward their proprietor, exclaimed—

"Now, captain, what's the worth of your authority? Be off now in a hurry, or I shall fire upon you in short order!"

We may not describe the furious anger of the Georgian. Irritated beyond the control of a proper caution, he precipitately—and without that due degree of deliberation which must have taught him the madness and inefficacy of any assault by his present force upon an enemy so admirably disposed of—gave the command to fire; and after the ineffectual discharge, which had no other result than to call forth a shout of derision from the besieged, he proceeded to charge the barrier, himself fearlessly leading the way. The first effort to break through the barricades was sufficient to teach him the folly of the design; and a discharge from the defences bringing down two of his men, warned him of the necessity of duly retrieving his error. He saw the odds, and retreated with order and in good conduct, until he sheltered the whole troop under a long hill, within rifle-shot of the enemy, whence, suddenly filing a detachment obliquely to the left, he made his arrangements for the passage of a narrow gorge, having something of the character of a road, and, though excessively broken and uneven, having been frequently used as such. It wound its way to the summit of a large hill, which stood parallel with the defences, and fully commanded them; and the descent of the gorge, on the opposite side, afforded him as good an opportunity, in a charge, of riding the squatters down, as the summit for picking them off singly with his riflemen.

He found the necessity of great circumspection, however, in the brief sample of controversy already given him; and with a movement in front, therefore, of a number of his force—sufficient, by employing the attention of the enemy in that quarter, to cover and disguise his present endeavor—he marshalled fifteen of his force apart from the rest, leading them himself, as the most difficult enterprise, boldly up the narrow pass. The skirmishing was still suffered, therefore, to continue on the ground where it had begun, whenever a momentary exposure of the person of besieged or besieger afforded any chance for a successful shot. Nor was this game very hazardous to either party. The beleaguered force, as we have seen, was well protected. The assailants, having generally dismounted, their horses being placed out of reach of danger, had, in the manner of their opponents, taken the cover of the rising ground, or the fallen tree, and in this way, awaiting the progress of events, were shielded from unnecessary exposure. It was only when a position became awkward or irksome, that the shoulder or the leg of the unquiet man thrust itself too pertinaciously above its shelter, and got barked or battered by a bullet; and as all parties knew too well the skill of their adversaries, it was not often that a shoulder or leg became so indiscreetly prominent.

As it was, however, the squatters, from a choice of ground, and a perfect knowledge of it, together with the additional guards and defences which they had been enabled to place upon it, had evidently the advantage. Still, no event, calculated to impress either party with any decisive notion of the result, had yet taken place; and beyond the injury done to the assailants in their first ill-advised assault, they had suffered no serious harm. They were confident in themselves and their leader—despised the squatters heartily—and, indeed, did not suffer themselves for a moment to think of the possibility of their defeat.

Thus the play proceeded in front of the defences, while Fullam silently and industriously plied his way up the narrow gorge, covered entirely from sight by the elevated ridges of rock, which, rising up boldly on either side of the pass, had indeed been the cause of its formation. But his enemy was on the alert; and the cunning of Munro—whom his companions, with an Indian taste, had entitled the "Black Snake"—had already prepared for the reception of the gallant Georgian. With a quick eye he had observed the diminished numbers of the force in front, and readily concluded, from the sluggishness of the affair in that quarter, that a finesse was in course of preparation. Conscious, too, from a knowledge of the post, that there was but a single mode of enfilading his defences, he had made his provision for the guardianship of the all-important point. Nothing was more easy than the defence of this pass, the ascent being considerable, rising into a narrow gorge, and as suddenly and in like manner descending on the point opposite that on which Fullam was toiling up his way. In addition to this, the gulley was winding and brokenly circuitous—now making a broad sweep of the circle—then terminating in a zig-zag and cross direction, which, until the road was actually gained, seemed to have no outlet; and at no time was the advancing force enabled to survey the pass for any distance ahead.

Everything in the approach of the Georgian was conducted with the profoundest silence: not the slightest whisper indicated to the assailants the presence or prospect of any interruption; and, from the field of strife below, nothing but an occasional shot or shout gave token of the business in which at that moment all parties were engaged. This quiet was not destined to continue long. The forlorn hope had now reached midway of the summit—but not, as their leader had fondly anticipated, without observation from the foe—when the sound of a human voice directly above warned him of his error; and, looking up, he beheld, perched upon a fragment of the cliff, which hung directly over the gorge, the figure of a single man. For the first time led to anticipate resistance in this quarter, he bade the men prepare for the event as well as they might; and calling out imperatively to the individual, who still maintained his place on the projection of the rock as if in defiance, he bade him throw down his arms and submit.

"Throw down my arms! and for what?" was the reply. "I'd like to know by what right you require us to throw down our arms. It may do in England, or any other barbarous country where the people don't know their rights yet, to make them throw down their arms; but I reckon there's no law for it in these parts, that you can show us, captain."

"Pick that insolent fellow off, one of you," was the order; and in an instant a dozen rifles were lifted, but the man was gone. A hat appearing above the cliff, was bored with several bullets; and the speaker, who laughed heartily at the success of his trick, now resumed his position on the cliff, with the luckless hat perched upon the staff on which it had given them the provocation to fire. He laughed and shouted heartily at the contrivance, and hurled the victim of their wasted powder down among them. Much chagrined, and burning with indignation, Fullam briefly cried out to his men to advance quickly. The person who had hitherto addressed him was our old acquaintance Forrester, to whom, in the division of the duties, this post had been assigned. He spoke again:—

"You'd better not, captain, I advise you. It will be dangerous if you come farther. Don't trouble us, now, and be off, as soon as you can, out of harm's way. Your bones will be all the better for it; and I declare I don't like to hurt such a fine-looking chap if I can possibly avoid it. Now take a friend's advice; 'twill be all the better for you, I tell you."

The speaker evidently meant well, so far as it was possible for one to mean well who was commissioned to do, and was, in fact, doing ill. The Georgian, however, only the more indignant at the impertinence of the address, took the following notice of it, uttered in the same breath with an imperative command to his own men to hasten their advance:—

"Disperse yourselves, scoundrels, and throw down your arms!—on the instant disperse! Lift a hand, or pull a trigger upon us, and every man shall dangle upon the branches of the first tree!"

As he spoke, leading the way, he drove his rowels into the sides of his animal; and, followed by his troop, bounded fearlessly up the gorge.

Chapter Fourteen

Catastrophe—Colleton's Discovery

It is time to return to Ralph Colleton, who has quite too long escaped our consideration. The reader will doubtless remember, with little difficulty, where and under what circumstances we left him. Provoked by the sneer and sarcasm of the man whom at the same moment he most cordially despised, we have seen him taking a position in the controversy, in which his person, though not actually within the immediate sphere of action, was nevertheless not a little exposed to some of its risks. This position, with fearless indifference, he continued to maintain, unshrinkingly and without interruption, throughout the whole period and amid all the circumstances of the conflict. There was something of a boyish determination in this way to assert his courage, which his own sense inwardly rebuked; yet such is the nature of those peculiarities in southern habits and opinions, to which we have already referred, on all matters which relate to personal prowess and a masculine defiance of danger, that, even while entertaining the most profound contempt for those in whose eye the exhibition was made, he was not sufficiently independent of popular opinion to brave its current when he himself was its subject. He may have had an additional motive for this proceeding, which most probably enforced its necessity. He well knew that fearless courage, among this people, was that quality which most certainly won and secured their respect; and the policy was not unwise, perhaps, which represented this as a good opportunity for a display which might have the effect of protecting him from wanton insult or aggression hereafter. To a certain extent he was at their mercy; and conscious, from what he had seen, of the unscrupulous character of their minds, every exhibition of the kind had some weight in his favor.

It was with a lively and excited spirit that he surveyed, from the moderate eminence on which he stood, the events going on around him. Though not sufficiently near the parties (and scrupulous not to expose himself to the chance of being for a moment supposed to be connected with either of them) to ascertain their various arrangements, from what had met his observation, he had been enabled to form a very correct inference as to the general progress of affairs. He had beheld the proceedings of each array while under cover, and contending with one another, to much the same advantage as the spectator who surveys the game in which two persons are at play. He could have pointed out the mistakes of both in the encounter he had witnessed, and felt assured that he could have ably and easily amended them. His frame quivered with the "rapture of the strife," as Attila is said to have called the excitation of battle; and his blood, with a genuine southern fervor, rushed to and from his heart with a bounding impulse, as some new achievement of one side or the other added a fresh interest to, and in some measure altered the face of, the affair. But when he beheld the new array, so unexpectedly, yet auspiciously for Munro, make its appearance upon the field, the excitement of his spirit underwent proportionate increase; and with deep anxiety, and a sympathy now legitimate with the assailants, he surveyed the progress of an affray for which his judgment prepared him to anticipate a most unhappy termination. As the strife proceeded, he half forgot his precaution, and unconsciously continued, at every moment, to approach more nearly to the scene of strife. His heart was now all impulse, his spirit all enthusiasm; and with an unquiet eye and restless frame, he beheld the silent passage of the little detachment under the gallant Georgian, up the narrow gorge. At some distance from the hill, and on an eminence, his position enabled him to perceive, when the party had made good their advance nearly to the summit, the impending danger. He saw the threatening cliff, hanging as it were in mid air above them; and all his sympathies, warmly excited at length by the fearfulness of the peril into a degree of active partisanship which, at the beginning, a proper prudence had well counselled him to avoid, he put spurs to his steed, and rushing forward to the foot of the hill, shouted out to the advancing party the nature of the danger which awaited them. He shouted strenuously, but in vain—and with a feeling almost amounting to agony, he beheld the little troop resolutely advance beneath the ponderous rock, which, held in its place by the slightest purchase, needed but the most moderate effort to upheave and unfix it for ever.

It was fortunate for the youth that the situation in which he stood was concealed entirely from the view of those in the encampment. It had been no object with him to place himself in safety, for the consideration of his own chance of exposure had never been looked to in his mind, when, under the noble impulse of humanity, he had rushed forward, if possible, to recall the little party, who either did not or were unwilling to hear his voice of warning and prevention. Had he been beheld, there would have been few of the squatters unable, and still fewer unwilling, to pick him off with their rifles; and, as the event will show, the good Providence alone which had hitherto kept with him, rather than the forbearance of his quondam acquaintance, continued to preserve his life.

Apprized of the ascent of the pass, and not disposed to permit of the escape of those whom the defenders of it above might spare, unobserved by his assailants in front, Dexter, with a small detachment, sallying through a loophole of his fortress, took an oblique course toward the foot of the gorge, by which to arrest the flight of the fugitives. This course brought him directly upon, and in contact with, Ralph, who stood immediately at its entrance, with uplifted eye, and busily engaged in shouting, at intervals, to the yet advancing assailants. The squatters approached cautiously and unperceived; for so deeply was the youth interested in the fate of those for whom his voice and hands were alike uplifted, that he was conscious of nothing else at that moment of despair and doubt. The very silence which at that time hung over all things, seemed of itself to cloud and obstruct, while they lulled the senses into a corresponding slumber.

It was well for the youth, and unlucky for the assassin, that, as Dexter, with his uplifted hatchet—for fire-arms at that period he dared not use, for fear of attracting the attention of his foes—struck at his head, his advanced foot became entangled in the root of a tree which ran above the surface, and the impetus of his action occurring at the very instant in which he encountered the obstruction, the stroke fell short of his victim, and grazed the side of his horse; while the ruffian himself, stumbling forward and at length, fell headlong upon the ground.

The youth was awakened to consciousness. His mind was one of that cast with which to know, to think, and to act, are simultaneous. Of ready decision, he was never at a loss, and seldom surprised into even momentary incertitude. With the first intimation of the attack upon himself, his pistol had been drawn, and while the prostrate ruffian was endeavoring to rise, and before he had well regained his feet, the unerring ball was driven through his head, and without word or effort he fell back among his fellows, the blood gushing from his mouth and nostrils in unrestrained torrents.

The whole transaction was the work of a single instant; and before the squatters, who came with their slain leader, could sufficiently recover from the panic produced by the event to revenge his death, the youth was beyond their reach; and the assailing party of the guard, in front of the post, apprized of the sally by the discharge of the pistol, made fearful work among them by a general fire, while obliquing to the entrance of the pass just in time to behold the catastrophe, now somewhat precipitated by the event which had occurred below. Ralph, greatly excited, regained his original stand of survey, and with feelings of unrepressed horror beheld the catastrophe. The Georgian had almost reached the top of the hill—another turn of the road gave him a glimpse of the table upon which rested the hanging and disjointed cliff of which we have spoken, when a voice was heard—a single voice—in inquiry:—

"All ready?"

The reply was immediate—

"Ay, ay; now prize away, boys, and let go."

The advancing troop looked up, and were permitted a momentary glance of the terrible fate which awaited them before it fell. That moment was enough for horror. A general cry burst from the lips of those in front, the only notice which those in the rear ever received of the danger before it was upon them. An effort, half paralyzed by the awful emotion which came over them, was made to avoid the down-coming ruin; but with only partial success; for, in an instant after, the ponderous mass, which hung for a moment like a cloud above them, upheaved from its bed of ages, and now freed from all stays, with a sudden, hurricane-like and whirling impetus, making the solid rock tremble over which it rushed, came thundering down, swinging over one half of the narrow trace, bounding from one side to the other along the gorge, and with the headlong fury of a cataract sweeping everything from before its path until it reached the dead level of the plain below. The involuntary shriek from those who beheld the mass, when, for an instant impending above them, it seemed to hesitate in its progress down, was more full of human terror than any utterance which followed the event. With the exception of a groan, wrung forth here and there from the half-crushed victim, in nature's agony, the deep silence which ensued was painful and appalling; and even when the dust had dissipated, and the eye was enabled to take in the entire amount of the evil deed, the prospect failed in impressing the senses of the survivors with so distinct a sentiment of horror, as when the doubt and death, suspended in air, were yet only threatened.

Though prepared for the event, in one sense of the word, the great body of the squatters were not prepared for the unusual emotions which succeeded it in their bosoms. The arms dropped from the hands of many of them—a speechless horror was the prevailing feature of all, and all fight was over, while the scene of bloody execution was now one of indiscriminate examination and remark with friend and foe. Ralph was the first to rush up the fatal pass, and to survey the horrible prospect.

One half of the brave little corps had been swept to instant death by the unpitying rock, without having afforded the slightest obstacle to its fearful progress. In one place lay a disembowelled steed panting its last; mangled in a confused and unintelligible mass lay beside him another, the limbs of his rider in many places undistinguishable from his own. One poor wretch, whom he assisted to extricate from beneath the body of his struggling horse, cried to him for water, and died in the prayer. Fortunately for the few who survived the catastrophe—among whom was their gallant but unfortunate young leader—they had, at the first glimpse of the danger, urged on their horses with redoubled effort, and by a close approach to the surface of the rock, taking an oblique direction wide of its probable course, had, at the time of its precipitation, reached a line almost parallel with the place upon which it stood, and in this way achieved their escape without injury. Their number was few, however; and not one half of the fifteen, who commenced the ascent, ever reached or survived its attainment.

Ralph gained the summit just in time to prevent the completion of the foul tragedy by its most appropriate climax. As if enough had not yet been done in the way of crime, the malignant and merciless Rivers, of whom we have seen little in this affair, but by whose black and devilish spirit the means of destruction had been hit upon, which had so well succeeded, now stood over the body of the Georgian, with uplifted hand, about to complete the deed already begun. There was not a moment for delay, and the youth sprung forward in time to seize and wrest the weapon from his grasp. With a feeling of undisguised indignation he exclaimed, as the outlaw turned furiously upon him—

"Wretch—what would you? Have you not done enough? would you strike the unresisting man?"

Rivers, with undisguised effort, now turned his rage upon the intruder. His words, choked by passion, could scarce find utterance; but he spoke with furious effort at length, as he directed a wild blow with a battle-axe at the head of the youth.

"You come for your death, and you shall have it!"

"Not yet," replied Ralph, adroitly avoiding the stroke and closing with the ruffian—"you will find that I am not unequal to the struggle, though it be with such a monster as yourself."

What might have been the event of this combat may not be said. The parties were separated in a moment by the interposition of Forrester, but not till our hero, tearing off in the scuffle the handkerchief which had hitherto encircled the cheeks of his opponent, discovered the friendly outlaw who collected toll for the Pony Club, and upon whose face the hoof of his horse was most visibly engraven—who had so boldly avowed his design upon his life and purse, and whom he had so fortunately and successfully foiled on his first approach to the village.

The fight was over after this catastrophe; the survivors of the guard, who were unhurt, had fled; and the parties with little stir were all now assembled around the scene of it. There was little said upon the occasion. The wounded were taken such care of as circumstances would permit; and wagons having been provided, were all removed to the village. Begun with too much impulse, and conducted with too little consideration, the struggle between the military and the outlaws had now terminated in a manner that left perhaps but little satisfaction in the minds of either party. The latter, though generally an unlicensed tribe—an Ishmaelitish race—whose hands were against all men, were not so sure that they had not been guilty of a crime, not merely against the laws of man and human society, but against the self-evident decrees and dictates of God; and with this doubt, at least, if not its conviction, in their thoughts, their victory, such as it was, afforded a source of very qualified rejoicing.

CHAPTER FIFTEEN

Close Quarters

Colleton was by no means slow in the recognition of the ruffian, and only wondered at his own dullness of vision in not having made the discovery before. Nor did Rivers, with all his habitual villany, seem so well satisfied with his detection. Perceiving himself fully known, a momentary feeling of inquietude came over him; and though he did not fear, he began to entertain in his mind that kind of agitation and doubt which made him, for the first time, apprehensive of the consequences. He was not the cool villain like Munro—never to be taken by surprise, or at disadvantage; and his eye was now withdrawn, though but for a moment, beneath the stern and searching glance which read him through.

That tacit animal confession and acknowledgment were alone sufficient to madden a temper such as that of Rivers. Easily aroused, his ferocity was fearless and atrocious, but not measured or methodical. His mind was not marked—we had almost said tempered—by that wholesome indifference of mood which, in all matters of prime villany, is probably the most desirable constituent. He was, as we have seen, a creature of strong passions, morbid ambition, quick and even habitual excitement; though, at times, endeavoring to put on that air of sarcastic superiority to all emotion which marked the character of the ascetic philosopher—a character to which he had not the slightest claim of resemblance, and the very affectation of which, whenever he became aroused or irritated, was completely forgotten. Without referring—as Munro would have done, and, indeed, as he subsequently did—to the precise events which had already just taken place and were still in progress about him, and which made all parties equally obnoxious with himself to human punishment, and for an offence far more criminal in its dye than that which the youth laid to his charge—he could not avoid the momentary apprehension, which—succeeding with the quickness of thought the intelligent and conscious glance of Colleton—immediately came over him. His eye, seldom distinguished by such a habit, quailed before it; and the deep malignity and festering hatred of his soul toward the youth, which it so unaccountably entertained before, underwent, by this mortification of his pride, a due degree of exaggeration.

Ralph, though wise beyond his years, and one who, in a thought borrowed in part from Ovid, we may say, could rather compute them by events than ordinary time, wanted yet considerably in that wholesome, though rather dowdyish virtue, which men call prudence. He acted on the present occasion precisely as he might have done in the college campus, with all the benefits of a fair field and a plentiful crowd of backers. Without duly reflecting whether an accusation of the kind he preferred, at such a time, to such men, and against one of their own accomplices, would avail much, if anything, toward the punishment of the criminal—not to speak of his own risk, necessarily an almost certain consequence from such an implied determination not to be *particeps criminis* with any of them, he approached, and boldly denounced Rivers as a murderous villain; and urgently called upon those around him to aid in his arrest.

But he was unheard—he had no auditors; nor did this fact result from any unwillingness on their part to hear and listen to the charge against one so detested as the accused. They could see and hear but of one subject—they could comprehend no other. The events of such fresh and recent occurrence were in all minds and before all eyes; and few, besides Forrester, either heard to understand, or listened for a moment to the recital.

Nor did the latter and now unhappy personage appear to give it much more consideration than the rest. Hurried on by the force of associating circumstances, and by promptings not of himself or his, he had been an active performer in the terrible drama we have already witnessed, and the catastrophe of which he could now only, and in vain, deplore. Leaning with vacant stare and lacklustre vision against the neighboring rock, he seemed indifferent to, and perhaps ignorant of, the occurrences taking place around him. He had interfered when the youth and Rivers were in contact, but so soon after the event narrated, that time for reflection had not then been allowed. The dreadful process of thinking himself into an examination of his own deeds was going on; and remorse, with its severe but salutary stings, was doing, without restraint, her rigorous duties.

Though either actually congregated or congregating around him, and within free and easy hearing of his voice, now stretched to its utmost, the party were quite too busily employed in the discussion of the events—too much immersed in the sudden stupor which followed, in nearly all minds, their termination—to know or care much what were the hard words which our young traveller bestowed upon the detected outlaw. They had all of them (their immediate leaders excepted) been hurried on, as is perfectly natural and not unfrequently the case, by the rapid succession of incidents (which in their progress of excitement gave them no time for reflection), from one act to another; without perceiving, in a single pause, the several gradations by which they insensibly passed on from crime to crime;—and it was only now, and in a survey of the several foot-prints in their progress, that they were enabled to perceive the vast and perilous leaps which they had taken. As in the ascent of the elevation, step by step, we can judge imperfectly of its height, until from the very summit we look down upon our place of starting, so with the wretched outcasts of society of whom we speak. Flushed with varying excitements, they had deputed the task of reflection to another and a calmer time; and with the reins of sober reason relaxed, whirled on by their passions, they lost all control over their own impetuous progress, until brought up and checked, as we have seen, by a catastrophe the most ruinous—the return of reason being the signal for the rousing up of those lurking furies—terror, remorse, and many and maddening regrets. From little to large events, we experience or behold this every day. It is a history, and all read it. It belongs to human nature and to society; and until some process shall be discovered by which men shall be compelled to think by rule and under regulation, as in a penitentiary their bodies are required to work, we despair of having much improvement in the general condition of human affairs. The ignorant and uneducated man is quite too willing to depute to others the task of thinking for him and furnishing his opinions. The great mass are gregarious, and whether a lion or a log is chosen for their guidance, it is still the same—they will follow the leader, if regularly recognised as such, even though he be an ass. As if conscious of their own incapacities, whether these arise from deficiencies of education or denials of birth, they forego the only habit—that of self-examination—which alone can supply the deficiency; and with a blind determination, are willing, on any terms, to divest themselves of the difficulties and responsibilities of their own government. They crown others with all command, and binding their hands with cords, place themselves at the disposal of those, who, in many cases, not satisfied with thus much, must have them hookwinked also. To this they also consent, taking care, in their great desire to be slaves, to be foremost themselves in trying on the bandage which keeps them in darkness and in chains for ever. Thus will they be content to live, however wronged, if not absolutely bruised and beaten; happy to escape from the cares of an independent mastery of their own conduct, if, in this way, they can also escape from the noble responsibilities of independence.

The unhappy men, thus led on, as we have seen, from the commission of misdemeanor to that of crime, in reality, never for a moment thought upon the matter. The landlord, Dexter, and Rivers, had, time out of mind, been their oracles; and, without referring to the distinct condition of those persons, they reasoned in a manner not uncommon with the ignorant. Like children at play, they did not perceive the narrow boundaries which separate indulgence from licentiousness; and in the hurried excitement of the mood, inspired by the one habit, they had passed at once, unthinkingly and unconsciously, into the excesses of the other. They now beheld the event in its true colors, and there were but few among the squatters not sadly doubtful upon the course taken, and suffering corresponding dismay from its probable consequences. To a few, such as Munro and Rivers, the aspect of the thing was unchanged—they had beheld its true features from the outset, and knew the course, and defied the consequences. They had already made up their minds upon it—had regarded the matter in all its phases, and suffered no surprise accordingly. Not so with the rest—with Forrester in particular, whose mental distress, though borne with manliness, was yet most distressing. He stood apart, saying nothing, yet lamenting inwardly, with the self-upbraidings of an agonized spirit, the easy facility with which he had been won, by the cunning of others, into the perpetration of a crime so foul. He either for a time heard not or understood not the charges made by Ralph against his late coadjutor, until brought to his consciousness by the increased stir among the confederates, who now rapidly crowded about the spot, in time to hear the denial of the latter to the accusation, in language and a manner alike fierce and unqualified.

"Hear me!" was the exclamation of the youth—his voice rising in due effect, and illustrating well the words he uttered, and the purpose of his speech:—"I charge this born and branded villain with an attempt upon my life. He sought to rob and murder me at the Catcheta pass but a few days ago. Thrown between my horse's feet in the struggle, he received the brand of his hoof, which he now wears upon his cheek. There he stands, with the well-deserved mark upon him, and which, but for the appearance of his accomplices, I should have made of a yet deeper character. Let him deny it if he can or dare."

The face of Rivers grew alternately pale and purple with passion, and he struggled in vain, for several minutes, to speak. The words came from him hoarsely and gratingly. Fortunately for him, Munro, whose cool villany nothing might well discompose, perceiving the necessity of speech for him who had none, interfered with the following inquiry, uttered in something like a tone of surprise.

"And what say you to this accusation, Guy Rivers? Can you not find an answer?"

"It is false—false as hell! and you know it, Munro, as well as myself. I never saw the boy until at your house."

"That I know, and why you should take so long to say it I can't understand. It appears to me, young gentleman," said Munro, with most cool and delightful effrontery, "that I can set all these matters right. I can show you to be under a mistake; for I happen to know that, at the very time of which you speak, we were both of us up in the Chestatee fork, looking for a runaway slave—you know the fellow, boys—Black Tom—who has been *out* for six months and more, and of whom I got information a few weeks ago. Well, as everybody knows, the Chestatee fork is at least twenty miles from the Catcheta pass; and if we were in one place, we could not, I am disposed to think, very well be in another."

"An *alibi*, clearly established," was the remark of Counsellor Pippin, who now, peering over the shoulders of the youth, exhibited his face for the first time during the controversies of the day. Pippin was universally known to be possessed of an admirable scent for finding out a danger when it is well over, and when the spoils, and not the toils, of the field are to be reaped. His appearance at this moment had the effect of arousing, in some sort, the depressed spirits of those around him, by recalling to

memory and into exercise the jests upon his infirmities, which long use
had made legitimate and habitual. Calculating the probable effect of
such a joke, Munro, without seeming to observe the interruption, looking significantly round among the assembly, went on to say—

"If you have been thus assaulted, young man, and I am not disposed to say it is not as you assert, it can not have been by any of our village, unless it be that Counsellor Pippin and his fellow Hob were the
persons: they were down, now I recollect, at the Catcheta pass, somewhere about the time; and I've long suspected Pippin to be more dangerous than people think him."

"I deny it all—I deny it. It's not true, young man. It's not true, my
friends; don't believe a word of it. Now, Munro, how can you speak so?
Hob—Hob—Hob—I say—where the devil are you? Hob—say, you
rascal, was I within five miles of the Catcheta pass to-day?" The negro,
a black of the sootiest complexion, now advanced:—

"No, maussa."

"Was I yesterday?"

The negro put his finger to his forehead, and the lawyer began to
fret at this indication of thought, and, as it promised to continue,
exclaimed—

"Speak, you rascal, speak out; you know well enough without
reflecting." The slave cautiously responded—

"If maussa want to be dere, maussa dere—no 'casion for ax Hob."

"You black rascal, you know well enough I was not there—that I
was not within five miles of the spot, either to-day, yesterday, or for ten
days back!"

"Berry true, maussa; if you no dere, you no dere. Hob nebber say
one ting when maussa say 'noder."

The unfortunate counsellor, desperate with the deference of his
body-servant, now absolutely perspired with rage; while, to the infinite
amusement of all, in an endeavor to strike the pliable witness, who
adroitly dodged the blow, the lawyer, not over-active of frame, plunged
incontinently forward, and paused not in his headlong determination
until he measured himself at length upon the ground. The laugh which
succeeded was one of effectual discomfiture, and the helpless barrister
made good his retreat from a field so unpromising by a pursuit of the
swift-footed negro, taking care not to return from the chase.

Colleton, who had regarded this interlude with stern brow and
wrathful spirit, now spoke, addressing Munro:—

"You affirm most strongly for this villain, but your speech is vain if its object be to satisfy my doubts. What effect it may have upon our hearers is quite another matter. You can not swear me out of my conviction and the integrity of my senses. I am resolute in the one belief, and do not hesitate here, and in the presence of himself and all of you, to pronounce him again all the scoundrel I declared him to be at first— in the teeth of all your denials not less than of his! But, perhaps—as you answer for him so readily and so well—let us know, for doubtless you can, by what chance he came by that brand, that fine impress which he wears so happily upon his cheek. Can you not inform him where he got it—on what road he met with it, and whether the devil's or my horse's heel gave it him!"

"If your object be merely to insult me, young man, I forgive it. You are quite too young for me to punish, and I have only pity for the indiscretion that moves you to unprofitable violence at this time and in this place, where you see but little respect is shown to those who invade us with harsh words or actions. As for your charge against Rivers, I happen to know that it is unfounded, and my evidence alone would be sufficient for the purpose of his defence. If, however, he were guilty of the attempt, as you allege, of what avail is it for you to make it? Look around you, young man!"—taking the youth aside as he spoke in moderated terms—"you have eyes and understanding, and can answer the question for yourself. Who is here to arrest him? Who would desire, who would dare to make the endeavor? We are all here equally interested in his escape, were he a criminal in this respect, because we are all here"—and his voice fell in such a manner as to be accommodated to the senses of the youth alone—"equally guilty of violating the same laws, and by an offence in comparison with which that against you would be entirely lost sight of. There is the courthouse, it is true—and there the jail; but we seldom see sheriff, judge, or jailer. When they do make their appearance, which is not often, they are glad enough to get away again. If we here suffer injury from one another, we take justice into our own hands—as you allege yourself partly to have done in this case—and there the matter generally ends. Rivers, you think, assaulted you, and had the worst of it. You got off with but little harm yourself, and a reasonable man ought to be satisfied. Nothing more need be said of it. This is the wisest course, let me advise you. Be quiet about the matter, go on your way, and leave us to ourselves. Better suffer a little wrong, and seem to know nothing of it, than risk a quarrel with those who, having once put themselves out of the shelter of the laws, take every opportunity of putting them at defiance. And what if you were to push the matter, where will the sheriff or the military find us? In a week and the judge will arrive, and the court will be in session. For that week we shall be out of the way. Nobody shall know—nobody can find us. This day's work will most probably give us all a great itch for travel."

Munro had, in truth, made out a very plain case; and his representations, in the main, were all correct. The youth felt their force, and his reason readily assented to the plain-sense course which they pointed out. Contenting himself, therefore, with reiterating the charge, he concluded with saying that, for the present, he would let the affair rest. "Until the ruffian"—thus he phrased it—"had answered the penalties of the laws for his subsequent and more heinous offence against them, he should be silent."

"But I have not done with *you*, young sir," was the immediate speech of Rivers—his self-confidence and much of his composure returned, as, with a fierce and malignant look, and a quick stride, he approached the youth. "You have thought proper to make a foul charge against me, which I have denied. It has been shown that your assertion is unfounded, yet you persist in it, and offer no atonement. I now demand redress—the redress of a gentleman. You know the custom of the country, and regard your own character, I should think, too highly to refuse me satisfaction. You have pistols, and here are rifles and dirks. Take your choice."

The youth looked upon him with ineffable scorn as he replied—

"You mistake me, sirrah, if you think I can notice your call with anything but contempt."

"What! will you not fight—not fight? not back your words?"

"Not with you!" was the calm reply.

"You refuse me satisfaction, after insulting me!"

"I always took him for a poor chicken, from the first time I set eyes on him," said one of the spectators.

"Yes, I didn't think much of him, when he refused to join us," was the remark of another.

"This comes of so much crowing; Brag is a good dog, but Holdfast is better," went on a third, and each man had his remark upon Colleton's seeming timidity. Scorn and indignation were in all faces around him; and Forrester, at length awakened from his stupor by the tide of fierce comment setting in upon his friend from all quarters, now thought it time to interfere.

"Come, 'squire, how's this? Don't give way—give him satisfaction, as he calls it, and send the lead into his gizzard. It will be no harm done, in putting it to such a creature as that. Don't let him crow over old Carolina—don't, now, squire! You can hit him as easy as a barndoor, for I saw your shot today; don't be afraid, now—stand up, and I'll back you against the whole of them."

"Ay, bring him forward, Forrester. Let him be a man, if he can," was the speech of one of the party.

"Come, 'squire, let me say that you are ready. I'll mark off the ground, and you shall have fair play," was the earnest speech of the woodman in terms of entreaty.

"You mistake me greatly, Forrester, if you suppose for a moment that I will contend on equal terms with such a wretch. He is a common robber and an outlaw, whom I have denounced as such, and whom I can not therefore fight with. Were he a gentleman, or had he any pretensions to the character, you should have no need to urge me on, I assure you."

"I know that, 'squire, and therefore it provokes me to think that the skunk should get off. Can't you, now, lay aside the gentleman just long enough to wing him? Now, do try!"

The youth smiled as he shook his head negatively. Forrester, with great anxiety, proceeded:—

"But, 'squire, they won't know your reason for refusing, and they will set you down as afear'd. They will call you a coward!"

"And what if they do, Forrester? They are not exactly the people about whose opinions I give myself any concern. I am not solicitous to gain credit for courage among them. If any of them doubt it, let him try me. Let one of them raise a hand or lift a finger upon me, and make the experiment. They will then find me ready and willing enough to defend myself from any outrage, come from what quarter it may."

"I'm afraid, 'squire, they can't be made to understand the difference between a gentleman and a squatter. Indeed, it isn't reasonable that they should, seeing that such a difference puts them out of any chance of dressing a proud fellow who carries his head too high. If you don't fight, 'squire, I must, if it's only for the honor of old Carolina. So here goes."

The woodman threw off his coat, and taking up his rifle, substituted

a new for the old flint, and furnishing the pan with fresh priming, before
our hero could well understand the proposed and novel arrangement so
as to interpose in its arrest, he advanced to the spot where Rivers stood,
apparently awaiting the youth's decision, and, slapping him upon the
shoulder, thus addressed him:—

"I say, Guy Rivers, the 'squire thinks you too great a blackguard for
him to handle, and leaves all the matter to me. Now, you see, as I've
done *that* to-day which makes me just as great a blackguard as yourself,
I stand up in his place. So here's for you. You needn't make any excuse,
and say you have no quarrel with me, for, as I am to handle you in his
place, you will consider me to say everything that he has said—every
word of it; and, in addition to that, if more be necessary, you must know
I think you a mere skunk, and I've been wanting to have a fair lick at
you for a monstrous long season."

"You shall not interfere, Forrester, and in this manner, on any pretence, for the shelter of the coward, who, having insulted me, now
refuses to give me satisfaction. If you have anything to ask at my hands,
when I have done with him, I shall be ready for you," was the reply of
Rivers.

"You hear that 'squire? I told you so. He has called you a coward,
and you will have to fight him at last."

"I do not see the necessity for that, Forrester, and beg that you will
undertake no fighting on my account. When my honor is in danger, I
am man enough to take care of it myself; and, when I am not, my friend
can do me no service by taking my place. As for this felon, the hangman
for him—nobody else."

Maddened, not less by the cool determination of Colleton than by
the contemptuous conclusion of his speech, Rivers, without a word,
sprang fiercely upon him with a dirk, drawn from his bosom with con-
certed motion as he made the leap—striking, as he approached, a blow
at the unguarded breast of the youth, which, from the fell and fiendish
aim and effort, must have resulted fatally had he not been properly prepared for some such attempt. Ralph was in his prime, however, of vigorous make and muscle, and well practised in the agile sports and
athletic exercises of woodland life. He saw the intent in the mischievous
glance of his enemy's eye, in time to guard himself against it; and, suddenly changing his position, as the body of his antagonist was nearly
upon him, he eluded the blow, and the force and impetus employed in
the effort bore the assassin forward. Before he could arrest his own

progress, the youth had closed in upon him, and by a dexterous use of his foot, in a manner well known to the American woodman, Rivers, without being able to interpose the slightest obstacle to the new direction thus given him, was forcibly hurled to the ground.

Before he could recover, the youth was upon him. His blood was now at fever-heat, for he had not heard the taunts upon his courage, from all around him, with indifference, though he had borne them with a laudable show of patience throughout. His eye shot forth fires almost as malignant as those of his opponent. One of his hands was wreathed in the neckcloth of his prostrate foe, while the other was employed in freeing his own dirk from the encumbrances of his vest. This took little time, and he would not have hesitated in the blow, when the interposition of those present bore him off, and permitted the fallen and stunned man to recover his feet. It was at this moment that the honest friendship of Forrester was to be tried and tested. The sympathies of those around were most generally with the ruffian; and the aspect of affairs was something unlucky, when the latter was not only permitted to recommence the attack, but when the youth was pinioned to the ground by others of the gang, and disarmed of all defence. The moment was perilous; and, whooping like a savage, Forrester leaped in between, dealing at the same time his powerful blows from one to the other, right and left, and making a clear field around the youth.

"Fair play is all I ask, boys—fair play, and we can lick the whole of you. Hurra for old Carolina. Who's he says a word against her? Let him stand up, and be knocked down. How's it, 'squire—you an't hurt, I reckon? I hope not; if you are, I'll have a shot with Rivers myself on the spot."

But Munro interposed: "We have had enough outcry, Forrester. Let us have no more. Take this young man along with you, or it will be worse for him."

"Well, Wat Munro, all the 'squire wants is fair play—fair play for both of us, and we'll take the field, man after man. I tell you what, Munro, in our parts the chickens are always hatched with spurs, and the children born with their eye-teeth. We know something, too, about whipping our weight in wildcats; and until the last governor of our state had all the bears killed, because they were getting civilized, we could wrestle with 'em man for man, and throw seven out of ten."

CHAPTER SIXTEEN

Conspiracy—Warning

Ralph was not permitted to return to the village that night—his sturdy friend Forrester insisting upon his occupying with him the little lodge of his own, resting on the borders of the settlement, and almost buried in the forest. Here they conversed until a late hour, previous to retiring; the woodman entering more largely into his own history than he had done before. He suffered painfully from the occurrences of the day: detailed the manner in which he had been worked upon by Munro to take part in the more fearful transaction with the guard—how the excitement of the approaching conflict had defeated his capacities of thought, and led him on to the commission of so great a part of the general offence. Touching the initial affair with the squatters, he had no compunctious scruples. That was all fair game in his mode of thinking, and even had blood been spilled more freely than it was, he seemed to think he should have had no remorse. But on the subject of the murder of the guard, for so he himself called his crime, his feeling was so intensely agonizing that Ralph, though as much shocked as himself at the events, found it necessary to employ sedative language, and to forbear all manner of rebuke.

At an early hour of the morning, they proceeding in company to the village—Forrester having to complete certain arrangements prior to his flight; which, by the advice of Colleton, he had at once determined upon. Such, no doubt, was the determination of many among them not having those resources, in a familiarity with crime and criminal associations, which were common to Munro and Rivers.

The aspect of the village was somewhat varied from its wont. Its people were not so far gone in familiarity with occurrences like those of the preceding day, as to be utterly insensible to their consequences; and a chill inertness pervaded all faces, and set at defiance every endeavor on the part of the few who had led, to put the greater number in better spirits, either with themselves or those around them. They were men habituated, it may be, to villainies; but of a petty description, and far beneath that which we have just recorded. It is not, therefore, to be wondered at, if, when the momentary impulse had passed away, they felt numerous misgivings. They were all assembled, as on the day before—their new allies with them—arms in their hands, but seemingly without much disposition for their use. They sauntered unconsciously about the village, in little groups or individually, without concert or combination, and with suspicious or hesitating eye. Occasionally, the accents of a single voice broke the general silence, though but for a moment; and then, with a startling and painful influence, which imparted a still deeper sense of gloom to the spirits of all. It appeared to come laden with a mysterious and strange terror, and the speaker, aptly personifying the Fear in Collins's fine "Ode on the Passions," "shrunk from the sound himself had made."

Ralph, in company with Forrester, made his appearance among the squatters while thus situated. Seeing them armed as on the previous day, he was apprehensive of some new evil; and as he approached the several stray groups, made known his apprehensions to his companion in strong language. He was not altogether assured of Forrester's own compunction, and the appearance of those around almost persuaded him to doubt his sincerity.

"Why are these people assembled, Forrester—is there anything new—is there more to be done—more bloodletting—more crime and violence—are they still unsatisfied?"

The earnestness of the inquirer was coupled with a sternness of eye and warmth of accent which had in them much, that, under other circumstances and at other times, would have been sorely offensive to the sturdy woodman; whose spirit, anything in the guise of rebuke would have been calculated to vex. But he was burdened with thoughts at the moment, which, in a sufficiently monitorial character, humbled him with a scourge that lacerated at every stroke.

"God forbid, 'squire, that more harm should be done. There has been more done already than any of us shall well get rid of. I wish to heaven I had taken caution from you. But I was mad, 'squire, mad to the heart, and became the willing tool of men not so mad, but more evil than I! God forbid, sir, that there should be more harm done."

"Then why this assembly? Why do the villagers, and these ragged and savage fellows whom you have incorporated among you—why do they lounge about idly, with arms in their hands, and faces that still seem bent on mischief?"

"Because, 'squire, it's impossible to do otherwise. We can't go to work, for the life of us, if we wished to; we all feel that we have gone too far, and those, whose own consciences do not trouble them, are yet too much troubled by fear of the consequences to be in any hurry to take up handspike or hammer again in this quarter of the world."

The too guilty man had indeed spoken his own and the condition of the people among whom he lived. They could now see and feel the fruits of that rash error which had led them on; but their consciousness came too late for retrieval, and they now wondered, with a simplicity truly surprising to those who know with what facility an uneducated and warm people may be led to their own ruin, that this consciousness had not come to them before. Ralph, attended by Forrester, advanced among the crowd. As he did so, all eyes were turned upon him, and a sullen conference took place, having reference to himself, between Munro and a few of the ringleaders. This conference was brief, and as soon as it was concluded, the landlord turned to the youth, and spoke as follows:—

"You were a witness, Mr. Colleton, of this whole transaction, and can say whether the soldiers were not guilty of the most unprovoked assault upon us, without reason or right."

"I can say no such thing, sir," was his reply. "On the contrary, I am compelled to say, that a more horrible and unjustifiable transaction I never witnessed. I must say that they were not the aggressors."

"How unjustifiable, young sir?" quickly and sternly retorted the landlord. "Did you not behold us ridden down by the soldiery? did they not attack us in our trenches—in our castle, as it were? and have we not a right to defend our castle from assailants? They took the adventure at their peril, and suffered accordingly."

"I know not what your title may be to the grounds you have defended so successfully, and which you have styled your castle, nor shall I stop to inquire. I do not believe that your right either gave you possession or authorized your defence in this cruel manner. The matter, however, is between you and your country. My own impressions are decidedly against you; and were I called upon for an opinion as to your mode of asserting your pretended right, I should describe it as brutal and barbarous, and wholly without excuse or justification, whether examined by divine or human laws."

"A sermon, a sermon from the young preacher, come, boys, give him Old Hundred. Really, sir, you promise almost as well as the parson you heard yesterday; and will take lessons from him, if advised by me. But go on—come to a finish—mount upon the stump, where you can be better seen and heard."

The cheek of the youth glowed with indignation at the speech of the ruffian, but he replied with a concentrated calmness that was full of significance:—

"You mistake me greatly, sir, if you imagine I am to be provoked into contest with you by any taunt which you can utter. I pride myself somewhat in the tact with which I discover a ruffian, and having, at an early period of your acquaintance, seen what you were, I can not regard you in any other than a single point of view. Were you not what I know you to be, whatever might have been the difference of force between us, I should ere this have driven my dirk into your throat."

"Why, that's something like, now—that's what I call manly. You do seem to have some pluck in you, young sir, though you might make more use of it. I like a fellow that can feel when he's touched; and don't think a bit the worse of you that you think ill of me, and tell me so. But that's not the thing now. We must talk of other matters. You must answer a civil question or two for the satisfaction of the company. We want to know, sir, if we may apprehend any interference on your part between us and the state. Will you tell the authorities what you saw?"

The youth made no answer to this question, but turning contemptuously upon his heel, was about to leave the circle, around which the assembly, in visible anxiety for his reply, was now beginning to crowd.

"Stay, young master, not so fast. You must give us some answer before you are off. Let us know what we are to expect. Whether, if called upon by any authority, you would reveal what you know of this business?" was the further inquiry of Munro.

"I certainly should—every word of it. I should at once say that you were all criminal, and describe you as the chief actor and instigator in this unhappy affair."

The response of Colleton had been unhesitating and immediate; and having given it, he passed through the throng and left the crowd, which, sullenly parting, made way for him in front. Guy Rivers, in an under tone, muttered in the ear of Munro as he left the circle:—

"That, by the eternal God, he shall never do. Are you satisfied now of the necessity of silencing him?"

Munro simply made a sign of silence, and took no seeming note of his departure; but his determination was made, and there was now no obstacle in that quarter to the long-contemplated vengeance of his confederate.

While this matter was in progress among the villagers, Counsellor Pippin vexed himself and his man Hob not a little with inquiries as to the manner in which he should contrive to make some professional business grow out of it. He could not well expect any of the persons concerned, voluntarily to convict themselves; and his thoughts turned necessarily upon Ralph as the only one on whom he could rest his desire in this particular. We have seen with what indifferent success his own adventure on the field of action, and when the danger was all well over, was attended; but he had heard and seen enough to persuade himself that but little was wanting, without appearing in the matter himself, to induce Ralph to prosecute Rivers for the attempt upon his life, a charge which, in his presence, he had heard him make. He calculated in this way to secure himself in two jobs—as magistrate, to institute the initial proceedings by which Rivers was to be brought to trial, and the expense of which Ralph was required to pay—and, as an attorney-at-law, and the only one of which the village might boast, to have the satisfaction of defending and clearing the criminal.

Such being the result of his deliberations, he despatched Hob with a note to Ralph, requesting to see him at the earliest possible moment, upon business of the last importance. Hob arrived at the inn just at the time when, in the court in front, Ralph, in company with the woodman, had joined the villagers there assembled. Hob, who from long familiarity with the habits of his master, had acquired something of a like disposition, felt exceedingly anxious to hear what was going on; but knowing his situation, and duly valuing his own importance as the servant of so great a man as the village-lawyer, he conceived it necessary to proceed with proper caution.

It is more than probable that his presence would have been unregarded had he made his approaches freely and with confidence; but Hob was outrageously ambitious, and mystery was delightful. He went to work in the Indian manner, and what with occasionally taking the cover, now of a bush, now of a pine tree, and now of a convenient hillock, Hob had got himself very comfortably lodged in the recess of an old ditch, originally cut to carry off a body of water which rested on what was now in part the public mall. Becoming interested in the proceedings, and hearing of the departure of Ralph, to whom he had been despatched, his head gradually assumed a more elevated position—he soon forgot his precaution, and the shoulders of the spy, neither the most diminutive nor graceful, becoming rather too protuberant, were saluted with a smart assault, vigorously kept up by the assailant, to whom the use of the hickory appeared a familiar matter. Hob roared lustily, and was dragged from his cover. The note was found upon him, and still further tended to exaggerate the hostile feeling which the party now entertained for the youth. Under the terrors of the lash, Hob confessed a great deal more than was true, and roused into a part forgetfulness of their offence by the increased prospect of its punishment, which the negro had unhesitatingly represented as near at hand, they proceeded to the office of the lawyer.

It was in vain that Pippin denied all the statements of his negro—his note was thrust into his face; and without scruple, seizing upon his papers, they consigned to the flames, deed, process, and document—all the fair and unfair proceedings alike, of the lawyer, collected carefully through a busy period of twenty years' litigation. They would have proceeded in like manner to the treatment of Ralph, but that Guy Rivers himself interposed to allay, and otherwise direct their fury. The cunning ruffian well knew that Forrester would stand by the youth, and unwilling to incur any risk, where the game in another way seemed so secure, he succeeded in quieting the party, by claiming to himself the privilege, on the part of his wounded honor, of a fair field with one who had so grievously assailed it. Taking the landlord aside, therefore, they discussed various propositions for taking the life of one hateful to the one person and dangerous to them all. Munro was now not unwilling to recognise the necessity of taking him off; and without entering into the feelings of Rivers, which were almost entirely personal, he gave his assent to the deed, the mode of performing which was somewhat to depend upon circumstances. These will find their due development as we proceed.

In the meanwhile, Ralph had returned to the village-inn, encountering, at the first step, upon entering the threshold, the person of the very interesting girl, almost the only redeeming spirit of that establishment. She had heard of the occurrence—as who, indeed, had not—and the first expression of her face as her eyes met those of Ralph, though with a smile, had in it something of rebuke for not having taken the counsel which she had given him on his departure from the place of prayer. With a gentleness strictly in character, he conversed with her for some time on indifferent topics—surprised at every uttered word from her lips—so musical, so true to the modest weaknesses of her own, yet so full of the wisdom and energy which are the more legitimate characteristics of the other sex. At length she brought him back to the subject of the recent strife.

"You must go from this place, Mr. Colleton—you are not safe in this house—in this country. You can now travel without inconvenience from your late injuries, which do not appear to affect you; and the sooner you are gone the better for your safety. There are those here"— and she looked around with a studious caution as she spoke, while her voice sunk into a whisper—"who only wait the hour and the opportunity to—" and here her voice faltered as if she felt the imagined prospect—"to put you to a merciless death. Believe me, and in your confident strength do not despise my warnings. Nothing but prudence and flight can save you."

"Why," said the youth, smiling, and taking her hand in reply, "why should I fear to linger in a region, where one so much more alive to its sternnesses than myself may yet dare to abide? Think you, sweet Lucy, that I am less hardy, less fearless of the dangers and the difficulties of this region than yourself? You little know how much at this moment my spirit is willing to encounter," and as he spoke, though his lips wore a smile, there was a stern sadness in his look, and a gloomy contraction of his brow, which made the expression one of the fullest melancholy.

The girl looked upon him with an eye full of a deep, though unconscious interest. She seemed desirous of searching into that spirit which he had described as so reckless. Withdrawing her hand suddenly, however, as if now for the first time aware of its position, she replied hastily:—

"Yet, I pray you, Mr. Colleton, let nothing make you indifferent to the warning I have given you. There is danger—more danger here to you than to me—though, to me—" the tears filled in her eyes as she spoke, and her head sunk down on her breast with an air of the saddest self-abandonment—"there is more than death."

The youth again took her hand. He understood too well the signification of her speech, and the sad sacrifice which it referred to; and an interest in her fate was awakened in his bosom, which made him for a moment forget himself and the gentle Edith of his own dreams.

"Command me, Miss Munro, though I peril my life in your behalf; say that I can serve you in anything, and trust me to obey."

She shook her head mournfully, but without reply. Again he pressed his services, which were still refused. A little more firmly, however, she again urged his departure.

"My solicitations have no idle origin. Believe me, you are in danger, and have but little time for delay. I would not thus hurry you, but that I would not have you perish. No, no! you have been gentle and kind, as few others have been, to the poor orphan; and, though I would still see and hear you, I would not that you should suffer. I would rather suffer myself."

Much of this was evidently uttered with the most childish unconsciousness. Her mind was obviously deeply excited with her fears, and when the youth assured her, in answer to her inquiries, that he should proceed in the morning on his journey, she interrupted him quickly—

"To-day—to-day—now—do not delay, I pray you. You know not the perils which a night may bring forth."

When assured that he himself could perceive no cause of peril, and when, with a manner sufficiently lofty, he gave her to understand that a feeling of pride alone, if there were no other cause, would prevent a procedure savoring so much of flight, she shook her head mournfully, though saying nothing. In reply to his offer of service, she returned him her thanks, but assuring him he could do her none, she retired from the apartment.

CHAPTER SEVENTEEN

Remorse

During the progress of the dialogue narrated in the conclusion of our last chapter, Forrester had absented himself, as much probably with a delicate sense of courtesy, which anticipated some further results than came from it, as with the view to the consummation of some private matters of his own. He now returned, and signifying his readiness to Ralph, they mounted their horses and proceeded on a proposed ride out of the village, in which Forrester had promised to show the youth a pleasanter region and neighborhood.

This ride, however, was rather of a gloomy tendency, as its influences were lost in the utterance and free exhibition to Ralph of the mental sufferings of his companion. Naturally of a good spirit and temper, his heart, though strong of endurance and fearless of trial, had not been greatly hardened by the world's circumstance. The cold droppings of the bitter waters, however they might have worn into, had not altogether petrified it; and his feelings, coupled with and at all times acted upon by a southern fancy, did not fail to depict to his own sense, and in the most lively colors, the offence of which he had been guilty.

It was with a reproachful and troublesome consciousness, therefore, that he now addressed his more youthful companion on the subject so fearfully presented to his thought. He had already, in their brief acquaintance, found in Ralph a firm and friendly adviser, and acknowledging in his person all the understood superiorities of polished manners and correct education, he did not scruple to come to him for advice in his present difficulties. Ralph, fully comprehending his distress, and conscious how little of his fault had been premeditated,— estimating, too, the many good qualities apparent in his character—did not withhold his counsel.

"I can say little to you now, Forrester, in the way of advice, so long as you continue to herd with the men who have already led you into so much mischief. You appear to me, and must appear to all men, while coupled with such associates, as voluntarily choosing your ground, and taking all the consequences of its position. As there would seem no necessity for your dwelling longer among them, you certainly do make your choice in thus continuing their associate."

"Not so much a matter of choice, now, 'squire, as you imagine. It was, to be sure, choice at first, but then I did not know the people I had to deal with; and when I did, you see, the circumstances were altered."

"How,—by what means?"

"Why, then, 'squire, you must know, and I see no reason to keep the thing from you, I took a liking, a short time after I came here, to a young woman, the daughter of one of our people, and she to me—at least so she says, and I must confess I'm not unwilling to believe her; though it is difficult to say—these women you know—" and as he left the unfinished sentence, he glanced significantly to the youth's face, with an expression which the latter thus interpreted—

"Are not, you would say, at all times to be relied on."

"Why, no, 'squire—I would not exactly say that—that might be something too much of a speech. I did mean to say, from what we see daily, that it isn't always they know their own minds."

"There is some truth, Forrester, in the distinction, and I have thought so before. I am persuaded that the gentler sex is far less given to deceit than our own; but their opinions and feelings, on the other hand, are formed with infinitely more frequency and facility, and are more readily acted upon by passing and occasional influences. Their very susceptibility to the most light and casual impressions, is, of itself, calculated to render vacillating their estimate of things and characters. They are creatures of such delicate construction, and their affections are of such like character, that, like all fine machinery, they are perpetually operated on by the atmosphere, the winds, the dew, and the night. The frost blights and the sun blisters; and a kind of stern accent elevates or depresses, where, with us, it might pass unheeded or unheard.

"We are more cunning—more shy and cautious; and seldom, after a certain age, let our affections out of our own custody. We learn very soon in life—indeed, we are compelled to learn, in our own defence, at a very early period—to go into the world as if we were going into battle. We send out spies, keep sentinels on duty, man our defences, carry arms in our bosoms, which we cover with a buckler, though, with the policy of a court, we conceal that in turn with a silken and embroidered vestment. We watch every erring thought—we learn to be equivocal of speech; and our very hearts, as the Indians phrase it, are taught to speak their desires with a double tongue. We are perpetually on the lookout for enemies and attack; we dread pitfalls and circumventions, and we feel that every face which we encounter is a smiling deceit—every honeyed word a blandishment meant to betray us. These are lessons which society, as at present constituted, teaches of itself.

"With women the case is essentially different. They have few of these influences to pervert and mislead. They have nothing to do in the market-place—they are not candidates for place or power—they have not the ambition which is always struggling for state and for self; but, with a wisdom in this, that might avail us wonderfully in all other respects, they are kept apart, as things for love and worship—domestic divinities, whose true altar-place is the fireside; whose true sway is over fond hearts, generous sensibilities, and immaculate honor. Where should they learn to contend with guile—to acquire cunning and circumspection—to guard the heart—to keep sweet affections locked up coldly, like mountain waters? Shall we wonder that they sometimes deceive themselves rather than their neighbors—that they sometimes misapprehend their own feelings, and mistake for love some less absorbing intruder, who but lights upon the heart for a single instant, as a bird upon his spray, to rest or to plume his pinions, and be off with the very next zephyr. But all this is wide of the mark, Forrester, and keeps you from your story."

"My story isn't much, Master Colleton, and is easily told. I love Kate Allen, and as I said before, I believe Kate loves me; and though it be scarcely a sign of manliness to confess so much, yet I must say to you, 'squire, that I love her so very much that I can not do without her."

"I honor your avowal, Forrester, and see nothing unmanly or unbecoming in the sentiment you profess. On the contrary, such a feeling, in my mind, more truly than any other, indicates the presence and possession of those very qualities out of which true manhood is made. The creature who prides himself chiefly upon his insensibilities, has no more claim to be considered a human being than the trees that gather round us, or the rocks over which we travel."

"Well, 'squire, I believe you are right, and I am glad that such is your opinion, for now I shall be able to speak to you more freely upon this subject. Indeed, you talk about the thing so knowingly, that I should not be surprised, 'squire, to find out that you too had something of the same sort troubling your heart, though here you are travelling far from home and among strangers."

The remark of Forrester was put with an air of arch inquiry. A slight shadow passed over and clouded the face of the youth, and for a moment his brow was wrinkled into sternness; but hastily suppressing the awakened emotion, whatever its origin might have been, he simply replied, in an indirect rebuke, which his companion very readily comprehended:—

"You were speaking of your heart, I believe, Forrester, and not of mine. If you please, we will confine ourselves to the one territory, particularly as it promises to find us sufficient employment of itself, without rendering it necessary that we should cross over to any other."

"It's a true word, 'squire—the business of the one territory is sufficient for me at this time, and more than I shall well get through with: but though I know this, somehow or other I want to forget it all, if possible; and sometimes I close my eyes in the hope to shut out ugly thoughts."

"The feeling is melancholy enough, but it is just the one which should test your manhood. It is not for one who has been all his life buffeting with the world and ill-fortune, to despond at every mischance or misdeed. Proceed with your narrative; and, in providing for the future, you will be able to forget not a little of the past."

"You are right, 'squire; I will be a man, and stand my chance, whether good or ill, like a man, as I have always been. Well, as I was saying, Kate is neither unkind nor unwilling, and the only difficulty is with her father. He is now mighty fond of the needful, and won't hear to our marriage until I have a good foundation, and something to go upon. It is this, you see, which keeps me here, shoulder to shoulder with these men, whom I like just as little perhaps as yourself; and it was because the soldiers came upon us just as I was beginning to lay up a little from my earnings, that made me desperate. I dreaded to lose what I had been so long working for; and whenever the thought of Kate came through my brain, I grew rash and ready for any mischief—and this is just the way in which I ran headlong into this difficulty."

"It is melancholy, Forrester, to think that, with such a feeling as that you profess for this young woman, you should be so little regardful of her peace or your own; that you should plunge so madly into strife and crime, and proceed to the commission of acts which not only embitter your life, but must defeat the very hopes and expectations for which you live."

"It's the nature of the beast," replied the woodman, with a melancholy shake of the head, in a phrase which has become a proverb of familiar use in the South. "It's the nature of the beast, 'squire: I never seem to think about a thing until it's all over, and too late to mend it. It's a sad misfortune to have such a temper, and so yesterday's work tells me much more forcibly than I can ever tell myself. But what am I to do, 'squire? that's what I want to know. Can you say nothing to me which will put me in better humor—can you give me no advice, no consolation? Say anything—anything which will make me think less about this matter."

The conscience of the unhappy criminal was indeed busy, and he spoke in tones of deep, though suppressed emotion and energy. The youth did not pretend to console—he well knew that the mental nature would have its course, and to withstand or arrest it would only have the effect of further provoking its morbidity. He replied calmly, but feelingly—

"Your situation is unhappy, Forrester, and calls for serious reflection. It is not for me to offer advice to one so much more experienced than myself. Yet my thoughts are at your service for what they are worth. You can not, of course, hope to remain in the country after this; yet, in flying from that justice to which you will have made no atonement, you will not necessarily escape the consequences of your crime, which, I feel satisfied, will, for a long season, rest heavily upon a spirit such as yours. Your confederates have greatly the advantage of you in this particular. The fear of human penalties is with them the only fear. Your severest judge will be your own heart, and from that you may not fly. With regard to your affections, I can say little. I know not what may be your resources—your means of life, and the nature of those enterprises which, in another region, you might pursue. In the West you would be secure from punishment; the wants of life in the wilderness are few, and of easy attainment; why not marry the young woman, and let her fly with you to happiness and safety?"

"And wouldn't I do so, 'squire?—I would be a happy fellow if I could. But her father will never consent. He had no hand in yesterday's business, and I wonder at that too, for he's mighty apt at all such scrapes; and he will not therefore be so very ready to perceive the necessity of my flight—certainly not of hers, she being his only child; and, though a tough old sort of chap, he's main fond of her."

"See him about it at once, then; and, if he does not consent, the only difficulty is in the delay and further protraction of your union. It would be very easy, when you are once well settled, to claim her as your wife."

"That's all very true and very reasonable, 'squire; but it's rather hard, this waiting. Here, for five years, have I been playing this sort of game, and it goes greatly against the grain to have to begin anew and in a new place. But here's where the old buck lives. It's quite a snug farm, as you may see. He's pretty well off, and, by one little end or the other, contrives to make it look smarter and smarter every year; but then he's just as close as a corkscrew, and quite mean in his ways. And—there's Kate, 'squire, looking from the window. Now, an't she a sweet creature? Come, 'light—you shall see her close. Make yourself quite at home, as I do. I make free, for you see the old people have all along looked upon me as a son, seeing that I am to be one at some time or other."

They were now at the entrance of as smiling a cottage as the lover of romance might well desire to look upon. Everything had a cheery, sunshiny aspect, looking life, comfort, and the "all in all content;" and, with a feeling of pleasure kindled anew in his bosom by the prospect, Ralph complied readily with the frank and somewhat informal invitation of his companion, and was soon made perfectly at home by the freedom and ease which characterized the manners of the young girl who descended to receive them. A slight suffusion of the cheek and a downcast eye, upon the entrance of her lover, indicated a gratified consciousness on the part of the maiden which did not look amiss. She was seemingly a gentle, playful creature, extremely young, apparently without a thought of guile, and altogether untouched with a solitary presentiment of the unhappy fortunes in store for her.

Her mother, having made her appearance, soon employed the youth in occasional discourse, which furnished sufficient opportunity to the betrothed to pursue their own conversation, in a quiet corner of the same room, in that under-tone which, where lovers are concerned, is of all others the most delightful and emphatic. True love is always timid: he, too, as well as fear, is apt to "shrink back at the sound himself has made." His words are few and the tones feeble. He throws his thoughts into his eyes, and they speak enough for all his purposes. On the present occasion, however, he was dumb from other influences, and the hesitating voice, the guilty look, the unquiet manner, sufficiently spoke, on the part of her lover, what his own tongue refused to whisper in the ears of the maiden. He strove, but vainly, to relate the melancholy event to which we have already sufficiently alluded. His words were broken and confused, but she gathered enough, in part, to comprehend the affair, though still ignorant of the precise actors and sufferers.

The heart of Katherine was one of deep-seated tenderness, and it may not be easy to describe the shock which the intelligence gave her. She did not hear him through without ejaculations of horror, sufficiently fervent and loud to provoke the glance of her mother, who did not, however, though turning her looks frequently upon the two, venture upon any inquiry, or offer any remark. The girl heard her lover patiently; but when he narrated the catastrophe, and told of the murder of the guard, she no longer struggled to restrain the feeling, now too strong for suppression. Her words broke through her lips quickly, as she exclaimed—

"But you, Mark—you had no part in this matter—you lent no aid—you gave no hand. You interfered, I am sure you did, to prevent the murder of the innocent men. Speak out, Mark, and tell me the truth, and relieve me from these horrible apprehensions."

As she spoke, her small hand rested upon his wrist with a passionate energy, in full accordance with the spirit of her language. The head of the unhappy man sank upon his breast; his eyes, dewily suffused, were cast upon the floor, and he spoke nothing, or inarticulately, in reply.

"What means this silence—what am I to believe—what am I to think, Mark Forrester? You can not have given aid to those bad men, whom you yourself despise. You have not so far forgotten yourself and me as to go on with that wicked man Rivers, following his direction, to take away life—to spill blood as if it were water! You have not done this, Mark. Tell me at once that I am foolish to fear it for an instant—that it is not so."

He strove, but in vain, to reply. The inarticulate sounds came forth chokingly from his lips without force or meaning. He strode impatiently up and down the apartment, followed by the young and excited maiden, who unconsciously pursued him with repeated inquiries;

while her mother, awakened to the necessity of interference, vainly strove to find a solution of the mystery, and to quiet both of the parties.

"Will you not speak to me, Mark? Can you not, will you now answer?"

The unhappy man shook his head, in a perplexed and irritated manner, indicating his inability to reply—but concluding with pointing his finger impatiently to Ralph, who stood up, a surprised and anxious spectator of the scene. The maiden seemed to comprehend the intimation, and with an energy and boldness that would not well describe her accustomed habit—with a hurried step, crossed the apartment to where stood the youth. Her eye was quick and searching—her words broken, but with an impetuous flow, indicating the anxiety which, while it accounted for, sufficiently excused the abruptness of her address, she spoke:—

"Do, sir, say that he had no hand in it—that he is free from the stain of blood! Speak for him, sir, I pray you; tell me—he will not tell himself!"

The old lady now sought to interpose, and to apologize for her daughter.

"Why, Kate, Katharine—forgive her, sir; Kate—Katharine, my dear—you forget. You ask questions of the stranger without any consideration."

But she spoke to an unconscious auditor; and Forrester, though still almost speechless, now interposed:—

"Let her ask, mother—let her ask—let her know it all. He can say what I can not. He can tell all. Speak out, 'squire—speak out; don't fear for me. It must come, and who can better tell of it than you, who know it all?"

Thus urged, Ralph, in a few words, related the occurrence. Though carefully avoiding the use of epithet or phrase which might color with an increased odium the connection and conduct of Forrester with the affair, the offence admitted of so little apology or extenuation, that the delicacy with which the details were narrated availed but little in its mitigation; and an involuntary cry burst from mother and daughter alike, to which the hollow groan that came from the lips of Forrester furnished a fitting echo.

"And this is all true, Mark—must I believe all this?" was the inquiry of the young girl, after a brief interval. There was a desperate precipitance in the reply of Forrester:—

"True—Katherine—true; every word of it is true. Do you not see it written in my face? Am I not choked—do not my knees tremble? and my hands—look for yourself—are they not covered with blood?"

The youth interposed, and for a moment doubted the sanity of his companion. He had spoken in figure—a mode of speech, which it is a mistake in rhetoricians to ascribe only to an artificial origin, during a state of mental quiet. Deep passion and strong excitements, we are bold to say, employ metaphor largely; and, upon an inspection of the criminal records of any country, it will be found that the most common narrations from persons deeply wrought upon by strong circumstances are abundantly stored with the evidence of what we assert.

"And how came it, Mark?" was the inquiry of the maiden; "and why did you this thing?"

"Ay, you may well ask, and wonder. I can not tell you. I was a fool— I was mad! I knew not what I did. From one thing I went on to another, and I knew nothing of what had been done until all was done. Some devil was at my elbow—some devil at my heart. I feel it there still; I am not yet free. I could do more—I could go yet farther. I could finish the damned work by another crime; and no crime either, since I should be the only victim, and well deserving a worse punishment."

The offender was deeply excited, and felt poignantly. For some time it tasked all the powers of Ralph's mind, and the seductive blandishments of the maiden herself, to allay the fever of his spirit; when, at length, he was something restored, the dialogue was renewed by an inquiry of the old lady as to the future destination of her anticipated son-in-law, for whom, indeed, she entertained a genuine affection.

"And what is to be the end of all this, Mark? What is it your purpose to do—where will you fly?"

"To the nation, mother—where else? I must fly somewhere—give myself up to justice, or—" and he paused in the sentence so unpromisingly begun, while his eyes rolled with unaccustomed terrors, and his voice grew thick in his throat.

"Or what—what mean you by that word, that look, Mark? I do not understand you; why speak you in this way, and to me?" exclaimed the maiden, passionately interrupting him in a speech, which, though strictly the creature of his morbid spirit and present excitement, was perhaps unnecessarily and something too wantonly indulged in.

"Forgive me, Katharine—dear Katharine—but you little know the madness and the misery at my heart."

"And have you no thought of mine, Mark? this deed of yours has brought misery, if not madness, to it too; and speech like this might well be spared us now!"

"It is this very thought, Kate, that I have made you miserable, when I should have striven only to make you happy. The thought, too, that I must leave you, to see you perhaps never again—these unman—these madden me, Katharine; and I feel desperate like the man striving with his brother upon the plank in the broad ocean."

"And why part, Mark? I see not this necessity!"

"Would you have me stay and perish? would you behold me, dragged perhaps from your own arms before the stern judge, and to a dreadful death? It will be so if I stay much longer. The state will not suffer this thing to pass over. The crime is too large—too fearful. Besides this, the Pony Club have lately committed several desperate offences, which have already attracted the notice of the legislature. This very guard had been ordered to disperse them; and this affair will bring down a sufficient force to overrun all our settlements, and they may even penetrate the nation itself, where we might otherwise find shelter. There will be no safety for me."

The despondence of the woodman increased as he spoke; and the young girl, as if unconscious of all spectators, in the confiding innocence of her heart, exclaimed, while her head sunk upon his shoulder:—

"And why, Mark, may we not all fly together? There will be no reason now to remain here, since the miners are all to be dispersed."

"Well said, Kate—well said—" responded a voice at the entrance of the apartment, at the sound of which the person addressed started with a visible trepidation, which destroyed all her previous energy of manner; "it is well thought on, Kate; there will, sure enough, be very little reason now for any of us to remain, since this ugly business; and the only question is as to what quarter we shall go. There is, however, just as little reason for our flight in company with Mark Forrester."

It was the father of the maiden who spoke—one who was the arbiter of her destinies, and so much the dictator in his household and over his family, that from his decision and authority there was suffered no appeal. Without pausing for a reply, he proceeded:—

"Our course, Mark, must now lie separate. You will take your route, and I mine; we can not take them together. As for my daughter, she can not take up with you, seeing your present condition. Your affairs are not as they were when I consented to your engagement; therefore, the least said and thought about past matters, the better."

"But—" was the beginning of a reply from the sad and discarded lover, in which he was not suffered to proceed. The old man was firm, and settled further controversy in short order.

"No talk, Mark—seeing that it's no use, and there's no occasion for it. It must be as I say. I cannot permit of Kate's connection with a man in your situation, who the very next moment may be brought to the halter and bring shame upon her. Take your parting, and try to forget old times, my good fellow. I think well of, and am sorry for you, Mark, but I can do nothing. The girl is my only child, and I must keep her from harm if I can."

Mark battled the point with considerable warmth and vigor, and the scene was something further protracted, but need not here be prolonged. The father was obdurate, and too much dreaded by the members of his family to admit of much prayer or pleading on their part. Apart from this, his reason, though a stern, was a wise and strong one. The intercession of Colleton, warmly made, proved equally unavailing; and after a brief but painful parting with the maiden, Forrester remounted his horse, and, in company with the youth, departed for the village. But the adieus of the lovers, in this instance, were not destined to be the last. In the narrow passage, in which, removed from all sight and scrutiny, she hung droopingly, like a storm-beaten flower, upon his bosom, he solicited, and not unsuccessfully, a private and a parting interview.

"To-night, then, at the old sycamore, as the moon rises," he whispered in her ear, as sadly and silently she withdrew from his embrace.

CHAPTER EIGHTEEN

Parting and Flight

With Ralph, the unhappy woodman, thus even denied to hope, returned, more miserable than before, to the village of Chestatee. The crowd there had been largely diminished. The more obnoxious among the offenders—those who, having taken the most prominent part in the late affair, apprehended the severest treatment—had taken themselves as much out of sight as possible. Even Munro and Rivers, with all their hardihood, were no longer to be seen, and those still lingering in the village were such as under no circumstances might well provoke suspicion of "subtle deed and counter enterprise." They were the fat men, the beef of society—loving long speeches and goodly cheer. The two friends, for so we may call them, were left almost in the exclusive possession of the hotel, and without observation discussed their several plans of departure. Forrester had determined to commence his journey that very night; while Ralph, with what might seem headstrong rashness, chose the ensuing day for a like purpose.

But the youth was not without his reasons for this determination. He knew perfectly well that he was in peril, but felt also that this peril would be met with much more difficulty by night than by day. Deeming himself secure, comparatively speaking, while actually in the village, he felt that it would be safer to remain there another night, than by setting off at mid-day, encounter the unavoidable risk of either pursuing his course through the night in that dangerous neighborhood, where every step which he took might be watched, or be compelled to stop at some more insulated position, in which there must be far less safety. He concluded, therefore, to set off at early dawn on the ensuing morning, and calculated, with the advantage of daylight all the way, through brisk riding, to put himself by evening beyond the reach of his enemies. That he was not altogether permitted to pursue this course, was certainly not through any neglect of preparatory arrangement.

The public table at the inn on that day was thinly attended; and the repast was partaken by all parties in comparative silence. A few words were addressed by Colleton to Lucy Munro, but they were answered, not coldly, but sparingly, and her replies were entirely wanting in their usual spirit. Still, her looks signified for him the deepest interest, and a significant motion of the finger, which might have been held to convey a warning, was all that he noted of that earnest manner which had gratified his self-esteem in her habit heretofore. The day was got through with difficulty by all parties; and as evening approached, Forrester, having effected all his arrangements without provoking observation, in the quiet and privacy of the youth's chamber, bade him farewell, cautioning him at the same time against all voluntary risk, and reminding him of the necessity, while in that neighborhood, of keeping a good lookout. Their courses lay not so far asunder but that they might, for a time, have proceeded together, and with more mutual advantage; but the suggestions and solicitations of Forrester on this subject were alike disregarded by Ralph, with what reason we may not positively say, but it is possible that it arose from a prudential reference to the fact that the association of one flying from justice was not exactly such as the innocent should desire. And this was reason enough.

They separated, and the youth proceeded to the preparation for his own contemplated departure. His pistols were in readiness, with his dirk, on the small table by the side of his bed; his portmanteau lay alike contiguous; and before seeking his couch, which he did at an early hour, he himself had seen that his good steed had been well provided with corn and fodder. The sable groom, too, whose attentions to the noble animal from the first, stimulated by an occasional bit of silver, had been unremitted, was now further rewarded, and promised faithfully to be in readiness at any hour. Thus, all things arranged, Ralph returned to his chamber, and without removing his dress, wrapping his cloak around him, he threw himself upon his couch, and addressed himself to those slumbers which were destined to be of no very long continuance.

Forrester, in the meanwhile, had proceeded with all the impatience of a lover to the designated place of *tryst*, under the giant sycamore, the sheltering limbs and leaves of which, on sundry previous occasions, had ministered to a like purpose. The place was not remote, or at least would not be so considered in country estimation, from the dwelling of the maiden; and was to be reached from the latter spot by a circuitous passage through a thick wood, which covered the distance between entirely. The spot chosen for the meeting was well known to both parties, and we shall not pretend, at this time of day, to limit the knowledge of its sweet fitness for the purposes of love, to them alone. They had tasted of its sweets a thousand times, and could well understand and appreciate that air of romantic and fairy-like seclusion which so much distinguished it, and which served admirably in concert with the uses to which it was now appropriated. The tree grew within and surmounted a little hollow, formed by the even and combined natural descents, to that common centre, of four hills, beautifully grouped, which surrounded and completely fenced it in. Their descents were smooth and even, without a single abruptness, to the bottom, in the centre of which rose the sycamore, which, from its own situation, conferred the name of Sycamore Hollow on the sweet spot upon which it stood. A spring, trickling from beneath its roots, shaded by its folding branches from the thirsty heats of the summer sun, kept up a low and continuous prattle with the pebbles over which it made its way, that consorted sweetly with the secluded harmonies that overmantled, as with a mighty wing, the sheltered place.

Scenes like these are abundant enough in the southern country; and by their quiet, unobtrusive, and softer beauties, would seem, and not inefficiently or feebly, to supply in most respects the wants of those bolder characteristics, in which nature in those regions is confessedly deficient. Whatever may be the want of southern scenery in stupendousness or sublimity, it is, we are inclined to believe, more than made up in those thousand quiet and wooing charms of location, which seem designed expressly for the hamlet and the cottage—the evening dance—the mid-day repose and rural banquet—and all those numberless practices of a small and well-intentioned society, which win the affections into limpid and living currents, touched for ever, here and there, by the sunshine, and sheltered in their repose by overhanging leaves and flowers, for ever fertile and for ever fresh. They may not occasion a feeling of solemn awe, but they enkindle one of admiring affection; and where the mountain and the bald rock would be productive of emotions only of strength and sternness, their softer featurings of brawling brook, bending and variegated shrubbery, wild flower, gadding vine, and undulating hillock, mould the contemplative spirit into gentleness and love. The scenery of the South below the mountain regions, seldom impresses at first, but it grows upon acquaintance; and in a little while, where once all things looked monotonous and unattractive, we learn to discover sweet influences that ravish us from ourselves at every step we take, into worlds and wilds, where all is fairy-like, wooing, and unchangingly sweet.

The night, though yet without a moon, was beautifully clear and cloudless. The stars had come out with all their brightness—a soft zephyr played drowsily and fitfully among the tops of the shrubbery, that lay, as it were, asleep on the circling hilltops around; while the odors of complicated charm from a thousand floral knots, which had caught blooms from the rainbows, and dyed themselves in their stolen splendors, thickly studding the wild and matted grass which sustained them; brought along with them even a stronger influence than the rest of the scene, and might have taught a ready lesson of love to much sterner spirits than the two, now so unhappy, who were there to take their parting and last embrace.

The swift motion of a galloping steed was heard, and Forrester was at the place and hour of appointment. In mournful mood, he threw himself at the foot of one of the hills, upon one of the tufted roots of the huge tree which sheltered the little hollow, and resigned himself to a somewhat bitter survey of his own condition, and of the privations and probable straits into which his rash thoughtlessness had so unhappily involved him. His horse, docile and well-trained, stood unfastened in the thicket, cropping the young and tender herbage at some little distance; but so habituated to rule that no other security than his own will was considered by his master necessary for his continued presence. The lover waited not long. Descending the hill, through a narrow pathway one side of the wood, well known and frequently trodden by both, he beheld the approach of the maiden, and hurried forward to receive her.

The terms upon which they had so long stood forbade constraint, and put at defiance all those formalities which, under other circumstances, might have grown out of the meeting. She advanced without hesitancy, and the hand of her lover grasped that which she extended, his arm passed about her, his lip was fastened to her own without hinderance, and, in that one sweet embrace, in that one moment of blissful forgetfulness, all other of life's circumstances had ceased to afflict.

But they were not happy even at that moment of delight and illusion. The gentler spirit of the maiden's sex was uppermost, and the sad story of his crime, which at their last meeting had been told her, lay with heavy influence at her heart. She was a gentle creature, and though dwelling in a wilderness, such is the prevailing influence upon female character, of the kind of education acquirable in the southern,—or, we may add, and thus perhaps furnish the reason for any peculiarity in this respect, the slave-holding states—that she partook in a large degree of that excessive delicacy, as well of spirit as of person, which, while a marked characteristic of that entire region, is apt to become of itself a disease, exhibiting itself too frequently in a nervousness and timidity that unfit its owner for the ruder necessities of life, and permit it to abide only under its more serene and summer aspects. The tale of blood, and its awful consequences, were perpetually recurring to her imagination. Her fancy described and dwelt upon its details, her thoughts wove it into a thousand startling tissues, until, though believing his crime unpremeditated, she almost shrank from the embrace of her lover, because of the blood so recently upon his hands. Placing her beside him upon the seat he had occupied, he tenderly rebuked her gloomy manner, while an inward and painful consciousness of its cause gave to his voice a hesitating tremor, and his eye, heretofore unquailing at any glance, no longer bold, now shrank downcast before the tearful emphasis of hers.

"You have come, Kate—come, according to your promise, yet you wear not loving looks. Your eye is vacant—your heart, it beats sadly and hurriedly beneath my hand, as if there were gloomy and vexatious thoughts within."

"And should I not be sad, Mark, and should you not be sad? Gloom and sorrow befit our situations alike; though for you I feel more than for myself. I think not so much of our parting, as of your misfortune in having partaken of this crime. There is to me but little occasion for grief in the temporary separation which I am sure will precede our final union. But this dreadful deed, Mark—it is this that makes me sad. The knowledge that you, whom I thought too gentle wantonly to crush the crawling insect, should have become the slayer of men—of innocent men, too—makes my heart bleed within, and my eyes fill; and when I think of it, as indeed I now think of little else, and feel that its remorse and all its consequences must haunt you for many years, I almost think, with my father, that it would be better we should see each other no more. I think I could see you depart, knowing that it was for ever, without a tear, were this sin not upon your head."

"Your words are cruel, Kate; but you can not speak to my spirit in language more severe than it speaks momentarily to itself. I never knew anything of punishment before; and the first lesson is a bitter one. Your words touch me but little now, as the tree, when the axe has once girdled it, has no feeling for any further stroke. Forbear then, dear Kate, as you love yourself. Brood not upon a subject that brings pain with it to your own spirit, and has almost ceased, except in its consequences, to operate upon mine. Let us now speak of those things which concern you nearly, and me not a little—of the only thing, which, besides this deed of death, troubles my thought at this moment. Let us speak of our future hope—if hope there may be for me, after the stern sentence which your lips uttered in part even now."

"It was for you—for your safety, believe me, Mark, that I spoke; my own heart was wrung with the language of my lips—the language of my cooler thought. I spoke only for your safety and not for myself. Could—I again repeat—could this deed be undone—could you be free from the reproach and the punishment, I would be content, though the strings of my heart cracked with its own doom, to forego all claim upon you—to give you up—to give up my own hope of happiness for ever."

Her words were passionate, and at their close her head sunk upon his shoulder, while her tears gushed forth without restraint, and in defiance of all her efforts. The heart of the woodman was deeply and painfully affected, and the words refused to leave his lips, while a kindred anguish shook his manly frame, and rendered it almost a difficulty with him to sustain the slight fabric of hers. With a stern effort, however, he recovered himself, and reseating her upon the bank from which, in the agitation of the moment, they had both arisen, he endeavored to soothe her spirit, by unfolding his plan of future life.

"My present aim is the nation—I shall cross the Chestatee river tomorrow, and shall push at once for the forest of Etowee, and beyond the Etowee river. I know the place well, and have been through it before. There I shall linger until I hear all the particulars of this affair in its progress, and determine upon my route accordingly. If the stir is great, as I reckon it will be, I shall push into Tennessee, and perhaps go for the

Mississippi. Could I hope that your father would consent to remove, I should at once do this and make a settlement, where, secure from interruption and all together, we might live happily and honorably for the future."

"And why not do so now—why stop at all among the Cherokees? Why not go at once into Mississippi, and begin the world, as you propose in the end to do?"

"What! and leave you for ever—now Kate, you are indeed cruel. I had not thought to have listened to such a recommendation from one who loved me as you profess."

"As I do, Mark—I say nothing which I do not feel. It does not follow that you will be any nigher your object, if my father continue firm in his refusal, though nigher to me, by lingering about in the nation. On the contrary, will he not, hearing of you in the neighborhood, be more close in his restraints upon me? Will not your chance of exposure, too, be so much the greater as to make it incumbent upon him to pursue his determination with rigor? while, on the other hand, if you remove yourself out of all reach of Georgia, in the Mississippi, and there begin a settlement, I am sure that he will look upon the affair with different notions."

"It can not be, Kate—it can not be. You know I have had but a single motive for living so long among this people and in these parts. I disliked both, and only lingered with a single hope, that I might be blessed with your presence always, and in the event of my sufficient success, that I might win you altogether for myself. I have not done much for this object, and this unhappy affair forbids me for the present to do more. Is not this enough, Katharine, and must I bury myself from you a thousand miles in the forest, ignorant of what may be going on, and without any hope, such as I have lived for before? Is the labor I have undergone—the life I have led—to have no fruits? Will you too be the first to recommend forgetfulness; to overthrow my chance of happiness? No—it must not be. Hear me, Kate—hear me, and say I have not worked altogether in vain. I have acquired some little by my toils, and can acquire more. There is one thing now, one blessing which you may afford, and the possession of which will enable me to go with a light heart and a strong hand into any forests, winning comforts for both of us—happiness, if the world have it—and nothing to make us afraid."

He spoke with deep energy, and she looked inquiringly into his face. The expression was satisfactory, and she replied without hesitation:—

"I understand you, Mark Forrester—I understand you, but it must not be. I must regard and live for affections besides my own. Would you have me fly for ever from those who have been all to me—from those to whom I am all—from my father—from my dear, my old mother! Fy, Mark."

"And are you not all to me, Katharine—the one thing for which I would live, and wanting which I care not to live? Ay, Katharine, fly with me from all—and yet not for ever. They will follow you and our end will then be answered. Unless you do this, they would linger on in this place without an object, even if permitted, which is very doubtful, to hold their ground—enjoying life as a vegetable, and dead before life itself is extinct."

"Spare your speech, Mark—on this point you urge me in vain," was the firm response of the maiden. "Though I feel for you as I feel for none other, I also feel that I have other ties and other obligations, all inconsistent with the step which you would have me take. I will not have you speak of it further—on this particular I am immoveable."

A shade of mortification clouded the face of Forrester as she uttered these words, and for a moment he was silent. Resuming, at length, with something of resignation in his manner, he continued—

"Well, Kate, since you will have it so, I forbear; though, what course is left for you, and what hope for me, if your father continues in his present humor, I am at a loss to see. There is one thing, however—there is one pledge that I would exact from you before we part."

He took her hand tenderly as he spoke, and his eyes, glistening with tearful expectation, were fixed upon her own; but she did not immediately reply. She seemed rather to await the naming of the pledge of which he spoke. There was a struggle going on between her mind and her affections; and though, in the end, the latter seemed to obtain the mastery, the sense of propriety, the moral guardianship of her own spirit battled sternly and fearlessly against their suggestions. She would make no promise which might, by any possibility, bind her to an engagement inconsistent with other and primary obligations.

"I know not, Mark, what may be the pledge which you would have from me, to which I could consent with propriety. When I hear your desires, plainly expressed to my understanding, I shall better know how to reply. You heard the language of my father: I must obey his wishes as far as I know them. Though sometimes rough, and irregular in his habits, to me he has been at all times tender and kind: I would not now disobey his commands. Still, in this matter, my heart inclines too much in your favor not to make me less scrupulous than I should otherwise desire to be. Besides, I have so long held myself yours, and with his sanction, that I can the more easily listen to your entreaties. If, then, you truly love me, you will, I am sure, ask nothing that I should not grant. Speak—what is the pledge?"

"It shall come with no risk, Kate, believe me, none. Heaven forbid that I should bring a solitary grief to your bosom; yet it may adventure in some respects both mind and person, if you be not wary. Knowing your father, as you know him too, I would have from you a pledge—a promise, here, solemnly uttered in the eye of Heaven, and in the holy stillness of this place, which has witnessed other of our vows no less sacred and solemn, that, should he sanction the prayer of another who seeks your love, and command your obedience, that you will *not* obey—that you will not go quietly a victim to the altar—that you will not pledge to another the same vow which has been long since pledged to me."

He paused a moment for a reply, but she spoke not; and with something like impetuosity he proceeded:—

"You make no reply, Katharine? You hear my entreaty—my prayer. It involves no impropriety; it stands in the way of no other duty, since, I trust, the relationship between us is as binding as any other which may call for your regard. All that I ask is, that you will not dispose of yourself to another, your heart not going with your hand, whatever may be the authority which may require it; at least, not until you are fully assured that it is beyond my power to claim you, or I become unworthy to press the claim."

"It is strange, Mark, that you should speak in a manner of which there is so little need. The pledge long since uttered as solemnly as you now require, under these very boughs, should satisfy you."

"So it should, Kate—and so it would, perhaps, could I now reason on any subject. But my doubts are not now of your love, but of your firmness in resisting a control at variance with your duty to yourself. Your words reassure me, however; and now, though with no glad heart, I shall pass over the border, and hope for the better days which are to make us happy."

"Not so fast, Master Forrester," exclaimed the voice of old Allen, emerging from the cover of the sycamore, to the shelter of which he had advanced unobserved, and had been the unsuspected auditor of the dialogue from first to last. The couple, with an awkward consciousness, started up at the speech, taken by surprise, and neither uttering a word in reply to this sudden address.

"You must first answer, young man, to the charge of advising my daughter to disobedience, as I have heard you for the last half hour; and to elopement, which she had the good sense to refuse. I thought, Master Forrester, that you were better bred than to be guilty of such offences."

"I know them not as such, Mr. Allen. I had your own sanction to my engagement with Katharine, and do not see that after that you had any right to break it off."

"You do not—eh? Well, perhaps, you are right, and I have thought better of the matter myself; and, between us, Kate has behaved so well, and spoken so prettily to you, and obeyed my orders, as she should have done, that I'm thinking to look more kindly on the whole affair."

"Are you, dear father?—Oh, I am so happy!"

"Hush, minx! the business is mine, and none of yours.—Hark you, Mark. You must fly—there's no two ways about that; and, between us, there will be a devil of a stir in this matter. I have it from good authority that the governor will riddle the whole nation but he'll have every man, woman, and child, concerned in this difficulty: so that'll be no place for you. You must go right on to the *Massassippi*, and enter lands enough for us all. Enter them in Kate's name, and they'll be secure. As soon as you've fixed that business, write on, say where you are, and we'll be down upon you, bag and baggage, in no time and less."

"Oh, dear father—this is so good of you!"

"Pshaw, get away, minx! I don't like kisses *jest* after supper; it takes the taste all out of my mouth of what I've been eating."

Forrester was loud in his acknowledgments, and sought by eulogistic professions to do away the ill effect of all that he might have uttered in the previous conversation; but the old man cut him short with his wonted querulousness:—

"Oh, done with your blarney, boy! 'It's all my eye and Betty Martin!' Won't you go in and take supper? There's something left, I reckon."

But Forrester had now no idea of eating, and declined accordingly, alleging his determination to set off immediately upon his route—a determination which the old man highly approved of.

"You are right, Mark—move's the word, and the sooner you go about it the better. Here's my hand on your bargain, and good-by—I reckon you'll have something more to say to Kate, and I suppose you don't want me to help you in saying it—so I leave you. She's used to the way; and, if she's at all afraid, you can easily see her home."

With a few more words the old man took his departure, leaving the young people as happy now as he had before found them sad and sorrowful. They did not doubt that the reason of this change was as he alleged it, and gave themselves no thought as to causes, satisfied as they were with effects. But old Allen had not proceeded without his host: he had been advised of the contemplated turn-out of all the squatters from the gold-region; and, having no better tenure than any of his neighbors, he very prudently made a merit of necessity, and took his measures as we have seen. The lovers were satisfied, and their interview now wore, though at parting, a more sunshiny complexion.

But why prolong a scene admitting of so little variety as that which describes the sweets, and the strifes, and the sorrows, of mortal love? We take it there is no reader of novels so little conversant with matters of this nature as not to know how they begin and how they end; and, contenting ourselves with separating the parties—an act hardhearted enough, in all conscience—we shall not with idle and questionable sympathy dwell upon the sorrows of their separation. We may utter a remark, however, which the particular instance before us occasions, in relation to the singular influence of love upon the mental and moral character of the man. There is no influence in the world's circumstance so truly purifying, elevating, and refining. It instils high and generous sentiments; it enobles human endeavor; it sanctifies defeat and denial; it polishes manners; it gives to morals a tincture of devotion; and, as with the spell of magic, such as Milton describes in "Comus," it dissipates with a glance the wild rout of low desires and insane follies which so much blur and blot up the otherwise fair face of human society. It permits of no meanness in its train; it expels vulgarity, and, with a high stretch toward perfected humanity, it unearths the grovelling nature, and gives it aspirations of soul and sunshine.

Its effect upon Forrester had been of this description. It had been his only tutor, and had taught him nobly in numberless respects. In every association with the maiden of his affections, his tone, his language, his temper, and his thoughts, seemed to undergo improvement and purification. He seemed quite another man whenever he came into her presence, and whenever the thought of her was in his heart. Indeed, such was the effect of this passion upon both of them; though this may have been partially the result of other circumstances, arising from their particular situation. For a long time they had known few enjoyments that were not intimately connected with the image of one another; and thus, from having few objects besides of contemplation or concern, they refined upon each other. As the minute survey in the forest of the single leaf, which, for years, may not have attracted the eye, unfolds the fine veins, the fanciful outline, the clear, green, and transparent texture, and the delicate shadowings of innumerable hues won from the skies and the sunshine—so, day by day, surveying the single object, they had become familiar with attractions in one another which the passing world would never have supposed either of them to possess. In such a region, where there are few competitors for human love and regard, the heart clings with hungering tenacity to the few stray affections that spring up, here and there, like flowers dropped by some kindly, careless hand, making a bloom and a blessing for the untrodden wilderness. Nor do they blossom there in vain, since, as the sage has told us, there is no breeze that wafts not life, no sun that brings not smiles, no water that bears not refreshment, no flower that has not charms and a solace, for some heart that would not well hope to be happy without them.

They separated on the verge of the copse to which he had attended her, their hands having all the way been passionately linked, and a seal having been set upon their mutual vows by the long, loving embrace which concluded their interview. The cottage was in sight; and, from the deep shade which surrounded him, he beheld her enter its precincts in safety; then, returning to the place of tryst, he led forth his steed, and, with a single bound, was once more in his saddle, and once more a wanderer. The cheerlessness of such a fate as that before him, even under the changed aspect of his affairs, to those unaccustomed to the rather too migratory habits of our southern and western people, would seem somewhat severe; but the only hardship in his present fortune, to the mind of Forrester, was the privation and protraction of his love-arrangements. The wild, woodland adventure common to the habits of the people of this class, had a stimulating effect upon his spirit at all other times; and, even now—though perfectly legitimate for a lover to move slowly from his mistress—the moon just rising above the trees, and his horse in full gallop through their winding intricacies, a warm and bracing energy came to his aid, and his heart grew cheery under its inspiriting influences. He was full of the future, rich in anticipation, and happy in the contemplation of a thousand projects. With a free rein he plunged forward into the recesses of the forest, dreaming of a cottage in the Mississippi, a heart at ease, and Katharine Allen, with all her beauties, for ever at hand to keep it so.

CHAPTER NINETEEN

Midnight Surprise

The night began to wane, and still did Lucy Munro keep lonely vigil in her chamber. How could she sleep? Threatened with a connection so dreadful as to her mind was that proposed with Guy Rivers— deeply interested as she now felt herself in the fortunes of the young stranger, for whose fate and safety, knowing the unfavorable position in which he stood with the outlaws, she had everything to apprehend—it can cause no wonder when we say sleep grew a stranger to her eyes, and without retiring to her couch, though extinguishing her light, she sat musing by the window of her chamber upon the thousand conflicting and sad thoughts that were at strife in her spirit. She had not been long in this position when the sound of approaching horsemen reached her ears, and after a brief interval, during which she could perceive that they had alighted, she heard the door of the hall gently unclosed, and footsteps, set down with nice caution, moving through the passage. A light danced for a moment fitfully along the chamber, as if borne from the sleeping apartment of Munro to that adjoining the hall in which the family were accustomed to pursue their domestic avocations. Then came an occasional murmur of speech to her ears, and then silence.

Perplexed with these circumstances, and wondering at the return of Munro at an hour something unusual—prompted too by a presentiment of something wrong, and apprehensive on the score of Ralph's safety—a curiosity not, surely, under these circumstances, discreditable, to know what was going on, determined her to ascertain something more of the character of the nocturnal visitation. She felt assured, from the strangeness of the occurrence, that evil was afoot, and solicitous for its prevention, she was persuaded to the measure solely with the view to good.

Hastily, but with trembling hands, undoing the door of her apartment, she made her way into the long, dark gallery, with which she was perfectly familiar, and soon gained the apartment already referred to. The door fortunately stood nearly closed, and she successfully passed it by and gained the hall, which immediately adjoined, and lay in perfect darkness. Without herself being seen, she was enabled, through a crevice in the partition dividing the two rooms, to survey its inmates, and to hear distinctly everything that was uttered.

As she expected, there were the two conspirators, Rivers and Munro, earnestly engaged in discourse; to which, as it concerns materially our progress, we may well be permitted to lend our attention. They spoke on a variety of topics entirely foreign to the understanding of the half-affrighted and nervously-susceptible, but still resolute young girl who heard them; and nothing but her deep anxieties for one, whose own importance in her eyes at that moment she did not conjecture, could have sustained her while listening to a dialogue full of atrocious intention, and larded throughout with a familiar and sometimes foul phraseology that certainly was not altogether unseemly in such association.

"Well, Blundell's gone too, they say. He's heartily frightened. A few more will follow, and we must both be out of the way. The rest could not well be identified, and whether they are or not does not concern us, except that they may blab of their confederates. Such as seem likely to suffer detection must be frightened off; and this, by the way, is not so difficult a matter. Pippin knows nothing of himself. Forrester is too much involved to be forward. It was for this that I aroused and set him on. His hot blood took fire at some little hints that I threw out, and the fool became a leader in the mischief. There's no danger from him; besides, they say, he's off too. Old Allen has broken off the match between him and his daughter, and the fellow's almost mad on the strength of it. There's but one left who might trouble us, and it is now understood that but one mode offers for his silence. We are perfectly agreed as to this, and no more scruples."

The quick sense of the maiden readily taught her who was meant;

and her heart trembled convulsively within her, as, with a word, Munro, replying to Rivers, gave his assent.

"Why, yes—it must be done, I suppose, though somehow or other I would it could be got rid of in any other way."

"You see for yourself, Wat, there can be no other way; for as long as he lives, there is no security. The few surviving guard will be seen to, and they saw too little to be dangerous. They were like stunned and stupified men. This boy alone was cool and collected, and is so obstinate in what he knows and thinks, that he troubles neither himself nor his neighbors with doubt or difficulty. I knew him a few years ago, when something more of a boy than now; and even then he was the same character."

"But why not let him start, and take the woods for it? How easy to settle the matter on the roadside, in a thousand different ways. The accumulation of these occurrences in the village, as much as anything else, will break us up. I don't care for myself for I expect to be off for a time; but I want to see the old woman and Lucy keep quiet possession here—"

"You are becoming an old woman yourself, Wat, and should be under guardianship. All these scruples are late; and, indeed, even were they not, they would be still useless. We have determined on the thing, and the sooner we set about it the better. The night wanes, and I have much to see to before daylight. To-morrow I must sleep—sleep—" and for a moment Rivers seemed to muse upon the word sleep, which he thrice repeated; then suddenly proceeding, as if no pause had taken place, he abruptly placed his hand upon the shoulder of Munro, and asked—

"You will bear the lantern; this is all you need perform. I am resolute for the rest."

"What will you use—dirk?"

"Yes—it is silent in its office, and not less sure. Are all asleep, think you—your wife?"

"Quite so—sound when I entered the chamber."

"Well, the sooner to business the better. Is there water in that pitcher? I am strangely thirsty to-night; brandy were not amiss at such a time."

And speaking this to himself, as it were, Rivers approached the side-table, where stood the commodities he sought. In this approach the maiden had a more perfect view of the malignities of his savage face;

and as he left the table, and again commenced a brief conversation in an under-tone with Munro, no longer doubting the dreadful object which they had in view, she seized the opportunity with as much speed as was consistent with caution and her trembling nerves, to leave the place of espionage, and seek her chamber.

But to what purpose had she heard all this, if she suffered the fear-ful deed to proceed to execution? The thought was momentary, but car-ried to her heart, in that moment, the fullest conviction of her duty.

She rushed hurriedly again into the passage—and, though appre-hending momentarily that her knees would sink from under her, took her way up the narrow flight of steps leading into the second story, and to the youth's chamber. As she reached the door, a feminine scruple came over her. A young girl seeking the apartment of a man at mid-night—she shrunk back with a new feeling. But the dread necessity drove her on, and with cautious hand undoing the latch securing the door by thrusting her hand through an interstice between the logs—wondering at the same time at the incautious manner in which, at such a period and place, the youth had provided for his sleeping hours—she stood tremblingly within the chamber.

Wrapped in unconscious slumbers, Ralph Colleton lay dreaming upon his rude couch of a thousand strange influences and associations. His roving fancies had gone to and fro, between his uncle and his bewitching cousin, until his heart grew softened and satisfied, not less with the native pleasures which they revived in his memory, than of the sweet oblivion which they brought of the many painful and perilous prospects with which he had more recently become familiar. He had no thought of the present, and the pictures of the past were all rich and rav-ishing. To his wandering sense at that moment there came a sweet vision of beauty and love—of an affection warmly cherished—green as the summer leaves—fresh as its flowers—flinging odors about his spirit, and re-awakening in its fullest extent the partially slumbering passion—reviving many a hope, and provoking with many a delicious anticipa-tion. The form of the one, lovely beyond comparison, flitted before him, while her name, murmured with words of passion by his parted lips, car-ried with its utterance a sweet promise of a pure faith, and an unforget-ting affection. Never once, since the hour of his departure from home, had he, in his waking moments, permitted that name to find a place upon his lips, and now syllabled into sound by them in his unconscious dreams, it fell with a stunning influence upon an auditor, whose heart grew colder in due proportion with the unconscious but warm tenderness of epithet with which his tongue coupled its utterance.

The now completely unhappy Lucy stood sad and statue-like. She heard enough to teach her the true character of her own feelings for one, whose articulated dreams had revealed the secret of his passion for another; and forgetting for a while the office upon which she had come, she continued to give ear to those sounds which brought to her heart only additional misery.

How long Ralph, in his mental wanderings, would have gone on, as we have seen, incoherently developing his heart's history, may not be said. Gathering courage at last, with a noble energy, the maiden proceeded to her proposed duty, and his slumbers were broken. With a half-awakened consciousness he raised himself partially up in his couch, and sought to listen. He was not deceived; a whispered sentence came to his ears, addressed to himself, and succeeded by a pause of several moments' continuance. Again his name was uttered. Half doubting his senses, he passed his hand repeatedly over his eyes, and again listened for the repetition of that voice, the identity of which he had as yet failed utterly to distinguish. The sounds were repeated, and the words grew more and more distinct. He now caught in part the tenor of the sentence, though imperfectly heard. It seemed to convey some warning of danger, and the person who spoke appeared, from the tremulous accents, to labor under many apprehensions. The voice proceeded with increased emphasis, advising his instant departure from the house—speaking of nameless dangers—of murderous intrigue and conspiracy, and warning against even the delay of a single instant.

The character of Ralph was finely marked, and firmness of purpose and a ready decision were among its most prominent attributes. Hastily leaping from his couch, therefore, with a single bound he reached the door of his chamber, which, to his astonishment, he found entirely unfastened. The movement was so sudden and so entirely unlooked-for, that the intruder was taken by surprise; and beheld, while the youth closed securely the entrance, the hope of escape entirely cut off. Ralph advanced toward his visiter, the dim outline of whose person was visible upon the wall. Lifting his arm as he approached, what was his astonishment to perceive the object of his assault sink before him upon the floor, while the pleading voice of a woman called upon him for mercy.

"Spare me, Mr. Colleton—spare me"—she exclaimed, in undisguised terror.

"You here, Miss Munro, and at this hour of the night!" was the wondering inquiry, as he lifted her from the floor, her limbs, trembling with agitation, scarcely able to support even her slender form.

"Forgive me, sir, forgive me. Think not ill of me, I pray you. I come to save you,—indeed, Mr. Colleton, I do—and nothing, believe me, would have brought me here but the knowledge of your immediate danger."

She felt the delicacy of her situation, and recognising her motive readily, we will do him the justice to say, Ralph felt it too in the assurance of her lips. A respectful delicacy pervaded his manner as he inquired earnestly:—

"What is this danger, Miss Munro? I believe you fear for me, but may you not have exaggerated the cause of alarm to yourself? What have I to fear—from what would you save me?"

"Nay, ask me not, sir, but fly. There is but little time for explanation, believe me. I know and do not imagine the danger. I can not tell you all, nor can you with safety bestow the time to hear. Your murderers are awake—they are in this very house, and nothing but instant flight can save you from their hands."

"But from whom, Miss Munro, am I to fear all this? What has given you this alarm, which, until you can give me some clue to this mystery, I must regard as unadvised and without foundation. I feel the kindness and interest of your solicitude—deeply feel, and greatly respect it; but, unless you can give me some reasonable ground for your fears, I must be stubborn in resisting a connection which would have me fly like a midnight felon, without having seen the face of my foe."

"Oh, heed not these false scruples. There is no shame in such a flight, and believe me, sir, I speak not unadvisedly. Nothing, but the most urgent and immediate danger would have prompted me, at this hour, to come here. If you would survive this night, take advantage of the warning and fly. This moment you must determine—I know not, indeed, if it be not too late even now for your extrication. The murderers, by this time, may be on the way to your chamber, and they will not heed your prayers, and they will scorn any defence which you might offer."

"But who are they of whom you speak, Miss Munro? If I must fly, let me at least know from what and whom. What are my offences, and whom have I offended?"

"That is soon told, though I fear, sir, we waste the time in doing so. You have offended Rivers, and you know but little of him if you think it possible for him to forget or forgive where once injured, however slightly. The miners generally have been taught to regard you as one whose destruction alone can insure their safety from punishment for their late aggressions. My uncle too, I grieve to say it, is too much under the influence of Rivers, and does indeed just what his suggestions prescribe. They have plotted your death, and will not scruple at its performance. They are even now below meditating its execution. By the merest good fortune I overheard their design, from which I feel persuaded nothing now can make them recede. Rely not on their fear of human punishment. They care perhaps just as little for the laws of man as of God, both of which they violate hourly with impunity, and from both of which they have always hitherto contrived to secure themselves. Let me entreat, therefore, that you will take no heed of that manful courage which would be honorable and proper with a fair enemy. Do not think that I am a victim to unmeasured and womanly fears. I have seen too much of the doings of these men, not to feel that no fancies of mine can do them injustice. They would murder you in your bed, and walk from the scene of their crime with confidence into the very courts of justice."

"I believe you, Miss Munro, and nothing doubt the correctness of your opinion with regard to the character of these men. Indeed, I have reason to know that what you say of Rivers, I have already realized in my own person. This attempt, if he makes it, will be the second in which he has put my life in hazard, and I believe him, therefore, not too good for any attempt of this evil nature. But why may I not defend myself from the assassins? I can make these logs tenable till daylight from all their assaults, and then I should receive succor from the villagers without question. You see, too, I have arms which may prove troublesome to an enemy."

"Trust not these chances; let me entreat that you rely not upon them. Were you able, as you say, to sustain yourself for the rest of the night in this apartment, there would be no relief in the morning, for how would you make your situation understood? Many of the villagers will have flown before to-morrow into the nation, until the pursuit is well over, which will most certainly be commenced before long. Some of them have already gone, having heard of the approach of the residue of the Georgia guard, to which the survivors at the late affair bore the particulars. Those who venture to remain will not come nigh this house, dreading to be involved in the difficulties which now threaten its occupants. Their caution would only be the more increased on hearing of any commotion. Wait not, therefore, I implore you, for the dawning of the day: it could never dawn to you. Rivers I know too well; he would overreach you by some subtlety or other; and how easy, even while we speak, to shoot you down through these uneven logs. Trust not, trust not, I entreat you; there is a sure way of escape, and you still have time, if at once you avail yourself of it."

The maid spoke with earnestness and warmth, for the terrors of her mind had given animation to her anxiety, while she sought to persuade the somewhat stubborn youth into the proposed and certainly judicious flight she contemplated for him. Her trepidation had made her part with much of that retreating timidity which had usually distinguished her manner; and perfectly assured herself of the causes of her present apprehension, she did not scruple to exhibit—indeed she did not seem altogether conscious of—the deep interest which she took in the fate and fortunes of him who stood beside her.

Flattered as he must have been by the marked feeling, which she could neither disguise nor he mistake, the youth did not, however, for a moment seek to abuse it; but with a habit at once gentle and respectful, combated the various arguments and suggestions which, with a single eye to his safety, she urged for his departure. In so doing, he obtained from her all the particulars of her discovery, and was at length convinced that her apprehensions were by no means groundless. She had accidentally come upon the conspirators at an interesting moment in their deliberations, which at once revealed their object and its aim; and he at length saw that, except in flight, according to her proposition, the chances were against his escape at all. While they thus deliberated, the distant sound of a chair falling below, occurring at an hour so unusual, gave an added force to her suggestions, and while it prompted anew her entreaties, greatly diminished his reluctance to the flight.

"I will do just as you advise. I know not, Miss Munro, why my fate and fortune should have provoked in you such an interest, unless it be that yours being a less selfish sex than ours, you are not apt to enter into calculations as to the loss of quiet or of personal risk, which, in so doing, you may incur. Whatever be the motive, however, I am grateful for its effects, and shall not readily forget the gentleness of that spirit which has done so much for the solace and the safety of one so sad in its aspect and so much a stranger in all respects."

The youth spoke with a tone and manner the most tender yet

respectful, which necessarily relieved from all perplexity that feeling of propriety and maiden delicacy which otherwise must have made her situation an awkward one. Ralph was not so dull, however, as not to perceive that to a livelier emotion he might in justice attribute the conduct of his companion; but, with a highly-honorable fastidiousness, he himself suggested a motive for her proceeding which her own delicacy rendered improper for her utterance. Still the youth was not marble exactly: and, as he spoke, his arm gently encircled her waist; and her form, as if incapable of its own support, hung for a moment, with apathetic lifelessness, upon his bosom; while her head, with an impulse not difficult to define, drooped like a bending and dewy lily upon his arm. But the passive emotion, if we may so style it, was soon over; and, with an effort, in which firmness and feebleness strongly encountered, she freed herself from his hold with an erect pride of manner, which gave a sweet finish to the momentary display which she had made of womanly weakness. Her voice, as she called upon him to follow her into the passage, was again firm in a moment, and pervaded by a cold ease which seemed to him artificial:—

"There is but little time left you now, sir, for escape: it were criminal not to use it. Follow me boldly, but cautiously—I will lead the way—the house is familiar to me, in night and day, and there must be no waste of time."

He would have resisted this conduct, and himself taken the lead in the advance; but, placing her small and trembling hand upon his arm, she insisted upon the course she had prescribed, and in a manner which he did not venture to resist. Their steps were slow into the open space which, seeming as an introduction to, at the same time separated the various chambers of the dwelling, and terminated in the large and cumbrous stairway which conducted to the lower story, and to which their course was now directed. The passage was of some length, but with cautious tread they proceeded in safety and without noise to the head of the stairway, when the maiden, who still preserved the lead, motioned him back, retreating herself, as she did so, into the cover of a small recess, formed by the stairs, which it partially overhung, and presenting a doubtful apology for a closet. Its door hung upon a broken and single hinge, unclosed—leaving, however, so small an aperture, that it might be difficult to account for their entrance.

There, amid the dust and mystery of time-worn household trumpery, old saddles, broken bridles, and more than one dismembered harness, they came to a pause, and were enabled now to perceive the realization in part of her apprehensions. A small lantern, the rays of light from which feebly made their way through a single square in front, disclosed to the sight the dim forms of the two assassins, moving upward to the contemplated deed of blood.

The terrors of Lucy, as she surveyed their approach, were great; but, with a mind and spirit beyond those commonly in the possession of her sex, she was enabled to conquer and rise above them; and, though her heart beat with a thick and hurried apprehension, her soul grew calmer the more closely approached the danger. Her alarm, to the mind of Ralph, was now sufficiently justified, as, looking through a crevice in the narrow apartment in which he stood, he beheld the malignant and hell-branded visage of Rivers, peering like a dim and baleful light in advance of his companion, in whose face a partial glimmer of the lamp revealed a something of reluctance, which rendered it doubtful how far Munro had in reality gone willingly on the task.

It was, under all the circumstances, a curious survey for the youth. He was a man of high passions, sudden of action, impetuous and unhesitating. In a fair field, he would not have been at a loss for a single moment; but here, the situation was so new, that he was more and more undetermined in his spirit. He saw them commissioned with his murder—treading, one by one the several steps below him—approaching momently nigher and nigher—and his heart beat audibly with conflicting emotions; while with one hand he grasped convulsively and desperately the handle of his dirk, the other being fully employed in sustaining the almost fainting form of his high-souled but delicate companion. He felt that, if discovered, he could do little in his defence and against assault; and though without a thought but that of fierce struggle to the last, his reason taught him to perceive with how little hope of success.

As the assassins continued to advance, he could distinctly trace every change of expression in their several countenances. In that of Rivers, linked with the hideousness that his wound conferred upon it, he noted the more wicked workings of a spirit, the fell character of whose features received no moderate exaggeration from the dim and flickering glare of the lamp which his hand unsteadily carried. The whole face had in it something awfully fearful. He seemed, in its expression, already striking the blow at the breast of his victim, or rioting with a fiendish revenge in his groaned agonies. A brief dialogue between his companion and himself more fully describes the character of the monster.

"Stay—you hurry too much in this matter," said Munro, putting his hand on that of Rivers, and restraining his steps for a moment as he paused, seemingly to listen. He continued—

"Your hand trembles, Rivers, and you let your lamp dance about too much to find it useful. Your footstep is unsteady, and but now the stairs creaked heavily beneath you. You must proceed with more caution, or we shall be overheard. These are sleepless times, and this youth, who appears to trouble you more than man ever troubled you before, may be just as much awake as ourselves. If you are determined in this thing, be not imprudent."

Rivers, who, on reaching the head of the flight, had been about to move forward precipitately, now paused, though with much reluctance; and to the speech of his companion, with a fearful expression of the lips, which, as they parted, disclosed the teeth white and closely clinched beneath them, replied, though without directly referring to its import—

"If I am determined—do you say!—But is not that the chamber where he sleeps?"

"No, old Barton sleeps there—*he* sleeps at the end of the gallery. Be calm—why do you work your fingers in that manner?"

"See you not my knife is in them? I thought at that moment that it was between his ribs, and working about in his heart. It was a sweet fancy, and, though I could not hear his groans as I stooped over him to listen, I almost thought I felt them."

The hand of the maiden grasped that of Ralph convulsively as these muttered words came to their ears, and her respiration grew more difficult and painful. *He* shuddered at the vindictive spirit which the wretch exhibited, while his own, putting on a feller and a fiercer temper, could scarcely resist the impulse which would have prompted him at once to rush forth and stab him where he stood. But the counsels of prudence had their influence, and he remained quiet and firm. The companion of the ruffian felt no less than his other hearers the savage nature of his mood, as thus, in his own way, he partially rebuked it:

"These are horrid fancies, Rivers—more like those which we should look to find in a panther than in a man; and you delight in them quite too much. Can you not kill your enemy without drinking his blood?"

"And where then would be the pleasure of revenge?"—he muttered, between his closed teeth. "The soldier who in battle slays his opponent, hates him not—he has no personal animosity to indulge. The man has never crossed his path in love or in ambition—yet he shoots him down, ruthlessly and relentlessly. Shall *he* do no more who hates, who fears, who sickens at the sight of the man who has crossed his path in love and in ambition? I tell you, Munro, I hate this boy—this beardless, this overweening and insolent boy. He has overthrown, he has mortified me, where I alone should have stood supreme and supereminent. He has wronged me—it may be without intention; but, what care I for that qualification. Shall it be less an evil because he by whom it is perpetrated has neither the soul nor the sense to be conscious of his error. The child who trifles with the powder-match is lessoned by the explosion which destroys him. It must be so with him. I never yet forgave a wrong, however slight and unimportant—I never will. It is not in my nature to do so; and so long as this boy can sleep at night, I can not. I will not seek to sleep until he is laid to rest for ever!"

The whole of this brief dialogue, which had passed directly beside the recess in which the maiden and youth had taken shelter, was distinctly audible to them both. The blood of Ralph boiled within him at this latter speech of the ruffian, in which he avowed a spirit of such dire malignity, as, in its utter disproportionateness to the supposed offence of the youth, could only have been sanctioned by the nature which he had declared to have always been his prompter; and, at its close, the arm of the youth, grasping his weapon, was involuntarily stretched forth, and an instant more would have found it buried in the bosom of the wretch—but the action did not escape the quick eye of his companion, who, though trembling with undiminished terror, was yet mistress of all her senses, and perceived the ill-advised nature of his design. With a motion equally involuntary and sudden with his own, her taper fingers grasped his wrist, and her eyes bright with dewy lustres, were directed upward, sweetly and appealingly to those which now bent themselves down upon her. In that moment of excitement and impending terror, a consciousness of her situation and a sense of shame which more than ever agitated her, rushed through her mind, and she leaned against the side of the closet for that support for which her now revived and awakened scruples forbade any reference to him from whom she had so recently received it. Still, there was nothing abrupt or unkind in her manner, and the youth did not hesitate again to place his arm around and in support of the form which, in reality, needed his strength. In doing so, however, a slight noise was the consequence, which the quick sense of Rivers readily discerned.

"Hark!—heard you nothing, Munro—no sound? Hear you no breathing?—It seems at hand—in that closet."

"Thou hast a quick ear to-night, Guy, as well as a quick step. I heard, and hear nothing, save the snorings of old Barton, whose chamber is just beside you to the left. He has always had a reputation for the wild music which his nose contrives, during his sleep, to keep up in his neighborhood."

"It came from the opposite quarter, Munro, and was not unlike the suppressed respiration of one who listens."

"Pshaw! that can not be. There is no chamber there. That is but the old closet in which we store away lumber. You are quite too regardful of your senses. They will keep us here all night, and the fact is, I wish the business well over."

"Where does Lucy sleep?"

"In the off shed-room below. What of her?"

"Of her—oh nothing!" and Rivers paused musingly in the utterance of this reply, which fell syllable by syllable from his lips. The landlord proceeded:—

"Pass on, Rivers; pass on: or have you determined better about this matter? Shall the youngster live? Indeed, I see not that his evidence, even if he gives it, which I very much doubt, can do us much harm, seeing that a few days more will put us out of the reach of judge and jury alike."

"You would have made a prime counsellor and subtle disputant, Munro, worthy of the Philadelphia lawyers," returned the other, in a sneer. "You think only of one part of this subject, and have no passions, no emotions: you can talk all day long on matters of feeling, without showing any. Did I not say but now, that while that boy slept I could not?"

"Are you sure that when he ceases to sleep the case will be any better?"

The answer to this inquiry was unheard, as the pair passed on to the tenantless chamber. Watching their progress, and under the guidance of the young maiden, who seemed endued with a courage and conduct worthy of more experience and a stronger sex, the youth emerged from his place of precarious and uncomfortable concealment, and descended to the lower floor. A few moments sufficed to throw the saddle upon his steed, without arousing the sable groom; and having brought him under the shadow of a tree at some little distance from the house, he found no further obstruction in the way of his safe and sudden flight.

He had fastened the door of his chamber on leaving it, with much more caution than upon retiring for the night; and having withdrawn the key, which he now hurled into the woods, he felt assured that, unless the assassins had other than the common modes of entry, he should gain a little time from the delay that would experience from this interruption; and this interval, returning to the doorway, he employed in acknowledgments which were well due to the young and trembling woman who stood beside him.

"Take this little token, sweet Lucy," said he, throwing about her neck the chain and casket which he had unbound from his own—"take this little token of Ralph Colleton's gratitude for this night's good service. I shall redeem it, if I live, at a more pleasant season, but you must keep it for me now. I will not soon forget the devotedness with which, on this occasion, you have perilled so much for a stranger. Should we never again meet, I pray you to remember me in your prayers, and I shall always remember you in mine."

He little knew, while he thus spoke in a manner so humbly of himself, of the deep interest which his uniform gentleness of manner and respectful deference, so different from what she had been accustomed to encounter, had inspired in her bosom; and so small at this period was his vanity, that he did not trust himself for a moment to regard the conjecture—which ever and anon thrust itself upon him—that the fearless devotion of the maiden in his behalf and for his safety, had in reality a far more selfish origin than the mere general humanity of her sex and spirit. We will not say that she would not have done the same by any other member of the human family in like circumstances; but it is not uncharitable to believe that she would have been less anxiously interested, less warm in her interest, and less pained in the event of an unfortunate result.

Clasping the gorgeous chain about her neck, his arm again gently encircled her waist, her head drooped upon her bosom—she did not speak—she appeared scarcely to feel. For a moment, life and all its pulses seemed resolutely at a stand; and with some apprehensions, the youth drew her to his bosom, and spoke with words full of tenderness. She made no answer to his immediate speech; but her hands, as if unconsciously, struck the spring which locked the casket that hung upon the chain, and the miniature lay open before her, the dim light of the moon shining down upon it. She reclosed it suddenly, and undoing it from the chain, placed it with a trembling hand in his own; and with an effort of calm and quiet playfulness, reminded him of the unintended gift. He received it, but only to place it again in her hand, reuniting it to the chain.

"Keep it," said he, "Miss Munro—keep it until I return to reclaim it. It will be as safe in your hands—much safer, indeed, than in mine. She whose features it describes will not chide, that, at a moment of peril, I place it in the care of one as gentle as herself."

Her eyes were downcast, as, again receiving it, she inquired with a girlish curiosity, "Is her name Edith, Mr. Colleton, of whom these features are the likeness!"

The youth, surprised by the question, met the inquiry with another.

"How know you?—wherefore do you ask?"

She saw his astonishment, and with a calm which had not, during the whole scene between them, marked her voice or demeanor, she replied instantly:—

"No matter—no matter, sir. I know not well why I put the question—certainly with no object; and am now more than answered."

The youth pondered over the affair in silence for a few moments, but desirous of satisfying the curiosity of the maiden, though on a subject and in relation to one of whom he had sworn himself to silence—wondering, at the same time, not less at the inquiry than the knowledge which it conveyed, of that which he had locked up, as he thought, in the recesses of his own bosom—was about to reply, when a hurried step, and a sudden noise from the upper apartment of the house, warned them of the dangers of further delay. The maiden interrupted with rapid tones the speech he was about to commence:—

"Fly, sir—fly. There is no time to be lost. You have lingered too long already. Do not hesitate longer—you have heard the determination of Rivers—this disappointment will only make him more furious. Fly, then, and speak not. Take the left road at the fork: it leads to the river. It is the dullest, and if they pursue, they will be most likely to fall into the other."

"Farewell, then, my good, my protecting angel—I shall not forget you—have no apprehensions for me—I have now but few for myself. Yet, ere I go—" and he bent down, and before she was conscious of his design, his lips were pressed warmly to her pale and beautiful forehead. "Be not vexed—chide me not," he murmured—"regard me as a brother—if I live I shall certainly become one. Farewell!"

Leaping with a single bound to his saddle, he stood erect for a moment, then vigorously applying his spurs, he had vanished in an instant from the sight. She paused in the doorway until the sounds of his hurrying progress had ceased to fall upon her ears; then, with a mournful spirit and heavy step, slowly reentered the apartment.

CHAPTER TWENTY

The Outlaw and His Victim

L ucy Munro re-entered the dwelling at a moment most inopportune. It was not less her obvious policy than desire—prompted as well by the necessity of escaping the notice and consequent suspicions of those whom she had defrauded of their prey, as by a due sense of that delicate propriety which belonged to her sex, and which her education, as the reader will have conjectured, had taught her properly to estimate—that made her now seek to avoid scrutiny or observation at the moment of her return. Though the niece, and now under the sole direction and authority of Munro, she was the child of one as little like that personage in spirit and pursuit as may well be imagined. It is not necessary that we should dwell more particularly upon this difference. It happened with the two brothers, as many of us have discovered in other cases, that their mental and moral make, though seemingly under the same tutorship, was widely dissimilar. The elder Munro, at an early period in life, broke through all restraints—defied all responsibilities—scorned all human consequences—took no pride or pleasure in any of its domestic associations—and was only known as a vicious profligate, with whom nothing might be done in the way of restraint or reformation. When grown to manhood, he suddenly left his parental home, and went, for a time, no one could say whither. When heard of, it appeared from all accounts that his licentiousness of habit had not deserted him: still, however, it had not, as had been anticipated, led to any fearful or very pernicious results. Years passed on, the parents died, and the brothers grew more than ever separate; when, in different and remote communities, they each took wives to themselves.

The younger, Edgar Munro, the father of Lucy, grew prosperous in business—for a season at least—and, until borne down by a rush of unfavorable circumstances, he spared neither pains nor expense in the culture of the young mind of that daughter whose fortunes are now somewhat before us. Nothing which might tend in the slightest to her personal improvement had been withheld; and the due feminine grace and accomplishment which followed these cares fitted the maiden for the most refined intellectual converse, and for every gentle association. She was familiar with books; had acquired a large taste for letters; and a vein of romantic enthusiasm, not uncommon to the southern temperament, and which she possessed in a considerable degree, was not a little sharpened and exaggerated by the works which fell into her hands.

Tenderly loved and gently nurtured by her parents, it was at that period in her life in which their presence and guardianship were most seriously needed, that she became an orphan; and her future charge necessarily devolved upon an uncle, between whom and her father, since their early manhood, but little association of any kind had taken place. The one looked upon the other as too licentious, if not criminally so, in his habits and pursuits; he did not know their extent, or dream of their character, or he had never doubted for an instant; while he, in turn, so estimated, did not fail to consider and to style his more sedate brother an inveterate and tedious proser; a dull sermonizer on feelings which he knew nothing about, and could never understand—one who prosed on to the end of the chapter, without charm or change, worrying all about him with exhortations to which they yielded no regard.

The parties were fairly quits, and there was no love lost between them. They saw each other but seldom, and, when the surviving brother took up his abode in the new purchase, as the Indian acquisitions of modern times have been usually styled, he was lost sight of, for a time, entirely, by his more staid and worthy kinsman.

Still, Edgar Munro did not look upon his brother as utterly bad. A wild indifference to social forms, and those staid customs which in the estimation of society become virtues, was, in his idea, the most serious error of which Walter had been guilty. In this thought he persisted to the last, and did not so much feel the privations to which his death must subject his child, in the belief and hope that his brother would not only be able but willing to supply the loss.

In one respect he was not mistaken. The afflictions which threw the niece of Walter a dependant upon his bounty, and a charge upon his attention, revived in some measure his almost smothered and in part forgotten regards of kindred; and with a tolerably good grace he came forward to the duty, and took the orphan to the asylum, such as it was, to which his brother's death-bed prayer had recommended her. At first, there was something to her young mind savoring of the romance to which she had rather given herself up, in the notion of a woodland cottage, and rural sports, and wild vines gadding fantastically around secluded bowers; but the reality—the sad reality of such a home and its associations—pressed too soon and heavily upon her to permit her much longer to entertain or encourage the dream of that glad fancy in which she originally set out.

The sphere to which she was transferred, it was soon evident, was neither grateful to the heart nor suited to the mind whose education had been such as hers; and the spirit of the young maiden, at all times given rather to a dreamy melancholy than to any very animated impulses, put on, in its new abiding-place, a garb of increased severity, which at certain moments indicated more of deep and settled misanthropy than any mere constitutionality of habit.

Munro was not at all times rude of speech and manner; and, when he pleased, knew well how so to direct himself as to sooth such a disposition. He saw, and in a little while well understood, the temper of his niece; and, with a consideration under all circumstances rather creditable, he would most usually defer, with a ready accommodation of his own, to her peculiarities. He was pleased and proud of her accomplishments; and from being thus proud, so far as such an emotion could consistently comport with a life and a licentiousness such as his, he had learned, in reality, to love the object who could thus awaken a sentiment to much beyond those inculcated by all his other habits. To her he exhibited none of the harsh manner which marked his intercourse with all other persons; and in his heart sincerely regretted, and sought to avoid the necessity which, as we have elsewhere seen, had made him pledge her hand to Rivers—a disposition of it which he knew was no less galling and painful to her than it was irksome yet unavoidable to himself.

Unhappily, however, for these sentiments, he was too much under the control and at the mercy of his colleague to resist or refuse his application for her person; and though for a long time baffling, under various pretences, the pursuit of that ferocious ruffian, he felt that the time was at hand, unless some providential interference willed it otherwise, when the sacrifice would be insisted on and must be made; or probably her safety, as well as his own, might necessarily be compromised. He knew too well the character of Rivers, and was too much in his power, to risk much in opposition to his will and desires: and, as we have already heard him declare, from having been at one time, and in some respects, the tutor, he had now become, from the operation of circumstances, the mere creature and instrument of that unprincipled wretch.

Whatever may have been the crimes of Munro beyond those already developed—known to and in the possession of Rivers—and whatever the nature of those ties, as well of league as of mutual risk, which bound the parties together in such close affinity, it is not necessary that we should state, nor, indeed, might it be altogether within our compass or capacity to do so. Their connection had, we doubt not, many ramifications; and was strengthened, there is little question, by a thousand mutual necessities, resulting from their joint and frequently-repeated violations of the laws of the land. They were both members of an irregular club, known by its constituents in Georgia as the most atrocious criminal that ever offended society or defied its punishments; and the almost masonic mysteries and bond which distinguished the members provided them with a pledge of security, which gave an added impetus to their already reckless vindictiveness against man and humanity. In a country, the population of which, few and far between, is spread over a wide, wild, and little-cultivated territory, the chances of punishment for crime, rarely realized, scarcely occasioned a thought among offenders; and invited, by the impunity which marked their atrocities, their reiterated commission. We have digressed, however, somewhat from our narrative, but thus much was necessary to the proper understanding of the portions immediately before us, and to the consideration of which we now return.

The moment was inopportune, as we have already remarked, at which Lucy Munro endeavored to effect her return to her own apartment. She was compelled, for the attainment of this object, to cross directly over the great hall, from the room adjoining and back of which the little shed-room projected in which she lodged. This hall was immediately entered upon from the passage-way, leading into the court in front, and but a few steps were necessary for its attainment. The hall had but a single outlet besides that through which she now entered, and this led at once into the adjoining apartment, through which only could she make her way to her own. Unhappily, this passage also contained the stairway flight which led into the upper story of the building; and, in her haste to accomplish her return, she had penetrated too far to effect her retreat, when a sudden change of direction in the light which Rivers carried sufficed to develop the form of that person, at the foot of the stairs, followed by Munro, just returning from the attempt which she had rendered fruitless, and now approaching directly toward her.

Conscious of the awkwardness of her situation, and with a degree of apprehension which now for the first time seemed to paralyze her faculties, she endeavored, but with some uncertainty and hesitation of manner, to gain the shelter of the wall which stretched dimly beside her; a hope not entirely vain, had she pursued it decisively, since the lamp which Rivers carried gave forth but a feeble ray, barely adequate to the task of guiding the footsteps of those who employed it. But the glance of the outlaw, rendered, it would seem, more malignantly penetrating from his recent disappointment, detected the movement; and though, from the imperfectness of the light, uncertain of the object, with a ready activity, the result of a conviction that the long-sought-for victim was now before him, he sprang forward, flinging aside the lamp as he did so, and grasping with one hand and with rigid gripe the almost-fainting girl: the other, brandishing a bared knife, was uplifted to strike, when her shrieks arrested the blow.

Disappointed in not finding the object he sought, the fury of the outlaw was rather heightened than diminished when he discovered that his arm only encircled a young and terrified female; and his teeth were gnashed in token of the bitter wrath in his bosom, and angry curses came from his lips in the undisguised vexation of his spirit. In the meantime, Munro advanced, and the lamp having been dashed out in the onset of Rivers, they were still ignorant of the character of their prisoner, until, having somewhat recovered from her first alarm, and struggling for deliverance from the painful gripe which secured her arm, she exclaimed—

"Unhand me, sir—unhand me, on the instant. What mean you by this violence?"

"Ha! it is you then, fair mistress, that have done this work. It is you that have meddled in the concerns of men, prying into their plans, and arresting their execution. By my soul, I had not thought you so ready or so apt; but how do you reconcile it to your notions of propriety to be abroad at an hour which is something late for a coy damsel? Munro, you must look to these rare doings, or they will work you some difficulty in time to come."

Munro advanced and addressed her with some sternness—"Why are you abroad, Lucy, and at this hour? why this disquietude, and what has alarmed you?—why have you left your chamber?"

The uncle did not obtain, nor indeed did he appear to expect, any answer to his inquiries. In the meanwhile, Rivers held possession of her arm, and she continued fruitlessly struggling for some moments in his grasp, referring at length to the speaker for that interference which he now appeared slow to manifest.

"Oh, sir! will you suffer me to be treated thus—will you not make this man undo his hold, and let me retire to my chamber?"

"You should have been there long before this, Lucy," was the reply, in a grave, stern accent. "You must not complain, if, found thus, at midnight, in a part of the building remote from your chamber, you should be liable to suspicions of meddling with things which should not concern you."

"Come, mistress—pray answer to this. Where have you been tonight—what doing—why abroad? Have you been eavesdropping—telling tales—hatching plots?"

The natural ferocity of Rivers's manner was rather heightened by the tone which he assumed. The maiden, struggling still for the release for which her spirit would not suffer her to implore, exclaimed:—

"Insolent! By what right do you ask me these or any questions? Unhand me, coward—unhand me. You are strong and brave only where the feeble are your opponents."

But he maintained his grasp with even more rigidity than before; and she turned towards the spot at which stood her uncle, but he had left the apartment for a light.

"Your speech is bold, fair mistress, and ill suits my temper. You must be more chary of your language, or you will provoke me beyond my own strength of restraint. You are my property—my slave, if I so please it, and all your appeals to your uncle will be of no effect. Hark you! you have done that to-night for which I am almost tempted to put this dagger into your heart, woman as you are! You have come between me and my victim—between me and my enemy. I had summed up all my wrongs, intending their settlement to-night. You have thwarted all my hopes—you have defrauded me of all my anticipations. What is it prevents me from putting you to death on the spot? Nothing. I have no fears, no loves, to hold and keep me back. I live but for revenge, and that which stays and would prevent me from its enjoyment, must also become its victim."

At this moment, Munro returned with a lamp. The affrighted girl again appealed to him, but he heeded her not. He soon left the passage, and the outlaw proceeded:—

"You love this youth—nay, shrink not back; let not your head droop in shame; he is worthy of your love, and for this, among other things, I hate him. He is worthy of the love of others, and for this, too, I hate him. Fool that you are, he cares not for you. 'Spite of all your aid to-night, he will not remember you to-morrow—he has no thought of you—his hope is built upon—he is wedded to another.

"Hear me, then! your life is in my hands, and at my mercy. There are none present who could interfere and arrest the blow. My dagger is even now upon your bosom—do you not feel it? At a word—a single suggestion of my thought—it performs its office, and for this night's defeat I am half revenged. You may arrest my arm—you may procure your release—even more—you may escape from the bondage of that union with me for which your uncle stands pledged, if you please."

"Speak—say—how!" was the eager exclamation of the maiden when this last suggestion met her ears.

"Put me on the scent—say on what route have you sent this boy, that I may realize the revenge I so often dream of."

"Never, never, as I hope to live. I would rather you should strike me dead on the spot."

"Why, so I will," he exclaimed furiously, and his arm rose and the weapon descended, but he arrested the stroke as it approached her.

"No! not yet. There will be time enough for this, and you will perhaps be more ready and resigned when I have got rid of this youth in whom you are so much interested. I need not disguise my purpose to you—you must have known it, when conspiring for its defeat; and now, Lucy, be assured, I shall not slumber in pursuit of him. I may be delayed, my revenge may be protracted, but I shall close with him at last. Withholding the clue which you may unfold, can not serve him very greatly; and having it in your hands, you may serve yourself and me. Take my offer—put me on his route, so that he shall not escape me, and be free henceforward from pursuit, or, as you phrase it, from persecution of mine."

"You offer highly, very highly, Guy Rivers, and I should be tempted to anything, save this. But I have not taken this step to undo it. I shall give you no clue, no assistance which may lead to crime and to the murder of the innocent. Release my hand, sir, and suffer me to retire."

"You have the means of safety and release in your own hands—a single condition complied with, and, so far as I am concerned, they are yours. Where is he gone—where secreted? What is the route which you have advised him to take? Speak, and to the point, Lucy Munro, for I may not longer be trifled with."

"He is safe, and by this time, I hope, beyond your reach. I tell you thus much, because I feel that it can not yield you more satisfaction than it yields to me."

"It is in vain, woman, that you would trifle with and delay me; he can not escape me in the end. All these woods are familiar to me, in night as in day, as the apartment in which we stand; and towards this boy I entertain a feeling which will endue me with an activity and energy as unshrinking in the pursuit as the appetite for revenge is keen which gives them birth and impulse. I hate him with a sleepless, an unforgiving hate, that can not be quieted. He has dishonored me in the presence of these men—he has been the instrument through which I bear this badge, this brand-stamp on my cheek—he has come between my passion and its object—nay, droop not—I have no reference now to you, though you, too, have been won by his insidious attractions, while he gives you no thought in return—he has done more than this, occasioned more than this, and wonder not that I had it in my heart at one moment to-night to put my dagger into your bosom, since through you it had been defrauded of its object. But why tremble—do you not tell me he is safe?"

"I do! and for this reason I tremble. I tremble with joy, not fear. I rejoice that through my poor help he is safe. I did it all. I sought him— hear me, Guy Rivers, for in his safety I feel strong to speak—I sought him even in his chamber, and felt no shame—I led the way—I guided him through all the avenues of the house—when you ascended the stairs we stood over it in the closet which is at its head. We beheld your progress—saw, and counted every step you took; heard every word you uttered; and more than once, when your fiend soul spoke through your lips, in horrible threatenings, my hand arrested the weapon with which the youth whom you now seek would have sent you to your long account, with all your sins upon your head. I saved you from his blow; not because you deserved to live, but because, at that moment, you were too little prepared to die."

It would be difficult to imagine—certainly impossible to describe, the rage of Rivers, as, with an excited spirit, the young girl, still trembling, as she expressed it, from joy, not fear, avowed all the particulars of Colleton's escape. She proceeded with much of the fervor and manner of one roused into all the inspiration of a holy defiance of danger:—

"Wonder not, therefore, that I tremble—my soul is full of joy at his escape. I heed not the sneer and the sarcasm which is upon your lips and in your eyes. I went boldly and confidently even into the chamber of the youth—I aroused him from his slumbers—I defied, at that moment of peril, what were far worse to me than your suspicions—I defied such as might have been his. I was conscious of no sin—no improper thought—and I called upon God to protect and to sanction me in what I had undertaken. He has done so, and I bless him for the sanction."

She sunk upon her knees as she spoke, and her lips murmured and parted as if in prayer, while the tears—tears of gladness—streamed warmly and abundantly from her eyes. The rage of the outlaw grew momently darker and less governable. The white foam collected about his mouth—while his hands, though still retaining their gripe upon hers, trembled almost as much as her own. He spoke in broken and bitter words.

"And may God curse you for it! You have dared much, Lucy Munro, this hour. You have bearded a worse fury than the tiger thirsting after blood. What madness prompts you to this folly? You have heard me avow my utter, uncontrollable hatred of this man—my determination, if possible, to destroy him, and yet you interpose. You dare to save him in my defiance. You teach him our designs, and labor to thwart them yourself. Hear me, girl! you know me well—you know I never threaten without execution. I can understand how it is that a spirit, feeling at this moment as does your own, should defy death. But, bethink you—is there nothing in your thought which is worse than death, from the terrors of which, the pure mind, however fortified by heroic resolution, must still shrink and tremble? Beware, then, how you chafe me. Say where the youth has gone, and in this way retrieve, if you can, the error which taught you to connive at his escape."

"I know not what you mean, and have no fears of anything you can do. On this point I feel secure, and bid you defiance. To think now, that, having chiefly effected the escape of the youth, I would place him again within your power, argues a degree of stupidity in me that is wantonly insulting. I tell you he has fled, by this time, beyond your reach. I say no more. It is enough that he is in safety; before a word of mine puts him in danger, I'll perish by your hands, or any hands."

"Then shall you perish, fool!" cried the ruffian; and his hand, hurried by the ferocious impulse of his rage, was again uplifted, when, in her struggles at freedom, a new object met his sight in the chain and portrait which Ralph had flung about her neck, and which, now falling from her bosom, arrested his attention, and seemed to awaken some recognition in his mind. His hold relaxed upon her arm, and with eager haste he seized the portrait, tearing it away with a single wrench from the rich chain to which it was appended, and which now in broken fragments was strewed upon the floor.

Lucy sprang towards him convulsively, and vainly endeavored at its recovery. Rivers broke the spring, and his eyes gazed with serpent-like fixedness upon the exquisitely-beautiful features which it developed. His whole appearance underwent a change. The sternness had departed from his face, which now put on an air of abstraction and wandering, not usually a habit with it. He gazed long and fixedly upon the portrait, unheeding the efforts of the girl to obtain it, and muttering at frequent intervals detached sentences, having little dependence upon one another:—

"Ay—it is she," he exclaimed—"true to the life—bright, beautiful, young, innocent—and I—But let me not think!"

Then turning to the maid—

"Fond fool—see you the object of adoration with him whom you so unprofitably adore. He loves *her*, girl—she, whom I—but why should I tell it you? is it not enough that we have both loved and loved in vain; and, in my revenge, you too shall enjoy yours."

"I have nothing to revenge, Guy Rivers—nothing for you, above all others, to revenge. Give me the miniature; I have it in trust, and it must not go out of my possession."

She clung to him as she spoke, fruitlessly endeavoring at the recovery of that which he studiously kept from her reach. He parried her efforts for a while with something of forbearance; but ere long his original temper returned, and he exclaimed, with all the air of the demon:—

"Why will you tempt me, and why longer should I trifle? You cannot have the picture—it belongs, or should belong, as well as its original, to me. My concern is now with the robber from whom you obtained it. Will you not say upon what route he went? Will you not guide me—and, remember well—there are some terrors greater to your mind than any threat of death. Declare, for the last time—what road he took."

The maiden was still, and showed no sign of reply. Her eye wandered—her spirit was in prayer. She was alone with a ruffian, irresponsible and reckless, and she had many fears.

"Will you not speak?" he cried—"then you must hear. Disclose the fact, Lucy—say, what is the road, or what the course you have directed for this youth's escape, or—mark me! I have you in my power—my fullest power—with nothing to restrain my passion or my power, and—"

She struggled desperately to release herself from his grasp, but he renewed it with all his sinewy strength, enforcing, with a vicelike gripe, the consciousness, in her mind, of the futility of all her physical efforts.

"Do you not hear!" he said. "Do you comprehend me."

"Do your worst!" she cried. "Kill me! I defy your power and your malice!"

"Ha! but do you defy my passions. Hark ye, if ye fear not death, there is something worse than death to so romantic a damsel, which shall teach ye fear. Obey me, girl—report the route taken by this fugitive, or by all that is black in hell or bright in heaven, I—"

And with a whisper, he hissed the concluding and cruel threat in the ears of the shuddering and shrinking girl. With a husky horror in her voice, she cried out:—

"You dare not! monster as you are, you dare not!" then shrieking, at the full height of her voice—"Save me, uncle! save me! save me!"

"Save you! It is he that dooms you! He has given you up to any fate that I shall decree!"

"Liar! away! I defy you. You dare not, ruffian! Your foul threat is but meant to frighten me."

The creeping terrors of her voice, as she spoke, contradicted the tenor of her speech. Her fears—quite as extreme as he sought to make them—were fully evinced in her trembling accents.

"Frighten you!" answered the ruffian. "Frighten you! why, not so difficult a matter either! But it is as easy to do, as to threaten—to make you feel as to make you fear—and why not? why should you not become the thing at once for which you have been long destined? Once certainly mine, Lucy Munro, you will abandon the silly notion that you can be anything to Ralph Colleton! Come!—"

Her shrieks answered him. He clapped his handkerchief upon her mouth.

"Uncle! uncle! save me!"

She was half stifled—she felt breath and strength failing. Her brutal assailant was hauling her away, with a force to which she could no longer oppose resistance; and with a single half-ejaculated prayer— "Oh, God! be merciful!" she sunk senselessly at his feet; even as a falling corse.

CHAPTER TWENTY-ONE

"Thou Shalt Do No Murder!"

Even at this moment, Munro entered the apartment. He came not a moment too soon. Rivers had abused his opportunity thus far; and it is not to be doubted that he would have forborne none of the advantages which his brute strength afforded him over the feeble innocent, were it not for the interposition of the uncle. He *had* lied, when he had asserted to the girl the sanction of the uncle for his threatened crime. Munro was willing that his niece should become the *wife* of the outlaw, and barely willing to consent even to this; but for anything less than this—base as he was—he would sooner have braved every issue with the ruffian, and perished himself in defence of the girl's virtue. He had his pride of family, strange to say, though nursed and nestled in a bosom which could boast no other virtue.

The moment he saw the condition of Lucy, with the grasp of Rivers still upon her, he tore her away with the strength of a giant.

"What have you been doing, Guy?"

His keen and suspicious glance of eye conveyed the question more significantly.

"Nothing! she is a fool only!"

"And you have been a brute! Beware! I tell you, Guy Rivers, if you but ruffle the hair of this child in violence, I will knife you, as soon as I would my worst enemy."

"Pshaw! I only threatened her to make her confess where she had
sent Colleton or hidden him."

"Ay, but there are some threats, Guy, that call for throat-cutting.
Look to it. We know each other; and you know that, though I'm willing
you should *marry* Lucy, I'll not stand by and see you harm her; and,
with my permission you lay no hands on her, until you are married."

"Very well!" answered the ruffian sullenly, and turning away, "see
that you get the priest soon ready. I'll wait upon neither man nor
woman over long! You sha'n't trifle with me much longer."

To this speech Munro made no answer. He devoted himself to his
still insensible niece, whom he raised carefully from the floor, and laid
her upon a rude settee that stood in the apartment. She meanwhile
remained unconscious of his care, which was limited to fanning her face
and sprinkling water upon it.

"Why not carry her to her chamber—put her in bed, and let us be
off?" said Rivers.

"Wait awhile!" was the answer.

The girl had evidently received a severe shock. Munro shook his
head, and looked at Rivers angrily.

"See to it, Guy, if any harm comes to her."

"Pshaw!" said the other, "she is recovering now."

He was right. The eyes of the sufferer unclosed, but they were
vacant—they lacked all intelligence. Munro pulled a flask of spirits
from his pocket, and poured some into her lips. They were livid, and
her cheeks of ashy paleness.

"She recovers—see!"

The teeth opened and shut together again with a sudden spasmodic
energy. The eyes began to receive light. Her breathing increased.

"She will do now," muttered Munro. "She will recover directly. Get
yourself ready, Guy, and prepare to mount, while I see that she is put to
bed. It's now a necessity that we should push this stranger to the wall,
and silence him altogether. I don't oppose you now, seeing that we've
got to do it."

"Ay," quoth Rivers, somewhat abstractedly—for he was a person of
changing and capricious moods—"ay! ay! it has to be done! Well! we
will do it!—as for her!"

Here he drew nigh and grasped the hand of the only half-conscious
damsel, and stared earnestly in her face. Her eyes opened largely and

wildly upon him, then closed again; a shudder passed over her form, and her hand was convulsively withdrawn from his grasp.

"Come, come, let her alone, and be off," said Munro. "As long as you are here, she'll be in a fit! See to the horses. There's no use to wait. You little know Lucy Munro if you reckon to get anything out of her. You may strike till doomsday at her bosom, but, where she's fixed in principle, she'll perish before she yields. Nothing can move her when she's resolved. In that she's the very likeness of her father, who was like a rock when he had sworn a thing."

"Ha! but the rock may be split, and the woman's will must be made to yield to a superior. I could soon—"

He took her hand once more in his iron grasp.

"Let her go, Guy!" said Munro sternly. "She shall have no rough usage while I'm standing by. Remember that! It's true, she's meddled in matters that didn't concern her, but there is an excuse. It was woman-like to do so, and I can't blame her. She's a true woman, Guy—all heart and soul—as noble a young thing as ever broke the world's bread—too noble to live with such as we, Guy; and I only wish I had so much man's strength as to be worthy of living with such as she."

"A plague on her nobility! It will cut all our throats, or halter us; and your methodistical jargon only encourages her. Noble or not, she has been cunning enough to listen to our private conversation; has found out all our designs; has blabbed everything to this young fellow, and made him master of our lives. Yes! would you believe it of her nobleness and delicacy, that she has this night visited him in his very chamber?"

"What!"

"Yes! indeed! and she avows it boldly."

"Ah! if she avows it, there's no harm!"

"What! no harm?"

"I mean to *her*. She's had no bad purpose in going to his chamber. I see it all!"

"Well, and is it not quite enough to drive a man mad, to think that the best designs of a man are to be thwarted, and his neck put in danger, by the meddling of a thing like this? She has blabbed all our secrets—nay, made him listen to them—for, even while we ascended the stairs to his chamber, they were concealed in the closet above the stairway, watched all our movements, and heard every word we had to say."

"And you *would* be talking," retorted the landlord. The other glared at him ferociously, but proceeded:—

"I heard the sound—their breathing—I told you at the time that I heard something stirring in the closet. But you had your answer. For an experienced man, Munro, you are duller than an owl by daylight."

"I'm afraid so," answered the other coolly. "But it's too late now for talk. We must be off and active, if we would be doing anything. I've been out to the stable, and find that the young fellow has taken off his horse. He has been cool enough about it, for saddle and bridle are both gone. He's had time enough to gear up in proper style, while you were so eloquent along the stairs. I reckon there was something to scare him off at last, however, for here's his dirk—I suppose it's his—which I found at the stable-door. He must have dropped it when about to mount."

"'Tis his!" said Rivers, seizing and examining it. "It is the weapon he drew on me at the diggings."

"He has the start of us—"

"But knows nothing of the woods. It is not too late. Let us be off. Lucy is recovering, and you can now leave her in safety. She will find the way to her chamber—or to *some* chamber. It seems that she has no scruples in going to any."

"Stop that, Guy! Don't slander the girl."

"Pooh! are you going to set up for a sentimentalist?"

"No: but if you can't learn to stop talking, I shall set you down as a fool! For a man of action, you use more of an unnecessary tongue than any living man I ever met. For God's sake, sink the lawyer when you're out of court! It will be high time to brush up for a speech when you are in the dock, and pleading with the halter dangling in your eyes. On, don't glare upon me! He who flings about his arrows by the handful mustn't be angry if some of them are flung back."

"Are you ready?"

"Ay, ready!—She's opening her eyes. We can leave her now.—What's the course?"

"We can determine in the open air. He will probably go west, and will take one or other of the two traces at the fork, and his hoofs will soon tell us which. Our horses are refreshed by this, and are in readiness. You have pistols: see to the flints and priming. There must be no scruples now. The matter has gone quite too far for quiet, and though the affair was all mine at first, it is now as perfectly yours."

As Rivers spoke, Munro drew forth his pistols and looked carefully at the priming. The sharp click of the springing steel, as the pan was thrown open, now fully aroused Lucy to that consciousness which had been only partial in the greater part of this dialogue. Springing to her feet with an eagerness and energy that was quite astonishing after her late prostration, she rushed forward to her uncle, and looked appealingly into his face, though she did not speak, while her hand grasped tenaciously his arm.

"What means the girl?" exclaimed Munro, now apprehensive of some mental derangement. She spoke, with a deep emphasis, but a single sentence:—

"It is written—thou shalt do no murder!"

The solemn tone—the sudden, the almost fierce action—the peculiar abruptness of the apostrophe—the whitely-robed, the almost spiritual elevation of figure—all so dramatic—combined necessarily to startle and surprise; and, for a few moments, no answer was returned to the unlooked-for speech. But the effect could not be permanent upon minds made familiar with the thousand forms of human and strong energies. Munro, after a brief pause, replied—

"Who speaks of murder, girl? Why this wild, this uncalled-for exhortation?"

"Not wild, not uncalled-for, uncle, but most necessary. Wherefore would you pursue the youth, arms in your hands, hatred in your heart, and horrible threatenings upon your lips? Why put yourself into the hands of this fierce monster, as the sharp instrument to do his vengeance and gratify his savage malignity against the young and the gentle? If you would do no murder, not so he. He will do it—he will make you do it, but he will have it done. Approach me not—approach me not—let me perish, rather! O God—my uncle, let him come not near me, if you would not see me die upon the spot!" she exclaimed, in the most terrified manner, and with a shuddering horror; as Rivers, toward the conclusion of her speech, had approached her with the view to an answer. To her uncle she again addressed herself, with an energy which gave additional emphasis to her language:—

"Uncle—you are my father now—you will not forget the dying prayer of a brother! My prayer is his. Keep that man from me—let me not see him—let him come not near me with his polluted and polluting breath! You know not what he is—you know him but as a stabber—as a hater—as a thief! But were my knowledge yours—could I utter in your ears the foul language, the fiend-threatenings which his accursed lips uttered in mine!—but no—save me from him is all I ask—protect the poor orphan—the feeble, the trampled child of your brother! Keep me from the presence of that bad man!"

As she spoke, she sank at the feet of the person she addressed, her hands were clasped about his knees, and she lay there shuddering and shrinking, until he lifted her up in his arms. Somewhat softened by his kindness of manner, the pressure upon her brain of that agony was immediately relieved, and a succession of tears and sobs marked the diminished influence of her terrors. But, as Rivers attempted something in reply, she started—

"Let me go—let me not hear him speak! His breath is pollution— his words are full of foul threats and dreadful thoughts. If you knew all that I know—if you feared what I fear, uncle—you would nigh slay him on the spot."

This mental suffering of his niece was not without its influence upon her uncle, who, as we have said before, had a certain kind and degree of pride—pride of character we may almost call it—not inconsistent with pursuits and a condition of life wild and wicked even as his. His eye sternly settled upon that of his companion, as, without a word, he bore the almost lifeless girl into the chamber of his wife, who, aroused by the clamor, had now and then looked forth upon the scene, but was too much the creature of timidity to venture entirely amid the disputants. Placing her under the charge of the old lady, Munro uttered a few consolatory words in Lucy's ear, but she heard him not. Her thoughts evidently wandered to other than selfish considerations at that moment, and, as he left the chamber, she raised her finger impressively:—

"Do no murder, uncle! let him not persuade you into crime; break off from a league which compels you to brook a foul insult to those you are bound in duty to protect."

"Would I could!" was his muttered sentence as he left the chamber. He felt the justice of the counsel, but wore the bewildered expression of countenance of one conscious of what is right, but wanting courage for its adoption.

"She has told you no foolish story of me?" was the somewhat anxious speech of Rivers upon the reappearance of the landlord.

"She has said nothing in plain words, Guy Rivers—but yet quite enough to make me doubt whether you, and not this boy we pursue, should not have my weapon in your throat. But beware! The honor of that child of Edgar Munro is to me what would have been my own; and let me find that you have gone a little beyond the permitted point, in speech or action, and we cut asunder. I shall then make as little bones of putting a bullet through your ribs as into those of the wild bullock of the hills. *I* am what I am: my hope is that *she* may always be the pure creature which she now is, if it were only that she might pray for me."

"She has mistaken me, Munro—"

"Say no more, Guy. She has not *much* mistaken you, or I have. Let us speak no more on this subject; you know my mind, and will be advised.—Let us now be off. The horses are in readiness, and waiting, and a good spur will bring us up with the game. The youth, you say, has money about him, a gold watch, and—"

The more savage ruffian grinned as he listened to these words. They betrayed the meaner motives of action in the case of the companion, who could acknowledge the argument of cupidity, while insensible to that of revenge.

"Ay! enough to pay you for your share in the performance. Do your part well, and you shall have all that he carries—gold, watch, trinkets, horse, everything. I shall be quite content to take—his life! Are you satisfied? Are there any scruples now?"

"No! none! I have no scruples! But to cut a throat, or blow out a man's liver with a brace of bullets, is a work that should be well paid for. The performance is by no means so agreeable that one should seek to do it for nothing."

Guy Rivers fancied himself a nobler animal than his companion, as he felt that he needed not the mercenary motive for the performance of the murderous action.

They were mounted, the horses being ready for them in the rear of the building.

"Round the hollow. We'll skirt the village, and not go through it," said Munro. "We may gain something on the route to the fork of the roads by taking the blind track by the red hill."

"As you will. Go ahead!"

A few more words sufficed to arrange the route, and regulate their pursuit, and a few moments sufficed to send them off in full speed over the stony road, both with a common and desperate purpose, but each moved by arguments and a passion of his own.

In her lonely chamber, Lucy Munro, now recovered to acutest consciousness, heard the tread of their departing hoofs; and, clasping her hands, she sank upon her knees, yielding up her whole soul to silent prayer. The poor girl never slept that night.

CHAPTER TWENTY-TWO

The Bloody Deed

L et us leave the outlaws to their progress for a brief space, while we gather up and pursue for awhile some other clues of our story.

We have witnessed the separation of Mark Forrester from his sweetheart, at the place of trysting. The poor fellow had recovered some of his confidence in himself and fortune, and was now prepared to go forth with a new sentiment of hope within his bosom. The sting was in a degree taken from his conscience—his elastic and sanguine temperament contributed to this—and with renewed impulses to adventure, and with new anticipations of the happiness that we all dream to find in life; the erring, but really honest fellow, rode fearlessly through the dim forests, without needing more auspicious lights than those of the kindling moon and stars. The favor of old Allen, the continued love of Kate, the encouragements of young Colleton, his own feeling of the absence of any malice in his heart, even while committing his crime, and the farther fact that he was well-mounted, and speeding from the region where punishment threatened—all these were influences which conspired to lessen, in his mind, the griefs of his present privation, and the lonely emotions which naturally promised to accompany him in his solitary progress.

His course lay for the great Southwest—the unopened forests, and mighty waters of the Mississippi valley. Here, he was to begin a new life. Unknown, he would shake off the fears which his crime necessarily inspired. Respited from death and danger, he would atone for it by penitence and honest works. Kate Allen should be his solace, and there would be young and lovely children smiling around his board. Such were the natural dreams of the young and sanguine exile.

"But who shall ride from his destiny?" saith the proverb. The wing of the bird is no security against the shaft of the fowler, and the helmet and the shield keep not away the draught that is poisoned. He who wears the greaves, the gorget, and the coat-of-mail, holds defiance to the storm of battle; but he drinks and dies in the hall of banqueting. What matters it, too, though the eagle soars and screams among the clouds, half-way up to heaven—flaunting his proud pinions, and glaring with audacious glance in the very eye of the sun—death waits for him in the quiet of his own eyry, nestling with his brood. These are the goodly texts of the Arabian sage, in whose garden-tree, so much was he the beloved of heaven, the birds came and nightly sang for him those solemn truths—those lessons of a perfect wisdom—which none but the favored of the Deity are ever permitted to hear. They will find a sufficient commentary in the fortune of the rider whom we have just beheld setting out from his parting with his mistress, on his way of new adventure—his heart comparatively light, and his spirit made buoyant with the throng of pleasant fancies which continually gathered in his thought.

The interview between Forrester and his mistress had been somewhat protracted, and his route from her residence to the road in which we find him, being somewhat circuitous, the night had waned considerably ere he had made much progress. He now rode carelessly, as one who mused—his horse, not urged by its rider, became somewhat careful of his vigor, and his gait was moderated much from that which had marked his outset. He had entered upon the trace through a thick wood, when the sound of other hoofs came down upon the wind; not to his ears, for, swallowed up in his own meditations, his senses had lost much of their wonted acuteness. He had not been long gone from the point of the road in which we found him, when his place upon the same route was supplied by the pursuing party, Rivers and Munro. They were both admirably mounted, and seemed little to regard, in their manner of using them, the value of the good beasts which they bestrode—driving them as they did, resolutely over fallen trees and jutting rocks, their sides already dashed with foam, and the flanks bloody with the repeated application of the rowel. It was soon evident that farther pursuit at such a rate would be impossible: and Munro, as well for the protection of the horses, as with a knowledge of this necessity, insisted upon a more moderated and measured pace.

Much against his own will, Rivers assented, though his impatience frequent found utterance in words querulously sarcastic. The love of gain was a besetting sin of the landlord, and it was by this passion that his accomplice found it easy, on most occasions, to defeat the suggestions of his better judgment. The tauntings of the former, therefore, were particularly bestowed upon this feature in his character, as he found himself compelled to yield to the requisition of the latter, with whom the value of the horses was no small consideration.

"Well, well," said Rivers, "if you say so, it must be so; though I am sure, if we push briskly ahead, we shall find our bargain in it. You too will find the horse of the youth, upon which you had long since set your eyes and heart, a full equivalent, even if we entirely ruin the miserable beasts we ride."

"The horse you ride is no miserable beast," retorted the landlord, who had some of the pride of a southron in this particular, and seemed solicitous for the honor of his stud—"you have jaded him by your furious gait, and seem entirely insensible to the fact that our progress for the last half hour, continued much longer, would knock up any animal. I'm not so sure, too, Guy, that we shall find the youngster, or that we shall be able to get our own bargain out of him when found. He's a tough colt, I take it, and will show fight unless you surprise him."

"Stay—hear you nothing now, as the wind sets up from below? Was not that the tramping of a horse?"

They drew up cautiously as the inquiry was put by Rivers, and pausing for a few minutes, listened attentively. Munro dismounted, and laying his ear to the ground, endeavored to detect and distinguish the distant sounds, which, in that way, may be heard with far greater readiness; but he arose without being satisfied.

"You hear nothing?"

"Not a sound but that which we make ourselves. Your ears to-night are marvellous quick, but they catch nothing. This is the third time to-night you have fancied sounds, and heard what I could not; and I claim to have senses in quite as high perfection as your own."

"And without doubt you have; but, know you not, Munro, that wherever the passions are concerned, the senses become so much more acute; and, indeed, are so many sentinels and spies—scouring about perpetually, and with this advantage over all other sentinels, that they then never slumber. So, whether one hate or love, the ear and the eye take heed of all that is going on—they minister to the prevailing passion, and seem, in their own exercise, to acquire some of the motive and impulse which belong to it."

"I believe this in most respects to be the case. I have observed it on more than one occasion myself, and in my own person. But, Guy, in all that you have said, and all that I have seen, I do not yet understand why it is that you entertain such a mortal antipathy to this young man, more than to many others who have at times crossed your path. I now understand the necessity for putting him out of the way; but this is another matter. Before we thought it possible that he could injure us, you had the same violent hatred, and would have destroyed him at the first glance. There is more in this, Guy, than you have been willing to let out; and I look upon it as strange, to say nothing more, that I should be kept so much in the dark upon the subject."

Rivers smiled grimly at the inquiry, and replied at once, though with evident insincerity,—

"Perhaps my desire to get rid of him, then, arose from a presentiment that we should have to do it in the end. You know I have a gift of foreseeing and foretelling."

"This won't do for me, Guy; I know you too well to regard you as one likely to be influenced by notions of this nature—you must put me on some other scent."

"Why, so I would, Wat, if I were assured that I myself knew the precise impulse which sets me on this work. But the fact is, my hate to the boy springs from certain influences which may not be defined by name—which grow out of those moral mysteries of our nature, for which we can scarcely account to ourselves; and, by the operation of which, we are led to the performance of things seemingly without any adequate cause or necessity. A few reflections might give you the full force of this. Why do some men shrink from a cat? There is an instance now in John Bremer; a fellow, you know, who would make no more ado about exchanging rifle-shots with his enemy at twenty paces, than at taking dinner; yet a black cat throws him into fits, from which for two days he never perfectly recovers. Again—there are some persons to whom the perfume of flowers brings sickness, and the song of a bird sadness. How are we to account for all these things, unless we do so by a reference to the peculiar make of the man? In this way you may understand why it is that I hate this boy, and would destroy him. He is my black cat, and his presence for ever throws me into fits."

"I have heard of the things of which you speak, and have known some of them myself; but I never could believe that the *nature* of the person had been the occasion. I was always inclined to think that circumstances in childhood, of which the recollection is forgotten—such as great and sudden fright to the infant, or a blow which affected the brain, were the operating influences. All these things, however, only affect the fancies—they beget fears and notions—never deep and abiding hatred—unquiet passion, and long-treasured malignity, such as I find in you on this occasion."

"Upon this point, Munro, you may be correct. I do not mean to say that hatred and a desire to destroy are consequent to antipathies such as you describe; but still, something may be said in favor of such a notion. It appears to me but natural to seek the destruction of that which is odious or irksome to any of our senses. Why do you crush the crawling spider with your heel? You fear not its venom; inspect it, and the mechanism of its make, the architecture of its own fabrication, are, to the full, as wonderful as anything within your comprehension; but yet, without knowing why, with an impulse given you, as it would seem, from infancy, you seek its destruction with a persevering industry, which might lead one to suppose you had in view your direst enemy."

"This is all very true; and from infancy up we do this thing, but the cause can not be in any loathsomeness which its presence occasions in the mind, for we perceive the same boy destroying with measured tortures the gaudiest butterfly which his hat can encompass."

"*Non sequitur*," said Rivers.

"What's that? some of your d——d law gibberish, I suppose. If you want me to talk with you at all, Guy, you must speak in a language I understand."

"Why, so I will, Wat. I only meant to say, in a phrase common to the law, and which your friend Pippin makes use of a dozen times a day, that it did not follow from what you said, that the causes which led to the death of the spider and the butterfly were the same. This we may know by the manner in which they are respectively destroyed. The boy, with much precaution and an aversion he does not seek to disguise, in his attempts on the spider, employs his shoe or a stick for the purpose of slaughter. But, with the butterfly, the case is altogether different. He first catches, and does not fear to hold it in his hand. He inspects it closely, and proceeds to analyze that which his young thought has already taught him is a beautiful creation of the insect world. He strips it, wing by wing, of its gaudy covering; and then, with a feeling of ineffable scorn, that so wealthy a noble should go unarmed and unprotected, he dashes him to the ground, and terminates his sufferings without further scruple. The spider, having a sting, he is compelled to fear, and consequently taught to respect. The feelings are all perfectly natural, however, which prompt his proceedings. The curiosity is common and innate which impels him to the inspection of the insect; and that feeling is equally a natural impulse which prompts him to the death of the spider without hesitation. So with me—it is enough that I hate this boy, though possessed of numberless attractions of mind and person. Shall I do him the kindness to inquire whether there be reason for the mood which prompts me to destroy him?"

"You were always too much for me, Guy, at this sort of argument, and you talk the matter over ingeniously enough, I grant; but still I am not satisfied, that a mere antipathy, without show of reason, originally induced your dislike to this young man. When you first sought to do him up, you were conscious of this, and gave, as a reason for the desire, the cut upon your face, which so much disfigured your loveliness."

Rivers did not appear very much to relish or regard this speech, which had something of satire in it; but he was wise enough to restrain his feelings, as, reverting back to their original topic, he spoke in the following manner:—

"You are unusually earnest after reasons and motives for action, to-night: is it not strange, Munro, that it has never occasioned surprise in your mind, that one like myself, so far superior in numerous respects to the men I have consented to lead and herd with, should have made such my profession?"

"Not at all," was the immediate and ready response of his companion. "Not at all. This was no mystery to me, for I very well knew that you had no choice, no alternative. What else could you have done? Outlawed and under sentence, I knew that you could never return, in any safety or security, whatever might be your disguise, to the society which had driven you out—and I'm sure that your chance would be but a bad one were you to seek a return to the old practice at Gwinnett courthouse. Any attempt there to argue a fellow out of the halter would be only to argue yourself into it."

"Pshaw, Munro, that is the case now—that is the necessity and difficulty of to-day. But where, and what was the necessity, think you, when, in the midst of good practice at Gwinnett bar, where I ruled without competitor, riding roughshod over bench, bar, and jury, dreaded alike by all, I threw myself into the ranks of these men, and put on their habits? I speak not now in praise of myself, more than the facts, as you yourself know them, will sufficiently warrant. I am now above those idle vanities which would make me deceive myself as to my own mental merits; but, that such was my standing there and then, I hold indisputable."

"It is true. I sometimes look back and laugh at the manner in which you used to bully the old judge, and the gaping jury, and your own brother lawyers, while the foam would run through your clenched teeth and from your lips in very passion; and then I wondered, when you were doing so well, that you ever gave up there, to undertake a business, the very first job in which put your neck in danger."

"You may well wonder, Munro, I could not well explain the mystery to myself, were I to try; and it is this which made the question and doubt which we set out to explain. To those who knew me well from the first, it is not matter of surprise that I should be for ever in excitements of one kind or another. From my childhood up, my temper was of a restless and unquiet character—I was always a peevish, a fretful and discontented person. I looked with scorn and contempt upon the humdrum ways of those about me, and longed for perpetual change, and wild and stirring incidents. My passions, always fretful and excitable, were never satisfied except when I was employed in some way which enabled me to feed and keep alive the irritation which was their and my very breath of life. With such a spirit, how could I be what men style and consider a good man? What folly to expect it. Virtue is but a sleepy, in-door, domestic quality—inconsistent with enterprise or great activity. There are no drones so perfect in the world as the truly orthodox. Hence the usual superiority of a dissenting, over an established church. It is for this reason, too, and from this cause, that a great man is seldom, if ever, a good one. It is inconsistent with the very nature of things to expect it, unless it be from a co-operation of singular circumstances, whose return is with the comets. Vice, on the contrary, is endowed with strong passions—a feverish thirst after forbidden fruits and waters—a bird-nesting propensity, that carries it away from the haunts of the crowded city, into strange wilds and interminable forests. It lives upon adventure—it counts its years by incidents, and has no other mode of computing time or of enjoying life. This fact—and it is undeniable with

respect to both the parties—will furnish a sufficient reason why the best
heroes of the best poets are always great criminals. Were this not the
case, from what would the interest be drawn?—where would be the
incident, if all men, pursuing the quiet paths of non-interference with
the rights, the lives, or the liberties of one another, spilt no blood,
invaded no territory, robbed no lord of his lady, enslaved and made no
captives in war? A virtuous hero would be a useless personage both in
play and poem—and the spectator or reader would fall asleep over the
utterance of stale apothegms. What writer of sense, for instance, would
dream of bringing up George Washington to figure in either of these
forms before the world—and how, if he did so, would he prevent reader
or auditor from getting excessively tired, and perhaps disgusted, with
one, whom all men are now agreed to regard as the hero of civilization?
Nor do I utter sentiments which are subjects either of doubt or disputa-
tion. I could put the question in such a form as would bring the million
to agree with me. Look, for instance, at the execution of a criminal. See
the thousands that will assemble, day after day, after travelling miles for
that single object, to gape and gaze upon the last agonizing pangs and
paroxsyms of a fellow-creature—not regarding for an instant the
fatigue of their position, the press of the crowd, or the loss of a dinner—
totally insusceptible, it would seem, of the several influences of heat and
cold, wind and rain, which at any other time would drive them to their
beds or firesides. The same motive which provokes this desire in the
spectator, if the parent, to a certain extent, of the very crime which has
led to the exhibition. It is the morbid appetite, which sometimes grows
to madness—the creature of unregulated passions, ill-judged direction,
and sometimes, even of the laws and usages of society itself, which is so
much interested in the promotion of characteristics the very reverse. It
may be that I have more of this perilous stuff about me than the gener-
ality of mankind; but I am satisfied there are few of them, taught as I
have been, and the prey of like influences, whose temper had been very
different from mine. The early and operating circumstances under
which I grew up, all tended to the rank growth and encouragement of
the more violent and vexing passions. I was the victim of a tyranny,
which, in the end, made me too a tyrant. To feel, myself, and exercise
the temper thus taught me, I had to acquire power in order to secure
victims; and all my aims in life, all my desires, tended to this one pursuit. Indifferent to me, alike, the spider who could sting, or the harmless
butterfly whose only offensiveness is in the folly of his wearing a glitter

which he can not take care of. I was a merciless enemy, giving no quarter; and with an Ishmaelitish spirit, lifting my hand against all the tribes that were buzzing around me."

"I believe you have spoken the truth, Guy, so far as your particular qualities of temper are concerned; for, had I undertaken to have spoken for you in relation to this subject, I should probably have said though not to the same degree, the same thing; but the wonder with me is, how, with such feelings, you should have so long remained in quiet, and in some respects, perfectly harmless."

"There is as little mystery in the one as in the other. You may judge that my sphere of action—speaking of *action* in a literal sense—was rather circumscribed at Gwinnett courthouse: but, the fact is, I was then but acquiring my education. I was, for the first time, studying rogues, and the study of rogues is not unaptly fitted to make one take up the business. *I*, at least, found it to have that effect. But, even at Gwinnett courthouse, learning as I did, and what I did, there was one passion, or perhaps a modified form of the ruling passion, which might have swallowed up all the rest had time been allowed it. I was young, and not free from vanity; particularly as, for the first time, my ears had been won with praise and gentle flatteries. The possession of early, and afterward undisputed talents, acquired for me deference and respect; and I was soon tempted to desire the applauses of the swinish multitude, and to feel a thirsting after public distinction. In short, I grew ambitious. I soon became sick and tired of the applauses, the fame, of my own ten-mile horizon; its origin seemed equivocal, its worth and quality questionable, at the best. My spirit grew troubled with a wholesale discontent, and roved in search of a wider field, a more elevated and extensive empire. But how could I, the petty lawyer of a county court, in the midst of a wilderness, appropriate time, find means and opportunities even for travel? I was poor, and profits are few to a small lawyer, whose best cases are paid for by a bale of cotton or a negro, when both of them are down in the market. In vain, and repeatedly, did I struggle with circumstances that for ever foiled me in my desires; until, in a rash and accursed hour when chance, and you, and the devil, threw the opportunity for crime in my path! It did not escape me, and—but you know the rest."

"I do, but would rather hear you tell it. When you speak thus, you put me in mind of some of the stump-speeches you used to make when you ran for the legislature."

"Ay, that was another, and not the least of the many reverses which my ambition was doomed to meet with. You knew the man who opposed me; you know that a more shallow and insignificant fop and fool never yet dared to thrust his head into a deliberative assembly. But, he was rich, and I poor. He a potato, the growth of the soil; I, though generally admitted a plant of more promise and pretension—I was an exotic! He was a patrician—one of the small nobility—a growth, *sui generis,* of the place—"

"Damn your law-phrases! stop with that, if you please."

"Well, well! he was one of the great men; I was a poor plebeian, whose chief misfortune, at that time, consisted in my not having a father or a great-grandfather a better man than myself! His money did the work, and I was bought and beat out of my election, which I considered certain. I then acquired knowledge of two things. I learned duly to estimate the value of the democratic principle, when I beheld the vile slaves, whose votes his money had commanded, laughing in scorn at the miserable creature they had themselves put over them. They felt not—not they—the double shame of their doings. They felt that he was King Log, but never felt how despicable they were as his subjects. This taught me, too, the value of money—its wonderful magic and mystery. In the mood occasioned by all these things, you found me, for the first time, and in a ready temper for any villany. You attempted to console me for my defeats, but I heard you not until you spoke of revenge. I was not then to learn how to be vindictive: I had always been so. I knew, by instinct, how to lap blood; you only taught me how to scent it! My first great crime proved my nature. Performed under your direction, though without your aid, it was wantonly cruel in its execution, since the prize desired might readily have been obtained without the life of its possessor. You, more merciful than myself, would have held me back, and arrested my stroke; but that would have been taking from the repast its finish: the pleasure, for it was such to me in my condition of mind, would have been lost entirely. It may sound strangely even in your ears when I say so, but I could no more have kept my knife from that man's throat than I could have taken wing for the heavens. He was a poor coward; made no struggle, and begged most piteously for his life; had the audacity to talk of his great possessions, his rank in society, his wife and children. These were enjoyments all withheld from me; these were the very things the want of which had made me what I was—what I am— and furiously I struck my weapon into his mouth, silencing his insulting speech. Should such a mean spirit as his have joys which were denied to me? I spurned his quivering carcass with my foot. At that moment I felt myself; I had something to live for. I knew my appetite, and felt that it was native. I had acquired a knowledge of a new luxury, and ceased to wonder at the crimes of a Nero and a Caligula. Think you, Munro, that the thousands who assemble at the execution of a criminal trouble themselves to inquire into the merits of his case—into the justice of his death and punishment? Ask they whether he is the victim of justice or of tyranny? No! they go to see a show—they love blood, and in this way have the enjoyment furnished to their hands, without the risk which must follow the shedding of it for themselves."

"There is one thing, Guy, upon which I never thought to ask you. What became of that beautiful young girl from Carolina, on a visit to the village, when you lost your election? You were then cavorting about her in great style, and I could see that you were well nigh as much mad after her as upon the loss of the seat."

Rivers started at the inquiry in astonishment. He had never fancied that, in such matters, Munro had been so observant, and for a few moments gave no reply. He evidently winced beneath the inquiry; but he soon recovered himself, however—for, though at times exhibiting the passions of a demoniac, he was too much of a proficient not to be able, in the end, to command the coolness of the villain.

"I had thought to have said nothing on this subject. Munro, but there are few things which escape your observation. In replying to you on this point, you will now have all the mystery explained of my rancorous pursuit of this boy. That girl—then a mere girl—refused me, as perhaps you know; and when, heated with wine and irritated with rejection, I pressed the point rather too warmly, she treated me with contempt and withdrew from the apartment. This youth is the favored, the successful rival. Look upon this picture, Walter—now, while the moon streams through the branches upon it—and wonder not that it maddened, and still maddens me, to think that, for his smooth face and aristocratic airs of superiority, I was to be sacrificed and despised. She was probably a year younger than himself; but I saw at the time, though both of them appeared unconscious of the fact, that she loved him then. What with her rejection and scorn, coming at the same time with my election defeat, I am what I am. These defeats were wormwood to my soul; and, if I am criminal, the parties concerned in them have been the cause of the crime."

"A very consoling argument, if you could only prove it!"

"Very likely—you are not alone. The million would say with yourself.

But hear the case as I put it, and not as it is put by the majority. Providence endowed me with a certain superiority of mind over my fellows. I had capacities which they had not—talents to which they did not aspire, and the possession of which they readily conceded to me. These talents fitted me for certain stations in society, to which, as I had the talents pre-eminently for such stations, the inference is fair that Providence intended me for some such stations. But I was denied my place. Society, guilty of favoritism and prejudice, gave to others, not so well fitted as myself for its purposes or necessities, the station in all particulars designed for me. I was denied my birthright, and rebelled. Can society complain, when prostituting herself and depriving me of my rights, that I resisted her usurpation and denied her authority? Shall she, doing wrong herself in the first instance, undertake to punish? Surely not. My rights were admitted—my superior capacity: but the people were rotten to the core; they had not even the virtue of truth to themselves. They made their own governors of the vilest and the worst. They willingly became slaves, and are punished in more ways than one. They first create the tyrants—for tyrants are the creatures of the people they sway, and never make themselves; they next drive into banishment their more legitimate rulers; and the consequence, in the third place, is, that they make enemies of those whom they exile. Such is the case with me, and such— but hark! That surely is the tread of a horse. Do you hear it? there is no mistake now—" and as he spoke, the measured trampings were heard resounding at some distance, seemingly in advance of them.

"We must now use the spur, Munro; your horses have had indulgence enough for the last hour, and we may tax them a little now."

"Well, push on as you please; but do you know anything of this route, and what course will you pursue in doing him up?"

"Leave all that to me. As for the route, it is an old acquaintance, and the blaze on this tree reminds me that we can here have a short cut which will carry us at a good sweep round this hill, bringing us upon the main trace about two miles farther down. We must take this course, and spur on, that we may get ahead of him, and be quietly stationed when he comes. We shall gain it, I am confident, before our man, who seems to be taking it easily. He will have three miles at the least to go, and over a road that will keep him in a walk half the way. We shall be there in time."

They reached the point proposed in due season. Their victim had not yet made his appearance, and they had sufficient time for all their arrangements. The place was one well calculated for the successful accomplishment of a deed of darkness. The road at the foot of the hill narrowed into a path scarcely wide enough for the passage of a single horseman. The shrubbery and copse on either side overhung it, and in many places were so thickly interwoven, that when, as at intervals of the night, the moon shone out among the thick and broken clouds which hung upon and mostly obscured her course, her scattered rays scarcely penetrated the dense enclosure.

At length the horseman approached, and in silence. Descending the hill, his motion was slow and tedious. He entered the fatal avenue; and, when in the midst of it, Rivers started from the side of his comrade, and, advancing under the shelter of a tree, awaited his progress. He came—no word was spoken—a single stroke was given, and the horseman, throwing up his hands, grasped the limb which projected over, while his horse passed from under him. He held on for a moment to the branch, while a groan of deepest agony broke from his lips, when he fell supine to the ground. At that moment, the moon shone forth unimpeded and unobscured by a single cloud. The person of the wounded man was fully apparent to the sight. He struggled, but spoke not; and the hand of Rivers was again uplifted, when Munro rushed forward.

"Stay—away, Guy!—we are mistaken—this is not our man!"

The victim heard the words, and, with something like an effort at a laugh, though seemingly in great agony, exclaimed—

"Ah, Munro, is that you?—I am so glad! but I'm afraid you come too late. This is a cruel blow; and—for what? What have I done to you, that—oh!—"

The tones of the voice—the person of the suffering man—were now readily distinguishable.

"Good God! Rivers, what is to be the end of all this blundering?"

"Who would have thought to find him here?" was the ferocious answer; the disappointed malice of the speaker prompting him to the bitterest feelings against the unintended victim—"why was he in the way? he is always in the way!"

"I am afraid you've done for him."

"We must be sure of it."

"Great God! would you kill him?"

"Why not? It must be done now."

The wounded man beheld the action of the speaker, and heard the discussion. He gasped out a prayer for life:—

"Spare me, Guy! Save me, Wat, if you have a man's heart in your bosom. Save me! spare me! I would live! I—oh, spare me!"

And the dying man threw up his hands feebly, in order to avert the blow; but it was in vain. Munro would have interposed, but, this time, the murderer was too quick for him, if not too strong. With a sudden rush he flung his associate aside, stooped down, and smote—smote fatally.

"Kate!—ah!—O God, have mercy!"

The wretched and unsuspecting victim fell back upon the earth with these last words—dead—sent to his dread account, with all his sins upon his head! And what a dream of simple happiness in two fond, feeble hearts, was thus cruelly and terribly dispersed for ever!

CHAPTER TWENTY-THREE

What Followed the Murder

There was a dreadful pause, after the commission of the deed, in which no word was spoken by either of the parties. The murderer, meanwhile, with the utmost composure wiped his bloody knife in the coat of the man whom he had slain. Boldly and coolly then, he broke the silence which was certainly a painful one to Munro if not to himself.

"We shall hear no more of his insolence. I owed him a debt. It is paid. If fools will be in the way of danger, they must take the consequences."

The landlord only groaned.

The murderer laughed.

"It is your luck," he said, "always to groan with devout feeling, when you have *done* the work of the devil! You may spare your groans, if they are designed for repentance. They are always too late!"

"It is a sad truth, though the devil said it."

"Well, rouse up, and let's be moving. So far, our ride has been for nothing. We must leave this carrion to the vultures. What next? Will it be of any use to pursue this boy again to-night? What say you? We must pursue and silence him of course; but we have pushed the brutes already sufficiently to-night. They would be of little service to-night, in a longer chase."

The person addressed did not immediately reply, and when he spoke, did not answer to the speech of his companion. His reply, at length, was framed in obedience to the gloomy and remorseful course of his thought.

"It will be no wonder, Guy, if the whole country turn out upon us. You are too wanton in your doings. Wherefore, when I told you of your error, did you strike the poor wretch again."

The landlord, it will be seen, spoke simply with reference to policy and expediency, and deserved as little credit for humanity as the individual he rebuked. In this particular lay the difference between them. Both were equally ruffianly, but the one had less of passion, less of feeling, and more of profession in the matter. With the other, the trade of crime was adopted strictly in subservience to the dictates of ill-regulated desires and emotions, suffering defeat in their hope of indulgence, and stimulating to a morbid action which became a disease. The references of Munro were always addressed to the petty gains; and the miserly nature, thus perpetually exhibiting itself, at the expense of all other emotions, was, in fact, the true influence which subjected him almost to the sole dictation of his accomplice, in whom a somewhat lofty distaste for such a peculiarity had occasioned a manner and habit of mind, the superiority of which was readily felt by the other. Still, we must do the landlord the justice to say that he had no such passion for bloodshed as characterized his companion.

"Why strike again!" was the response of Rivers. "You talk like a child. Would you have had him live to blab? Saw you not that he knew us both? Are you so green as to think, if suffered to escape, his tongue or hands would have been idle? You should know better. But the fact is, he could not have lived. The first blow was fatal; and, if I had deliberated for an instant, I should have followed the suggestions of your humanity—I should have withheld the second, which merely terminated his agony."

"It was a rash and bloody deed, and I would we had made sure of your man before blindly rushing into these unnecessary risks. It is owing to your insane love of blood, that you so frequently blunder in your object."

"Your scruples and complainings, Wat, remind me of that farmyard philosopher, who always locked the door of his stable after the steed had been stolen. You have your sermon ready in time for the funeral, but not during the life for whose benefit you make it. But whose fault was it that we followed the wrong game? Did you not make certain of the fresh track at the fork, so that there was no doubting you?"

"I did—there was a fresh track, and our coming upon Forrester proves it. There may have been another on the other prong of the fork, and doubtless the youth we pursue has taken that; but you were in such an infernal hurry that I had scarce time to find out what I did."

"Well, you will preach no more on the subject. We have failed, and accounting for won't mend the failure. As for this bull-headed fellow, he deserves his fate for his old insolence. He was for ever putting himself in my way, and may not complain that I have at last put him out of it. But come, we have no further need to remain here, though just as little to pursue further in the present condition of our horses."

"What shall we do with the body? we can not leave it here."

"Why not?—What should we do with it, I pray? The wolves may want a dinner to-morrow, and I would be charitable. Yet stay—where is the dirk which you found at the stable? Give it me."

"What would you do?"

"You shall see. Forrester's horse is off—fairly frightened, and will take the route back to the old range. He will doubtless go to old Allen's clearing, and carry the first news. There will be a search, and when they find the body, they will not overlook the weapon, which I shall place beside it. There will then be other pursuers than me; and if it bring the boy to the gallows, I shall not regret our mistake to night."

As he spoke, he took the dagger, the sheath of which he threw at some distance in advance upon the road, then smeared the blade with the blood of the murdered man, and thrust the weapon into his garments, near the wound.

"You are well taught in the profession, Guy, and, if you would let me, I would leave it off, if for no other reason than the very shame of being so much outdone in it. But we may as well strip him. If his gold is in his pouch, it will be a spoil worth the taking, for he has been melting and running for several days past at Murkey's furnace."

Rivers turned away, and the feeling which his countenance exhibited might have been that of disdainful contempt as he replied,

"Take it, if you please—I am in no want of his money. *My* object was not his robbery."

The scorn was seemingly understood; for, without proceeding to do as he proposed, Munro retained his position for a few moments, appearing to busy himself with the bridle of his horse, having adjusted which he returned to his companion.

"Well, are you ready for a start? We have a good piece to ride, and should be in motion. We have both of us much to do in the next three days, or rather nights; and need not hesitate what to take hold of first. The court will sit on Monday, and if you are determined to stand and see it out—a plan which I don't altogether like—why, we must prepare to get rid of such witnesses as we may think likely to become troublesome."

"That matter will be seen to. I have ordered Dillon to have ten men in readiness, if need be for so many, to carry off Pippin, and a few others, till the adjournment. It will be a dear jest to the lawyer, and one not less novel than terrifying to him, to miss a court under such circumstances. I take it, he has never been absent from a session for twenty years; for, if sick before, he is certain to get well in time for business, spite of his physician."

The grim smile which disfigured still more the visage of Rivers at the ludicrous association which the proposed abduction of the lawyer awakened in his mind, was reflected fully back from that of his companion, whose habit of face, however, in this respect, was more notorious for gravity than any other less stable expression. He carried out, in words, the fancied occurrence; described the lawyer as raving over his undocketed and unargued cases, and the numberless embryos lying composedly in his pigeonholes, awaiting, with praiseworthy patience, the moment when they should take upon them a local habitation and a name; while he, upon whom they so much depended, was fretting with unassuaged fury in the constraints of his prison, and the absence from that scene of his repeated triumphs which before had never been at a loss for his presence.

"But come—let us mount," said the landlord, who did not feel disposed to lose much time for a jest. "There is more than this to be done yet in the village; and, I take it, you feel in no disposition to waste more time to-night. Let us be off."

"So say I, but I go not back with you, Wat. I strike across the woods into the other road, where I have much to see to; besides going down the branch to Dixon's Ford, and Wolf's Neck, where I must look up our men and have them ready. I shall not be in the village, therefore, until late to-morrow night—if then."

"What—you are for the crossroads, again," said Munro. "I tell you what, Guy, you must have done with that girl before Lucy shall be yours. It's bad enough—bad enough that she should be compelled to look to you for love. It were a sad thing if the little she might expect to find were to be divided between two or more."

"Pshaw—you are growing Puritan because of the dark. I tell you I have done with *her*. I can not altogether forget what she was, nor what I have made her; and just at this time she is in need of my assistance. Good-night! I shall see Dillon and the rest of them by morning, and prepare for the difficulty. My disguise shall be complete, and if you are wise you will see to your own. I would not think of flight, for much may be made out of the country, and I know of none better for our purposes. Good-night!"

Thus saying, the outlaw struck into the forest, and Munro, lingering until he was fairly out of sight, proceeded to rifle the person of Forrester—an act which the disdainful manner and language of his companion had made him hitherto forbear. The speech of Rivers on this subject had been felt; and, taken in connection with the air of authority which the mental superiority of the latter had necessarily imparted to his address, there was much in it highly offensive to the less adventurous ruffian. A few moments sufficed to effect the lightening of the woodman's purse of the earnings which had been so essential a feature in his dreams of cottage happiness; and while engaged in this transfer, the discontent of the landlord with his colleague in crime, occasionally broke out into words—

"He carries himself highly, indeed; and I must stand reproved whenever it pleases his humor. Well, I am in for it now, and there is no chance of my getting safely out of the scrape just at this moment; but the day will come, and, by G——d! I will have a settlement that'll go near draining his heart of all the blood in it."

As he spoke in bitterness he approached his horse, and flinging the bridle over his neck, was in a little while a good distance on his way from the scene of blood; over which Silence now folded her wings, brooding undisturbed, as if nothing had taken place below; so little is the sympathy which the transient and inanimate nature appears, at any time, to exhibit, with that to the enjoyment of which it yields the bloom and odor of leaf and flower, soft zephyrs and refreshing waters.

CHAPTER TWENTY-FOUR

The Fates Favor the Fugitive

L et us now return to our young traveller, whose escape we have already narrated.

Utterly unconscious of the melancholy circumstance which had diverted his enemies from the pursuit of himself, he had followed studiously the parting directions of the young maiden, to whose noble feeling and fearless courage he was indebted for his present safety; and taken the almost *blind* path which she had hastily described to him. On this route he had for some time gone, with a motion not extravagantly free, but sufficiently so, having the start, and with the several delays to which his pursuers had been subjected, to have escaped the danger—while the vigor of his steed lasted—even had they fallen on the proper route. He had proceeded in this way for several miles, when, at length, he came upon a place whence several roads diverged into opposite sections of the country. Ignorant of the localities, he reined in his horse, and deliberated with himself for a few moments as to the path he should pursue. While thus engaged, a broad glare of flame suddenly illumined the woods on his left hand, followed with the shrieks, equally sudden, seemingly of a woman.

There was no hesitation in the action of the youth. With unscrupulous and fearless precipitation, he gave his horse the necessary direction, and with a smart application of the rowel, plunged down the narrow path toward the spot from whence the alarm had arisen. As he approached, the light grew more intense, and he at length discovered a little cottage-like dwelling, completely embowered in thick foliage, through the crevices of which the flame proceeded, revealing the cause of terror, and illuminating for some distance the dense woods around. The shrieks still continued; and throwing himself from his horse, Ralph darted forward, and with a single and sudden application of his foot, struck the door from its hinges, and entered the dwelling just in time to save its inmates from the worst of all kinds of death.

The apartment was in a light blaze—the drapery of a couch which stood in one corner partially consumed, and, at the first glance, the whole prospect afforded but little hope of a successful struggle with the conflagration. There was no time to be lost, yet the scene was enough to have paralyzed the nerves of the most heroic action.

On the couch thus circumstanced lay an elderly lady, seemingly in the very last stages of disease. She seemed only at intervals conscious of the fire. At her side, in a situation almost as helpless as her own, was the young female whose screams had first awakened the attention of the traveller. She lay moaning beside the couch, shrieking at intervals, and though in momentary danger from the flames, which continued to increase, taking no steps for their arrest. Her only efforts were taken to raise the old woman from the couch, and to this, the strength of the young one was wholly unequal. Ralph went manfully to work, and had the satisfaction of finding success in his efforts. With a fearless hand he tore down the burning drapery which curtained the windows and couch; and which, made of light cotton stuffs, presented a ready auxiliar to the progress of the destructive element. Striking down the burning shutter with a single blow, he admitted the fresh air, without which suffocation must soon have followed, and throwing from the apartment such of the furniture as had been seized upon by the flames, he succeeded in arresting their farther advance.

All this was the work of a few moments. There had been no word of intercourse between the parties, and the youth now surveyed them with looks of curious inquiry, for the first time. The invalid, as we have said, was apparently struggling with the last stages of natural decay. Her companion was evidently youthful, in spite of those marks which even the unstudied eye might have discerned in her features, of a temper and a spirit subdued and put to rest by the world's strife and trial, and by afflictions which are not often found to crowd and to make up the history and being of the young. Their position was peculiarly insulated, and Ralph wondered much at the singularity of a scene to which his own experience could furnish no parallel. Here were two lone women—living on the borders of a savage nation, and forming the frontier of a class of whites little less savage, without any protection, and, to his mind, without any motive for making such their abiding-place. His wonder might possibly have taken the shape of inquiry, but that there was something of oppressive reserve and shrinking timidity in the air of the young woman, who alone could have replied to his inquiries. At this time an old female negro entered, now for the first time alarmed by the outcry, who assisted in removing such traces of the fire as still remained about the room. She seemed to occupy a neighboring outhouse, to which, having done what seemed absolutely necessary, she immediately retired.

Colleton, with a sentiment of the deepest commiseration, proceeded to reinstate things as they might have been before the conflagration, and having done so, and having soothed, as far as he well might, the excited apprehensions of the young girl, who made her acknowledgments in a not unbecoming style, he ventured to ask a few questions as to the condition of the old lady and of herself; but, finding from the answers that the subject was not an agreeable one, and having no pretence for further delay, he prepared to depart. He inquired, however, his proper route to the Chestatee river, and thus obtained a solution of the difficulty which beset him in the choice of roads at the fork.

While thus employed, however, and just at the conclusion of his labors, there came another personage upon the scene, to whom it is necessary that we should direct our attention.

It will be remembered that Rivers and Munro, after the murder of Forrester, had separated—the latter on his return to the village—the other in a direction which seemed to occasion some little dissatisfaction in the mind of his companion. After thus separating, Rivers, to whom the whole country was familiar, taking a shorter route across the forest, by which the sinuosities of the main road were generally avoided, entered, after the progress of a few miles, into the very path pursued by Colleton, and which, had it been chosen by his pursuers in the first instance, might have entirely changed the result of the pursuit. In taking this course it was not the thought of the outlaw to overtake the individual whose blood he so much desired; but, with an object which will have its development as we continue, he came to the cottage at the very time when, having succeeded in overcoming the flames, Ralph was employed in a task almost as difficult—that of reassuring the affrighted inmates, and soothing them against the apprehension of farther danger.

With a caution which old custom had made almost natural in such cases, Rivers, as he approached the cross-roads, concealed his horse in the cover of the woods, advanced noiselessly, and with not a little surprise, to the cottage, whose externals had undergone no little alteration from the loss of the shutter, the blackened marks, visible enough in the moonlight, around the window-frame, and the general look of confusion which hung about it. A second glance made out the steed of our traveller, which he approached and examined. The survey awakened all those emotions which operated upon his spirit when referring to his successful rival; and, approaching the cottage with extreme caution, he took post for a while at one of the windows, the shutter of which, partially unclosed, enabled him to take in at a glance the entire apartment.

He saw, at once, the occasion which had induced the presence, in this situation, of his most hateful enemy; and the thoughts were strangely discordant which thronged and possessed his bosom. At one moment he had drawn his pistol to his eye—his finger rested upon the trigger, and the doubt which interposed between the youth and eternity, though it sufficed for his safety then, was of the most slight and shadowy description. A second time did the mood of murder savagely possess his soul, and the weapon's muzzle fell pointblank upon the devoted bosom of Ralph; when the slight figure of the young woman passing between, again arrested the design of the outlaw, who, with muttered curses, uncocking, returned the weapon to his belt.

Whatever might have been the relationship between himself and these females, there was an evident reluctance on the part of Rivers to exhibit his ferocious hatred of the youth before those to whom he had just rendered a great and unquestioned service; and, though untroubled by any feeling of gratitude on their behalf, or on his own, he was yet unwilling, believing, as he did, that his victim was now perfectly secure, that they should undergo any further shock, at a moment too of such severe suffering and trial as must follow in the case of the younger, from those fatal pangs which were destroying the other.

Ralph now prepared to depart; and taking leave of the young woman, who alone seemed conscious of his services, and warmly acknowledged them, he proceeded to the door. Rivers, who had watched his motions attentively, and heard the directions given him by the girl for his progress, at the same moment left the window, and placed himself under the shelter of a huge tree, at a little distance on the path which his enemy was directed to pursue. Here he waited like the tiger, ready to take the fatal leap, and plunge his fangs into the bosom of his victim. Nor did he wait long.

Ralph was soon upon his steed, and on the road; but the Providence that watches over and protects the innocent was with him, and it happened, most fortunately, that just before he reached the point at which his enemy stood in watch, the badness of the road had compelled those who travelled it to diverge aside for a few paces into a little by-path, which, at a little distance beyond, and when the bad places had been rounded, brought the traveller again into the proper path. Into this bypath, the horse of Colleton took his way; the rider neither saw the embarrassments of the common path, nor that his steed had turned aside from them. It was simply providential that the instincts of the horse were more heedful than the eyes of the horseman.

It was just a few paces ahead, and on the edge of a boggy hollow that Guy Rivers had planted himself in waiting. The tread of the young traveller's steed, diverging from the route which he watched, taught the outlaw the change which it was required that he should also make in his position.

"Curse him!" he muttered. "Shall there be always something in the way of my revenge?"

Such was his temper, that everything which baffled him in his object heightened his ferocity to a sort of madness. But this did not prevent his prompt exertion to retrieve the lost ground. The "turn-out" did not continue fifty yards, before it again wound into the common road, and remembering this, the outlaw hurried across the little copse which separated the two routes for a space. The slow gait at which Colleton now rode, unsuspicious of danger, enabled his enemy to gain the position which he sought, close crouching on the edge of the thicket, just where the roads again united. Here he waited—not many seconds.

The pace of our traveller, we have said, was slow. We may add that his mood was also inattentive. He was not only unapprehensive of present danger, but his thoughts were naturally yielded to the condition of the two poor women, in that lonely abode of forest, whom he had just rescued, in all probability, from a fearful death. Happy with the pleasant

consciousness of a good action well performed, and with spirits naturally rising into animation, freed as they were from a late heavy sense of
danger—he was as completely at the mercy of the outlaw who awaited
him, pistol in hand, as if he lay, as his poor friend, Forrester, so recently
had done, directly beneath his knife.

And so thought Rivers, who heard the approaching footsteps, and
now caught a glimpse of his approaching shadow.

The outlaw deliberately lifted his pistol. It was already cocked. His
form was sheltered by a huge tree, and as man and horse gradually drew
nigh, the breathing of the assassin seemed almost suspended in his ferocious anxiety for blood.

The dark shadow moved slowly along the path. The head of the
horse is beside the outlaw. In a moment the rider will occupy the same
spot—and then! The finger of the outlaw is upon the trigger—the
deadly aim is taken!—what arrests the deed? Ah! surely there is a
Providence—a special arm to save—to interpose between the criminal
and his victim—to stay the wilful hands of the murderer, when the deed
seems already done, as it has been already determined upon.

Even in that moment, when but a touch is necessary to destroy the
unconscious traveller—a sudden rush is heard above the robber. Great
wings sweep away, with sudden clatter, and the dismal hootings of an
owl, scared from his perch on a low shrub-tree, startles the cold-
blooded murderer from his propriety. With the nervous excitement of
his mind, and his whole nature keenly interested in the deed, to break
suddenly the awful silence, the brooding hush of the forest, with unexpected sounds, and those so near, and so startling—for once the outlaw
ceased to be the master of his own powers!

The noise of the bird scared the steed. He dashed headlong forward,
and saved the life of his rider!

Yet Ralph Colleton never dreamed of his danger—never once conjectured how special was his obligations to the interposing hand of
Providence! And so, daily, with the best of us—and the least fortunate.
How few of us ever dream of the narrow escapes we make, at moments
when a breath might kill us, when the pressure of a "bare bodkin" is all
that is necessary to send us to sudden judgment!

And the outlaw was again defeated. He had not, perhaps, been
scared. He had only been surprised—been confounded. In the first cry
of the bird, the first rush of his wings, flapping through the trees, it

seemed as if they had swept across his eyes. He lowered the pistol involuntarily—he forgot to pull the trigger, and when he recovered himself,
steed and rider had gone beyond his reach.

"Is there a devil," he involuntarily murmured, "that stands between
me and my victim? am I to be baffled always? Is there, indeed, a God?"

He paused in stupor and vexation. He could hear the distant tramp
of the horse, sinking faintly out of hearing.

"That I, who have lived in the woods all my life, should have been
startled by an owl, and at such a moment!"

Cursing the youth's good fortune, not less than his own weakness,
the fierce disappointment of Guy Rivers was such that he fairly gnashed
his teeth with vexation. At first, he thought to dash after his victim, but
his own steed had been fastened near the cottage, several hundred yards
distant, and he was winded too much for a further pursuit that night.

Colleton was, meanwhile, a mile ahead, going forward swimmingly,
never once dreaming of danger. He was thus far safe. So frequently and
completely had his enemy been baffled in the brief progress of a single
night, that he was almost led to believe—for, like most criminals, he was
not without his superstition—that his foe was under some special
guardianship. With ill-concealed anger, and a stern impatience, he
turned away from the spot in which he had been just foiled, and soon
entered the dwelling, to which we propose also to return.

CHAPTER TWENTY-FIVE

Subdued Agonies

The entrance of Guy Rivers awakened no emotion among the inmates of the dwelling; indeed, at the moment, it was almost unperceived. The young woman happened to be in close attendance upon her parent, for such the invalid was, and did not observe his approach, while he stood at some little distance from the couch, surveying the scene. The old lady was endeavoring, though with a feebleness that grew more apparent with every breath, to articulate something, to which she seemed to attach much importance, in the ears of the kneeling girl, who, with breathless attention, seemed desirous of making it out, but in vain; and, signifying by her countenance the disappointment which she felt, the speaker, with something like anger, shook her skinny finger feebly in her face, and the broken and incoherent words, with rapid effort but like success, endeavored to find their way through the half-closed aperture between her teeth. The tears fell fast and full from the eyes of the kneeling girl, who neither sobbed nor spoke, but, with continued and yet despairing attention, endeavored earnestly to catch the few words of one who was on the eve of departure, and the words of whom, at such a moment, almost invariably acquire a value never attached to them before: as the sounds of a harp, when the chords are breaking, are said to articulate a sweet sorrow, as if in mourning for their own fate.

The outlaw, all this while, stood apart and in silence. Although perhaps but little impressed with the native solemnity of the scene before him, he was not so ignorant of what was due to humanity, and not so unfeeling in reference to the parties here interested, as to seek to disturb its progress or propriety with tone, look, or gesture, which might make either of them regret his presence. Becoming impatient, however, of a colloquy which, as he saw that it had not its use, and was only productive of mortification to one of the parties, he thought only prudent to terminate, he advanced toward them; and his tread, for the first time, warned them of his presence.

With an effort which seemed supernatural, the dying woman raised herself with a sudden start in the bed, and her eyes glared upon him with a threatening horror, and her lips parting, disclosed the broken and decayed teeth beneath, ineffectually gnashing, while her long, skinny fingers warned him away. All this time she appeared to speak, but the words were unarticulated, though, from the expression of every feature, it was evident that indignation and reproach made up the entire amount of everything she had to express. The outlaw was not easily influenced by anger so impotent as this; and, from his manner of receiving it, it appeared that he had been for some time accustomed to a reception of a like kind from the same person. He approached the young girl, who had now risen from her knees, and spoke to her in words of comparative kindness:—

"Well, Ellen, you have had an alarm, but I am glad to see you have suffered no injury. How happened the fire?"

The young woman explained the cause of the conflagration, and narrated in brief the assistance which had been received from the stranger.

"But I was so terrified, Guy," she added, "that I had not presence of mind enough to thank him."

"And what should be the value of your spoken thanks, Ellen? The stranger, if he have sense, must feel that he has them, and the utterance of such things had better be let alone. But, how is the old lady now? I see she loves me no better than formerly."

"She is sinking fast, Guy, and is now incapable of speech. Before you came, she seemed desirous of saying something to me, but she tried in vain to speak, and now I scarcely think her conscious."

"Believe it not, Ellen: she is conscious of all that is going on, though her voice may fail her. Her eye is even now fixed upon me, and with the old expression. She would tear me if she could."

"Oh, think not thus of the dying, Guy—of her who has never harmed, and would never harm you, if she had the power. And yet, Heaven knows, and we both know, she has had reason enough to hate, and, if she could, to destroy you. But she has no such feeling now."

"You mistake, Ellen, or would keep the truth from me. You know she has always hated me; and, indeed, as you say, she has had cause enough to hate and destroy me. Had another done to me as I have done to her, I should not have slept till my hand was in his heart."

"She forgives you all, Guy, I know she does, and God knows I forgive you—I, who, above all others, have most reason to curse you for ever. Think not that she can hate upon the brink of the grave. Her mind wanders, and no wonder that the wrongs of earth press upon her memory, her reason being gone. She knows not herself of the mood which her features express. Look not upon her, Guy, I pray you, or let me turn away my eyes."

"Your spirit, Ellen, is more gentle and shrinking than hers. Had you felt like her, I verily believe that many a night, when I have been at rest within your arms, you would have driven a knife into my heart."

"Horrible, Guy! how can you imagine such a thing? Base and worthless as you have made me, I am too much in your power, I fear— I love you still too much; and, though like a poison or a firebrand you have clung to my bosom, I could not have felt for you a single thought of resentment. You say well when you call me shrinking. I am a creature of a thousand fears; I am all weakness and worthlessness."

"Well, well—let us not talk further of this. When was the doctor here last?"

"In the evening he came, and left some directions, but told us plainly what we had to expect. He said she could not survive longer than the night; and she looks like it, for within the last few hours she has sunk surprisingly. But have you brought the medicine?"

"I have, and some drops which are said to stimulate and strengthen."

"I fear they are now of little use, and may only serve to keep up life in misery. But they may enable her to speak, and I should like to hear what she seems so desirous to impart."

Ellen took the cordial, and hastily preparing a portion in a wineglass, according to the directions, proceeded to administer it to the gasping patient; but, while the glass was at her lips, the last paroxysm of death came on, and with it something more of that consciousness now fleeting for ever. Dashing aside the nostrum with one hand, with the other she drew the shrinking and half-fainting girl to her side, and, pressing her down beside her, appeared to give utterance to that which, from the action, and the few and audible words she made out to articulate, would seem to have been a benediction.

Rivers, seeing the motion, and remarking the almost supernatural strength with which the last spasms had endued her, would have taken the girl from her embrace; but his design was anticipated by the dying woman, whose eyes glared upon him with an expression rather demoniac than human, while her paralytic hand, shaking with ineffectual effort, waved him off. A broken word escaped her lips here and there, and—"sin"—"forgiveness"—was all that reached the ears of her grandchild, when her head sank back upon the pillow, and she expired without a groan.

A dead silence followed this event. The girl had no uttered anguish—she spoke not her sorrows aloud; yet there was that in the wobegone countenance, and the dumb grief, that left no doubt of the deep though suppressed and half-subdued agony of soul within. She seemed one to whom the worst of life had been long since familiar, and who would not find it difficult herself to die. She had certainly outlived pride and hope, if not love; and if the latter feeling had its place in her bosom, as without doubt it had, then was it a hopeless lingerer, long after the sunshine and zephyr had gone which first awakened it into bloom and flower. She knelt beside the inanimate form of her old parent, shedding no tear, and uttering no sigh. Tears would have poorly expressed the wo which at that moment she felt; and the outlaw, growing impatient of the dumb spectacle, now ventured to approach and interrupt her. She rose, meekly and without reluctance, as he spoke; with a manner which said as plainly as words could have said— 'Command, and I obey. Bid me go, even now, at midnight, on a perilous journey, over and into foreign lands, and I go without murmur or repining.' She was a heart-stricken, a heart-broken, and abused woman—and yet she loved still, and loved her destroyer.

"Ellen," said he, taking her hand, "your mother was a Christian—a strict worshipper—one who, for the last few years of her life, seldom put the Bible out of her hands; and yet she cursed me in her very soul as she went out of the world."

"Guy, Guy, speak not so, I pray you. Spare me this cruelty, and say not for the departed spirit what it surely never would have said of itself."

"But it did so say, Ellen, and of this I am satisfied. Hear me, girl. I know something of mankind, and womankind too, and I am not often mistaken in the expression of human faces, and certainly was not mistaken in hers. When, in the last paroxysm, you knelt beside her with your head down upon her hand and in her grasp, and as I approached her, her eyes, which feebly threw up the film then rapidly closing over them, shot out a most angry glare of hatred and reproof; while her lips parted—I could see, though she could articulate no word—with involutions which indicated the curse that she could not speak."

"Think not so, I pray you. She had much cause to curse, and often would she have done so, but for my sake she did not. She would call me a poor fool, that so loved the one who had brought misery and shame to all of us; but her malediction was arrested, and she said it not. Oh, no! she forgave you—I know she did—heard you not the words which she uttered at the last?"

"Yes, yes—but no matter. We must now talk of other things, Ellen; and first of all, you must know, then, I am about to be married."

Had a bolt from the crossbow at that moment penetrated into her heart, the person he addressed could not have been more transfixed than at this speech. She started—an inquiring and tearful doubt rose into her eyes, as they settled piercingly upon his own; but the information they met with there needed no further word of assurance from his lips. He was a stern tyrant—one, however, who did not trifle.

"I feared as much, Guy—I have had thoughts which as good as told me this long before. The silent form before me has said to me, over and over again, you would never wed her whom you have dishonored. Oh, fool that I was!—spite of her forebodings and my own, I thought—I still think, and oh, Guy, let me not think in vain—that there would be a time when you would take away the reproach from my name and the sin from my soul, by making me your wife, as you have so often promised."

"You have indeed thought like a child, Ellen, if you suppose that, situated as I am, I could ever marry simply because I loved."

"And will you not love her whom you are now about to wed?"

"Not as much as I have loved you—not half so much as I love you now—if it be that I have such a feeling at this moment in my bosom."

"And wherefore then would you wed, Guy, with one whom you do not, whom you can not love? In what have I offended—have I ever reproached or looked unkindly on you, Guy, even when you came to me, stern and full of reproaches, chafed with all things and with everybody?"

"There are motives, Ellen, governing my actions into which you must not inquire—"

"What, not inquire, when on these actions depend all my hope—all my life! Now indeed you are the tyrant which my old mother said, and all people say, you are."

The girl for a moment forgot her submissiveness, and her words were tremulous, less with sorrow than the somewhat strange spirit which her wrongs had impressed upon her. But she soon felt the sinking of the momentary inspiration, and quickly sought to remove the angry scowl which she perceived coming over the brow of her companion.

"Nay, nay—forgive me, Guy—let me not reproach—let me not accuse you. I have not done so before: I would not do so now. Do with me as you please; and yet, if you are bent to wed with another, and forget and overlook your wrongs to me, there is one kindness which would become your hands, and which I would joy to receive from them. Will you do for me this kindness, Guy? Nay, now be not harsh, but say that you will do it."

She seized his hand appealingly as she spoke, and her moist but untearful eyes were fixed pleadingly upon his own. The outlaw hesitated for a moment before he replied.

"I propose, Ellen, to do for you all that may be necessary—to provide you with additional comforts, and carry you to a place of additional security, where you shall live to yourself, and have good attendance."

"This is kind—this is much, Guy; but not much more than you have been accustomed to do for me. That which I seek from you now is something more than this; promise me that it shall be as I say."

"If it breaks not into my arrangements—if it makes me not go aside from my path, I will certainly do it, Ellen. Speak, therefore; what is it I can do for you?"

"It will interfere with none of your arrangements, Guy, I am sure; it can not take you from your path, for you could not have provided for that of which you knew not. I have your pledge, therefore—have I not?"

"You have," was the reply, while the manner of Rivers was tinctured with something like curiosity.

"That is kind—that is as you ought to be. Hear me now, then," and her voice sunk into a whisper, as if she feared the utterance of her own words; "take your knife, Guy—pause not, do it quickly, lest I fear and tremble—strike it deep into the bosom of the poor Ellen, and lay her beside the cold parent, whose counsels she despised, and all of whose predictions are now come true. Strike—strike quickly, Guy Rivers; I have your promise—you can not recede; if you have honor, if you have truth, you must do as I ask. Give me death—give me peace."

"Foolish girl, would you trifle with me—would you have me spurn and hate you? Beware!"

The outlaw well knew the yielding and sensitive material out of which his victim had been made. His stern rebuke was well calculated to effect in her bosom that revulsion of feeling which he knew would follow any threat of a withdrawal, even of the lingering and frail fibres of that affection, few, and feeble as they were, which he might have once persuaded her to believe had bound him to her. The consequence was immediate, and her subdued tone and resigned action evinced the now entire supremacy of her natural temperament.

"Oh, forgive me, Guy, I know not what I ask or what I do. I am so worn and weary, and my head is so heavy, that I think it were far better if I were in my grave with the cold frame whom we shall soon put there. Heed not what I say—I am sad and sick, and have not the spirit of reason, or a healthy will to direct me. Do with me as you will—I will obey you—go anywhere, and, worst of all, behold you wed another; ay, stand by, if you desire it, and look on the ceremony, and try to forget that you once promised me that I should be yours, and yours only."

"You speak more wisely, Ellen; and you will think more calmly upon it when the present grief of your grandmother's death passes off."

"Oh, that is no grief, now, Guy," was the rather hasty reply. "That is no grief now: should I regret that she has escaped these tidings—should I regret that she has ceased to feel trouble, and to see and shed tears—should I mourn, Guy, that she who loved me to the last, in spite of my follies and vices, has ceased now to mourn over them? Oh, no! this is no grief, now; it was grief but a little while ago, but now you have made it matter of rejoicing."

"Think not of it,—speak no more in this strain, Ellen, lest you anger me."

"I will not—chide me not—I have no farther reproaches. Yet, Guy, is she, the lady you are about to wed—is she beautiful, is she young— has she long raven tresses, as I had once, when your fingers used to play in them?" and with a sickly smile, which had in it something of an old vanity, she unbound the string which confined her own hair, and let it roll down upon her back in thick and beautiful volumes, still black, glossy, and delicately soft as silk.

The outlaw was moved. For a moment his iron muscles relaxed—a gentler expression overspread his countenance, and he took her in his arms. That single, half-reluctant embrace was a boon not much bestowed in the latter days of his victim, and it awakened a thousand tender recollections in her heart, and unsealed a warm spring of gushing waters. An infantile smile was in her eyes, while the tears were flowing down her cheeks.

But, shrinking or yielding, at least to any great extent made up very little of the character of the dark man on whom she depended; and the more than feminine weakness of the young girl who hung upon his bosom like a dying flower, received its rebuke, after a few moments of unwonted tenderness, when, coldly resuming his stern habit, he put her from his arms, and announced to her his intention of immediately taking his departure.

"What," she asked, "will you not stay with me through the night, and situated as I am?"

"It is impossible; even now I am waited for, and should have been some hours on my way to an appointment which I must not break. It is not with me as with you; I have obligations to others who depend on me, and who might suffer injury were I to deceive them."

"But this night, Guy—there is little of it left, and I am sure you will not be expected before the daylight. I feel a new terror when I think I shall be left by all, and here, too, alone with the dead."

"You will not be alone, and if you were, Ellen, you have been thus lonely for many months past, and should be now accustomed to it."

"Why, so I should, for it has been a fearful and a weary time, and I went not to my bed one night without dreading that I should never behold another day."

"Why, what had you to alarm you? you suffered no affright—no injury? I had taken care that throughout the forest your cottage should be respected."

"So I had your assurance, and when I thought, I believed it. I knew you had the power to do as you assured me you would, but still there were moments when our own desolation came across my mind; and what with my sorrows and my fears, I was sometimes persuaded, in my madness, to pray that I might be relieved of them, were it even by the hands of death."

"You were ever thus foolish, Ellen, and you have as little reason now to apprehend as then. Besides, it is only for the one night, and in the morning I shall send those to you who will attend to your own removal to another spot, and to the interment of the body."

"And where am I to go?"

"What matters it where, Ellen? You have my assurance that it shall be a place of security and good attendance to which I shall send you."

"True, what matters it where I go—whether among the savage or the civilized? They are to me all alike, since I may not look them in the face, or take them by the hand, or hold communion with them, either at the house of God or at the family fireside."

The gloomy despondence of her spirit was uppermost; and she went on, in a series of bitter musings, denouncing herself as an outcast, a worthless something, and, in the language of the sacred text, calling on the rocks and mountains to cover her. The outlaw, who had none of those fine feelings which permitted of even momentary sympathy with that desolation of heart, the sublime agonies of which are so well calculated to enlist and awaken it, cut short the strain of sorrow and complaint by a fierce exclamation, which seemed to stun every sense of her spirit.

"Will you never have done?" he demanded. "Am I for ever to listen to this weakness—this unavailing reproach of yourself and everything around you? Do I not know that all your complaints and reproaches, though you address them in so many words to yourself, are intended only for my use and ear? Can I not see through the poor hypocrisy of such a lamentation? Know I not that when you curse and deplore the sin, you only withhold the malediction from him who tempted and partook of it, in the hope that his own spirit will apply it all to himself? Away, girl; I thought you had a nobler spirit—I thought you felt the love that I now find existed only in expression."

"I do feel that love; I would, Guy, that I felt it not—that it did exist only in my words. I were then far happier than I am now, since stern look or language from you would then utterly fail to vex and wound as it does now. I can not bear your reproaches; look not thus upon me, and speak not in those harsh sentences—not now—not now, at least, and in this melancholy presence."

Her looks turned upon the dead body of her parent as she spoke; and with convulsive effort she rushed toward and clasped it round. She threw

herself beside the corpse and remained inanimate, while the outlaw, leaving the house for an instant, called the negro servant and commanded
her attendance. He now approached the girl, and taking up her hand,
which lay supine upon the bosom of the dead body, would have soothed
her grief; but though she did not repulse, she yet did not regard him.

"Be calm, Ellen," he said, "recover and be firm. In the morning you
shall have early and good attention, and with this object, in part, am I
disposed to hurry now. Think not, girl, that I forget you. Whatever may
be my fortune, I shall always have an eye to yours. I leave you now, but
shall see you before long, when I shall settle you permanently and comfortably. Farewell."

He left her in seeming unconsciousness of the words whispered in
her ears, yet she heard them all, and duly estimated their value. To her
to whom he had once pledged himself entirely, the cold boon of his
attention and sometime care was painfully mortifying. She exhibited
nothing, however, beyond what we have already seen, of the effect of
this consolation upon her heart. There is a period in human emotions,
when feeling itself becomes imperceptible—when the heart (as it were)
receives the *coup de grace,* and days, and months, and years, before the
body expires, shows nothing of the fire which is consuming it.

We would not have it understood to be altogether the case with the
young destitute before us; but, at least, if she still continued to feel these
still-occurring influences, there was little or no outward indication of
their power upon the hidden spirit. She said nothing to him on his
departure, but with a half-wandering sense, that may perhaps have
described something of the ruling passion of an earlier day, she rose
shortly after he had left the house, and placing herself before the small
mirror which surmounted the toilet in the apartment, rearranged with
studious care, and with an eye to its most attractive appearance, the
long and flowing tresses of that hair, which, as we have already
remarked, was of the most silky and raven-like description. Every
ringlet was adjusted to its place, as if nothing of sorrow was about her—
none of the badges and evidences of death and decay in her thought.
She next proceeded to the readjustment of the dress she wore, taking
care that a string of pearl, probably the gift of her now indifferent lover,
should leave its place in the little cabinet, where, with other trinkets of
the kind, it had been locked up carefully for a long season, and once
more adorned with it the neck which it failed utterly to surpass in delicacy or in whiteness. Having done this, she again took her place on the

couch, along with the corpse; and with a manner which did not appear to indicate a doubt of the still lingering spirit, she raised the lifeless head, with the gentlest effort placing her arm beneath, then laid her own quietly on the pillow beside it.

CHAPTER TWENTY-SIX

The Camp

Ignorant, as we have already said, of his late most providential escape from the weapon of his implacable enemy, Ralph Colleton was borne forward by his affrighted steed with a degree of rapidity which entirely prevented his rider from remarking any of the objects around him, or, indeed, as the moon began to wane amid a clustering body of clouds, of determining positively whether he were still in the road or not. The *trace* (as public roads are called in that region) had been rudely cut out by some of the earlier travellers through the Indian country, merely *traced* out—and hence, perhaps, the term—by a *blaze*, or white spot, made upon the trees by hewing from them the bark; which badge, repeated in succession upon those growing immediately upon the line chosen for the destined road, indicated its route to the wayfarer. It had never been much travelled, and from the free use at the present time of other and more direct courses, it was left almost totally unemployed, save by those living immediately in its neighborhood. It had, therefore, become, at the time of which we speak, what, in backwood phrase, is known as a *blind-path*.

Such being the case, it is not difficult to imagine that, when able to restrain his horse, Ralph, as he feared, found himself entirely out of its guidance—wandering without direction among the old trees of the forest. Still, as for the night, now nearly over, he could have no distinct point in view, and saw just as little reason to go back as forward, he gave himself but little time for scruple or hesitation. Resolutely, though with a cautious motion, he pricked his steed forward through the woods, accommodating his philosophy, as well as he could, to the various interruptions which the future, as if to rival the past, seemed to have treasured up in store for him.

He had not proceeded far in this manner when he caught the dim rays of a distant fire, flickering and ascending among the trees to the left of the direction he was taking. The blaze had something in it excessively cheering, and, changing his course, he went forward under its guidance. In this effort, he stumbled upon something like a path, which pursuing, brought him at length to a small and turbid creek, into which he plunged fearlessly, and soon found himself in swimming water. The ford had been little used, and the banks were steep, so that he got out with difficulty upon the opposite side. Having done so, his eye was enabled to take a full view of the friendly fire which had just attracted his regard, and which he soon made out to proceed from the encampment of a wagoner, such as may be seen every day, or every night, in the wild woods of the southern country.

He was emigrating, with all his goods and gods, to that wonderfully winning region, in the estimation of this people, the valley of the Mississippi. The emigrant was a stout, burly, bluff old fellow, with full round cheeks, a quick, twinkling eye, and limbs rather Herculean than human. He might have been fifty-five years or so; and his two sons, one of them a man grown, the other a tall and goodly youth of eighteen, promised well to be just such vigorous and healthy-looking personages as their father. The old woman, by whom we mean—in the manner of speech common to the same class and region—to indicate the spouse of the wayfarer, and mother of the two youths, was busied about the fire, boiling a pot of coffee, and preparing the family repast for the night. A somewhat late hour for supper and such employment, thought our wanderer; but the difficulty soon explained itself in the condition of their wagon, and the conversation which ensued among the travellers. There was yet another personage in the assembly, who must be left to introduce himself to the reader.

The *force* of the traveller—for such is the term by which the number of his slaves are understood—was small; consisting of some six *workers*, and three or four little negro children asleep under the wagon. The workers were occupied at a little distance, in replacing boxes, beds, and some household trumpery, which had been taken out of the wagon, to enable them to effect its release from the slough in which it had cast one of its wheels, and broken its axle, and the restoration of which had made their supper so late in the night. The heavier difficulties of their labor had been got over, and with limbs warmed and chafed by the extra exercise they had undergone, the whites had thrown themselves under a tree, at a little distance from the fire at which the supper was in preparation, while a few pine torches, thrown together, gave them sufficient light to read and remark the several countenances of their group.

"Well, by dogs, we've had a tough 'bout of it, boys; and, hark'ye, strannger, gi' us your hand. I don't know what we should have done without you, for I never seed man handle a little poleaxe as you did that same affair of your'n. You must have spent, I reckon, a pretty smart time at the use of it, now, didn't ye?"

To this speech of the farmer, a ready reply was given by the stranger, in the identical voice and language of our old acquaintance, the pedler, Jared Bunce, of whom, and of whose stock in trade, the reader will probably have some recollection.

"Well, now, I guess, friend, you an't far wide of your reckoning. I've been a matter of some fifteen or twenty years knocking about, off and on, in one way or another, with this same instrument, and pretty's the service now, I tell ye, that it's done me in that bit of time."

"No doubt, no doubt; but what's your trade, if I may be so bold, that made you larn the use of it so nicely?"

"Oh, what—my trade? Why, to say the truth, I never was brought up to any trade in particular, but I am a pretty slick hand, now, I tell you, at all of them. I've been in my time a little of a farmer, a little of a merchant, a little of a sailor, and, somehow or other, a little of everything, and all sort of things. My father was jest like myself, and swore, before I was born, that I should be born jest like him—and so I was. Never were two black peas more alike. He was a 'cute old fellow, and swore he'd make me so too—and so he did. You know how he did that?—now, I'll go a York shilling against a Louisiana bit, that you can't tell to save you."

"Why, no, I can't—let's hear," was the response of the wagoner, somewhat astounded by the volubility of his new acquaintance.

"Well, then, I'll tell you. He sent me away, to make my fortin, and git my edication, 'mongst them who was 'cute themselves, and maybe that an't the best school for larning a simple boy ever went to. It was sharp edge agin sharp edge. It was the very making of me, so far as I was made."

"Well, now, that is a smart way, I should reckon, to get one's edication. And in this way I suppose you larned how to chop with your little poleaxe. Dogs! but you've made me as smart a looking axle as I ever tacked to my team."

"I tell you, friend, there's nothing like sich an edication. It does everything for a man, and he larns to make everything out of nothing. I could make my bread where these same Indians wouldn't find the skin of a hoe-cake; and in these woods, or in the middle of the sea, t'ant anything for me to say I can always fish up some notion that will sell in the market."

"Well, now, that's wonderful, strannger, and I should like to see how you would do it."

"You can't do nothing, no how, friend, unless you begin at the beginning. You'll have to begin when you're jest a mere boy, and set about getting your edication as I got mine. There's no two ways about it. It won't come to you; you must go to it. When you're put out into the wide world, and have no company and no acquaintance, why, what are you to do? Suppose, now, when your wagon mired down, I had not come to your help, and cut out your wood, and put in the spoke, wouldn't you have had to do it yourself?"

"Yes—to be sure; but then I couldn't have done it in a day. I an't handy at these things."

"Well, that was jest the way with me when I was a boy. I had nobody to help me out of the mud—nobody to splice my spokes, or assist me any how, and so I larned to do it myself. And now, would you think it, I'm sometimes glad of a little turn-over, or an accident, jest that I may keep my hand in, and not forget to be able to help myself or my neighbors."

"Well, you're a cur'ous person, and I'd like to hear something more about you. But it's high time we should wet our whistles, and it's but dry talking without something to wash a clear way for the slack. So, boys, be up, and fish up the jemmi-john—I hope it hain't been thumped to bits in the rut. If it has, I shall be in a tearing passion."

"Well, now, that won't be reasonable, seeing that it's no use, and jest wasting good breath that might bring a fair price in the market."

"What, not get in a passion if all the whiskey's gone? That won't do, strannger, and though you have helped me out of the ditch, by dogs, no man shall prevent me from getting in a passion if I choose it."

"Oh, to be sure, friend—you an't up to my idee. I didn't know that it was for the good it did you that you got in a passion. I am clear that when a man feels himself better from a passion, he oughtn't to be shy in getting into it. Though that wasn't a part of my edication, yet I guess, if such a thing would make me feel more comfortable, I'd get in a passion fifty times a day."

"Well, now, strannger, you talk like a man of sense. 'Drot the man, says I, who hain't the courage to get in a passion! None but a miserable, shadow-skinning Yankee would refuse to get in a passion when his jug of whiskey was left in the road!"

"A-hem—" coughed the dealer in small wares—the speech of the old wagoner grating harshly upon his senses; for if the Yankee be proud of anything, it is of his country—its enterprise, its institutions; and of these, perhaps, he has more true and unqualified reason to be pleased and proud than any other one people on the face of the globe. He did not relish well the sitting quietly under the harsh censure of his companion, who seemed to regard the existence of a genuine emotion among the people down east as a manifest absurdity; and was thinking to come out with a defence, in detail, of the pretensions of New England, when, prudence having first taken a survey of the huge limbs of the wagoner, and calling to mind the fierce prejudices of the uneducated southrons generally against all his tribe, suggested the convenient propriety of an evasive reply.

"A-hem—" repeated the Yankee, the *argumentum ad hominem* still prominent in his eyes—"well, now, I take it, friend, there's no love to spare for the people you speak of down in these parts. They don't seem to smell at all pleasant in this country."

"No, I guess not, strannger, as how should they—a mean, tricky, catchpenny, skulking set—that makes money out of everybody, and hain't the spirit to spend it! I do hate them, now, worse than a polecat!"

"Well, now, friend, that's strange. If you were to travel for a spell, down about Boston or Salem in Massachusetts, or at Meriden in Connecticut, you'd hear tell of the Yankees quite different. If you believe what the people say thereabouts, you'd think there was no sich people on the face of the airth."

"That's jist because they don't know anything about them; and it's not because they can't know them neither, for a Yankee is a varmint you can nose anywhere. It must be that none ever travels in those parts—selling their tin-kettles, and their wooden clocks, and all their notions."

"Oh, yes, they do. They make 'em in those parts. I know it by this same reason, that I bought a lot myself from a house in Connecticut, a town called Meriden, where they make almost nothing else but clocks—where they make 'em by steam, and horse-power, and machinery, and will turn you out a hundred or two to a minute."

The pedler had somewhat "overleaped his shoulders," as they phrase it in the West, when his companion drew himself back over the blazing embers, with a look of ill-concealed aversion, exclaiming, as he did so—

"Why, you ain't a Yankee, air you?"

The pedler was a special pleader in one sense of the word, and knew the value of a technical distinction as well as his friend, Lawyer Pippin. His reply was prompt and professional:—

"Why, no, I ain't a Yankee according to your idee. It's true, I was born among them; but that, you know, don't make a man one on them?"

"No, to be sure not. Every man that's a freeman has a right to choose what country he shall belong to. My dad was born in Ireland, yet he always counted himself a full-blooded American."

The old man found a parallel in his father's nativity, which satisfied himself of the legitimacy of the ground taken by the pedler, and helped the latter out of his difficulty.

"But here's the whiskey standing by us all the time, waiting patiently to be drunk. Here, Nick Snell, boy, take your hands out of your breeches-pocket, and run down with the calabash to the branch. The water is pretty good thar, I reckon; and, strannger, after we've taken a sup, we'll eat a bite, and then lie down. It's high time, I reckon, that we do so."

It was in his progress to the branch that Ralph Colleton came upon this member of the family.

Nick Snell was no genius, and did not readily reply to the passing inquiry which was put to him by the youth, who advanced upon the main party while the dialogue between the pedler and the wagoner was in full gust. They started, as if by common consent, to their feet, as his horse's tread smote upon their ears; but, satisfied with the appearance of a single man, and witnessing the jaded condition of his steed, they were content to invite him to partake with them of the rude cheer which the good-woman was now busied in setting before him.

The hoe-cakes and bacon were smoking finely, and the fatigue of the youth engaged his senses, with no unwillingness on their part, to detect a most savory attraction in the assault which they made upon his sight and nostrils alike. He waited not for a second invitation, but in a few moments—having first stripped his horse, and put the saddle, by direction of the emigrant, into his wagon—he threw himself beside them upon the ground, and joined readily and heartily in the consumption of the goodly edibles which were spread out before them.

They had not been long at this game, when a couple of fine watch-dogs which were in the camp, guarding the baggage, gave the alarm, and the whole party was on the alert, with sharp eye and cocked rifle. They commenced a survey, and at some distance could hear the tread of horsemen, seemingly on the approach. The banditti, of which we have already spoken, were well known to the emigrant, and he had already to complain of divers injuries at their hands. It is not, therefore, matter of surprise, that he should place his sentinels, and prepare even for the most audacious attack.

He had scarcely made this disposition of his forces, which exhibited them to the best advantage, when the strangers made their appearance. They rode cautiously around, without approaching the defences sufficiently nigh to occasion strife, but evidently having for their object originally an attack upon the wayfarer. At length, one of the party, which consisted of six persons, now came forward, and, with a friendly tone of voice, bade them good-evening in a manner which seemed to indicate a desire to be upon a footing of the most amiable sort with them. The old man answered dryly, with some show of sarcastic indifference in his speech—

"Ay, good evening enough, if the moon had not gone down, and if the stars were out, that we might pick out the honest men from the rogues."

"What, are there rogues in these parts, then, old gentleman?" asked the new-comer.

"Why do you ask me?" was the sturdy reply. "You ought to be able to say, without going farther than your own pockets."

"Why, you are tough to-night, my old buck," was the somewhat crabbed speech of the visiter.

"You'll find me troublesome, too, Mr. Nightwalker: so take good counsel, and be off while you've whole bones, or I'll tumble you now in half a minute from your crittur, and give you a sharp supper of pine-knots."

"Well, that wouldn't be altogether kind on your part, old fellow, and I mightn't be willing to let you; but, as you seem not disposed to be civil, I suppose the best thing I can do is to be off."

"Ay, ay, be off. You get nothing out of us; and we've no shot that we want to throw away. Leave you alone, and Jack Ketch will save us shot."

"Ha, ha!" exclaimed the outlier, in concert, and from the deeper emphasis which he gave it, in chorus to the laughter which followed, among the party, the dry expression of the old man's humor—

"Ha, ha! old boy—you have the swing of it to-night," continued the visiter, as he rode off to his companions; "but, if you don't mind, we shall smoke you before you get into Alabam!"

The robber rejoined his companions, and a sort of council for deliberation was determined upon among them.

"How now, Lambert! you have been at dead fault," was his sudden address, as he returned, to one of the party. "You assured me that old Snell and his two sons were the whole force that he carried, while I find two stout, able-bodied men besides, as well armed, and ready for the attack. The old woman, too, standing with the gridiron in her fists, is equal of herself to any two men, hand to hand."

Lambert, a short, sly, dogged little personage, endeavored to account for the error, if such it was—"but he was sure, that at starting, there were but three—they must have had company join them since. Did the lieutenant make out the appearance of the others?"

"I did," said the officer in command, "and, to say truth, they do not seem to be of the old fellow's party. They must have come upon him since the night. But how came you, Lambert, to neglect sawing the axle? You had time enough when it stood in the farmyard last night, and you were about it a full hour. The wagon stands as stoutly on its all-fours as the first day it was built."

"I did that, sir, and did it, I thought, to the very mark. I calculated to leave enough solid to bear them to the night, when in our circuit we should come among them just in time to finish the business. The wood is stronger, perhaps, than I took it to be, but it won't hold out longer than to-morrow, I'm certain, when, if we watch, we can take our way with them."

"Well, I hope so, and we must watch them, for it won't do to let the old fellow escape. He has, I know, a matter of three or four hundred hard dollars in his possession, to buy lands in Mississippi, and it's a pity to let so much good money go out of the state."

"But why may we not set upon them now?" inquired one of the youngest of the party.

"For a very good reason, Briggs—they are armed, ready, and nearly equal in number to ourselves; and though I doubt not we should be able to ride over them, yet I am not willing to leave one or more of us behind. Besides, if we keep the look-out to-morrow, as we shall, we can settle the business without any such risk."

This being the determination, the robbers, thus disappointed of their game, were nevertheless in better humor than might have been well expected; but such men are philosophers, and their very reckless-ness of human life is in some respects the result of a due estimate of its vicissitudes. They rode on their way laughing at the sturdy bluntness of the old wagoner, which their leader, of whom we have already heard under the name of Dillon, related to them at large. With a whoop and halloo, they cheered the travellers as they rode by, but at some distance from, the encampment. The tenants of the encampment, thus strangely but fortunately thrown together, having first seen that everything was quiet, took their severally assigned places, and laid themselves down for repose. The pedler contenting himself with guessing that "them 'ere chaps did not make no great deal by that speculation."

CHAPTER TWENTY-SEVEN

The Outlaws

It was in the wildest and least-trodden recesses of the rock and forest, that the band of outlaws, of which Rivers was the great head and leader, had fixed their place of abode and assemblage. A natural cavity, formed by the juxtaposition of two huge rocks, overhung by a third, with some few artificial additions, formed for them a cavern, in which—so admirably was it overgrown by the surrounding forest, and so finely situated among hills and abrupt ridges yielding few inducements for travel—they found the most perfect security.

It is true such a shelter could not long have availed them as such, were the adjacent country in the possession of a civilized people; but the near neighborhood of the Cherokees, by keeping back civilization, was, perhaps, quite as much as the position they had chosen, its protection from the scrutiny of many, who had already, prompted by their excesses, endeavored, on more than one occasion, to find them out. The place was distant from the village of Chestatee about ten miles, or perhaps more. No highway—no thoroughfare or public road passed in its neighborhood, and it had been the policy of the outlaws to avoid the use of any vehicle, the traces of which might be followed. There was, besides, but little necessity for its employment. The place of counsel and assemblage was not necessarily their place of abode, and the several members of the band found it more profitable to reside, or keep stations, in the adjacent hamlets and *stands* (for by this latter name in those regions, the nightly stopping-places of wayfarers are commonly designated) where, in most cases, they put on the appearance, and in many respects bore the reputation, of staid and sober working men.

This arrangement was perhaps the very best for the predatory life they led, as it afforded opportunities for information which otherwise must have been lost to them. In this way they heard of this or that traveller—his destination—the objects he had in view, and the wealth he carried about with him. In one of these situations the knowledge of old Snell's journey, and the amount of wealth in his possession, had been acquired; and in the person of the worthy stable-boy who brought corn to the old fellow's horses the night before, and whom he rewarded with a *thrip* (the smallest silver coin known in the southern currency, the five-cent issue excepted) we might, without spectacles, recognise the active fugleman of the outlaws, who sawed half through his axle, cleaned his wheels of all their grease, and then attempted to rob him the very night after.

Though thus scattered about, it was not a matter of difficulty to call the outlaws together upon an emergency. One or more of the most trustworthy among them had only to make a tour over the road, and through the hamlets in which they were harbored within the circuit of ten or twenty miles, and as they kept usually with rigid punctuality to their several stations, they were soon apprized, and off at the first signal. A whisper in the ear of the hostler who brought out your horse, or the drover who put up the cattle, was enough; and the absence of a colt from pasture, or the missing of a stray young heifer from the flock, furnished a sufficient reason to the proprietor for the occasional absence of Tom, Dick, or Harry: who, in the meanwhile, was, most probably, crying "stand" to a true man, or cutting a trunk from a sulkey, or, in mere wantonness, shooting down the traveller who had perhaps given him a long chase, yet yielded nothing by way of compensation for the labor.

Dillon, or, to speak more to the card, Lieutenant Dillon, arrived at the place of assemblage just as the day was breaking. He was a leader of considerable influence among the outlaws, and, next to Rivers, was most popular. Indeed, in certain respects, he was far more popular; for, though perhaps not so adroit in his profession, nor so well fitted for its command, he was possessed of many of those qualities which are apt to be taking with "the fierce democratie!" He was a prince of hail fellows— was thoroughly versed in low jest and scurvy anecdote—could play at pushpins, and drink at every point in the game; and, strange to say, though always drinking, was never drunk. Nor, though thus accomplished, and thus prone to these accomplishments, did he ever neglect those duties which he assumed to perform. No indulgence led him away from his post, and, on the other hand, no post compelled or constrained him into gravity. He was a careless, reckless blade, indifferent alike, it would seem, to sun and storm—and making of life a circle, that would not inaptly have illustrated the favorite text of Sardanapalus.

He arrived at the cave, as we have said, just as the day was breaking. A shrill whistle along the ridges of wood and rock, as he passed them, denoted the various stations of the sentinels, as studiously strewed along the paths by which their place of refuge might be assailed, as if they were already beleaguered by an assailing army. Without pausing to listen to the various speeches and inquiries which assailed his ears upon his arrival he advanced to the cavern, and was told that the captain had been for some time anxiously awaiting his arrival—that he had morosely kept the inner recess of the cave, and since his return, which had not been until late in the night, had been seen but two or three times, and then but for a moment, when he had come forth to make inquiries for himself.

Leaving his men differently disposed, Dillon at once penetrated into the small apartment in which his leader was lodged, assured of the propriety of the intrusion, from what had just been told him.

The recess, which was separated from the outer hall by a curtain of thick coarse stuff, falling to the floor from a beam, the apertures for the reception of which had been chiselled in the rock, was dimly illuminated by a single lamp, hanging from a chain, which was in turn fastened to a pole that stretched directly across the apartment. A small table in the centre of the room, covered with a piece of cotton cloth, a few chairs, a broken mirror, and on a shelf that stood trimly in the corner, a few glasses and decanters, completed the furniture of the apartment.

On the table at which the outlaw sat, lay his pistols—a huge and unwieldy, but well-made pair. A short sword, a dirk, and one or two other weapons of similar description, contemplated only for hand-to-hand purposes, lay along with them; and the better to complete the picture, now already something *outré*, a decanter of brandy and tumblers were contiguous.

Rivers did not observe the slide of the curtain to the apartment, nor the entrance of Dillon. He was deeply absorbed in contemplation; his head rested heavily upon his two palms, while his eyes were deeply fixed upon the now opened miniature which he had torn from the neck of Lucy Munro, and which rested before him. He sighed not—he spoke not, but ever and anon, as if perfectly unconscious all the while of what he did, he drank from the tumbler of the compounded draught that stood before him, hurriedly and desperately, as if to keep the strong emotion from choking him. There was in his look a bitter agony of expression, indicating a vexed spirit, now more strongly than ever at work in a way which had, indeed, been one of the primest sources of his miserable life. It was a spirit ill at rest with itself—vexed at its own feebleness of execution—its incapacity to attain and acquire the realization of its own wild and vague conceptions. His was the ambition of one who discovers at every step that nothing can be known, yet will not give up the unprofitable pursuit, because, even while making the discovery, he still hopes vainly that he may yet, in his own person, give the maxim the lie. For ever soaring to the sun, he was for ever realizing the fine Grecian fable of Icarus; and the sea of disappointment into which he perpetually fell, with its tumultuous tides and ever-chafing billows, bearing him on from whirlpool to whirlpool, for ever battling and for ever lost. He was unconscious, as we have said, of the entrance and approach of his lieutenant, and words of bitterness, in soliloquy, fell at brief periods from his lips.—

"It is after all the best—" he mused. "Despair is the true philosophy, since it begets indifference. Why should I hope? What prospect is there now, that these eyes, that lip, these many graces, and the imperial pride of that expression, which looks out like a high soul from the heaven that men talk and dream of—what delusion is there now to bid me hope they ever can be more to me than they are now? I care not for the world's ways—nor feel I now the pang of its scorn and its outlawry; yet I would it were not so, that I might, upon a field as fair as that of the most successful, assert my claim, and woo and win her—not with those childish notes of commonplace—that sickly cant of sentimental stuff which I despise, and which I know she despises no less than I.

"Yet, when this field was mine, as I now desire it, what more did it avail me? Where was the strong sense—the lofty reason that should then have conquered with an unobstructed force, sweeping all before it, as the flame that rushes through the long grass of the prairies? Gone— prostrate—dumb. The fierce passion was upward, and my heart was then more an outlaw than I myself am now.

"Yet there is one hope—one chance—one path, if not to her affections, at least to her. It shall be done, and then, most beautiful witch, cold, stern, and to me heartless, as thou hast ever been—thou shalt not always triumph. I would that I could sleep on this—I would that I could sleep. There is but one time of happiness—but one time when the thorn has no sting—when the scorn bites not—when the sneer chafes not—when the pride and the spirit shrink not—when there is no wild passion to make everything a storm and a conflagration among the senses—and that is—when one forgets!—I would that I could sleep!"

As he spoke, his head sunk upon the table with a heavy sound, as if unconsciousness had really come with the articulated wish. He started quickly, however, as now, for the first time, the presence of Dillon became obvious, and hurriedly thrusting the portrait into his vest, he turned quickly to the intruder, and sternly demanded the occasion of his interruption. The lieutenant was prepared, and at once replied to the interrogatory with the easy, blunt air of one who not only felt that he might be confided in, but who was then in the strict performance of his duties.

"I came at your own call, captain. I have just returned from the river, and skirting down in that quarter, and was kept something later than I looked for; hearing, on my arrival, that you had been inquiring for me, I did not hesitate to present myself at once, not knowing but the business might be pressing."

"It is pressing," responded the outlaw, seemingly well satisfied with the tacit apology. "It is pressing, Dillon, and you will have little time for rest before starting again. I myself have been riding all night, and shall be off in another hour. But what have you to report? What's in the wind now?"

"I hear but little, sir. There is some talk about a detachment of the Georgia guard, something like a hundred men, to be sent out expressly for our benefit; but I look upon this as a mistake. Their eye is rather upon the miners, and the Indian gold lands and those who dig it, and not upon those who merely take it after it is gathered. I have heard, too, of something like a brush betwixt Fullam's troop and the miners at Tracy's diggings, but no particulars, except that the guard got the worst of it."

"On that point I am already advised. That is well for us, since it will turn the eye of the authorities in a quarter in which we have little to do. I had some hand in that scrape myself, and set the dogs on with this object; and it is partly on this matter that I would confer with you, since there are some few of our men in the village who had large part in it, who must not be hazarded, and must yet stay there."

"If the brush was serious, captain, that will be a matter of some difficulty; for of late, there has been so much of our business done, that government, I believe, has some thought of taking it up, and in order to do so without competition, will think of putting us down. Uncle Sam and the states, too, are quarrelling in the business, and, as I hear, there is like to be warm work between them. The Georgians are quite hot on the subject, and go where I will, they talk of nothing else than hanging the president, the Indians, and all the judges. They are brushing up their rifles, and they speak out plain."

"The more sport for us—but this is all idle. It will all end in talk, and whether it do or not, we, at least, have nothing to do with it. But, there is drink—fill—and let us look to business before either of us sleep."

The lieutenant did as suggested by Rivers, who, rising from his seat, continued for some time to pace the apartment, evidently in deep meditation. He suddenly paused, at length, and resuming his seat, inquired of Dillon as to the manner in which he had been employed through the last few days.

A narration, not necessary to repeat, followed from the officer, in which the numerous petty details of frontier irregularity made up the chief material. Plots and counterplots were rife in his story, and more than once the outlaw interrupted his officer in the hope of abridging the petty particulars of some of their attenuated proportions—an aim not always successful, since, among the numerous virtues of Lieutenant Dillon, that of precision and niceness in his statements must not be omitted. To this narration, however, though called for by himself, the superior yielded but little attention, until he proceed to describe the adventure of the night, resulting so unsuccessfully, with the emigrating farmer. When he described the persons of the two strangers, so unexpectedly lending their aid in defence of the traveller, a new interest was awakened in the features and manner of his auditor, who here suddenly and with energy interrupted him, to make inquiries with regard to their dress and appearance, which not a little surprised Dillon, who had frequently experienced the aversion of his superior to all seemingly unnecessary minutiæ. Having been satisfied on these points, the outlaw rose, and pacing the apartment with slow steps, seemed to meditate some design which the narrative had suggested. Suddenly pausing, at length, as if all the necessary lights had shone in upon his deliberations at once, he turned to Dillon, who stood in silent waiting, and thus proceeded:—

"I have it," said he, half-musingly, "I have it, Dillon—it must be so. How far, say you, is it from the place where the man—what's his name—encamped last night?"

"Nine or ten miles, perhaps, or more."

"And you know his route for to-day?"

"There is not but one which he can take, pursuing the route which he does."

"And upon that he will not go more than fifteen or twenty miles in the day. But not so with *him*—not so with *him*. He will scarcely be content to move at that pace, and there will be no hope in that way to overtake him."

Rivers spoke in soliloquy, and Dillon, though accustomed to many of the mental irregularities of his superior, exhibited something like surprise as he looked upon the lowering brows and unwonted indecision of the outlaw.

"Of whom does the captain speak?" was his inquiry.

"Of *whom?*—of *him*—of *him!*" was the rather abrupt response of the superior, who seemed to regard the ignorance of his lieutenant as to the object in view, with almost as much wonder as that worthy entertained at the moment for the hallucinations of his captain.

"Of whom should I speak—of whom should I think but the one—accursed, fatal and singular, who—" and he stopped short, while his mind, now comprehending the true relationship between himself and the person beside him, which, in his moody self-examination, he had momentarily forgotten, proceeded to his designs with all his wonted coherence.

"I wander, Dillon, and am half-asleep. The fact is, I am almost worn out with this unslumbering motion. I have not been five hours out of the saddle in the last twenty-four, and it requires something more of rest, if I desire to do well what I have on hand—what, indeed, we both have on hand."

There was something apologetic in the manner, if not in the language, of the speaker; and his words seemed to indicate, if possible, an excuse for the incoherence of his address, in the physical fatigue which he had undergone—in this way to divert suspicion from those mental causes of excitement, of which, in the present situation, he felt somewhat ashamed. Pouring out a glass of liquor, and quaffing it without pause, he motioned to the lieutenant to do the same—a suggestion not possible for that person to misunderstand—and then proceeded to narrate such portions of the late occurrences in and about the village as it was necessary he should know. He carefully suppressed his own agency in any of these events, for, with the policy of the ancient, he had learned, at an early period in his life, to treat his friend as if he might one day become his enemy; and, so far as such a resolution might consistently be maintained, while engaged in such an occupation as his, he rigidly observed it.

"The business, Dillon, which I want you to execute, and to which you will give all your attention, is difficult and troublesome, and requires ingenuity. Mark Forrester was killed last night, as is supposed, in a fray with a youth named Colleton, like himself a Carolinian. If such is not the opinion yet, I am determined such shall be the opinion; and have made arrangements by which the object will be attained. Of course the murderer should be taken, and I have reasons to desire that this object too should be attained. It is on this business, then, that you are to go. You must be the officer to take him."

"But where is he? if within reach, you know there is no difficulty."

"Hear me; there is difficulty though he is within reach. He is one of the men whom you found with the old farmer you would otherwise have attacked last night. There is difficulty, for he will fight like a wild beast, and stick to his ground like a rattlesnake; and, supported by the old fellow whom you found him with, he will be able to resist almost any force which you could muster on the emergency. The only fear I have is, that being well-mounted, he will not keep with the company, but as they must needs travel slowly, he will go on and leave them."

"Should it not rather be a source of satisfaction than otherwise—will it not put him more completely at our disposal?"

"No; for having so much the start of you, and a good animal, he will soon leave all pursuit behind him. There is a plan which I have been thinking of, and which will be the very thing, if at once acted upon. You know the sheriff, Maxson, lives on the same road; you must take two of the men with you, pick fresh and good horses, set off to Maxson's at once with a letter which I shall give you, and he will make you special deputies for the occasion of this young man's arrest. I have arranged it so that the suspicion shall take the shape of a legal warrant, sufficient to authorize his arrest and detention. The proof of his offence will be matter of after consideration."

"But will Maxson do this—may he not refuse? You know he has been once before threatened with being brought up for his leaning toward us, in that affair of the Indian chief, Enakamon."

"He can not—he dare not refuse!" said the outlaw, rising impatiently. "He holds his place and his life at my disposal, and he knows it. He will not venture to refuse me!"

"He has been very scrupulous of late in all his dealings with us, you know, and has rather kept out of our way. Besides that, he has been thorough-going at several camp-meetings lately, and, when a man begins to appear over-honest, I think it high time he should be looked after by all parties."

"You are right, Dillon, you are right. I should not trust it to paper either. I will go myself. But you shall along with me, and on the way I will put you in a train for bringing out certain prisoners whom it is necessary that we should secure before the sitting of the court, and until it is over. They might be foolish enough to convict themselves of being more honest than their neighbors, and it is but humane to keep them from the commission of an impropriety. Give orders for the best two of your troop, and have horses saddled for all four of us. We must be on the road."

Dillon did as directed, and returned to the conference, which was conducted, on the part of his superior, with a degree of excitation, mingled with a sharp asperity of manner, something unwonted for him in the arranging of any mere matter of business.

"Maxson will not refuse us; if he do, I will hang him by my saddle-straps. The scoundrel owes his election to our votes, and shall he refuse us what we ask? He knows his fate too well to hesitate. And then, Dillon, when you have his commission for the arrest of this boy, spare not the spur: secure him at all hazards of horseflesh or personal inconvenience. He will not resist the laws, or anything having their semblance; nor, indeed, has he any reason—"

"No reason, sir! why, did you not say he had killed Forrester?" inquired his companion.

"Your memory is sharp, master lieutenant; I did say, and I say so still. But he affects to think not, and I should not be at all surprised if he not only deny it to you, but in reality disbelieve it himself. Have you not heard of men who have learned in time to believe the lies of their own invention? Why not men doubt the truth of their own doings? There are such men, and he may be one of them. He may deny stoutly and solemnly the charge, but let him not deceive you or baffle your pursuit. We shall prove it upon him, and he shall hang, Dillon—ay, hang, hang, hang—though it be under her very eyes!"

It was in this way that, in the progress of the dialogue which took place between the chief and his subordinate, the rambling malignity would break through the cooler counsels of the villain, and dark glimpses of the mystery of the transaction would burst upon the senses of the latter. Rivers had the faculty, however, of never exhibiting too much of himself; and when hurried on by a passion seemingly too fierce to furious for restraint, he would suddenly curb himself in, while a sharp and scornful smile would curl his lips, as if he felt a consciousness, not only of his own powers of command, but of his impenetrability to all analysis.

The horses being now ready, the outlaw, buckling on his pistols, and hiding his dirk in his bosom, threw a huge cloak over his shoulders, which fully concealed his person; and, in company with his lieutenant, and two stout men of his band, all admirably and freshly mounted, they proceeded to the abode of the sheriff.

This man, connected, though secretly, with Rivers and Munro, was indebted to them and the votes which in that region they could throw into the boxes, for his elevation to the office which he held, and was, as might reasonably have been expected, a mere creature under their management. Maxson, of late days, however, whether from a reasonable apprehension, increasing duly with increasing years, that he might become at last so involved in the meshes of those crimes of his colleagues, from which, while he was compelled to share the risk, he was denied in great part the profit, had grown scrupulous—had avoided as much as possible their connexion; and, the better to strengthen himself in the increasing favor of public opinion, had taken advantage of all those externals of morality and virtue which, unhappily, too frequently conceal qualities at deadly hostility with them. He had, in the popular phrase of the country, "got religion;" and, like the worthy reformers of the Cromwell era, everything which he did, and everything which he said, had Scripture for its authority. Psalm-singing commenced and ended the day in his house, and graces before meat and graces before sleep, prayers and ablutions, thanksgivings and fastings, had so much thinned the animal necessities of his household, that a domestic war was the consequence, and the sheriff and the sheriff's lady held separate sway, having equally divided the dwelling between them, and ruling each their respective sovereignties with a most jealous watchfulness. All rights, not expressly delegated in the distribution of powers originally, were insisted on even to blood; and the arbitration of the sword, or rather the poker, once appealed to, most emphatically, by the sovereign of the gentler sex, had cut off the euphonious utterance of one of the choicest paraphrases of Sternhold and Hopkins in the middle; and by bruising the scull of the reformed and reforming sheriff, had nearly rendered a new election necessary to the repose and well-being of the county in which they lived.

But the worthy convert recovered, to the sore discomfiture of his spouse, and to the comfort and rejoicing of all true believers. The breach in his head was healed, but that which separated his family remained the same—

"As rocks that had been rent asunder."

They knew the fellowship of man and wife only in so much as was absolutely essential to the keeping up of appearances to the public eye—a matter necessary to maintaining her lord in the possession of his dignity; which, as it conferred honor and profit, through him, upon her also, it was of necessity a part of her policy to continue.

There had been a brush—a small gust had passed over that fair region of domestic harmony—on the very morning upon which the outlaw and his party rode up the untrimmed and half-overgrown avenue, which led to the house of the writ-server. There had been an amiable discussion between the two, as to which of them, with propriety, belonged the duty of putting on the breeches of their son, Tommy, preparatory to his making his appearance at the breakfast-table. Some extraneous influence had that morning prompted the sheriff to resist the performance of a task which had now for some time been imposed upon him, and for which, therefore, there was the sanction of prescription and usage. It was an unlucky moment for the assertion of his manhood: for, a series of circumstances operating just about that time unfavorably upon the mind of his wife, she was in the worst possible humor upon which to try experiments.

She heard the refusal of her liege to do the required duty, therefore, with an astonishment, not unmingled with a degree of pleasure, as it gave a full excuse for the venting forth upon him of those splenetic humors, which, for some time, had been growing and gathering in her system. The little sheriff, from long attendance on *courts* and *camps,* had acquired something more, perhaps, of the desire and disposition, than the capacity, to make long speeches and longer sermons, in the performance of both of which labors, however, he was admirably fortified by the technicals of the law, and the Bible phraseology. The quarrel had been waged for some time, and poor Tommy, the bone of contention, sitting all the while between the contending parties in a state of utter nudity, kept up a fine running accompaniment to the full tones of the wranglers, by crying bitterly for his breeches.

For the first time for a long period of years, the lady found her powers of tongue fail in the proposed effect upon the understanding of her loving and legal lord; and knowing but of one other way to assail it, her hand at length grappling with the stool, from which she tumbled the breechless babe without scruple, seized upon an argument to which her adversary could oppose neither text nor technical; when, fortunately for him, the loud rapping of their early visiters at the outer door of the dwelling interposed between her wrath and its object, and spared the life of the devout sheriff for other occurrences. Bundling the naked child out of sight, the mother rushed into an inner apartment, shaking the stool in the pale countenance of her lord as she retreated, in a manner and with a look which said, as plainly as words could say, that this temporary delay would only sharpen her appetite for vengeance, and exaggerate its terrors when the hour did arrive. It was with a hesitating step and wobegone countenance, therefore, that the officer proceeded to his parlor, where a no less troublesome, but less awkward, trial awaited him.

Chapter Twenty-eight

Arrest

The high-sheriff made his appearance before his early and well-known visiters with a desperate air of composure and unconcern, the effort to attain which was readily perceptible to his companions. He could not, in the first place, well get rid of those terrors of the domestic world from which their interruption had timely shielded him; nor, on the other hand, could he feel altogether assured that the visit now paid him would not result in the exaction of some usurious interest. He had recently, as we have said, as much through motives of worldly as spiritual policy, become an active religionist, in a small way, in and about the section of country in which he resided; and knowing that his professions were in some sort regarded with no small degree of doubt and suspicion by some of his brethren holding the same faith, he felt the necessity of playing a close and cautious game in all his practices. He might well be apprehensive, therefore, of the visits of those who never came but as so many omens of evil, and whose claims upon, and perfect knowledge of, his true character, were such, that he felt himself, in many respects, most completely at their mercy.

Rivers did not give much time to preliminaries, but, after a few phrases of commonplace, coming directly to the point, he stated the business in hand, and demanded the assistance of the officer of justice for the arrest of one of its fugitives. There were some difficulties of form in the matter, which saved the sheriff in part, and which the outlaw had in great part overlooked. A warrant of arrest was necessary from some officer properly empowered to issue one, and a new difficulty was thus presented in the way of Colleton's pursuit. The sheriff had not the slightest objections to making deputies of the persons recommended by the outlaw, provided they were fully empowered to execute the commands of some judicial officer; beyond this, the scrupulous executioner of justice was unwilling to go; and having stood out so long in the previous controversy with his spouse, it was wonderful what a vast stock of audacious courage he now felt himself entitled, and ventured, to manifest.

"I can not do it, Master Guy—it's impossible—seeing, in the first place, that I ha'n't any right by the laws to issue any warrant, though it's true, I has to serve them. Then, agin, in the next place, 'twont do for another reason that's jist as good, you see. It's only the other day, Master Guy, that the fear of the Lord come upon me, and I got religion; and now I've set myself up as a worker in other courts, you see, than those of man; and there be eyes around me that would see, and hearts to rejoice at the backslidings of the poor laborer. Howbeit, Master Guy, I am not the man to forget old sarvice; and if it be true that this man has been put to death in this manner, though I myself can do nothing at this time, I may put you in the way—for the sake of old time, and for the sake of justice, which requires that the slayer of his brother should also be slain—of having your wish."

Though something irritated still at the reluctance of his former creature to lend himself without scruple to his purposes, the outlaw did not hesitate to accept the overture, and to press for its immediate accomplishment. He had expostulated with the sheriff for some time on the point, and, baffled and denied, he was very glad, at the conclusion of the dialogue with that worthy, to find that there was even so much of a prospect of concert, though falling far short of his original anticipations, from that quarter. He was too well aware, also, of the difficulty in the way of any proceeding without something savoring of authority in the matter; for, from a previous and rather correct estimate of Colleton's character, he well foresaw that, knowing his enemy, he would fight to the last against an arrest; which, under the forms of law and with the sanction of a known officer, he would otherwise readily recognise and submit to. Seizing, therefore, upon the speech of the sheriff, Rivers eagerly availed himself of its opening to obtain those advantages in the affair, of which, from the canting spirit and newly-awakened morality of his late coadjutor, he had utterly begun to despair. He proceeded to reply to the suggestion as follows:—

"I suppose, I must content myself, Maxson, with doing in this thing as you say, though really I see not why you should now be so particular, for there are not ten men in the county who are able to determine upon any of your powers, or who would venture to measure their extent. Let us hear your plan, and I suppose it will be effectual in our object, and this is all I want. All I desire is, that our people, you know, should not be murdered by strangers without rhyme or reason."

The sheriff knew well the hypocrisy of the sentiment with which Rivers concluded, but made no remark. A single smile testified his knowledge of the nature of his colleague, and indicated his suspicion of a deeper and different motive for this new activity. Approaching the outlaw closely, he asked, in a half whisper:—

"Who was the witness of the murder—who could swear for the magistrate? You must get somebody to do that."

This was another point which Rivers, in his impatience, had not thought to consider. But fruitful in expedient, his fertile mind suggested that ground of suspicion was all that the law required for apprehension at least, and having already arranged that the body of the murdered man should be found under certain circumstances, he contented himself with procuring commissions, as deputies, for his two officers, and posted away to the village.

Here, as he anticipated, the intelligence had already been received—the body of Forrester had been found, and sufficient ground for suspicion to authorize a warrant was recognised in the dirk of the youth, which, smeared with blood as it had been left by Rivers, had been found upon the body. Rivers had but little to do. He contrived, however, to do nothing himself. The warrant of Pippin, as magistrate, was procured, and the two officers commissioned by the sheriff went off in pursuit of the supposed murderer, against whom the indignation of all the village was sufficiently heightened by the recollection of the close intimacy existing between Ralph and Forrester, and the nobly characteristic manner in which the latter had volunteered to do his fighting with Rivers. The murdered man had, independent of this, no small popularity of his own, which brought out for him a warm and active sympathy highly creditable to his memory. Old Allen, too, suffered deeply, not less on his own than his daughter's account. She, poor girl, had few words, and her sorrow, silent, if not tearless, was confined to the solitude of her own chamber.

In the prosecution of the affair against Ralph, there was but one person whose testimony could have availed him, and that person was Lucy Munro. As the chief particular in evidence, and that which established the strong leading presumption against him, consisted in the discovery of his dagger alongside the body of the murdered man, and covered with his blood; it was evident that she who could prove the loss of the dagger by the youth, and its finding by Munro, prior to the event, and unaccompanied by any tokens of crime, would not only be able to free the person suspected, at least from this point of suspicion, but would be enabled to place its burden elsewhere, and with the most conclusive distinctness.

This was a dilemma which Rivers and Munro did not fail to consider. The private deliberation, for an hour, of the two conspirators, determined upon the course which for mutual safety they were required to pursue; and Munro gave his niece due notice to prepare for an immediate departure with her aunt and himself, on some plausible pretence, to another portion of the country.

To such a suggestion, as Lucy knew not the object, she offered no objection; and a secret departure was effected of the three, who, after a lonely ride of several hours through a route circuitously chosen to mislead, were safely brought to the sheltered and rocky abiding-place of the robbers, as we have already described it. Marks of its offensive features, however, had been so modified as not to occasion much alarm. The weapons of war had been studiously put out of sight, and apartments, distinct from those we have seen, partly the work of nature, and partly of man, were assigned for the accommodation of the new-comers. The outlaws had their instructions, and did not appear, though lurking and watching around in close and constant neighborhood.

Nor, in this particular alone, had the guilty parties made due provision for their future safety. The affair of the guard had made more stir than had been anticipated in the rash moment which had seen its consummation; and their advices warned them of the approach of a much larger force of state troops, obedient to the direction of the district-attorney, than they could well contend with. They determined, therefore, prudently for themselves, to keep as much out of the way of detection as they could; and to avoid those risks upon which a previous conference had partially persuaded them to adventure. They were also apprized of the greater excitement attending the fate of Forrester, than could possibly have followed the death, in his place, of the contemplated victim; and, adopting a habit of caution, heretofore but little considered in that region, they prepared for all hazards, and, at the same time, tacitly determined upon the suspension of their numerous atrocities—at least, while a controlling force was in the neighborhood. Previous impunity had led them so far, that at length the neighboring country was aroused, and all the better classes, taking advantage of the excitement, grew bolder in the expression of their anger against those who had beset them so long. The sheriff, Maxson, had been something tutored by these influences, or, it had been fair to surmise that his scruples would have been less difficult to overcome.

In the meantime, the pursuit of Ralph Colleton, as the murderer of Forrester, had been hotly urged by the officers. The pursuers knew the route, and having the control of new horses as they proceeded, at frequent intervals, gained of course at every step upon the unconscious travellers. We have seen the latter retiring to repose at a late hour of the night. Under the several fatigues which all parties had undergone, it is not strange that the sun should have arisen some little time before those who had not retired quite so early as himself. At a moderately late hour they breakfasted together—the family of the wagoner, and Ralph, and our old friend the pedler. Pursuing the same route, the two latter, after the repast, separated, with many acknowledgments on both sides, from the emigrating party, and pursued their way together.

On their road, Bunce gave the youth a long and particular account of all those circumstances at the village-inn by which he had been deprived of his chattels, and congratulated himself not a little on the adroit thought which had determined him to retain the good steed of the Lawyer Pippin in lieu of his losses. He spoke of it as quite a clever and creditable performance, and one as fully deserving the golden honors of the medal as many of those doings which are so rewarded.

On this point his companion said little; and though he could not altogether comprehend the propriety of the pedler's morals, he certainly did not see but that the necessity and pressing danger of his situation somewhat sanctioned the deceit. He suggested this idea to Bunce, but when he came to talk of the propriety of returning the animal the moment he was fairly in safety, the speculator failed entirely to perceive the moral of his philosophy.

The sheriff's officers came upon the wagoner a few hours after the two had separated from him. The intelligence received from him quickened their pace, and toward noon they descried our travellers ascending a hill a few hundred yards in advance of them. A repeated application of the spur brought them together, and, as had been anticipated by Rivers, Ralph offered not the slightest objection, when once satisfied of the legality of his arrest, to becoming their prisoner. But the consternation of Bunce was inexpressible. He endeavored to shelter himself in the adjoining woods, and was quietly edging his steed into the covert for that purpose, on the first alarm, but was not permitted by the sharp eyes and ready unscrupulosity of the robber representatives of the law. They had no warrant, it is true, for the arrest of any other person than "the said Ralph Colleton"—but the unlucky color of Pippin's horse, and their perfect knowledge of the animal, readily identifying him, did the business for the pedler.

Under the custody of the laws, therefore, we behold the youth retracing his ground, horror-stricken at the death of Forrester—indignant at the suspicions entertained of himself as the murderer, but sanguine of the result, and firm and fearless as ever. Not so Bunce; there were cruel visions in his sight of seven-sided pine-rails—fierce regulators—Lynch's law, and all that rude and terrible sort of punishment, which is studiously put in force in those regions for the enjoyment of evil-doers. The next day found them both securely locked up in the common jail of Chestatee.

CHAPTER TWENTY-NINE

Chub Williams

The young mind of Colleton, excursive as it was, could scarcely realize to itself the strange and rapidly succeeding changes of the last few days. Self-exiled from the dwelling in which so much of his heart and hope had been stored up—a wanderer among the wandering—assaulted by ruffians—the witness of their crimes—pursued by the officers of justice, and finally the tenant of a prison, as a criminal himself! After the first emotions of astonishment and vexation had subsided—ignorant of the result of this last adventure, and preparing for the worst—he called for pen and paper, and briefly, to his uncle, recounted his adventures, as we have already related them, partially acknowledging his precipitance in departing from his house, but substantially insisting upon the propriety of those grounds which had made him do so.

To Edith, what could he say? Nothing—everything. His letter to her, enclosed in that to her uncle, was just such as might be expected from one with a character such as we have endeavored to describe— that of the genuine aristocrat of Carolina—gentle, but firm—soothing, but manly—truly, but loftily affectionate—the rock touched, if not softened by the sunbeam; warm and impetuous, but generally just in his emotions—liberal in his usual estimate of mankind, and generous, to a fault, in all his associations;—ignorant of any value in money, unless for high purposes—as subservient to taste and civilization—a graceful humanity and an honorable affection.

With a tenderness the most respectful, Ralph reiterated his love—
prayed for her prayers—frankly admitted his error in his abrupt flight,
and freely promised atonement as soon as he should be freed from his
difficulties; an event which, in speaking to her, he doubted not. This
duty over, his mind grew somewhat relieved, and, despatching a note by
the jailer's deputy to the lawyer Pippin, he desired immediately to see
him.

Pippin had looked for such an invitation, and was already in attendance. His regrets were prodigious, but his gratification not less, as it
would give him an opportunity, for some time desired, for serving so
excellent a gentleman. But the lawyer shook his head with most professional uncertainty at every step of his own narration of the case, and
soon convinced Ralph that he really stood in a very awkward predicament. He described the situation of the body of Forrester when found;
the bloody dirk which lay beside it, having the initials of his name plainly
carved upon it; his midnight flight; his close companionship with
Forrester on the evening of the night in which he had been murdered—
a fact proved by old Allen and his family; the intimate freedom with
which Forrester had been known to confide his purposes to the youth,
deducible from the joint call which they had made upon the sweetheart
of the former; and many other smaller details, unimportant in themselves, but linked together with the rest of the particulars, strengthening
the chain of circumstances against him to a degree which rendered it
improbable that he should escape conviction.

Pippin sought, however, to console his client, and, after the first
development of particulars, the natural buoyancy of the youth
returned. He was not disposed readily to despair, and his courage and
confidence rose with the pressure of events. He entered into a plain
story of all the particulars of his flight—the instrumentality of Miss
Munro in that transaction, and which she could explain, in such a manner as to do away with any unfavorable impression which that circumstance, of itself, might create. Touching the dagger, he could say
nothing. He had discovered its loss, but knew not at what time he had
lost it. The manner in which it had been found was, of course, fatal,
unless the fact which he alleged of its loss could be established; and of
this the consulting parties saw no hope. Still, they did not despair, but
proceeded to the task of preparing the defence for the day of trial, which
was at hand. The technical portions of the case were managed by the
lawyer, who issued his subpœnas—made voluminous notes—wrote

out the exordium of his speech—and sat up all night committing it to memory.

Having done all that the occasion called for in his interview with Ralph, the lawyer proceeded to visit, uncalled for, one whom he considered a far greater criminal than his client. The cell to which the luckless pedler, Bunce, had been carried, was not far from that of the former, and the rapid step of the lawyer soon overcame the distance between.

Never was man seemingly so glad to see his neighbor as was Bunce, on this occasion, to look upon Pippin. His joy found words of the most honeyed description for his visiter, and his delight was truly infectious. The lawyer was delighted too, but his satisfaction was of a far different origin. He had now some prospect of getting back his favorite steed— that fine animal, described by him elsewhere to the pedler, as docile as the dog, and fleet as the deer. He had heard of the safety of his horse, and his anger with the pedler had undergone some abatement; but, with the consciousness of power common to inferior minds, came a strong desire for its use. He knew that the pedler had been guilty in a legal sense of no crime, and could only be liable in a civil action for his breach of trust. But he suspected that the dealer in wares was ignorant of the advantageous distinctions in morals which the law had made, and consequently amused himself with playing upon the fears of the offender. He put on a countenance of much commiseration, and, drawing a long sigh, regretted the necessity which had brought him to prepare the mind of his old friend for the last terrors of justice.

But Bunce was not a man easily frightened. As he phrased it himself, he had been quite too long knocking about among men to be scared by shadows, and replied stoutly—though really with some internal misgivings—to the lachrymalities of the learned counsel. He gave him to understand that, if he got into difficulty, he knew some other persons whom his confessions would make uncomfortable; and hinted pretty directly at certain practices of a certain professional gentleman, which, though the pedler knew nothing of the technical significant, might yet come under the head of barratry, and so forth.

The lawyer was the more timid man of the two, and found it necessary to pare down his potency. He soon found it profitable to let the matter rest, and having made arrangements with the pedler for bringing suit for damages against two of the neighboring farmers concerned in the demolition of his wares—who, happening to be less guilty than their accessaries, had ventured to remain in the country—Bunce found no difficulty in making his way out of the prison. There had been no right originally to detain him; but the consciousness of guilt, and some other ugly misgivings, had so relaxed the nerves of the tradesman, that he had never thought to inquire if his name were included in the warrant of arrest. It is probable that his courage and confidence would have been far less than they appear at present, had not Pippin assured him that the regulators were no longer to be feared; that the judge had arrived; that the grand-jury had found bills against several of the offenders, and were still engaged in their labors; that a detachment of the state military had been ordered to the station; and that things looked as civil as it was altogether possible for such warlike exhibition to allow. It is surprising to think how fearlessly uncompromising was the conduct of Bunce under this new condition of affairs.

But the pedler, in his own release from custody, was not forgetful of his less-fortunate companion. He was a frequent visiter in the dungeon of Ralph Colleton; bore all messages between the prisoner and his counsel; and contributed, by his shrewd knowledge of human kind, not a little to the material out of which his defence was to be made.

He suggested the suspicion, never before entertained by the youth, or entertained for a moment only, that his present arrest was the result of a scheme purposely laid with a reference to this end; and did not scruple to charge upon Rivers the entire management of the matter.

Ralph could only narrate what he knew of the malignant hatred of the outlaw to himself—another fact which none but Lucy Munro could establish. Her evidence, however, would only prove Rivers to have meditated one crime; it would not free him from the imputation of having committed another. Still, so much was important, and casualties were to be relied upon for the rest.

But what was the horror of all parties when it was known that neither Lucy nor any of the landlord's family were to be found! The process of subpœna was returned, and the general opinion was, that alarmed at the approach of the military in such force, and confident that his agency in the late transactions could not long remain concealed in the possession of so many, though guilty like himself, Munro had fled to the west.

The mental agony of the youth, when thus informed, can not well be conceived. He was, for a time, utterly prostrate, and gave himself up to despair. The entreaties of the pedler, and the counsels and exhortings of the lawyer, failed equally to enliven him; and they had almost come to adopt his gloomy resignation, when, as he sat on his low bench, with head drooping on his hand, a solitary glance of sunshine fell through the barred window—the only one assigned to his cell.

The smile of God himself that solitary ray appeared to the diseased spirit of the youth, and he grew strong in an instant. Talk of the lessons of the learned, and the reasonings of the sage!—a vagrant breeze, a rippling water, a glance of the sweet sunlight, have more of consolation in them for the sad heart than all the pleadings of philosophy. They bring the missives of a higher teacher.

Bunce was an active coadjutor with the lawyer in this melancholy case. He made all inquiries—he went everywhere. He searched in all places, and spared no labor; but at length despaired. Nothing could be elicited by his inquiries, and he ceased to hope himself, and ceased to persuade Ralph into hope. The lawyer shook his head in reply to all questions, and put on a look of mystery which is the safety-valve to all swollen pretenders.

In this state of affairs, taking the horse of the youth, with a last effort at discoveries, Bunce rode forth into the surrounding country. He had heretofore taken all the common routes, to which, in his previous intercourse with the people, he had been accustomed; he now determined to strike into a path scarcely perceptible, and one which he never remembered to have seen before. He followed, mile after mile, its sinuosities. It was a wild, and, seemingly, an untrodden region. The hills shot up jaggedly from the plain around him—the fissures were rude and steep—more like embrasures, blown out by sudden power from the solid rock. Where the forest appeared it was dense and intricate—abounding in brush and underwood; where it was deficient, the blasted heath chosen by the witches in Macbeth would have been no unfit similitude.

Hopeless of human presence in this dreary region, the pedler yet rode on as if to dissipate the unpleasant thoughts, following upon his frequent disappointment. Suddenly, however, a turn in the winding path brought him in contact with a strange-looking figure, not more than five feet in height, neither boy nor man, uncouthly habited, and seemingly one to whom all converse but that of the trees and rocks, during his whole life, had been unfamiliar.

The reader has already heard something of the Cherokee pony—it was upon one of these animals he rode. They are a small, but compactly made and hardy creature—of great fortitude, stubborn endurance, and an activity, which, in the travel of day after day, will seldom subside from the gallop. It was the increasing demand for these animals that had originally brought into existence and exercise a company, which, by a transition far from uncommon, passed readily from the plundering of horses to the cutting of throats and purses; scarcely discriminating in their reckless rapacity between the several degrees of crime in which such a practice involved them.

Though somewhat uncouth in appearance, the new-comer seemed decidedly harmless—nay, almost idiotic in appearance. His smile was pleasant, though illuminating features of the ruggedest description, and the tones of his voice were even musical in the ears of the pedler, to whom any voice would probably have seemed so in that gloomy region. He very sociably addressed Bunce in the *patois* of that section; and the ceremonial of introduction, without delay or difficulty, was overcome duly on both sides. In the southern wilderness, indeed, it does not call for much formality, nor does a strict adherence to the received rules of etiquette become at all necessary, to make the traveller "hail fellow, well met." Anything in that quarter, savoring of reserve or stiffness, is punished with decided hostility or openly-avowed contempt; and, in the more rude regions, the refusal to partake in the very social employments of wrestling or whiskey-drinking, has brought the scrupulous personage to the more questionable enjoyments of a regular gouging match and fight. A demure habit is the most unpopular among all classes. Freedom of manner, on the other hand, obtains confidence readily, and the heart is won, at once, by an off-handed familiarity of demeanor, which fails to recognise any inequalities in human condition. The society and the continued presence of Nature, as it were, in her own peculiar abode, put aside all merely conventional distinctions, and men meet upon a common footing. Thus, even when perfect strangers to one another, after the usual preliminaries of "how are you, friend," or "stranger?"—"*whar* from?"—"*whar* going?"—"fair" or "foul weather"—as the case may be—the acquaintance is established, and familiarity well begun. Such was the case in the present instance. Bunce knew the people well, and exhibited his most unreluctant manner. The horses of the two, in like manner with their masters, made similar overtures; and, in a little while, their necks were drawn in parallel lines together.

Bunce was less communicative, however, than the stranger. Still his head and heart, alike, were full, and he talked more freely than was altogether consistent with his Yankee character. He told of Ralph's predicament, and the clown sympathized; he narrated the quest which had brought him forth, and of his heretofore unrewarded labors; concluded with naming the ensuing Monday as the day of the youth's trial, when, if nothing in the meantime could be discovered of the true criminal—for the pedler never for a moment doubted that Ralph was innocent—he "mortally feared things would go agin him."

"That will be hard, too—a mighty touch difficulty, now, strannger—to be hanged for other folks' doings. But, I reckon, he'll have to make up his mind to it."

"Oh, no! don't say so, now, my friend, I beg you. What makes you think so?" said the anxious pedler.

"Why, only from what I *heer'd* you say. You said so yourself, and I believed it as if I had seed it," was the reply of the simple countryman.

"Oh, yes. It's but a poor chance with him now, I guess. I'd a notion that I could find out some little particular, you see—"

"No, I don't see."

"To be sure you don't, but that's my say. Everybody has a say, you know."

"No, I don't know."

"To be sure of course you don't know, but that's what I tell you. Now you must know—"

"Don't say *must* to me, strannger, if you want that we shall keep hands off. I don't let any man say *must* to me."

"No harm, my friend—I didn't mean no harm," said the worried pedler, not knowing what to make of his acquaintance, who spoke shrewdly at times, but occasionally in a speech, which awakened the doubts of the pedler as to the safety of his wits. Avoiding all circumlocution of phrase, and dropping the "you sees," and "you knows" from his narration, he proceeded to state his agency in procuring testimony for the youth, and of the ill-success which had hitherto attended him. At length, in the course of his story, which he contrived to tell with as much caution as came within the scope of his education, he happened to speak of Lucy Munro; but had scarcely mentioned her name when his queer companion interrupted him:—

"Look you, strannger, I'll lick you now, off-hand, if you don't put Miss for a handle to the gal's name. She's Miss Lucy. Don't I know her, and han't I seen her, and isn't it I, Chub Williams, as they calls me, that loves the very airth she treads?"

"You know Miss Lucy?" inquired the pedler, enraptured even at this moderate discovery, though carefully coupling the prefix to her name while giving it utterance—"now, do you know Miss Lucy, friend, and will you tell me where I can find her?"

"Do you think I will, and you may be looking arter her too? 'Drot my old hat, strannger, but I do itch to git at you."

"Oh, now, Mr. Williams—"

"I won't answer to that name. Call me Chub Williams, if you wants to be perlite. Mother always calls me Chub, and that's the reason I like it."

"Well, Chub,"—said the other, quite paternally—"I assure you I don't love Miss Munro—and—"

"What! you don't love Miss Lucy. Why, everybody ought to love her. Now, if you don't love her, I'll hammer you, strannger, off-hand."

The poor pedler professed a proper sort of love for the young lady—not exactly such as would seek her for a wife, however, and succeeded in satisfying, after a while, the scruples of one who, in addition to deformity, he also discovered to labor under the more serious curse of partial idiocy. Having done this, and flattered, in sundry other ways, the peculiarities of his companion, he pursued his other point with laudable pertinacity.

He at length got from Chub his own history: how he had run into the woods with his mother, who had suffered from the ill-treatment of her husband: how, with his own industry, he had sustained her wants, and supplied her with all the comforts which a long period had required; and how, dying at length, she had left him—the forest boy—alone, to pursue those toils which heretofore had an object, while she yielded him in return for them society and sympathy. These particulars got from him in a manner the most desultory, were made to preface the more important parts of the narrative.

It appears that his harmlessness had kept him undisturbed, even by the wild marauders of that region, and that he still continued to procure a narrow livelihood by his woodland labors, and sought no association with that humanity which, though among fellow-creatures, would still have lacked of fellowship for him. In the transfer of Lucy from the village to the shelter of the outlaws, he had obtained a glimpse of her person and form, and had ever since been prying in the neighborhood for a second and similar enjoyment. He now made known to the pedler her place of concealment, which he had, some time before this event, himself discovered; but which, through dread of Rivers, for whom he seemed to entertain an habitual fear, he had never ventured to penetrate.

"Well, I must see her," exclaimed Bunce. "I a'n't afraid, 'cause you see, Mr. Williams—Chub, I mean, it's only justice, and to save the poor young gentleman's life. I'm sure I oughtn't to be afraid, and no more I a'n't. Won't you go there with me, Chub?"

"Can't think of it, strannger. Guy is a dark man, and mother said I must keep away when he rode in the woods. Guy don't talk—he shoots."

The pedler made sundry efforts to procure a companion for his adventure; but finding it vain, and determined to do right, he grew more resolute with the necessity, and, contenting himself with claiming the guidance of Chub, he went boldly on the path. Having reached a certain point in the woods, after a very circuitous departure from the main track, the guide pointed out to the pedler a long and rude ledge of rocks, so rude, so wild, that none could have ever conjectured to find them the abode of anything but the serpent and the wolf. But there, according to the idiot, was Lucy Munro concealed. Chub gave the pedler his directions, then alighting from his nag, which he concealed in a clump of neighboring brush, hastily and with the agility of a monkey ran up a neighboring tree which overhung the prospect.

Bunce, left alone, grew somewhat staggered with his fears. He now half-repented of the self-imposed adventure; wondered at his own rash humanity, and might perhaps have utterly forborne the trial, but for a single consideration. His pride was concerned, that the deformed Chub should not have occasion to laugh at his weakness. Descending, therefore, from his horse, he fastened him to the hanging branch of a neighboring tree, and with something of desperate defiance in his manner, resolutely advanced to the silent and forbidding mass of rocks, which rose up so sullenly around him. In another moment, and he was lost to sight in the gloomy shadow of the entrance-passage pointed out to him by the half-witted, but not altogether ignorant dwarf.

CHAPTER THIRTY

The Rock Castle of the Robbers

B ut the preparations of Bunce had been foreseen and provided for by
those most deeply interested in his progress; and scarcely had the
worthy tradesman effected his entrance fairly into the forbidden territory, when he felt himself grappled from behind. He struggled with an
energy, due as much to the sudden terror as to any exercise of the free
will; but he struggled in vain. The arms that were fastened about his
own bound them down with a grasp of steel; and after a few moments
of desperate effort, accompanied with one or two exclamations, half-
surprise, half-expostulation, of "Hello, friend, what do you mean?" and
"I say, now, friend, you'd better have done—" the struggle ceased, and
he lay supine in the hold of the unseen persons who had secured him.

These persons he could not then discern; the passage was cav-
ernously dark, and had evidently been as much the work of nature as of
art. A handkerchief was fastened about his eyes, and he felt himself carried on the shoulders of those who made nothing of the burden. After
the progress of several minutes, in which the anxiety natural to his situation led Bunce into frequent exclamations and entreaties, he was set
down, the bandage was removed from his eyes, and he was once more
permitted their free exercise.

To his great wonder, however, nothing but women, of all sizes and
ages, met his sight. In vain did he look around for the men who brought
him. They were no longer to be seen, and so silent had been their passage

out, that the unfortunate pedler was compelled to satisfy himself with the belief that persons of the gentler sex had been in truth his captors.

Had he, indeed, given up the struggle so easily? The thought was mortifying enough; and yet, when he looked around him, he grew more satisfied with his own efforts at resistance. He had never seen such strongly-built women in his life: scarcely one of them but could easily have overthrown him, without stratagem, in single combat. The faces of many of them were familiar to him; but where had he seen them before? His memory failed him utterly, and he gave himself up to his bewilderment.

He looked around, and the scene was well calculated to affect a nervous mind. It was a fit scene for the painter of the supernatural. The small apartment in which they were, was formed in great part from the natural rock; where a fissure presented itself, a huge pine-tree, overthrown so as to fill the vacuity, completed what nature had left undone; and, bating the one or two rude cavities left here and there in the sides—themselves so covered as to lie hidden from all without—there was all the compactness of a regularly-constructed dwelling. A single and small lamp, pendent from a beam that hung over the room, gave a feeble light, which, taken in connection with that borrowed from without, served only to make visible the dark indistinct of the place. With something dramatic in their taste, the old women had dressed themselves in sombre habiliments, according to the general aspect of all things around them; and, as the unfortunate pedler continued to gaze in wonderment, his fear grew with every progressive step in his observation. One by one, however, the old women commenced stirring, and, as they moved, now before and now behind him—his eyes following them on every side—he at length discovered, amid the group, the small and delicate form of the very being for whom he sought.

There, indeed, were Lucy Munro and her aunt, holding a passive character in the strange assembly. This was encouraging; and Bunce, forgetting his wonder in the satisfaction which such a prospect afforded him, endeavored to force his way forward to them, when a salutary twitch of the arm from one of the beldam troop, by tumbling him backward upon the floor of the cavern, brought him again to a consideration of his predicament. He could not be restrained from speech, however—though, as he spoke, the old women saluted his face on all hands with strokes from brushes of fern, which occasioned him no small inconvenience. But he had gone too far now to recede; and, in a broken manner—broken as much by his own hurry and vehemence as by the interruptions to which he was subjected—he contrived to say enough to Lucy of the situation of Colleton, to revive in her an interest of the most painful character. She rushed forward, and was about to ask more from the beleaguered pedler; but it was not the policy of those having both of them in charge to permit such a proceeding. One of the stoutest of the old women now came prominently upon the scene, and, with a rough voice, which it is not difficult to recognise as that of Munro, commanded the young girl away, and gave her in charge to two attendants. But she struggled still to hear, and Bunce all the while speaking, she was enabled to gather most of the particulars in his narration before her removal was effected.

The mummery now ceased, and Bunce having been carried elsewhere, the maskers resumed their native apparel, having thrown aside that which had been put on for a distinct purpose. The pedler, in another and more secure department of the robbers' hiding-place, was solaced with the prospect of a long and dark imprisonment.

In the meantime, our little friend Chub Williams had been made to undergo his own distinct punishment for his share in the adventure. No sooner had Bunce been laid by the heels, than Rivers, who had directed the whole, advanced from the shelter of the cave, in company with his lieutenant, Dillon, both armed with rifles, and, without saying a word, singling out the tree on which Chub had perched himself, took deliberate aim at the head of the unfortunate urchin. He saw the danger in an instant, and his first words were characteristic: "Now don't—don't, now, I tell you, Mr. Guy—you may hit Chub!"

"Come down, then, you rascal!" was the reply, as, with a laugh, lowering the weapon, he awaited the descent of the spy. "And now, Bur, what have you to say that I shouldn't wear out a hickory or two upon you?"

"My name ain't Bur, Mr. Guy; my name is Chub, and I don't like to be called out of my name. Mother always called me Chub."

"Well, Chub—since you like it best, though at best a bur—what were you doing in that tree? How dare you spy into my dwelling, and send other people there? Speak, or I'll skin you alive!"

"Now, don't, Mr. Guy! Don't, I beg you! 'Taint right to talk so, and I don't like it!—But is that your dwelling, Mr. Guy, in truth?—you really live in it, all the year round? Now, you don't, do you?"

The outlaw had no fierceness when contemplating the object before him. Strange nature! He seemed to regard the deformities of mind and body, in the outcast under his eyes, as something kindred. Was there anything like sympathy in such a feeling? or was it rather that perversity of temper which sometimes seems to cast an ennobling feature over violence, and to afford here and there, a touch of that moral sunshine which can now and then give an almost redeeming expression to the countenance of vice itself? He contemplated the idiot for a few moments with a close eye, and a mind evidently busied in thought. Laying his hand, at length, on his shoulder, he was about to speak, when the deformed started back from the touch as if in horror—a feeling, indeed, fully visible in every feature of his face.

"Now, don't touch Chub, Mr. Guy! Mother said you were a dark man, and told me to keep clear of you. Don't touch me agin, Mr. Guy; I don't like it."

The outlaw, musingly, spoke to his lieutenant: "And this is education. Who shall doubt its importance? who shall say that it does not overthrow and altogether destroy the original nature? The selfish mother of this miserable outcast, fearing that he might be won away from his service to her, taught him to avoid all other persons, and even those who had treated her with kindness were thus described to this poor dependant. To him the sympathies of others would have been the greatest blessing; yet she so tutored him, that, at her death, he was left desolate. You hear his account of me, gathered, as he says, and as I doubt not, from her own lips. That account is true, so far as my other relationships with mankind are concerned; but not true as regards my connection with her. I furnished that old creature with food when she was starving, and when this boy, sick and impotent, could do little for her service. I never uttered a harsh word in her ears, or treated her unkindly; yet this is the character she gives of me—and this, indeed, the character which she has given of all others. A feeling of the narrowest selfishness has led her deliberately to misrepresent all mankind; and has been productive of a more ungracious result, in driving one from his species, who, more than any other, stands in need of their sympathy and association."

While Rivers spoke thus, the idiot listened with an air of the most stupid attention. His head fell on one shoulder, and one hand partially sustained it. As the former concluded his remarks, Chub recovered a posture as nearly erect as possible, and remarked, with as much significance as could comport with his general expression—

"Chub's mother was good to Chub, and Mr. Guy mustn't say nothing agin her."

"But, Chub, will you not come and live with me? I will give you a good rifle—one like this, and you shall travel everywhere with me."

"You will beat Chub when you are angry, and make him shoot people with the rifle. I don't want it. If folks say harm to Chub, he can lick 'em with his fists. Chub don't want to live with you."

"Well, as you please. But come in and look at my house, and see where I live."

"And shall I see the strannger agin? I can lick *him,* and I told him so. But he called me Chub, and I made friends with him."

"Yes, you shall see him, and—"

"And Miss Lucy, too—I want to see Miss Lucy—Chub saw her, and she spoke to Chub yesterday."

The outlaw promised him all, and after this there was no further difficulty. The unconscious idiot scrupled no longer, and followed his conductors into—prison. It was necessary, for the further safety of the outlaws in their present abode, that such should be the case. The secret of their hiding-place was in the possession of quite too many; and the subject of deliberation among the leaders was now as to the propriety of its continued tenure. The country, they felt assured, would soon be overrun with the state troops. They had no fears of discovery from this source, prior to the affair of the massacre of the guard, which rendered necessary the secretion of many in their retreat, who, before that time, were perfectly unconscious of its existence. In addition to this, it was now known to the pedler and the idiot, neither of whom had any reason for secrecy on the subject in the event of their being able to make it public. The difficulty, with regard to the two latter, subjected them to no small risk of suffering from the ultimate necessities of the rogues, and there was a sharp and secret consultation as to the mode of disposing of the two captives; but so much blood had been already spilled, that the sense of the majority revolted at the further resort to that degree of violence—particularly, too, when it was recollected that they could only hold their citadel for a certain and short period of time. It was determined, therefore, that so long as they themselves continued in their hiding-place, Bunce and Chub should, perforce, continue prisoners. Having so determined, and made their arrangements accordingly, the two last-made captives were assigned a cell, chosen with reference to its greater security than the other portions of their hold—one sufficiently tenacious of its trust, it would seem, to answer well its purpose.

In the meantime, the sufferings of Lucy Munro were such as may well be understood from the character of her feelings, as we have heretofore beheld their expression. In her own apartment—her cell, we may style it, for she was in a sort of honorable bondage—she brooded with deep melancholy over the narrative given by the pedler. She had no reason to doubt its correctness, and, the more she meditated upon it, the more acute became her misery. But a day intervened, and the trial of Ralph Colleton must take place; and, without her evidence, she was well aware there could be no hope of his escape from the doom of felony— from the death of shame and physical agony. The whole picture grew up before her excited fancy. She beheld the assembled crowd—she saw him borne to execution—and her senses reeled beneath the terrible conjurations of her fancy. She threw herself prostrate upon her couch, and strove not to think, but in vain. Her mind, growing hourly more and more intensely excited, at length almost maddened, and she grew conscious herself—the worst of all kinds of consciousness—that her reason was no longer secure in its sovereignty. It was with a strong effort of the still-firm will that she strove to meditate the best mode of rescuing the victim from the death suspended above him; and she succeeded, while deliberating on this object, in quieting and more subtle workings of her imagination.

Many were the thoughts which came into her brain in this examination. At one time she thought it not impossible to convey a letter, in which her testimony should be carefully set down; but the difficulty of procuring a messenger, and the doubt that such a statement would prove of any avail, decided her to seek for other means. An ordinary mind, and a moderate degree of interest in the fate of the individual, would have contented itself with some such step; but such a mind and such affections were not those of the high-souled and spirited Lucy. She dreaded not personal danger; and to rescue the youth, whom she so much idolized, from the doom that threatened him, she would have willingly dared to encounter that doom itself in its darkest forms. She determined, therefore, to rely chiefly upon herself in all efforts which she should make for the purpose in view; and her object, therefore, was to effect a return to the village in time to appear at the trial.

Yet how should this be done? She felt herself to be a captive; she knew the restraints upon her—and did not doubt that all her motions were sedulously observed. How then should she proceed? An agent was necessary; and, while deliberating with herself upon the difficulty thus assailing her at the outset, her ears were drawn to the distinct utterance of sounds, as of persons engaged in conversation, from the adjoining section of the rock.

One of the voices appeared familiar, and at length she distinctly made out her own name in various parts of the dialogue. She soon distinguished the nasal tones of the pedler, whose prison adjoined her own, separated only by a huge wall of earth and rock, the rude and jagged sides of which had been made complete, where naturally imperfect, for the purposes of a wall, by the free use of clay, which plastered in huge masses into the crevices and every fissure, was no inconsiderable apology for the more perfect structures of civilization.

Satisfied, at length, from what she heard, that the two so confined were friendly, she contrived to make them understand her contiguity, by speaking in tones sufficiently low as to be unheard beyond the apartment in which they were. In this way she was enabled to converse with the pedler, to whom all her difficulties were suggested, and to whom she did not hesitate to say that she knew that which would not fail to save the life of Colleton.

Bunce was not slow to devise various measures for the further promotion of the scheme, none of which, however, served the purpose of showing to either party how they should get out, and, but for the idiot, it is more than probable, despairing of success, they would at length have thrown aside the hope of doing anything for the youth as perfectly illusory.

But Chub came in as a prime auxiliar. From the first moment in which he heard the gentle tones of Lucy's voice, he had busied himself with his long nails and fingers in removing the various masses of clay which had been made to fill up sundry crevices of the intervening wall, and had so far succeeded as to detach a large square of the rock itself, which, with all possible pains and caution, he lifted from the embrasure. This done, he could distinguish objects, though dimly, from one apartment in the other, and thus introduced the parties to a somewhat nearer acquaintance with one another. Having done so much, he reposed from his labors, content with a sight of Lucy, on whom he continued to gaze with a fixed and stupid admiration.

He had pursued this work so noiselessly, and the maiden and Bunce had been so busily employed in discussing their several plans, that they had not observed the vast progress which Chub had made toward furnishing them with a better solution of their difficulties than any of their own previous cogitations. When Bunce saw how much had been done in one quarter, he applied himself resolutely to similar experiments on the opposite wall: and had the satisfaction of discovering that, as a dungeon, the dwelling in which they were required to remain was sadly deficient in some few of the requisites of security. With the aid of a small pick of iron, which Lucy handed him from her cell, he pierced the outer wall in several places, in which the clay had been required to do the offices of the rock, and had the satisfaction of perceiving, from the sudden influx of light in the apartment, succeeding his application of the instrument, that, with a small labor and in little time, they should be enabled to effect their escape, at least into the free air, and under the more genial vault of heaven.

Having made this discovery, it was determined that nothing more should be done until night, and having filled up the apertures which they had made, with one thing or another, they proceeded to consult, with more deliberate composure, on the future progress. It was arranged that the night should be permitted to set in fairly—that Lucy should retire early, having first taken care that Munro and her aunt, with whom she more exclusively consorted—Rivers having kept very much out of sight since her removal—should see her at the evening meal, without any departure from her usual habits. Bunce undertook to officiate as guide, and as Chub expressed himself willing to do whatever Miss Lucy should tell him, it was arranged that he should remain, occasionally making himself heard in his cell, as if in conversation, for as long a period after their departure as might be thought necessary to put them sufficiently in advance of pursuit—a requisition to which Chub readily gave his consent. He was the only one of the party who appeared to regard the whole matter with comparative indifference. He knew that a man was in danger of his life—he felt that he himself was in prison, and he said he would rather be out among the pine-trees—but there was no rush of feeling, such as troubled the heart of the young girl, whose spirit, clothing itself in all the noblest habiliments of humanity, lifted her up into the choicest superiority of character—nor had the dwarf that anxiety to do a service to his fellow, which made the pedler throw aside some of his more worldly characteristics—he did simply as he was bid, and had no further care.

Miss Lucy, he said, talked sweetly, like his mother, and Chub would do for Miss Lucy anything that she asked him. The principle of his government was simple, and having chosen a sovereign, he did not withhold his obedience. Thus stood the preparations of the three prisoners, when darkness—long-looked-for, and hailed with trembling emotions—at length came down over the silent homestead of the outlaws.

CHAPTER THIRTY-ONE

Escape

The night gathered apace, and the usual hour of repose had come. Lucy retired to her apartment with a trembling heart, but a courageous spirit, full of a noble determination to persevere in her project. Though full of fear, she never for a moment thought of retreat from the decision which she had made. Her character afforded an admirable model for the not unfrequent union that we find in woman, of shrinking delicacy with manly and efficient firmness.

Munro and Rivers, having first been assured that all was quiet, by a ramble which they took around their hiding-place, returned to the little chamber of the latter, such as we have described it in a previous portion of our narrative, and proceeded to the further discussion of their plans. The mind of the landlord was very ill at ease. He had arrived at that time of life when repose and a fixed habitation became necessary; and when, whatever may have been the habits of earlier manhood, the mind ceases to crave the excitements of adventure, and foregoes, or would fain forego, all its roving characteristics. To this state of feeling had he come, and the circumstances which now denied him the fruition of that prospect of repose which he had been promising himself so long, were regarded with no little restlessness and impatience. At the moment, the colleagues could make no positive arrangements for the future. Munro was loth to give up the property which, in one way or other, he had acquired in the neighborhood, and which it was impossible for him to remove to any other region; and, strange to say, a strong feeling of inhabitiveness—the love of home—if home he could be thought to have anywhere—might almost be considered a passion with his less scrupulous companion.

Thus situated, they lingered on in the hope that the military would soon be withdrawn from the neighborhood, as it could only be maintained at great expense by the state; and then, as the country was but nominally settled, and so sparsely as to scarcely merit any consideration, they felt assured that they might readily return to their old, or any practices, and without any further apprehension. The necessity, however, which made them thus deliberate, had the effect, at the same time, of impressing them with a gloomy spirit, not common to either of them.

"Let us see, Munro," said the more desperate ruffian; "there is, after all, less to apprehend than we first thought. In a week, and the court will be over; in another week, and the guard will be withdrawn; and for this period only will it be necessary that we should keep dark. I think we are now perfectly safe where we are. The only persons who know of our retreat, and might be troublesome, are safe in our possession. They will hardly escape until we let them, and before we do so we shall first see that they can give us no further necessity for caution. Of our own party, none are permitted to know the secrets of our hiding-place, but those in whom we may trust confidently. I have taken care to provide for the doubtful at some distance in the adjoining woods, exaggerating so greatly the danger of exposure, that they will hardly venture to be seen under any circumstances by anybody. Once let these two weeks go over, and I have no fears; we shall have no difficulties then."

"And what's to be done with the pedler and the fool? I say, Guy, there must be no more blood—I will not agree to it. The fact is, I feel more and more dismal every day since that poor fellow's death; and now that the youngster's taken, the thought is like fire in my brain, which tells me he may suffer for our crime."

"Why, you are grown parson. Would you go and save him, by giving up the true criminal? I shall look for it after this, and consider myself no longer in safety. If you go on in this manner, I shall begin to meditate an off-hand journey to the Mississippi."

"Ay, and the sooner we all go the better—though, to be plain, Guy, let this affair once blow over, and I care not to go with *you* any longer. We must then cut loose for ever, I am not a good man, I know—anything but that; but you have carried me on, step by step, until I am what I am afraid to name to myself. You found me a rogue—you have made me a—"

"Why do you hesitate? Speak it out, Munro; it is a large step gained toward reform when we learn to name truly our offences to ourselves."

"I dare not. The thought is sufficiently horrible without the thing. I hear some devil whispering it too frequently in my ears, to venture upon its utterance myself. But you—how you can live without feeling it, after your experience, which has been so much more dreadful than mine, I know not."

"I do feel it, Munro, but have long since ceased to fear it. The reiteration takes away the terror which is due rather to the novelty than to the offence. But when I began, I felt it. The first sleep I had after the affair of Jessup was full of tortures. The old man, I thought, lay beside me in my bed; his blood ran under me, and clotted around me, and fastened me there, while his gashed face kept peering into mine, and his eyes danced over me with the fierce light of a threatening comet. The dream nearly drove me mad, and mad I should have been had I gone to my prayers. I knew that, and chose a different course for relief."

"What was that?"

"I sought for another victim as soon after as I conveniently could. The one spectre superseded the other, until all vanished. They never trouble me now, though sometimes, in my waking moments, I have met them on the roadside, glaring at me from bush or tree, until I shouted at them fiercely, and then they were gone. These are my terrors, and they do sometimes unman me."

"They would do more with me; they would destroy me on the spot. But, let us have no more of this. Let us rather see if we can not do something towards making our visions more agreeable. Do you persevere in the sacrifice of this youngster? Must he die?"

"Am I a child, Walter Munro, that you ask me such a question? Must I again tell over the accursed story of my defeat and of his success? Must I speak of my thousand defeats—of my overthrown pretensions—my blasted hopes, where I had set my affections—upon which every feeling of my heart had been placed? Must I go over a story so full of pain and humiliation—must I describe my loss, in again placing before your eyes a portraiture like this? Look, man, look—and read my answer in the smile, which, denying me, teaches me, in this case, to arm myself with a denial as immutable as hers."

He placed before his companion the miniature of Edith, which he took from his bosom, where he seemed carefully to treasure it. He was again the envenomed and the excited savage which we have elsewhere seen him, and in which mood Munro knew well that nothing could be done with him in the shape of argument or entreaty. He went on:—

"Ask me no questions, Munro, so idle, so perfectly unnecessary as this. Fortune has done handsomely here. He falls through *me*, yet falls by the common hangman. What a double blow is this to both of them. I have been striving to imagine their feelings, and such a repast as that effort has procured me—I would not exchange it—no—not for worlds—for nothing less, Munro, than my restoration back to that society—to that place in society, from which my fierce passions, and your cruel promptings, and the wrongs of society itself, have for ever exiled me."

"And would you return, if you could do so?"

"To-morrow—to-night—this instant. I am sanguinary, Munro—revengeful—fierce—all that is bad, because I am not permitted to be better. My pride, my strong feelings and deeply absorbing mood—these have no other field for exercise. The love of home, the high ambition, which, had society done due common justice, and had not, in enslaving itself, dishonored and defrauded me—would, under other circumstances, have made me a patriot. My pride is even now to command the admiration of men—I never sought their love. Their approbation would have made me fearless and powerful in their defence and for their rights—their injustice makes me their enemy. My passions, unprovoked and unexaggerated by mortifying repulses, would have only been a warm and stimulating influence, perpetually working in their service—but, pressed upon and irritated as they have been they grew into so many wild beasts, and preyed upon the cruel or the careless keepers, whose gentle treatment and constant attention had tamed them into obedient servants. Yet, would I could, even now, return to that condition in which there might be hope. The true spectre of the criminal—such as I am—the criminal chiefly from the crimes and injustice of society, not forgetting the education of my boyhood, which grew out of the same crimes, and whose most dreadful lesson is selfishness—is despair! The black waters once past, the blacker hills rise between, and there is no return to those regions of hope, which, once lost, are lost for ever. This is the true punishment—the worst punishment which man inflicts upon his fellow—the felony of public opinion. The curse of society is no unfit illustration of that ban which its faith holds forth as the penal doom of the future. There is no return!"

The dialogue, mixed up thus, throughout, with the utterance of opinions on the part of the outlaw, many of which were true or founded in truth, yet coupled with many false deductions—was devoted, for some little while longer, to the discussion of their various necessities and plans for the future. The night had considerably advanced in this way, when, of a sudden, their ears were assailed with an eldritch screech, like that of the owl, issuing from one of the several cells around them.

The quick sense of Rivers immediately discerned the voice of the idiot, and without hesitation he proceeded to that division of the rock which contained the two prisoners. To each of these apartments had been assigned a sentinel, or watch, whose own place of abode—while covered completely and from sight, and in all respects furnishing a dwelling, though rather a confined one for himself—enabled him to attend the duty assigned him without himself being seen. The night had been fairly set in, when Bunce, with the aid of Chub Williams, with all due caution proceeded to his task, and with so much success, that, in the course of a couple of hours, they had succeeded, not only in making a fair outlet for themselves, but for Lucy Munro too.

The watchman, in the meantime, holding his duty as merely nominal, gave himself as little trouble as possible; and believing all things quiet, had, after a little while, insinuated himself into the good graces of as attractive a slumber as may usually be won in the warm summer season in the south, by one to whom a nightwatch is a peculiarly ungracious exercise. Before this conclusion, however, he looked forth every now and then, and deceived by the natural stillness of earth and sky, he committed the further care of the hours, somewhat in anticipation of the time, to the successor who was to relieve him on the watch.

Without being conscious of this decision in their favor, and ignorant entirely of the sentinel himself, the pedler fortunately chose this period for his own departure with the young lady whom he was to escort; and who, with probably far less fear than her gallant, did not scruple, for a single instant, to go forth under his guidance. Chub took his instructions from the lips of Lucy, and promised the most implicit obedience.

They had scarcely been well gone when the sentinels were changed, and one something more tenacious of discipline, or something less drowsy than his predecessor, took his place. After muttering at intervals, as directed, for the space of an hour, probably, from the time at which his companion had departed, Chub thought it only prudent to sally forth too. Accordingly, ascending to the break in the wall, through which his companion had made his way, the urchin emerged from the cavern at the unlucky moment, when, at some ten or fifteen paces in front of him, the sentinel came forth from his niche to inspect the order of his watch. Chub saw his adversary first, and his first impulse originated the scream which drew the attention of Rivers, as already narrated. The outlaw rushed quickly to the scene of difficulty, and before the sentinel had well recovered from the astonishment occasioned by the singularly sudden appearance and wild screech of the urchin.

"Why, what is this, Briggs; what see you?" was the hasty inquiry of Rivers.

"There, sir, there," exclaimed the watch, still half bewildered, and pointing to the edge of the hill, where, in a condition seemingly of equal incertitude with himself, stood the imbecile.

"Seize upon him—take him at once—let him not escape you!" were the hasty orders of the outlaw. Briggs set forward, but his approach had the effect of giving determination also to Chub; who, just as the pursuer thought himself sure of his captive, and was indeed indirectly upon him, doubled himself up, as it were into a complete ball, and without effort rolled headlong down the hill; gathering upon his feet as he attained the level, seemingly unhurt, and with all the agility of the monkey.

"Shall I shoot, sir?" was the inquiry of Briggs, as the urchin stood off, laughing wildly at his good fortune.

"Now, don't"—was the cry—"Now, don't"—was the exclamation of Chub himself, who, however, trusting nothing to the effect of his entreaty, ran vigorously on his way.

"Yes, shoot him down," was the sudden exclamation of Munro; but Rivers struck the poised weapon upward in the hands of the sentinel, to the astonishment, not less of him than of the landlord.

"No—let him live, Munro. Let him live. Such as he should be spared. Is he not alone—without fellowship—scorned—an outcast—without sympathy—like myself. Let him live, let him live!"

The word of mercy from his lips utterly confounded his companion. But, remembering that Rivers was a monster of contradictions, Munro turned away, and gave directions to see after the other prisoners.

A few moments sufficed for this, and the panic was universal among the inmates of the rock. The secret was now lost unless immediate pursuit could avail in the recovery of the fugitives. This pursuit was immediately undertaken, and both Rivers and Munro, taking different directions, and dispersing their whole force about the forest, set off on the search.

Apprehensive of pursuit, the policy of Bunce, to whom Lucy gave up the entire direction of their flight, was determined upon with not a little judgment. Assured that his pursuers would search chiefly on the direct route between their abode and the village, to which they would necessarily surmise the flight was directed, he boldly determined upon a course, picked sinuously out, obliquing largely from the true direction, which, while it would materially lengthen the distance, would at least secure them, he thought, from the danger of contact with the scouring party.

By no means ignorant of the country, in and about which he had frequently travelled in the pursuit of trade, he contrived, in this way, completely to mislead the pursuers; and the morning found them still some distance from the village, but in a direction affording few chances of interruption in their contemplated approach to it.

Lucy was dreadfully fatigued, and a frequent sense of weariness almost persuaded her to lay down life itself in utter exhaustion: but the encouraging words of the pedler, and the thought of *his* peril, for whose safety—though herself hopeless of all besides—she would willingly peril all, restored her, and invigorated her to renewed effort.

At the dawn of day they approached a small farmhouse, some of the inmates of which happened to know Lucy; and, though they looked somewhat askant at her companion, and wondered not a little at the circumstance of her travelling at such a time of night, yet, as she was generally well respected, their surmises and scruples were permitted to sleep; and, after a little difficulty, they were persuaded to lend her the family pony and side-saddle, with the view to the completion of her journey. After taking some slight refreshment, she hurried on; Bunce, keeping the road afoot, alongside, with all the patient docility of a squire of the middle ages; and to the great satisfaction of all parties, they arrived in sight of the village just as Counsellor Pippin, learned in the law, was disputing with the state attorney upon the non-admissibility of certain points of testimony, which it was the policy of the former to exclude.

CHAPTER THIRTY-TWO

Doom

The village of Chestatee was crowded with visiters of all descriptions. Judges and lawyers, soldiers and citizens and farmers—all classes were duly represented, and a more wholesome and subordinate disposition in that quarter, may be inferred as duly resulting from the crowd. Curiosity brought many to the spot from portions of country twenty, thirty, and even forty miles off—for, usually well provided with good horses, the southron finds a difference of ten or twenty miles no great matter.

Such had been the reputation of the region here spoken of, not less for its large mineral wealth than for the ferocious character of those in its neighborhood, that numbers, who would not otherwise have adventured, now gladly took advantage of the great excitement, and the presence of so many, to examine a section of country of which they had heard so much. There came the planter, of rather more wealth than his neighbors, solicitous for some excitement and novelty to keep himself from utter stagnation. There came the farmer, discontented with his present abiding-place, and in search of a new spot of more promise, in which to drive stakes and do better. The lawyer, from a neighboring county, in search of a cause; the creditor in search of his runaway debtor—the judge and the jury also adding something, not less to the number than the respectability of the throng.

The grand-jury had found several bills, and most of them for the more aggravated offences in the estimation of the law. Rivers, Munro, Blundell, Forrester, were all severally and collectively included in their inquiries; but as none of the parties were to be found for the present at least, as one of them had been removed to another and higher jurisdiction, the case of most importance left for trial was that which charged Colleton with Forrester's murder.

There was no occasion for delay; and, in gloomy and half-desponding mood, though still erect and unshrinking to the eye of the beholder, Ralph refused the privilege of a traverse, and instructed Pippin to go on with the case. The lawyer himself had not the slightest objection to this procedure, for, not to be harsh in our estimate of his humanities, there is no reason to believe that he regarded for a single instant the value of his client's life, but as its preservation was to confer credit upon his capacity as his legal friend and adviser. The issue was consequently made up without delay—the indictment was read—the prisoner put himself upon God and the country, according to the usual forms, and the case proceeded.

The general impression of the spectators was decidedly in favor of the accused. His youth—the noble bearing—the ease, the unobtrusive confidence—the gentle expression, pliant and, though sad, yet entirely free from anything like desponding weakness—all told in his favor. He was a fine specimen of the southern gentleman—the true nobleman of that region, whose pride of character is never ostentatiously displayed and is only to be felt in the influence which it invariably exercises over all with whom it may have contact or connection. Though firm in every expression, and manly in every movement, there was nothing in the habit and appearance of Ralph, which, to the eye of those around, savored of the murderer. There was nothing ruffianly or insincere. But, as the testimony proceeded—when the degree of intimacy was shown which had existed between himself and the murdered man—when they heard that Forrester had brought him wounded and fainting to his home—had attended him—had offered even to fight for him with Rivers; when all these facts were developed, in connection with the sudden flight of the person so befriended—on the same night with him who had befriended him—he having a knowledge of the proposed departure of the latter—and with the finding of the bloody dagger marked with the youth's initials—the feeling of sympathy very perceptibly underwent a change. The people, proverbially fickle, and, in the present instance justifiably so, veered round to the opposite extreme of opinion, and a confused buzz around, sometimes made sufficiently audible to all senses, indicated the unfavorable character of the change. The witnesses were closely examined, and the story was complete and admirably coherent. The presumptions, as they were coupled together, were conclusive; and, when it was found that not a solitary witness came forward even to say that the accused was a man of character and good connections—a circumstance which could not materially affect the testimony as it stood, but which, wanting, gave it additional force— the unhappy youth, himself, felt that all was over.

A burning flush, succeeded by a deathlike paleness, came over his face for a moment—construed by those around into a consciousness of guilt; for, where the prejudices of men become active, all appearances of change, which go not to affect the very foundation of the bias, are only additional proofs of what they have before believed. He rested his head upon his hands in deep but momentary agony. What were his feelings then? With warm, pure emotions; with a pride only limited by a true sense of propriety; with an ambition whose eye was sunward ever; with affections which rendered life doubly desirable, and which made love a high and holy aspiration: with these several and predominating feelings struggling in his soul, to be told of such a doom; to be stricken from the respect of his fellows; to forfeit life, and love, and reputation; to undergo the punishment of the malefactor, and to live in memory only as a felon—ungrateful, foolish, fiendish—a creature of dishonest passions, and mad and merciless in their exercise!

The tide of thought which bore to his consciousness all these harrowing convictions, was sudden as the wing of the lightning, and nearly shattered, in that single instant, the towering manhood whose high reachings had attracted it. But the pride consequent to his education, and the society in which he had lived, came to his relief; and, after the first dreadful agony of soul, he again stood erect, and listened, seemingly unmoved, to the defences set up by his counsel.

But how idle, even to his mind, desirous as he must have been of every species of defence, were all the vainglorious mouthings of the pettifogger! He soon discovered that the ambition of Pippin chiefly consisted in the utterance of his speech. He saw, too, in a little while, that the nonsense of the lawyer had not even the solitary merit—if such it be—of being extemporaneous; and in the slow and monotonous delivery of a long string of stale truisms, not bearing any analogy to the case in hand, he perceived the dull elaborations of the closet.

But such was not the estimate of the lawyer himself. He knew what he was about; and having satisfied himself that the case was utterly hopeless, he was only solicitous that the people should see that he could still make a speech. He well knew that his auditory, perfectly assured with himself of the hopelessness of the defence, would give him the credit of having made the most of his materials, and this was all he wanted. In the course of his exhortations, however, he was unfortunate enough to make an admission for his client which was, of itself, fatal; and his argument thence became unnecessary. He admitted that the circumstances sufficiently established the charge of killing, but proceeded, however, to certain liberal assumptions, without any ground whatever, of provocation on the part of Forrester, which made his murder only matter of self-defence on the side of the accused, whose crime therefore became justifiable: but Ralph, who had for some time been listening with manifest impatience to sundry other misrepresentations, not equally evil with this, but almost equally annoying, now rose and interrupted him; and, though the proceeding was something informal, proceeded to correct the statement.

"No one, may it please your honor, and you, gentlemen, now presiding over my fate, can be more conscious than myself from the nature of the evidence given in this case, of the utter hopelessness of any defence which may be offered on my behalf. But, while recognising, in their fullest force, the strong circumstantial proofs of crime which you have heard, I may be permitted to deny for myself what my counsel has been pleased to admit for me. To say that I have *not* been guilty of this crime, is only to repeat that which was said when I threw myself upon the justice of the country. I denied any knowledge of it then—I deny any knowledge of, or participation in it, now. I am *not* guilty of this killing, whether with or without justification. The blood of the unfortunate man Forrester is *not* upon my hands; and, whatever may be your decree this day, of this sweet consciousness nothing can deprive me.

"I consider, may it please your honor, that my counsel, having virtually abandoned my cause, I have the right to go on with it myself—"

But Pippin, who had been dreadfully impatient heretofore, started forward with evident alarm.

"Oh, no—no, your honor—my client—Mr. Colleton—how can you think such a thing? I have not, your honor, abandoned the case. On the contrary, your honor will remember that it was while actually proceeding with the case that I was interrupted."

The youth, with a singular degree of composure, replied:—

"Your honor will readily understand me, though the gentleman of the bar does not. I conceive him not only to have abandoned the case, your honor, but actually to have joined hand and hand with the prosecuting counsel. It is true, sir, that he still calls himself *my* counsel—and still, under that name, presumes to harangue, as he alleges, in my behalf; but, when he violates the truth, not less than my instructions—when he declares all that is alleged against me in that paper *to be true,* all of which *I* declare *to be false*—when he admits me to be guilty of a crime of which I am *not* guilty—I say that he has not only abaodoned my case, but that he has betrayed the trust reposed in him. What, your honor, must the jury infer from the confession which he has just made?—what, but that in my conference with him *I* have made the same confession? It becomes necessary, therefore, may it please your honor, not only that I take from him, thus openly, the power which I confided to him, but that I call upon your honor to demand from him, upon oath, whether such an admission was ever made to him by me. I know that my own words will avail me nothing here—I also know why they should not—but I am surely entitled to require that he should speak out, as to the truth, when *his* misrepresentations are to make weight against me in future. His oath, that I made no such confession to him, will avail nothing for my defence, but will avail greatly with those who, from present appearances, are likely to condemn me. I call upon him, may it please your honor, as matter of right, that he should be *sworn* to this particular. This, your honor will perceive, if my assertion be true, is the smallest justice which he can do me; beyond this I will ask and suggest nothing—leaving it to your own mind how far the license of his profession should be permitted to one who thus not only abandons, but betrays and misrepresents his client."

The youth was silent, and Pippin rose to speak in his defence. Without being sworn, he admitted freely that such a confession had not been made, but that he had inferred the killing from the nature of the testimony, which he thought conclusive on the point; that his object had been to suggest a probable difficulty between the parties, in which he would have shown Forrester as the aggressor. He bungled on for some time longer in this manner, but, as he digressed again into the defence of the accused, Ralph again begged to interrupt him.

"I think it important, may it please your honor, that the gentleman should be sworn as to the simple fact which he has uttered. *I want it on record*, that, at some future day, the few who have any interest in my fate should feel no mortifying doubts of my innocence when reminded of the occurrence—which this strange admission, improperly circulated, might otherwise occasion. Let him swear, your honor, to the fact: this, I think, I may require."

After a few moments of deliberation, his honor decided that the demand was one of right, strictly due, not merely to the prisoner and to the abstract merits of the case, but also to the necessity which such an event clearly occasioned, of establishing certain governing principles for restraining those holding situations so responsible, who should so far wilfully betray their trusts. The lawyer was made to go through the humiliating process, and then subjected to a sharp reprimand from the judge; who, indeed, might have well gone further, in actually striking his name from the rolls of court.

It was just after this interesting period in the history of the trial— and when Pippin, who could not be made to give up the case, as Ralph had required, was endeavoring to combat with the attorney of the state some incidental points of doctrine, and to resist their application to certain parts of the previously, recorded testimony—that our heroine, Lucy Munro, attended by her trusty squire, Bunce, made her appearance in the courthouse.

She entered the hall more dead than alive. The fire was no longer in her eye—a thick haze had overspread its usually rich and lustrous expression; her form trembled with the emotion—the strong and struggling emotion of her soul; and fatigue had done much toward the general enervation of her person. The cheek was pale with the innate consciousness; the lips were blanched, and slightly parted, as if wanting in the muscular exercise which could bring them together. She tottered forward to the stand upon which the witnesses were usually assembled, and to which her course had been directed, and for a few moments after her appearance in the courtroom her progress had been as one stunned by a sudden and severe blow.

But, when roused by the confused hum of human voices around her, she ventured to look up, and her eye, as if by instinct, turned upon the dark box assigned for the accused—she again saw the form, in her mind and eye, of almost faultless mould and excellence—then there was no more weakness, no more struggle. Her eye kindled, the color rushed into her cheeks, a sudden spirit reinvigorated her frame; and, with clasped hands, she boldly ascended the small steps which led to the stand from which her evidence was to be given, and declared her ability, in low tones, almost unheard but by the judge, to furnish matter of interest and importance to the defence. Some little demur as to the formality of such a proceeding, after the evidence had been fairly closed, took place between the counsel; but, fortunately for justice, the judge was too wise and too good a man to limit the course of truth to prescribed rules, which could not be affected by a departure, in the present instance, from their restraints. The objection was overruled, and the bold but trembling girl was called upon for her testimony.

A new hope had been breathed into the bosoms of the parties most concerned, on the appearance of this interruption to the headlong and impelling force of the circumstances so fatally arrayed against the prisoner. The pedler was overjoyed, and concluded that the danger was now safely over. The youth himself felt his spirit much lighter in his bosom, although he himself knew not the extent of that testimony in his favor which Lucy was enabled to give. He only knew that she could account for his sudden flight on the night of the murder, leading to a fair presumption that he had not premeditated such an act; and knew not that it was in her power to overthrow the only fact, among the circumstances arrayed against him, by which they had been so connected as to make out his supposed guilt.

Sanguine, herself, that the power was in her to effect the safety of the accused, Lucy had not for a moment considered the effect upon others, more nearly connected with her than the youth, of the development which she was prepared to make. These considerations were yet to come.

The oath was administered; she began her narration, but at the very outset, the difficulties of her situation beset her. How was she to save the man she loved? How, but by showing the guilt of her uncle? How was she to prove that the dirk of the youth was not in his possession at the time of the murder? By showing that, just before that time, it was in the possession of Munro, who was setting forth for the express purpose of murdering the very man, now accused and held guilty of the same crime. The fearful gathering of thoughts and images, thus, without preparation, working in her mind, again destroyed the equilibrium by which her truer senses would have enforced her determination to proceed. Her head swam, her words were confused and incoherent, and perpetually contradictory. The hope which her presence had inspired as suddenly departed; and pity and doubt were the prevailing sentiments of the spectators.

After several ineffectual efforts to proceed, she all at once seemed informed of the opinions around her, and gathering new courage from the dreadful thought now forcing itself upon her mind, that what she had said had done nothing toward her object, she exclaimed impetuously, advancing to the judge, and speaking alternately from him to the jury and the counsel—

"He is *not* guilty of this crime, believe me. I may not say what I know—I can not—you would not expect me to reveal it. It would involve others whom I dare not name. I must not say *that*—but, believe me, Mr. Colleton is not guilty—he did not commit the murder—it was somebody else—I know, I will swear, he had no hand in the matter."

"Very well, my young lady, I have no doubt you think, and honestly believe, all that you say; but what reasons have you for this bold assertion in the teeth of all the testimony which has already been given? You must not be surprised, if we are slow in believing what you tell us, until you can show upon what grounds you make your statement. How know you that the prisoner did not commit this crime? Do you know who did? Can you reveal any facts for our knowledge? This is what you must do. Do not be terrified—speak freely—officer! a chair for the lady—tell us all that you know—keep nothing back—remember, you are sworn to speak *the truth*—the *whole truth*."

The judge spoke kindly and encouragingly, while, with considerable emphasis, he insisted upon a full statement of all she knew. But the distress of the poor girl increased with every moment of thought, which warned her of the predicament in which such a statement must necessarily involve her uncle.

"Oh, how can I speak all this? How can I tell that which must destroy him—"

"Him?—Of whom do you speak, lady? Who is *he*?" inquired the attorney of the state.

"He—who?—Oh, no, I can say nothing. I can tell you nothing. I know nothing but that Mr. Colleton is *not* guilty. He struck no blow at Forrester. I am sure of it—some other hand—some other person. How can you believe that he would do so?"

There was no such charitable thought for him, however, in the minds of those who heard—as how should there be? A whispering dialogue now took place between the judge and the counsel, in which, while they evidently looked upon her as little better than demented with her love for the accused, they still appeared to hold it due to justice, not less than to humanity, to obtain from her every particular of testimony bearing on the case, which, by possibility, she might really have in her possession. Not that they really believed that she knew anything which might avail the prisoner. Regarding her as individually and warmly interested in his life, they looked upon her appearance, and the evidence which she tendered—if so it might be styled—as solely intended to provoke sympathy, gain time, or, possibly, as the mere ebullition of feelings so deeply excited as to have utterly passed the bounds of all restraining reason. The judge, who was a good, not less than a sensible man, undertook, in concluding this conference, to pursue the examination himself, with the view to bringing out such portions of her information as delicacy or some other more influential motive might persuade her to conceal.

"You are sure, Miss Munro, of the innocence of the prisoner so sure that you are willing to swear to it. Such is *your* conviction, at least; for, unless you saw the blow given by another hand, or could prove Mr. Colleton to have been elsewhere at the time of the murder, of course you could not, of a certainty, swear to any such fact. You are not now to say whether you believe him *capable* of such an act or not. You are to say whether you *know* of any circumstances which shall acquit him of the charge, or furnish a plausible reason, why others, not less than yourself, should have a like reason with yourself to believe him innocent. Can you do this, Miss Munro? Can you show anything, in this chain of circumstances, against him, which, of your own knowledge, you can say to be untrue? Speak out, young lady, and rely upon every indulgence from the court."

Here the judge recapitulated all the evidence which had been furnished against the prisoner. The maiden listened with close attention, and the difficulties of her situation became more and more obvious. Finding her slow to answer, though her looks were certainly full of meaning, the presiding officer took another course for the object which he had in view. He now proceeded to her examination in the following form:—

"You know the prisoner?"

"I do."

"You knew the murdered man?"

"Perfectly."

"Were they frequently together since the appearance of the prisoner in these regions?"

"Frequently."

"At the house in which you dwell?"

"Yes."

"Were they together on the day preceding the night of the murder?"

"They were—throughout the better portion of it."

"Did they separate at your place of residence, and what was the employment of the prisoner subsequently on the same day?"

"They did separate while at our house, Mr. Colleton retiring at an early hour of the evening to his chamber."

"So far, Miss Munro, your answers correspond directly with the evidence, and now come the important portions. You will answer briefly and distinctly. After that, did you see anything more of the prisoner, and know you of his departure from the house—the hour of the night—the occasion of his going—and the circumstances attending it?"

These questions were, indeed, all important to the female delicacy of the maiden, as well as to the prisoner, and as her eye sunk in confusion, and as her cheek paled and kindled with the innate consciousness, the youth, who had hitherto been silent, now rose, and without the slightest hesitancy of manner, requested of the maiden that she would say no more.

"See you not, your honor, that her mind wavers—that she speaks and thinks wildly? I am satisfied that though she might say something, your honor, in accounting for my strange flight, yet, as that constitutes but a small feature in the circumstances against me, what she can allege will avail me little. Press her no farther, therefore, I entreat you. Let her retire. Her word can do me no good, and I would not, that, for my sake and life, she should feel, for a single instant an embarrassment of spirit, which, though it be honorable in its character, must necessarily be distressing in its exercise. Proceed with your judgment, I pray you—whatever it may be; I am now ready for the worst, and though innocent as the babe unborn of the crime urged against me, I am not afraid to meet its consequences. I am not unwilling to die."

"But you must *not* die—they will not—they *can not* find you guilty! How know they you are guilty? Who dares say you are guilty, when *I* know you are innocent? Did I not see you fly? Did I not send you on your way—was it not to escape from murder yourself that you flew, and how should you have been guilty of that crime of which you were the destined victim yourself? Oh, no—no! you are not guilty—and the dagger—I heard that!—that is not true—oh, no, the dagger—you dropt it—"

The eye of the inspired girl was caught by a glance—a single glance—from one at the opposite corner of the court-room, and that glance brought her back to the full consciousness of the fearful development whe was about to make. A decrepit old woman, resting with bent form upon a staff, which was planted firmly before her, seemed wrapped in the general interest pervading the court. The woman was huge of frame and rough of make; her face was large and swollen, and the tattered cap and bonnet, the coarse and soiled materials which she wore, indicated one of the humblest caste in the country. Her appearance attracted no attention, and she was unmarked by all around; few having eyes for anything but the exciting business under consideration.

But the disguise did not conceal her uncle from the glance of his niece. That one look had the desired effect—the speech was arrested before its conclusion, and the spectators, now more than ever assured of the partial sanity of the witness, gave up any doubts which had previously begun to grow in behalf of the accused. A second look of the landlord was emphatic enough for the purpose of completely silencing her farther evidence. She read in its fearful expression, as plainly as if spoken in words—"The next syllable you utter is fatal to your uncle—your father. Now speak, Lucy, if you can."

For a single moment she was dumb and stationary—her eye turned from her uncle to the prisoner. Horror, and the agonies natural to the strife in her bosom, were in its wild expression, and, with a single cry of "I can not—I must not save him!" from her pallid lips, she sunk down senseless upon the floor, and was borne out by several of the more sympathizing spectators.

There was nothing now to delay the action of the court. The counsel had closed with the argument, and the judge proceeded in his charge to the jury. His remarks were rather favorable than otherwise to the prisoner. He dwelt upon his youth—his manliness—the seeming excellence of his education, and the propriety which had marked his whole behavior on trial. These he spoke of as considerations which must, of course, make the duty, which they had to perform, more severely painful to all. But they could not do away with the strong and tenacious combination of circumstances against him. These were all closely knit, and all tended strongly to the conviction of the guilt of the accused. Still they were circumstantial; and the doubts of the jury were, of course, so many arguments on the side of mercy. He concluded.

But the jury had no doubts. How should they doubt? They deliberated, indeed, for form's sake, but not long. In a little while they returned to their place, and the verdict was read by the clerk.

"Guilty."

"Guilty," responded the prisoner, and for a moment his head dropped upon his clasped hands, and his frame shivered as with an ague.

"Guilty—guilty—Oh, my father—Edith—Edith—have I lived for this?"

There was no other sign of human weakness. He arose with composure, and followed, with firm step, the officer to his dungeon. His only thought was of the sorrows and the shame of others—of those of whom he had been the passion and the pride—of that father's memory and name, of whom he had been the cherished hope—of that maiden of whom he had been the cherished love. His firm, manly bearing won the esteem of all those who, nevertheless, at the same moment, had few if any doubts of the justice of his doom.

CHAPTER THIRTY-THREE

Prayers and Promises

Ralph Colleton was once more in his dungeon—alone—and without hope. For a moment during the progress of his trial, and at the appearance of Lucy, he deemed it possible that some providential fortune might work a change in the aspect of things, favorable to his escape from what, to his mind, was far worse than any thought of death, in the manner of his death. But when, after a moment of reflection, he perceived that the feminine delicacy of the maiden must suffer from any further testimony from her lips—when he saw that, most probably, in the minds of all who heard her narration, the circumstance of her appearance in his chamber and at such an hour of the night, and for any object, would be fatal to her reputation—when he perceived this consciousness, too, weighing down even to agony the soul of the still courageous witness—the high sense of honor which had always prompted him, not less than that chivalrous consideration of the sex taught in the south among the earliest lessons of society to its youth—compelled him to interpose, and prevent, if possible, all further utterance, which, though possibly all-important to him, would be fatally destructive to her.

He did so at his own self-sacrifice! We have seen how the poor girl was silenced. The result was, that Ralph Colleton was again in his dungeon—hope shut out from its walls, and a fearful death and ignominy written upon them. When the officers attending him had retired—

when he heard the bolt shot, and saw that the eyes of curiosity were excluded—the firm spirit fled which had supported him. There was a passing weakness of heart which overcame its energies and resolve, and he sank down upon the single chair allotted to his prison. He buried his face in his hands, and the warm tears gushed freely through his fingers. While thus weeping, like a very child, he heard the approach of footsteps without. In a moment he recovered all his manliness and calm. The traces of his weakness were sedulously brushed from his cheeks, and the handkerchief employed for the purpose studiously put out of sight. He was not ashamed of the pang, but he was not willing that other eyes should behold it. Such was the nature of his pride—the pride of strength, moral strength, and superiority over those weaknesses, which, however natural they may be, are nevertheless not often held becoming in the man.

It was the pedler, Bunce, who made his appearance—choosing, with a feature of higher characteristic than would usually have been allotted him, rather to cheer the prison hours of the unfortunate, than to pursue his own individual advantages; which, at such a time, might not have been inconsiderable. The worthy pedler was dreadfully disappointed in the result of his late adventure. He had not given himself any trouble to inquire into the nature of those proofs which Lucy Munro had assured him were in her possession; but satisfied as much by his own hope as by her assurance, that all would be as he wished it, he had been elevated to a pitch of almost indecorous joy, which strongly contrasted with his present depression. He had little now to say in the way of consolation, and that little was coupled with so much that was unjust to the maiden, as to call forth, at length, the rebuke of Colleton.

"Forbear on this subject, my good sir—she did what she could, and what she might have said would not have served me much. It was well she said no more. Her willingness—her adventuring so much in my behalf—should alone be sufficient to protect her from everything like blame. But tell me, Bunce, what has become of her—where is she gone, and who is now attending her?"

"Why, they took her back to the old tavern. A great big woman took her there, and looked after her. I did go and had a sight on her, and there, to be sure, was Munro's wife, though her I did see, I'll be sworn in among the rocks where they shut us up."

"And was Munro there?"

"Where—in the rocks?"

"No—in the tavern?—You say his wife had come back—did he trust himself there?"

"I rather guess not—seeing as how he'd stand a close chance of 'quaintance with the rope. No, neither him, nor Rivers, nor any of the regulators—thank the powers—ain't to be seen nowhere. They're all off—up into the nation, I guess, or off, down in Alabam by this time, clear enough."

"And who did you see at the rocks, and what men were they that made you prisoners?"

"Men—if I said men, I was 'nation out, I guess. Did I say men?"

"I understood you so."

"'Twan't men at all. Nothing better than women, and no small women neither. Didn't see a man in the neighborhood, but Chub, and he ain't no man neither."

"What is he?"

"Why, for that matter, he's neither one thing nor another—nothing, no how. A pesky little creature! What they call a hobbe-de-hoy will suit for his name sooner than any other that I know on. For he ain't a man and he ain't a boy; but jest a short, half-grown up chunk of a fellow, with bunchy shoulders, and a big head, with a mouth like an oven, and long lap ears like saddle flaps."

In this manner the pedler informed Ralph of all those previous particulars with which he had not till then been made acquainted. This having been done, and the dialogue having fairly reached its termination—and the youth exhibiting some strong symptoms of weariness—Bunce took his departure for the present, not, however, without again proffering his services. These Ralph did not scruple to accept—giving him, at the same time, sundry little commissions, and among them a message of thanks and respectful consideration to Miss Munro.

She, in the meanwhile, had, upon fainting in the court-room, been borne off in a state of utter insensibility, to the former residence of Munro, to which place, as the pedler has already informed us, the wife of the landlord had that very morning returned, resuming, precisely as before, all the previous order of her domestic arrangements. The reason for this return may be readily assigned. The escape of the pedler and of Lucy from their place of temporary confinement had completely upset all the prior arrangements of the outlaws. They now conceived it no longer safe as a retreat; and failing as they did to overtake the fugitives, it was determined that, in the disguises which had been originally suggested for their adoption, they should now venture into the village, as many of them as were willing, to obtain that degree of information which would enable them to judge what further plans to adopt.

As Rivers had conjectured, Chub Williams, so far from taking for the village, had plunged deeper into the woods, flying to former and well-known haunts, and regarding the face of man as that of a natural enemy. The pedler had seen none but women, or those so disguised as such as to seem none other than what they claimed to be—while Lucy had been permitted to see none but her uncle and aunt, and one or two persons she had never met before.

Under these circumstances, Rivers individually felt no apprehensions that his wild refuge would be searched; but Munro, something older, less sanguine, and somewhat more timid than his colleague, determined no longer to risk it; and having, as we have seen, effectually checked the utterance of that evidence which, in the unconscious excitation of his niece, must have involved him more deeply in the meshes of the law, besides indicating his immediate and near neighborhood, he made his way, unobserved, from the village, having first provided for her safety, and as he had determined to keep out of the way himself, having brought his family back to their old place of abode.

He had determined on this course from a variety of considerations. Nothing, he well knew, could affect his family. He had always studiously kept them from any participation in his offences. The laws had no terror for them; and, untroubled by any process against him, they could still remain and peaceably possess his property, of which he well knew, in the existing state of society in the South, no legal outlawry of himself would ever avail to deprive them. This could not have been his hope in their common flight. Such a measure, too, would only have impeded his progress, in the event of his pursuit, and have burdened him with encumbrances which would perpetually involve him in difficulty. He calculated differently his chances. His hope was to be able, when the first excitements had overblown, to return to the village, and at least quietly to effect such a disposition of his property, which was not inconsiderable, as to avoid the heavy and almost entire loss which would necessarily follow any other determination.

In all this, however, it may be remarked that the reasonings of Rivers, rather than his own, determined his conduct. That more adventurous ruffian had, from his superior boldness and greater capacities in general, acquired a singular and large influence over his companion: he governed him, too, as much by his desire of gain as by any distinct superiority which he himself possessed; he stimulated his avarice with the promised results of their future enterprises in the same region after the passing events were over; and thus held him still in that fearful bondage of subordinate villany whose inevitable tendency is to make the agent the creature, and finally the victim. The gripe which, in a moral sense, and with a slight reference to character, Rivers had upon the landlord, was as tenacious as that of death—but with this difference, that it was death prolonged through a fearful, and, though not a protracted, yet much too long a life.

The determination of Munro was made accordingly; and, following hard upon the flight of Lucy from the rocks, we find the landlady quietly reinstated in her old home as if nothing had happened. Munro did not, however, return to the place of refuge; he had no such confidence in circumstances as Rivers; his fears had grown active in due proportion with his increase of years; and, with the increased familiarity with crime, had grown up in his mind a corresponding doubt of all persons, and an active suspicion which trusted nothing. His abode in all this time was uncertain: he now slept at one deserted lodge, and now at another; now in the disguise of one and now of another character; now on horseback, now on foot—but in no two situations taking the same feature or disguise. In the night-time he sometimes adventured, though with great caution, to the village, and made inquiries. On all hands, he heard of nothing but the preparations making against the clan of which he was certainly one of the prominent heads. The state was roused into activity, and a proclamation of the governor, offering a high reward for the discovery and detention of any persons having a hand in the murder of the guard, was on one occasion put into his own hands. All these things made caution necessary, and, though venturing still very considerably at times, he was yet seldom entirely off his guard.

Rivers kept close in the cover of his den. That den had numberless ramifications, however, known only to himself; and his calm indifference was the result of a conviction that it would require two hundred men, properly instructed, and all at the same moment, to trace him through its many sinuosities. He too, sometimes, carefully disguised, penetrated into the village, but never much in the sight of those who were not bound to him by a common danger. To Lucy he did not appear on such occasions, though he did to the old lady, and even at the family fireside.

Lucy, indeed, had eyes for few objects, and thoughts but for one.

She sat as one stupified with danger, yet sufficiently conscious of it as to be conscious of nothing besides. She was bewildered with the throng of horrible circumstances which had been so crowded on her mind and memory in so brief a space of time. At one moment she blamed her own weakness in suffering the trial of Ralph to progress to a consummation which she shuddered to reflect upon. Had she a right to withhold her testimony—testimony so important to the life and the honor of one person, because others might suffer in consequence—those others the real criminals, and he the innocent victim? and loving him as she did, and hating or fearing his enemies? Had she performed her duty in suffering his case to go to judgment? and such a judgment—so horrible a doom! Should she now suffer it to go to its dreadful execution, when a word from her would stay the hand of the officer, and save the life of the condemned? But would such be its effect? What credence would be given now to one who, in the hall of justice, had sunk down like a criminal herself—withholding the truth, and contradicting every word of her utterance? To whom, then, could she apply? who would hear her plea, even though she boldly narrated all the truth, in behalf of the prisoner? She maddened as she thought on all these difficulties; her blood grew fevered, a thick haze overspread her senses, and she raved at last in the most wild delirium.

Some days went by in her unconsciousness, and when she at length grew calm—when the fever of her mind had somewhat subsided—she opened her eyes and found, to her great surprise, her uncle sitting beside her couch. It was midnight; and this was the hour he had usually chosen when making his visits to his family. In these stolen moments, his attendance was chiefly given to that hapless orphan, whose present sufferings he well knew were in great part attributable to himself.

The thought smote him, for, in reference to her, all feeling had not yet departed from his soul. There was still a lurking sensibility—a lingering weakness of humanity—one of those pledges which nature gives of her old affiliation, and which she never entirely takes away from the human heart. There are still some strings, feeble and wanting in energy though they be, which bind even the most reckless outcast in some little particular to humanity; and, however time, and the world's variety of circumstance, may have worn them and impaired their firm hold, they still sometimes, at unlooked-for hours, regrapple the long-rebellious subject, and make themselves felt and understood as in the first moments of their creation.

Such now was their resumed sway with Munro. While his niece—the young, the beautiful, the virtuous—so endowed by nature—so improved by education—so full of those fine graces, beyond the reach of any art—lay before him insensible—her fine mind spent in incoherent ravings—her gentle form racked with convulsive shudderings—the still, small, monitorial voice, unheard so long, spoke out to him in terrible rebukings. He felt in those moments how deeply he had been a criminal; how much, not of his own, he had appropriated to himself and sacrificed; and how sacred a trust he had abused, in the person of the delicate creature before him, by a determination the most cruel and perhaps unnecessary.

Days had elapsed in her delirium; and such were his newly-awakened feelings, that each night brought him, though at considerable risk, an attendant by her bed. His hand administered—his eyes watched over; and, in the new duties of the parent, he acquired a new feeling of duty and domestic love, the pleasures of which he had never felt before. But she grew conscious at last, and her restoration relieved his mind of one apprehension which had sorely troubled it. Her condition, during her illness, was freely described to her. But she thought not of herself—she had no thought for any other than the one for whom thoughts and prayers promised now to avail but little.

"Uncle—" she spoke at last—"you are here, and I rejoice to see you. I have much to say, much to beg at your hands: oh, let me not beg in vain! Let me not find you stubborn to that which may not make me happy—I say not that, for happy I never look to be again—but make me as much so as human power can make me. When—" and she spoke hurriedly, while a strong and aguish shiver went through her whole frame—"when it is said that he must die?"

He knew perfectly of whom she spoke, but felt reluctant to indulge her mind in a reference to the subject which had already exercised so large an influence over it. But he knew little of the distempered heart, and fell into an error by no means uncommon with society. She soon convinced him of this, when his prolonged silence left it doubtful whether he contemplated an answer.

"Why are you silent? do you fear to speak? Have no fears now. We have no time for fear. We must be active—ready—bold. Feel my hand: it trembles no longer. I am no longer a weak-hearted woman."

He again doubted her sanity, and spoke to her soothingly, seeking to divert her mind to indifferent subjects; but she smiled on the endeavor, which she readily understood, and putting aside her aunt, who began to prattle in a like strain, and with a like object, she again addressed her uncle.

"Doubt me not, uncle: I rave no longer. I am now calm—calm as it is possible for me to be, having such a sorrow as mine struggling at my heart. Why should I hide it from you? It will not be hidden. I love him—love him as woman never loved man before—with a soul and spirit all unreservedly his, and with no thought in which he is not always the principal. I know that he loves another; I know that the passion which I feel I must feel and cherish alone; that it must burn itself away, though it burn away its dwelling-place. I am resigned to such a fate; but I am not prepared for more. I can not bear that he too should die—and such a death! He must not die—he must not die, my uncle; though we save him—ay, save him—for another."

"Shame on you, my daughter! how can you confess so much? Think on your sex—you are a woman—think on your youth!" Such was the somewhat strongly-worded rebuke of the old lady.

"I have thought on all—on everything. I feel all that you have said, and the thought and the feeling have been my madness. I must speak, or I shall again go mad. I am not the tame and cold creature that the world calls woman. I have been differently made. I can love in the world's despite. I can feel through the world's freeze. I can dare all, when my soul is in it, though the world sneer in scorn and contempt. But what I have said, is said to *you*. I would not—no, not for worlds, that he should know I said it—not for worlds!" and her cheeks were tinged slightly, while her head rested for a single instant upon the pillow.

"But all this is nothing!" she started up, and again addressed herself to the landlord. "Speak, uncle! tell me, is there yet time—yet time to save him? When is it they say he must die?"

"On Friday next, at noon."

"And this—?"

"Is Monday."

"He must not die—no, not die, then, my uncle! You must save him—you *must* save him! You have been the cause of his doom: you must preserve him from his execution. You owe it him as a debt—you owe it me—you owe it to yourself. Believe not, my uncle, that there is no other day than this—no other world—no other penalties than belong to this. You read no bible, but you have a thought which must tell you that there are worlds—there is a life yet to come. I know you can not doubt—you must not doubt—you must believe. Have a fear of its punishments, have a hope of its rewards, and listen to my prayer. You must save Ralph Colleton; ask me not how—talk not of difficulties. You must save him—you must—you must!"

"Why, you forget, Lucy, my dear child—you forget that I too am in danger. This is midnight: it is only at this hour that I can steal into the village; and how, and in what manner, shall I be able to do as you require?"

"Oh, man!—man!—forgive me, dear uncle, I would not vex you! But if there were gold in that dungeon—broad bars of gold, or shining silver, or a prize that would make you rich, would you ask me the how and the where? Would that clumsy block, and those slight bars, and that dull jailer, be an obstacle that would keep you back? Would you need a poor girl like me to tell you that the blocks might be pierced—that the bars might be broken—that the jailer might be won to the mercy which would save? You have strength—you have skill—you have the capacity, the power—there is but one thing wanting to my prayer—the will, the disposition!"

"You do me wrong, Lucy—great wrong, believe me. I feel for this young man, and the thought has been no less painful to me than to you, that my agency has contributed in great measure to his danger. But what if I were to have the will, as you say—what if I went forward to the jailer and offered a bribe—would not the bribe which the state has offered for my arrest be a greater attraction than any in my gift? To scale the walls and break the bars, or in any forcible manner to effect the purpose, I must have confederates, and in whom could I venture to confide? The few to whom I could intrust such a design are, like myself, afraid to adventure or be seen, and such a design would be defeated by Rivers himself, who so much hates the youth, and is bent on his destruction."

"Speak not of *him*—*say to him nothing*—you must do it yourself if you do it all. You can effect much if you seriously determine. You can design, and execute all, and find ready and able assistance, if you once willingly set about it. I am not able to advise, nor will you need my counsel. Assure me that you will make the effort—that you will put your whole heart in it—and I have no fears—I feel confident of his escape."

"You think too highly of my ability in this respect. There was a time, Lucy, when such a design had not been so desperate, but now—"

"Oh, not so desperate now, uncle, uncle—I could not live—not a moment—were he to perish in that dreadful manner! Have I no claim upon your mercy—will you not do for me what you would do for money—what you have done at the bidding of that dreadful wretch, Rivers? Nay, look not away, I know it all—I know that you had the dagger of Colleton—that you put it into the hands of the wretch who struck the man—that you saw him strike—that you strove not to stop his hand. Fear you not I shall reveal it? Fear you not?—but I will not— I can not! Yet this should be enough to make you strive in this service. Heard you not, too, when he spoke and stopped my evidence, knowing that my word would have saved him—rather than see me brought to the dreadful trial of telling what I knew of that night—that awful night—when you both sought his life? Oh, I could love him for this— for this one thing—were there nothing else besides worthy of my love!"

The incident to which she referred had not been unregarded by the individual she addressed, and while she spoke, his looks assumed a meditative expression, and he replied as in soliloquy, and in broken sentences:—

"Could I pass to the jail unperceived—gain admittance—then— but who would grapple with the jailer—how manage that?—let me see—but no—no—that is impossible!"

"What is impossible?—nothing is impossible in this work, if you will but try. Do not hesitate, dear uncle—it will look easier if you will reflect upon it. You will see many ways of bringing it about. You can get aid if you want it. There's the pedler, who is quite willing, and Chub— Chub will do much, if you can only find him out."

The landlord smiled as she named these two accessaries. "Bunce— why, what could the fellow do?—he's not the man for such service; now Chub might be of value, if he'd only follow orders: but that he won't do. I don't see how we're to work it, Lucy—it looks more difficult the more I think on it."

"Oh, if it's only difficult—if it's not impossible—it will be done. Do not shrink back, uncle; do not scruple. The youth has done you no wrong—you have done him much. You have brought him where he is, he would have been safe otherwise. You must save him. Save him, uncle—and hear me as I promise. You may then do with me as you please. From that moment I am your slave, and then, if it must be so— if you will then require it, I am willing then to become *his* slave too— him whom you have served so faithfully and so unhappily for so long a season."

"Of whom speak you?"

"Guy Rivers! yes—I shall then obey you, though the funeral come with the bridal."

"Lucy!"

"It is true. I hope not to survive it. It will be a worse destiny to me than even the felon death to the youth whom I would save. Do with me as you please then, but let him not perish. Rescue him from the doom you have brought upon him—and oh, my uncle, in that other world— if there we meet—the one good deed shall atone, in the thought of my poor father, for the other most dreadful sacrifice to which his daughter now resigns herself."

The stern man was touched. He trembled, and his lips quivered convulsively as he took her hand into his own. Recovering himself, in a firm tone, as solemn as that which she had preserved throughout the dialogue, he replied—

"Hear me, Lucy, and believe what I assure you. I *will* try to save this youth. I will do what I can, my poor child, to redeem the trust of your father. I have been no father to you heretofore, not much of one, at least, but it is not too late, and I will atone. I will do my best for Colleton—the thing is full of difficulty and danger, but I will try to save him. All this; however, must be unknown—not a word to anybody; and Rivers must not see you happy, or he will suspect. Better not be seen— still keep to your chamber, and rest assured that all will be done, in my power, for the rescue of the youth."

"Oh, now you are, indeed, my father—yet—uncle, shall I see you at the time when it is to be done? Tell me at what moment you seek his deliverance, that I may be upon my knees. Yet say not to him that I have done anything or said anything which has led to your endeavors. He will not think so well of me if you do; and, though he may not love, I would have him think always of me as if—as if I were a woman."

She was overcome with exertion, and in the very revival of her hope, her strength was exhausted; but she had sunk into a sweet sleep ere her uncle left the apartment.

CHAPTER THIRTY-FOUR

New Parties on the Stage

A day more had elapsed, and the bustle in the little village was increased by the arrival of other travellers. A new light came to the dungeon of Ralph Colleton, in the persons of his uncle and cousin Edith, whom his letters, at his first arrest, had apprized of his situation. They knew that situation only in part, however; and the first intimation of his doom was that which he himself gave them.

The meeting was full of a painful pleasure. The youth himself was firm—muscle and mind all over; but deeply did his uncle reproach himself for his precipitation and sternness, and the grief of Edith, like all deep grief, was dumb, and had no expression. There was but the sign of wo—of wo inexpressible—in the ashy lip, the glazed, the tearless and half-wandering eye, and the convulsive shiver, that at intervals shook her whole frame, like strong and sudden gusts among the foliage. The youth, if he had any at such an hour, spared his reproaches. He narrated in plain and unexaggerated language, as if engaged in the merest narration of commonplace, all the circumstances of his trial. He pointed out the difficulties of his situation, to his mind insuperable, and strove to prepare the minds of those who heard, for the final and saddest trial of all, even as his own mind was prepared. In that fearful work of preparation, the spirit of love could acknowledge no restraining influence, and never was embrace more fond than that of Ralph and the maiden. Much of his uncle's consolation was found in the better disposition which he now entertained, though at too late a day, in favor of their passion. He would now willingly consent to all.

"Had you not been so precipitate, Ralph—" he said, "had you not been so proud—had you thought at all, or given me time for thought, all this trial had been spared us. Was I not irritated by other things when I spoke to you unkindly? You knew not how much I had been chafed— you should not have been so hasty."

"No more of this, uncle, I pray you. I was wrong and rash, and I blame you not. I have nobody but myself to reproach. Speak not of the matter; but, as the best preparation for all that is to come, let your thought banish me rather from contemplation. Why should the memory of so fair a creature as this be haunted by a story such as mine? Why should she behold, in her mind's eye, for ever, the picture of my dying agonies—the accursed scaffold—the—" and the emotion of his soul, at the subject of his own contemplation, choked him in his utterance, while Edith, half-fainting in his arms, prayed his forbearance.

"Speak not thus—not of this, Ralph, if you would not have me perish. I am fearfully sick now, my head swims, and all is commotion at my heart. Not water—not water—give me hope—consolation. Tell me that there is still some chance—some little prospect—that somebody is gone in search of evidence—in search of hope. Is there no circumstance which may avail? Said you not something of—did you not tell me of a person who could say for you that which would have done much towards your escape? A woman, was it not—speak, who is she—let me go to her—she will not refuse to tell me all, and do all, if she be a woman."

Ralph assured her in the gentlest manner of the hopelessness of any such application; and the momentary dream which her own desires had conjured into a promise, as suddenly subsided, leaving her to a full consciousness of her desolation. Her father at length found it necessary to abridge the interview. Every moment of its protraction seemed still more to unsettle the understanding of his daughter. She spoke wildly and confusedly, and in that thought of separation which the doom of her lover perpetually forced upon her, she contemplated, in all its fearful extremities, her own. She was borne away half delirious—the feeling of wo something blunted, however, by the mental unconsciousness following its realization.

Private apartments were readily found them in the village, and having provided good attendance for his daughter, Colonel Colleton set out, though almost entirely hopeless, to ascertain still farther the particulars of the case, and to see what might be done in behalf of one of whose innocence he felt perfectly assured. He knew Ralph too well to suspect him of falsehood; and the clear narrative which he had given, and the manly and unhesitating account of all particulars having any bearing on the case which had fallen from his lips, he knew, from all his previous high-mindedness of character, might safely be relied on. Assured of this himself, he deemed it not improbable that something might undergo development, in a course of active inquiry, which might tend to the creation of a like conviction in the minds of those in whom rested the control of life and judgment.

His first visit was to the lawyer, from whom, however, he could procure nothing, besides being compelled, without possibility of escape, to listen to a long string of reproaches against his nephew.

"I could, and would have saved him, Colonel Colleton, if the power were in mortal," was the self-sufficient speech of the little man; "but he would not—he broke in upon me when the very threshold was to be passed, and just as I was upon it. Things were in a fair train, and all might have gone well but for his boyish interruption. I would have come over the jury with a settler. I would have made out a case, sir, for their consideration, which every man of them would have believed he himself saw. I would have shown your nephew, sir, riding down the narrow trace, like a peaceable gentleman; anon, sir, you should have seen Forrester coming along full tilt after him. Forrester should have cried out with a whoop and a right royal oath; then Mr. Colleton would have heard him and turned round to receive him. But Forrester is drunk, you know, and will not understand the young man's civilities. He blunders out a volley of curses right and left, and bullies Master Colleton for a fight, which he declines. But Forrester is too drunk to mind all that. Without more ado, he mounts the young gentleman, and is about to pluck out his eyes, when he feels the dirk in his ribs, and then they cut loose. He gets the dirk from Master Colleton, and makes at him; but he picks up a hatchet that happens to be lying about, and drives at his head, and down drops Forrester, as he ought to, dead as a door-nail."

"Good heavens! and why did you not bring these facts forward? They surely could not have condemned him under these circumstances."

"Bring them forward! To be sure, I would have done so; but, as I tell you, just when on the threshold, at the very entrance into the transaction, up pops this hasty young fellow—I'm sorry to call your nephew so, Colonel Colleton—but the fact is, he owes his situation entirely to himself. I would have saved him, but he was obstinately bent on not being saved; and just as I commenced the affair, up he pops and tells me, before all the people, that I know nothing about it. A pretty joke, indeed. I know nothing about it, and it my business to know all about it. Sir, it ruined him. I saw, from that moment, how the cat would jump. I pitied the poor fellow, but what more could I do?"

"But it is not too late—we can memorialize the governor, we can put these facts in form, and by duly showing them with the accompanying proofs, we can obtain a new trial—a respite."

"Can't be done now—it's too late. Had I been let alone—had not the youth come between me and my duty—I would have saved him, sir, as under God, I have saved hundreds before. But it's too late now."

"Oh, surely not too late! with the facts that you mention, if you will give me the names of the witnesses furnishing them, so that I can obtain their affidavits—"

"Witnesses!—what witnesses?"

"Why, did you not tell me of the manner in which Forrester assaulted my nephew, and forced upon him what he did as matter of self-defense? Where is the proof of this?"

"Oh, proof! Why, you did not think that was the true state of the case—that was only the case I was to present to the jury."

"And there is, then, no evidence for what you have said?"

"Not a tittle, sir. Evidence is scarcely necessary in a case like this, sir, where the state proves more than you can possibly disprove. Your only hope, sir, is to present a plausible conjecture to the jury. Just set their fancies to work, and they have a taste most perfectly dramatic. What you leave undone, they will do. Where you exhibit a blank, they will supply the words wanting. Only set them on trail, and they'll tree the 'possum. They are noble hands at it, and, as I now live and talk to you, sir, not one of them who heard the plausible story which I would have made out, but would have discovered more common sense and reason in it than in all the evidence you could possibly have given them. Because, you see, I'd have given them a reason for everything. Look, how I should have made out the story. Mr. Colleton and Forrester are excellent friends, and both agree to travel together. Well, they're to meet at the forks by midnight. In the meantime, Forrester goes to see his sweetheart, Kate Allen—a smart girl, by the way, colonel, and well to look on. Parting's a very uncomfortable thing, now, and they don't altogether like it. Kate cries, and

Forrester storms. Well, *must* come comes at last. They kiss, and are off—different ways. Well, grief's but a dry companion, and to get rid of him, Forrester takes a drink; still grief holds on, and then he takes another and another, until grief gets off at last, but not before taking with him full half, and not the worst half either, of the poor fellow's senses. What then? Why, then he swaggers and swears at everything, and particularly at your nephew, who, you see, not knowing his condition, swears at him for keeping him waiting—"

"Ralph Colleton never swears, Mr. Pippin," said the colonel, grimly.

"Well, well, if he didn't swear then, he might very well have sworn, and I'll be sworn but he did on that occasion; and it was very pardonable too. Well, he swears at the drunken man, not knowing his condition, and the drunken man rolls and reels like a rowdy, and gives it to him back, and then they get at it. Your nephew, who is a stout colt, buffets him well for a time, but Forrester, who is a mighty, powerful built fellow, he gets the better in the long run, and both come down together in the road. Then Forrester, being uppermost, sticks his thumb into Master Colleton's eye—the left eye, I think, it was—yes, the left eye it was—and the next moment it would have been out, when your nephew, not liking it, whipped out his dirk, and, 'fore Forrester could say Jack Robinson, it was playing about in his ribs; and, then comes the hatchet part, just as I told it you before."

"And is none of this truth?"

"God bless your soul, no! Do you suppose, if it was the truth, it would have taken so long a time in telling? I wouldn't have wasted the breath on it. The witnesses would have done that, if it were true; but in this was the beauty of my art, and had I been permitted to say to the jury what I've said to you, the young man would have been clear. It wouldn't have been gospel, but where's the merit of a lawyer, if he can't go through a bog? This is one of the sweetest and most delightful features of the profession. Sir, it is putting the wings of fiction to the lifeless and otherwise immovable body of the fact."

Colonel Colleton was absolutely stunned by the fertility and volubility of the speaker, and after listening for some time longer, as long as it was possible to procure from him anything which might be of service, he took his departure, bending his way next to the wigwam, in which, for the time being, the pedler had taken up his abode. It will not be necessary that we should go with him there, as it is not probable that anything materially serving his purpose or ours will be adduced from the narrative of Bunce.

In the meantime, we will turn our attention to a personage, whose progress must correspond, in all respects, with that of our narrative.

Guy Rivers had not been unapprized of the presence of the late comers at the village. He had his agents at work, who marked the progress of things, and conveyed their intelligence to him with no qualified fidelity. The arrival of Colonel Colleton and his daughter had been made known to him within a few hours after its occurrence, and the feelings of the outlaw were of a nature the most complex and contradictory. Secure within his den, the intricacies of which were scarcely known to any but himself, he did not study to restrain those emotions which had prompted him to so much unjustifiable outrage. With no eye to mark his actions or to note his speech, the guardian watchfulness which had secreted so much, in his association with others, was taken off; and we see much of that heart and those wild principles of its government, the mysteries of which contain so much that it is terrible to see. Slowly, and for a long time after the receipt of the above-mentioned intelligence, he strode up and down the narrow cell of his retreat; all passions at sway and contending for the mastery—sudden action and incoherent utterance occasionally diversifying the otherwise monotonous movements of his person. At one moment, he would clinch his hands with violence together, while an angry malediction would escape through his knitted teeth—at another, a demoniac smile of triumph, and a fierce laugh of gratified malignity would ring through the apartment, coming bark upon him in an echo, which would again restore him to consciousness, and bring back the silence so momentarily banished.

"They are here; they have come to witness his degradation—to grace my triumph—to feel it, and understand my revenge. We will see if the proud beauty knows me now—if she yet continues to discard and to disdain me. I have her now upon my own terms. She will not refuse; I am sure of her; I shall conquer her proud heart; I will lead her in chains, the heaviest chains of all—the chains of a dreadful necessity. He must die else! I will howl it in her ears with the voice of the wolf; I will paint it before her eyes with a finger dipped in blood and in darkness! She shall see him carried to the gallows; I shall make her note the halter about his neck—that neck, which, in her young thought, her arms were to have encircled only; nor shall she shut her eyes upon the last scene, nor close her ears to the last groan of my victim! She shall see and hear all, or comply with all that I demand! It must be done: but how? How shall I see her? how obtain her presence? how command her attention?

Pshaw! shall a few beardless soldiers keep me back, and baffle me in this? Shall I dread the shadow now, and shrink back when the sun shines out that makes it? I will not fear. I will see her. I will bid defiance to them all! She shall know my power, and upon one condition only will I use it to save him. She will not dare to refuse the condition; she will consent; she will at last be mine: and for this I will do so much—go so far—ay, save him whom I would yet be so delighted to destroy!"

Night came; and in a small apartment of one of the lowliest dwellings of Chestatee, Edith and her father sat in the deepest melancholy, conjuring up perpetually in their minds those images of sorrow so natural to their present situation. It was somewhat late, and they had just returned from an evening visit to the dungeon of Ralph Colleton. The mind of the youth was in far better condition than theirs, and his chief employment had been in preparing them for a similar feeling of resignation with himself. He had succeeded but indifferently. They strove to appear firm, in order that he should not be less so than they found him; but the effort was very perceptible, and the recoil of their dammed-up emotions was only so much more fearful and overpowering. The strength of Edith had been severely tried, and her head now rested upon the bosom of her father, whose arms were required for her support, in a state of feebleness and exhaustion, leaving it doubtful, at moments, whether the vital principle had not itself utterly departed.

At this period the door opened, and a stranger stood abruptly before them. His manner was sufficiently imposing, though his dress was that of the wandering countryman, savoring of the jockey, and not much unlike that frequently worn by such wayfarers as the stagedriver and carrier of the mails. He had on an overcoat made of buckskin, an article of the Indian habit; a deep fringe of the same material hung suspended from two heavy capes that depended from the shoulder. His pantaloons were made of buckskin also; a foxskin cap rested slightly upon his head, rather more upon one side than the other; while a whip of huge dimensions occupied one of his hands. Whiskers, of a bushy form and most luxuriant growth, half-obscured his cheek, and the mustaches were sufficiently small to lead to the inference that the wearer had only recently decided to suffer the region to grow wild. A black-silk handkerchief, wrapped loosely about his neck, completed the general outline; and the *tout ensemble* indicated one of those dashing blades, so frequently to be encountered in the southern country, who, despising the humdrum monotony of regular life, are ready for adventure—lads of the turf, the muster-ground, the general affray—the men who can whip their weight in wild-cats—whose general rule it is to knock down and drag out.

Though startling at first to both father and daughter, the manner of the intruder was such as to forbid any further alarm than was incidental to his first abrupt appearance. His conduct was respectful and distant— closely observant of the proprieties in his address, and so studiously guarded as to satisfy them, at the very outset, that nothing improper was intended. Still, his entrance without any intimation was sufficiently objectionable to occasion a hasty demand from Colonel Colleton as to the meaning of his intrusion.

"None, sir, is intended, which may not be atoned for," was the reply. "I had reason to believe, Colonel Colleton, that the present melancholy circumstances of your family were such as might excuse an intrusion which may have the effect of making them less so; which, indeed, may go far toward the prevention of that painful event which you now con- template as certain."

The words were electrical in their effect upon both father and daughter. The former rose from his chair, and motioned the stranger to be seated; while the daughter, rapidly rising also, with an emotion which gave new life to her form, inquired breathlessly—

"Speak, sir! say—how!"—and she lingered and listened with figure bent sensibly forward, and hand uplifted and motionless, for reply. The person addressed smiled with visible effort, while slight shades of gloom, like the thin clouds fleeting over the sky at noonday, obscured at intervals the otherwise subdued and even expression of his counte- nance. He looked at the maiden while speaking, but his words were addressed to her father.

"I need not tell you, sir, that the hopes of your nephew are gone. There is no single chance upon which he can rest a doubt whereby his safety may be secured. The doom is pronounced, the day is assigned, and the executioner is ready."

"Is your purpose insult, sir, that you tell us this?" was the rather fierce inquiry of the colonel.

"Calmly, sir," was the response, in a manner corresponding well with the nature of his words; "my purpose, I have already said, is to bring, or at least to offer, relief; to indicate a course which may result in the safety of the young man whose life is now at hazard; and to con- tribute, myself to the object which I propose."

"Go on—go on, sir, if you please, but spare all unnecessary reference to his situation," said the colonel, as a significant pressure of his
arm on the part of his daughter motioned him to patience. The stranger
proceeded:—

"My object in dwelling upon the youth's situation was, if possible, by
showing its utter hopelessness in every other respect, to induce you the
more willingly to hear what I had to offer, and to comply with certain conditions which must be preparatory to any development upon my part."

"There is something strangely mysterious in this. I am willing to do
anything and everything, in reason and without dishonor, for the safety
of my nephew; the more particularly as I believe him altogether innocent of the crime laid to his charge. More than this I dare not; and I shall
not be willing to yield to unknown conditions, prescribed by a stranger,
whatever be the object: but speak out at once, sir, and keep us no longer
in suspense. In the meantime, retire, Edith, my child; we shall best
transact this business in your absence. You will feel too acutely the consideration of this subject to listen to it in discussion. Go, my daughter."

But the stranger interposed, with a manner not to be questioned:—

"Let her remain, Colonel Colleton; it is, indeed, only to her that I
can reveal the mode and the conditions of the assistance which I am to
offer. This was the preliminary condition of which I spoke. To her alone
can my secret be revealed, and my conference must be entirely with her."

"But, sir, this is so strange—so unusual—so improper."

"True, Colonel Colleton; in the ordinary concerns, the everyday
offices of society, it would be strange, unusual, and improper; but these
are not times, and this is not a region of the world, in which the common forms are to be insisted upon. You forget, sir, that you are in the
wild abiding-place of men scarcely less wild—with natures as stubborn
as the rocks, and with manners as uncouth and rugged as the woodland
growth which surrounds us. I know as well as yourself that my demand
is unusual; but such is my situation—such, indeed, the necessities of the
whole case, that there is no alternative. I am persuaded that your
nephew can be saved; I am willing to make an effort for that purpose,
and my conditions are to be complied with: one of them you have
heard—it is for your daughter to hear the rest."

The colonel still hesitated. He was very tenacious of those forms of
society, and of intercourse between the sexes, which are rigidly insisted
upon in the South, and his reluctance was manifest. While he yet hesitated, the stranger again spoke:

"The condition which I have proposed, sir, is unavoidable, but I ask you not to remove from hearing: the adjoining room is not so remote but that you can hear any appeal which your daughter may be pleased to make. Her call would reach your ears without effort. My own security depends, not less than that of your nephew, upon your compliance with the condition under which only will I undertake to save him."

These suggestions prevailed. Suspecting the stranger to be one whose evidence would point to the true criminal, himself an offender, he at length assented to the arrangement, and, after a few minutes' further dialogue, he left the room. As he retired, the stranger carefully locked the door, a movement which somewhat alarmed the maiden; but the respectful manner with which he approached her, and her own curiosity not less than interest in the progress of the event, kept her from the exhibition of any apprehensions.

The stranger drew nigh her. His glances, though still respectful, were fixed, long and searchingly, upon her face. He seemed to study all its features, comparing them, as it would seem, with his own memories. At length, as with a sense of maidenly propriety, she sternly turned away, he addressed her:—

"Miss Colleton has forgotten me, it appears, though I have some claim to be an old acquaintance. I, at least, have a better memory for my friends—I have not forgotten *her*."

Edith looked up in astonishment, but there was no recognition in her glance. A feeling of mortified pride might have been detected in the expression of his countenance, as, with a tone of calm unconsciousness, she replied—

"You are certainly unremembered, if ever known, by me, sir. I am truly sorry to have forgotten one who styles himself my friend."

"Who was—who is—or, rather, who is now willing again to be your friend, Miss Colleton," was the immediate reply.

"Yes, and so I will gladly call you, sir, if you succeed in what you have promised."

"I have yet promised nothing, Miss Colleton."

"True, true! but you say you have the power, and surely would not withhold it at such a time. Oh, speak, sir! tell me how you can serve us all, and receive my blessings and my thanks for ever."

"The reward is great—very great—but not greater—perhaps not as great, as I may demand for my services. But we should not be ignorant of one another in such an affair, and at such a time as this. Is it true, then, that Miss Colleton has no memory which, at this moment, may spare me from the utterance of a name, which perhaps she herself would not be altogether willing to hear, and which it is not my policy to have uttered by any lips, and far less by my own? Think—remember— lady, and let me be silent still on that one subject. Let no feeling of pride influence the rejection of a remembrance which perhaps carries with it but few pleasant reflections."

Again were the maiden's eyes fixed searchingly upon the speaker, and again, conflicting with the searching character of his own glance, were they withdrawn, under the direction of a high sense of modest dignity. She had made the effort at recognition—that was evident even to him—and had made it in vain.

"Entirely forgotten—well! better that than to have been remembered as the thing I was. Would it were possible to be equally forgotten by the rest—but this, too, is vain and childish. She must be taught to remember me."

Thus muttered the stranger to himself; assuming, however, an increased decision of manner at the conclusion, he approached her, and tearing from his cheeks the huge whiskers that had half-obscured them, he spoke in hurried accents:—

"Look on me now, Miss Colleton—look on me now, and while you gaze upon features once sufficiently well known to your glance, let your memory but retrace the few years when it was your fortune, and my fate, to spend a few months in Gwinnett county. Do you remember the time—do you remember that bold, ambitious man, who, at that time, was the claimant for a public honor—who was distinguished by you in a dance, at the ball given on that occasion—who, maddened by wine, and a fierce passion which preyed upon him then, like a consuming fire, addressed you, though a mere child, and sought you for his bride, who—but I see you remember all!"

"And are you then Creighton—Mr. Edward Creighton—and so changed!" And she looked upon him with an expression of simple wonder.

"Ay, that was the name once—but I have another now. Would you know me better—I am Guy Rivers, where the name of Creighton must not again be spoken. It is the name of a felon—of one under doom of outlawry—whom all men are privileged to slay. I have been hunted from society—I can no longer herd with my fellows—I am without kin, and am almost without kind. Yet, base and black with crime—doomed

by mankind—banished all human abodes—the slave of fierce passions—the leagued with foul associates, I dared, in your girlhood, to
love you; and, more daring still, I dare to love you now. Fear not, lady—
you are Edith Colleton to me; and worthless, and vile, and reckless,
though I have become, for you I can hold no thought which would
behold you other than you are—a creature for worship rather than for
love. As such I would have you still; and for this purpose do I seek you
now. I know your feeling for this young man—I saw it then, when you
repulsed me. I saw that you loved each other, though neither of you
were conscious of the truth. You love him now—you would not have
him perish—I know well how you regard him, and I come, knowing
this, to make hard conditions with you for his life."

"Keep me no longer in suspense—speak out, Mr. Creighton"—she
cried, gaspingly.

"Rivers—Rivers—I would not hear the other—it was by that name
I was driven from my fellows."

"Mr. Rivers, say what can be done—what am I to do—money—
thanks, all that we can give shall be yours, so that you save him from this
fate."

"And who would speak thus for me? What fair pleader, fearless of
man's opinion—that blights or blesses, without reference to right or
merit—would so far speak for me!"

"Many—many, Mr. Rivers—I hope there are many. Heaven knows,
though I may have rejected in my younger days, your attentions, I know
not many for whom I would more willingly plead and pray than yourself. I do remember now your talents and high reputation, and deeply
do I regret the unhappy fortune which has denied them their
fulfilment."

"Ah, Edith Colleton, these words would have saved me once—now
they are nothing, in recompense for the hopes which are for ever gone.
Your thoughts are gentle, and may sooth all spirits but my own. But
sounds that lull others, lull me no longer. It is not the music of a rich
dream, or of a pleasant fancy, which may beguile me into pleasure. I am
dead—dead as the cold rock—to their influence. The storm which
blighted me has seared, and ate into the very core. I am like the tree
through which the worm has travelled—it still stands, and there is
foliage upon it, but the heart is eaten out and gone. Your words touch
me no longer as they did—I need something more than words and
mere flatteries—flatteries so sweet even as those which come from your

lips—are no longer powerful to bind me to your service. I can save the youth—I will save him, though I hate him; but the conditions are fatal to your love for him."

There was much in this speech to offend and annoy the hearer; but she steeled herself to listen, and it cost her some effort to reply.

"I can listen—I can hear all that you may say having reference to him. I know not what you may intend; I know not what you may demand for your service. But name your condition. All in honor—all that a maiden may grant and be true to herself, all—all, for his life and safety."

"Still, I fear, Miss Colleton—your love for him is not sufficiently lavish to enable your liberality to keep pace with the extravagance of my demand—"

"Hold, sir—on this particular there is no need of further speech. Whatever may be the extent of my regard for Ralph, it is enough that I am willing to do much, to sacrifice much—in return for his rescue from this dreadful fate. Speak, therefore, your demand—spare no word—delay me, I pray, no longer."

"Hear me, then. As Creighton, I loved you years ago—as Guy Rivers I love you still. The life of Ralph Colleton is forfeit—for ever forfeit—and a few days only interpose between him and eternity. I alone can save him—I can give him freedom; and, in doing so, I shall risk much, and sacrifice not a little. I am ready for this risk—I am prepared for every sacrifice—I will save him at all hazards from his doom, upon one condition!"

"Speak! speak!"

"That you be mine—that you fly with me—that in the wild regions of the west, where I will build you a cottage and worship you as my own forest divinity, you take up your abode with me, and be my wife. My wife!—all forms shall be complied with, and every ceremony which society may call for. Nay, shrink not back thus—" seeing her recoil in horror and scorn at the suggestion—"beware how you defy me—think, that I have his life in my hands—think, that I can speak his doom or his safety—think, before you reply!"

"There is no time necessary for thought, sir—none—none. It can not be. I can not comply with the conditions which you propose. I would die first."

"And he will die too. Be not hasty, Miss Colleton—remember—it is not merely your death but his—his death upon the gallows—"

"Spare me! spare me!"

"The halter—the crowd—the distorted limb—the racked frame—"

"Horrible—horrible!"

"Would you see this—know this, and reflect upon the shame, the mental agony, far greater than all, of such a death to him?"

With a strong effort, she recovered her composure, though but an instant before almost convulsed—

"Have you no other terms, Mr. Rivers?"

"None—none. Accept them, and he lives—I will free him, as I promise. Refuse them—deny me, and he must die, and nothing may save him then."

"Then he must die, sir!—we must both die—before we choose such terms. Sir, let me call my father. Our conference must end here. You have chosen a cruel office, but I can bear its infliction. You have tantalized a weak heart with hope, only to make it despair the more. But I am now strong, sir—stronger than ever—and we speak no more on this subject."

"Yet pause—to relent even to-morrow may be too late. To-night you must determine, or never."

"I have already determined. It is impossible that I can determine otherwise. No more, sir!"

"There is one, lady—one young form—scarcely less beautiful than yourself, who would make the same—ay, and a far greater—sacrifice than this, for the safety of Ralph Colleton. One far less happy in his love than you, who would willingly die for him this hour. Would you be less ready than she is for such a sacrifice?"

"No, not less ready for death—as I live—not less willing to free him with the loss of my own life. But not ready for a sacrifice like this—not ready for this."

"You have doomed him!"

"Be it so, sir. Be it so. Let me now call my father."

"Yet think, ere it be too late—once gone, not even your words shall call me back."

"Believe me, I shall not desire it."

The firmness of the maiden was finely contrasted with the disappointment of the outlaw. He was not less mortified with his own defeat than awed by the calm and immoveable bearing, the sweet, even dignity, which the discussion of a subject so trying to her heart, and the overthrow of all hope which her own decision must have occasioned, had failed utterly to affect. He would have renewed his suggestions, but while repeating them, a sudden commotion in the village—the trampling of feet—the buzz of many voices, and sounds of wide-spread confusion, contributed to abridge an interview already quite too long. The outlaw rushed out of the apartment, barely recognising, at his departure, the presence of Colonel Colleton, whom his daughter had now called in. The cause of the uproar we reserve for another chapter.

CHAPTER THIRTY-FIVE

Proposed Rescue

The pledge which Munro had given to his niece in behalf of Colleton was productive of no small inconvenience to the former personage. Though himself unwilling—we must do him the justice to believe—that the youth should perish for a crime so completely his own, he had in him no great deal of that magnanimous virtue, of itself sufficiently strong to have persuaded him to such a risk, as that which he had undertaken at the supplication of Lucy. The more he reflected upon the matter, the more trifling seemed the consideration. With such a man, to reflect is simply to *calculate*. Money, now—the spoil or the steed of the traveller—would have been a far more decided stimulant to action. In regarding such an object, he certainly would have overlooked much of the danger, and have been less heedful of the consequences. The selfishness of the motive would not merely have sanctioned, but have smoothed the enterprise; and he thought too much with the majority—allowing for any lurking ambition in his mind—not to perceive that where there is gain there must be glory.

None of these consolatory thoughts came to him in the contemplation of his present purpose. To adventure his own life—perhaps to exchange places with the condemned he proposed to save—though, in such a risk, he only sought to rescue the innocent from the doom justly due to himself—was a flight of generous impulse somewhat above the usual aim of the landlord; and, but for the impelling influence of his niece—an influence which, in spite of his own evil habits, swayed him beyond his consciousness—we should not now have to record the almost redeeming instance in the events of his life at this period—the *one* virtue, contrasting with, if it could not lessen or relieve, the long tissue of his offences.

There were some few other influences, however—if this were not enough—coupled with that of his niece's entreaty, which gave strength and decision to his present determination. Munro was not insensible to the force of superior character, and a large feeling of veneration led him, from the first, to observe the lofty spirit and high sense of honor which distinguished the bearing and deportment of Ralph Colleton. He could not but admire the native superiority which characterized the manner of the youth, particularly when brought into contrast with that of Guy Rivers, for whom the same feeling had induced a like, though not a parallel respect, on the part of the landlord.

It may appear strange to those accustomed only to a passing and superficial estimate of the thousand inconsistencies which make up that contradictory creation, the human mind, that such should be a feature in the character of a ruffian like Munro; but, to those who examine for themselves, we shall utter nothing novel when we assert, that a respect for superiority of mental and even mere moral attribute, enters largely into the habit of the ruffian generally. The murderer is not unfrequently found to possess benevolence as well as veneration in a high degree; and the zealots of all countries and religions are almost invariably creatures of strong and violent passions, to which the extravagance of their zeal and devotion furnishes an outlet, which is not always innocent in its direction or effects. Thus, in their enthusiasm—which is only a minor madness—whether the Hindoo bramin or the Spanish bigot, the English roundhead or the follower of the "only true faith" at Mecca, he understood, it is but a word and a blow—though the word be a hurried prayer to the God of their adoration, and the blow be aimed with all the malevolence of hell at the bosom of a fellow-creature. There is no greater inconsistency in the one character than in the other. The temperament which, under false tuition, makes the zealot, and drives him on to the perpetration of wholesale murder, while uttering a prayer to the Deity, prompts the same individual who, as an assassin or a highwayman, cuts your throat, and picks your pocket, and at the next moment bestows his ill-gotten gains without reservation upon the starving beggar by the wayside.

There was yet another reason which swayed Munro not a little in his determination, if possible, to save the youth—and this was a lurking sentiment of hostility to Rivers. His pride, of late, on many occasions, had taken alarm at the frequent encroachments of his comrade upon its boundaries. The too much repeated display of that very mental superiority in his companion, which had so much fettered him, had aroused his own latent sense of independence; and the utterance of sundry pungent rebukes on the part of Rivers had done much towards provoking within him a new sentiment of dislike for that person, which gladly availed itself of the first legitimate occasion for exercise and development. The very superiority which commanded, and which he honored, he hated for that very reason; and, in our analysis of moral dependence, we may add, that, in Greece, and the mere Hob of the humble farmhouse, Munro might have been the countryman to vote Aristides into banishment because of his reputation for justice. The barrier is slight, the space short, the transition easy, from one to the other extreme of injustice; and the peasant who voted for the banishment of the just man, in another sphere and under other circumstances, would have been a Borgia or a Catiline. With this feeling in his bosom, Munro was yet unapprized of its existence. It is not with the man, so long hurried forward by his impulses as at last to become their creature, to analyze either their character or his own. Vice, though itself a monster, is yet the slave of a thousand influences, not absolutely vicious in themselves; and their desires it not uncommonly performs when blindfolded. It carries the knife, it strikes the blow, but is not always the chooser of its own victim.

But, fortunately for Ralph Colleton, whatever and how many or how few were the impelling motives leading to this determination, Munro had decided upon the preservation of his life; and with that energy of will, which, in a rash office, or one violative of the laws, he had always heretofore displayed, he permitted no time to escape him unemployed for the contemplated purpose. His mind immediately addressed itself to its chosen duty, and, in one disguise or another, and those perpetually changing, he perambulated the village, making his arrangements for the desired object. The difficulties in his way were not trifling in character nor few in number; and the greatest of these was that of finding coadjutors willing to second him. He felt assured that he could confide in none of his well-known associates, who were to a man the creatures of Rivers; that outlaw, by a liberality which seemed to disdain money, and yielding every form of indulgence, having acquired over them an influence almost amounting to personal affection. Fortunately for his purpose, Rivers dared not venture much into the village or its neighborhood; therefore, though free from any fear of obstruction from one in whose despite his whole design was undertaken, Munro was yet not a little at a loss for his co-operation. To whom, at that moment, could he turn, without putting himself in the power of an enemy? Thought only raised up new difficulties in his way, and in utter despair of any better alternative, though scarcely willing to trust to one of whom he deemed so lightly, his eyes were compelled to rest, in the last hope, upon the person of the pedler, Bunce.

Bunce, if the reader will remember, had, upon his release from prison, taken up his abode temporarily in the village. Under the protection now afforded by the presence of the judge, and the other officers of justice—not to speak of the many strangers from the adjacent parts, whom one cause or another had brought to the place—he had presumed to exhibit his person with much more audacity and a more perfect freedom from apprehension than he had ever shown in the same region before. He now—for ever on the go—thrust himself fearlessly into every cot and corner. No place escaped the searching analysis of his glance; and, in a scrutiny so nice, it was not long before he had made the acquaintance of everybody and everything at all worthy, in that region, to be known. He could now venture to jostle Pippin with impunity; for, since the trial in which he had so much blundered, the lawyer had lost no small portion of the confidence and esteem of his neighbors. Accused of the abandonment of his client—an offence particularly monstrous in the estimation of those who are sufficiently interested to acquire a personal feeling in such matters—and compelled, as he had been—a worse feature still in the estimation of the same class—to "eat his own words"—he had lost caste prodigiously in the last few days, and his fine sayings lacked their ancient flavor in the estimation of his neighbors. His speeches sunk below par along with himself; and the pedler, in his contumelious treatment of the disconsolate jurist, simply obeyed and indicated the direction of the popular opinion. One or two rude replies, and a nudge which the elbow of Bunce, effected in the ribs of the lawyer, did provoke the latter so far as to repeat his threat on the subject of the prosecution for the horse; but the pedler snapped his fingers in his face as he did so, and bade him defiance. He also reminded Pippin of the certain malfeasances to which he had referred previously, and the consciousness of the truth was sufficiently strong and awkward to prevent his proceeding to any further measure of disquiet with the offender. Thus, without fear, and with an audacity of which he was not a little proud, Bunce perambulated the village and its neighborhood, in a mood and with a deportment he had never ventured upon before in that quarter.

He had a variety of reasons for lingering in the village seemingly in a state of idleness. Bunce was a long-sighted fellow, and beheld the promise which it held forth, at a distance, of a large and thriving business in the neighborhood; and he had too much sagacity not to be perfectly aware of the advantage, to a tradesman, resulting from a prior occupation of the ground. He had not lost everything in the conflagration which destroyed his cart-body and calicoes; for, apart from sundry little debts due him in the surrounding country, he had carefully preserved around his body, in a black silk handkerchief, a small wallet, holding a moderate amount of the best bank paper. Bunce, among other things, had soon learned to discriminate between good and bad paper, and the result of his education in this respect assured him of the perfect integrity of the three hundred and odd dollars which kept themselves snugly about his waist—ready to be expended for clocks and calicoes, horn buttons, and wooden combs, knives, and negro-handkerchiefs, whenever their proprietor should determine upon a proper whereabout in which to fix himself. Bunce had grown tired of peddling—the trade was not less uncertain than fatiguing. Besides, travelling so much among the southrons, he had imbibed not a few of their prejudices against his vocation, and, to speak the truth, had grown somewhat ashamed of his present mode of life. He was becoming rapidly aristocratic, as we may infer from a very paternal and somewhat patronizing epistle, which he despatched about this time to his elder brother and copartner, Ichabod Bunce, who carried on his portion of the business at their native place in Meriden, Connecticut. He told him, in a manner and vein not less lofty than surprising to his coadjutor, that it "would not be the thing, no how, to keep along, lock and lock with him, in the same gears." It was henceforward his "idee to drive on his own hook. Times warn't as they used to be;" and the fact was—he did not say it in so many words—the firm of Ichabod Bunce and Brother was scarcely so creditable to the latter personage as he should altogether desire among his southern friends and acquaintances. He "guessed, therefore, best haul off," and each—here Bunce showed his respect for his new friends by quoting their phraseology—"must paddle his own canoe."

We have minced this epistle, and have contented ourselves with providing a scrap, here and there, to the reader—despairing, as we utterly do, to gather from memory a full description of a performance so perfectly unique in its singular compound of lofty vein, with the patois and vulgar contractions of his native, and those common to his adopted country.

It proved to his more staid and veteran brother, that Jared was the only one of his family likely to get above his bread and business; but, while he lamented the wanderings and follies of his brother, he could not help enjoying a sentiment of pride as he looked more closely into the matter. "Who knows," thought the clockmaker to himself, "but that Jared, who is a monstrous sly fellow, will pick up some southern heiress, with a thousand blackies, and an hundred acres of prime cotton-land to each, and thus ennoble the blood of the Bunces by a rapid ascent, through the various grades of office in a sovereign state, until a seat in Congress—in the cabinet itself—receives him;"—and Ichabod grew more than ever pleased and satisfied with the idea, when he reflected that Jared had all along been held to possess a goodly person, and a very fair development of the parts of speech. He even ventured to speculate upon the possibility of Jared passing into the White House—the dawn of that era having already arrived, which left nobody safe from the crowning honors of the republic.

Whether the individual of whom so much was expected, himself entertained any such anticipations or ideas, we do not pretend to say; but, certain it is, that the southern candidate for the popular suffrage could never have taken more pains to extend his acquaintance or to ingratiate himself among the people, than did our worthy friend the pedler. In the brief time which he had passed in the village after the arrest of Colleton, he had contrived to have something to say or do with almost everybody in it. He had found a word for his honor the judge; and having once spoken with that dignitary, Bunce was not the man to fail at future recognition. No distance of manner, no cheerless response, to the modestly urged or moderate suggestion, could prompt him to forego an acquaintance. With the jurors he had contrived to enjoy a sup of whiskey at the tavern bar-room, and had actually, and with a manner the most adroit, gone deeply into the distribution of an entire packet of steelpens, one of which he accommodated to a reed, and to the fingers of each of the worthy twelve, who made the panel on that occasion— taking care, however, to assure them of the value of the gift, by saying, that if he were to sell the article, twenty-five cents each would be his lowest price, and he could scarcely save himself at that. But this was not all. Having seriously determined upon abiding at the south, he ventured upon some few of the practices prevailing in that region, and on more than one occasion, a gallon of whiskey had circulated "free gratis," and "*pro bono publico*," he added, somewhat maliciously, at the cost of our worthy tradesman. These things, it may not be necessary to say, had elevated that worthy into no moderate importance among those around him; and, that he himself was not altogether unconscious of the change, it may be remarked that an ugly *kink*, or double in his back— the consequence of his pack and past humility—had gone down wonderfully, keeping due pace in its descent with the progress of his upward manifestations.

Such was the somewhat novel position of Bunce, in the village and neighborhood of Chestatee, when the absolute necessity of the case prompted Munro's application to him for assistance in the proposed extrication of Ralph Colleton. The landlord had not been insensible to the interest which the pedler had taken in the youth's fortune, and not doubting his perfect sympathy with the design in view, he felt the fewer scruples in approaching him for the purpose. Putting on, therefore, the disguise, which, as an old woman, had effectually concealed his true person from Bunce on a previous occasion, he waited until evening had set in fairly, and then proceeded to the abode of him he sought.

The pedler was alone in his cottage, discussing, most probably, his future designs, and calculating to a nicety the various profits of each premeditated branch of his future business. Munro's disguise was intended rather to facilitate his progress without detection through the village, than to impose upon the pedler merely; but it was not unwise that he should be ignorant also of the person with whom he dealt. Affecting a tone of voice, therefore, which, however masculine, was yet totally unlike his own, the landlord demanded a private interview, which was readily granted, though, as the circumstance was unusual, with some few signs of trepidation. Bunce was no lover of old women, nor, indeed, of young ones either. He was habitually and constitutionally cold and impenetrable on the subject of all passions, save that of trade, and would rather have sold a dress of calico, than have kissed the prettiest damsel in creation. His manner, to the old woman who appeared before him, seemed that of one who had an uncomfortable suspicion of having pleased rather more than he intended; and it was no small relief, therefore, the first salutation being over, when the masculine tones reassured him. Munro, without much circumlocution, immediately proceeded to ask whether he was willing to lend a hand for the help of Colleton, and to save him from the gallows?

"Colleton!—save Master Colleton!—do tell—is that what you mean?"

"It is. Are you the man to help your friend—will you make one along with others who are going to try for it?"

"Well, now, don't be rash; give a body time to consider. It's pesky full of trouble; dangerous, too. It's so strange!—" and the pedler showed himself a little bewildered by the sudden manner in which the subject had been broached.

"There's little time to be lost, Bunce: if we don't set to work at once, we needn't set to work at all. Speak out, man! will you join us, now or never, to save the young fellow?"

With something like desperation in his manner, as if he scrupled to commit himself too far, yet had the will to contribute considerably to the object, the pedler replied:—

"Save the young fellow? well, I guess I will, if you'll jest say what's to be done. I'll lend a hand, to be sure, if there's no trouble to come of it. He's a likely chap, and not so stiff neither, though I did count him rather high-headed at first; but after that, he sort a smoothed down, and now I don't know nobody I'd sooner help jest now out of the slush: but I can't see how we're to set about it."

"Can you fight, Bunce? Are you willing to knock down and drag out, when there's need for it?"

"Why, if I was fairly listed, and if so be there's no law agin it. I don't like to run agin the law, no how; and if you could get a body clear on it, why, and there's no way to do the thing no other how, I guess I shouldn't stand too long to consider when it's to help a friend."

"It may be no child's play, Bunce, and there must be stout heart and free hand. One mustn't stop for trifles in such cases; and as for the law, when a man's friend's in danger, he must make his own law."

"That wan't my edication, no how; my principles goes agin it. I must think about it, I must have a little time to consider." But the landlord saw no necessity for consideration, and, fearful that the scruples of Bunce would be something too strong, he proceeded to smooth away the difficulty.

"After all, Bunce, the probability is, we shall be able to manage the affair without violence: so we shall try, for I like blows just as little as anybody else; but it's best, you know, to make ready for the worst. Nobody knows how things will turn up; and if it comes to the scratch, why, one mustn't mind knocking a fellow on the head if he stands in the way."

"No, to be sure not. 'Twould be foolish to stop and think about what's law, and what's not law, and be knocked down yourself."

"Certainly, you're right, Bunce; that's only reason."

"And yet, mister, I guess you wouldn't want that I should know your real name, now, would you? or maybe you're going to tell it to me now? Well—"

"To the business: what matters it whether I have a name or not? I have a fist, you see, and—"

"Yes, yes, I see," exclaimed he of the notions, slightly retreating, as Munro, suiting the action to the word, thrust, rather more closely to the face of his companion than was altogether encouraging, the ponderous mass which courtesy alone would consider a fist—

"Well, I don't care, you see, to know the name, mister; but some-how it raally aint the thing, no how, to be mistering nobody knows who. I see you aint a woman plain enough from your face, and I pretty much conclude you must be a man; though you have got on—what's that, now? It's a kind of calico, I guess; but them's not fast colors, friend. I should say, now, you had been taken in pretty much by that bit of goods. It aint the kind of print, now, that's not afeard of washing."

"And if I have been taken in, Bunce, in these calicoes, you're the man that has done it," said the landlord, laughing. "This piece was sold by you into my own hands, last March was a year, when you came back from the Cherokees."

"Now, don't! Well, I guess there must be some mistake; you aint sure, now, friend: might be some other dealer that you bought from?"

"None other than yourself, Bunce. You are the man, and I can bring a dozen to prove it on you."

"Well, I 'spose what you say's true, and that jest let's me know how to mister you now, 'cause, you see, I do recollect now all about who I sold that bit of goods to that season."

The landlord had been overreached; and, amused with the ingenu-ity of the trader, he contented himself with again lifting the huge fist in a threatening manner, though the smile which accompanied the action fairly deprived it of its terrors.

"Well, well," said the landlord, "we burn daylight in such talk as this. I come to you as the only man who will or can help me in this matter; and Lucy Munro tells me you will—you made her some such promise."

"Well, now, I guess I must toe the chalk, after all; though, to say truth, I don't altogether remember giving any such promise. It must be right, though, if she says it; and sartain she's a sweet body—I'll go my length for her any day."

"You'll not lose by it; and now hear my plan. You know Brooks, the jailer, and his bulldog brother-in-law, Tongs? I saw you talking with both of them yesterday."

"Guess you're right. Late acquaintance, though; they aint neither on 'em to my liking."

"Enough for our purpose. Tongs is a brute who will drink as long as he can stand, and some time after it. Brooks is rather shy of it, but he will drink enough to stagger him, for he is pretty weak-headed. We have only to manage these fellows, and there's the end of it. They keep the jail."

"Yes, I know; but you don't count young Brooks?"

"Oh, he's a mere boy. Don't matter about him. He's easily managed. Now hear to my design. Provide your jug of whiskey, with plenty of eggs and sugar, so that they shan't want anything, and get them here. Send for Tongs at once, and let him only know what's in the wind; then ask Brooks, and he will be sure to force him to come. Say nothing of the boy; let him stay or come, as they think proper. To ask all might make them suspicious. They'll both come. They never yet resisted a spiritual temptation. When here, ply them well, and then we shall go on according to circumstances. Brooks carries the keys along with him: get him once in for it, and I'll take them from him. If he resists, or any of them—"

"Knock 'em down?"

"Ay, quickly as you say it!"

"Well, but how if they do not bring the boy, and they leave him in the jail?"

"What then! Can't we knock him down too?"

"But, then, they'll fix the whole business on my head. Won't Brooks and Tongs say where they got drunk, and then shan't I be in a scant fixin'?"

"They dare not. They won't confess themselves drunk—it's as much as their place is worth. They will say nothing till they get sober, and then they'll get up some story that will hurt nobody."

"But—"

"But what? will you never cease to but against obstacles? Are you a man—are you ready—bent to do what you can? Speak out, and let me know if I can depend on you," exclaimed the landlord, impatiently.

"Now, don't be in a passion! You're as soon off as a fly-machine, and a thought sooner. Why, didn't I say, now, I'd go my length for the young gentleman? And I'm sure I'm ready, and aint at all afeared, no how. I only did want to say that, if the thing takes wind, as how it raaly stood, it spiles all my calkilations. I couldn't 'stablish a consarn here, I guess, for a nation long spell of time after."

"And what then? where's your calculations? Get the young fellow clear, and what will his friends do for you? Think of that, Bunce. You go off to Carolina with him, and open store in his parts, and he buys from you all he wants—his negro-cloths, his calicoes, his domestics, and stripes, and everything. Then his family, and friends and neighbors, under his recommendation—they all buy from you; and then the presents they will make you—the fine horses—and who knows but even a plantation and negroes may all come out of this one transaction?"

"To be sure—who knows? Well, things do look temptatious enough, and there's a mighty deal of reason, now, in what you say. Large business that, I guess, in the long run. Aint I ready? Let's see—a gallon of whiskey—aint a gallon a heap too much for only three people?"

"Better have ten than want. Then there must be pipes, tobacco, cigars; and mind, when they get well on in drinking, I shall look to you through that window. Be sure and come to me then. Make some pretence, for, as Brooks may be slow and cautious, I shall get something to drop into his liquor—a little mixture which I shall hand you."

"What mixture? No pizen, I hope! I don't go that, not I—no pizening for me."

"Pshaw! fool—nonsense! If I wanted their lives, could I not choose a shorter method, and a weapon which I could more truly rely upon than I ever can upon you? It is to make them sleep that I shall give you the mixture."

"Oh, laudnum. Well, now, why couldn't you say laudnum at first, without frightening people so with your mixtures?—There's no harm in laudnum, for my old aunt Tabitha chaws laudnum-gum jest as other folks chaws tobacco."

"Well, that's all—it's only to get them asleep sooner. See now about your men at once. We have no time to lose; and, if this contrivance fails,

I must look about for another. It must be done to-night, or it can not be done at all. In an hour I shall return; and hope, by that time, to find you busy with their brains. Ply them well—don't be slow or stingy—and see that you have enough of whiskey. Here's money—have everything ready."

The pedler took the money—why not? it was only proper to spoil the Egyptians—and, after detailing fully his plans, Munro left him. Bunce gave himself but little time and less trouble for reflection. The prospects of fortune which the landlord had magnified to his vision, were quite too enticing to be easily resisted by one whose *morale* was not of a sort to hold its ground against his habitual cupidity and newly-awakened ambition; and having provided everything, as agreed upon, necessary for the accommodation of the jailer and his assistant, Bunce sallied forth for the more important purpose of getting his company.

CHAPTER THIRTY-SIX

Sack and Sugar

The task of getting the desired guests, as Munro had assured him, was by no means difficult, and our pedler was not long in reporting progress. Tongs, a confirmed toper, was easily persuaded to anything that guaranteed hard drinking. He luxuriated in the very idea of a debauch. Brooks, his brother-in-law, was a somewhat better and less pregnable person; but he was a widower, had been a good deal with Tongs, and, what with the accustomed loneliness of the office which he held, and the gloomy dwelling in which it required he should live, he found it not such an easy matter to resist the temptation of social enjoyment, and all the pleasant associations of that good-fellowship, which Bunce had taken care to depict before the minds of both parties. The attractions of Bunce himself, by-the-way, tended, not less than the whiskey and cigars, to persuade the jailer, and to neutralize most of the existing prejudices current among those around him against his tribe. He had travelled much, and was no random observer. He had seen a great deal, as well of human nature as of places; could tell a good story, in good spirit; and was endowed with a dry, sneaking humor, that came out unawares upon his hearers, and made them laugh frequently in spite of themselves.

Bunce had been now sufficiently long in the village to enable those about him to come at a knowledge of his parts; and his accomplishments, in the several respects referred to, were by this time generally well understood. The inducement was sufficiently strong with the jailer; and, at length, having secured the main entrance of the jail carefully, he strapped the key to a leathern girdle, which he wore about him, lodging it in the breast-pocket of his coat, where he conceived it perfectly safe, he prepared to go along with his worthy brother-in-law. Nor was the younger Brooks forgotten. Being a tall, good-looking lad of sixteen, Tongs insisted it was high time he should appear among men; and the invitation of the pedler was opportune, as affording a happy occasion for his initiation into some of those practices, esteemed, by a liberal courtesy, significant of manliness.

With everything in proper trim, Bunce stood at the entrance of his lodge, ready to receive them. The preliminaries were soon despatched, and we behold them accordingly, all four, comfortably seated around a huge oaken table in the centre of the apartment. There was the jug, and there the glasses—the sugar, the peppermint, the nutmegs—the pipes and tobacco—all convenient, and sufficiently tempting for the unscrupulous. The pedler did the honors with no little skill, and Tongs plunged headlong into the debauch. The whiskey was never better, and found, for this reason, anything but security where it stood. Glass after glass, emptied only to be replenished, attested the industrious hospitality of the host, not less than its own excellence. Tongs, averaging three draughts to one of his companion's, was soon fairly under way in his progress to that state of mental self-glorification in which the world ceases to have vicissitudes, and the animal realizes the abstractions of an ancient philosophy, and denies all pain to life.

Brooks, however, though not averse to the overcoming element, had more of that vulgar quality of prudence than his brother-in-law, and far more than was thought amiable in the opinion of the pedler. For some time, therefore, he drank with measured scrupulousness; and it was with no small degree of anxiety that Bunce plied him with the bottle—complaining of his unsociableness, and watching, with the intensity of any other experimentalist, the progress of his scheme upon him. As for the lad—the younger Brooks—it was soon evident that, once permitted, and even encouraged to drink, as he had been, by his superiors, he would not, after a little while, give much if any inconvenience to the conspirators. The design of the pedler was considerably advanced by Tongs, who, once intoxicated himself, was not slow in the endeavor to bring all around him under the same influence.

"Drink, Brooks—drink, old fellow," he exclaimed; "as you are a

true man, drink, and don't fight shy of the critter! Whiskey, my boy—
old Monongahely like this, I say—whiskey is wife and children—house
and horse—lands and niggers—liberty and [hiccup] plenty to live on!
Don't you see how I drive ahead, and don't care for the hind wheels? It's
all owing to whiskey! Grog, I say—Hark ye, Mr. Pedler—grog, I say, is
the wheels of life: it carries a man *for'ad*. Why don't men go *for'ad* in the
world? What's the reason now? I'll tell you. They're afeared. Well, now,
who's afeared when he's got a broadside of whiskey in him? Nobody—
nobody's afeared but you—you, Ben Brooks, you're a d———d crick—
crick—you're always afeared of something, or nothing; for, after all,
whenever you're afeared of something, it turns out to be nothing! All
'cause you don't drink like a man. That's his cha-cha-*rack*-ter, Mr.
Bunce; and it's all owing 'cause he won't drink!"

"Guess there's no sparing of reason in that bit of argument, now, I
tell you, Mr. Tongs. Bless my heart—it's no use talking, no how, but I'd
a been clean done up, dead as a door-nail, if it hadn't been for drink.
Strong drink makes strong. Many's the time, and the freezing cold, and
the hard travelling in bad roads, and other dreadful fixins I've seed,
would soon ha' settled me up, if it hadn't been for that same good stuff
there, that Master Brooks does look as if he was afeared on. Now, don't
be afeared, Master Brooks. There's no teeth in whiskey, and it never
bites nobody."

"No," said Brooks, with the utmost simplicity; "only when they take
too much."

"How?" said the pedler, looking as if the sentence contained some
mysterious meaning. Brooks might have explained, but for Tongs, who
dashed in after this fashion:—

"And who takes too much? You don't mean to say I takes too much,
Ben Brooks. I'd like to hear the two-legged critter, now, who'd say I
takes more of the stuff than does me good. I drinks in reason, for the
benefit of my health; and jest, you see, as a sort of medicine, Mr. Bunce;
and, Brooks, you knows I never takes a drop more than is needful."

"Sometimes—sometimes, Tongs, you know you ain't altogether
right under it—now and then you take a leetle too much for your
good," was the mild response of Brooks, to the almost fierce speech of
his less scrupulous brother-in-law. The latter, thus encountered,
changed his ground with singular rapidity.

"Well, by dogs!—and what of that?—and who is it says I shan't, if
it's my notion? I'd like now to see the boy that'll stand up agin me and

make such a speech. Who says I shan't take what I likes—and that I takes more than is good for me? Does you say so, Mr. Bunce?"

"No, thank ye, no. How should I say what ain't true? You don't take half enough, now, it's my idee, neither on you. It's all talk and no cider, and that I call monstrous dry work. Come, pass round the bottle. Here's to you, Master Tongs—Master Brooks, I drink your very good health. But fill up, fill up—you ain't got nothing in your tumbler."

"No, he's a sneak—you're a sneak, Brooks, if you don't fill up to the hub. Go the whole hog, boy, and don't twist your mouth as if the stuff was physic. It's what I call nation good, now; no mistake in it, I tell you."

"Hah! that's a true word—there's no mistake in this stuff. It is jest now what I calls ginywine."

"True Monongahely, Master Bunce. Whoever reckoned to find a Yankee pedler with a *raal* good taste for Monongahely? Give us your fist, Mr. Bunce; I see you know's what's what. You ain't been among us for nothing. You've larned something by travelling; and, by dogs! you'll come to be something yit, if you live long enough—if so be you can only keep clear of the *old range*."

The pedler winced under the equivocal compliments of his companion, but did not suffer anything of this description to interfere with the vigorous prosecution of his design. He had the satisfaction to perceive that Brooks had gradually accommodated himself not a little to the element in which his brother-in-law, Tongs, was already floating happily; and the boy, his son, already wore the features of one over whose senses the strong liquor was momentarily obtaining the mastery. But these signs did not persuade him into any relaxation of his labors; on the contrary, encouraged by success, he plied the draughts more frequently and freely than before, and with additional evidence of the influence of the potations upon those who drank, when he found that he was enabled, unperceived, to deposit the contents of his own tumbler, in most instances, under the table around which they gathered. In the cloud of smoke encircling them, and sent up from their several pipes, Bunce could perceive the face of his colleague in the conspiracy peering in occasionally upon the assembly, and at length, on some slight pretence, he approached the aperture agreeably to the given signal, and received from the hands of the landlord a vial containing a strong infusion of opium, which he placed cautiously in his bosom, and awaited the moment of more increased stupefaction to employ it. So favorably had the liquor operated by this time upon the faculties of all, that the elder Brooks grew garrulous and full of jest at the expense of his son—who now, completely overcome, had sunk down with his head upon the table in a profound slumber. The pedler joined, as well as Tongs, in the merriment—this latter personage, by the way, having now put himself completely under the control of the ardent spirit, and exhibiting all the appearance of a happy madness. He howled like the wolf, imitated sundry animals, broke out into catches of song, which he invariably failed to finish, and, at length, grappling his brother-in-law, Brooks, around the neck, with both arms, as he sat beside him, he swore by all that was strong in *Monongahely,* he should give them a song.

"That's jest my idee, now, Master Tongs. A song is a main fine thing, now, to fill up the chinks. First a glass, then a puff or two, and then a song."

Brooks, who, in backwood parlance, was "considerably up a stump"—that is to say, half drunk—after a few shows of resistance, and the utterance of some feeble scruples, which were all rapidly set aside by his companions, proceeded to pour forth the rude melody which follows:—

The How-d'ye-do Boy.

"For a how-d'ye-do boy, 'tis pleasure enough
To have a sup of such goodly stuff—
To float away in a sky of fog,
And swim the while in a sea of grog;
        So, high or low,
        Let the world go,
The how-d'ye-do boy don't care for it—no—no—no—no."

Tongs, who seemed to be familiar with the uncouth dithyrambic, joined in the chorus, with a tumultuous discord, producing a most admirable effect; the pedler dashing in at the conclusion, and shouting the *finale* with prodigious compass of voice. The song proceeded:—

"For a how-d'ye-do boy, who smokes and drinks,
He does not care who cares or thinks;
Would Grief deny him to laugh and sing,
He knocks her down with a single sling—
        So, high or low,
        Let the world go,
The how-d'ye-do boy don't care for it—no—no—no—no."

"For a how-d'ye-do boy is a boy of the night—

It brings no cold, and it does not fright;
He buttons his coat and laughs at the shower,
And he has a song for the darkest hour—
  So, high or low,
  Let the world go,
The how-d'ye-do boy don't care for it—no—no—no—no."

The song gave no little delight to all parties. Tongs shouted, the pedler roared applause, and such was the general satisfaction, that it was no difficult thing to persuade Brooks to the demolition of a bumper, which Bunce adroitly proposed to the singer's own health. It was while the hilarity thus produced was at its loudest, that the pedler seized the chance to pour a moderate portion of the narcotic into the several glasses of his companions, while a second time filling them; but, unfortunately for himself, not less than the design in view, just at this moment Brooks grew awkwardly conscious of his own increasing weakness, having just reason enough left to feel that he had already drunk too much. With a considerable show of resolution, therefore, he thrust away the glass so drugged for his benefit, and declared his determination to do no more of that business. He withstood all the suggestions of the pedler on the subject, and the affair began to look something less than hopeless when he proceeded to the waking up of his son, who, overcome by the liquor, was busily employed in a profound sleep, with his head upon the table.

Tongs, who had lost nearly all the powers of action, though retaining not a few of his parts of speech, now came in fortunately to the aid of the rather-discomfited pedler. Pouring forth a volley of oaths, in which his more temperate brother-in-law was denounced as a mean-spirited critter, who couldn't drink with his friend or fight with his enemy, he made an ineffectual effort to grapple furiously with the offender, while he more effectually arrested his endeavor to waken up his son. It is well, perhaps, that his animal man lacked something of its accustomed efficiency, and resolutely refused all co-operation with his mood; or, it is more than probable, such was his wrath, that his more staid brother-in-law would have been subjected to some few personal tests of blow and buffet. The proceedings throughout suggested to the mind of the pedler a mode of executing his design, by proposing a bumper all round, with the view of healing the breach between the parties, and as a final draught preparatory to breaking up.

A suggestion so reasonable could not well be resisted; and, with the best disposition in the world toward sobriety, Brooks was persuaded to assent to the measure. Unhappily, however, for the pedler, the measure was so grateful to Tongs, that, before the former could officiate, the latter, with a desperate effort, reached forward, and, possessing himself of his own glass, he thrust another, which happened to be the only undrugged one, and which Bunce had filled for himself, into the grasp of the jailer. The glass designed for Brooks was now in the pedler's own hands, and no time was permitted him for reflection. With a doubt as to whether he had not got hold of the posset meant for his neighbor, Bunce was yet unable to avoid the difficulty; and, in a moment, in good faith, the contents of the several glasses were fairly emptied by their holders. There was a pause of considerable duration; the several parties sank back quietly into their seats; and, supposing from appearances that the effect of the drug had been complete, the pedler, though feeling excessively stupid and strange, had yet recollection enough to give the signal to his comrade. A moment only elapsed, when Munro entered the apartment, seemingly unperceived by all but the individual who had called him; and, as an air of considerable vacancy and repose overspread all the company, he naturally enough concluded the potion had taken due hold of the senses of the one whom it was his chief object to overcome. Without hesitation, therefore, and certainly asking no leave, he thrust one hand into the bosom of the worthy jailer, while the other was employed in taking a sure hold of his collar. To his great surprise, however, he found that his man suffered from no lethargy, though severely bitten by the drink. Brooks made fierce resistance; though nothing at such a time, or indeed at any time, in the hands of one so powerfully built as Munro.

"Hello! now—who are you, I say? Hands off!—Tongs! Tongs!—Hands off!—Tongs, I say—"

But Tongs heard not, or heeded not, any of the rapid exclamations of the jailer, who continued to struggle. Munro gave a single glance to the pedler, whose countenance singularly contrasted with the expression which, in the performance of such a duty, and at such a time, it might have been supposed proper for it to have worn. There was a look from his eyes of most vacant and elevated beatitude; a simper sat upon his lips, which parted ineffectually with the speech that he endeavored to make. A still lingering consciousness of something to be done, prompted him to rise, however, and stumble toward the landlord, who, while scuffling with the jailer, thus addressed him:—

"Why, Bunce, it's but half done!—you've bungled. See, he's too sober by half!"

"Sober? no, no—guess he's drunk—drunk as a gentleman. I say, now—what must I do?"

"Do?" muttered the landlord, between his teeth, and pointing to Tongs, who reeled and raved in his seat, "do as I do!" And, at the word, with a single blow of his fist, he felled the still refractory jailer with as much ease as if he had been an infant in his hands. The pedler, only half conscious, turned nevertheless to the half-sleeping Tongs, and resolutely drove his fist into his face.

It was at that moment that the nostrum, having taken its full effect, deprived him of the proper force which alone could have made the blow available for the design which he had manfully enough undertaken. The only result of the effort was to precipitate him, with an impetus not his own, though deriving much of its effect from his own weight, upon the person of the enfeebled Tongs: the toper clasped him round with a corresponding spirit, and they both rolled upon the floor in utter imbecility, carrying with them the table around which they had been seated, and tumbling into the general mass of bottles, pipes, and glasses, the slumbering youth, who, till that moment, lay altogether ignorant of the catastrophe.

Munro, in the meanwhile, had possessed himself of the desired keys; and throwing a sack, with which he had taken care to provide himself, over the head of the still struggling but rather stupified jailer, he bound the mouth of it with cords closely around his body, and left him rolling, with more elasticity and far less comfort than the rest of the party, around the floor of the apartment.

He now proceeded to look at the pedler; and seeing his condition, though much wondering at his falling so readily into his own temptation—never dreaming of the mistake which he had made—he did not waste time to rouse him up, as he plainly saw he could get no further service out of him. A moment's reflection taught him, that, as the condition of Bunce himself would most probably free him from any suspicion of design, the affair told as well for his purpose as if the original arrangement had succeeded. Without more pause, therefore, he left the house, carefully locking the doors on the outside, so as to delay egress, and hastened immediately to the release of the prisoner.

Chapter Thirty-seven

Freedom—Flight

The landlord lost no time in freeing the captive. A few minutes sufficed to find and fit the keys; and, penetrating at once to the cell of Ralph Colleton, he soon made the youth acquainted with as much of the circumstances of his escape as might be thought necessary for the satisfaction of his immediate curiosity. He wondered at the part taken by Munro in the affair, but hesitated not to accept his assistance. Though scrupulous, and rigidly so, not to violate the laws, and having a conscientious regard to all human and social obligations, he saw no immorality in flying from a sentence, however agreeable to law, in all respects so greatly at variance with justice. A second intimation was not wanting to his decision; and, without waiting until the landlord should unlock the chain which secured him, he was about to dart forward into the passage, when the restraining check which it gave to his forward movement warned him of the difficulty.

Fortunately, the obstruction was small: the master-key, not only of the cells, but of the several locks to the fetters of the prison, was among the bunch of which the jailer had been dispossessed; and, when found, it performed its office. The youth was again free; and a few moments only had elapsed, after the departure of Munro from the house of the pedler, when both Ralph and his deliverer were upon the high-road, and bending their unrestrained course toward the Indian nation.

"And now, young man," said the landlord, "you are free. I have performed my promise to one whose desire in this matter jumps full with my own. I should have been troubled enough had you perished for the death of Forrester, though, to speak the truth, I should not have risked myself, as I have done tonight, but for my promise to her."

"Who?—of whom do you speak? To whom do I owe all this, if it comes not of your own head?"

"And you do not conjecture? Have you not a thought on the subject? Was it likely, think you, that the young woman, who did not fear to go to a stranger's chamber at midnight, in order to save him from his enemy, would forget him altogether when a greater danger was before him?"

"And to Miss Munro again do I owe my life? Noble girl! how shall I requite—how acknowledge my deep responsibility to her?"

"You can not! I have not looked on either of you for nothing; and my observation has taught me all your feelings and hers. You can not reward her as she deserves to be rewarded—as, indeed, she only can be rewarded by you, Mr. Colleton. Better, therefore, that you seek to make no acknowledgments."

"What mean you? Your words have a signification beyond my comprehension. I know that I am unable to requite services such as hers, and such an endeavor I surely should not attempt; but that I feel gratitude for her interposition may not well be questioned—the deepest gratitude; for in this deed, with your aid, she relieves me, not merely from death, but the worse agony of that dreadful form of death. My acknowledgments for this service are nothing, I am well aware; but these she shall have: and what else have I to offer, which she would be likely to accept?"

"There is, indeed, one thing, Mr. Colleton—now that I reflect—which it may be in your power to do, and which may relieve you of some of the obligations which you owe to her interposition, here and elsewhere."

The landlord paused for a moment, and looked hesitatingly in Ralph's countenance. The youth saw and understood the expression, and replied readily:—

"Doubt not, Mr. Munro, that I shall do all things consistent with propriety, in my power to do, that may take the shape and character of requital for this service; anything for Miss Munro, for yourself or others, not incompatible with the character of the gentleman. Speak, sir: if you can suggest a labor of any description, not under this head, which would be grateful to yourself or her, fear not to speak, and rely upon my gratitude to serve you both."

"I thank you, Mr. Colleton; your frankness relieves me of some heavy thoughts, and I shall open my mind freely to you on the subject which now troubles it. I need not tell you what my course of life has been. I need not tell you what it is now. Bad enough, Mr. Colleton—bad enough, as you must know by this time. Life, sir, is uncertain with all persons, but far more uncertain with him whose life is such as mine. I know not the hour, sir, when I may be knocked on the head. I have no confidence in the people I go with; I have nothing to hope from the sympathies of society, or the protection of the laws; and I have now arrived at that time of life when my own experience is hourly repeating in my ears the words of scripture: 'The wages of sin is death.' Mine has been a life of sin, Mr. Colleton, and I must look for its wages. These thoughts have been troubling me much of late, and I feel them particularly heavy now. But, don't think, sir, that fear for myself makes up my suffering. I fear for that poor girl, who has no protector, and may be doomed to the control of one who would make a hell on earth for all under his influence. He has made a hell of it for me."

"Who is he? whom do you mean?"

"You should know him well enough by this time, for he has sought your life often enough already—who should I mean, if not Guy Rivers?"

"And how is she at the mercy of this wretch?"

The landlord continued as if he had not heard the inquiry:

"Well, as I say, I know not how long I shall be able to take care of and provide for that poor girl, whose wish has prompted me this night to what I have undertaken. She was my brother's child, Mr. Colleton, and a noble creature she is. If I live, sir, she will have to become the wife of Rivers; and, though I love her as my own—as I have never loved my own—yet she must abide the sacrifice from which, *while I live,* there is no escape. But something tells me, sir, I have not long to live. I have a notion which makes me gloomy, and which has troubled me ever since you have been in prison. One dream comes to me every night—whenever I sleep—and I wake, all over perspiration, and with a terror I'm ashamed of. In this dream I see my brother always, and always with the same expression. He looks at me long and mournfully, and his finger is uplifted, as if in warning. I hear no word from his lips, but they are in motion as if he spoke, and then he walks slowly away. Thus, for several nights, has my mind been haunted, and I'm sure it is not for nothing. It warns me that the time is not very far distant when I shall receive the wages of a life like mine—the wages of sin—the death, perhaps—who knows?—the death of the felon!"

"These are fearful fancies, indeed, Mr. Munro; and, whether we think on them or not, will have their influence over the strongest-minded, of us all: but the thoughts which they occasion to your mind, while they must be painful enough, may be the most useful, if they awaken regret of the past, and incite to amendment in the future. Without regarding them as the presentiments of death, or of any fearful change, I look upon them only as the result of your own calm reflections upon the unprofitable nature of vice; its extreme unproductiveness in the end, however enticing in the beginning; and the painful privations of human sympathy and society, which are the inevitable consequences of its indulgence. These fancies are the sleepless thoughts, the fruit of an active memory, which, at such a time, unrestrained by the waking judgment, mingles up the counsels and the warnings of your brother and the past, with all the images and circumstances of the present time. But—go on with your suggestion. Let me do what I can for the good of those in whom you are interested."

"You are right: whatever may be my apprehensions, life is uncertain enough, and needs no dreams to make it more so. Still, I can not rid myself of this impression, which sticks to me like a shadow. Night after night I have seen him—just as I saw him a year before he died. But his looks were full of meaning; and when his lips opened, though I heard not a word, they seemed to me to say, 'The hour is at hand!' I am sure they spoke the truth, and I must prepare for it. *If I live,* Mr. Colleton, Lucy must marry Rivers: there's no hope for her escape. If I die, there's no reason for the marriage, for she can then bid him defiance. She is willing to marry him now merely on my account; for, to say in words, what you no doubt understand, *I* am at his mercy. If I perish before the marriage take place, it will not take place; and she will then need a protector—"

"Say no more," exclaimed the youth, as the landlord paused for an instant—"say no more. It will be as little as I can say, when I assure you, that all that my family can do for her happiness—all that I can do—shall be done. Be at ease on this matter, and believe me that I promise you nothing which my heart would not strenuously insist upon my performing. She shall be a sister to me."

As he spoke, the landlord warmly pressed his hand, leaning forward from his saddle as he did so, but without a single accompanying word. The dialogue was continued, at intervals, in a desultory form, and without sustaining, for any length of time, any single topic. Munro seemed heavy with gloomy thoughts; and the sky, now becoming lightened with the glories of the ascending moon, seemed to have no manner of influence over his sullen temperament. Not so with the youth. He grew elastic and buoyant as they proceeded; and his spirit rose, bright and gentle, as if in accordance with the pure lights which now disposed themselves, like an atmosphere of silver, throughout the forest. The thin clouds, floating away from the parent-orb, and no longer obscuring her progress, became tributaries, and were clothed in their most dazzling draperies—clustering around her pathway, and contributing not a little to the loveliness of that serene star from which they received so much. But the contemplations of the youth were not long permitted to run on in the gladness of his newly-found liberty. On a sudden, the action of his companion became animated: he drew up his steed for an instant, then applying the rowel, exclaimed in a deep but suppressed tone—

"We are pursued—ride, now—for your life, Mr. Colleton; it is three miles to the river, and our horses will serve us well. They are chosen—ply the spur, and follow close after me."

Let us return to the village. The situation of the jailer, Brooks, and of his companions, as the landlord left them, will be readily remembered by the reader. It was not until the fugitives were fairly on the road, that the former, who had been pretty well stunned by the severe blow given him by Munro, recovered from his stupor; and he then laboured under the difficulty of freeing himself from the bag about his head and shoulders, and his incarceration in the dwelling of the pedler.

The blow had come nigh to sobering him, and his efforts, accordingly, were not without success. He looked round in astonishment upon the condition of all things around him, ignorant of the individual who had wrested from him his charge, besides subjecting his scull to the heavy test which it had been so little able to resist or he to repel; and, almost ready to believe, from the equally prostrate condition of the pedler and his brother, that, in reality, the assailant by which he himself was overthrown was no other than the potent bottle-god of his brother's familiar worship.

Such certainly would have been his impression but for the sack in which he had been enveloped, and the absence of his keys. The blow, which he had not ceased to feel, might have been got by a drunken man in a thousand ways, and was no argument to show the presence of an enemy; but the sack, and the missing keys—they brought instant conviction, and a rapidly increasing sobriety, which as it duly increased his capacity for reflection, was only so much more unpleasant than his drunkenness.

But no time was to be lost, and the first movement—having essayed, though ineffectually, to kick his stupid host and snoring brother-in-law into similar consciousness with himself—was to rush headlong to the jail, where he soon realized all the apprehensions which assailed him when discovering the loss of his keys. The prisoner was gone, and the riotous search which he soon commenced about the village collected a crowd, whose clamors, not less than his own, had occasioned the uproar, which concluded the conference between Miss Colleton and Guy Rivers, as narrated in a previous chapter.

The mob, approaching the residence of Colonel Colleton, as a place which might probably have been resorted to by the fugitive, brought the noise more imperiously to the ears of Rivers, and compelled his departure. He sallied forth, and in a little while ascertained the cause of the disorder. By this time the dwelling of Colonel Colleton had undergone the closest scrutiny. It was evident to the crowd, that, so far from harboring the youth, they were not conscious of the escape; but of this Rivers was not so certain. He was satisfied in his own mind that the stern refusal of Edith to accept his overtures for the rescue, arose only from the belief that they could do without him. More than ever irritated by this idea, the outlaw was bold enough, relying upon his disguise, to come forward, and while all was indecisive in the multitude, to lay plans for a pursuit. He did not scruple to instruct the jailer as to what course should be taken for the recovery of the fugitive; and by his cool, strong sense and confidence of expression, he infused new hope into that much-bewildered person. Nobody knew who he was, but as the village was full of strangers, who had never been seen there before, this fact occasioned neither surprise nor inquiry.

His advice was taken, and a couple of the Georgia guard, who were on station in the village, now making their appearance, he suggested the course which they should pursue, and in few words gave the reasons which induced the choice. Familiar himself with all the various routes of the surrounding country, he did not doubt that the fugitive, under whatever guidance, for as yet he knew nothing of Munro's agency in the business, would take the most direct course to the Indian nation.

All this was done, on his part, with an excited spirit, the result of that malignant mood which now began to apprehend the chance of being deprived of all its victims. Had this not been the case—had he not been present—the probability is, that, in the variety of counsel, there would have been a far greater delay in the pursuit; but such must always be the influence of a strong and leading mind in a time of trial and popular excitement. Such a mind concentrates and makes effective the power which otherwise would be wasted in air. His superiority of character was immediately manifest—his suggestions were adopted without dissent; and, in a few moments the two troopers, accompanied by the jailer, were in pursuit upon the very road taken by the fugitives.

Rivers, in the meanwhile, though excessively anxious about the result of the pursuit, was yet too sensible of his own risk to remain much longer in the village. Annoyed not a little by the apprehended loss of that revenge which he had described as so delicious in contemplation to his mind, he could not venture to linger where he was, at a time of such general excitement and activity. With a prudent caution, therefore, more the result of an obvious necessity than of any accustomed habit of his life, he withdrew himself as soon as possible from the crowd, at the moment when Pippin—who never lost a good opportunity—had mounted upon a stump in order to address them. Breaking away just as the lawyer was swelling with some old truism, and perhaps no truth, about the rights of man and so forth, he mounted his horse, which he had concealed in the neighborhood, and rode off to the solitude and the shelter of his den.

There was one thing that troubled his mind along with its other troubles, and that was to find out who were the active parties in the escape of Colleton. In all this time, he had not for a moment suspected Munro of connection with the affair—he had too much overrated his own influence with the landlord to permit of a thought in his mind detrimental to his conscious superiority. He had no clue, the guidance of which might bring him to the trail; for the jailer, conscious of his own irregularity, was cautious enough in suppressing everything like a detail of the particular circumstances attending the escape; contenting himself, simply, with representing himself as having been knocked down by some persons unknown, and rifled of the keys while lying insensible.

Rivers could only think of the pedler, and yet, such was his habitual contempt for that person, that he dismissed the thought the moment it came into his mind. Troubled thus in spirit, and filled with a thousand conflicting notions, he had almost reached the rocks, when he was surprised to perceive, on a sudden, close at his elbow, the dwarfish figure of our old friend Chub Williams. Without exhibiting the slightest show of apprehension, the urchin resolutely continued his course along with the outlaw, unmoved by his presence, and with a degree of cavalier indifference which he had never ventured to manifest to that dangerous personage before.

"Why, how now, Chub—do you not see me?" was the first inquiry of Rivers.

"Can the owl see?—Chub is an owl—he can't see in the moonlight."

"Well, but, Chub—why do you call yourself an owl? You don't want to see me, boy, do you?"

"Chub wants to see nobody but his mother—there's Miss Lucy now—why don't you let me see her? she talks jest like Chub's mother."

"Why, you dog, didn't you help to steal her away? Have you forgotten how you pulled away the stones? I should have you whipped for it, sir—do you know that I can whip—don't the hickories grow here?"

"Yes, so Chub's mother said—but you can't whip Chub. Chub laughs—he laughs at all your whips. *That* for your hickories. Ha! ha! ha! Chub don't mind the hickories—you can't catch Chub, to whip him with your hickories. Try now, if you can. Try—" and as he spoke he darted along with a rickety, waddling motion, half earnest in his flight, yet seemingly, partly with the desire to provoke pursuit. Something irritated with what was so unusual in the habit of the boy, and what he conceived only so much impertinence, the outlaw turned the horse's head down the hill after him, but, as he soon perceived, without any chance of overtaking him in so broken a region. The urchin all the while, as if encouraged by the evident hopelessness of the chase on the part of the pursuer, screeched out volley after volley of defiance and laughter— breaking out at intervals into speeches which he thought most like to annoy and irritate.

"Ha, ha, ha! Chub don't mind your hickories—Chub's fingers are long—he will pull away all the stones of your house, and then you will have to live in the tree-top."

But on a sudden his tune was changed, as Rivers, half-irritated by the pertinacity of the dwarf, pull[ed] out a pistol, and directed it at his head. In a moment, the old influence was predominant, and in undisguised terror he cried out—

"Now don't—don't, Mr. Guy—don't you shoot Chub—Chub won't laugh again—he won't pull away the stones—he won't."

The outlaw now laughed himself at the terror which he had inspired, and beckoning the boy near him, he proceeded, if possible, to persuade him into a feeling of amity. There was a strange temper in him with reference to this outcast. His deformity—his desolate condition—his deficient intellect, inspired, in the breast of the fierce man, a feeling of sympathy, which he had not entertained for the whole world of humanity beside.

Such is the contradictory character of the misled and the erring spirit. Warped to enjoy crime—to love the deformities of all moral things—to seek after and to surrender itself up to all manner of perversions, yet now and then, in the long tissue, returning, for some moments, to the original temper of that first nature not yet utterly departed; and few and feeble though the fibres be which still bind the heart to her worship, still strong enough at times to remind it of the *true,* however it may be insufficient to restrain it in its wanderings after the *false.*

But the language and effort of the outlaw, though singularly kind, failed to have any of the desired effect upon the dwarf. With an unhesitating refusal to enter the outlaw's dwelling-place in the rocks, he bounded away into a hollow of the hills, and in a moment was out of sight of his companion. Fatigued with his recent exertions, and somewhat more sullen than usual, Rivers entered the gloomy abode, into which it is not our present design to follow him.

CHAPTER THIRTY-EIGHT

Pursuit—Death

The fugitives, meanwhile, pursued their way, with the speed of men conscious that life and death hung upon their progress. There needed no exhortations from his companion to Ralph Colleton. More than life, with him, depended upon his speed. The shame of such a death as that to which he had been destined was for ever before his eyes, and with a heart nerved to its utmost by a reference to the awful alternative of flight, he grew reckless in the audacity with which he drove his horse forward in defiance of all obstacle and over every impediment. Nor were the present apprehensions of Munro much less than those of his companion. To be overtaken, as the participant of the flight of one whose life was forfeit, would necessarily invite such an examination of himself as must result in the development of his true character, and such a discovery must only terminate in his conviction and sentence to the same doom. His previously-uttered presentiment grew more than ever strong with the growing consciousness of his danger; and with an animation, the fruit of an anxiety little short of absolute fear, he stimulated the progress of Colleton, while himself driving the rowel ruthlessly into the smoking sides of the animal he bestrode.

"On, sir—on, Mr. Colleton—this is no moment for graceful attitude. Bend forward—free rein—rashing spur. We ride for life—for life. They must not take us alive—remember *that*. Let them shoot—strike, if they please—but they must put no hands on us as living men. If we must die, why—any death but a dog's. Are you prepared for such a finish to your ride?"

"I am—but I trust it has not come to that. How much have we yet to the river?"

"Two miles at the least, and a tough road. They gain upon us—do you not hear them—we are slow—very slow. These horses—on, Syphax, dull devil—on—on!"

And at every incoherent and unconnected syllable, the landlord struck his spurs into his animal, and incited the youth to do the same.

"There is an old mill upon the branch to our left, where for a few hours we might lie in secret, but daylight would find us out. Shall we try a berth there, or push on for the river?" inquired Munro.

"Push on, by all means—let us stop nowhere—we shall be safe if we make the nation," was the reply.

"Ay, safe enough, but that's the rub. If we could stretch a mile or two between us, so as to cross before they heave in sight, I could take you to a place where the whole United States would never find us out—but they gain on us—I hear them every moment more and more near. The sounds are very clear to-night—a sign of rain, perhaps to-morrow. On, sir! Push! The pursuers must hear us, as we hear them."

"But I hear them not—I hear no sounds but our own—" replied the youth.

"Ah, that's because you have not the ears of an outlaw. There's a necessity for using our ears, one of the first that we acquire, and I can hear sounds farther, I believe, than any man I ever met, unless it be Guy Rivers. He has the ears of the devil, when his blood's up. Then he hears further than I can, though I'm not much behind him even then. Hark! they are now winding the hill not more than half a mile off, and we hear nothing of them now until they get round—the hill throws the echo to the rear, as it is more abrupt on that side than on this. At this time, if they heard us before, they can not hear us. We could now make the old mill with some hope of their losing our track, as we strike into a blind path to do so. What say you, Master Colleton—shall we turn aside or go forward?"

"Forward, I say. If we are to suffer, I would suffer on the high road, in full motion, and not be caught in a crevice like a lurking thief. Better be shot down—far better—I think with you—than risk recapture."

"Well—it's the right spirit you have, and we may beat them yet! We cease again to hear them. They are driving through the close grove where the trees hang so much over. God—it is but a few moments since we went through it ourselves—they gain on us—but the river is not far—speed on—bend forward, and use the spur—a few minutes more close pushing, and the river is in sight. Kill the beasts—no matter—but make the river."

"How do we cross?" inquired the youth, hurriedly, though with a confidence something increased by the manner of his companion.

"Drive in—drive in—there are two fords, each within twenty yards of the other, and the river is not high. You take the path and ford to the right, as you come in sight of the water, and I'll keep the left. Your horse swims well—so don't mind the risk; and if there's any difficulty, leave him, and take to the water yourself. The side I give you is the easiest; though it don't matter which side I take. I've gone through worse chances than this, and, if we hold on for a few moments, we are safe. The next turn, and we are on the banks."

"The river—the river," exclaimed the youth, involuntarily, as the broad and quiet stream wound before his eyes, glittering like a polished mirror in the moonlight.

"Ay, there it is—now to the right—to the right! Look not behind you. Let them shoot—let them shoot! but lose not an instant to look. Plunge forward and drive in. They are close upon us, and the flat is on the other side. They can't pursue, unless they do as we, and they have no such reason for so desperate a course. It is swimming and full of snags! They will stop—they will not follow. In—in—not a moment is to be lost—" and speaking, as they pursued their several ways, he to the left, and Ralph Colleton to the right ford, the obedient steeds plunged forward under the application of the rowel, and were fairly in the bosom of the stream, as the pursuing party rode headlong up the bank.

Struggling onward, in the very centre of the stream, with the steed, which, to do him all manner of justice, swam nobly, Ralph Colleton could not resist the temptation to look round upon his pursuers. Writhing his body in the saddle, therefore, a single glance was sufficient; and, in the full glare of the moonlight, unimpeded by any interposing foliage, the prospect before his eyes was imposing and terrible enough. The pursuers were four in number—the jailer, two of the Georgia guard, and another person unknown to him.

As Munro had predicted, they did not venture to plunge in as the fugitives had done—they had no such fearful motive for the risk; and the few moments which they consumed in deliberation as to what they should do, contributed not a little to the successful experiment of the swimmers.

But the youth at length caught a fearful signal of preparation; his ear noted the sharp click of the lock, as the rifle was referred to in the final resort; and his ready sense conceived but of one, and the only mode of evading the danger so immediately at hand. Too conscpicuous in his present situation to hope for escape, short of a miracle, so long as he remained upon the back of the swimming horse, he relaxed his hold, carefully drew his feet from the stirrups, resigned his seat, and only a second before the discharge of the rifle, was deeply buried in the bosom of the Chestatee.

The steed received the bullet in his head, plunged forward madly, to the no small danger of Ralph, who had now got a little before him, but in a few moments lay supine upon the stream, and was borne down by its current. The youth, practised in such exercises, pressed forward under the surface for a sufficient time to enable him to avoid the present glance of the enemy, and at length, in safety, rounding a jutting point of the shore, which effectually concealed him from their eyes, he gained the dry land, at the very moment in which Munro, with more success, was clambering, still mounted, up the steep sides of a neighboring and slippery bank.

Familiar with such scenes, the landlord had duly estimated the doubtful chances of his life in swimming the river directly in sight of the pursuers. He had, therefore, taken the precaution to oblique consider-ably to the left from the direct course, and did not, in consequence, appear in sight, owing to the sinuous windings of the stream, until he had actually gained the shore.

The youth beheld him at this moment, and shouted aloud his own situation and safety. In a voice indicative of restored confidence in him-self, no less than in his fate, the landlord, by a similar shout, recognised him, and was bending forward to the spot where he stood, when the sharp and joint report of three rifles from the opposite banks, attested the discovery of his person; and, in the same instant, the rider tottered forward in his saddle, his grasp was relaxed upon the rein, and, without a word, he toppled from his seat, and was borne for a few paces by his horse, dragged forward by one of his feet, which had not been released from the stirrup.

He fell, at length, and the youth came up with him. He heard the groans of the wounded man, and, though exposing himself to the same chance, he could not determine upon flight. He might possibly have saved himself by taking the now freed animal which the landlord had ridden, and at once burying himself in the nation. But the noble weakness of pity determined him otherwise; and, without scruple or fear, he resolutely advanced to the spot where Munro lay, though full in the sight of the pursuers, and prepared to render him what assistance he could. One of the troopers, in the meantime, had swum the river; and, freeing the flat from its chains, had directed it across the stream for the passage of his companions. It was not long before they had surrounded the fugitives, and Ralph Colleton was again a prisoner, and once more made conscious of the dreadful doom from which he had, at one moment, almost conceived himself to have escaped.

Munro had been shockingly wounded. One ball had pierced his thigh, inflicting a severe, though probably not a fatal wound. Another, and this had been enough, had penetrated directly behind the eyes, keeping its course so truly across, as to tear and turn the bloody orbs completely out upon the cheek beneath. The first words of the dying man were—

"Is the moon gone down—lights—bring lights!"

"No, Munro; the moon is still shining without a cloud, and as brightly as if it were day," was the reply of Ralph.

"Who speaks—speak again, that I may know how to believe him."

"It is I, Munro—I, Ralph Colleton."

"Then it is true—and I am a dead man. It is all over, and he came not to me for nothing. Yet, can I have no lights—no lights?—Ah!" and the half-reluctant reason grew more terribly conscious of his situation, as he thrust his fingers into the bleeding sockets from which the fine and delicate conductor of light had been so suddenly driven. He howled aloud for several moments in his agony—in the first agony which came with that consciousness—but, recovering, at length, he spoke with something of calm and coherence.

"Well, Mr. Colleton, what I said was true. I knew it would be so. I had warning enough to prepare, and I did try, but it's come over soon and nothing is done. I have my wages, and the text spoke nothing but the truth. I can not stand this pain long—it is too much—and—"

The pause in his speech, from extreme agony, was filled up by a shriek that rung fearfully amid the silence of such a scene, but it lasted not long. The mind of the landlord was not enfeebled by his weakness, even at such a moment. He recovered and proceeded:—

"Yes, Mr. Colleton, I am a dead man. I have my wages—but my death is your life! Let me tell the story—and save you, and save Lucy—and thus—(oh, could I believe it for an instant)—save myself! But, no matter—we must talk of other things. Is that Brooks—is that Brooks beside me?"

"No, it is I—Colleton."

"I know—I know," impatiently—"who else?"

"Mr. Brooks, the jailer, is here—Ensign Martin and Brincle, of the Georgia guard," was the reply of the jailer.

"Enough, then, for your safety, Mr. Colleton. They can prove it all, and then remember Lucy—poor Lucy! You will be in time—save her from Guy Rivers—Guy Rivers—the wretch—not Guy Rivers—no—there's a secret—there's a secret for you, my men, shall bring you a handsome reward. Stoop—stoop, you three—where are you?—stoop, and hear what I have to say! It is my dying word!—and I swear it by all things, all powers, all terrors, that can make an oath solemn with a wretch whose life is a long crime! Stoop—hear me—heed all—lose not a word—not a word—not a word! Where are you?"

"We are here, beside you—we hear all that you say. Go on!"

"Guy Rivers is not his name—he is not Guy Rivers—hear now—Guy Rivers is the outlaw for whom the governor's proclamation gives a high reward—a thousand dollars—the man who murdered Judge Jessup. Edward Creighton, of Gwinnett courthouse—he is the murderer of Jessup—he is the murderer of Forrester, for whose death the life of Mr. Colleton here is forfeit! I saw him kill them both!—I saw more than that, but that is enough to save the innocent man and punish the guilty! Take down all that I have said. I, too, am guilty! would make amends, but it is almost too late—the night is very dark, and the earth swings about like a cradle. Ah!—have you taken down on paper what I said? I will tell you nothing more till all is written—write it down—on paper—every word—write that before I say any more!"

They complied with his requisition. One of the troopers, on a sheet of paper furnished by the jailer, and placed upon the saddle of his horse, standing by in the pale light of the moon, recorded word after word, with scrupulous exactness, of the dying man's confession. He proceeded duly to the narration of every particular of all past occurrences, as we ourselves have already detailed them to the reader, together with many more, unnecessary to our narrative, of which we had heretofore no cognizance. When this was done, the landlord required it to be read, commenting, during its perusal, and dwelling, with more circumstantial minuteness, upon many of its parts.

"That will do—that will do! Now swear me, Brooks!—you are in the commission—lift my hand and swear me, so that nothing be wanting to the truth! What if there is no bible?" he exclaimed, suddenly, as some one of the individuals present suggested a difficulty on this subject.

"What!—because there is no bible, shall there be no truth? I swear—though I have had no communion with God—I swear to the truth—by him! Write down my oath—he is present—they say he is always present! I believe it now—I only wish I had always believed it! I swear by him—he will not falsify the truth!—write down my oath, while I lift my hand to him! Would it were a prayer—but I can not pray—I am more used to oaths than prayers, and I can not pray! Is it written—it is written? Look, Mr. Colleton, look—you know the law. If you are satisfied, I am. Will it do?"

Colleton replied quickly in the affirmative, and the dying man went on:—

"Remember Lucy—the poor Lucy! You will take care of her. Say no harsh words in her ears—but, why should I ask this of you, whom— Ah!—it goes round—round—round—swimming—swimming. Very dark—very dark night, and the trees dance—Lucy—"

The voice sunk into a faint whisper whose sounds were unsyllabled—an occasional murmur escaped them once after, in which the name of his niece was again heard; exhibiting, at the last, the affection, however latent, which he entertained in reality for the orphan trust of his brother. In a few moments, and the form stiffened before them in all the rigid sullenness of death.

CHAPTER THIRTY-NINE

Wolf's Neck—Capture

The cupidity of his captors had been considerably stimulated by the dying words of Munro. They were all of them familiar with the atrocious murder which, putting a price upon his head, had driven Creighton, then a distinguished member of the bar in one of the more civilized portions of the state, from the pale and consideration of society; and their anxieties were now entirely addressed to the new object which the recital they had just heard had suggested to them. They had gathered from the narrative of the dying man some idea of the place in which they would most probably find the outlaw; and, though without a guide to the spot, and altogether ignorant of its localities, they determined—without reference to others, who might only subtract from their own share of the promised reward, without contributing much, if any, aid, which they might not easily dispense with—at once to attempt his capture. This was the joint understanding of the whole party, Ralph Colleton excepted.

In substance, the youth was now free. The evidence furnished by Munro only needed the recognition of the proper authorities to make him so; yet, until this had been effected, he remained in a sort of understood restraint, but without any actual limitations. Pledging himself that they should suffer nothing from the indulgence given him, he mounted the horse of Munro, whose body was cared for, and took his course back to the village; while, following the directions given them, the guard and jailer pursued their way to the Wolf's Neck in their search after Guy Rivers.

The outlaw had been deserted by nearly all his followers. The note of preparation and pursuit, sounded by the state authorities, had inspired the depredators with a degree of terror, which the near approximation of the guard, in strong numbers, to their most secluded place, had not a little tended to increase; and accordingly, at the period of which we now speak, the outlaw, deserted by all but one or two of the most daring of his followers—who were, however, careful enough of themselves to keep in no one place long, and cautiously to avoid their accustomed haunts—remained in his rock, in a state of gloomy despondency, not usually his characteristic. Had he been less stubborn, less ready to defy all chances and all persons, it is not improbable that Rivers would have taken counsel by their flight, and removed himself, for a time at least, from the scene of danger. But his native obstinacy, and that madness of heart which, as we are told, seizes first upon him whom God seeks to destroy, determined him, against the judgment of others, and in part against his own, to remain where he was; probably in the fallacious hope that the storm would pass over, as on so many previous occasions it had already done, and leave him again free to his old practices in the same region. A feeling of pride, which made him unwilling to take a suggestion of fear and flight from the course of others, had some share in this decision; and, if we add the vague hungering of his heart toward the lovely Edith, and possibly the influence of other pledges, and the imposing consideration of other duties, we shall not be greatly at a loss in understanding the injudicious indifference to the threatening dangers which appears to have distinguished the conduct of the otherwise politic and circumspect ruffian.

That night, after his return from the village, and the brief dialogue with Chub Williams, as we have already narrated it, he retired to the deepest cell of his den, and, throwing himself into a seat, covering his face with his hands, he gave himself up to a meditation as true in its philosophy as it was humiliating throughout in its application to himself. Dillon, his lieutenant—if such a title may be permitted in such a place, and for such a person—came to him shortly after his arrival, and in brief terms, with a blunt readiness—which, coming directly to the point, did not offend the person to whom it was addressed—demanded to know what he meant to do with himself.

"We can't stay here any longer," said he; "the troops are gathering all round us. The country's alive with them, and in a few days we shouldn't be able to stir from the hollow of a tree without popping into the gripe of some of our hunters. In the Wolf's Neck they will surely seek us; for, though a very fine place for us while the country's thin, yet even its old owners, the wolves, would fly from it when the horn of the hunter rings through the wood. It won't be very long before they pierce to the very 'nation,' and then we should have but small chance of a long grace. Jack Ketch would make mighty small work of our necks, in his hurry to go to dinner."

"And what of all this—what is all this to me?" was the strange and rather phlegmatic response of the outlaw, who did not seem to take in the full meaning of his officer's speech, and whose mind, indeed, was at that moment wandering to far other considerations. Dillon seemed not a little surprised by this reply, and looked inquiringly into the face of the speaker, doubting for a moment his accustomed sanity. The stern look which his glance encountered directed its expression elsewhere, and, after a moment's pause, he replied—

"Why, captain, you can't have thought of what I've been saying, or you wouldn't speak as you do. I think it's a great deal to both you and me, what I've been telling you; and the sooner you come to think so too, the better. It's only yesterday afternoon that I narrowly missed being seen at the forks by two of the guard, well mounted, and with rifles. I had but the crook of the fork in my favor, and the hollow of the creek at the old ford where it's been washed away. They're all round us, and I don't think we're safe here another day. Indeed, I only come to see if you wouldn't be off with me, at once, into the 'nation.'"

"You are considerate, but must go alone. I have no apprehensions where I am, and shall not stir for the present. For yourself, you must determine as you think proper. I have no further hold on your service. I release you from the oath. Make the best of your way into the 'nation'—ay, go yet farther; and, hear me, Dillon, go where you are unknown—go where you can enter society; seek for the fireside, where you can have those who, in the dark hour, will have no wish to desert you. I have no claim now upon you, and the sooner you 'take the range' the better."

"And why not go along with me, captain? I hate to go alone, and hate to leave you where you are. I shan't think you out of danger while you stay here, and don't see any reason for you to do so."

"Perhaps not, Dillon; but there is reason, or I should not stay. We may not go together, even if I were to fly—our paths lie asunder. They may never more be one. Go you, therefore, and heed me not; and think of me no more. Make yourself a home in the Mississippi, or on the Red river, and get yourself a fireside and family of your own. These are the things that will keep your heart warm within you, cheering you in hours that are dark, like this."

"And why, captain," replied the lieutenant, much affected—"why should you not take the course which you advise for me? Why not, in the Arkansas, make yourself a home, and with a wife—"

"Silence, sir!—not a word of that! Why come you to chafe me here in my den? Am I to be haunted for ever with such as you, and with words like these?" and the brow of the outlaw blackened as he spoke, and his white teeth knit together, fiercely gnashing for an instant, while the foam worked its way through the occasional aperture between them. The ebullition of passion, however, lasted not long, and the outlaw himself, a moment after, seemed conscious of its injustice.

"I do you wrong, Dillon; but on this subject I will have no one speak. I can not be the man you would have me; I have been schooled otherwise. My mother has taught me a different lesson: her teachings have doomed me, and these enjoyments are now all beyond my hope."

"Your mother?" was the response of Dillon, in unaffected astonishment.

"Ay, man—my mother! Is there anything wonderful in that? She taught me the love of evil with her milk—she sang it in lullabies over my cradle—she gave it me in the playthings of my boyhood; her schoolings have made me the morbid, the fierce criminal, the wilful, vexing spirit, from whose association all the gentler virtues must always desire to fly. If, in the doom which may finish my life of doom, I have any one person to accuse of all, that person is—my mother!"

"Is this possible? Can it be true? It is strange—very strange!"

"It is not strange; we see it every day—in almost every family. She did not *tell* me to lie, or to swindle, or to stab—no! oh, no! she would have told me that all these things were bad; but she *taught* me to perform them all. She roused my *passions,* and not my *principles,* into activity. She provoked the one, and suppressed the other. Did my father reprove my improprieties, she petted me, and denounced him. She crossed his better purposes, and defeated all his designs, until, at last, she made my passions too strong for my government, not less than hers, and left me, knowing the true, yet the victim of the false. Thus it was that, while my intellect, in its calmer hours, taught me that virtue is the only source of true felicity, my ungovernable passions set the otherwise sovereign reason at defiance, and trampled it under foot. Yes, in that last hour of eternal retribution, if called upon to denounce or to accuse, I can point but to one as the author of all—the weakly-fond, misjudging, misguiding woman who gave me birth!

"Within the last hour I have been thinking over all these things. I have been thinking how I had been cursed in childhood by one who surely loved me beyond all other things besides. I can remember how sedulously she encouraged and prompted my infant passions, uncontrolled by her authority and reason, and since utterly unrestrainable by my own. How she stimulated me to artifices, and set me the example herself, by frequently deceiving my father, and teaching me to disobey and deceive him! She told me not to lie; and she lied all day to him, on my account, and to screen me from his anger. She taught me the catechism, to say on Sunday, while during the week she schooled me in almost every possible form of ingenuity to violate all its precepts. She bribed me to do my duty, and hence my duty could only be done under the stimulating promise of a reward; and, without the reward, I went counter to the duty. She taught me that God was superior to all, and that he required obedience to certain laws; yet, as she hourly violated those laws herself in my behalf, I was taught to regard myself as far superior to him! Had she not done all this, I had not been here and thus: I had been what now I dare not think on. It is all her work. The greatest enemy my life has ever known has been my mother!"

"This is a horrible thought, captain; yet I can not but think it true."

"It is true! I have analyzed my own history, and the causes of my character and fortunes now, and I charge it all upon her. From one influence I have traced another, and another, until I have the sweeping amount of twenty years of crime and sorrow, and a life of hate, and probably a death of ignominy—all owing to the first ten years of my infant education, where the only teacher that I knew was the woman who gave me birth!—But this concerns not you. In my calm mood, Dillon, you have the fruit of my reason: to abide its dictate, I should fly with you; but I suffer from my mother's teachings even in this. My passions, my pride, my fierce hope—the creature of a maddening passion—

will not let me fly; and I stay, though I stay alone, with a throat bare for the knife of the butcher, or the halter of the handman. I will not fly!"

"And I will stay with you. I can dare something, too, captain; and you shall not say, when the worst comes to the worst, that Tom Dillon was the man to back out. I will not go either, and, whatever is the chance, you shall not be alone."

Rivers, for a moment, seemed touched by the devotion of his follower, and was silent for a brief interval; but suddenly the expression of his eye was changed, and he spoke briefly and sternly:—

"You shall not stay with me, sir! What! am I so low as this, that I may not be permitted to be alone when I will? Will my subordinates fly in my face, and presume to disobey my commands? Go, Dillon—have I not said that you *must* fly—that I no longer need your services? Why linger, then, where you are no longer needed? I have that to perform which requires me to be alone, and I have no further time to spare you. Go—away!"

"Do you really speak in earnest, captain?" inquired the lieutenant, doubtingly, and with a look of much concern.

"Am I so fond of trifling, that my officer asks me such a question?" was the stern response.

"Then I am your officer still—you will go with me, or I shall remain."

"Neither, Dillon. The time is past for such an arrangement. You are discharged from my service, and from your oath. The club has no further existence. Go—be a happy, a better man, in another part of the world. You have some of the weaknesses of your better nature still in you. You had no mother to change them into scorn, and strife, and bitterness. Go—you may be a better man, and have something, therefore, for which to live. I have not—my heart can know no change. It is no longer under the guidance of reason. It is quite ungovernable now. There was a time when—but why prate of this?—it is too late to think of, and only maddens me the more. Besides, it makes not anything with you, and would detain you without a purpose. Linger no longer, Dillon—speed to the west, and, at some future day, perhaps you shall see me when you least expect, and perhaps least desire it."

The manner of the outlaw was firm and commanding, and Dillon no longer had any reason to doubt his desires, and no motive to disobey his wishes. The parting was brief, though the subordinate was truly affected. He would have lingered still, but Rivers waved him off with a farewell, whose emphasis was effectual, and, in a few moments, the latter sat once more alone.

His mood was that of one disappointed in all things, and, consequently, displeased and discontented with all things—querulously so. In addition to this temper, which was common to him, his spirit, at this time, labored under a heavy feeling of despondency, and its gloomy sullenness was perhaps something lighter to himself while Dillon remained with him. We have seen the manner in which he had hurried that personage off. He had scarcely been gone, however, when the inconsistent and variable temper of the outlaw found utterance in the following soliloquy:—

"Ay, thus it is—they all desert me; and this is human feeling. They all fly the darkness, and this is human courage. They love themselves only, or you only while you need no love; and this is human sympathy. I need all of these, yet I get none; and when I most need, and most desire, and most seek to obtain, I am the least provided. These are the fruits which I have sown, however; should I shrink to gather them?

"Yet, there is one—but one of all—whom no reproach of mine could drive away, or make indifferent to my fate. But I will see her no more. Strange madness! The creature, who, of all the world, most loves me, and is most deserving of my love, I banish from my soul as from my sight. And this is another fruit of my education—another curse that came with a mother—this wilful love of the perilous and the passionate—this scorn of the gentle and the soft—this fondness for the fierce contradiction—this indifference to the thing easily won—this thirst after the forbidden. Poor Ellen—so gentle, so resigned, and so fond of her destroyer; but I will not see her again. I must not; she must not stand in the way of my anxiety to conquer that pride which had ventured to hate or to despise me. I shall see Munro, and he shall lose no time in this matter. Yet, what can he be after—he should have been here before this; it now wants but little to the morning, and ah! I have not slept. Shall I ever sleep again!"

Thus, striding to and fro in his apartment, the outlaw soliloquized at intervals. Throwing himself at length upon a rude couch that stood in the corner, he had disposed himself as it were for slumber, when the noise as of a falling rock, attracted his attention, and without pausing, he cautiously took his way to the entrance, with a view to ascertain the cause. He was not easily surprised, and the knowledge of surrounding danger made him doubly observant, and more than ever watchful.

Let us now return to the party which had pursued the fugitives, and which, after the death of the landlord, had, as we have already narrated, adopting the design suggested by his dying words, immediately set forth in search of the notorious outlaw, eager for the reward put upon his head. Having already some general idea of the whereabouts of the fugitive, and the directions given by Munro having been of the most specific character, they found little difficulty, after a moderate ride of some four or five miles, in striking upon the path directly leading to the Wolf's Neck.

At this time, fortunately for their object, they were encountered suddenly by our old acquaintance, Chub Williams, whom, but little before, we have seen separating from the individual in whose pursuit they were now engaged. The deformed quietly rode along with the party, but without seeming to recognise their existence—singing all the while a strange woodland melody of the time and region—probably the production of some village wit:—

"Her frock it was a *yaller,*
   And she was *mighty sprigh*
And she bounced at many a *feller*
   Who came *a-fighting shy.*

"Her eye was like a *sarpent's eye.*
   Her cheek was like a flower,
But her tongue was like a pedler's clock,
   'Twas a-striking every hour.

"And wasn't she the gal for me,
   And wasn't she, I pray, sir,
And I'll be *drot,* if you say not,
   We'll fight this very day, sir,
   We'll fight this very day, sir."

Having delivered himself of this choice morsel of song, the half-witted fellow conceitedly challenged the attention of the group whom he had not hitherto been disposed to see.

"'Spose you reckon I don't see you, riding 'longside of me, and say-ing nothing, but listening to my song. I'm singing for my own self, and

you oughtn't to listen—I didn't ax you, and I'd like to know what you're
doing so nigh Chub's house."

"Why, where's your house, Chub?" asked one of the party.

"You ain't looking for it, is you? 'cause you can't think to find it a-
looking down. I lives in the tree-top when weather's good like to-night,
and when it ain't, I go into the hollow. I've a better house than Guy
Rivers—he don't take the tree at all, no how."

"And where is his house, Chub?" was the common inquiry of all the
party. The dwarf looked at them for a few moments without speech,
then with a whisper and a gesture significant of caution, replied—

"If you're looking for Guy, 'tain't so easy to find him if he don't want
to be found, and you must speak softly if you hunt him, whether or no.
He's a dark man, that Guy Rivers—mother always said so—and he lives
a long way under the ground."

"And can't you show us where, Chub? We will give you money for
your service."

"Hain't you got 'tatoes? Chub's hungry—hain't eat nothing to-
night. Guy Rivers has plenty to eat, but he cursed Chub's mother."

"Well, show us where he is, and we'll give you plenty to eat. Plenty
of potatoes and corn," was the promise of the party.

"And build up Chub's house that the fire burnt? Chub lives in the
tree now. Guy Rivers' man burnt Chub's house, 'cause he said Chub was
sassy."

"Yes, my boy, we'll build up your house, and give you a plenty to go
upon for a year. You shall have potatoes enough for your lifetime, if you
will show us how to come upon Guy Rivers tonight. He *is* a bad fellow,
as you say; and we won't let him trouble you any more, if you'll only
show us where he is to be found."

"Well—I reckon I can," was the response, uttered in a confidential
whisper, and much more readily given than was the wont of the speaker.
"Chub and Guy talked together to-night, and Guy wanted Chub to go
with him into his house in Wolf's Neck. But Chub don't love the wolf,
and he don't love the Wolf's Neck, now that Miss Lucy's gone away from
it. It's a mighty dark place, the Wolf's Neck, and Chub's afear'd in the
dark places, where the moon and stars won't shine down."

"But you needn't be afraid now, little Chub. You're a good little fellow, and we'll keep with you and follow close, and there shall be no danger to you. We'll fight Guy Rivers for you, so that he can't hurt you any
more."

"You'll fight Guy! You! Guy kin fight to kill!"

"Yes, but we'll kill *him;* only you show us where he is, so that we can catch him and tie him, and he'll never trouble Chub any more."

"What! you'll tie Guy? How I'd like to see anybody tie Guy! You kain't tie Guy. He'd break through the ropes, he would, if he on'y stretched out his arms."

"You'll see! only show us how to find him, and we'll tie him, and we'll build you a new house, and you shall have more potatoes and corn than you can shake a stick at, and we'll give you a great jug of whiskey into the bargain."

"Now will you! And a jug of whiskey too, and build a new house for Chub's mother—and the corn, and the 'tatoes."

"All! you shall have all we promise."

"Come! come! saftly! put your feet down saftly, for Guy's got great white owls that watch for him, and they hoot from the old tree when the horses are coming. Saftly! saftly!"

There is an idiocy that does not lack the vulgar faculty of mere shrewdness—that can calculate selfishly, and plan coolly—in short, can show itself cunning, whenever it has a motive. Find the motive for the insane and the idiotic, always, if you would see them exercise the full extent of their little remaining wits.

Chub Williams had a sagacity of this sort. His selfishness was appealed to, and all his faculties were on the alert. He gave directions for the progress of the party—after his own manner, it is true—but with sufficient promptness and intelligence to satisfy them that they might rely upon him. Having reached a certain lonely spot among the hills, contiguous to the crag, or series of crags, called the Wolf's Neck, Chub made the party all dismount, and hide their horses in a thicket into which they found it no easy matter to penetrate. This done, he led them out again, cautiously moving along under cover, but near the margin of the road. He stept as lightly himself as a squirrel, taking care, before throwing his weight upon his foot, to feel that there was no rotting branch or bough beneath, the breaking of which might occasion noise.

"Saftly! saftly!" he would say in a whisper, turning back to the party, when he found them treading hurriedly and heavily upon the brush. Sometimes, again, he ran ahead of all of them, and for a few moments would be lost to sight; but he usually returned, as quickly and quietly as he went, and would either lead them forward on the same route with confidence, or alter it, according to his discoveries. He was literally feeling

his way; the instincts and experience of the practised scout finding no
sort of obstacle in the deficiency of his reasoning powers.

His processes did not argue any doubts of his course; only a choice
of direction—such as would promise more ease and equal security.
Some of his changes of movement, he tried to explain, in his own fashion, when he came back to guide them on other paths.

"Saftly back—saftly now, this way. Guy's in his dark house in the
rock, but there's a many rooms, and 't mout be, we're a walking jest
now, over his head. Then he mout hear, you see, and Guy's got ears like
the great owl. He kin hear mighty far in the night, and see too: and you
mustn't step into his holes. There's heap of holes in Guy's dark house.
Saftly, now—and here away."

Briefly, the rocky avenues were numerous in the Wolf's Neck, and
some of them ran near the surface. There were sinks upon the surface
also, covered with brush and clay, into which the unthinking wayfarer
might stumble, perhaps into the very cavern where the outlaw at that
moment housed himself. The group around the idiot did not fail to
comprehend the reasons for all his caution. They confided to his skill
implicitly; having, of themselves, but small knowledge of the wild
precincts into which they desired to penetrate.

Having, at length; brought them to points and places, which
afforded them the command of the avenues to the rock, the next object
of their guide was to ascertain where the outlaw was at that moment
secreted. It was highly important to know *where* to enter—where to
look—and not waste time in fruitless search of places in which a single
man might have a dozen blind seekers at his mercy. The cunning of the
idiot conceived this necessity himself.

His policy made each of the party hide himself out of sight, though
in a position whence each might see.

All arranged as he desired, the urchin armed himself with a rock,
not quite as large as his own head, but making a most respectable
approach to it. This, with the aid of coat and kerchief he secured upon
his back, between his shoulders; and thus laden, he yet, with the agility
of the opossum, her young ones in her pouch, climbed up a tree which
stood a little above that inner chamber which Guy Rivers had appropriated for himself, and where, on more occasions than one, our idiot had
peeped in upon him. Perched in his tree securely, and shrouded from
sight among its boughs, the urchin disengaged the rock from his shoulders, took it in both his hands, and carefully selecting its route, he

pitched it, with all his might, out from the tree, and in such a direction, that, after it had fairly struck the earth, it continued a rolling course down the declivity of the rocks, making a heavy clatter all the way it went.

The *ruse* answered its purpose. The keen senses of the outlaw caught the sound. His vigilance, now double keen, awakened to its watch. We have seen, in previous pages, the effect that the rolling stone had upon the musing and vexed spirit of Guy Rivers, after the departure of Dillon. He came forth, as we have seen, to look about for the cause of alarm; and, as if satisfied that the disturbance was purely accidental, had retired once more to the recesses of his den.

Here, throwing himself upon his couch, he seemed disposed to sleep. Sleep, indeed! He himself denied that he ever slept. His followers were all agreed that when he did sleep, it was only with half his faculties shut up. One eye, they contended, was always open!

Chub Williams, and one of the hunters had seen the figure of the outlaw as he emerged from the cavern. The former instantly identified him. The other was too remote to distinguish anything but a slight human outline, which he could only determine to be such, as he beheld its movements. He was too far to assault, the light was too imperfect to suffer him to shoot with any reasonable certainty of success, and the half of the reward sought by his pursuers, depended upon the outlaw being taken alive!

But, there was no disappointment among the hunters. Allowing the outlaw sufficient time to return to his retreats, Chub Williams slipped down his tree—the rest of the party slowly emerged from their several places of watch, and drew together for consultation.

In this matter, the idiot could give them little help. He could, and did, describe, in some particulars, such of the interior as he had been enabled to see on former occasions, but beyond this he could do nothing; and he was resolute not to hazard himself in entering the dominion of a personage, so fearful as Guy Rivers, in such companionship as would surely compel the wolf to turn at bay. Alone, his confidence in his own stealth and secresy, would encourage him to penetrate; but, *now!*—he only grinned at the suggestion of the hunters; saying shrewdly: "No! thank you! I'll stay out here and keep Chub's company."

Accordingly, he remained without, closely gathered up into a lump, behind a tree, while the more determined Georgians penetrated with cautious pace into the dark avenue, known in the earlier days of

the settlement as a retreat for the wolves when they infested that portion of the country, and hence distinguished by the appellation of the
Wolf's Neck.

For some time they groped onward in great uncertainty as to their
course; but a crevice in the wall, at one point, gave them a glimmer of
the moonlight, which, falling obliquely upon the sides of the cavern,
enabled them to discern the mouth of another gorge diverging from
that in which they were. They entered; and followed this new route,
until their farther progress was arrested by a solid wall which seemed to
close them in, hollowly caved from all quarters, except the one narrow
point from which they had entered it.

Here, then, they were at a stand; but, according to Chub's directions, there must be a mode of ingress to still another chamber from
this; and they prepared to seek it in the only possible way; namely, by
feeling along the wall for the opening which their eye had failed to
detect. They had to do this on hands and knees, so low was the rock
along the edges of the cavern.

The search was finally successful. One of the party found the wall to
give beneath his hands. There was an aperture, a mere passage-way for
wolf or bear, lying low in the wall, and only closed by a heavy curtain of
woollen.

This was an important discovery. The opening led directly into the
chamber of the outlaw. How easily it could be defended, the hunters
perceived at a glance. The inmate of the cavern, if wakeful and courageous, standing above the gorge with a single hatchet, could brain every
assailant on the first appearance of his head. How serious, then, the
necessity of being able to know that the occupant of the chamber
slept—that occupant being Guy Rivers. The pursuers well knew what
they might expect at his hands, driven to his last fastness, with the spear
of the hunter at his throat. Did he sleep, then—the man who never
slept, according to the notion of his followers, or with one eye always
open!

He did sleep, and never more soundly than now, when safety
required that he should be most on the alert. But there is a limit to the
endurance of the most iron natures, and the outlaw had overpassed his
bounds of strength. He was exhausted by trying and prolonged excitements, and completely broken down by physical efforts which would
have destroyed most other men outright. His subdued demeanor—his
melancholy—were all due to this condition of absolute exhaustion. He

slept, not a refreshing sleep, but one in which the excited spirit kept up
its exercises, so as totally to neutralize what nature designed as compensation in his slumbers. His sleep was the drowse of incapacity, not
the wholesome respite of elastic faculties. It was actual physical imbecility, rather than sleep; and, while the mere animal man, lay incapable,
like a log, the diseased imagination was at work, conjuring up its spec-
tres as wildly and as changingly, as the wizard of the magic-lanthorn
evokes his monsters against the wall.

His limbs writhed while he slept. His tongue was busy in audible
speech. He had no secrets, in that mysterious hour, from night, and
silence, and his dreary rocks. His dreams told him of no other auditors.

The hunter, who had found and raised the curtain that separated
his chamber from the gloomy gorges of the crag, paused, and motioned
his comrades back, while he listened. At first there was nothing but a
deep and painful breathing. The outlaw breathed with effort, and the
sigh became a groan, and he writhed upon the bed of moss which
formed his usual couch in the cavern. Had the spectator been able to
see, the lamp suspended from a ring in the roof of the cavern, though
burning very dimly, would have shown him the big-beaded drops of
sweat that now started from the brows of the sleeper. But he could hear;
and now a word, a name, falls from the outlaw's lips—it is followed by
murmured imprecations. The feverish frame, tortured by the restless
and guilt-goading spirit, writhed as he delivered the curses in broken
accents. These, finally, grew into perfect sentences.

"Dying like a dog in her sight! Ay, she shall see it! I will hiss in her
ears as she gazes—'It is *my* work! this is *my* revenge!' Ha! ha! where her
pride then?—her high birth and station?—wealth, family? Dust, shame,
agony, and death!"

Such were the murmured accents of the sleeping man, when they
were distinguishable by the hunter, who, crouching beneath the curtain, listened to his sleeping speech. But all was not exultation. The
change from the voice of triumph to that of wo was instantaneous; and
the curse and the cry, as of one in mortal agony, pain or terror, followed
the exulting speech.

The Georgian, now apprehensive that the outlaw would awaken,
crept forward, and, still upon his hands and knees, was now fairly
within the vaulted chamber. He was closely followed by one of his companions. Hitherto, they had proceeded with great caution, and with a
stealth and silence that were almost perfect. But the third of the party to

enter—who was Brooks, the jailer—more eager, or more unfortunate, less prudent certainly—not sufficiently stooping, as the other two had done, or rising too soon—contrived to strike with his head the pole which bore the curtain, and which, morticed in the sides of the cavern, ran completely across the awkward entrance. A ringing noise was the consequence, while Brooks himself was precipitated back into the passage, with a smart cut over his brows.

The noise was not great, but quite sufficient to dissipate the slumbers of the outlaw, whose sleep was never sound. With that decision and fierce courage which marked his character, he sprang to his feet in an instant, grasped the dirk which he always carried in his bosom, and leaped forward, like a tiger, in the direction of the narrow entrance. Familiar with all the sinuosities of his den, as well in daylight as in darkness, the chances might have favored him even with two powerful enemies within it. Certainly, had there been but one, he could have dealt with him, and kept out others. But the very precipitation of the jailer, while it occasioned the alarm, had the effect, in one particular, of neutralizing its evil consequences. The two who had already penetrated the apartment, had not yet risen from their knees—in the dim light of the lamp, they remained unseen—they were crouching, indeed, directly under the lamp, the rays of which lighted dimly the extremes, rather than the centre of the cell. They lay in the way of the outlaw, as he sprang, and, as he dashed forward from his couch toward the passageway, his feet were caught by the Georgian who had first entered, and so great was the impetus of his first awakening effort, that he was precipitated with a severe fall over the second of the party; and, half stunned, yet still striking furiously, the dirk of Rivers found a bloodless sheath in the earthen floor of the cell. In a moment, the two were upon him, and by the mere weight of their bodies alone, they kept him down.

"Surrender, Guy! we're too much for you, old fellow!"

There was a short struggle. Meanwhile, Brooks, the jailer, joined the party.

"We're *three* on you, and there's more without."

The outlaw was fixed to the ground, beneath their united weight, as firmly as if the mountain itself was on him. As soon as he became conscious of the inutility of further struggle—and he could now move neither hand nor foot—he ceased all further effort; like a wise man economizing his strength for future occasions. Without difficulty the captors bound him fast, then dragged him through the narrow entrance, the long rocky gorges which they had traversed, until they all emerged into the serene light of heaven, at the entrance of the cavern.

Here the idiot boy encountered them, now coming forward boldly, and staring in the face of the captive with a confidence which he had never known before. He felt that his fangs were drawn; and his survey of the person his mother had taught him so to dread, was as curious as that which he would have taken of some foreign monster. As he continued this survey, Rivers, with a singular degree of calmness for such a time, and such circumstances, addressed him thus:—

"So, Chub, this is your work;—you have brought enemies to my home, boy! Why have you done this? What have I done to you, but good? I gave bread to your mother and yourself!"

"Psho! Chub is to have his own bread, his own corn, and 'taters, too, and a whole jug of whiskey."

"Ah! you have sold yourself for these, then, to my enemies. You are a bad fellow, Chub—a worse fellow than I thought you. As an idiot, I fancied you might be honest and grateful."

"You're bad yourself, Mr. Guy. You cursed Chub, and you cursed Chub's mother; and your man burnt down Chub's house, and you wanted to shoot Chub on the tree."

"But I didn't shoot, Chub; and I kept the men from shooting you when you ran away from the cave."

"You can't shoot now," answered the idiot, with an exulting chuckle; "and they'll keep you in the ropes, Mr. Guy; they've got you on your back, Mr. Guy; and I'm going to laugh at you all the way as you go. Ho! ho! ho! See if I don't laugh, till I scares away all your white owls from the roost."

The outlaw looked steadily in the face of the wretched urchin, with a curious interest, as he half murmured to himself:—

"And that I should fall a victim to such a thing as this! The only creature, perhaps, whom I spared or pitied—so wretched, yet so ungrateful. But there is an instinct in it. It is surely in consequence of a law of nature. He hates in proportion as he fears. Yet he has had nothing but protection from me, and kindness. Nothing! I spared him, when—but—" as if suddenly recollecting himself, and speaking aloud and with recovered dignity:—

"I am your prisoner, gentlemen. Do with me as you please."

"Hurrah!" cried the urchin, as he beheld the troopers lifting and securing the outlaw upon the horse, while one of the party leaped up behind him—one of his hands managing the bridle, and the other grasping firmly the rope which secured the captive; "hurrah! Guy's in the rope! Guy's in the rope!"

Thus cried the urchin, following close behind the party, upon his mountain-tacky. That cry, from such a quarter, more sensibly than anything besides, mocked the outlaw with the fullest sense of his present impotence. With a bitter feeling of humiliation, his head drooped upon his breast, and he seemed to lose all regard to his progress. Daylight found him safely locked up in the jail of Chestatee, the occupant of the very cell from which Colleton had escaped.

But no such prospect of escape was before him. He could command none of the sympathies that had worked for his rival. He had no friends left. Munro was slain, Dillon gone, and even the miserable idiot had turned his fangs upon the hand that fed him. Warned, too, by the easy escape of Colleton, Brooks attended no more whiskey-parties, nor took his brother-in-law Tongs again into his friendly counsels. More—he doubly ironed his prisoner, whose wiles and resources he had more reason to fear than those which his former captive could command. To cut off more fully every hope which the outlaw might entertain of escape from his bonds and durance, a detachment of the Georgia guard, marching into the village that very day, was put in requisition, by the orders of the judge, for the better security of the prisoner, and of public order.

CHAPTER FORTY

Quiet Passages and New Relations

We have already reported the return of Lucy Munro to the village-inn of Chestatee. Here, to her own and the surprise of all other parties, her aunt was quietly reinstated in her old authority—a more perfect one now—as housekeeper of that ample mansion. The reasons which determined her liege upon her restoration to the household have been already reported to the reader. His prescience as to his own approaching fate was perhaps not the least urgent among them. He fortunately left her in possession, and we know how the law estimates this advantage. Of her trials and sorrows, when she was made aware of her widowhood, we will say nothing. Sensitive natures will easily conjecture their extent and intensity. It is enough for the relief of such natures, if we say that the widow Munro was not wholly inconsolable. As a good economist, a sensible woman, with an eye properly regardful of the future, we are bound to suppose that she needed no lessons from Hamlet's mother to make the cold baked funeral-meats answer a double purpose.

But what of her niece? We are required to be something more full and explicit in speaking to her case. The indisposition of Lucy was not materially diminished by the circumstances following the successful effort to persuade the landlord to the rescue of Ralph Colleton. The feverish excitements natural to that event, and even the fruit of its fortunate issue, in the death of Munro, for whom she really had a grateful regard, were not greatly lessened, though certainly something relieved, by the capture of Rivers, and his identification with the outlawed Creighton. She was now secure from him: she had nothing further to apprehend from the prosecution of his fearful suit; and the death of her uncle, even if the situation of Rivers had left him free to urge it further, would, of itself, have relieved her from the only difficulty in the way of a resolute denial.

So far, then, she was at peace. But a silent sorrow had made its way into her bosom, gnawing there with the noiselessness and certainty of the imperceptible worm, generated by the sunlight, in the richness of the fresh leaf, and wound up within its folds. She had no word of sorrow in her speech—she had no tear of sorrow in her eye—but there was a vacant sadness in the vague and wan expression of her face, that needed neither tears nor words for its perfect development. She was the victim of a passion which—as hers was a warm and impatient spirit—was doubly dangerous; and the greater pang of that passion came with the consciousness, which now she could no longer doubt, that it was entirely unrequited. She had beheld the return of Ralph Colleton; she had heard from other lips than his of his release, and of the atoning particulars of her uncle's death, in which he furnished all that was necessary in the way of testimony to the youth's enlargement and security; and though she rejoiced, fervently and deeply, at the knowledge that so much had been done for him, and so much by herself, she yet found no relief from the deep sadness of soul which necessarily came with her hopelessness. Busy tongues dwelt upon the loveliness of the Carolina maiden who had sought him in his prison—of her commanding stature, her elegance of form, her dignity of manner and expression, coupled with the warmth of a devoted love and a passionate admiration of the youth who had also so undesiringly made the conquest of her own heart. She heard all this in silence, but not without thought. She thought of nothing besides. The forms and images of the two happy lovers were before her eyes at all moments; and her active fancy pictured their mutual loves in colors so rich and warm, that, in utter despondency at last, she would throw herself listlessly upon her couch, with sometimes an unholy hope that she might never again rise from it.

But she was not forgotten. The youth she had so much served, and so truly saved, was neither thoughtless nor ungrateful. Having just satisfied those most near and dear to him of his safety, and of the impunity which, after a few brief forms of law, the dying confession of the landlord would give him; and having taken, in the warm embrace of a true love, the form of the no-longer withheld Edith to his arms, he felt that his next duty was to her for whom his sense of gratitude soon discovered that every form of acknowledgment must necessarily prove weak.

At an early hour, therefore—these several duties having been done—Ralph made his appearance at the village-inn, and the summons of the youth soon brought Lucy from her chamber.

She came freely and without hesitation, though her heart was tremulous with doubt and sorrow. She had nothing now to learn of her utter hopelessness, and her strength was gathered from her despair. Ralph was shocked at the surprising ravages which a few days of indisposition had made upon that fine and delicate richness of complexion and expression which had marked her countenance before. He had no notion that she was unhappy beyond the cure of time. On the contrary, with a modesty almost akin to dullness—having had no idea of his own influence over the maiden—he was disposed to regard the recent events—the death of Munro and the capture of Rivers—as they relieved her from a persecution which had been cruelly distressing, rather calculated to produce a degree of relief, to which she had not for a long time been accustomed; and which, though mingled up with events that prevented it from being considered matter for rejoicing, was yet not a matter for one in her situation very greatly to deplore.

Her appearance, however, only made him more assiduously gentle and affectionate in the duties he had undertaken to perform. He approached her with the freedom of one warranted by circumstances in recognizing in her person a relation next to the sweetest and the dearest in life. With the familiar regard of a brother, he took her hand, and placing her beside him on the rude sofa of the humble parlor, he proceeded to those little inquiries after her health, and of those about her, which usually form the opening topics of all conversation. He proceeded then to remind her of that trying night, when, in defiance of female fears, and laudably regardless of those staid checks and restraints by which her sex would conceal or defend its weaknesses, she had dared to save his life.

His manner, generally warm and eager, dilated something beyond its wont; and if ever gratitude had yet its expression from human lips and in human language, it was poured forth at that moment from his into the ears of Lucy Munro.

And she felt its truth; she relied upon the uttered words of the speaker; and her eyes grew bright with a momentary kindling, her cheek flushed under his glance, while her heart, losing something of the chillness which had so recently oppressed it, felt lighter and less desolate in that abode of sadness and sweetness, the bosom in which it dwelt.

Yet, after all, when thought came again under the old aspect—when she remembered his situation and her own, she felt the shadow once more come over her with an icy influence. It was not gratitude which her heart craved from that of Ralph Colleton. The praise and the approval and the thanks of others might have given her pleasure, but these were not enough from him; and she sighed that he from whom alone love would be precious, had nothing less frigid than gratitude to offer. But even that was much, and she felt it deeply. His approbation was not a little to a spirit whose reference to him was perpetual; and when—her hand in his—he recounted the adventures of that night—when he dwelt upon her courage—upon her noble disregard of opinions which might have chilled in many of her sex the fine natural currents of that godlike humanity which conventional forms, it is well to think, can not always fetter or abridge—when he expatiated upon all these things with all the fervor of his temperament—she with a due modesty, shrinking from the recital of her own performances—she felt every moment additional pleasure in his speech of praise. When, at length, relating the particulars of the escape and death of Munro, he proceeded, with all the tender caution of a brother, softening the sorrow into sadness, and plucking from grief as much of the sting as would else have caused the wound to rankle, she felt that though another might sway his heart and its richer affections, she was not altogether destitute of its consideration and its care.

"And now, Lucy—my sweet sister—for my sister you are now—you will accede to your uncle's prayer and mine—you will permit me to be your brother, and to provide for you as such. In this wild region it fits not that you should longer abide. This wilderness is uncongenial—it is foreign to a nature like yours. You have been too long its tenant—mingling with creatures not made for your association, none of whom are capable of appreciating your worth. You must come with us, and live with my uncle—with my cousin Edith—"

"Edith?"—and she looked inquiringly, while a slight flush of the cheek and kindling of the eye in him followed the utterance of the single word by her, and accompanied his reply.

"Yes, Edith—Edith Colleton, Lucy, is the name of my cousin, and the relationship will soon be something closer between us. You will love her, and she, I know, will love you as a sister, and as the preserver of one so very humble as myself. It was a night of danger when you first heard her name, and saw her features; and when you and she will converse over that night and its events, I feel satisfied that it will bring you both only the closer to one another."

"We will not talk of it farther, Mr. Colleton—I would not willingly hear of it again. It is enough that you are now free from all such danger—enough that all things promise well for the future. Let not any thought of past evil, or of risk successfully encountered, obscure the prospect—let no thought of me produce an emotion; hostile, even for a moment, to your peace."

"And why should you think, my sweet girl, and with an air of such profound sorrow, that such a thought must be productive of such an emotion. Why should the circumstances so happily terminating, though perilous at first, necessarily bring sorrow with remembrance. Surely you are now but exhibiting the sometimes coy perversity which is ascribed to your sex. You are now, in a moment of calm, but assuming those winning playfulnesses of a sex, conscious of charm and power, which, in a time of danger, your more masculine thought had rejected as unbecoming. You forget, Lucy, that I have you in charge—that you are now my sister—that my promise to your departed uncle, not less than my own desire to that effect, makes me your guardian for the future—and that I am now come hopeful of success, to take you with me to my own country, and to bring you acquainted with her—(I must keep no secret from you, who are my sister)—who has my heart—who—but you are sick, Lucy. What means this emotion?"

"Nothing, nothing, Mr. Colleton. A momentary weakness from my late indisposition—it will soon be over. Indeed, I am already well. Go on, sir—go on!"

"Lucy, why these titles? Why such formality? Speak to me as if I were the new friend, at least, if you will not behold in me an old one. I have received too much good service from you to permit of this constraint. Call me Ralph—or Colleton—or—or—nay, look not so coldly—why not call me your brother?"

"Brother—brother be it then, Ralph Colleton—brother—brother. God knows, I need a brother now!" and the ice of her manner was thawed quickly by his appeal, in which her accurate sense, sufficiently unclouded usually by her feelings, though themselves at all times strong, discovered only the honest earnestness of truth.

"Ah, now, you look—and now you are indeed my sister. Hear me, then, Lucy, and listen to all my plans. You have not seen Edith—my Edith now—you must be *her* sister too. She is now, or will be soon, something nearer to me than a sister—she is something dearer already. We shall immediately return to Carolina, and you will go along with us."

"It may not be, Ralph—I have determined otherwise. I will be your sister—as truly so as sister possibly could be—but I can not go with you. I have made other arrangements."

The youth looked up in astonishment. The manner of the maiden was very resolute, and he knew not what to understand. She proceeded, as she saw his amazement:—

"It may not be as you propose, Mr.—Ralph—my brother—circumstances have decreed another arrangement—another, and perhaps a less grateful destiny for me."

"But why, Lucy, if a less pleasant, or at least a doubtful arrangement, why yield to it—why reject my solicitation? What is the plan to which, I am sad to see, you so unhesitatingly give the preference?"

"Not unhesitatingly—not unhesitatingly, I assure you. I have thought upon it deeply and long, and the decision is that of my cooler thought and calmer judgment. It may be in a thousand respects a less grateful arrangement than that which you offer me; but, at least, it will want one circumstance which would couple itself with your plan, and which would alone prompt me to deny myself all its other advantages."

"And what is that one circumstance, dear Lucy, which affrights you so much? Let me know. What peculiarity of mine—what thoughtless impropriety—what association, which I may remove, thus prevents your acceptance of my offer, and that of Edith? Speak—spare me not in what you shall say—but let your thoughts have their due language, just as if you were—as indeed you are—my sister."

"Ask me not, Ralph, I may not utter it. It must not be whispered to myself, though I perpetually hear it. It is no impropriety—no peculiarity—no wrong thought or deed of yours, that occasions it. The evil is in me; and hence you can do nothing which can possibly change my determination."

"Strange, strange girl! What mystery is this? Where is now that feeling of confidence, which led you to comply with my prayer, and consider me as your brother? Why keep this matter from me—why withhold any particular, the knowledge of which might be productive of a remedy for all the difficulty."

"Never—never. The knowledge of it would be destructive of all beside. It would be fatal—seek not, therefore, to know it—it would profit you nothing, and me it would crush for ever to the earth. Hear me, Ralph—my brother!—hear me. Hitherto you have known me—I am proud to think—as a strong-minded woman, heedless of all things in her desire for the good—for the right. In a moment of peril to you or to another, I would be the same woman. But the strength which supports through the trial, subsides when it is over. The ship that battles with the storms and the seas, with something like a kindred buoyancy, goes down with the calm that follows their violence. It is so with me. I could do much—much more than woman generally—in the day of trial, but I am the weakest of my sex when it is over. Would you have the secret of these weaknesses in your possession, when you must know that the very consciousness, that it is beyond my own control, must be fatal to that pride of sex which, perhaps, only sustains me now? Ask me not further, Ralph, on this subject. I can tell you nothing; I *will* tell you nothing; and to press me farther must only be to estrange me the more. It is sufficient that I call you brother—that I pledge myself to love you as a sister—as sister never loved brother before. This is as much as I can do, Ralph Colleton—is it not enough?"

The youth tried numberless arguments and entreaties, but in vain, to shake her purpose; and the sorrowful expression of his voice and manner, not less than of his language, sufficiently assured her of the deep mortification which he felt upon her denial. She soothed his spirit with a gentleness peculiarly her own, and, as if she had satisfied herself that she had done enough for the delicacy of her scruples in one leading consideration, she took care that her whole manner should be that of the most confiding and sisterly regard. She even endeavored to be cheerful, seeing that her companion, with her unlooked-for denial, had lost all his elasticity; but without doing much to efface from his countenance the traces of dissatisfaction.

"And what are your plans, Lucy? Let me know them, at least. Let me see how far they are likely to be grateful to your character, and to make you happy."

"Happy! happy!" and she uttered but the two words, with a brief interval between them, while her voice trembled, and the gathering suffusion in her large and thickly-fringed blue eyes attested, more than anything besides, the prevailing weakness of which she had spoken.

"Ay, happy, Lucy! That is the word. You must not be permitted to choose a lot in life, in which the chances are not in favor of your happiness."

"I look not for that now, Ralph," was her reply, and with such hopeless despondency visible in her face as she spoke, that, with a deeper interest, taking her hand, he again urged the request she had already so recently denied.

"And why not, my sweet sister? Why should you not anticipate happiness as well as the rest of us? Who has a better right to happiness than the young, the gentle, the beautiful, the good?—and you are all of these, Lucy! You have the charms—the richer and more lasting charms—which, in the reflective mind, most always awaken admiration! You have animation, talent, various and active—sentiment, the growth of truth, propriety, and a lofty aim—no flippancy, no weak vanity—and a gentle beauty, that woos while it warms."

Her face became very grave, as she drew back from him.

"Nay, my sweet Lucy! why do you repulse me? I speak nothing but the truth."

"You mock me!—I pray you, mock me not. I have suffered much, Mr. Colleton—very much, in the few last years of my life, from the sneer, and the scorn, and the control of others! But I have been taught to hope for different treatment, and a far gentler estimate. It is ill in you to take up the speech of smaller spirits, and when the sufferer is one so weak, so poor, so very wretched as I am now! I had not looked for such scorn from you!"

Ralph was confounded. Was this caprice? He had never seen any proof of the presence of such an infirmity in her. And yet, how could he account for those strange words—that manner so full of offended pride? What had he been saying? How had she misconceived him? He took her hand earnestly in his own. She would have withdrawn it; but no!—he held it fast, and looked pleadingly into her face, as he replied:—

"Surely, Lucy, you do me wrong! How could you think that I would design to give you pain? Do you really estimate me by so low a standard, that my voice, when it speaks in praise and homage, is held to be the voice of vulgar flattery, and designing falsehood?"

"Oh, no, Ralph! not that—anything but that!"

"That I should sneer at *you*, Lucy—feel or utter scorn—*you*, to whom I owe so much! Have I then been usually so flippant of speech—a trifler—when we have spoken together before?—the self-assured fopling, with fancied superiority, seeking to impose upon the vain spirit and the simple confidence? Surely, I have never given you cause to think of me so meanly!"

"No! no! forgive me! I know not what I have said! I meant nothing so unkind—so unjust!"

"Lucy, your esteem is one of my most precious desires. To secure it, I would do much—strive earnestly—make many sacrifices of self. Certainly, for this object, I should be always truthful."

"You are, Ralph! I believe you."

"When I praised you, I did not mean merely to praise. I sought rather to awaken you to a just appreciation of your own claims upon a higher order of society than that which you can possibly find in this frontier region. I have spoken only the simple truth of your charms and accomplishments. I have *felt* them, Lucy, and paint them only as they are. Your beauties of mind and person—"

"Oh, do not, I implore you!"

"Yes, I must, Lucy! though of these beauties I should not have spoken—should not now speak—were it not that I feel sure that your superior understanding would enable you to listen calmly to a voice, speaking from my heart to yours, and speaking nothing but a truth which it honestly believes! And it is your own despondency, and humility of soul, that prompts me thus to speak in your praise. There is no good reason, Lucy, why you should not be happy—why fond eyes should not look gladly and gratefully for the smiles of yours! You carry treasures into society, Lucy, which society will everywhere value as beyond price!"

"Ah! why will you, sir—why, Ralph?—"

"You must not sacrifice yourself, Lucy. You must not defraud society of its rights. In a more refined circle, whose chances of happiness will be more likely to command than yours? You must go with me and Edith—go to Carolina. There you will find the proper homage. You will see the generous and the noble;—they will seek you—honorable gentlemen, proud of your favor, happy in your smiles—glad to offer you homes and hearts, such as shall be not unworthy of your own."

The girl heard him, but with no strengthening of self-confidence. The thought which occurred to her, which spoke of her claims, was that *he* had not found them so coercive. But, of course, she did not breathe the sentiment. She only sighed, and shook her head mournfully; replying, after a brief pause:—

"I must not hear you, Ralph. I thank you, I thank Miss Colleton, for the kindness of this invitation, but I dare not accept it. I can not go with you to Carolina. My lot is here, with my aunt, or where she goes. I must not desert her. She is now even more destitute than myself."

"Impossible! Why, Lucy, your aunt tells me that she means to continue in this establishment. How can you reconcile it to yourself to remain here, with the peril of encountering the associations, such as we have already known them, which seem naturally to belong to such a border region."

"You forget, Ralph, that it was here I met with you," was the sudden reply, with a faint smile upon her lips.

"Yes; and I was driven here by a fate, against my will—that we *should* meet, Lucy. But though we are both here, now, the region is unseemly to both, and neither need remain an hour longer than it is agreeable. Why should you remain out of your sphere, and exposed to every sort of humiliating peril."

"You forget—my aunt."

"Ay, but what security is there that she will not give you another uncle?"

"Oh, fie, Ralph!"

"Ay, she is too feeble of will, too weak, to be independent. She will marry again, Lucy, and is not the woman to choose wisely. Besides, she is not your natural aunt. She is so by marriage only. The tie between you is one which gives her no proper claim upon you."

"She has been kind to me, Ralph."

"Yet she would have seen you sacrificed to this outlaw!"

Lucy shuddered. He continued:—

"Her kindness, lacking strength and courage, would leave you still to be sacrificed, whenever a will, stronger than her own, should choose to assert a power over you. She can do nothing for you—not even for your security. You must not remain here, Lucy."

"Frankly, then, Ralph, I do not mean to do so long; nor does my aunt mean it. She is feeble, as you say; and, knowing it, I shall succeed in persuading her to sell out here, and we shall then remove to a more civilized region, to a better society, where, indeed, if you knew it, you would find nothing to regret, and see no reason to apprehend either for my securities or tastes. We shall seek refuge among my kindred—among the relatives of my mother—and I shall there be as perfectly at home, and quite as happy, as I can be any where."

"And where is it that you go, Lucy?"

"Forgive me, Ralph, but I must not tell you."

"Not tell me!"

"Better that I should not—better, far better! The duties for which the high Providence brought us together have been, I think, fairly accomplished. I have done my part, and you, Mr. Colleton—Ralph, I mean—you have done yours. There is nothing more that we may not do apart. Here, then, let our conference end. It is enough that you have complied with the dying wish of my uncle—that I have not, is not your fault."

"Not my fault, Lucy, but truly my misfortune. But I give not up my hope so easily. I still trust that you will think better of your determination, and conclude to go with us. We have a sweet home, and should not be altogether so happy in it, with the thought of your absence for ever in our minds."

"What!—not happy, and she with you!"

"Happy!—yes!—but far happier with both of you. You, my sister, and—"

"Say no more—"

"No more now, but I shall try other lips, perhaps more persuasive than mine. Edith shall come—"

His words were suddenly arrested by the energetic speech and action of his companion. She put her hand on his wrist—grasped it—and exclaimed—

"Let her not come! Bring her not here, Ralph Colleton! I have no wish to see her—*will not* see her, I tell you—would not have her see *me* for the world!"

Ralph was confounded, and recoiled from the fierce, spasmodic energy of the speaker, so very much at variance with the subdued tone of her previous conversation. He little knew what an effort was required hitherto, on her part, to maintain that tone, and to speak coolly and quietly of those fortunes, every thought of which brought only disappointment and agony to her bosom.

She dropped his hand as she concluded, and with eyes still fixed upon him, she half turned round, as if about to leave the room. But the crisis of her emotions was reached. She sickened with the effort. Her limbs grew too weak to sustain her; a sudden faintness overspread all her faculties—her eyes closed—she gasped hysterically, and tottering forward, she sank unconscious into the arms of Ralph, which were barely stretched out in time to save her from falling to the floor. He bore her to the sofa, and laid her down silently upon it.

He was struck suddenly with the truth to which he had hitherto shown himself so blind. He would have been the blindest and most obtuse of mortals, did he now fail to see. That last speech, that last look, and the fearful paroxysm which followed it, had revealed the poor girl's secret. Its discovery overwhelmed him, at once with the consciousness of his previous and prolonged dullness—which was surely mortifying—as with the more painful consciousness of the evil which he had unwittingly occasioned. But the present situation of the gentle victim called for immediate attention; and, hastily darting out to another apartment, he summoned Mrs. Munro to the succor of her niece.

"What is the matter, Mr. Colleton?"

"She faints," answered the other hoarsely, as he hurried the widow into the chamber.

"Bless my soul, what *can* be the matter!"

The wondering of the hostess was not permitted to consume her time and make her neglectful; Colleton did not suffer this. He hurried her with the restoratives, and saw them applied, and waiting only till he could be sure of the recovery of the patient, he hurried away, without giving the aunt any opportunity to examine him in respect to the cause of Lucy's illness.

Greatly excited, and painfully so, Ralph hastened at once to the lodgings of Edith. She was luckily alone. She cried out, as he entered—

"Well, Ralph, she will come with us?"

"No!"

"No!—and why not, Ralph! I must go and see her."

"She will not see you, Edith."

"Not see me!"

"No! She positively declines to see you."

"Why, Ralph, that is very strange. What can it mean?"

"Mean, Edith, it means that I am very unfortunate. I have been a blind fool if nothing worse."

"Why, what can *you* mean, Ralph. What is this new mystery? This is, surely, a place of more marvels than—"

"Hear me, Edith, my love, and tell me what you think. I am bewildered, mortified, confounded."

He proceeded, as well as he could to relate what had occurred; to give, not only the words, but to describe the manner of Lucy—so much of it had been expressed in this way—and he concluded, with a warm suffusion of his cheeks, to mention the self-flattering conclusion to which he had come:—

"Now, Edith, you who know me so well, tell me, can you think it possible that I have done, or said anything which has been calculated to make her suppose that I loved her—that I sought her. In short, do you think me capable of playing the scoundrel. I feel that I have been blind—something of a fool, Edith—but, on my soul, I can not recall a moment in which I have said or shown anything to this poor girl which was unbecoming in the gentleman."

The maiden looked at him curiously. At first there was something like an arch smile playing upon her lips and in her light lively eyes. But when she noted how real was his anxiety—how deeply and keenly he felt his own doubt—she felt that the little jest which occurred to her fancy, would be unseemly and unreasonable. So, she answered promptly, but quietly—

"Pshaw, Ralph, how can you afflict yourself with any such notions? I have no doubt of the perfect propriety of your conduct, and I will venture to say that Miss Munro entertains no reproaches."

"Yet, feeling so grateful to her, Edith—and when I first came here, lonely, wounded and suffering every way—feeling so much the want of sympathy—I may have shown to her—almost the only being with whom I could sympathize—I may have shown to her a greater degree of interest, than—"

"My dear Ralph, you are certainly one of the most modest young men of the present generation; that is, if you do not deceive yourself now, in your conjectures touching the state of Miss Munro's affections. After all, it may be a sudden illness from exhaustion, excitement, terror—which you have undertaken to account for by supposing her desperately in love."

"Heaven grant it be so," answered Ralph.

"Well, whether so or not, do not distress yourself. I will answer for it, you are not to blame. And here, let me whisper a little secret in your ears. However forbidden by all the wise, solemn, staid regulations of good society, there are young women—very few I grant you—who will, without the slightest call for it, or provocation, suffer their little hearts to go out of their own keeping—who will—I am ashamed to confess it—

positively suffer themselves to love even where the case is hopeless—where no encouragement is given to them—where they can have no rights at all, and where they can only sigh, and mourn, and envy the better fortunes of other people. I have no doubt that Miss Munro is one of these very unsophisticated persons; and that you have been all the while, and only the innocent cause of all her troubles. I acquit you of *lèse majesté*, Ralph, so put off your doleful faces."

"Don't speak so carelessly of the matter, Edith. We owe this girl a heavy debt—I do, at least."

"And we shall try and pay it, Ralph. But you must leave this matter to me. I will go and see Lucy."

"But she refuses to see you."

"I will not be refused. I *will* see her, and she *shall* see me, and I trust we shall succeed in taking her home with us. It may be, Ralph, that she will feel shy in thinking of you as a brother, but I will do my best to make her adopt me as a sister."

"My own, my generous Edith—it was ever thus—you are always the noble and the true. Go, then—you are right—you must go alone. Relieve me from this sorrow if you can. I need not say to you, persuade her, if in your power; for much I doubt whether her prospects are altogether so good as she has represented them to me. So fine a creature must not be sacrificed."

Edith lost no time in proceeding to the dwelling and into the chamber of Lucy Munro. She regarded none of the objections of the old lady, the aunt of her she sought, who would have denied her entrance. Edith's was a spirit of the firmest mould—tenacious of its purpose, and influenced by no consideration which would have jostled with the intended good. She approached the sufferer, who lay half-conscious only on her couch. Lucy could not be mistaken as to the person of her visiter. The noble features, full of generous beauty and a warm spirit, breathing affection for all human things, and doubly expanded with benevolent sweetness when gazing down upon one needing and deserving of so much—all told her that the beloved and the betrothed of Ralph Colleton was before her. She looked but once; then, sighing deeply, turned her head upon the pillow, so as to shut out a presence so dangerously beautiful.

But Edith was a woman whose thoughts—having deeply examined the minute structure of her own heart—could now readily understand that of another which so nearly resembled it. She perceived the true course for adoption; and, bending gently over the despairing girl, she possessed herself of one of her hands, while her lips, with the most playful sweetness of manner, were fastened upon those of the sufferer. The speech of such an action was instantaneous in its effect.

"Oh, why are you here—why did you come?" was the murmured inquiry of the drooping maiden.

"To know you—to love you—to win you to love me, Lucy. I would be worthy of your love, dear girl, if only to be grateful. I know how worthy you are of all of mine. I have heard all."

"No! no! not all—not all, or you never would be here."

"It is for that very reason that I am here. I have discovered more than Ralph Colleton could report, and love you all the better. Lucy, as you can feel with me how worthy he is of the love of both."

A deep sigh escaped the lips of the lovely sufferer, and her face was again averted from the glance of her visiter. The latter passed her arm under her neck, and, sitting on the bedside, drew Lucy's head to her bosom.

"Yes, Lucy, the woman has keener instincts than the man, and feels even where he fails to see. Do not wonder, therefore, that Edith Colleton knows more than her lover ever dreamed of. And now I come to entreat you to love *me* for *his* sake. You shall be my sister, Lucy, and in time you may come to love me for my own sake. My pleasant labor, Lucy, shall be to win your love—to force you to love me, whether you will or no. We can not alter things, can not change the courses of the stars; can not force nature to our purposes in the stubborn heart or the wilful fancy: and the wise method is to accommodate ourselves to the inevitable, and see if we can not extract an odor from the breeze no matter whence it blows. Now, I am an only child, Lucy. I have neither brother nor sister, and want a friend, and need a companion, one whom I can love—"

"You will have—have—your husband."

"Yes, Lucy, and as a husband! But I am not content. I must have *you*, also, Lucy."

"Oh, no, no! I can not—can not!"

"You *must!* I can not and will not go without you. Hear me. You have mortified poor Ralph very much. He swore to your uncle, in his dying moments—an awful moment—that you should be his sister— that you should enjoy his protection. His own desires—mine—my father's—all concur to make us resolute that Ralph shall keep his oath!

And he must! and you must consent to an arrangement upon which we have set our hearts."

"To live with *him*—to see *him* daily!" murmured the suffering girl.

"Ay, Lucy," answered the other boldly; "and to love him, and honor him, and sympathize with him in his needs, as a true, devoted woman and sister, so long as he shall prove worthy in your eyes and mine. I know that I am asking of you, Lucy, what I would ask of no ordinary woman. If I held you to be an ordinary woman, to whom we simply owe a debt of gratitude, I should never dream to offer such an argument. But it is because you *do* love him, that I wish you to abide with us; your love hallowed by its own fires, and purifying itself, as it will, by the exercise of your mind upon it."

The cheeks of Lucy flushed suddenly, but she said nothing. Edith stooped to her, and kissed her fondly. Then she spoke again, so tenderly, so gently, with such judicious pleading—appealing equally to the exquisite instincts of the loving woman and the thoughtful mind—that the suffering girl was touched.

But she struggled long. She was unwilling to be won. She was vexed that she was so weak: she was so weary of all struggle, and she needed sympathy and love so much!

How many various influences had Edith to combat! how many were there working in her favor! What a conflict was it all in the poor heart of the sorrowful and loving Lucy!

Edith was a skilful physician for the heart—skilful beyond her years.

Love was the great want of Lucy.

Edith soon persuaded her that she knew how to supply it. She was so solicitous, so watchful, so tender, so—

Suddenly the eyes of Lucy gushed with a volume of tears, and she buried her face in Edith's bosom; and she wept—how passionately!—the sobbings of an infant succeeding to the more wild emotions of the soul, and placing her, like a docile and exhausted child, at the entire control of her companion, even as if she had been a mother.

"Do with me as you will, Edith, my sister."

There was really no argument, there were no reasons given, which could persuade any mind, having first resolved on the one purpose, to abandon it for the other. How many reasons had Lucy for being firm in the first resolution she had made!

But the ends of wisdom do not depend upon the reasons which

enforce conviction. Nay, conviction itself, where the heart is concerned, is rarely to be moved by any efforts, however noble, of the simply reasoning faculty.

Shall we call them *arts*—the processes by which Edith Colleton had persuaded Lucy Munro to her purposes? No! it was the sweet nature, the gentle virtues, the loving tenderness, the warm sympathies, the delicate tact—these, superior to art and reason, were made evident to the suffering girl, in the long interview in which they were together; and her soul melted under their influence, and the stubborn will was subdued, and again she murmured lovingly—

"Do with me as you will, my sister."

CHAPTER FORTY-ONE

"Last Scene of All"

There was no little stir in the village of Chestatee on the morning following that on which the scene narrated in the preceding chapter had taken place. It so happened that several of the worthy villagers had determined to remove upon that day; and Colonel Colleton and his family, consisting of his daughter, Lucy Munro, and his future son-in-law, having now no further reason for delay, had also chosen it as their day of departure for Carolina. Nor did the already named constitute the sum total of the cavalcade setting out for that region. Carolina was about to receive an accession in the person of the sagacious pedler, who, in a previous conversation with both Colonel Colleton and Ralph, had made arrangements for future and large adventures in the way of trade—having determined, with the advice and assistance of his newly-acquired friends, to establish one of those wonders of various combinations, called a country store, among the good people of Sumter district. Under their direction, and hopeful of the Colleton patronage and influence, Bunce never troubled himself to dream of unprofitable speculations; but immediately drawing up letters for his brother and some other of his kinsmen engaged in the manufacture, in Connecticut, of one kind of *notion* or other, he detailed his new designs, and furnished liberal orders for the articles required and deemed necessary for the wants of the free-handed backwoodsmen of the South. Lest our readers should lack any information on the subject of these wants, we shall narrate a brief dialogue between the younger Colleton and our worthy merchant, which took place but a few hours before their departure:—

"Well, Bunce, are you ready? We shall be off now in a couple of hours or so, and you must not keep us waiting. Pack up at once, man, and make yourself ready."

"I guess you're in a little bit of a small hurry, Master Colleton, 'cause, you see, you've some reason to be so. You hain't had so easy a spell on it, no how, and I don't wonder as how you're no little airnest to get off. Well, you won't have to wait for me. I've jest got through mending my little go-cart—though, to be sure, it don't look, no how, like the thing it was. The rigilators made awful sad work of the box and body, and, what with patching and piecing, there's no two eends on it alike."

"Well, you're ready, however, and we shall have no difficulty at the last hour?"

"None to speak on. Jared Bunce aint the chap for burning daylight; and whenever you're ready to say, 'Go,' he's gone. But, I say, Master Ralph, there's one little matter I'd like to look at."

"What's that? Be quick, now, for I've much to see to."

"Only a minute. Here, you see, is a letter I've jest writ to my brother, Ichabod Bunce, down to Meriden. He's a 'cute chap, and quite a Yankee, now, I tell you; and as I knows all his ways, I've got to keep a sharp look-out to see he don't come over me. Ah, Master Ralph, it's a hard thing to say one's own flesh and blood aint the thing, but the truth's the truth to be sure, and, though it does hurt in the telling, that's no reason it shouldn't be told."

"Certainly not!"

"Well, as I say, Ichabod Bunce is as close and 'cute in his dealings as any man in all Connecticut, and that's no little to say, I'm sartin. He's got the trick, if anybody's got it, of knowing how to make your pocket his, and squaring all things coming in by double multiplication. If he puts a shilling down, it's sure to stick to another; and if he picks one up, it never comes by itself—there's always sure to be two on 'em."

"A choice faculty for a tradesman."

"You've said it."

"Just the man for business, I take it."

"Jest so; you're right there, Master Colleton—there's no mistake about that. Well, as I tell'd you now, though he's my own brother, I have to keep a raal sharp look out over him in all our dealings. If he says two and two makes four, I sets to calkilate, for when he says so, I'm sure there's something wrong in the calkilation; and tho' to be sure I do know, when the thing stands by itself, that two and two does make four; yet, somehow, whenever he says it, I begin to think it not altogether so sartain. Ah, he's a main hand for trade, and there's no knowing when he'll come over you."

"But, Bunce, without making morals a party to this question, as you are in copartnership with your brother, you should rather rejoice that he possesses so happy a faculty; it certainly should not be a matter of regret with you."

"Why, how—you wouldn't have me to be a mean-spirited fellow, who would live all for money, and not care how it comes. I can't, sir— 'tain't my way, I assure you. I do feel that I wasn't born to live nowhere except in the South; and so I thought when I wrote Ichabod Bunce my last letter. I told him every man on his own hook, now—for, you see, I couldn't stand his close-fisted contrivances no longer. He wanted me to work round the ring like himself, but I was quite too up-and-down for that, and so I squared off from him soon as I could. We never did agree when we were together, you see—'cause naterally, being brothers and partners, he couldn't shave me as he shaved other folks, and so, 'cause he couldn't by nature and partnership come 'cute over me, he was always grumbling, and for every yard of prints, he'd make out to send two yards of grunt and growls, and that was too much, you know, even for a pedler to stand; so we cut loose, and now as the people say on the river—every man paddle his own canoe."

"And you are now alone in the way of trade, and this store which you are about to establish is entirely on your own account?"

"Guess it is; and so, you see, I must pull with single oar up stream, and shan't quarrel with no friend that helps me now and then to send the boat ahead."

"Rely upon us, Bunce. You have done too much in my behalf to permit any of our family to forget your services. We shall do all that we can toward giving you a fair start in the stream, and it will not be often that you shall require a helping-hand in paddling your canoe."

"I know'd it, Master Colleton. 'Tain't in Carolina, nor in Georgy, nor Virginny, no—nor down in Alabam, that a man will look long for provisions, and see none come. That's the people for me. I guess I must ha' been born by nature in the South, though I did see daylight in Connecticut."

"No blarney, Bunce. We know you—what you are and what you are not!—good and bad in fair proportions. But what paper is that in your hand?"

"Oh, that? That's jest what I was going now to ax you about. That's my bill of particulars, you see, that I'm going to send on by the post, to Ichabod Bunce. He'll trade with me, now we're off partnership, and be as civil as a lawyer jest afore court-time. 'Cause, you see, he'll be trying to come over me, and will throw as much dust in my eyes as he can. But I guess he don't catch me with mouth ajar. I know his tricks, and he'll find me up to them."

"And what is it you require of me in this matter?"

"Oh, nothing, but jest to look over this list, and tell me how you 'spose the things will suit your part of the country. You see I must try and larn how to please my customers, that is to be. Now, you see, here's, in the first place—for they're a great article now in the country, and turn out well in the way of sale—here's—"

But we need not report the catalogue. Enough, that he proceeded to unfold (dwelling with an emphatic and precise description of each article in turn) the immense inventory of wares and merchandises with which he was about to establish. The assortment was various enough. There were pen-knives, and jack-knives, and clasp-knives, and dirk-knives, horn and wooden combs, calicoes and clocks, and tin-ware and garden-seeds; everything, indeed, without regard to fitness of association, which it was possible to sell in the region to which he was going.

Ralph heard him through his list with tolerable patience; but when the pedler, having given it a first reading, proposed a second, with passing comments on the prospects of sale of each separate article, by way of recapitulation, the youth could stand it no longer. Apologizing to the tradesman, therefore, in good set terms, he hurried away to the completion of those preparations called for by his approaching departure. Bunce having no auditor, was compelled to do the same; accordingly, a few hours after, the entire party made its appearance in the court of the village-inn, where the carriages stood in waiting.

About this time another party left the village, though in a different direction. It consisted of old Allen, his wife, and daughter Kate. In their company rode the lawyer Pippin, who, hopeless of elevation in his present whereabouts, was solicitous of a fairer field for the exhibition of his powers of law and logic than that which he now left had ever afforded him. He made but a small item in the caravan. His goods and chattels required little compression for the purposes of carriage, and a small

Jersey—a light wagon in free use in that section, contained all his wardrobe, books, papers, &c.—the heirlooms of a long and carefully economized practice. We may not follow his fortunes after his removal to the valley of the Mississippi. It does not belong to the narrative; but, we may surely say to those in whom his appearance may have provoked some interest, that subsequently he got into fine practice—was notorious for his stump-speeches; and a random sheet of the "Republican Star and Banner of Independence" which we now have before us, published in the town of "Modern Ilium," under the head of the "Triumph of Liberty and Principle," records, in the most glowing language, the elevation of Peter Pippin, Esq., to the state legislature, by seven votes majority over Colonel Hannibal Hopkins, the military candidate—Pippin 39, Hopkins 32. Such a fortunate result, if we have rightly estimated the character of the man, will have easily salved over all the hurts which, in his earlier history, his self-love may have suffered.

But the hour of departure was at hand, and assisting the fair Edith into the carriage, Ralph had the satisfaction of placing her beside the sweetly sad, the lovely, but still deeply suffering girl, to whom he owed so much in the preservation of his life. She was silent when he spoke, but she looked her replies, and he felt that they were sufficiently expressive. The aunt had been easily persuaded to go with her niece, and we find her seated accordingly along with Colonel Colleton in the same carriage with the young ladies. Ralph rode, as his humor prompted, sometimes on horseback, and sometimes in a light gig—a practice adopted with little difficulty, where a sufficient number of servants enabled him to transfer the trust of one or the other conveyance to the liveried outriders. Then came the compact, boxy, buggy, buttoned-up vehicle of our friend the pedler—a thing for which the unfertile character of our language, as yet, has failed to provide a fitting name—but which the backwoodsman of the west calls a go-cart; a title which the proprietor does not always esteem significant of its manifold virtues and accommodations. With a capacious stomach, it is wisely estimated for all possible purposes; and when opened with a mysterious but highly becoming solemnity, before the gaping and wondering woodsman, how "awful fine" do the contents appear to Miss Nancy and the little whiteheads about her. How grand are its treasures, of tape and toys, cottons and calicoes, yarn and buttons, spotted silks and hose—knives and thimbles—scissors and needles—wooden clocks, and coffee-mills, &c.—not to specify a closely-packed and various assortment of tin-ware and japan, from the tea-kettle and coffee-pot to the drinking mug for the pet boy and the shotted rattle for the infant. A judicious distribution of the two latter, in the way of presents to the young, and the worthy pedler drives a fine bargain with the parents in more costly commodities.

The party was now fairly ready, but, just at the moment of departure, who should appear in sight but our simple friend, Chub Williams. He had never been a frequent visiter to the abodes of men, and of course all things occasioned wonder. He seemed fallen upon some strange planet, and was only won to the attention by the travellers, on hearing the voice of Lucy Munro calling to him from the carriage window. He could not be made to understand the meaning of her words when she told him where she was going, but contented himself with saying he would come for her, as soon as they built up his house, and she should be his mother. It was for this purpose he had come to the village, from which, though surprised at all things he saw, he was anxious to get away. He had been promised, as we remember, the rebuilding of his cabin, by the men who captured Rivers; together with sundry other little acquisitions, which, as they were associated with his animal wants, the memory of the urchin did not suffer to escape him. Ralph placed in his hands a sum of money, trifling in itself, but larger in amount than Chub had ever seen at any one time before; and telling him it was his own, rejoined the party which had already driven off. The pedler still lingered, until a bend in the road put his company out of sight; when, driving up to the idiot, who stood with open mouth wondering at his own wealth, he opened upon him the preliminaries of trade, with a respectful address, duly proportioned to the increased finances of the boy.

"I say, now, Chub—seeing you have the raal grit, if it ain't axing too much, what do you think to do with all that money? I guess you'd like to lay out a little on't in the way of trade; and as I ain't particular where I sell, why, the sooner I begin, I guess, the better. You ain't in want of nothing, eh? No knife to cut the saplings, and pare the nails, nor nothing of no kind? Now I has everything from—"

Bunce threw up the lid of his box, and began to display his wares.

"There's a knife for you, Chub Williams—only two bits. With that knife you could open the stone walls of any house, even twice as strong as Guy Rivers's. And there's a handkerchief for your neck, Chub— Guy'll have to wear one of rope, my lad: and look at the suspenders, Chub—fit for the king; and—"

Where the pedler would have stopped, short of the display and enu-
meration of all the wares in his wagon, it is not easy to say, but for an
unexpected interruption. One of the outsiders of the Colleton party,
galloped back at this moment, no other indeed, than our former
acquaintance, the blacky, Cæsar, the fellow whose friendship for Ralph
was such that he was reluctant to get him the steed upon which he left
his uncle's house in dudgeon. Ralph had sent him back to see what
detained the pedler, and to give him help in case of accident.

Cæsar at once divined the cause of the pedler's delay, as he saw the
box opened, and its gaudy contents displayed before the eyes of the
wondering idiot. He was indignant. The negro of the South has as little
reverence for the Yankee pedler as his master, and Cæsar was not slow
to express the indignation which he felt.

"Ki! Misser Bunce, aint you shame for try for draw de money out
ob the boy pocket, wha' massa gee um?"

"Why Cæsar, he kaint eat the money, old fellow, and he kaint wear
it; and he'll have to buy something with it, whenever he wants to use it."

"But gee um time, Misser Bunce—gee um time! De money aint fair
git warm in de young man pocket. Gee um time! Le' em look 'bout um,
and see wha' he want; and ef you wants to be friendly wid um, gee um
somet'ing youse'f—dat knife burn bright in he eye! Gee um dat, and le's
be moving! Mausa da wait! Ef you's a coming for trade in we country,
you mus' drop de little bizness—'taint 'spectable in Car'lina."

The pedler was rebuked. He looked first at Cæsar, then at Chub,
and finally handed the boy the knife.

"You're right. There, Chub, there's a knife for you. You're a good little fellow, as well as you knows how to be."

Chub grinned, took the knife, opened both blades, and nodding his
head, made off without a word.

"The etarnal little heathen! Never to say so much as thank ye."

"Nebber mind, Misser Bunce; dat's de 'spectable t'ing wha' you do.
Always 'member, ef you wants to be gempleman's, dat you kaint take no
money from nigger and poor buckrah. You kin gib um wha' you please,
but you mustn't 'speck dem to be gibbing you."

"But in the way of *trade,* Cæsar," said the pedler, putting his horse
in motion.

"Der's a time for *trade,* and a time for *gib,* and you must do de genteel t'ing, and nebber consider wha's de 'spense of it, or de profit. De
nigger hab he *task* in de cornfiel', and he hab for do um; but 'spose

maussa wants he nigger to do somet'ing dat aint in he task—dat's to say in de nigger own time—wha' den? He *pays* um han'some for it. When you's a trading, trade and git you pay, but when you's a trabelling with gemplemans and he family, da's no time for trade. Ef you open you box at dem times, you must jest put in you hand, and take out de t'ing wha' you hab for gib, and say, 'Yer Cæsar—somet'ing for you, boy!'"

"Hem! that's the how, is it?" said the pedler with a leer that was good-humoredly knowing. "Well, old fellow, as you've given me quite a lesson how to behave myself, I guess I must show you that I understand how to prove that I'm thankful—so here, Cæsar, is a cut for you from one of my best goods."

He accompanied the words with a smart stroke of his whip, a totally unexpected salutation, over the shoulders, which set the negro off in a canter. Bunce, however, called him back, holding up a flaming handkerchief of red and orange, as a means of reconciliation. Cæsar was soon pacified, and the two rode on together in a pleasant companionship, which suffered no interruptions on the road; Cæsar all the way continuing to give the pedler a proper idea of the processes through which he might become a respectable person in Carolina.

There are still other parties to our story which it is required that we should dispose of according to the rules of the novel.

Let us return to the dungeon of the outlaw, where we behold him in a situation as proper to his deserts as it is new to his experience. Hitherto, he has gone free of all human bonds and penalties, save that of exile from society, and a life of continued insecurity. He has never prepared his mind with resignation to endure patiently such a condition. What an intellect was here allowed to go to waste—what fine talents have been perverted in this man. Endowments that might have done the country honor, have been made to minister only in its mischiefs.

How sad a subject for contemplation! The wreck of intellect, of genius, of humanity. Fortunate for mankind, if, under the decree of a saving and blessing Providence, there be no dark void on earth—when one bright star falls from its sphere, if there is another soon lighted to fill its place, and to shine more purely than that which has been lost. May we not believe this—nay, we must, and exult, on behalf of humanity—that, in the eternal progress of change, the nature which is its aliment no less than its element, restores not less than its destiny removes. Yet, the knowledge that we lose not, does not materially lessen the pang when we behold the mighty fall—when we see the great mind, which, as a star, we have almost worshipped, shooting with headlong precipitance through the immense void from its place of eminence, and defrauding the eye of all the glorious presence and golden promise which had become associated with its survey.

The intellect of Guy Rivers had been gigantic—the mistake—a mistake quite too common to society—consisted in an education limited entirely to the mind, and entirely neglectful of the *morale* of the boy. He was taught, like thousands of others; and the standards set up for his moral government, for his passions, for his emotions, were all false from the first. The capacities of his mind were good as well as great—but they had been restrained, while the passions had all been brought into active, and at length ungovernable exercise. How was it possible that reason, thus taught to be subordinate, could hold the strife long, when passion—fierce passion—the passion of the querulous infant, and the peevish boy, only to be bribed to its duty by the toy and the sugarplum—is its uncompromising antagonist?

But let us visit him in his dungeon—the dungeon so lately the abode of his originally destined, but now happily safe victim. What philosophy is there to support *him* in *his* reverse—what consolation of faith, or of reflection, the natural result of the due performance of human duties? none! Every thought was self-reproachful. Every feeling was of self-rebuke and mortification. Every dream was a haunting one of terror, merged for ever in the deep midnight cry of a fateful voice which bade him despair. "Curse God and die!"

In respect to his human fortunes, the voice was utterly without pity. He had summed up for himself, as calmly as possible, all his chances of escape. There was no hope left him. No sunlight, human or divine, penetrated the crevices of his dungeon, as in the case of Ralph Colleton, cheering him with promise, and lifting his soul with faith and resignation. Strong and self-relying as was his mind by nature, he yet lacked all that strength of soul which had sustained Ralph even when there seemed no possible escape from the danger which threatened his life. But Guy Rivers was not capable of receiving light or warmth from the simple aspects of nature. His soul, indurated by crime, was as insusceptible to the soothing influence of such aspects, as the cold rocky cavern where he had harbored, was impenetrable to the noonday blaze. The sun-glance through the barred lattice, suddenly stealing, like a friendly messenger, with a sweet and mellow smile upon his lips, was hailed as an angelic visiter, by the enthusiastic nature of the one, without guile in his own heart. Rivers would have regarded such a visiter as an intruder; the smile in his eyes would have been a sneer, and he would have turned away from it in disgust. The mind of the strong man is the medium through which the eyes see, and from which life takes all its color. The heart is the prismatic conductor, through which the affections show; and that which is seared, or steeled, or ossified—perverted utterly from its original make—can exhibit no rainbows—no arches of a sweet promise, linking the gloomy earth with the bright and the beautiful and the eternal heavens.

The mind of Guy Rivers had been one of the strongest make—one of large and leading tendencies. He could not have been one of the mere ciphers of society. He must be something, or he must perish. His spirit would have fed upon his heart otherwise, and, wanting a field and due employment, his frame must have worn away in the morbid repinings of its governing principles. Unhappily, he had not been permitted a choice. The education of his youth had given a fatal direction to his manhood; and we find him, accordingly, not satisfied with his pursuit, yet resolutely inflexible and undeviating in the pursuit of error. Such are the contradictions of the strong mind, to which, wondering as we gaze, with unreasonable and unthinking astonishment, we daily see it subject. Our philosophers are content with declaiming upon effects— they will not permit themselves or others to trace them up to their causes. To heal the wound, the physician may probe and find out its depth and extent; the same privilege is not often conceded to the physician of the mind or of the morals, else numberless diseases, now seemingly incurable, had been long since brought within the healing scope of philosophical analysis. The popular cant would have us forbear even to look at the history of the criminal. Hang the wretch, say they, but say nothing about him. Why trace his progress?—what good can come out of the knowledge of those influences and tendencies, which have made him a criminal? Let them answer the question for themselves!

The outlaw beheld the departing cavalcade of the Colletons, from the grated window. He saw the last of all those in whose fortunes he might be supposed to have an interest. He turned from the sight with a bitter pang at his heart, and, to his surprise, discovered that he was not alone in the solitude of his prison. One ministering spirit sat beside him upon the long bench, the only article of furniture afforded to his dungeon.

The reader has not forgotten the young woman to whose relief, from fire, Ralph Colleton so opportunely came while making his escape from his pursuers. We remember the resignation—the yielding weakness of her broken spirit to the will of her destroyer. We have seen her left desolate by the death of her only relative, and only not utterly discarded by him, to whose fatal influence over her heart, at an earlier period, we may ascribe all her desolation. She then yielded without a struggle to his will, and, having prepared her a new abiding-place, he had not seen her after, until, unannounced and utterly unlooked-for, certainly uninvited, she appeared before him in the cell of his dungeon.

Certainly, none are utterly forgotten! There are some who remember—some who feel with the sufferer, however lowly in his suffering—some who can not forget. No one perishes without a tearful memory becoming active when informed of his fate; and, though the world scorns and despises, some one heart keeps a warm sympathy, that gives a sigh over the ruin of a soul, and perhaps plants a flower upon its grave.

Rivers had not surely looked to see, in his dungeon, the forsaken and the defrauded girl, for whom he had shown so little love. He knew now, at first, how to receive her. What offices could she do for him—what influence exercise—how lighten the burden of his doom—how release him from his chains? Nothing of this could she perform—and what did she there? For sympathy, at such a moment, he cared little—for such sympathy, at least, as he could command. His pride and ambition, heretofore, had led him to despise and undervalue the easy of attainment. He was always grasping after the impossible. The fame which he had lost for ever, grew doubly attractive to his mind's eye from the knowledge of this fact. The society, which had expelled him from its circle and its privileges, was an Eden in his imagination, simply on that account. The love of Edith Colleton grew more desirable from her scorn;—and the defeat of hopes so daring, made his fierce spirit writhe within him, in all the pangs of disappointment, only neutralized by his hope of revenge. And that hope was now gone; the dungeon and the doom were all that met his eyes;—and what had she, his victim, to do in his prison-cell, and with his prison feelings—she whom Providence, even in her own despite, was now about to avenge? No wonder he turned away from her in the bitterness of the thought which her appearance must necessarily have inspired.

"Turn not away!—speak to me, Guy—speak to me, if you have pity in your soul! You shall not drive me from you—you shall not dismiss me now. I should have obeyed you at another time, though you had sent me to my death—but I can not obey you now. I am strong now, strong—very strong since I can say so much. I am come to be with you to the last, and, if it be possible, to die with you; and you shall not refuse me. You shall not—oh, you will not—you can not—"

And, as she spoke, she clung to him as one pleading herself for life to the unrelenting executioner. He replied, in a sarcasm, true to his general course of life.

"Yes, Ellen! your revenge for your wrongs would not be well complete, unless your own eyes witnessed it; and you insist upon the privilege as if you duly estimated the luxury. Well!—you may stay. It needed but this, if anything had been needed, to show me my own impotence."

"Cruel to the last, Guy—cruel to the last! Surely the few hours between this and that of death, are too precious to be employed in bitterness. Were not prayer better—if you will not pray, Guy, let me. My prayer shall be for you; and, in the forgiveness which my heart shall truly send to my lips for the wrongs you have done to me and mine, I shall not altogether despair, so that you join with me, of winning a forgiveness far more important and precious! Guy, will you join me in prayer?"

"My knees are stiff, Ellen. I have not been taught to kneel."

"But it is not too late to learn. Bend, bow with me, Guy—if you have ever loved the poor Ellen, bow with her now. It is her prayer; and, oh, think, how weak is the vanity of this pride in a situation like yours. How idle the stern and stubborn spirit, when men can place you in bonds—when men can take away life and name—when men can hoot and hiss and defile your fettered and enfeebled person! It was for a season and a trial like this, Guy, that humility was given us. It was in order to such an example that the Savior died for us."

"He died not for me. I have gained nothing by his death. Men are as bad as ever, and wrong—the wrong which deprived me of my right in society—has been as active and prevailing a principle of human action as before he died. It is in his name now that they do the wrong, and in his name, since his death, they have contrived to find a sanction for all manner of crime. Speak no more of this, Ellen; you know nothing about it. It is all folly."

"To you, Guy, it may be. To the wise all things are foolish. But to the humble heart there is a truth, even in what are thought follies, which brings us the best of teachings. That is no folly which keeps down, in the even posture of humility, the spirit which circumstances would only bind and crush in every effort to rise. That is no folly which prepares us for reverses, and fortifies us against change and vicissitude. That is no folly which takes away the sting from affliction—which has kept me, Guy, as once before you said, from driving a knife into your heart, while it lay beating against the one to which yours had brought all manner of affliction. Oh, believe me, the faith and the feeling and the hope, not less than the fear, which has made me what I am now—which has taught me to rely only on the one—which has made me independent of all things and all loves—ay, even of yours, when I refer to it—is no idle folly. It is the only medicine by which the soul may live. It is that which I bring to you now. Hear me, then—Guy, hear the prayer of the poor Ellen, who surely has some right to be heard by you. Kneel for me, and with me, on this dungeon floor, and pray—only pray."

"And what should I pray for, and what should I say—and whom should I curse?"

"Oh, curse none!—say anything you please, so that it have the form of a prayer. Say, though but a single sentence, but say it in the spirit which is right."

"Say what?"

"Say—'the Lord's will be done,' if nothing more; but say it in the true feeling—the feeling of humble reliance upon God."

"And wherefore say this? His will must be done, and will be done, whether I say it or not. This is all idle—very idle—and to my mind excessively ridiculous, Ellen."

"Not so, Guy, as your own sense will inform you. True, his will must be done; but there is a vast difference between desiring that it be done, and in endeavoring to resist its doing. It is one thing to pray that his will have its way without stop, but quite another to have a vain wish in one's heart to arrest its progress. But I am a poor scholar, and have no words to prove this to your mind, if you are not willing to think upon the subject. If the danger is not great enough in your thought—if the happiness of that hope of immortality be not sufficiently impressive to you—how can I make it seem different? The great misfortune of the learned and the wise is, that they will not regard the necessity. If they did—if they could be less self-confident—how much more readily would all these lights from God shine out to them, than to us who want the far sense so quickly to perceive and to trace them out in the thick darkness. But it is my prayer, Guy, that you kneel with me in prayer; that you implore the feeling of preparedness for all chances which can only come from Heaven. Do this for me, Guy—Guy, my beloved—the destroyer of my youth, of all my hope, and of all of mine, making me the poor destitute and outcast that you find me now—do this one, one small kindness for the poor Ellen you have so much wronged, and she forgives you all. I have no other prayer than this—I have no other wish in life."

As she spoke, she threw herself before him, and clasped his knees firmly with her hands. He lifted her gently from the floor, and for a few moments maintained her in silence in his arms. At length, releasing her from grasp, and placing her upon the bench, on which, until that moment, he had continued to sit, he replied:—

"The prayer is small—very small, Ellen—which you make, and I know no good reason why I should not grant it. I have been to you all that you describe me. You have called me truly your destroyer, and the forgiveness you promise in return for this prayer is desirable even to one so callous as myself. I will do as you require."

"Oh, will you? then I shall be so happy!—" was her exclamation of rejoicing. He replied gravely—

"We shall see. I will, Ellen, do as you require, but you must turn away your eyes—go to the window and look out. I would not be seen in such a position, nor while uttering such a prayer."

"Oh, be not ashamed, Guy Rivers. Give over that false sentiment of pride which is now a weakness. Be the man, the—"

"Be content, Ellen, with my terms. Either as I please, or not at all. Go to the window."

She did as he directed, and a few moments had elapsed only when he called her to him. He had resumed his seat upon the bench, and his features were singularly composed and quiet.

"I have done something more than you required, Ellen, for which you will also have to forgive me. Give me your hand, now."

She did so, and he placed it upon his bosom, which was now streaming with his blood! He had taken the momentary opportunity afforded him by her absence at the window to stab himself to the heart with a penknife which he had contrived to conceal upon his person. Horror-struck, the affrighted woman would have called out for assistance, but, seizing her by the wrist, he sternly stayed her speech and action.

"Not for your life, Ellen—not for your life! It is all useless. I first carefully felt for the beatings of my heart, and then struck where they were strongest. The stream flows now which will soon cease to flow, and but one thing can stop it."

"Oh, what is that, Guy?—let me—"

"Death—which is at hand! Now, Ellen, do you forgive me? I ask no forgiveness from others."

"From my heart I do, believe me."

"It is well. I am weak. Let me place my head upon your bosom. It is some time, Ellen, since it has been there. How wildly does it struggle! Pray, Ellen, that it beat not long. It has a sad office! Now—lips—give me your lips, Ellen. You have forgiven me—all—everything?"

"All, all!"

"It grows dark—but I care not. Yet, throw open the window—I will not rest—I will pursue! He shall not escape me!—Edith—Edith!" He was silent, and sunk away from her embrace upon the floor. In the last moment his mind had wandered to the scene in which, but an hour before, he had witnessed the departure of Edith with his rival, Colleton.

The jailer, alarmed by the first fearful cry of Ellen succeeding this event, rushed with his assistants into the cell, but too late. The spirit had departed; and they found but the now silent mourner, with folded arms, and a countenance that had in it volumes of unutterable wo, bending over the inanimate form of one whose life and misnamed love had been the bane of hers.

The end.

Afterword

Even as a young man, before his marriage into the gentry and ascension to the planter class, Simms shared the tidewater Southerner's "characteristic bias in favor of seaboard culture," viewing with "fundamental distrust" the "craving for land [and] wealth" that fostered the migration westward over the Appalachians.[1] In 1831, for instance, he voiced suspicion that "the possession of so much territory" was "greatly inimical to the well being of this country." The constant "pull[ing] up [of] stakes and boom[ing] off for the new Canaan," Simms contended, not only "prevents the formation of society" but also "destroys that which is already well established" (*L*, I, 37). Despite his personal preference to remain in the South Carolina low country (he rejected the offer by his father to make him wealthy and politically prominent in Mississippi), the realistic-minded Simms recognized the inevitability of westward expansion in the development of the nation. Furthermore, in demonstration of a literary progressiveness in contrast with his conservatism in politics and economics, he identified the frontier as a dynamic, increasingly important topic with which to capture the imagination of the largely urban-based reading public. His timing in 1834 was perfect; *Guy Rivers* came off the press in New York just when America-in-literature was becoming a national demand; and the gold rush in the outlaw-dominated Georgia backwoods provided strikingly different subject matter.

That Simms himself had traveled through the Georgia gold-mining region and talked with prospectors and settlers who gave him first-hand accounts helped him catch the excitement of the frontier. In addition to his observations as traveler, Simms prepared for the writing of *Guy Rivers* by learning all he could about the notorious "Western Land Pirate," John A. Murrell, upon whose syndicate he loosely modeled the Pony Club. He read all versions of Murrell's exploits that he could lay hands on; and he later claimed to have interviewed Murrell's captor, Virgil Stewart. But since *Guy Rivers* was published before most of the printed material on Murrell became available, and since the author's alleged meeting with Stewart was perhaps a hoax,[2] in his first Border novel Simms could not have relied so heavily upon the Murrell legend—part history and part folklore—as he afterwards did in *Richard Hurdis* and, to a lesser extent, in *Border Beagles* and *Helen Halsey*. But the strength of *Guy Rivers* lies in its realistic delineation of an ugly, untamed frontier, not in its re-creation of historical or mythical events however extravagant. Cooper's widely read frontier novels of the 1820s had glorified civilized man's entry into the virgin forests of the New World and his conquest of a redoubtable and worthy enemy, the once-mighty Indian nations. The "high romance" of civilized man's encounter with pristine wilderness and noble savage tapped, in the words of Louis Rubin, "a vein of myth and meaning" of "profound significance to the Western imagination."[3] But Cooper's was the sentimentalized frontier of the past—of the seventeenth and eighteenth century. The frontier of Cooper's and Simms's present—of the early nineteenth century—a backwoods now largely cleared of the threat of Indians but instead plagued by "a class of whites little less savage" (p. 258)—had until *Guy Rivers* never been realistically depicted in literature. Since the putting down of crime and corruption within a society never matches the grandeur of a victory in warfare against a formidable foe, the frontier of *Guy Rivers*—shed of idealism and imaginative appeal—produced a different, less clearly recognizable kind of heroism. There is no sense of tragedy in the defeat and death of a scoundrel; yet the outlaw-infested frontier of Simms's time and place imposed hardships and dangers equal to those faced by the early colonists. Under less flamboyant and picturesque circumstances, the courage of the borderer was as sorely tested as had been the fortitude of the early settler. The point might well be made that the frontier of the Old Southwest uniquely characterizes our national aspirations; yet to most Americans it possesses less glamour and glory than either the frontier of colonial times or the later frontier of the mountain and desert West. And though Simms's (as well as Cooper's) portrayals of the colonial frontier were from the beginning seen as being high-minded and idealistic, Simms's depiction of the frontier of his own day, curious to relate, was too often considered low-minded and vulgar. And it is a striking anomaly that even today Simms's Revolutionary Romances—like his Indian novels set in Colonial times—are thought of as being "lofty and idealistic," and his Border Romances "vulgar, sensational, and cheap" (Wimsatt, 100). Is there a difference in Simms's treatment of the "two" frontiers? is Frontier A innately lofty and Frontier B innately vulgar? or is the difference simply within the perception of the critic? Simms used the same techniques, the same descriptive and narrative abilities, the same theories of art and history, the same vision of America in writing both *Guy Rivers* (Frontier B) and the *Yemassee* (Frontier A). It must be recognized that Simms in writing of the frontier in America—regardless of the century—wrote "with his sleeves rolled up";[4] his tendency to speak in plain terms, to call things by their names, fostered in his works a robust prose style which unflinchingly portrayed (sometimes in graphic detail) the ugly as well as the beautiful. Despite an admiration for romanticism, intuitively and instinctively Simms was a realist, as remarked first by Vernon L. Parrington,[5] whose admiration for Simms has been noted, but unwisely and unaccountably ignored. But even Parrington acknowledged that Simms was not a consistent realist, any more than he was a consistent romantic. In the best of Simms—and, for that matter, in the worst of Simms—there is a propensity for realism under a deceiving romantic cover, the "romance" *Guy Rivers* itself being a striking example. Coming, as it did, as part of America's revolt from the literary dominance of England—the movement for intellectual independence to which Simms was fully committed—*Guy Rivers* fulfilled romantic expectations in its representation of a wild, yet starkly beautiful portion of America; but its plain-spoken vernacular and its explicit violence offended some readers who otherwise applauded. In 1834 genteel readers looked for a "higher seriousness" in literature, and *Guy River's* action-filled pages made good reading that belied the significance of what Simms had accomplished. The reader of Simms's day could not possibly have visualized that *Guy Rivers* was to fill a niche in what was to be our literature's most comprehensive portrayal of the development of America as a nation.

As we have seen, the physical and moral ugliness of the frontier of the Old Southwest is not an invention of Simms; he depicted faithfully what he saw, and his unfiltered vision revealed scenes of desolation and patterns of human behavior far from beautiful. Yet Simms responded to the lonely beauty of the wilderness with sensitivity both to its delicacy and to its stunning, intimidating power. A passage in the opening paragraphs of *Guy Rivers* illustrates:

Sun and sky do their work of beauty upon earth, without heeding
the ungracious return which she may make; and a rich warm sunset flung over the hills and woods a delicious atmosphere of
beauty, burnishing the dull heights and the gloomy pines with
golden hues, far more bright, if far less highly valued by men, than
the metallic treasures which lay beneath their masses. Invested by
the lavish bounties of the sun, so soft, yet bright, so mild, yet beautiful, the waste put on an appearance of sweetness, if it did not rise
into the picturesque. The very uninviting and unlovely character
of the landscape, rendered the sudden effect of the sunset doubly
effective .... The solitary group of pines, that, here and there, shot
up suddenly like illuminated spires;—the harsh and repulsive
hills, that caught, in differing gradations, a glow and glory from
the same bright fountain of light and beauty;—even the low copse,
uniform of height, and of dull hues, not yet quite caparisoned for
spring, yet sprinkled with gleaming eyes, and limned in pencilling
beams and streaks of fire; these, all, appeared suddenly to be subdued in mood, and appealed, with a freshening interest, to the eye
of the traveller whom at midday their aspects discouraged only.
[2–3]

Another display of Simms's close observation of nature and his keen
appreciation of its subtleties occurs in his description of Sycamore
Hollow, the meeting place of Mark Forrester and Kate Allen. After
recording the pleasing sounds, tastes, and sights of the setting's
secluded beauty, Simms comments:

Scenes like these are abundant enough in the southern country;
and by their quiet, unobtrusive, and softer beauties, would seem,
and not inefficiently or feebly, to supply in most respects the wants
of those bolder characteristics, in which nature in those regions is
confessedly deficient. Whatever may be the want of southern
scenery in stupendousness or sublimity, it is . . . more than made
up in those thousand quiet and wooing charms of location, which
seem designed expressly for the hamlet and the cottage . . . limpid
and living currents, touched for ever, here and there, by the sunshine, and sheltered in their repose by overhanging leaves and
flowers, for ever fertile and for ever fresh. They may not occasion
a feeling of solemn awe, but they enkindle one of admiring affection; and where the mountain and the bold rock would be productive of emotions only of strength and sternness, their softer
featurings of brawling brook, bending and variegated shrubbery,
wild flower, gadding vine, and undulating hillock, mould the con-

templative spirit into gentleness and love. The scenery of the South below the mountain regions, seldom impresses at first, but it grows upon acquaintance; and in a little while, where once all things looked monotonous and unattractive, we learn to discover sweet influences that ravish us from ourselves at every step we take, into worlds and wilds, where all is fairy-like, wooing, and unchangingly sweet. [191–92][6]

But, as if to clarify his intentions, early in the novel Simms is "fair to confess" that his protagonist, with "but small passion for that 'grassy couch,' and 'leafy bower,'" gave "the most unromantic preference" to "comfortable lodgings and a good roof" (7). Thus the reader learns in the initial chapter that Simms's "romance" of Georgia will be marked by realism.

One spectacular scene in particular captures the terrible violence that can result when lawless men disturb the balance of nature for their own evil purpose. The rock avalanche ingeniously engineered by Wat Munro to crash down from the hilltop upon the pursuing, unsuspecting Georgia Guard raised "feelings of unrepressed horror" in Ralph Colleton as he "beheld the catastrophe":

The advancing troop looked up, and were permitted a momentary glance of the terrible fate which awaited them before it fell. That moment was enough for horror. A general cry burst from the lips of those in front, the only notice that those in the rear ever received of the danger before it was upon them. An effort, half paralyzed by the awful emotion which came over them, was made to avoid the down-coming ruin; but with only partial success; for, in an instant after, the ponderous mass, which hung for a moment like a cloud above them, upheaved from its bed of ages, and now freed from all stays, with a sudden, hurricane-like and whirling impetus, making the solid rock tremble over which it rushed, came thundering down, swinging over one half of the narrow trace, bounding from one side to the other along the gorge, and with the headlong fury of a cataract sweeping everything from before its path until it reached the dead level of the plain below. The involuntary shriek from those who beheld the mass, when, for an instant impending above them, it seemed to hesitate in its progress down, was more full of human terror than any utterance which followed the event. With the exception of a groan, wrung forth here and there from the half-crushed victim, in nature's agony, the deep silence which ensued was painful and appalling;

and even when the dust had dissipated, and the eye was enabled to take in the entire amount of the evil deed, the prospect failed in impressing the senses of the survivors with so distinct a sentiment of horror, as when the doubt and death, suspended in air, were yet only threatened. [156–57]

There is much more detailing of the horrors of this "bloody execution," one of the scenes in *Guy Rivers* most unsettling to sensitive readers not prepared for the graphic description of a warfare unassociated with patriotic causes.

But Simms's predilection for realism is not limited to the portrayal of violence; it is also apparent in his full-bodied description of Chestatee, the gold-rush village on the frontier of the "wildest region of the then little-settled state of Georgia" (40). Forming "the debatable land between the savage and the civilized," the Chestatee area (Simms points out), was "doubly wild," partaking of "the ferocity of the one, and the skill, cunning, and cupidity of the other." The village itself resembles "some ten out of every dozen of the country towns in all the corresponding region." Consisting of some thirty or forty dwellings, chiefly of logs, Chestatee, like "all the interior settlements of the South and West," had no "very decided air of regularity and order," because the squatter "laid the foundation-logs of his dwelling" wherever suited him best. Thus there were no "public squares," and no "streets laid out by line and rule" as in "an orderly and methodical society." With "individual convenience" the only consideration, the squatters and gold-diggers randomly chose to build wherever there was elevated land "commanding a long reach of prospect"; where "a good spring" or "a fair branch" maintained "a perpetually clear and undiminishing current"; and where, "lastly, but not less important," the "agues and fevers came not" (44).

Simms exhibits an almost anthropological interest in the priorities observed "in the centre of the village"—prerogatives reflecting and molding the customs and habits of the inhabitants. Because, like "most southern and western" frontier towns, Chestatee had been founded on a gigantic scale, seemingly calculated to accommodate "a population of millions," there was "no want of room, no risk of narrow streets and pavements, no deficiency of area," and no crowding or congestion. Thus the custom of each house having its own huge wood-burning lamp "left few stirring apprehensions of their firing one another." Simms's account is succinct and distinct:

It was night, and the lamps of the village were all in full blaze, illuminating with an effect the most picturesque and attractive the fifty paces immediately encircling them. Each dwelling boasted of their auxiliar and attraction; and in this particular but few cities afford so abundantly the materials for a blaze as our country villages. Three or four posts are erected at convenient distances from each other in front of the building—a broad scaffold, sufficiently large for the purpose, is placed upon them, on which a thick coat of clay is plastered; at evening, a pile is built upon this, of dry timber and the rich pine which overruns and mainly marks the forest of the south. These piles, in a blaze, serve the nightly strollers of the settlement as guides and beacons. . . . [46–47]

The priorities of a frontier town are reflected in the "cluster of four huge fabrics," located in the "very centre" of Chestatee, that "in some sort sustained the pretension of the settlement." Simms's representation of this "ostentatious collection" consisting of the courthouse, the jail, the tavern, and the shop of the blacksmith brings to mind *The Scarlet Letter*'s delineation of the prison, the scaffold, and the cemetery as symbolic structures in seventeenth-century Boston. Though a comparison between a colonial Puritan town in Massachusetts and a nineteenth-century frontier village in Georgia hardly seems in order, it is interesting that each author should use the relative importance of certain man-made structures as a measure of the communities' priorities. Simms's portrait of a gold-rush town of the Old Southwest throws light on little known aspects of our social history; no other chronicle in our fiction can match it in validity or comprehensiveness. Simms's sly observation that "some of the members" of the Chestatee's structural Big Four (courthouse, jail, tavern, blacksmith shop) "appeared placed there rather for show than service" opens a long, but eminently quotable passage—

. . . the two last-mentioned being at all times the very first in course of erection, and the essential nucleus in the formation of the southern and western settlement. The courthouse and the jail, standing directly opposite each other, carried in their faces a family outline of sympathetic and sober gravity. There had been some effect at pretension in their construction, both being cumbrously large, awkward, and unwieldy; and occupying, as they did, the only portion of the village . . . stripped of its forest covering, bore an aspect of mutual and ludicrous wildness and vacancy. They had both been built upon a like plan and equal scale; and the only difference existing between them, but one that was immediately perceptible to the eye, was the superfluous abundance of windows in the former, and their deficiency in the latter. A moral agency had most probably prompted the architect to the distinction here hit upon—and he felt, doubtless, in admitting free access to the light in the house of justice, and in excluding it almost entirely from that of punishment, that he had recognised the proprieties of a most excellent taste and true judgment. . . . There was yet, however, another marked difference between the courthouse and jail . . . . The former had the advantage of its neighbor, in being surmounted by a small tower or cupula, in which a bell of moderate size hung suspended, permitted to speak only on such important occasions as the opening of court, sabbath service, and the respective anniversaries of the birthday of Washington and the Declaration of Independence. This building, thus distinquished above its fellows, served also all the purposes of a place of worship, whenever some preacher found his way into the settlement; an occurrence . . . of very occasional character. . . . Though neighbors in every substantial respect, the four fabrics were most uncharitably remote, and stood frowning gloomily at one another—scarcely relieved of the cheerless and sombre character . . . by the several blazes, flashing out upon the scene from the twin lamps in front of the tavern . . . warm indications of life and good lodgings within. . . . [the] broader glare from the smith's furnace streamed in bright lines . . . pouring through the unclayed logs of the hovel, in which, at his craft, the industrious proprietor was even then busily employed. Occasionally, the sharp click of his hammer, ringing upon and resounding from the anvil, and a full blast from the capacious bellows, indicated the busy animation, if not the sweet concert . . . of a more civilized and better regulated society. [47–49]

Far more central in the thoughts and habits of most residents of Chestatee was the tavern, which served as an eating place, a gathering place, and an inn, in addition to its main function as a drinking place. The multi-purposes of the dinner table draw the author's attention:

Many of the persons then present were not residents, but visiters in the village from the neighboring country. They had congregated there, as was usually the case, on each Saturday . . . with the view not less to the procuring of their necessaries, than the enjoyment of good company. Having attended in the first place to the ostensible objects of their visit, the village tavern, in the usual phrase, "brought them up;" and in social, yet wild carousal, they commonly spent the residue of the day. It was in this way that they met their acquaintance—found society, and obtained the news; objects of primary importance . . . with a people whose insulated positions . . . left them no alternative but to do this or rust altogether. The regular lodgers of the tavern were not numerous therefore, and consisted in the main of those laborers in the diggings who had not yet acquired the means of establishing households of their own. [88–89]

The fare at the "plentifully furnished" dinner table consisted of "eggs and ham, hot biscuits, hommony, milk, marmalade, venison, *Johnny*, or journey cakes and dried fruits stewed"—not properly "classed under the head of delicacies," but "served up in a style of neatness and cleanliness, that, after all, was perhaps the best of all possible recommendations." Little "form or ceremony" was observed, each guest being so busily engaged "in the destruction and overthrow of the tower of biscuits, the pile of eggs, and such other" that the appearance at the table of villager after villager went unnoticed. "[I]ndeed," Simms relates, "so busily were all employed, that he who should have made his *entrée* . . . with an emphasis commanding notice, might, not without reason, have been set down as truly and indefensibly impertinent" (90).

The "excessively rude" architecture of the building—both interior and exterior—is carefully delineated, in too much detail to be quoted. But a passage near the end of Simms's long description provides the atmosphere of a frontier tavern-inn:

The light on each side of the building was received through a few small windows, one of which only was allotted to each apartment, and this was generally found to possess as many modes of fastening as the jail opposite—a precaution referable to the great dread of the Indian outrages . . . . The furniture of the hotel amply accorded with all its other features. A single large and two small tables; a few old oaken chairs . . . with bottoms made of ox or deer skin . . . a broken mirror, that stood ostentatiously over the mantle, surmounted . . . by a well-smoked picture of the Washington family in a tarnished gilt frame—asserting the Americanism of the proprietor and place . . . . The tavern itself, in reference to the obvious pursuit of many of those who made it their home, was entitled "The Golden Egg"—a title made sufficiently notorious to the spectator, from a huge signboard . . . bearing upon a light-blue ground a monstrous egg of the deepest yellow . . . . Lest, however, his design in the painting itself should be at all questionable, [the artist] had taken the wise precaution of showing what was meant by printing the words "Golden Egg," in huge Roman letters, beneath it; these, in turn, being placed above another inscription, promising "Entertainment for man and horse." [93–95]

Simms's effectiveness in detailing minutiae revealing obscure, yet fascinating phases of the frontier environment extends to the characterization of its inhabitants. According to Simms, "the adventurers of which this wild congregation was made up" were motivated by "influences as various as the differing features of their several countenances." The "very *olla-podrida* of moral and mental combination," they had come to Chestatee "oddly and confusedly jumbled together" from all parts of the world. Comprised chiefly of those who possessed an "inordinate desire of a sudden to acquire wealth" and to whom "the ordinary operations of human trade or labor had proved tedious or unproductive," they were attracted to "the novel employment of gold-finding"—or, as Simms puts it, "gold-*seeking*." Nevertheless, the "very name of such a pursuit" carried with it to many "no small . . . charm of persuasion." In addition to the gold-seekers, many of those living on the "outskirts of civilization" had been "rejected" by society and "driven, like . . . refuse and . . . scum" to the backwoods. In Simms's words, "Here, alike, came the spendthrift and the indolent, the dreamer and the outlaw, congregating, though guided by contradictory impulses, in the formation of a common caste, and in the pursuit of a like object— some with the view to profit and gain; others, simply from no alternative being left them . . ." (45).

This down-to-earth assessment of the occupants of Chestatee is based upon Simms's own experiences, his extensive first-hand knowledge of frontier life. Yet the Georgia backwoods included another kind of person—the "rude but honest woodman"—upon whom the inevitable advance of civilization must depend. A love of adventure coupled with a "growing impatien[ce] of . . . confined boundaries" prompted people like Mark Forrester "to tread new regions and enjoy new pleasures and employments" in a spirit close to what "an earlier period of human history" had called chivalry. In *Guy Rivers* such characters as Forrester, Parson Witter, and Fullam, the leader of the Georgia Guard—as well as, of course, Ralph Colleton himself—represent inhabitants of the frontier concerned with human justice and service to community, not the exploitation of man and nature. Parson Witter, one of the novel's most effectively drawn minor characters, serves as an illustration of the beneficial effect of an unselfish individual upon even the roughest environment.

The practice of religion is an aspect of frontier life that greatly interested Simms. The following description—playful and ironic, yet meticulous and appreciative—apprehends the many nuances of the observance of religion in the backwoods:

> It was the sabbath—and though, generally speaking, very far from being kept holy in that region, yet, as a day of repose from labor—a holyday, in fact—it was observed, at all times, with more than religious scrupulosity. Such an event among the people of this quarter was always productive of a congregation. The occurence being unfrequent, its importance was duly and necessarily increased in the estimation of those, the remote and insulated portion of whom rendered society, whenever it could be found a leading and general attraction. No matter what the character of the auspices under which it was obtained, they yearned for its associations, and gathered where they were to be enjoyed. A field-preaching, too, is a legitimate amusement; and, though not intended as such, formed a genuine excuse and apology for those who desired it less for its teaching than its talk—who sought it less for the word which it brought of God than that which it furnished from the world of man. It was a happy cover for those who, cultivating a human appetite, and conscious of a human weakness, were solicitous, in respecting and providing for them, not to offend the Creator in the presence of his creatures. [116]

The field-preacher on this particular day was Parson Witter, who not only had "softened and delighted" the heart of Mark Forrester, but who also had "made the strongest impression upon his almost primitive and certainly only in part civilized hearers." With "merits of mind" of an "elevated order" far superior to "the current run of his fellow-laborers," Witter nevertheless kept "pace evenly with the precepts which he taught" so as "to be not unworthy of the faith which he professed":

> He was of the methodist persuasion—a sect which, among those who have sojourned in our southern and western forests, may confidently claim to have done more, and with motives as little questionable as any, toward the spread of civilization, good habits, and a proper morality, with the great mass, than all other known sects put together. . . . This, without exaggeration, applicable to the profession at large, was particularly due to the individual member

in question; and among the somewhat savage and always wild
people whom he exhorted, Parson Witter was in many cases an
object of sincere affection, and in all commanded their respect.
[117–18]

This is a remarkable, historically accurate tribute to an evangelical sect
coming from a non-church goer (nominally an Episcopalian) who nevertheless was a deeply religious man.

Not content with generalizing, Simms goes on to particularize the
workings of the good Parson Witter, including an insightful account of
the customs and traditions—one could almost say the politics—of the
practice of religion on the frontier. Close attention to detail marks the
author's description of Chestatee's "place of meeting and prayer":

> The sight is something goodly, as well to the man of the world
> as to the man of God, to behold the fairly-decked array of people,
> drawn from a circuit of some ten or even fifteen miles in extent, on
> the sabbath, neatly dressed in their choicest apparel . . . . No chim-
> ing and chattering bells warn them of the day or of the duty—no
> regularly-constituted and well-salaried priest—no time-honored
> fabric . . . reminding them regularly of the recurring sabbath . . . .
> The preacher comes when the spirit prompts, or as circumstances
> may impel or permit. The news of his arrival passes from farm to
> farm, from house to house; placards announce it from the trees on
> the roadside, parallel . . . with an advertisement for strayed oxen,
> as we have seen it numberless times; and a day does not well elapse
> before it is in possession of everybody who might well avail them-
> selves of its promise for the ensuing Sunday. The parson comes to
> the house of one of his auditory a night or two before; messages
> and messengers are despatched to this and that neighbor, who
> despatch in turn to other neighbors. . . . The place of worship and
> the preacher are duly designated, and, by the time appointed, as if
> the bell had tolled for their enlightenment, the country assembles
> at the stated place; and though the preacher may sometimes fail of
> attendance, the people never do. [118–19]

Parson Witter is indirectly responsible for advancing the relationship between Lucy Munro and Ralph Colleton, for it is while en route to
the prayer meeting that the two young outsiders to Chestatee—already
much drawn to each other—fall into extended conversation for the first
time. This conversation affords Simms the opportunity to satirize, if
ever so lightly, male chauvinism and at the same time to reveal the

ungracious role of an educated, intelligent woman in the backwoods (even the rustic Forrester perceives that Lucy "feels pretty clearly that this isn't the sort of country in which she has a right to live" [96]). Certainly the most appealing female character portrayed in *Guy Rivers*, Lucy Munro displays a sprightliness and wit that capture the fancy of traditional-minded Colleton[7] despite his betrothal to cousin Edith back in South Carolina. After polite preliminaries, with the confidence of his station and sex Colleton launches into a philosophical discourse intended to flatter his companion. "There is far more truth, my own experience tells me," he proclaims, "in the profession of your sex, whether in love or in religion, than in ours—and believe me, I mean this as no idle compliment. . . . Your existence being merged in that of the stronger sex, you lose all that general selfishness which is the strict result of our pursuits. Your impulses are narrowed to a single point or two, and there all your hopes . . . become concentrated. . . . You have but few aims, few hopes. With these your very existence is bound up, and if you lose these you are yourselves lost. Thus I find that your sex, to a certain age, are creatures of love . . . ."

Colleton's sexist remarks, though well-intentioned, elicit a courteous, though pointed rebuff from Lucy Munro: ". . . do you conceive it altogether fair in you thus to compliment us at our own expense? You give us the credit of truth . . . in matters . . . [of] the affections and the heart; but this is done by robbing us entirely of mental independence. You are . . . a moral Robin Hood, you compel us to give up everything we possess, in order that you may have the somewhat equivocal merit of restoring back a small portion of what you take" (120–21). Later in the conversation she dazzles the surprised yet admiring Colleton once more with her clever defense of intellectuality in women: "The gentlemen, nowadays, seldom look to us for intellectual gladiatorship; they are content that our weakness should shield us from the war. But, I conceive the reproach of our poverty to come unkindly from those who make us poor. It is, of this, sir, that I complain." When Colleton counters that his "clumsy . . . utterance" deserved her "graceful swordsmanship," Munro again responds with elegance and grace. "It was only with a degree of perversity, intended solely to establish our independence of opinion, at least for the moment, that I chose to mistake and misapprehend you. Your remark, clothed in any other language, could scarcely put on a form more consistent with your meaning." The comment of the author underlines the irony: "Ralph bowed at a compliment which had something equivocal in it . . ." (122). One unexpected thing that Simms occasionally does well, particularly for his time, is to espouse women's rights.

In addition to Lucy Munro, among the persons encountered by Forrester and Colleton on "the old *trace*" to the meeting were, near the front, gayly prancing, laughing "young of both sexes"; behind them, "the more staid, the antiques—and those rapidly becoming so"; on the roadside, "trimly dressed" slaves from nearby plantations; and— in anticipation of Mark Twain's depiction in *Huckleberry Finn*—some established white citizens with double-barrelled guns and rifles, "it being deemed politic, at that time, to prepare for all contingencies, for the Indian or for the buck, as well as for the more direct object of the journey" (119).[8] In a beautiful natural setting of venerable oaks, "far more grand, majestic" than a cathedral, the impressive sermon of Parson Witter was interrupted by the news that some gold-claim lands had been confiscated by outlaws. Immediately the guns and rifles flashed in view, joined quickly by pistols, cutlasses, and knives. "The words of peace," Simms writes with irony, "which [the congregation] had just heard seemed to have availed them but little, for every brow was blackened, and every tongue tipped with oaths and execrations" (p. 154).

Simms antedated the ironic, raucous humor of Mark Twain in ways other than religious satire. In fact, one chapter in *Guy Rivers* (chapter 7, "The Yankee Outwits the Lawyer") is in itself an early exemplar of the Southwest humor popularized through the writings of A. B. Longstreet (whose *Georgia Scenes* came out in 1835, one year after *Guy Rivers*), William Tappan Thompson, Thomas Bangs Thorpe, Johnson J. Hooper, and George Washington Harris—all well before Clemens. Though hardly in the class of the Duke and the Dauphin, Mark Twain's classic confidence men, Simms's Jared Bunce, Yankee pedler, and Lawyer Pippin, "disputatious civilian" in the words of the author, engage in a battle of wits in which the more entrepreneurial Bunce out-maneuvers the scheming practitioner in a confidence game.

In any unstable environment the presence of a few worthy individuals is not enough to change the odds favoring the dishonest and the unscrupulous. "The wild condition of the country—the absence of all civil authority, and almost of laws," Simms confirms, "may readily account for the frequency and impunity with which . . . desperate men committed crime and defied its consequences" (46). In short, with its "mass so heterogeneous in its origin and tendency," Chestatee was a hotbed of "[s]trife, discontent, and contention" in which even among the dishonest the spoils went to "the bold spirit and the strong hand" relying upon physical violence and intimidation. Such conditions inevitably promoted two things: the concept of frontier justice (an attempt by the people to control the lawless) and the concept of the crime syndicate (an attempt by the lawless to control the people). Once again, outlawry was at advantage, with the ability to manipulate even the concept designed by the people as protection from lawlessness. Both of these concepts merit further consideration.

Mark Forrester, in his colorful vernacular, indignantly enlightens Colleton concerning the inner workings of frontier justice, about to be administered in Chestatee to the fraudalent Yankee pedler, Jared Bunce:

> "What! you from Georgy, and never to hear tell of the regilators? Why, that's the very place, I reckon, where the breed begun. The regilators are jest then, you see, our own people. We hain't got much law and justice in these pairts, and when the rascals git too sassy and plentiful, we all turn out, few or many, and make a business of cleaning out the stables. We turn justices, and sheriffs, and lawyers, and settle scores with the growing sinners. We jine, hand in hand, agin such a chap as Jared Bunce, and set in judgment upon his evil-doings. It's a regilar court, though we make it up ourselves, and app'ints our own judges and juries, and pass judgment 'cordin' to the case. Ef it's the first offence, or only a small one, we let's the fellow off with only a taste of the hickory. Ef it's a tough case, and an old sinner, we give him a belly-full. Ef the whole country's roused, then Judge Lynch puts on his black cap, and the rascal takes a hard ride on a rail, a duck in the pond, and a perfect seasoning of hickories, tell thar ain't much left of him, or, may be, they don't stop to curry him, but jest halters him at once to the nearest swinging limb." [53]

Though Colleton's bright legal mind sees the irony of this kind of "sharp justice!" the essential correctness of Forrester's account is verified from a different perspective by Munro's more matter-of-fact explication of the administration of law in the backwoods: "There is the court-house, it is true—and there the jail; but we seldom see sheriff, judge, or jailer. When they do make their appearance, which is not often, they are glad enough to get away again. If we here suffer injury from one another, we take justice into our own hands . . . and there the matter generally ends" (165). The author himself avers that Munro "had in truth, made out a very plain case; and his representations, in the main, were all correct" (166).

Moreover, as indicated, conditions permitting the people to take the law in their own hands also breed the organization of crime—as illustrated historically by the terrorization of the Old Southwest by the John Murrell syndicate in the 1830s.[9] Simms draws upon this fact in *Guy Rivers* with the portrayal of the dreaded Pony Club, "an irregular club, known by its constituents in Georgia as the most atrocious criminal that ever offended society or defied its punishments; and the almost masonic mysteries and bond which distinguised the members provided them with a pledge of security, which gave an added impetus to their already reckless vindictiveness against man and humanity." A secret and powerful syndicate in a "wide, wild, and little-cultivated territory" ran even less risk than an individual of ever being punished for crime; the "impunity which marked [the] atrocities" of the Pony Club naturally "invited . . . their reiterated commission" (220). It was as an almost sure haven for the perpetration of crime that the Pony Club (anonymously headed by Wat Munro) managed to attract Guy Rivers from a thriving practice of law.

Simms's interest in the psychology of crime at least partly instigated his writing *Guy Rivers*. This interest is seen not only in the creation of the title character, but to a lesser extent in the characterization of Wat Munro and even the well-intentioned Mark Forrester. Munro, even more than Rivers, is the professional criminal, whose motivation is avarice, not hate—whose specialty is fraud and theft, not murder and acts of violence. Much more wary and cool-headed than Rivers, he is appalled by Rivers's lust for blood, considering it a foolhardiness incongruous with the successful perpetration of lucrative crime. "Can you not kill your enemy without drinking his blood?" Munro asks Rivers at one time. "And where then would be the pleasure of revenge?" is the reply (211–12). Though it was Munro who introduced Rivers to a career outside the law, Munro nevertheless concedes, "If I did give you the first lessons in your education, you have long since gone beyond your master" (113). Munro's fondness for Lucy, his abhorrence to any unnecesary shedding of blood, and his final rebellion against Rivers's lust for Lucy and implacable hatred for Colleton lead him to a kind of penitence— and some assumption of responsibility. He dies almost heroically, helping Colleton to escape and then, on his deathbed, testifying against Rivers. Forrester, uprooted from "'old So. Ca.' . . . in pursuit of his fortune among strangers" (82), allows his impetuosity and restlessness to lead him, under the instigation of Munro, to the senseless murder of a Georgia Guard during the fight over the gold claims. Later, Forrester acknowledges his error to Colleton, "I wish to heaven I had taken caution from you. But I was mad, 'squire, mad to the heart, and became the willing tool of men not so mad, but more evil than I!"; in the conversation he explains the plight of others like himself caught up in complicity with the Pony Club: "We can't go to work, for the life of us, if we wished to; we all feel that we have gone too far, and those, whose own consciences do not trouble them, are yet too much troubled by fear of the consequences to be in any hurry to take up handspike or hammer again in this quarter of the world" (172). At the urging of Colleton, who recognizes the essential innocence of the woodsman, Forrester makes plans to move further west, where, in Colleton's words, "you would be secure from punishment" and where "the wants of life . . . are of easy attainment" (182). The magic appeal of the frontier to honorable men with broken lives (but regenerated dreams) is fully captured in Simms's description of Mark Forrester's trek through the wilderness in search of a meaningful existence: "His course lay for the great Southwest—the unopened forests, and mighty waters of the Mississippi valley. Here, he was to begin a new life. Unknown, he would shake off the fears which his crime necessarily inspired. Respited from death and danger, he would atone for it by penitence and honest works" (237–38). That the "natural dreams of the young and sanguine exile" end with his brutal murder by Rivers does not diminish the significance of Simms's recognition of this potential of the frontier.

But the focal point of Simms's study of the criminal mind is Guy Rivers himself. One of the author's techniques in developing reader interest in Guy Rivers is the gradual revelation of what others know and think of him. Ralph Colleton, for instance, early confides to Mark Forrester that "there are few men whose looks I so little like, and whom I would more willingly avoid, than that man Rivers"; and after first mistaking as fear Colleton's dread of Rivers ("you mistake me, Forrester, I fear no man"), Forrester concedes that "Guy Rivers is not the right kind of man, and everybody here knows it, and keeps clear of him" (96). Colleton's identification of Rivers as the outlaw who had attempted to rob and murder him in the wilderness at Catcheta pass, coupled with his observation of Rivers's intended murder of a helpless, wounded member of the Georgia Guard, brings his revulsion toward Rivers to an apex. When the insulted outlaw challenges him to duel, Colleton looks at him "with ineffable scorn": "You mistake me, sirrah, if you think I can notice your call with anything but contempt" (166). Even at Forrester's coaxing, "Don't give way—give him satisfaction, as he calls it, and send the lead into his gizzard," Colleton does not budge in his resolution: "You mistake me greatly, Forrester, if you suppose for a moment that I will contend on equal terms with such a wretch," Colleton avows. "He is a common robber and an outlaw, whom I have denounced as such, and whom I can not therefore fight with. Were he a gentleman, or had he any pretensions to the character, you should have no need to urge me on, I assure you" (167). Neither Forrester, nor the spectators (who take Colleton as a "poor chicken" coward), can understand the rationale behind Colleton's refusal; but Rivers does not miss the significance of the affront. Indeed much of his seething resentment toward society stems from his perception of being discriminated against by the social aristocracy of his time and place.

It is in giving voice to Rivers's objections to being denied high place in society that Simms appears most sympathetic to the criminal's cause. In fact, the author attributes to Rivers words that reflect an attitude reminiscent of Simms's own as an ambitious young man trying to establish himself in Charleston. In a discussion with Munro, Rivers reveals the source of his societal rebelliousness: "Providence endowed me with a certain superiority of mind over my fellows. I had capacities which they had not . . . ," he proclaims. "These talents fitted me for certain stations in society . . . . But I was denied my place. Society, guilty of favoritism and prejudice, gave to others . . . the station in all particulars designed for me. I was denied my birthright, and rebelled" (248). Rivers's feeling of estrangement seems akin to Simms's recurring belief that "I could never be, in my native place, what I might be elsewhere" (*L*, I, 164);[10] and this parallel perhaps accounts for the fact that the author—even while registering repugnance at Rivers's cruelty and aversion to his life of crime—understands better than most of his contemporaries the role of society and environment in the making of a criminal. "Can society complain," Simms has Rivers ask Munro, "when prostituting herself and depriving me of my rights, that I resisted her usurpation and denied her authority?"

Since it is almost exclusively in the second half of *Guy Rivers* (i.e., volume II of the original edition) that the title character becomes intro-spective—begins to search inwardly for the causes of his criminal behavior—one might well hazard the guess that Simms's purpose in writing the novel changed before he completed its composition. Comments by Simms himself support this belief. In the preface to the "new and revised edition" issued by Redfield in 1855, Simms acknowl-edged (as was his wont) the existence of "mistakes and excesses" in the first edition; but he also lamented that "nothing now can be done toward the amendment of the halting portions, except to trim and pare away some of the cumbering foliage." But, as he had also done in the prefatory remarks to the Redfield re-issue of *The Yemassee* two years earlier, the author admitted his revulsion to the idea of extensive revi-sion, which he considered questionable in merit and unprofitable in use of time.[10] Thus, once again, as with *The Yemassee,* Simms's apology that more than some "pruning" of small defects "could not be attempted" probably should be considered at least partially tongue-in-cheek. But there is a difference. In the case of *Guy Rivers* Simms intimated that his *whole conception* of the novel underwent change from beginning to end: "I could wish now—were this proper or possible—to remould the whole of the first half of the story, both as respects plan and style; for this portion was written under a false, or, rather, an imperfect concep-tion of what was demanded of such a work." Such an admission invites speculation as to what "false, or, . . . imperfect" concept was modified during the process of the novel to the extent that "[t]he reader will, no doubt, readily detect the difference of manner which exists between the first and latter half of the story" (xxvii). Simms's comments are sufficiently vague to prohibit pinpointing, but in no way do they con-tradict the thesis that the mind of the criminal becomes increasingly the thematic concern of *Guy Rivers* as it moves from its first half (or vol-ume) to its second.

But to begin at the beginning, the novel opens with Ralph Colleton clearly the protagonist-hero about whom all the action revolves, the center of all attention; Guy Rivers has the subordinate role of hard-hearted villain, the avowed enemy of a hero for whom he has a vindic-tive hatred. In the first half of the novel, Guy Rivers is the almost inhuman blackguard that causes one to shudder and hiss. Early, how-ever, in the second volume—or, more precisely, what *was* the second volume in the 1834 edition—the focus of the novel shifts from pre-dominantly on Colleton to almost equally (perhaps even primarily) on

Rivers—whose mind we now look into with more and more interest. Almost for the first time the reader begins to recognize why the book is entitled *Guy Rivers,* not *Ralph Colleton.* Time and again, the author enters Rivers's consciousness, examining the motivations for even his most dastardly crimes; and providing hitherto unknown intimate details of his personal life. Though (as we have seen) early in the novel Rivers accuses Munro, "You taught me first to be the villain you now find me" (112), it is not until chapter 22 (chapter 4 of the second volume in the first edition) that Simms concentrates upon Rivers's own perception of the reason he exchanged a "good practice at Gwinnett bar" (243) for a career in crime. The very "possession of . . . undisputed talents" that encourage Rivers, in his own words, to grow "ambitious" also cause him to become "sick and tired" of the limitations of his "own ten-mile horizon." His spirit, already "troubled with a wholesale discontent," is even more oppressed by his unrequited love for Edith Colleton (who refused him in favor of her cousin Ralph) and by his unsuccessful venture into politics (an election won by an "insignificant fop and fool" with family name and money). "What with her rejection and scorn, coming at the same time with my election defeat, I am what I am," Rivers tells Munro. "These defeats were wormwood to my soul" (245–47). An even more damming denunciation by Rivers is his condemnation of his "weakly-fond, misjudging, misguiding" mother as his "greatest enemy," responsible for his "twenty years of crime and sorrow, and a life of hate, and probably a death of ignominy" (404). Denial of responsibility for wrongdoing Simms sees as characteristic of the selfish, self-centered criminal of high intelligence who seethes in resentment at his perceived rejection of society. But the question remains in the reader's mind: is the author portraying Rivers as an instinctively cruel person with a proclivity for crime who enjoys blaming others for his transgressions? or is the author at least partially supporting the thesis that education and environment produce the criminal? If *Guy Rivers* has weaknesses, certainly among them is Simms's ambivalence about the *born criminal vs. environmental criminal* dichotomy; he seems to come down on both sides of the question—heredity primarily in the first eighteen or so chapters; environment particularly in the closing chapters.

Unquestionably, however, as the novel progresses, Simms makes an effort to mitigate Rivers's cruelty by the occasional display of a gentler side of his nature. Witness, for instance, the sympathy of Guy

Rivers for the malformed dwarf, Chub Williams, whose life he spared although Munro would kill him as a security risk. "No—let him live, Munro," is Rivers's remark. "Let him live. Such as he should be spared. Is he not alone—without fellowship—scorned—an outcast—without sympathy—like myself. Let him live, let him live!" (324). (Simms's authorial comment: ". . . remembering that Rivers was a monster of contradictions, Munro turned away . . .") Another example that brutality and cruelty did not always dominate Rivers is his decision, just before his own capture at Wolf's Neck, to command his loyal lieutenant, Tom Dillon, to leave him to his fate: "Go you . . . and heed me not; and think of me no more. Make yourself a home in the Mississippi, or on the Red river, and get yourself a fireside and family of your own" (403). And even Rivers's relationship with Ellen, a woman he has abused and forsaken, but who nevertheless continues to love him, ends with a display of a quality close to self-reproach and tenderness. While still free but knowing he is doomed, Rivers reflects upon her: "Poor Ellen—so gentle, so resigned, and so fond of her destroyer; but I will not see her again" (406). Rivers's prophecy proves wrong: after his capture Ellen visits him in prison and is with him at his death. But it is during his title character's period of imprisonment that the author pictures in him the agony of despair: "Every thought was self-reproachful. Every feeling was of self-rebuke and mortification. Every dream was a haunting one of terror, merged for ever in the deep midnight cry of a fateful voice which bade him despair. 'Curse God and die!'" (442). Recognizing her faithless lover's spiritual plight, Ellen pleads to him to join her in prayer, for "it is not too late to learn": "Bend, bow with me, Guy—if you have ever loved the poor Ellen, bow with her now." Though Rivers asserts that the "Savior [who] died for us" in Ellen's religious belief "died not for me," the criminal is nevertheless moved to grant her request because "the forgiveness you promise in return for this prayer is desirable even to one so callous as myself." Rivers's actual prayer is problematical—"I have done something more than you required, Ellen"—but his suicide is not: "Death— . . . is at hand! Now, Ellen, do you forgive me? I ask no forgiveness from others" (445–48).

The dehumanized villain has become increasingly the object of psychological study—a human being who is a victim as well as an offender. In the end Simms's judgment of Rivers's career sounds almost naturalistic, as if the course of crime had been predetermined by forces beyond control: "Unhappily he had not been permitted a choice. The education of his youth had given a fateful direction to his manhood; and we find him, accordingly, not satisfied with his pursuit, yet resolutely inflexible and undeviating in the pursuit of error" (443).

As the novel shifts its emphasis from Colleton to Rivers, and the psychology of crime emerges as an important theme, the main thrust of *Guy Rivers* remains the portrayal of the hazards and hardships of the early nineteenth-century frontier. Since the suppression of lawlessness and the assertion of civic responsibility are essential to the development of civilization on the frontier, some understanding of the origins and motivations of crime is beneficial to enlightened law and order, a necessity in civilized society. That Simms himself thought the tragic conversion of a "gigantic . . . intellect" into a criminal mind germane to public interest is revealed in an ironic observation near the conclusion of *Guy Rivers*: "The popular cant would have us forbear even to look at the history of the criminal. Hang the wretch, say they, but say nothing about him. Why trace his progress?—What good can come out of the knowledge of those influences and tendencies, which have made him a criminal?" (443).

In conclusion, Simms at a relatively early age began developing a literary vision of America (which he fully articulated in 1845); and a close reading of his writings, particularly his fiction, reveals that he persistently and consistently adhered to that vision, with but small (if sometimes significant) concessions to social, political, and literary fashion. Simms could (and did) select his literary subjects with an eye to the literary market; but he stubbornly refused to drop what he considered important topics because they were unfashionable, and sooner or later he succeeded in completing, in a truly remarkable achievement, his entire saga of the development of America from its pre-colonial roots through its phenomenal growth into the trans-Mississippi West almost four centuries later.

Guy Rivers is first and foremost a novel to be read and enjoyed. But one's enjoyment is not lessened by the fact that in reading it, one becomes acquainted with a little known, fascinating time and place crucial to an understanding and appreciation of America's expansion from an Atlantic seaboard-bordered nation into one with an elastic western boundary that eventually stretched all the way to the Pacific. *Guy Rivers: A Tale of Georgia* is the definitive American novel in what it attempts to do.

NOTES

1. See Mary Ann Wimsatt, *The Major Fiction of William Gilmore Simms: Cultural Traditions and Literary Form* (Baton Rouge: Louisiana State University Press, 1989), 89, and James E. Kibler, Jr., "The First Simms Letters: 'Letters from the West' (1826)," *Southern Literary Journal* 19 (Spring 1987): 81–91.

2. Much has been written on the Murrell-Stewart-Simms connection, ranging from affirmations of its importance to questionings of its existence. See William P. Trent, *William Gilmore Simms* (Boston: Houghton Mifflin, 1892), 116; Hampton M. Jarrell, "Simms's Visits to the Southwest," *American Literature* 5 (March 1933): 33; William Stanley Hoole, "A Note on Simms's Visits to the Southwest," *American Literature* 6 (November 1934): 335; Wimsatt, *Major Fiction*, 93–98. Estimates of Stewart also vary, from his being hailed a hero to his being called an impostor: for the former, see Augustus Q. Walton, *A History of the Detection, Conviction, Life and Designs of John A. Murel, the Great Western Land Pirate . . .* (Cincinnati [1835]) and H. R. Howard (comp.), *The History of Virgil A. Stewart, and His Adventure in Capturing and Exposing the Great "Western Land Pirate" and His Gang . . .* (New York, 1836); for the latter, see J. F. H. Claiborne, *Life and Correspondence of John A. Quitman, Major-General, U.S.A., and Governor of the State of Mississippi* (New York, 1860), I, 138n, and James Lal Penick, Jr., *The Great Western Land Pirate: John A. Murrell in Legend and History* (Columbia: University of Missouri Press, 1981), 3, *passim.* Many others have written on the Murrell saga, the most useful account being Jonathan Daniels, *The Devil's Backbone: The Story of the Natchez Trace* (New York: McGraw-Hill, 1962), 240–46.

3. *The Edge of the Swamp: A Study in the Literature and Society of the Old South* (Baton Rouge: Louisiana State University Press, 1989), 104.

4. See John Caldwell Guilds, *Simms: A Literary Life* (Fayetteville: University of Arkansas Press, 1992), 339, 344.

5. See his *The Romantic Revolution in America* (Volume II of *Main Currents in American Thought: An Interpretation of American Literature from the Beginnings to 1920*, 3 vols.) New York: Harcourt, 1927, 125–36.

6. In his letters and other writings Simms often made similar observations about the sensuous, seductive beauty of low-country South Carolina. For other apt descriptions of nature in *Guy Rivers,* see 42, 283ff., 311.

7. Colleton remains intensely loyal and faithful to Edith, but Lucy's effect on him is also noted by the author: "Still the youth was not marble exactly: and, as he spoke, his arm gently encircled her waist . . ." (209).

8. Simms later observes: "Some of the party, it is true, had made their appearance at the place of prayer with rifles and fowling pieces, a practice which occasioned no surprise" (130).

9. In his contemporary account, Augustus Q. Walton (perhaps a pseudonym) states that "John A. Murel has never been surpassed in cold-blooded murders, by any other names recorded on the pages of history, and his other villainous feats have never been surpassed by any who have preceded him. He may justly claim the honor of reducing villany to an organized system . . ." (*Murel,* 17).

10. Simms sensed a "hostility" to the "claims of my intellect," which "would never be anywhere more jealously resisted" than in the "proud, wealthy & insulated community . . . in which I was born" (*L,* I, 164); and more than once he expressed the feeling of being "tempted, repudiated as I am here, to clear out . . ." (*L,* II, 208–9). Despite expressions of ambivalence toward his birthplace, which surfaced particularly during periods of despondency, in actuality Simms was devoted to Charleston and South Carolina.

11. The relevant passage in the preface to *Guy Rivers* reads: ". . . the mind, however willing and resolute, revolts at the alteration, whatever its promise of improvement. The labor of such a performance grows absolutely terrible even to contemplate; and, in very degree with the ability of the artist to repair or improve the ancient structure, is his capacity to design and build anew. It is also very questionable whether any attempt to amend or correct the errors in an old plan might not impose the whole fabric to the censure of rude and wretched journey" (xxviii). In *Simms: A Literary Life* I have discussed at some length the validity of Simms's self-knowledge concerning his habits of composition.

Historical Background

Though the 1930s saw a revival of interest in the gold-mining industry, the Georgia gold rush remains relatively unknown, remembered primarily as one of the causes for the removal of the Cherokee Indians to lands beyond the Mississippi River. Yet it was America's first gold rush, and many of the miners who took part in the California gold rush in 1849 had learned and perfected their alluvial mining techniques in Georgia.

The Georgia "gold belt" stretches for approximately 150 miles, due north-east and southwest, across the northern end of the state. By the late 1700s, gold had already been discovered in the piedmont region of North Carolina, and prospectors who traced this area to the southwest invaded the Cherokee lands in Georgia. Gold was not officially discovered in Georgia, however, until 1828 or 1829. Benjamin Parks, a young boy who literally stumbled onto a gold nugget in the Chestatee River while hunting deer, usually receives credit for the first find.

Soon after Parks's discovery, thousands poured into Georgia. Senator John C. Calhoun of South Carolina bought land and started mines in the Dahlonega area, the richest part of the gold belt. The mining industry in Georgia ranked second only to agriculture in the 1830s, and a branch mint had been established at Dahlonega by 1838. A decade later, most of the miners left for California. Many would subsequently return to Georgia with new mining techniques, but the Civil War ended all such endeavors. The citizens of the Dahlonega area describe in their memoirs a setting remarkably similar to Simms's Chestatee. Indeed, historical records suggest that Simms painted a vividly accurate portrait of frontier life in *Guy Rivers,* dramatizing the frequency of violence and conflict in Georgia during the 1830s. Federal troops were sent to Georgia to enforce government regulations with regard to the gold-mining regions. Native miners often fought with each other and with "intruders" from other states. The Georgia State Guard was formed in 1830 for the purpose of upholding state laws. Guard officers in counties bordering the Cherokee lands organized volunteer companies to make the Indians submit to Georgia law and to keep the whites from mining the Indian territory. Though the battle between the miners and the Georgia Guard as depicted in *Guy Rivers* is not based strictly on historical data, such conflicts were typical, and if they did not always occur on the large scale Simms portrays, it was not unusual for violence on the Georgia frontier to result in death.

Gold-mining towns, with their diverse population and persistent strife, provided ample business for professional men like Simms's lawyer Pippin; and, as historians indicate, the frontier was no less a haven for the notorious outlaw than for the professional businessman. It seems likely that the now-legendary John Murrell was a source of inspiration for the character of Guy Rivers. Born in Tennessee around 1804, Murrell was in fact a counterfeiter as well as a thief of horses and slaves. His crimes occurred in the 1820s and 1830s, when the frontier had advanced to the west and when the Arkansas Territory as well as the areas of western Tennessee and Mississippi had yet to be settled. Legend credits Murrell with virtually every offense imaginable, from developing and consolidating a network of criminals called the Mystic Clan of the Confederacy to plotting a slave revolt in the Southwest. The Murrell of this mythology is intelligent, merciless, and vain, taking special pride in his mother's teaching him to steal at an early age.

The legend of Murrell derives largely from the written narrative of Virgil A. Stewart. Stewart, a Tennessean who allegedly met and rode with Murrell, claimed to have secretly written down Murrell's stories about his own crimes. He turned Murrell over to the authorities and served as the main witness when Murrell was tried in July 1834 for stealing slaves. Seven months later, under the name of Augustus Q. Walton, Stewart published *A History of the Detection, Conviction, Life and Designs of John A. Murel, the Great Western Land Pirate.* The accuracy of this account has always been suspect, partly because Stewart and Murrell at one time lived within five miles of each other, supposedly without knowing one another, and also because there is evidence that Stewart was engaged in illegal business of his own before he met Murrell. It has been theorized that Stewart's narrative may have been fabricated primarily for financial exploitation. At the time of Murrell's trial, some believed that Stewart had been in league with Murrell before deciding to betray him.

Though Stewart's narrative was not published until 1835, Simms, during his earlier travels to the Southwest to see his father, had almost certainly read or heard about Murrell's crimes and about gangs of men who committed violent acts. Historians characterize Stewart's description of Murrell's gang as melodramatic and unreliable, but confirm that such networks terrorizing the

Old Southwest did exist, albeit probably not so tightly organized as Stewart's account suggests.

Following his conviction in July 1834, Murrell was placed in prison. As for what became of him following his early release in April 1844, accounts vary. Several report that he died in prison, and a few characterize him as a virtual imbecile by the time he completed his prison term. Most describe him as a model prisoner who became a respectable citizen of the community and worked as a blacksmith until he died in November 1844 of tuberculosis contracted in prison. According to some stories, his body was dug up after his death, and his head was removed and later displayed at carnivals and fairs for ten cents' admission.

References

Bryan, T. Conn. "The Gold Rush in Georgia," *Georgia Review* 9 (1955): 398–404.

Coulter, E. Merton. *Auraria: The Story of a Georgia Gold-Mining Town* (Athens: University of Georgia Press, 1956).

Green, Fletcher M. "Georgia's Forgotten Industry: Gold Mining," *Georgia Historical Quarterly* 19 (1935): 93–111, 211–28.

Penick, James Lal, Jr. *The Great Western Land Pirate: John A. Murrell in Legend and History* (Columbia: University of Missouri Press, 1981).

Explanatory Notes

CHAPTER TWO

p. 21, title *Chevalier d'industrie:* (French) adventurer, crook.

p. 14, lines 25–26 Pony Club: During the 1830s, in the parts of Georgia which bordered the Cherokee territory, "Pony Clubs" attempted to drive the Indians off by destroying their homes and property. The group Simms describes here is probably loosely based on the Mystic Clan of the Confederacy, a band of men known for stealing horses and slaves. According to legend, John Murrell was the leader of this gang, and the men committed crimes far more heinous than stealing.

p. 14, line 36 condign: deserved, appropriate.

p. 16, line 29 Baldwin and the Holy Cross: a reference to Baldwin I, king of Jerusalem from 1100 to 1118, and the Crusades.

p. 17, line 2 cravat: a reference, used in the nineteenth century, to a hangman's noose.

p. 19, line 18 banditti: (singular or plural) an outlaw, especially a member of a band of marauders, who lives by plunder.

CHAPTER THREE

p. 21, line 1 greensward: turf that is green with growing grass.

p. 27, line 7 conned: committed to memory.

CHAPTER FIVE

p. 41, line 18 stentorian: extremely loud.

p. 45, line 9 *olla-podrida:* (Spanish) melting pot.

p. 49 line 13 catch: a round for three or more unaccompanied and usually male voices, often with suggestive or obscene lyrics.

CHAPTER SIX

p. 52, line 17 regulators: vigilante groups which reestablished the social order in settlements on the frontier. According to historians, every town below

St. Louis on the Mississippi River had its own band of regulators in the 1830s.

p. 53, line 26 Judge Lynch: Though the word "lynch" in the 1830s referred to almost any sort of penalty imposed by mobs or vigilante groups, references to the Court of Judge Lynch meant the punishment of death.

p. 53, line 37 *fusee:* (French) rocket.

p. 58, line 32 Monongahela: whiskey, named after the river in northern West Virginia and southwest Pennsylvania which flows north, joining the Allegheny River at Pittsburgh to form the Ohio River.

p. 60, line 4 scratch: the devil.

p. 62, line 31 foundered: disabled, lame.

p. 63, lines 26–27 *ad captandum:* (Latin) designed to please or attract the crowd.

CHAPTER SEVEN

p. 72, line 12 quondam: former, sometime.

CHAPTER NINE

p. 88, line 2 *soi-disant medico:* (French, Spanish) so-called doctor.

p. 94, lines 35–36 "The Golden Egg": Fletcher M. Green lists "The Golden Egg" among the names of actual mining hotels and taverns in Georgia during the 1830s ("Georgia's Forgotten Industry: Gold Mining, Part Two," *Georgia Historical Quarterly* 19 [1935]: 213).

CHAPTER TEN

p. 101, line 11 Catcheta pass: located approximately twenty miles from the Chestatee forks.

p. 106, line 38 beef: brawn.

p. 108, line 31 Mammon: riches or material wealth, especially as having a debasing influence. In the New Testament, "mammon" is a personification of wealth, money, property, and profit. Through Christian folklore, the word became the name of a demon of avarice, equated with Lucifer and Satan. In Milton's *Paradise Lost,* Mammon is constantly bending over to admire the gold-paved floor of heaven; he is also the last spirit to fall from heaven. In DePlancy's *Dictionnair Infernal,* written in the nineteenth century, Mammon serves as the ambassador of hell to England.

Moloch: the name of a Canaanite idol to whom children were sacrificed as burnt offerings. Milton presents him as one of the devils in *Paradise Lost;* the name is broadly applied to any tyrannical power that is appeased by human subservience or sacrifice.

CHAPTER ELEVEN
p. 117, line 25 scrip: a bag or wallet.

CHAPTER TWELVE
p. 137, line 11 short sixes: a reference to pistols.

CHAPTER THIRTEEN
p. 143, line 10 The "Georgia Guard": The Georgia State Guard was formed by legislative act in December 1830. This group, which consisted of sixty men, had the responsibility of enforcing state law. With the help of volunteer companies, the Guard forced the Cherokee Indians to submit to Georgia law and tried to keep the whites from invading Cherokee lands to prospect for gold. The battle between the miners and the Guard in *Guy Rivers* is not based on an actual battle, but clashes like this one were fairly typical.

p. 150, line 25 enfilading: lining up in opposite and parallel rows.

CHAPTER SIXTEEN
p. 173, line 9 Old Hundred: a hymn.

CHAPTER TWENTY
p. 228, line 11 corse: a variation of "corpse."

CHAPTER TWENTY-ONE
p. 235, line 3 a tittle: a very small part.

CHAPTER TWENTY-TWO
p. 238, line 13 eyry: a variation of "aerie," a nest on a cliff or mountaintop.

p. 246, lines 7–8 *sui generis:* (Latin) constituting a class alone: unique, peculiar.

p. 250, lines 5–14. Apparently in response to objections to the depiction of excessive brutality in the original 1833 edition, Simms (or his editor) has altered the specific details of Rivers's murder of Forrester. See Textual Notes, pp. 486–87.

CHAPTER TWENTY-THREE
p. 251, lines 3–4. In contrast to the intent of softening (in the Redfield edition) the details of the murder of Forrester in the closing of the previous chapter, Simms seems to make Rivers a more unfeeling criminal in these lines than he had in the original version. See Textual Notes, pp. 486–87.

CHAPTER TWENTY-FOUR
p. 261, line 31 "bare bodkin": dagger (from Hamlet's famous soliloquy, III, i, 75–76).

CHAPTER TWENTY-SIX
p. 277, line 33 jemmijohn: a jug.
p. 278, line 29 catchpenny: designed to appeal to the ignorant or unwary through sensationalism or cheapness.
p. 279, line 25 calabash: bottle or dipper made from the gourd of the same name.
p. 281, line 5 Jack Ketch: a reference to the executioner.
p. 281, line 6 outlier: one who does not live where his office, business, or estate is.
p. 281, line 11 smoke: shoot.

CHAPTER TWENTY-SEVEN
p. 284, line 14 fugleman: one who heads a group.
p. 285, line 7 Sardanapalus: Though traditionally considered to be the last king of Assyria, Sardanapalus is actually a combination of three Assyrian rulers. According to legend, he was the last and most dissolute in a line of effete sovereigns. He is blamed for Assyria's downfall at the hands of an army of Medes, Persians, and Babylonians. He had defeated these forces three times, but when the Euphrates River flooded the royal capital, thus fulfilling a prophecy, he fled to his palace, where he burned himself, his treasures, and his concubines.

CHAPTER TWENTY-EIGHT
p. 295 There is no Chapter XXVIII in the Redfield edition, apparently the result of a careless misnumbering of chapters. Chapter XXVII of the Redfield edition is the equivalent of Chapter IX of the second volume of the original 1833 edition; Chapter XXIX is the equivalent of Chapter X of the second volume of the original printing. The error is an example of the slipshod proofreading and printing practices of the nineteenth century. The mistake has been corrected, and the chapters are correctly numbered in the Arkansas edition.

CHAPTER TWENTY-NINE
p. 306, line 14 *patois:* (French) the characteristic special language of an occupational or social group: jargon.

CHAPTER THIRTY-TWO

p. 327, line 9 traverse: a formal denial of a matter of fact alleged by the opposite party in a legal pleading.

p. 328, lines 33–34 pettifogger: a lawyer whose methods are petty, under-handed, or disreputable; a shyster.

CHAPTER THIRTY-THREE

p. 340, line 17 hobbe-de-hoy: (hobbledehoy) an awkward or gawky youth.

CHAPTER THIRTY-FIVE

p. 365, line 29 roundhead: a reference to a follower of Oliver Cromwell, who served as the lord protector of England from 1653 to 1658; a Puritan.

p. 367, line 33 contumelious: insolently abusive and humiliating.

CHAPTER THIRTY-SIX

p. 376, line 3 toper: one who drinks to excess.

p. 378, line 9 crick: probably a shortened form of "cricket," used here to refer to a small or timid person.

p. 381, line 10 bumper: a brimming cup or glass.

p. 382, line 9 posset: a hot drink of sweetened and spiced milk, curdled with ale or wine.

CHAPTER THIRTY-NINE

p. 403, lines 32–35 The notorious John Murrell credited his mother with teaching him to steal.

p. 413, line 7 lanthorn: variation of "lantern."

p. 416, line 5 tacky: a small pony or inferior horse.

CHAPTER FORTY

p. 430, lines 6–7 *lese majeste:* (French) a crime committed against a sovereign power.

CHAPTER FORTY-ONE

p. 438, line 36 whiteheads: those with light hair; also, those who are highly favored or fortunate, as in the current usage of "fair-haired."

p. 439, line 1 japan: work finished and decorated in the Japanese manner.

Textual Notes

Guy Rivers: A Tale of Georgia was first published in 1834 by Harper & Brothers in New York; because, however, Simms himself oversaw the publication of a "New and Revised Edition" by Redfield in 1855—in Simms's own words in late 1854, "the revised copy of 'Guy Rivers' . . . cost me a great deal of labour" (*Letters*, III, 240)—the 1855 Redfield printing is used as copy-text for the Arkansas Edition of *Guy Rivers*.

I. A Partial List of Substantive Changes

Listed below are the most important substantive changes Simms made in the 1834 edition in revising it for the 1855 Redfield edition (copy-text). Passages from the original edition revised by Simms are reproduced as they appear in the 1834 edition, followed by page and line reference to the revised passage as printed in the Arkansas Edition.

In the 1855 edition, chapter numbers appear as Roman numerals and periods follow the chapter titles. Throughout the Arkansas Edition, chapter numbers are spelled out and the periods following the chapter titles are omitted.

ORIGINAL EDITION
Chapter II, p. 24, line 36–p. 25, line 10
He knew the danger and hopelessness of a second encounter with men sufficiently odious, in common report, to make him doubly cautious, after the adventure so nearly fatal. Exiled from society, after having acquired a large taste for many of its enjoyments, they found in the frontier impunity for those crimes and offences, for the punishment of which it had imposed ineffectual and defrauded penalties; and conscious of no responsibility to divine or human spirit, the result of their tacit outlawry, had prompted them to retort upon men the stern severities of justice.

For the comparable passage as revised by Simms in 1854, see the Arkansas Edition, p. 20, lines 12–15.

ORIGINAL EDITION
Chapter III, p. 29, lines 29–33
He valued it not for itself, and not with any disposition simply to procure and to increase the quantities in his possession. He was by no means a miser or a mercenary, and his regards were given to it as the visible embodiment of power little less than divine. He was not, in short, that worst of all possible pretenders, the aristocrat, on the score of his property.

For the comparable passage as revised by Simms in 1854, see the Arkansas Edition, p. 23, lines 30–38.

ORIGINAL EDITION
Chapter III, p. 30, lines 5–16
A son, to the younger brother, had concentrated the affections of that exile, whose chief sorrows on the subject of his declining fortunes and fruitless endeavors, grew entirely out of those thoughts about the future which every look upon his boy was calculated to provoke; while, to William Colleton, the elder, the young and beautiful Edith, a few months older than her cousin Ralph, repaired greatly the absence of her mother, and neutralized in part, if in some respects she did not subdue, some few of the less favourable features in the character of the father.

For the comparable passage as revised by Simms in 1854, see the Arkansas Edition, p. 24, lines 4–11.

ORIGINAL EDITION
Chapter V, p. 53, lines 17–21
(His face was finely southern)—it wanted the calculating lines of cunning,—that false presentiment of wisdom, fatal to honesty, which so many, mistaking for the true object, fall down and worship.

Simms deleted this passage from the 1855 edition.

ORIGINAL EDITION
Chapter IX, p. 114, line 1–p. 116, line 35
It was a subject of much doubt and deliberation in our mind, whether or not to furnish to the reader a full and dainty detail of the viands spread out on the present occasion. A supper or dinner has at all times been a favourite theme for display among the romancers. They appear to have seized upon it for portraiture and description, with as much reckless avidity usually as the most hungry knight among them might be conjectured to exhibit towards the real banquet and the substantials, after the labour of a hard day's fight for his honour and his mistress. Regarding such a theme evidently with an eye of great favour—

possibly, as a common passage of arms, attesting the due degree of skill necessary for permission to enter upon the lists—there are few ——g our ablest
writers in this field that have withheld their whole strength from the subject.
Scott, following the example of Homer, always feeds his heroes well; and some
excellent lesson might be gleaned from his writings by those overdelicate novelists, who seldom furnish hero or heroine with an appetite at all. Cooper
keeps his adventurers well also, and is particular to have them fully supplied
when in the woods and among the Indians. We cannot say that Bulwer has
often admitted us to a regular dinner-party—Guloseton is no exception—
unless it be among the rogues associated with one of his heroes, in the stews of
——n; but enough for example, in this particular, as well as authority, may be
found in the industriously plied labours of the thousand and one followers and
rivals of these great leaders in the field we speak of. Nor have our purely
American writers—a tribe rather servilely dependent, we are constrained to
admit, upon the dicta of European authority—disdained imitation in this
respect. It is rather remarkable that the very best passages from sundry of their
works—so far as they appear to have been penned *con amore,* and under the
influence of a spirit highly susceptible to the operations of its own fancies—are
devoted to this sort of description. They have dilated with singular and conscious felicity, linked with a strange viand-like fascination of style, fitly illus-
trative of the subject,—upon the grace of gravies, the cream of custards, the
currency of currants—the fantasies, in short, of fish, flesh, and fowl alike; and
with a glorious hocus pocus, worthy of the weird sisters of Macbeth, they have
made the whole earth and every sea contribute their dainty delectabilities, as
indeed they should, to the pleasing of the palate of that hero, in whose fortunes, as in duty bound, the whole world must be so much interested. The
compounds and concatenations of Paris—that centre of soup and civilization—mingled on the same board with the more solid characteristics of John
Bull's refectory in London, exhibit a more beautiful national affinity, than, in
political matters, we can ever hope to see take place between them. To these we
may add the almost savage association of ponderosities and delicacies, in the
furnishing of which the generous purveyor has seemingly spared neither
labour nor expense, though sacrificing, most grievously we take it, all pretensions to good taste and a decent propriety, in the choice and distribution of his
various dishes.

It was therefore, as we have already said, with a deliberation certainly due
to, and imperatively demanded by the subject, that we debated with ourselves
as to what we should do in the furnishing our hero's dinner-table. What shall
we have, landlord—what's in the larder, most sweet hostess? Wanting in
—— Quickly, and the Mistress Ford, and sweet Anne Page, and that most
truculent and magnificent of all worthies, Sir John Falstaff, our apprehensions

as to the quality of our viands, by way of recompense for our other deficiencies, were only reasonable. We dreaded too, lest with a reference to what we have all this time been saying, we should not be able to provide our readers with that kind and quality of repast, to which it was but fair to infer their appetites had been accustomed; and, not without much hesitation, many misgivings, and a close examination into our right, as good chroniclers, to withhold any thing however humble in the progress of our story, we determined upon the seemingly rash step which in part we have taken. We perfectly well knew, that in our semi-barbarian region, south of the Potomac, or, in more familiar phrase, of Mason's and Dixon's line—we could not cater so widely or so variously for the dinner-table as in the land of notions and novelties, where the apples grow ready baked, in pies of goodly dimensions, and where Cape Cod, tendering its all bountiful aids and auxiliars, robs the sea-serpent of those delicate fins for which, it appears, in just revenge, he has pursued the smackmen into the very harbours of Yankee land. Our apprehensions may well be conceived, therefore, though it passes our ability to describe them, until, calling a council of war with our hostess, Mrs. Dorothy Munro,—whom your eyes —————— perceive doling out sundry capacious plates of soup from the corpulent vessel beside her,—we determined, in few words, rather with the view to the enlightenment than the temptation of the reader, to set the repast, such as it is, without further hesitation before him.

Simms deleted this passage from the 1855 edition.

ORIGINAL EDITION
Chapter XII, p. 190, lines 12–24
To understand the full force of this sarcasm, it is necessary that the reader should have some knowledge of the modes of thinking on the subject of the duello, and individual readiness for the *ultima ratio*, prevailing in the southern and western country. There is no imputation upon a man so formidable and destructive to his character and pretensions as any backwardness in this respect, and it is by no means unfrequent to hear the lawyer of the interior defending his client, in a prosecution for assault and battery, by alleging the pusillanimity of the person who suffered and submitted to it.

Simms deleted this passage from the 1855 edition.

ARKANSAS EDITION
Chapter Twenty, p. 227, lines 13–24
This passage does not appear in the original edition; Simms added it in his 1854 revision.

Arkansas Edition
Chapter Twenty, p. 227, lines 28–33
This passage does not appear in the original edition; Simms added it in his 1854 revision.

Original Edition
Volume II, Chapter II, p. 42, lines 9–14

"Ay, but by hell, and I dare even more!" was the instant response of the ruffian.

"Then heaven be merciful to thee and me," was all that she said, when she sank senselessly at his feet, just as his arms, with audacious grasp, were encircling her waist.

For the comparable passage as revised by Simms in 1854, see the Arkansas Edition, p. 227, line 37–p. 228, line 11.

Original Edition
Volume II, Chapter III, p. 42, line 1–p. 43, line 17

At this moment Munro re-entered the apartment, and his presence served to restrain the lawlessness of that fiercer passion which had no other restraint at that moment. The attention of the —————— ———— immediately called to the condition of his prostrate and much-abused niece; and reproving his companion for his violence, without comprehending or conjuring its extent, he raised her carefully from the floor and seated her in a chair that stood in a corner of the apartment.

For the comparable passage as revised by Simms in 1854, see the Arkansas Edition, p. 229, lines 1–14.

Arkansas Edition
Chapter Twenty-one, p. 229, line 15–p. 230, line 9
This passage does not appear in the original edition; Simms added it in his 1854 revision.

Arkansas Edition
Chapter Twenty-two, p. 235, line 14–p. 236, line 4
This passage does not appear in the original edition; Simms added it in his 1854 revision.

ORIGINAL EDITION
Volume II, Chapter IV, p. 66, lines 20–30

He threw up his hands with fearful energy as he beheld his murderer—from whom Munro had wrested the weapon originally used—aiming a second blow with the small hatchet which he always wore. The interposition of Munro was without avail; the sharp steel drove through, separating the extended fingers of the fallen man as he threw them up, and crushing and crunching deeply into the scull. The unhappy woodman sank back, without groan or further word, even as an ox beneath the stunning stroke of the butcher.

For the comparable passage as revised by Simms in 1854, see the Arkansas Edition, p. 250, lines 5–14.

ORIGINAL EDITION
Volume II, Chapter V, p. 67, lines 2–11

The murderer at length, with the utmost composure, wiping his bloody weapon upon the long grass on the road side, interrupted a silence which was certainly painful to the landlord, if not to himself, by exclaiming—

"Well, Munro, so far our ride has been for nothing, and so much time has been lost already, that I fear it is now hopeless to attempt further pursuit of the boy, at least for to-night. What say you?"

For the comparable passage as revised by Simms in 1854, see the Arkansas Edition, p. 251, lines 2–8.

ARKANSAS EDITION
Chapter Twenty-three, p. 251, lines 9–20

This passage does not appear in the original edition; Simms added it in his 1854 revision.

ORIGINAL EDITION
Volume II, Chapter VI, p. 79, lines 17–37

The outlaw coolly prepared his pistol as he approached—the huge tree, under the shelter of which he lurked, effectually concealed him, and his respiration grew restrained at every step in Ralph's advance. At length the form of man and horse grew fairly perceptible—it was almost beside him—the deadly aim was taken—the hand on the trigger, when suddenly, as the horseman passed beneath the fatal tree, a huge pair of wings, with a wild and flapping noise, rushed from among its branches. The steed took flight, and went headlong forward; while the outlaw, seized upon for the first time in his life with a nameless terror, in which his excited imagination took an active part, dropped the fatal weapon, and for a moment stood paralyzed. In a moment he was reassured, when the cause of his affright was explained in the uncouth hootings of the owl, whom the tread of the horse's hoofs had expelled from the quiet perch of his tree, and compelled to take shelter in another.

For the comparable passage as revised by Simms in 1854, see the Arkansas Edition, p. 260, line 33–p. 262, line 5.

ARKANSAS EDITION
Chapter Thirty-nine, p. 408, line 38–p. 409, line 21
This passage does not appear in the original edition; Simms added it in his 1854 revision.

ORIGINAL EDITION
Volume II, Chapter XXI, p. 280, line 16–p. 281, line 35
With a sagacity something inconsistent with his general idiocy, he gave some instructions for the party which indicated a perfect consciousness of the somewhat dangerous undertaking which they had in view; and, according to his directions, the troopers having reached a certain point contiguous to Wolf's Neck, were made to dismount by their idiot guide, and having fastened his, with their horses, in the shade of a small clump of brushwood, he bade them follow him with cautious tread along the margin of the road, studiously avoiding, as they did so, the dry leaves and withered branches and every movement productive of unnecessary noise. Sometimes, proceeding with the singularly rapid motion which belonged to him, they lost sight of him at moments, and preparing for this, he had advised them of the route to follow, by breaking a bush on such occasions, and leaving it at every point in the path in which a difficulty might be anticipated to occur. The great extent of the rock cavities generally styled the Wolf's Neck, diverging, as some of its ramifications did, to various and remote points from the centre, rendered such precaution necessary, since those on the outside could not well discover in many cases in which cavities were below, any external indications of the fact. Having now brought them to positions which gave them a commanding view of various points at the same moment, Chub instructed them to place themselves out of sight, and to await the result of the experiment he was about to try, to determine, without any risk to himself, the precise position of the outlaw at that moment. Accordingly, arming himself with a rock, scarcely smaller than his head, he contrived to secure it about his person, while, with the rapidity of a squirrel, he ascended a tree overlooking, like the others, the dwelling of the fugitive. Having first carefully ensconced himself within the sheltering branches, which he had so chosen as effectually to conceal him, he plunged the stone from his high perch in such a manner as to determine for it a rolling course down the declivity of the hill, even after it had fairly struck the earth. The stone did its duty precisely as required, and the pursuing party had the satisfaction, as we

have already narrated, to behold the object of their aim emerge from the cave, and closely scrutinize the scene around him. As if satisfied that the cause of the disturbance was purely occasional, and was not the effect of design, Rivers returned to his den, and again throwing himself upon the couch of his inner apartment, appeared disposed to yield himself up to sleep. Having allowed some little time to elapse after the re-ingress of the outlaw, his hunters descended from their several points of observation, and proceeded to arrange the circumstances of his capture.

For the comparable passage as revised by Simms in 1854, see the Arkansas Edition, p. 409, line 22–p. 411, line 27.

ORIGINAL EDITION
Volume II, Chapter XXII, p. 282, line 30–p. 283, line 10
Heretofore they had gone on in perfect secrecy. The individual who had discovered the curtain motioned to his companions, and raising its folds from the bottom, listened with suppressed respiration, while he endeavoured to gather whatever sound of life might be going on within. Rivers, half asleep, and enfeebled by exhaustion of one kind or other, breathed hard and quick—occasionally, a muttered monosyllable breaking from his lips would indicate the still restless mind, always at strife with the weaker clay in which it was imprisoned. Words might be distinguished, at moments, as his feverish form was thrown from one side to the other upon his couch—but such words—they were curses—imprecations upon himself, upon all, mingled too with an occasional lamenting—the tribute which vice invariably pays to virtue—for the high places from which he had for ever fallen.

For the comparable passage as revised by Simms in 1854, see the Arkansas Edition, p. 412, line 23–p. 413, line 34.

ORIGINAL EDITION
Volume II, Chapter XXI, p. 284, line 31–p. 285, line 13
"Guy Rivers cursed Chub's mother—Guy Rivers' man burnt down Chub's house, and Guy wanted to shoot Chub on the tree."

"But didn't I keep the man from shooting you when you run away from the cave—I would have been your friend, boy—and I did not curse your mother. But go—" and half muttering to himself, and half in the hearing of the boy, he went on, as it were, in soliloquy—"so wretched, yet so revengeful—desolate, I would have taken him to my kindness, as of kin in desolation, and this is the reward. He has had nothing but kindness from me, and yet—but I am your prisoner, gentlemen—I am not unwilling. Lead on."

For the comparable passage as revised by Simms in 1854, see the Arkansas Edition, p. 415, line 13–p. 416, line 18.

ORIGINAL EDITION
Volume II, Chapter XXII, p. 285, line 30–p. 286, line 7
The reasons have already been narrated to the reader, which had determined
the landlord upon this measure, and we are satisfied to say that all things, so far
as the law of householdery is concerned, now went on with the accustomed
economy; for the old lady, having some reputation in her way, could manage
the cold baked meats with most praiseworthy capacity.

*For the comparable passage as revised by Simms in 1854, see the Arkansas
Edition, p. 417, lines 4–16.*

ORIGINAL EDITION
Volume II, Chapter XXII, p. 296, line 298–p. 297, line 22
"I have not surely striven for such a character, and would not have you so
esteem me. What I have said, I have said truly. I think you what I have dared to
say you are. I have spoken of your beauty and your many charms, not simply
because of them, for, had you not, at the same time, been securely possessed of
a high intelligence and strong sense, I had said nothing, in your ears, of your
own praise. I am not used to this; and am sincerely honest when I say, that I
can see no reason why, with attractions like yours, you should speak so doubtingly of your chances for happiness. These chances will be yours. Come with
me—come with my Edith. Let me not speak in praise of my own country,
when I promise that in Carolina, your own various merits will not long want
for homage. They will come—believe me, Lucy—almost worthy of you—to
bend before you. The young and the gallant—our nobles—and nature's
nobles too, will be glad to love you, and will freely offer themselves for your
favour—".

"No more, Ralph; no more of this. It may not be. I have already determined. I shall still remain with my aunt, who is now destitute like myself. We
have money—my uncle has at least left us well provided in that respect. We
shall therefore be at no loss, nor find it difficult to leave this region. We shall
go to a section of the country more civilized in aspect than this; where indeed
your regards will find nothing to regret, and no reason to apprehend, for us."

*For the comparable passage as revised by Simms in 1854, see the Arkansas
Edition, p. 425, line 5–p. 427, line 1.*

ORIGINAL EDITION
Volume II, Chapter XXII, p. 301, line 10–p. 302, line 37
"I have come to win your love. I have come to ask—to beg—to implore you,
for him, not less than for myself. You know not how he suffers from your
denial. He had given a solemn pledge, which your refusal has defeated. He
thinks you offended with him—he feels deeply the debt you have conferred
upon us all, and while his feelings of affection—affection as true and more ten-

der than that of a brother—prompt the same thing, those of gratitude are no less strong and urgent in the desire that you will accept his offer—my offer, for indeed, dear Lucy, it is mine. But I have another argument beyond all these. He fears that a want of confidence in him, or a more delicate scruple yet, or indifference, or some other cause, inimical to his pride and character, prompts you in all this. My reason for the entreaty is founded on a persuasion the reverse of his. I know the true cause, and feel, that, but for me and the feeling in your bosom which neither of us may name, his proffer must have been accepted. It is for this very reason that I come to solicit. I would not that another should think as I have thought, and hence I would have you, Lucy, dwell with me as Ralph's sister and mine. Fear not that I shall give up your secret—come with me and be secure."

[five paragraphs omitted][1]

And the lips of the sisters met, and their arms were linked together in the most affectionate confidence, while the spirits of Lucy, if not more bouyant and elastic, were at least something more composed than before.

For the comparable passage as revised by Simms in 1854, see the Arkansas Edition, p. 431, line 21–p. 433, line 11.

ORIGINAL EDITION

Volume II, Chapter XXIII, p. 311, line 18–p. 312, line 11

Bunce would have gone on narrating, as we have already heard them, in detail, the name of every commodity in his wagon, but, at this stage of his speech, one of the outriders returned under the orders of Master Ralph, to see what delayed the worthy trafficker, and to render assistance if any were needed. The blacky, who was no other than our old friend Caesar, was urgent—for the profession of peddling wins as little respect from the southern slave as from the southern freeman—and did not hesitate to declaim against the burning shame of the attempt of Mr. Bunce to wheedle the poor boy out of the money "Mass Ralph been gib 'em." ...

Let us now give our attention to another person of our narrative. Let us go to the dungeon of Guy Rivers, and behold him in a situation so entirely new to him. What a fine mind was here ruined, and how melancholy the contemplation.

For the comparable passage as revised by Simms in 1854, see the Arkansas Edition, p. 439, line 34–p. 441, line 30.

Note

1. For passages of three or more paragraphs in the original edition, only the first and last paragraphs are reproduced for identification purposes.

II. Emendations

Listed below to the left of the brackets are accidentals as they appear in the 1855 Redfield edition; to the right of the brackets are emendations by the editor for the Arkansas Edition. The citation in the left-hand margin is to the page and line in the Arkansas Edition on which the emendation occurs.

Page: Line:

29.21   Ah] "Ah
34.16   understand] to understand
112.24-25 tempation] temptation
169.37   ten.] ten."
180.35   her.] her."
196.12   Though] "Though
203.30   dirk?] dirk?"
213.33-34 better?'] better?"
225.24   and and] and
267.17   married.] married."
267.36   bosom.] bosom."
287.22   mysent] myself
289.13   him.] him."
289.23   Of] "Of
290.29   disposal?] disposal?"
291.07   He] "He
295.00   Chapter XXIX] Chapter Twenty-eight (See Explanatory Notes)
301.00   Chapter XXX] Chapter Twenty-nine
308.06   you.'] you."
310.00   Chapter XXXI] Chapter Thirty
319.00   Chapter XXXII] Chapter Thirty-one
322.15   so?] so?"
326.00   Chapter XXXIII] Chapter Thirty-two
336.16   began] begun
338.00   Chapter XXXIV] Chapter Thirty-three
339.04   sunk] sank
340.02   there?] there?"
346.07   mander] manner
349.00   Chapter XXXV] Chapter Thirty-four
358.36   Colleton.] Colleton."
364.00   Chapter XXXVI] Chapter Thirty-five
376.00   Chapter XXXVII] Chapter Thirty-six
380.13   song.] song."
384.00   Chapter XXXVIII] Chapter Thirty-seven

393.00   Chapter XXXIX] Chapter Thirty-eight
394.12   birth] berth
394.35   Forward] "Forward
400.00   Chapter XL] Chapter Thirty-nine
417.00   Chapter XLI] Chapter Forty
427.35   disappointmont] disappointment
429.26   than—'] than—"
434.00   Chapter XLII] Chapter Forty-one
445.11   impotence.] impotence."

Select Bibliography

LETTERS

The Letters of William Gilmore Simms. Ed. Mary C. Simms Oliphant, Alfred Taylor Odell, and T. C. Duncan Eaves. 5 vols. Columbia: University of South Carolina Press, 1952–1956. (Cited in Introduction and Afterword as *L,* followed by volume and page number.)

The Letters of William Gilmore Simms. Ed. Mary C. Simms Oliphant and T. C. Duncan Eaves. Supplement, Vol. VI. Columbia: University of South Carolina Press, 1982.

MODERN COLLECTIONS

Selected Poems of William Gilmore Simms. Ed. James Everett Kibler, Jr. Athens: University of Georgia Press, 1990.

Stories and Tales. Ed. John Caldwell Guilds (Vol. V of *The Writings of William Gilmore Simms: Centennial Edition*). Columbia: University of South Carolina Press, 1974.

BIOGRAPHY

Guilds, John Caldwell. *Simms: A Literary Life.* Fayetteville: University of Arkansas Press, 1992.

Trent, William P. *William Gilmore Simms* (American Men of Letters Series). Boston: Houghton Mifflin, 1892.

GENERAL CRITICISM AND STUDIES

Davidson, Donald. "Introduction." In *The Letters of William Gilmore Simms*, Vol. I. Columbia: University of South Carolina Press, 1952. [see xxxi–clii; early, highly appreciative estimate of Simms's fiction]

Faust, Drew Gilpin. *A Sacred Circle: The Dilemma of the Intellectual in the Old South, 1840–1860*. Baltimore: Johns Hopkins University Press, 1977. [deals extensively and perceptively with Simms as Southern intellectual]

Gray, Richard. *Writing the South: Ideas of an American Region*. Cambridge: Cambridge University Press, 1986. [see "To Speak of Arcadia: William Gilmore Simms and Some Plantation Novelists," 45–62]

Guilds, John Caldwell, ed. *"Long Years of Neglect": The Work and Reputation of William Gilmore Simms*. Fayetteville: University of Arkansas Press, 1988. [evaluative essays by Guilds, James B. Meriwether, Anne M. Blythe, Linda E. McDaniel, Nicholas G. Meriwether, James E. Kibler, Jr., David Moltke-Hansen, Mary Ann Wimsatt, Rayburn S. Moore, Miriam J. Shillingsburg, John McCardell, and Louis D. Rubin, Jr.]

Hubbell, Jay B. *The South in American Literature, 1607–1900*. [Durham]: Duke University Press, 1954. [chapter on Simms, 572–602; still one of the best short essays on the author]

Kolodny, Annette. *The Lay of the Land: Metaphors as Experience and History in American Life and Letters*. Chapel Hill: University of North Carolina Press, 1975. [see 115–32; feminist study of Simms's depiction of landscape]

Kreyling, Michael. *Figures of the Hero in Southern Narrative*. Baton Rouge: Louisiana State University Press, 1987. [see "William Gilmore Simms: Writer and Hero," 30–51]

McHaney, Thomas L. "William Gilmore Simms." In *The Chief Glory of Every People: Essays on Classic American Writers*. Ed. Matthew J.

Bruccoli. Carbondale: Southern Illinois University Press, 1973, pp. 173–90. [notable for its recognition of the significance of Border novels such as *Guy Rivers*]

Parrington, Vernon L. *The Romantic Revolution in America, 1800–1860.* New York: Harcourt, Brace, 1927. Vol. II of *Main Currents in American Thought.* 3 vols. 1927–1930. [chapter on Simms, 125–36; an important early assessment of his achievements]

Ridgely, J. V. *William Gilmore Simms.* (Twayne's United States Authors Series). New York: Twayne, 1962.

Rubin, Louis D., Jr. *The Edge of the Swamp: A Study in the Literature and Society of the Old South.* Baton Rouge: Louisiana State University Press, 1989. [see "The Dream of the Plantation: Simms, Hammond, Charleston," 54–102; and "The Romance of the Frontier: Simms, Cooper, and the Wilderness," 103–26]

Wakelyn, Jon L. *The Politics of a Literary Man: William Gilmore Simms.* Westport, Conn.: Greenwood, 1973.

Wimsatt, Mary Ann. *The Major Fiction of William Gilmore Simms: Cultural Traditions and Literary Form.* Baton Rouge: Louisiana State University Press, 1989. [valuable study focussing on the Revolutionary Romances and Simms's use of humor throughout his fiction]

REFERENCE WORK

Butterworth, Keen and James E. Kibler, Jr. *William Gilmore Simms: A Reference Guide.* Boston: G. K. Hall, 1980. [contemporary reviews of *Guy Rivers* are listed and very briefly summarized, 24–27, 30–33, 37, 65–66, 101–2, 118]